E. HOFFMANN PRICE'S
PIERRE D'ARTOIS: OCCULT DETECTIVE & ASSOCIATES MEGAPACK®

E. HOFFMANN PRICE'S
PIERRE D'ARTOIS: OCCULT DETECTIVE & ASSOCIATES MEGAPACK®

WILDSIDE PRESS

COPYRIGHT INFO

Contents

INTRODUCTION, by Alexander Kreitner

Welcome to *E. Hoffmann Price's Pierre d'Artois: Occult Detective & Associates MEGAPACK®*! Wildside Press, in association with Mr. Price's heirs, are dedicated to making the extensive body of work of this pulpsmith extraordinaire accessible once again to the public through our line of MEGAPACK® collections.

Edgar Hoffman Price (July 3, 1898–June 18, 1988) was a prolific pulp writer who got his start writing for *Weird Tales* and became a peripheral member of the Lovecraft Circle of weird fiction writers. He served in the military during World War I and his time overseas and love of adventure and martial feats flavored his later pulp writings; an interest that was not at all hypothetical as his life story can attest. He started out as a hobbyist, selling two stories to *Weird Tales* in 1924, but after leaving his job at the Union Carbide Corporation in 1932, Price became a professional "fictioneer" as he called it, writing extensively for the pulps until they began to fold in the early 1950s. His biggest claim to fame was being the only individual who personally met the "triumvirate" of *Weird Tales* authors: H. P. Lovecraft, Robert E. Howard, and Clark Ashton Smith, all of whom he corresponded with for many years.

This collection contains all the stories featuring Price's swashbuckling, French occult detective Pierre d'Artois, as well as the adventures of Glenn Farrell, a character who is a compatriot of d'Artois. Price patterned his d'Artois character after a fencing instructor he knew (real name withheld to avoid comparisons to Price's creation). Sadly, because Pierre d'Artois and Jules de Grandin—Seabury Quinn's own French occult detective—premiered in *Weird Tales* at almost the same time, many came to believe that Price had copied Quinn's character. In order to avoid that impression, Price withdrew his character after only nine stories were published. As an interesting side note, the d'Artois story "Lord of the Fourth Axis" (not included here due to copyright issues) inspired Price's fourth-dimensional ideas that went into his initial draft of what became his collaboration with Lovecraft, "Through the Gates of the Silver Key" (available in *The 11th Golden Age of Weird Fiction MEGAPACK®: E. Hoffmann Price*). Also of note, this package contains the story "One Arabian Night," wherein d'Artois & Farrell enter another of Price's series milieu, the world of Ismeddin (if you enjoy that story, check out *E. Hoffmann Price's Fables of Ismeddin MEGAPACK®* for more of the series.)

It would be fair to say that Price's character Glenn Farrell is a fictional stand-in for Price himself: a world-wise, rough-and-tumble lover of exotic women. He also visits many of the foreign lands that Price was so fascinated with and, in the case of Bayonne, France (where d'Artois lives), Price actually served there in the military (along with a brief stint in the Phillipines, another of Price's favorite locales). Many of Price's later detective, adventure, and "spicy pulp" heroes bear a striking resemblance to Farrell and take place in similar locales and this pulp-friendly personality is what kept Price in business for so many years, eventually publishing—by his own calculations—over 500 stories for various pulp and slick magazines. Wildside Press is proud to make his work available again to readers. Due to the inaccessibility of much of Price's work (he kept no manuscript archive and so we must resort to those original publication copies we can track down) we have decided to package the material into themed Megapacks, highlighting specific genres he worked in. Later volumes will be released as we gather further material (any collectors interested in aiding our endeavors by supplying photocopies from their collections are urged to contact Wildside through our website, wildsidepress.com).

We hope you enjoy these occult adventures. Here is a list of other collections of Price's work in the MEGAPACK® series (some already available, others out shortly):

> *E. Hoffmann Price's Two-Fisted Detective MEGAPACK®*
> *E. Hoffmann Price's War And Western Action MEGAPACK®*
> *E. Hoffmann Price's Exotic Adventures MEGAPACK®*
> *The 11th Golden Age of Weird Fiction MEGAPACK®: E. Hoffmann Price*
> *E. Hoffmann Price's Fables of Ismeddin MEGAPACK®*
> *E. Hoffmann Price's Pierre d'Artois: Occult Detective & Associates MEGA-PACK®*
> *The E. Hoffmann Price Spicy-Adventure MEGAPACK®*

THE WORD OF SANTIAGO

Originally published in *Weird Tales*, February 1926.

In a sombre, black-tapestried room of a château perched high on a Pyreneean crest overlooking both France and Spain, was an altar, a block of teakwood whose thirty-three grotesquely carved panels depicted the thirty-three strange diversions of gods and men: age-old monstrosities, bold in their antique frankness; unsavory survivals of primitive fancies; the materialized visions of unhallowed Asian mysteries.

On either side of this altar stood the silver effigy of a peacock, whose outspread fan rose, and, drooping forward, joined that of its mate so as to form a canopy, a miniature shrine. Before this shrine smoldered two brazen censers whose pale fumes serpentined caressingly about the slim, three-edged *épée* whose keen point was embedded in the teakwood pedestal. The bell guard and grip of the blade were severely plain; but the pommel was crowned with the tiny image of a silver peacock whose painted fan was star-dusted with pale sapphires, cool emeralds, flaring rubies, and fiercely glittering diamonds. Such was the shrine, and such the deity thereof.

The heavy door of the room opened silently, admitting into the sombre twilight the tall, black-robed figure of Don Santiago, the acolyte of that strange altar. Moving as one who walks in a dream, the Spaniard advanced and struck light to the thirty-three black tapers about the altar. Their red, wavering flames filled the room with a flickering, sinister glow, revealing groups of grotesques embroidered in silver thread upon the room's black, silken draperies, each group marking one of the four cardinal points of the compass.

Retreating a pace, the Spaniard, arms extended, faced the four points, before each inclining his head as in salutation. Last of all he bowed low before the shrine, its silver peacocks, and slender, frosty white blade.

"I prefer Cain to Abel, and Nimrud to Javeh," he intoned sonorously; "I prefer Esau to Jacob and Iblis to Allah; and Thee, Malik Taûs, I exalt above gods and all powers; and to Thee, Omnipotent Rebel, I raise my prayer and lift my eyes."

He paused, touched with his fingertips first his temples, then his lips; then, crossing his arms on his breast, the Spaniard made obeisance once more before that gleaming shrine.

"Lord of the Outer Marches, Prince of the Borderland, hear my prayer and grant my desire! Grant me victory over the arrogant one, grant me the defeat of him who mocks at Thy servants, of him who made of me a show and a mockery. Thou who rulest the world, Thou who hast made the world Thine own, hear me, Malik Taûs, Lord Peacock, hear me and give me the strength to prevail over him who holdeth Thee in scorn, him who hath offended Thy servant. Hear me, High

9

Sovereign, Rebel Prince, Dark Lord! Thou who art power made absolute, Thousand-Eyed Malik Taûs, hear me and grant me victory!"

The flickering tapers rose to tall, sinuous flames; the censers fumed in heavy, twining serpents. With a final obeisance, Don Santiago turned from the altar. But ere he could gain the door, it opened to admit an intruder.

"And what may be your pleasure?" demanded Don Santiago, confronting his visitor.

Somewhere, at some time, he had seen those lean, haughty features, those cold, relentless eyes, that tall, erect form.

The intruder smiled with the cool reserve of the superior person in the presence of one almost his equal, then, looking the Spaniard squarely in the eye, made a curious, fleeting gesture with his left hand, as with his right he flung aside a fold of his cape.

"What? Am I then unknown to you, Don Santiago?"

Don Santiago started, blinked in amazement, then bowed low in recognition of the gesture and of the peacock that flamed on the stranger's breast.

"Welcome, Lord and Master! And my prayer... Will it be granted?"

"Don Santiago," began the Spaniard's visitor, "you have served me well, and I am appreciative. But your request passes the limits of reason. This one prayer I can not grant. You have challenged d'Artois to meet you in secret, by moonlight at the Spring of St. Leon, to engage in mortal combat; and now you pray for victory. Know then that this d'Artois serves me well, and as truly as you do; and I can not permit you to slay him."

"Serves you?" queried the Spaniard in amazement. "Master, he is not of the elect; he serves your Adversary, the Nazarene whom we defy and scorn."

The Master smiled sardonically.

"Nonsense, Santiago! Was it not once said by the Adversary, 'All that take the sword shall perish by the sword'? And has not this d'Artois fought several duels, in each meeting slaying his opponent, so that it is now unlawful for him to fight a duel in France? Now were I to permit him to fall by your hand, would I not be testifying to the truth of that which was spoken in Galilee a very long time ago?"

"But," protested Santiago, "d'Artois always has a just cause, defending that to which you are opposed. He is a true servant of the Nazarene."

The Lord Peacock smiled scornfully.

"It is also written, 'And to him that striketh thee on one cheek, offer also the other.' And therefore, d'Artois, though he never met me face to face as you have, yet serves me well; for instead of offering his other cheek, he draws a keen blade which he handles with a skill that even I could envy.

"Santiago," continued the Master, with a half-sorrowful, half-quizzical smile, "how I am misunderstood, even by my servants! Do you not yet know that all the strong, the proud, the haughty and willful serve me, whether or not they acknowledge me? Do you not know that many a man who leads a life of magnificent vice and monumental folly, instead of serving me, serves the Nazarene instead, seeing that he is an example whereof the priests avail themselves to seduce the world from me? And do you not know that those who forsake their luxurious sins to follow the Nazarene serve me best of all, since they, in telling of their redemption, entice those who dare sin only after having been assured of the efficacy of repentance, and of eventual forgiveness? Have you ever thought that this Nazarene in his humility is more arrogant than I in my colossal pride, which led me to prefer elemental fire and abysmal darkness to servitude and bondage? Santiago, even you, the most faithful and talented of my servants, do not understand me."

Malik Taûs sighed as does one burdened with the cares of a universe.

"No, Santiago, I can not turn against him who, though unwittingly, serves me as well as you. In a word, I forbid this meeting; for d'Artois is the more skilful, and will surely slay you. Nor can I let you slay him; for in either case, I lose, and my empery is diminished. In these degenerate days when civilization has nearly outlawed dueling, should I not prize those rare few who love the sword, and contrive to use it well?"

"But, Master," persisted the Spaniard, "I have given my word; I can not withdraw my challenge. Is then your promise of success in all my ventures thus to be canceled in my hour of need?"

"You can and you shall withdraw, Santiago," commanded the Master sternly, his dark eyes gleaming menacingly. "You shall not keep this rendezvous. I forbid it."

The Spaniard glared defiantly into the cold, fierce eyes of the Master.

"Malik Taûs, my word is good, even though you fail in yours. And therefore do I deny and disown you, and defy you to the uttermost. For whatever may be the penalty, in this world or the next, my word freely given must and shall be kept."

"And I, Don Santiago," came the cool response, "shall devise so that you shall not keep it. Therefore accept my warning, and beware my wrath. *Vaya con Dios*," he concluded with a mocking smile.

And with a courtly bow the Master turned and departed.

"Fraud! Impostor!" snarled Don Santiago.

Seizing from the tapestried wall an ancient battle-ax, he battered beyond all recognition the silver peacocks, and utterly defaced the obscenely carved altar of teak. But the slim sword remained true and straight and faultless, resisting his efforts to snap it across his knee.

Pierre d'Artois laid aside his mask and blade, regarding with a quizzical smile the perspiring features and shaking hand of his valet-secretary-fencing partner.

"Why such an effort? Is it then so difficult to touch me once in an afternoon? But listen, Jannicot: tonight at 12 I meet a friend by moonlight at the Spring of St. Leon. There will be no seconds, no director, not even a surgeon. One of us will remain there until his friends call for the vanquished."

"But this is folly!" protested Jannicot. "You may go into an ambush. Or for want of speedy attention, you may die of your wounds."

"Nonsense! For very good reasons we must meet in secret. The twentieth century frowns upon sword play, even here in France. Anyway, he is a man of honor. There will be no ambush. No surgeon will be required. I am no bungler; neither is he. One thrust, his or mine, will suffice. Surgery would be wasted effort. Therefore if I do not meet you at the appointed time…"

"But how do you know that he will be there? You have not heard from him for over a month. It is rumored that he is in Spain; others claim that he is in Morocco. He may fail you entirely."

"The word of Santiago is good. He will not fail me. Dead, drunk, or dying, he will be there."

"But these treacherous Spaniards! An ambush…"

"Bah! He is a man of honor. And moreover, I must keep my word, even as he will keep his. And now, Jannicot, I will sleep. Awaken me at 10."

At the stroke of 10, d'Artois arose, and dressed with as much care and deliberation as though he were about to make his customary morning promenade.

"Idiot!" reproved d'Artois, as Jannicot came tottering in under the weight of a great tray; "am I then a python? Assassin! Would you have me gorge myself? *À bas*! Bring me a cut of cold meat and a bit of sauterne. And by the way, Jannicot, if you will solemnly promise not to seek me until two hours after midnight, you may drive me to within a kilometer of the Spring of St. Leon. I must not the my hand or eye. You promise? *Eh bien, allons*!"

The powerful Issotta roadster leaped forward into the night like some great cat upon its prey. Kilometer after kilometer they sped, up grade and down, winding their way through the curves and dips of the great highway that, running through the Pyrenees, leads to Bayonne. Like a bird of prey they swooped into and through St. Jean de Luz. Then at a slower pace they picked their way on until the slim, silvery spires of the old cathedral of Bayonne appeared high above the dark blot of the groves surrounding the city.

"Park here, Jannicot, and await my return. And if in two hours I am not with you, seek me."

"But why two hours?"

"So that the survivor may be assured a fair departure."

Jannicot, depressed by the thought of that secret encounter, man to man on the green at the Spring of St. Leon, shivered as he saw his master draw from the tonneau a pair of slender *épées*. Their sinister gleam in moonlight made him shudder. He sought to grasp his master's hand.

"Nonsense, Jannicot! I could touch the devil himself tonight. Thus: the illogical parry, the uncanny *riposte*," he continued, as his blade flickered through its deceptive, sweeping *parades*. "It is timing, Jannicot. You are young and active, yet have you ever deceived my parry, or avoided my *riposte*? It can not be done; the man is not born who can escape me. And remember your word. *À bientôt*!"

D'Artois saluted with his blade, tucked it under his left arm to keep its mate company, then turned and picked his way across the street, and was lost in the black depths of the grove at whose opposite end was the Spring of St. Leon.

"I am early," reflected d'Artois, as he entered the empty clearing. He glanced at his watch. It lacked a minute of midnight. Alone…yet not entirely alone. A sinister, foreboding presence seemed to lurk about him. D'Artois shivered, toyed with the hilts of his *épées*, peered into the shadows, listened for the approach of his adversary. The great cathedral clock struck midnight.

And then a voice, soft, courteous.

"I trust that I have not kept you waiting long? I was detained in Spain."

D'Artois turned to confront Don Santiago.

"Not at all," he replied with a bow. "But your approach was silent."

"What? Would you expect a fanfare of trumpets? Are we not both outlaws, forbidden to meet on the field of honor in France?"

"Quite so, Don Santiago. But which end will you take? *Ça m'est égal*!"

With a gesture of his blade, d'Artois indicated the smooth, unbroken green before them.

"It is of no import, Monsieur d'Artois. The moon is almost overhead; the ground is level; and there are no shadows to favor either."

In silence the adversaries stripped to the waist, stamped on the short grass to try its footing, poised and flexed their blades, each selecting one of his pair. And each courteously declined to inspect the other's blade to see that it conformed to custom and regulation.

Pierre d'Artois, slim and erect as an obelisk, faced his adversary, his sword at the carry.

"For the mastery of the world, Don Santiago...e*n garde*!"

With sinuous, serpentine grace they went through the evolutions of the salute preliminary to a bout. Each recoiled a pace and out of reach, with that catlike, swift smoothness of a polished swordsman.

Don Santiago advanced warily, the point of his *épée* tracing fine, imperceptible circles in the air, a menacing, vibrant, silvery death. D'Artois, motionless, frozen in place, immobile as the pyramids, stood his ground, revealing the master who never wastes a move. And none but a master would dare await, cold-footed, the attack of that swift, hawk-like Spaniard; for immobility, while confounding the adversary, causes the passive, watchful one to "freeze", to lose the fine alertness of his nerves.

The Spaniard's vicious feint had no effect, drew not the sign of a parry. A fierce beat failed to shake the master's firm wrist. But the strain of immobility seemed to tell on d'Artois: his wrist, drooping slightly, shifted his guard, leaving his forearm exposed. Don Santiago's blade reached forth with the darting stab of a serpent's stroke, his arm fully extended. The sword of d'Artois enveloped that of his adversary, swept it aside, leaped forward in its deadly swift advance. But the subtle Spaniard, prepared for the trap, withdrew, so that the thrust fell short. In sheer bravado, he had dropped his guard in retreating, showing how well he had gauged his adversary's reach.

Again they came on guard. This time the play was light, swift, staccato, a dizzying interchange of attack, counterattack, parry and *riposte*. The honors were even; each recognized in the other a master, a cunning, deadly opponent, each with a wondrous sense of time, a keen eye, and a sure hand. Bird of prey and bird of prey had met, circling, swooping, awaiting that inevitable instant in every bout when one of the adversaries suffers a momentary dulling of the nerves, fatal relaxation of watchfulness. That moment, and that moment alone, could decide the day; for in skill they matched each other; in that cold, passionless, impersonal hatred begotten of the touch of steel upon steel they matched each other; master and master had met.

As *phrase* succeeded *phrase*, the Spaniard noted that, despite the wondrous succession of sweeping parries, infinitely varied and perfectly executed, d'Artois, when hard pressed, favored the double *contre sixte*. And this he bore in mind, and smiled his thin, crooked smile.

A pause in the fierceness of the fencing; a moment's slackening of tension. Then, without sign or warning, came the Spaniard's thrust, twice avoiding the flashing succession of double *contre sixte*, and home…but not for a touch; for the blade of d'Artois, point dropped, swept across his body from *sixte* to *prime*, brushing aside the blade of Santiago, then leaped forward in a *riposte* that was to impale the Spaniard: that wondrous, incredible parry and reply that none but a genius or madman would dare employ. But again the Spaniard withdrew, so that the advance of d'Artois fell short by the width of a finger.

Out of reach, d'Artois dropped his guard.

"Beautiful, Don Santiago! *Magnifique*! And I would have sworn that none but the devil himself could have escaped me."

The Spaniard smiled coolly, and bowed in acknowledgment.

"A truce, Don Santiago! The victor will never again find a worthy opponent."

"En garde!" snapped the Spaniard.

And once again the staccato click-click of the blades, the tinkle of blade on bell guards, the hoarse breathing of the contestants. Don Santiago with the ferocity of a tiger pressed his opponent to the utmost, ever watchful for that one fatal slip; but at last, tiring of his vain assaults, seeking a moment's respite, slackened the tension. Slowly, rhythmically, he advanced, retreated, feinted, parried, weaving backward, forward, in a steady march, a fixed cadence. Slowly but certainly d'Artois succumbed to the spell of that soporific rhythm as to the hypnotic passes of a mesmerist, replying with a lifeless parry to a languid feint, advancing. retreating in time to the cadence beat by the Spaniard's caressing movements, even as one who, listlessly, unconsciously beats time with his foot to the faint strains of distant music. It was not blade to blade, but will against will, the invisible matching of intangible weapons.

With a thrill of horror, with a shudder of sudden awakening, d'Artois realized his peril, realized that the Spaniard sought to lull him to sleep, then, with an abrupt change of pace, run him through ere he could accommodate himself to the shift in cadence.

On the trail of this revelation came inspiration: two could play at that game. There would be some instant wherein Don Santiago could be caught off his guard, lulled to sleep by his own mesmeric passes, lulled by the very response of d'Artois, the victim to be.

Another languid feint; to which Don Santiago replied with a *contre sixte*, a meaningless gesture, seeing that the thrust of d'Artois was no true menace, but merely the response to the Spaniard's hypnotic, caressing evolutions…and d'Artois, accelerating on the instant the speed of his advance, sank into a full lunge, chin almost on his knee, slipping under the Spaniard's guard, clear of the point which was a shade too high. No parry, no *coup d'arrêt*, no retreat could avoid the deadly swiftness of that lunge. The Spaniard was trapped in his own snare!

As d'Artois slipped forward, he knew that nothing on earth could halt his impaling blade.

A blinding, elemental flame flared before his eyes as his *épée* sank home; a blinding, consuming flame that seared and lashed him, enfolded him. Then blackness, Cimmerian, absolute, as he pitched forward, arm extended, face to the ground.

And meanwhile, Jannicot paced restlessly in circles about the Issotta roadster, smoking countless cigarettes, assuring himself that all would be well.

Half past 12… One o'clock… Perhaps Don Santiago had been delayed… Half past one… What duel could last that long, even between cunning, wary fencers, master opposed to master?

Forgetful of his promise, forgetful of all save his concern for d'Artois, Jannicot plunged into the blackness of the grove, picked the path, and, panic-stricken, stumbled toward the Spring of St. Leon. At the edge of the clearing he halted, stunned by the sight that confronted him. For an instant, dumb terror and dismay paralyzed him, blinded him. Then, closely examining the inert form of d'Artois, he searched, but in vain, for a wound.

"*Salaud*! Struck him down from ambush!" he growled as he scooped up from the spring a hatful of water, dashing it full into his master's face. Then, still seeking to revive d'Artois, he noted the trampled grass, the signs of prolonged combat.

D'Artois stirred, muttered incoherently. Jannicot, picking him bodily from the green, staggered back to the Issotta with his burden. D'Artois, somewhat recovered, though still muttering unintelligibly, took a draft of the cognac Jannicot offered.

"I'm all right. Drive on."

D'Artois shuddered, drew about himself his cloak. The terror of that moon-drenched clearing still overwhelmed him, dulled him, oppressed him with an indescribable horror. What had struck him? What had he touched? That abysmal flame still flared before his eyes.

The Issotta once more leaped into the darkness, speeding up that ribbon-like road with a full-throated roar. Clouds obscured the moon. A haze enveloped the car, so that its headlights could reach but a few yards ahead. Jannicot, sorely puzzled by the mystery of the evening, drove desperately. D'Artois slumped back in his seat, unnerved, still consumed with strange surmises.

Then the shrill scream of brakes: and the speeding Issotta, whipping and skidding, came to a halt but a few meters short of an obstacle, a wrecked car that blocked their path.

Jannicot leaped from the wheel, followed by d'Artois, who had partly recovered from his lethargy. Pinned under the wreckage was an apparently lifeless form, face to the ground.

D'Artois drew from his tool chest a jack with which he lifted the wreck.

"Nasty turn here… Poor devil…but he may not be dead," he murmured, as he drew the unconscious victim clear of the debris. Then, in utter astonishment, "Don Santiago!"

"Crapule!" flared Jannicot, likewise recognizing the battered features of the Spaniard. "Served him right, having you struck down from ambush. Coward, he fled too fast!"

"But we can't leave him here. Get a surgeon, Jannicot."

"Spare yourselves the trouble, *Messieurs*," counseled a calm, sonorous voice from behind them. "He has been dead over two hours…wrecked…driving out of Spain in great haste…"

"Two hours? Out of Spain?"

"Look at the tracks."

The stranger with a gesture indicated the trace of the wrecked car's wheels, then, disregarding their questions, continued his way down the road to Spain, speaking in a low tone, apparently to someone accompanying him.

"Santiago, though you defied me, you are a man after my own heart; for even Death, my servant, could not prevent you from keeping your word."

THE PEACOCK'S SHADOW

Originally published in *Weird Tales*, November 1926.

"*Mon vieux*, what do you say to a bit of housebreaking?"

This, from Pierre d'Artois, a gentleman of France and a master of the sword, seemed unusual, to say the least.

"Well, why not?" I agreed, not to be outdone by the d'Artois nonchalance. "But whose house do we invade? What the devil, do you fear I will become homesick if from time to time there is not something to remind me of my own native land of liberty?"

"*Mais non*! No, we are not going as prohibition agents. Not at all! And it is no ordinary house into which we are to break. We invade the château of Monsieur the Marquis de la Tour de Maracq," announced Pierre as he stepped on the accelerator of his favorite car, the Issotta roadster.

"But what of Monsieur the Marquis?" I suggested with what seemed to be a touch of reason.

"He is very busy at Biarritz at a fencing tournament."

Well, this solved one riddle: I now knew why d'Artois, that fierce old *ferrailleur*, had overlooked a chance to demonstrate his exquisite mastery of the sword.

"But, *mon Pierre*, what of the housebreaking? What loot are we after?" I ventured as we cleared Pont de Mousserole and left behind us the gray battlements of Bayonne.

"The truth of it is, I am playing what you call the hunch," he evaded, then continued: "But he is the good hunch. There has been an elopement, and it is for me to locate the lady."

Worse and worse yet! A quiet month in Bayonne…

"Who is the girl?"

D'Artois laughed.

"A princess, and the daughter of a king."

"Not bad for a marquis. And young and beautiful?" I retorted to the mockery I saw in his keen old eyes.

"Beautiful, yes; if you like such beauty. But young, no. In fact, older than I am."

"The devil!"

"The truth! Thirty-seven hundred years old at least."

This was too much!

"*Mais non.* I do not jest," continued Pierre. "She was stolen from the Guimet museum of Lyons and carried all the way to the château of the marquis."

"Well, and that is a case for the police, is it not?"

"No. For one is not really certain; it is but strongly suspected that he accomplished the almost impossible feat of looting the museum and carrying the mummy to his château. Monsieur the Prefect of Police, not being any too sure of himself, has taken me into his confidence and asked me to investigate unofficially. A false move would ruin him, since Monsieur the Marquis is a man of influence."

"But why should anyone steal a mummy, especially de la Tour de Maracq, who is rich as an Indian prince, and of a house as old as Charlemagne?"

"A scholar, a soldier, a man of letters," enumerated d'Artois, continuing my thought, "and a fantastic madman, if this report is correct. He is too talented for sanity."

"Even as yourself," I hinted.

"Touché." acknowledged d'Artois. "But I do not elope with ladies 3700 years old."

He fingered a pack of *Bastos*, but thinking better of so foul a deed, decided to light the Coronado I had given him.

"All very quaint. But let's get to facts," I urged. "What have you to work on in this love affair?"

"I have the good hunch. And it is more of a love affair than you realize."

Which was logical enough. Those whom gold could not tempt, might indeed steal objects of art, jewels over which to gloat in secret, a relic, an antique rug; but a shriveled mummy! Well, tastes vary.

And the case should be simple of solution, at least as regarded the marquis; for the missing lady could not be concealed with any degree of facility. A simple matter of walking or climbing into the château, and leaving again with our princess; or else reporting that she was not to be found, and that Monsieur the Marquis was not her abductor. A jewel could be hidden; but a mummy…

The château was perched upon a crest some hundred meters off the road. We parked the Issotta and proceeded on foot.

Instead of knocking at the door, as seemed to be his intent, despite his quip about housebreaking, d'Artois selected a key from his ring, tried it; selected another, picked at the lock, but to no avail. The third, however, was applied with more success; the heavy door yielded to his touch, admitting us into a vestibule, thence to a salon.

"Welcome to Tour de Maracq," murmured d'Artois with a courtly bow. "Quick about it, and we'll be out of here long before he has fought his last bout."

"But the servants?" I suggested.

"They are few in number. It seems the marquis has an aversion to women, so that there are no female domestics to contend with. Thus it is that one of the *ménage* has gone to Bayonne to negotiate with a stranger who sought to buy some rare vintages which are to be pilfered from the master's cellars. Another is keeping a rendezvous with a demoiselle who hailed him a week ago and made an engagement for today. Each has some illicit engagement whereof he will not babble. Now it would have been inconvenient to arrange on short order for lovers for any female servants…praise be to the eccentricity of Monsieur the Marquis!"

I noted the rich tapestries; the massive teakwood furniture; the floor of rare hardwoods partly masked by Chinese and Indian rugs. And on the walls were arms of infinite variety; wavy-bladed kresses, kampilans, scimitars; halberds, assegai, lances; maces and battle-axes in endless number, all grouped in clusters. Some of these arms were burnished; but many bore dark, ominous stains.

And thus we roamed through the house, from one apartment to another, I wondering at the beauty, the grotesquerie, the oddness of the furnishings and adornments, d'Artois regarding all with an appraising glance that revealed nothing of whatever interest he might have felt.

Strange gods in bronze and onyx and basalt glared at us, brandished their distorted arms in futile rage, mouthed threats with their twisted lips; resented our presence in every way possible to inanimate things; inanimate, yes, but enlivened with the spiritual essence absorbed from their centuries of devotees. But no mummies. Nevertheless, d'Artois studied his surroundings. But nothing seemed to arouse his interest, until…

"Ah…look!"

He indicated a tiny *darabukeh*, a small kettledrum whose body was of grotesque carven wood, its head of a strange hide; strange to me, at least.

"Curious, yes. But what has this to do with mummies?"

"Nothing at all. But I fancied that drumhead…"

A smile concluded his remark. Now what the devil significance had that little tom-tom?

"But no mummies, Pierre."

"True. But one can picture a man's mind from the house he keeps. Fancy then the odd brain that twists in the skull of de la Tour de Maracq!"

And thus, room by room, we searched the château proper, servants' quarters, basements, passages and all. Toward the end of our tour we stumbled upon a stairway which led to an apartment which we had overlooked.

It was a large room of contradictory appearance: a study, if one judged from its desk, table, bookcases; a bedroom, surely, if gauged by the lordly canopied bed of antique workmanship; or a museum, if one drew conclusions from the ornaments.

As we had done in the salon, we found again a collection of arms, armor, polycephalous gods with contorted limbs and features. And this time, mummies, two of them: one in its sycamore case, the other, not only encased, but enshrined in its massive granite sarcophagus.

Naturally I was exultant.

"Useless!" exclaimed Pierre. "See how they fit their cases; and see also that none of the cases would fit the princess we seek."

With a tape he laid off the dimensions of the mummy we sought, showing clearly that those present were of greater stature.

"Not so good, Pierre, not so good. Apparently we're stuck."

"Not entirely," muttered Pierre absent-mindedly.

I saw him examining an *épée*, a slim, three-edged dueling sword. The pommel, which was adorned with a tiny silver peacock, seemed to fascinate d'Artois. Which was natural enough, Pierre being a connoisseur of the sword, and its undisputed master. Still, business was business…

A dried, mummified human head, wrinkled and shrunken, a Patagonian relic, hung by its hair from a cluster of arrows. And this, attracting my eye to the library table over which that gruesome trophy hung, drew me to the table itself. I picked up from the inestimable Kurdish rug which covered its top a thick book, leather-bound, and emblazoned with a peacock.

"Hell's fire! It's bound in human skin!"

"So it is," agreed Pierre. "I wondered how long it would take you to recognize human hide when it was tanned. You passed up that little drum without noticing it."

And then Pierre thumbed the pages, began to read to himself. Glancing over his shoulder, I saw that he well spared himself the trouble of reading aloud. The book was either in Arabic or Persian, neither of which I could understand.

As Pierre read, and fumed, and muttered, apparently quite interested, I devoted myself to the one bright spot in that necrophagous apartment: a painting in oils, a portrait of a young woman, lovely beyond all description, with smoldering, Babylonic eyes, full, delicately sensuous lips; fine features whose every line and curve bespoke calm, aristocratic insolence. And this smiled from a cluster of swords, and was enshrined in an atmosphere of death and doom, and gruesome relics! Whether or not the kidnaper of a mummy, this marquis was surely a freak.

Pierre's smile, as he laid down the book he had been reading, resembled that of a cat who has just had a pleasant *tête-à-tête* with the canary. Whether the worthy marquis had expressed his unusual humor by having a book of Arabic jests bound in human hide, I couldn't say; but Pierre seemed on the inside of something which had been evading him.

The portrait caught his eye.

"Very lovely. Yes, I met her, twenty years ago, shortly before her untimely death. His last mistress..."

Death...death...even that loveliness enshrined by morbid trophies was itself a memento of death. I shuddered, chilled, despite the sun's slanting rays which warmed and illumined that necrophiliac room.

"And he sleeps here. Or is this but an antique, a decoration?"

I glanced again at the lordly bed, half expecting to find festoons of skulls about the canopy, fringes of scalp locks, strands of teeth. Then I noted an unnatural curvature of the drawn curtains, something which forced them forward, and out of their natural drape.

"*Que diable*! Another mummy! And no case to match."

D'Artois took from his vest pocket his tape-line, took measurements, compared them with his notebook; studied the wrappings, the markings.

"The very lady!"

I advanced to pick up the aged beauty. Simplicity, this quest. And this, after all Pierre's halo of mystery!

"*Jamais*! *Pas du tout*! We must locate the case; all or nothing. If we alarm him, who knows what may happen to the case? *Allons*!"

But before leaving, he paused to regard once more the portrait of the girl with the Babylonic eyes.

"That was a lovely little *épée*, that one with the peacock on its pommel. It seems strangely familiar...well, and since the marquis has probably fought his last bout and is on his way back, we leave opportunely," remarked d'Artois, as the Issotta's long nose headed toward Bayonne.

At Place de Théâtre we parked, found a table on the paving, well within the shade of the awning. D'Artois called for a weird favorite of his, whose two ingredients he himself mixed, and then diluted with charged water: a milky, curiously flavored drink, Anis del Oso and Cordiale Gentiane, a suave, insipid madhouse in a slim, tall glass. The springs of the Isle of Patmos must have flowed with Anis del Oso.

As we sipped and smoked, I noted the great limousine of Monsieur the Marquis de la Tour de Maracq draw up to the curbing, returning from Biarritz. Lean, aquiline-featured, elegant and courtly in bearing, and haughty as Lucifer was the marquis. Touching the brim of his high hat with the head of his stick, he acknowledged the salute of the footman, then handed from the limousine a woman whose features, to say the very least, startled me.

"What in—!"

"No, *mon cher*," murmured d'Artois, "she is no ghost, though she may be the reincarnation of the lady whose portrait we saw at Château Maracq. There is no telling what deviltry the marquis has worked in his day, but this is a flesh-and-blood woman. And now do you see a light?"

"A light? What in the world has she to do with this mummy?"

D'Artois laughed maliciously.

"I'll swear you have mummies on the brain! But just wait. Well, that is Mademoiselle Lili Allzaneau of 34 rue Lachepaillet. Like her scriptural counterpart, she lives on the city wall in an apartment overlooking the park."

Which last was of course superfluous: for the mention of her address was quite sufficient. Yet La Belle Allzaneau bore the stamp of the thoroughbred; the patrician insolence, the smoldering Babylonic eyes, long, narrow, veiled; the slim, gracious hands of a princess of the blood. And her dress, and her figure, and her bearing were all in accord. Behold the *grand dame* of the château, and her double, La Belle Allzaneau of rue Lachepaillet!

* * * *

A few days elapsed, during which Pierre left me to my own devices. And I then, emerging from his preoccupation, he sought relaxation in a stroll which took us along the Adour, around, and back to the ramparts of Lachepaillet.

To our right was the Gate of Spain, its drawbridge and guardhouse; far beneath us, at the foot of the city walls, on whose parapet we sat, was the bottom of the dry moat; while to our left front, across the moat and a hundred meters beyond its outer bank, was the Spring of St. Leon and the cluster of ancient trees that half concealed it. Though their crests almost met, their trunks were widely separated, so that the spring and its low, hemispherical cupola were in a small clearing.

The sun was setting. Long shadows marched slowly across the gently rolling ground beneath us, and to our front. Pierre d'Artois, as he took from his case and lit a villainous *Bastos*, stared at the Spring of St. Leon. And then he resumed the thread of his rambling discourse, continuing a tale he had so often before begun and abruptly abandoned.

"With that lunge I could have impaled the devil himself, for I had him swinging like a windmill, skilful swordsman though he was. Yes, and had it really been

Monsieur the Devil himself, and not Santiago with whom I crossed swords, I still hold that someone must have struck me down from the rear to save his lord and master!"

He spoke of his secret duel by moonlight with Santiago the Spaniard, two years ago, in the small clearing by this very Spring of St. Leon, and of the outcome of the affair: how, as after hard, fierce fighting he had slipped through the Spaniard's guard to impale him with a thrust to the chest, there had been an awful flare of elemental flame, followed by blackness and oblivion; how Jannicot, his servant, had come in search of him, carried him back to the car; and how, on the return trip, they had found Don Santiago dead beneath his own car, wrecked on the way *from* Spain, hurrying, apparently, to keep his rendezvous with d'Artois.

"Since Santiago never reached Bayonne to meet me, then who? A double? For that stout wrist was not that of an apparition, nor do illusions or phantoms leave footprints, nor can they beat one's blade so that one's arm tingles up to the shoulder. Impossible!"

"But then what did hit you?"

"Who knows? Perhaps a confederate, despite our having agreed to meet without seconds. But by the time I recovered full possession of my wits, several days later, any bruise the blow might have left had subsided. Yet something must have struck me..."

In the lengthening shadows, the Spring of St. Leon appeared less and less as a place for midnight trysts, either for love or war. And though listening to Pierre's dissertation, my thoughts were of Bayonne, this "pet" city of mine which is still girdled by walls and moats and earthworks; whose ground is steeped with blood spilled in centuries of warfare, and undermined with casements, and passages, and dungeons. Some of the passages had been built by Vauban when he fortified the town; but there were many others, of much greater antiquity; vaults wherein Roman legionaries had worshiped Mithra, Saracen emirs practiced necromancy, and medieval alchemists sought the immutable Azoth, and dabbled in thaumaturgy.

"A curious thing I noted," continued d'Artois, "was that a small silver peacock adorned the pommel of his *épée*...strange how one notes such details before a duel..."

Silver peacock...why, we had seen a similar sword at Château de la Tour de Maracq the other day!... I wondered...

And out of that network of passages, what might not have emerged from a mining casemate to strike Pierre from the rear and save the day for Santiago, or Santiago's double, or the devil, or what it was that d'Artois had met?

Something had loosened the ordinarily well-shackled d'Artois tongue. I marveled, and encouraged its wagging. And then he stopped short, pointing toward the Spring of St. Leon.

"By the belles of Hell!" he exclaimed, quaintly distorting a selection from the American doughboy's lexicon, which he strove most valiantly to master. "What is *she* doing there?"

A girl stood at the spring; a slim girl whose white arms and shoulders and iridescent gown gleamed boldly against the shadows of the grove and the dark cupola of the spring.

"La Belle Allzaneau," explained Pierre; for I lacked that old man's keen vision.

As he spoke, she rounded the cupola of St. Leon, its low gray mass hiding her from sight.

"But how can you recognize anyone at that distance and in this light, Pierre?"

"Her general outline, the gown she wears...which by the way is a trifle inappropriate for the locality... I have often seen her at the Casino at Biarritz."

That evening, as Jannicot brought our coffee, d'Artois, after theorizing for a while about the duel at St. Leon, abruptly switched to the mummy, poor neglected lady whom he seemed to have entirely forgotten.

"Your imagination, *mon cher*, is entirely dead," he declared. "And in this quest of the mummy case (for we have the lady herself located) one needs much imagination. *Alors*, to you shall fall the duty of private soldier; that of sentry-go, by night. Jannicot shall walk post during the day."

"What?"

"Yes. Sentry-go. You watch by night."

"Why pick on me?"

"You are too conspicuous in this small town. Jannicot, watching a cow staked on the city wall, would never be noted, for he will look like any other yokel similarly occupied. Whereas you..."

I bowed elaborately in appreciation of the compliment.

"Whereas you, under cover of darkness—but that is obvious."

"But how will watching 34 rue Lachepaillet assist you?"

"It will prevent your disturbing my meditations."

"Still, what has that girl to do with mummies?"

"Imbecile! You have no imagination. So take your post at sunset, watch until morning, and report to me all the exits, entries, and doings of La Belle Allzaneau, and her visitors as well. Though few but Monsieur the Marquis call at her apartment."

* * * *

And thus I spent a week, walking post by night. Not truly walking, but rather lounging on the parapet of the ancient battlements, always keeping an eye on the door of Lili Allzaneau, who lived on the city wall, who had ensnared a marquis; "a peer of France," as they used to put it.

And what was Pierre, *beau sabreur* and master of devices, doing as I frittered away my time, noting the princely cars which stopped at the door of Lili of the City Wall; listening to the sound of merriment subdued to a patrician pitch: an aristocratic reserve in keeping with the *lorette* who designed to accord only to the lords of the world the pleasure of her presence?

Each morning I rendered my report, usually with mocking formality, imitating the supposed manner of a private detective. I especially enjoyed the report of the fourth vigil: "Monsieur Pierre d'Artois, noted boulevardier and swordsman, was seen entering the apartment of Mademoiselle Allzaneau at about 11:30 P.M., apparently having returned with mademoiselle from the theater. When I quit my post at sunrise, he had not yet left."

"Idiot!" snapped Pierre, relishing the jest. "You slept on post."

"The devil I did; I watched most vigilantly."

"Well, since you must know it all, the apartment of Mademoiselle Allzaneau has an exit on 43 rue des Faures, the alley which parallels rue Lachepaillet. Now, are you ashamed of your base insinuations?"

I was properly squelched. Later, I checked up on rue des Faures and verified his claim. But what in all creation had Pierre been doing in the company of La Belle Allzaneau? A man of his age! Though I could well conceive that any lady of the world could take pride in being seen with Pierre d'Artois, that fine, courtly old master of the sword.

What a mess! Not a trace of connection between any of the diverse elements that danced before my eyes: a marquis, a mummy he had stolen, her still missing case; a duel, fought two years ago at St. Leon, and a *lorette* with Babylonic eyes…yes, and the lady of the portrait at the château, the double, the deceased original whose reincarnation La Belle Allzaneau seemed to be. Too much for me.

But one does not question d'Artois to any purpose.

A week, as I said, had passed: uneventful espionage. And then, just as I was to leave Pierre's house to resume my vigil, he detained me.

"A moment, *mon vieux*. I have again the hunch. It will happen tonight."

"What, for the Lord's sake, will happen? The mummy seek her case, or you elope with Lili? Or challenge your rival the marquis?"

"Anything is more than likely to happen tonight. I hear that Monsieur the Marquis has gone to Spain. And Mademoiselle Allzaneau will receive no visitors this evening, not even me. And so on… I have the hunch, as you so elegantly put it, the hell will be popping tonight."

"Well, where do I come in?"

"You? You shall follow her should she leave her apartment; follow her, and see it to a finish, whatever it be. It may be to a strange place, *mon vieux*; therefore take these with you."

He passed me a Luger automatic, a blackjack, and what appeared to be a left-handed, fingerless, mailed glove; strangely like a Roman cestus, at least as to its obvious purpose.

"Looks like trouble, Pierre," I remarked, as I strapped the Luger and its holster under my left arm. "But why this glove?…and…what the devil! A peacock decorating it!"

"Yes. It may serve you well. If you are accosted, exhibit the peacock, and you will be passed on without question."

"Lay off, Pierre, lay off! Have you a dime novel complex?"

"*Mais non*. Do not laugh. You may have no occasion to try it. But remember the peacock. A full moon will make your task easier, or more difficult…that depends… As for me…we may meet unexpectedly. But if not, see it to a finish, and do not fail me."

With this command firmly impressed upon me, I took my post, wondering at the assortment of junk which he had forced upon me. A Luger…well, that was sound judgment; a pistol is an excellent playmate. And a blackjack could conceivably come in handy. But that fingerless glove with its peacock!

* * * *

Nearly midnight. Not a car in front of her apartment all evening. La Belle Al-lzaneau evidently was carrying on reverie and not riot during the absence of her lover in Spain.

A copper kettle of a moon was rising.

"Do not fail me. Follow her and use your judgment."

Well, and into what sort of mess would Pierre be venturing in the meanwhile? Rich entertainment somewhere for someone.

Lord, what a sleepy night! Silence along rue Lachepaillet, and more silence in the park beneath me, beyond the dry moat that girdled the walls. The night before Christmas was fairly spiked to the mast for pure stillness.

Follow Lili…where? Why the pistol, the blackjack, the ornamental brass knuckles?…brass, the devil! I'd have sworn they were gold…or perhaps it was the moonlight.

A light in Lili's window, just for a moment. Then darkness again. And then the door on the *rez-de-chaussée* opened. Lili herself, in a gown of star-dusted, metallic luster stepped into the street, crossed, paused within a meter of my lurking place.

In the entire world had I never seen a woman half as lovely, as perfectly formed, as faultlessly arrayed as she was, from her silver slippers to her dusky hair…great Lord! A peacock tiara, all aflame with small rubies, and emeralds, and sapphires and diamonds glowed in the darkness of her coiffure! It began to seem as though I had but to step forth, show her my brass knuckles and their silver peacock, and claim her as a partner in whatever devil's dance was in store for us.

"Follow her, and use your judgment."

No, better not accost her; else he'd have said, "Accompany her."

All this in an instant; then she turned to a low, narrow entrance directly beneath my position on the parapet, and vanished into its opening.

Now what on earth was that faultlessly gowned girl doing in an ancient powder magazine or storeroom which used to serve the garrison in days past? I'd prowled around in many of them; all were crowded with rubbish, and filth, and the dust of centuries.

Now when should I begin to trail her? If immediately, I should betray my presence; if I paused, I'd lose the trail. And then I became aware of the aura of perfume she had left behind her, a rich, heavy, arabesque fragrance. The very scent a sample of which Pierre had let me smell the other evening. Now, by the rod, I could trail that persistent, curious perfume anywhere… So, after a pause of a few more moments, I leaped from the parapet and plunged into the magazine.

"Plunged" is the right word, though I didn't begin plunging until my third step into the darkness, when I stepped into vacancy. I came to a stop at a landing, ten steps down. With belated good judgment, I sized things up with my electric torch. More steps, steep, narrow, rubbish-laden, leading to abysmal blackness far below. And in darkness I edged my way down. The haunting, persistent fragrance of La Belle Allzaneau led me on.

I paused at the foot of the last flight. My feet were on sandy bottom. I listened, but heard nothing save the breathing of that fierce silence. And from the subterranean mustiness came the perfume of Lili, reaching from the blackness to enfold me. She had been there, and had not branched off into any lateral passages on her way down.

Luger in one hand, torch in the other, I stabbed the gloom. Vacancy. I was alone in that ancient vault, alone with the perfume of a girl who wore a jeweled peacock in her hair.

There were tiny footprints on the sand. And then I noted a low archway, an exit, which, being on the shadowed side of a bastion, had not had its presence betrayed by the entrance of outer moonlight. Lili had left the vault, whose bottom was on a level with the bottom of the dry moat; had left the enclosure of Bayonne, and was without the walls, somewhere.

Then I picked up the trail, tiny footprints in the sand. She had kept close to the wall, heading along toward Porte d'Espagne. But I knew she would not pass that point: for no woman would ruin her footgear in the slime and mud of the moat bottom past the Gate of Spain, the result of seepage from the locks of the Adour.

Beneath the drawbridge of Porte d'Espagne, I picked a lingering trace of perfume; and likewise her footprints, which for several paces I had lost. She had edged away from the wall, crossed the moat, ascended the steep bank.

Her destination? Logically, any place; she had choice of the whole countryside. Nor could I trail her any farther. Tracking in sand is the limit of my skill.

I took stock of my surroundings. If she continued in a straight line…

Hell's hinges! She was bound for the Spring of St. Leon, that unsavory spot where d'Artois, in his moment of victory over Santiago, had been struck from the rear.

Conceivably she might be keeping a rendezvous with the marquis, or more likely, some other lover. And we had seen her there a week ago, at sunset.

Things seemed to be pulling together, but leaving me still confused. The girl had some connection with this spot where Santiago, armed with a sword whose pommel was adorned with a peacock, had met d'Artois. The marquis had a similar sword; and the marquis was the girl's lover. And the girl was the living image of the former mistress of the marquis. She wore a peacock in her coiffure, and I wore one on my left hand. Well, what of it? Something, yes; but what?

A sequin glistened on the ground. In the stillness of the clearing, the heavy air still bore a trace of her perfume. But she was nowhere in sight.

I sized up the ground near the spring. There, in that small, flat space, Pierre and Santiago had crossed swords. There was the rock on which he had laid his hat and coat. Here he had taken his position, sword in hand, on guard…

I whirled in my tracks. Pure nervousness; a reflex occasioned by the memory of that something which had struck d'Artois from the rear. There, in the shadow of a small knoll, was the entrance to a casemate, seemingly at least. Another sequin gleamed on the ground. On her way, she had severed a thread of her gown, and was now shedding sequins every few paces. With her short start, she could scarcely have left my range of vision, unless she were deliberately hiding. Then…logically, she had entered the casemate; had at least paused at its entrance, as the sequin dropped from her gown indicated.

Without any excessive eagerness or exultation, I entered the casemate. Darkness, absolute. But a trace of her perfume! I smelled not only perfume, but trouble; here, for a fact, I was really getting into something.

A few steps, feeling my way in the dark. I dared not risk the torch. Ahead of me, apparently around a curve, was a faint glow, as of a dim light still farther beyond, a shadowy reflex of a half-concealed illuminant; so dim that I had not perceived it for a moment. Well…

"Halt!" snapped a voice.

The flare of an electric torch smote me full in the face, blinding me. But before I could draw the Luger…

"You are late," continued the voice, "and I doubt that the master will receive you in that garb…"

"Never mind my clothes," I temporized, catching my wits and also a glimpse of my accoster, now that the ray had left my face. "Has the lady of the peacock —?"

I touched my forehead with my left hand, a more instinctive than deliberate gesture to indicate Lili's coiffure. As I lowered my hand, the watcher bowed low, kissing the peacock's figure.

That was an excellent little blackjack I wielded with my right, smacking neatly across the inclined head of the warder.

"Well, and if the master is particular about costumes, perhaps this will answer."

After stripping the hood and cape from the sentry, I bound and gagged him, arranged him snugly against and parallel to the wall, and continued my way down the passage; down, literally, as it inclined at a rather quick slope, curving ever to the right, so that it led back toward the citadel of Bayonne, and far beneath its foundations. At regular intervals, candles cast a dim light.

I had noted the swarthy, foreign features of the warder I had blackjacked, and wondered still more. Almost anything was likely to happen…and where was Pierre?

Then came steps, winding, circular steps, leading to the very heart of the earth. Chilly dampness had displaced the outer warmth. To what strange festival was that girl bound? And what was that peacock which had such talismanic effect on the warder? Who the master? And why the costume?

At the foot of the winding stairs I found a twisting passage, this time level. Turns…more turns…a murmur of voices, chanting sonorously…and then…

A heavy iron grillwork, a gate, barred my progress. I flattened myself close against the door jamb, peering through the bars at a unique sight. Before me, at the end of the passage, was a great vaulted chamber, illumined with a deep red glow. As much of the walls as I could see was covered with black arras, figured grotesquely in silver embroidery, monstrous designs of intertwining forms and unheard-of creatures alternating with medallions inscribed in characters resembling Arabic. At the far end of the vault was an altar, behind which stood the enshrined image of a great peacock, his painted fan fully spread, and enameled in naturalistic colors. A bronze railing rose waist-high before the altar; and from a cleft in the platform between the railing and altar, two great black hands, palms uplifted, reached forth.

Kneeling on the floor in crescent formation were a dozen robed and hooded figures, worshipers at the peacock's shrine. The chanting had ceased; and from the group rose one who advanced to the altar steps, facing the image, extended

27

his arms, and began the recital of a ritual. At times he paused for the response of the communicants; resumed his chant, ceasing again to make gestures and genuflections. But not a word of it could I understand; neither of the priest, nor of the worshipers.

Well, and where was La Belle Allzaneau, she who wore on her forehead the unusual symbol, which seemed to be the key to this secret place into which I had wandered? And Pierre? Certainly he had not sent me on into this place and stayed off the scene himself; or had he miscalculated, sending me to real action instead of reserving it for himself?... And thus I wondered, wondered at the scene, at the rites, at the unholy tapestry of the walls, and the cornices which depicted in sculptured panorama the unsavory themes of Asian mysteries...the predecessors of the peacock.

Pierre?... No, Pierre could not have miscalculated so far as to send me into the midst of things and follow a false lead himself...great Lord, could it be Pierre who conducted the ritual? Absurd; but the audacity of the man knew no limits

On and on rolled the rich, resonant voice of the priest. Acolytes marched about the crescent of kneeling communicants, swinging censers and chanting; retired, grouped themselves about the altar. And then...

The priest turned to face the congregation. Not Pierre, but Etienne, Marquis de la Tour de Maracq! He who had stolen the mummy of a princess; he who lived surrounded by death's symbols, a servant of polycephalous idols, he who studied an obscure book bound in human hide, found time also to act as high priest of the silver peacock.

A sweeping gesture; another sonorous phrase; and the assemblage rose, bowed, backed out of the vault, toward the iron grating through which I peered.

I shrank back against the wall, becoming a shadow among the shadows, and waited for the grill to swing open and let the worshipers enter the passage so that, emerging from my angle, I could mingle with them, one of them, disguised in my hood and mask, and guarded by the peacock on my wrist. And once they had passed on, I could return.

And then I remembered the warder I had bound and gagged. Would they notice him lying in the shadows? Should I hasten on ahead of them, conceal the sentry outside the passage, and thus avoid the alarm caused by his discovery? Damn that sentry! Why had I left him where he dropped?

The door clicked. Too late to run on ahead to clear the way. The cloaked worshipers crowded even into my corner in that narrow passage, not even noticing me. One, however, seemed to mistake me for a comrade who had knelt beside him, and had left at his elbow.

"The master seemed hasty tonight, don't you think, Raoul?"

I shrugged my shoulders, mumbled a phrase in Tagalog. The ruse served well. Evidently men of all languages met there.

"Oh, pardon, Monsieur..."

And he went on through the passage in search of his comrade.

I mingled with the dozen who were leaving, contriving to fall back un-obtrusively, thus avoiding the appearance of lingering in a place from which all were departing. And as the tail of the file of hooded men rounded the first turn, I dropped back and resumed my post at one side of the grill, deep in the shadows, seeing, but unseen.

The marquis descended from the altar steps, halted in the center of the vault; stroked his black mustache; frowned... Three swift steps to his left brought him to the heavy black arras, which he parted.

"They have gone, *chérie*."

And from behind the embroidered hangings came La Belle Allzaneau, white arms and shoulders and iridescent gown agleam under that deep, lurid light.

"Etienne, I'm somewhat disappointed... I had expected—"

"To see something grotesque and awful, and outlandish? *Ma chère*, those whom you saw were neophytes, and the rites of the innermost shrine are not for their eyes," explained the marquis as he again parted the arras and drew from behind it a low table laden with refreshments.

He then drew up a chaise longue among whose cushions the girl enthroned herself. The marquis took his place opposite her, and facing me, so that while I could look him full in the eye, I could see but the profile of La Belle Allzaneau, Lili of Lachepaillet, the *lorette* who had the manner of a queen.

"No, petite," continued the marquis, "those were neophytes. But to you I shall reveal—"

"Yet am I not even more of a neophyte?" interrupted the girl as she selected a wafer from the tray before her.

"Nevertheless, I shall reveal to you, as I promised, the innermost secrets; you shall enter the adytum, the awful holy of holies."

"But, Etienne, you must explain. Who is this peacock, and what is his significance?"

Who, indeed, was the peacock? I forgot, for the moment, that the bound and gagged sentry might be discovered by the departing communicants, thus betraying the fact that someone had intruded. Still, it had taken me ten minutes to enter; and they, going upgrade, up flights of steps, would require more time. And should they return, they would search each passageway, taking their time, in all thoroughness, probably twenty minutes or half an hour.

Well then, and what was that glittering bird whose image had caused the warder to bow and kiss my left hand?

"The peacock," explained the marquis, answering the girl, as well as myself "is the symbol of him we serve: Malik Taûs, which in the Persian signifies 'Lord Peacock'."

"Which explains exactly nothing, Etienne!"

"Malik Taûs," he repeated, as one who humors a captivating but unruly child, "is none other than he whom they call Ahriman... Lucifer, the Morning Star... Satan, the outlaw, he whom we, the rebels, the battered but unvanquished ones serve. Now do you understand?"

Eavesdropping on devil-worship! What next?

And La Belle Allzaneau smiled her slow, enigmatic smile, unterrified at that which made me shudder.

Thus, as they ate and drank, the marquis explained the monstrous scenes depicted on the cornices, Oriental perversions antedating Malik Taûs, the girl interrupting from time to time. I watched, and wondered.

Very curious it was that their voices seemed to come from my right clearly, but as from a greater distance than the speakers seemed to be. It was as if I were watching some phantasmagoria. Her voice I heard as her lips parted; but it seemed to come not from her lips, but from my right.

And then it struck me as odd that they both were left-handed. Both ate left-handed, picked up their goblets with their left hands. The marquis, striking a match, struck it with his left. Was this left-handedness another manifestation of the rites of Malik Taûs, or was it but coincidence that both the girl and her host were left-handed?

"This is an ancient shrine," continued the marquis, his voice clear, but coming not from in front of me, down a long, narrow passage, but seemingly from my right. "This is an ancient shrine in which Mithra was worshiped by Roman legionaries; and renegade Moslems and those who followed the Moorish forces into Spain bowed here before Tanit, and Istar, Mylitta, and Anaïtis, all of whom are one, one goddess who came out of Egypt... Isis, the Great Goddess..."

I listened, fascinated by the rich voice of that strange, dark man; nor wondered that the girl was ensnared by his pagan chant, his intoned syllables which sang of monstrous rites and unheard-of lore. I forgot, remembered, and straightway dismissed the thought of the possible return of the departed neophytes. My Luger would serve me well, if necessary; and hand to hand, the brass knuckles.

As the marquis smoked and drank, and expounded, I saw that his gaze went past the girl, seeming to seek me in my alcove of blackness. But no, surely he could not see me, where I crouched in darkness. He frowned passingly, shook his head, made a fleeting gesture of annoyance, as of one who is irritated by the buzzing of a mosquito. Then, continuing his speech, he reached again behind the arras.

I heard a click, and at the same time a faint, droning, humming sound. For a moment the lights dimmed. And then, suddenly, I awoke to the significance of that which had occurred. In the darkness I saw very distinctly a bluish violet glow, an aureole which surrounded each of the bars of the gates before me. That click had been the sound of a latch slipping into place; and that glow was the leakage into the air of a high tension electrical current.

Hell's bells! Had he seen me? Did he know of my presence? Or...perhaps... most likely it was that he suspected the presence of some loitering neophyte, some eavesdropper who had paused, and who would, as he leaned against the grillage, be seared and scorched lifeless by the flaming death that lurked in that ironwork. My advance was barred beyond all hope.

Well, I could watch; and in case of a pinch, a shot from my Luger would reach down the passage. For I felt sure that the marquis designed some outlandish deed; not only the words of Pierre, but the atmosphere of the place, the very expression of the man himself so worked on my nerves that I sensed the presence of something hideous and unheard of. That lurid light, that glittering peacock, those black hands upraised toward the altar, and the hypnotic words and chanting tones of the marquis... I shuddered. It is not pleasant to consider shooting an unarmed man from ambush, but...as these French put it, *que voulez-vous*?

"Without evil, there could be no good," continued the sonorous rhythm of the marquis. "They are extremes of the same essence, even as heat and cold are of the same nature. And to serve the Lord of Evil (if evil indeed there is) is to pay a just tribute to him without whom there could be none of the so-called good, if good indeed there is. Thus in time to come, when Malik Taûs spreads his painted fan over all the earth, we who now serve him shall be princes and lords, and shall inherit the world. Look!" he commanded, his voice rising imperiously as he pointed to the shrine; "look and see his thousand eyes that watch over us!"

The girl turned, following with her eyes his compelling gesture. And in that instant the marquis, never pausing in his speech, dropped into her wine a tiny pellet.

The man was mad with a fearful, unspeakable madness. And here I was, barred from preventing what I now sensed to be impending, a sequel to the preliminary rites I had witnessed, a manifestation of demonolatry in which none but the high priest would officiate.

"Those black hands? They are the hands of Abbadon, the Dark Angel who serves Malik Taûs; and on them we lay that which we dedicate to the Lord Peacock," explained the marquis.

I loosened the Luger in its holster. At times one must shoot from ambush...but not yet.

"And so you are the only adept, Etienne?" queried the girl, resuming her wine.

"There was another, but he is dead. Through my fault. Don Santiago de las Torres Negras."

Lord, what a revelation! Here, in this awful place, I was about to learn another side of that uncanny duel fought by Pierre d'Artois at midnight, at the Spring of St. Leon.

"He challenged one Pierre d'Artois," continued the marquis, "to fight in secret, at midnight, at the Spring of St. Leon. And the Master forbade—"

"And why did you forbid, Etienne?"

"I didn't. No. The Master of Masters..." The marquis lowered his voice. "A stranger out of Kurdistan, one whom I recognized as a master of adepts, by the signs he gave...*the Master*, I now believe... Malik Taûs himself, the Lord Peacock incarnate as man! He forbade the duel. I feared for Santiago, and wished to prevent it, out of deference to the Master's wishes, and from fear of d'Artois, a swordsman without like or equal. So I invited Santiago to a château across the border, in Spain, set back all the clocks, sought to divert him, deceive him until, when at last he did sense my device, it would be too late for him to keep his rendezvous. Rob him of his honor, yes; make him fail in his word, yes; but I sought to spare him that meeting with d'Artois, and from the vengeance of the Master."

"And did you succeed?"

"No. Santiago detected the trick before it was absolutely too late, leaped into his car, and drove fiercely into the night, with still a chance to keep his word inviolate."

"So he fell in the duel?"

The marquis winced.

"No, *chérie*. He never reached the rendezvous. A storm arose; and he skidded on a dangerous turn, doubly dangerous on account of the rain. The wrecked car crushed the life out of him. Had I but let him go, he might have won; or at least died like a man...thus I killed Santiago, my friend... And this stranger from Kurdistan may have been an impostor, a fraud… Imbecile! I believed him to be the Lord Peacock incarnate!"

Christ, what a tale! Was it then the Kurdish stranger whom d'Artois had met, and almost vanquished? The devil who had inspired the marquis to meddle, and caused the death of Santiago on that lonely road from Spain? My brain reeled with the madness of it all…

And then I raised my eyes again to regard that marquis who chanted sonorously to that lovely girl, serene and calm, reclining among silken cushions in the Adytum of Darkness, in the very shrine of the Oriflamme of Iniquity, face to face with its high priest…and this without changing expression, save to shake her patrician head in pity…what a woman!

Had they discovered the gagged warder? Were they returning? I was in a devilish mess, literally. Devils on all sides, and in an atmosphere of demonolatry.

The girl nodded…sank back among the emblazoned cushions. Drugged. Inert. The tiny pill had done its work.

The marquis rose, thrust the table behind the arras; listened to the breathing of the sleeping madonna; straightened himself to his full height. Madness and despair flamed in his sombre eyes; his lips drooped; his lean cheeks were drawn. The muscles at the point of his jaw were knotted and quivering. If not the devil, then was this marquis his double: Satan overcome with sorrow, but unrelenting.

What now? Madness was his. But what form would it assume?

With swift, sure fingers he removed the silver slippers of La Belle Allzaneau; stripped from her the glittering, iridescent gown; and then the tenuous silk which clung to her form.

Cristo del Grao! What had that madman in mind?

And then he lifted her bodily from the chaise longue, strode up the cinnabar-strewn pathway toward the shrine, ascended the altar steps, and placed his burden upon the upraised, black palms of those great hands that reached for their prey.

Turning from the altar, he took a small mallet and struck a gong whose thin note shivered and hissed, with a rustling, lingering vibration, chilling, sighing, not full-throated as bronze should be. And from panels on either flank of the altar emerged those same hooded, sheeted figures that had passed me a short time ago, filed now to their places and knelt before the shrine, a vermilion crescent of demonolaters bowing before their chief and their god.

One of the number, after his salaam, arose and advanced to the altar steps, leaned over the brazen railing, and with a stick of rouge marked on the side of the unconscious girl; then a mark on her breast; and then on her forehead a mark. At the same time, coming from the right, just beyond my angle of vision, were four who pushed forward on rollers a massive stone trough; a trough over whose sides slopped some of the liquid it contained. Trough? No trough at all, but a sarcophagus, chiseled with Egyptian hieroglyphics! And as if by symmetry, there came from the left four others, each pair of whom bore a mummy case. These cases were placed on either side of the altar, standing upright. One, the mummy case of a man; the other, of a woman. This I knew from their sizes, and from the gilded masks which depicted the features of the deceased.

The case of the man seemed heavy. But those who carried the case of the woman bore it as though it were empty. And I wondered if indeed that could be the case we sought; Pierre and I.

The hooded figures, after putting their burdens into position, resumed their places in the crescent of devotees, leaving the marquis alone on the altar steps, facing the shrine.

Well, and at least I need fear no attack; for those who had passed me at the gate had but doubled back and waited behind the scenes for their signal to reappear. It had all been stage-setting. And it all apparently amounted to nothing more than an initiation of the girl into the secret order of demonolatry.

I relaxed and let the Luger sink into its holster.

And then I noticed what under normal circumstances I would have noted immediately; the solution of that which made both the marquis and the girl seem left-handed, and that which made the voices seem to come from my right, instead of from directly in front of me. I was looking into a mirror, into one, or three, or some odd number of mirrors which caused a reversal of left and right. Had I not shrunk back into my corner, against the door jamb, I would have noted that those who filed past me had not come directly toward me, but rather from one side. I could now distinguish my image before me, very faint, almost imperceptible, yet there, nevertheless.

So! And here I was to witness an initiation into the inner circle of demonolatry. My fears for the girl had been panic, and nerves, almost hysteria. And the mummy case, the smaller one, was doubtless that which Pierre sought.

But where was Pierre? No matter. In the morning we would return and loot the place...

The marquis, after bowing before the shrine of the peacock, extended his arms, chanted in a tongue unknown to me. Then, after tossing incense into the brazier on the altar, he began anew, this time in French.

"Malik Taûs, Standard-bearer of Iniquity, Lord of the Outer Marches, Prince of the Borderland, thee we revere, and before thee we bow! Hear then our prayer, Malik Taûs, Thousand-eyed Lord Peacock, Sovereign Rebel, Dark Prince! To thee we consecrate this sacrifice on behalf of Santiago who defied thee; and for him we crave pardon and peace, for him across the Border we raise our prayer!"

"Amin!" intoned the congregation, bowing their heads to the floor. "So be it!"

A pause. And again the marquis raised his voice.

"Santiago, Santiago my friend, whose death I caused, concede to me your pardon, and accept from me our prayer! I who sent you to your death, and these my servants alike seek to make atonement!"

"Amin!"

"And this woman without like or equal, I offer to you, Santiago; and to you I consecrate her, to be yours until the end of time. Santiago, you whom I sent to your death, accept her who is the very image and likeness of her I loved very long ago; accept as my peace offering this wondrous one who is my lost one incarnate. Santiago, in the name of Thousand-eyed Malik Taûs, I offer to you this woman whom I shall embalm in rich spices and wind in linen, and encase in sycamore and enshrine beside you to be yours for ever and ever!"

"Amin!"

Lord God! A poniard gleamed in his upraised hand. I drew and leveled the Luger...remembered I looked into a mirror...dropped my eyes, sick with horror...

A blinding, awful incandescence flared about me, illuminating that vault with the blue-white flame of noonday sun...a muffled, choked report...the mirror before me was clouded. A dense mist fogged the air. Hooded figures rushed to and fro, confused, colliding with each other, clawing and rubbing their eyes, blinded by that devastating flame.

And among them strode one not hooded, who moved with sure, swift certitude. Pierre d'Artois, wielding a blackjack! Each swing brought down a hooded figure; down they went before those cool, deliberately placed strokes...one stroke, one man...the cruel precision of machinery...the last man had taken the count. Pierre stepped to the wall, reached behind the arras; withdrew his hand, snatched from the wall an antique battle-ax, and dashed down the passage toward me.

"Don't touch that grill!" I shouted.

"The juice, he is turned off."

And to prove it, Pierre assaulted that grillwork with his massive ax, smiting fiercely, bending and deforming the sturdy bars. I crawled through, followed him back to the Adytum of Darkness.

"Take the girl," he commanded, as, true to his nature, and never forgetting his mission, he seized the mummy case, the one designed for a woman, and led the way to the exit.

As I leaped to the altar railing, lifted the still unconscious girl from the black hands, and wrapped her in my cape, I noted that the other mummy case was empty, and that its cover had been kicked aside.

One or two devil-worshipers stirred and twitched. Others groaned. Striding over that miniature battlefield, I followed in Pierre's trace. And we made good time, Pierre and I, for the devil, though down for the count of ten, still lurked in that awful vault.

No one accosted us as Pierre led the way across the park to his car. What a pair we were: a vermilion-robed figure embracing a mummy case, and I, likewise robed, bearing in my arms a girl whose hair streamed to the ground, whose limbs gleamed brightly in the moonlight.

* * * *

Well, the madman's jubilee ended in Pierre's apartment.

Lili, quite calm and magnificent in Pierre's silken lounge robe, sipped a bit of cognac and took the entire affair as a matter of course, though she did have certain regrets.

"Those lovely shoes! Monsieur Landon, perhaps you would return for them?" she mocked.

And then, to Pierre, "Do tell me what it all was about."

"*Chère petite*, it is a very long story. The stolen mummy would not interest you, directly; but my search for Madame the Princess and—what you call in English, her wooden negligee, *n'est-ce pas*?—her sycamore case is what made me cross your trail. *Voyez!*"

Pierre showed us a photograph.

"This, Mademoiselle, does it not resemble you?"

"Quelle bêtise!" flared Lili. "What a notion!"

And then she admitted the resemblance, acknowledged that that face of gilded sycamore, carved 3700 years ago, might pass as an Egyptianesque version of her own loveliness.

"So? It does resemble, yes? And the painting in the château, that of the mistress he adored twenty years ago, that could be your portrait of today, were not the lady's costume a shade out of date. Behold the succession of resemblances, partly real, partly fancied. That I noted, immediately. And moreover, I saw, as did you, *mon ami*, that book bound in human hide; but unlike you, I read therefrom, many strange things. Then those drums whose heads were of human hide, and the arms, and all the other trophies of death…death…death which has haunted Monsieur the Marquis, turned his brilliant mind, and made him do this madness which we witnessed.

"And the duel at St. Leon, two years ago. I knew that Don Santiago was the good friend of Monsieur the Marquis; and I knew also that there had been something very odd about that midnight meeting. Thus when I saw you, Mademoiselle, all so lovely in the sunset, I added the two and the two; by intuition. Very simple, *n'est-ce pas*?

"And this Santiago," continued the old man, "wore on the pommel of his sword a peacock; as also did Monsieur the Marquis on that sword at his château. None of which really proved anything; however, I began to think. Thus it was but a matter of having you watched, Mademoiselle, until things happened.

"And while you watched, *mon vieux*, I prowled around, and found the plans of Vauban's fortifications and engineering works, and saw that he had not built the passage leading to St. Leon. And as for last night, I attended the preliminary rites, having, as you so nicely put it, beaned one of the worshipers and assumed his costume."

"What the devil! You joined in their ceremonies?"

"Yes. It was I who spoke to you; but you did not take the tumble, so you missed some rare sport. I had but to put myself into the case which had contained the embalmed body of my ancient enemy, Santiago. And thus they carried me into position at the altar. Then, at the crucial moment, I kicked off the cover, and fired a press photographer's flashlight gun. Dazzled by that fearful light, they could see nothing. As for me, I closed my eyes as I fired, and then, after the flash…"

He affectionately caressed the blackjack.

"And with this wonderful little implement, I worked them over, as you might say it, while they still blinked and rubbed their eyes, utterly blinded by that sudden flare."

"He really was going to kill me?" queried the queen of Lachepaillet, who had scarcely grasped the entire sequence of events, and their significance.

"Exactly that, *chère petite*. In his way, he loved you, for yourself, and for the sake of his departed sweetheart; and therefore he was to sacrifice you, and embalm you, and set you up in state, in the mummy case of a princess, thus performing the supreme penance, making his peace with the Lord Peacock, and with

Santiago alike. An artistic soul, Monsieur the Marquis! He is leaving for Spain… unless unhappily I struck him too hard! But he will not annoy you again."

"These uncanny resemblances, Monsieur d'Artois…it is all so fantastic," suggested Lili. "I resemble his former mistress, and I resemble a mummy. Am I then a mere shadow?"

"That is really not so incredible. For you, Mademoiselle, are the niece of her whom Monsieur the Marquis loved twenty years ago; so that that resemblance is not at all a subject of wonder, even if extraordinary. This, however, he did not know, nor I either, until I investigated—nor did you know. As for the mummy, well, coincidence…and a stretch of fancy."

"But your duel, Pierre, at St. Leon?"

"Who knows? Illusion…a stranger from Kurdistan… I attempt no explanation. Santiago is dead, even as may be the marquis and some of his followers; but the Stranger still lives, and the Peacock's shadow still hangs over us."

THE BRIDE OF THE PEACOCK

Originally published in *Weird Tales*, August 1932.

"Mademoiselle," said Pierre d'Artois after a moment's reflection, "there is really no reason for your being alarmed at repeatedly dreaming that you are opening a grave. After all, a dream…"

"Monsieur," she demanded, "does one in a dream break one's fingernails? Just look!"

She thrust her hands, fingers extended, squarely before our eyes. The nails were ragged and broken, and beneath them was a distinct trace of verdigris.

"I left them just as they were this morning, verdigris and all, to show you how I've been pawing at that door again. My new slippers and gown were torn, and soiled with green mold from kneeling before it. It's driving me mad!"

In her eyes was a terrible, haunted look that made them a star-less, somber midnight.

Pierre d'Artois studied first the slim white fingers with their marred nails, and then the dark, surpassing loveliness of Diane Livaudais. "But where do you walk?"

She shrugged her faultless shoulders, and made a despairing gesture of the hand.

"If I only knew! But I don't. First there was someone talking to me in my sleep. Though I couldn't ever recollect, exactly, what the voice said to me, I always had the impression when I awoke that there was a grave that I was to open. And somehow I felt that it was Etienne who called me. You know, Monsieur d'Artois. I was very fond of Etienne, and living in that house he gave me, it was only natural that I'd have him on my mind."

"When," queried Pierre, "did Etienne give you that house on Rue Lachepaillet?"

"It's over two years ago. 1928. Several months after he disappeared, I received a letter from him, from Marrakesh, saying that he was seriously wounded, and that if he died, he wanted me to live in his house on Rue Lachepaillet. Then, a month or so later, I learned that he was dead. Just a clipping from a paper in Marrakesh—a French newspaper, you understand—and a note in Arabic, which I had Doctor Delaronde translate. It confirmed the clipping, saying that Etienne's last words had been that he wanted me to have his house in Bayonne and the personal effects in it.

"So," she continued, "living in that legacy, and missing him terribly, I would easily dream of him, and wake with the sense of having heard his voice. I felt his presence, as though he were seeking to speak some final thought that his friend had not included in that scrap of Arabic script."

"By the way, have you those bits of paper?"

And then, as Mademoiselle Livaudais took them from her handbag, d'Artois continued, "The voice became more insistent?"

"Yes. Though it wasn't really a voice. I would awake with the feeling that someone had given an order. An overpowering will forcing me to some vague task I couldn't quite remember except for somehow associating it always with a grave. A task I couldn't accomplish and couldn't evade."

"And always Etienne's presence?"

"Yes and no," she answered. "I don't know. An oppressing confusion. A dominant, crushing will. Not like Etienne at all. He was domineering—you may have known him—but not in that remorseless way. He loved me. Almost as much as I loved him. But this is relentless, inhuman. Yet I sense Etienne in it.

"And..." She again extended her fingers. "This proves that just last night I was trying to open the door of a vault. As on so many other nights. Gown tattered. Slippers soiled. Verdigris under my nails. I'm weary. Weary to death."

"You should have seen me sooner."

"It was so outrageous. So I kept it to myself. But now I want you to find out where I am going, and why, before I lose my mind entirely."

Pierre rose and from a drawer in his desk took a tiny vial, a part of whose amber-colored contents he poured into a small, stemmed glass.

"Drink," he suggested. "It is a sedative. It will make you relax. You must relax. Look me full in the eye...better yet, look intently at the ring on my finger... then think of nothing at all..."

I noted then that Pierre had seated his visitor so that she faced a strong, glaring light.

"You are weary from trying to remember... Cease trying, and it will come to you..."

Pierre's voice was droning monotonously. "Don't try to remember...you are weary...weary...weary of trying...think of nothing...nothing...nothing at all," he persisted in soporific accents.

Her eyes were staring fixedly at the stone that flamed and pulsed dazzlingly on Pierre's hand. I'd never known Pierre to wear a diamond of any kind, much less that obtrusive, massive clot of fire.

Her lips half parted, and her breath came very slowly and rhythmically in cadence to Pierre's measured, purring syllables.

She was in a trance, induced by a drop of a hypnotic, and Pierre's compelling will.

Again he spoke, still with that murmuring monotony. "You are sleeping... soundly...deeply...so deeply that you won't waken until I call you... Do you understand?"

"Yes," she murmured, "I won't awaken...until...you call."

Then Pierre spoke in a voice of command. "It is now last night. The voice is speaking. Repeat it to me!"

Pierre leaned forward. His long fingers gripped the carved arms of his chair. Perspiration cropped out on his brow, now cleft with a saber-slash of a frown. Diane stirred uneasily, made a gesture of protest.

"You will speak and tell me. I command and you must obey!" he said solemnly and deeply as the chanted ritual of a high priest.

I myself was ready to leap or yell from the terrific tension that moment by moment had been becoming more and more acute. I sensed a Power that was hammering at Pierre through Diane's resistance.

Then Pierre prevailed. The tension eased. She spoke in painfully clear-cut mechanical syllables: and in *Persian*! Not the colloquial Persian of which I knew a smattering, but the rich language of the old days.

"Now, answer," demanded Pierre, "as you have been answering."

"Etienne," she began in French, but as mechanical as before, "I can't find the spring. But I'll return tomorrow night and try again… I can't understand what you are saying…the drums are too loud, and they don't want me to understand…"

Etienne, Marquis de la Tour de Maracq, not dead in far-off Morocco, in some obscure tomb beyond the red walls of Marrakesh, but buried in one of the crypts that honeycomb the foundations of Bayonne. And she spent her nights answering him, and seeking him.

"But it couldn't be. The dead don't chant from their graves. It must be the hysteria of a woman mourning a dead lover," I insisted to myself as I heard those outrageous words.

And then I looked at Pierre. My insistence mocked me. He trembled violently. His lips moved soundlessly, and he swayed slightly. He was exerting his supreme effort; but not another word could he drag from Diane. Pierre was beaten to a standstill.

He relaxed, and sighed deeply.

"Never to be too much damned *revenant*, I will meet you face-to-face, and you will speak to me!" he exclaimed.

He smiled that grim cold smile I once saw on his face as he crossed blades one unforgotten night with one who on that night ceased to be the most deadly swordsman in France.

Pierre struck his hands sharply together. "Enough! Awaken!" he ordered.

And, as Diane started, and blinked, and looked confusedly about her: "Tell me, *mademoiselle*, do you understand Persian?"

"Of course not," replied Diane. "But why?"

"You spoke Persian when I asked you to repeat…"

"Oh, did I say anything?"

"*Mais, certainement*! I commanded, and you spoke. And half the population of hell's backyard fought to break my control. But you spoke. Listen!"

Pierre repeated Diane's words.

"Did *I* say that?" she demanded incredulously.

"Indeed you did, *mademoiselle*," I assured her.

"Why, whoever heard of such a thing?"

"I, for one," affirmed Pierre. "An illiterate servant girl, delirious from fever, chanted ancient Hebraic, to the mystification of the doctors. It developed, finally, that she had once lived with the family of a German savant, and used to hear him reciting Hebraic texts: and this was impressed upon her subconscious mind, which was released in her delirium.

"Similarly someone has spoken Persian, either to your ear or to your mind at some time. Tell me, did you ever hear this, in any language?"

And Pierre recited:

"When I am dead, open my grave and see
The smoke that curls about thy feet;
In my dead heart the fire still burns for thee:
Yea, the smoke rises from my winding sheet."

Diane shuddered. "Beautiful. But ghastly!"

As for me, I had heard and often admired that macabre Persian conceit. Yet this time an evil lurked in the amorous fancy that Hafiz chanted to some girl in a garden of Shiraz nine hundred years ago.

"And you replied, 'I can't find the spring.' You said that the drums kept you from understanding. You did well to come to me. I will fight this to a finish, *its* or mine."

"Do you really think it's Etienne calling from his grave?"

Diane asked this question in a hesitant voice, abashed at her outlandish query.

"Mademoiselle," replied Pierre, "I am an old man, and I am none too positive about the impossibility of anything. Yet if he is speaking from Satan's throne room I will find him and silence him, for no honest lover would haunt you this way."

Pierre rang for his man, Raoul.

"My good friend, Landon, will join me in this campaign. We will be your guardians. Raoul will drive you home. And this evening we may see you, Landon and I!"

Diane graciously offered her hand. "Monsieur d'Artois, and you, Monsieur Landon, have restored my courage. I feel ever so much better. And do call tonight if you wish. *À bientôt!*"

With a wave of her hand, and a smile for the moment free from the shadow of the grave, she followed Raoul to the Issotta coupe.

"Pierre," I said as the door clicked behind Diane, "when she was in that trance, you might have commanded her to ignore the voice."

"Not at all! That would be like putting a plaster cast over an ulcer. I must rather find and exterminate the cause of this outrageous thing that talks to her and makes her sleep a wandering nightmare. Never think that she told us more than a fraction of what she does and hears and says in her sleep. Something fought me face-to-face as I commanded her to speak: and as she spoke, I suddenly lost control."

"The devil you say! I felt it myself... Do you believe..."

"Anything is possible in Bayonne," replied Pierre. "Anything may thunder and whisper from the ancient night of the passages and labyrinths that undermine Bayonne. Bayonne was founded by the Romans, whose legionaries worshipped Mithra and Cybele in subterranean crypts. The Saracens, the Spanish, the French, the Bearnais have made this the playground of armies, and have enriched the earth with dead. This is all soil well raked over, and alive with strange seeds. Apostate priests have chanted the terrible foulness of the Black Mass, and mediaeval necromancers and thaumaturgists have pursued their crafts in those unremembered red passages and vaults.

"Sometimes the Church hounded them to the surface, and roasted them at the stake, good and evil alike: but more remained intact than ever were unearthed.

"I myself once saw a vault opened up when builders excavated for the foundation of a house, many years ago…"

Pierre shuddered.

"It is not so much what I saw as the inferences I was compelled to draw. Now from behind some brazen gate a Presence commands Diane to enter. Her dead lover calls her to God knows what terrible festival among the dead. Or Something impersonates the dead Marquis, for some purpose beyond imagining, some lingering trace of an ancient force that has come to life and strengthened itself through feeding on her susceptible mind.

"And now please dispense with my company while I study various things. Notably this clipping, and this scrap of a note. Those Partagas cigars are at your elbow, and there is a decanter of Armagnac."

So saying, Pierre left me to my own resources.

I prowled about his study, peering at the titles of books ranged row after row on their shelves; scrutinizing the clustered scimitars, ripple-edged kreeses, keen tulwars, and the sheaves of lances and assegais standing in a corner. And here and there were *epees*, with their bell guards and slim, three-cornered blades: each a trophy of some encounter of Pierre's younger days, when the duel was not the comic opera affair it is today in 193—

Raoul entered, presented Pierre's compliments, and left a tray of cold meats, cheese, and a bottle of thin, dry wine. Strange, how a fellow that keeps such excellent brandy would have such terrible sour wine! But it wasn't so bad…and neither was Bayonne…with a quiet month or so the most of which was to be devoted to acting as Pierre's second in fencing with a dead marquis who declaimed the *Diwan* of Hafiz from his grave in Marrakesh. But I didn't blame the marquis. That girl would make any one turn over in his grave!

And then Pierre reappeared. "I see that you have survived those sandwiches *a l'americain* which Raoul constructed. Good! But I have a task for you."

"Lead on," I replied.

"*Alors*, my good Raoul will drive you to Mademoiselle Diane's house, where you will take your post at the door of her bedroom. You will stand watch, and if she walks in her sleep, follow her, even to the fuming hinges of hell's back door, but by no means wake her. And here," he continued, "is a pistol and a clip of cartridges, and a flashlight."

I thrust the Luger into my hip-pocket, tested the flashlight and found it in good order. "It seems," I commented, "that we are not dealing entirely with dead men muttering in their graves."

"From what I learned—possibly I should say, inferred—while you were absorbing the most of that decanter of Armagnac," replied Pierre, "there is something in what you say. In the meanwhile, keep your mind strictly on your work, and do not be too free with that pistol. I will be on hand later to relive you, and I prefer not to have you riddle me in error."

"Shall we leave the door open?"

"No," answered Pierre, "I have a most accomplished pass key. *A tantot!*"

And Pierre returned to his holy of holies to answer the telephone as I followed Raoul to the Isotta.

"Monsieur Landon," greeted the lovely Livaudais as she admitted me, "you don't know how relieved I am that Monsieur d'Artois has taken things in hand. But what is he doing this evening?"

"Lord alone knows, beyond busily studying that clipping and that note from the marquis' unknown friend in Morocco. And his telephone rang continually. He's hot on the trail of something, or he wouldn't have sent me to stand guard at your door tonight."

"Good God! Am I then in such danger?"

"By no means. I am here merely to follow you if you wander tonight."

"Splendid. Then I shall bid you goodnight. Surely you'll forgive my being such an anything but gracious hostess? You know, it's been a trying day. There on the table is a decanter of Grenache, and cigarettes."

"Perhaps you might show me the switches that control the lights," I suggested. "I prefer to watch in the dark, but I may need light in a hurry."

After showing me the switch, Mademoiselle Livaudais bade me goodnight. I selected the most uncomfortable chair in the living-room: not such a difficult task, with that array of somber teak, carved by artisans who, since they sat cross-legged on the floor, had no conception of comfort as applied to chairs—and set it near the bedroom door. Then I took a length of heavy thread I'd brought for that purpose, and tied one end of it to the doorknob and the other to a heavy bronze ashtray which I set on a chair at the other side of the door. Thus if she opened the door, and caught me napping, the fall of the ashtray would arouse me. Not that I expected to doze; but rather that I didn't want to take any chances.

I settled down to watch. It wasn't like military sentry duty, where a moment of drowsiness might cost the lives of an entire outpost. There was nothing to do but sit there in that exquisitely carved teak straitjacket, with my reflections for company.

And I wasn't the least bit drowsy. My mission effectively prevented that. I wondered if the dead marquis materialized and led her to a hidden panel, or called from the street, or tapped on her window-pane. The whole thing was outrageous: so much so that the marquis murmuring in his grave occupied a much smaller place in my thoughts than this exceedingly lovely Diane.

In fact, I began to think with decided disapproval of the marquis; although, to be honest about it, he was handicapped, in a way.

And thus and thus…

Then I wondered at the sweetness that subtly pervaded the room. Strange I hadn't noticed it before. Well, those Partagas cigars of Pierre's had been heavy enough to dull my sense of smell for a while. Certainly I'd not notice that delicate perfume. Like the ghost of incense. The very ashes of an odor.

I'm sure I wasn't asleep, and hadn't been even for a moment of that watch. And yet as I look back at it all, I couldn't have been awake.

Something was emerging from the darkness of Diane's living room. I sat there, contemplating the shadow that materialized from the shadows, as though of all things in the world there was nothing more commonplace than that the blackness should coalesce into a shape.

I regarded with mild curiosity the silvery gleam that deliberately drew closer. I wondered what mummery was in progress. It might of course be a knife. Perhaps I should really shift a bit to one side, or else it would pin me to the back of my chair. It came nearer…

Then something within me snapped. I knew that I had been sleeping, with my eyes open and fully conscious. With a terrific start I moved, just in time to evade the stroke.

The intruder instinctively sought for an instant to wrench his dagger free from the unyielding hardwood which held it fast: so that I had him well by the throat before he abandoned his weapon and met me hand to hand.

He was lean as a serpent and long-armed as an ape. But I eluded his clutch, and drove a fast one to his jaw that sent him reeling back into the darkness. It shook him. It should have laid him out cold. But he came back for more.

As he recovered and closed in, a fresh poniard in hand, I drew my pistol and fired.

I saw him sag in the middle and crumple, riddled by that hail of lead at close range; saw another shape emerge from the darkness at my left. But before I could shift my fire, there was a heavy impact behind my ear: and then I saw nothing at all save abysmal blackness shot with livid streaks and dazzling flashes.

"Where's Pierre?" was my last thought as I met the floor, still clutching the pistol.

* * * *

I don't know how long I was out. My head was spinning crazily as I opened my eyes and saw Pierre regarding me with mingled solicitude and amusement.

"So," he railed, "I leave you on guard and here I find you, flat on your face. No matter! Your stout skull seems none the worse."

"But what happened to the corpse?" queried d'Artois, as I clambered to my feet and dropped into a chair.

"What corpse?"

He indicated the pistol lying on the floor where it had slipped from my fingers when my grip had relaxed, and pointed at the empty cartridge-cases glittering on the rug.

"Someone…how would you say it?…was polished off. You never miss."

Flattering, but true.

That dark splash that stained the polished hardwood floor at the edge of the rug did indicate some one seriously riddled.

It all came back to me.

"They crept up on me. I was asleep with my eyes open. I came to in the nick of time. And number two slugged me just as I accounted for number one."

I wrenched the poniard from the chair.

"Lucky I snapped out of it," I continued. "Good Lord, but I can't understand how I watched that fellow slip up on me without my moving until it was almost too late. I wonder if it could have been that perfume…"

"What perfume?" queried Pierre.

I sniffed, twice, thrice. "Be damned, Pierre, but it's gone. That must have been it."

But d'Artois was looking at the poniard, and had nothing to say about vanished doors. "*Mais regardez donc*! Here! Take the slant!"

He pointed at the inlay in delicate hair-lines of pale gold that decorated the slim, curved blade.

"Very pretty job of inlaying," I admitted. "Never saw a peacock more beautifully drawn."

"*Imbecile!*" fumed Pierre. "So it's only a pretty bit of engraving to you, this peacock! But it's a wonder Mademoiselle Diane hasn't been disturbed with all the rioting and shooting. Could she have walked out before our very eyes?"

"No. Look at that string knotted to the doorknob and the ashtray. It's not been disturbed. She's still asleep."

"Nevertheless, I must look." Pierre opened the door. "Death and damnation! She's gone!" he exclaimed. "Walked right out before your eyes!"

Gone she was. Not through the door I had watched. And not through the windows, between whose bars nothing larger than a cat could have crept.

"No, and not up the chimney," announced Pierre. "Then where?"

"Through the floor or the wall, perhaps," I hinted.

D'Artois took me at my word. On hands and knees he explored the floor and the tiled hearth, poking and thrusting about with the blade of his penknife, seeking for some trace of a catch or spring which would release a trapdoor or sliding panel. And then he devoted his attention to the paneled walls; but in vain. If there was any secret exit, secret indeed it was.

But Pierre was by no means discouraged. "Let this rest for the moment," he directed, "and we will search the rest of the apartment."

"But," I protested, "that isn't finding Diane."

"Finding Diane," he replied, "may not be the most important thing at present. She has been carrying on her nocturnal wanderings for some time, and from each trip she has returned. It is likely that she will return this time also."

"How about trailing those assassins that nearly polished me off?"

"Eminently sensible," admitted d'Artois. "If we could follow them the trail would doubtless lead to the source of the deviltry. Your letting moonlight through one of them must have been most disconcerting. Look! They left through the door, and none too deliberately."

"But this will have to be investigated by daylight," he continued. "And that would advertise our moves to the enemy. Finally, I suspect that the trail would be lost very soon after it is picked up in the street. Let us rather inspect this house of the dead marquis."

And while Pierre did the serious inspecting, I prowled about, admiring the antique Feraghan carpet that shimmered silkily under my feet, the floor lamp of saw-pierced damascene brasswork, the oddly carved teak statuettes from Tibet, curious bits of jade and lacquer: and on the mantel was a silver peacock with outspread fan.

"Look!" exclaimed Pierre, interrupting my contemplation of the rare and strange adornments of the room. "Behold! Unusual, *n'est-ce pas?*"

I took the book he offered me, thumbed its pages. "What's so unusual about that? Looks like Arabic or Persian... Good God, Pierre, it's bound...damned if it isn't! Human skin!"

"I saw that also. But I referred to the title."

"But that's the back cover."

"*Que voulez-vous?* Where would you have it in such language? But look at the title itself."

"You forget that I can't read this scratching," I reminded Pierre. "Try it yourself."

"*Pardon*! Well then, it is entitled, *Kitab ul Aswad.*"

"Of course. The Black Book. Manifestly appropriate. Title matches the color of the cover. Now this one," I continued, indicating a red-bound American best seller, "should be called *Kitab ul Abbmar.*"

"Idiot!" growled Pierre. "Have you ever heard of *THE* Black Book?"

And to forestall any further irrelevant replies, Pierre opened the book and read aloud in sonorous Arabic:

"Which is to say," he translated, knowing that the old, literary Arabic is too much for any but a scholar, *"God created of fire seven bright spirits, even as a man lights seven tapers one after the other: and the chief of these was Malik Tawus, to whom he gave the dominion of the world and all that therein is: so that God sleeps dreamlessly while his viceroy rules as seemeth good to him."*

"Odd enough," I admitted, "but what of it? Except that the evening is superabundant with peacocks. First they try to ream me out with a blade inlaid with a peacock; and then I stand here, admiring the silver image of a peacock on the mantel, and now you read me of Malik Tawus. Say, now, was that *malik* or *malaak?*"

"Malik," replied Pierre. "Although he has been called *Malaak* as well."

"And you end," I resumed, "by favoring me with a rich passage about the King, Lord, or Angel Peacock, according as the scribe splashed his reed or the tradition garbled the story…"

"I heard something in her room," Pierre interrupted. And Pierre, who had preceded me, halted and whirled to face me at Diane's door. "She has returned. While we babbled of black books."

"Impossible!"

"Then take a look," challenged Pierre.

I looked, and I saw.

Diane lay curled up in her great canopied bed, sound asleep. On her feet were satin boudoir slippers, torn and scarred and soiled.

"She went, and she returned, before our eyes."

And then Diane spoke: but not to us.

"I found the spring, Etienne. But I couldn't move the panel. I'll return tomorrow night…"

"Good Lord, it's got her!"

"Don't wake her," commanded Pierre. "Let her sleep. We've been outmaneuvered. *Alors*, we will retire in confusion, get ourselves some sleep, and tomorrow —we shall see what we shall see."

* * * *

After a later breakfast, Pierre and I drove across the river to the Third Guard's Cemetery, turned back to town and then through the Mousserole Gate, across the

45

drawbridge, and into the hills. D'Artois apparently was idling away his time; but having seen him open and smoke his way through the second pack of Bastos, which smelled no less of burning rags than the first pack, I knew that he was far from loafing. Whenever we passed the obsolete gun emplacements, casemates, or lunettes in the surrounding hills, Pierre would slow up, stare a moment, refer to a sketch, mutter to himself, and step on the gas again.

"Vauban built that...and that also was erected by Vauban..." was the sum of his comments.

We were retracing our course. The jovial, bearded and mitered statue of Cardinal Lavigerie welcomed us to Place de Theatre.

"Doubtless we should pause for a drink."

"The *anis del oso* is not so bad," I seconded.

But in vain.

Pierre drew away from the curb, and thence to the left, skirting the park that lies outside the walls and moat on the side toward the Biarritz road. Again to the left, turning our backs to Biarritz, we headed into Porte d'Espagne and the old guard house, driving across the causeway that at this point blocks the moat.

"Vauban, it seems, built the whole works," I remarked. And then, "Hello! What's this? Stop a moment..."

But d'Artois cleared the breach in the wall, utterly ignoring my desire to pause and look.

And then he spoke: "Jackass! Do you fancy that I didn't see those several men roaming about the green between the edge of the moat and the Spring of St. Leon with surveyor's instruments and the like? And need I impress upon you that they are by no means surveying, and that those instruments are by no means transits and levels? *Alors*, why need we pause and stare at those good men?"

All of which suggested that Pierre knew more about the goings on at the Spring of St. Leon than he cared to publish in the papers.

"Well, perhaps Vauban didn't build the whole works," I began, seeing that surveyors had been definitely dismissed. "I would imagine that we'd find the entrance somewhere near the ancient part of the city, not far from the cathedral. Possibly near that fountain..."

"Erected on the site of the castle of the Hastingues, taken by assault in the Eleventh Century by the Bayonnais," quoted Pierre mockingly from the guide book.

I ignored the jibe, and continued, "And to find it, we'll have to cover the ground stone by stone."

But Pierre was taking no hints that afternoon. "Impossible!" he exclaimed. "It would take weeks. And then we'd be too late."

"Very much what I say, *mon vieux*. In a word..."

Pierre's gesture was painfully expressive.

"Well," said I, "The whole thing sounds like a Chinese dream. All of it."

Un reve chinois, do you say? *Comment*? Was it a Mongolian vision that came so close to pinning you to the back of your chair after you, an old campaigner, went to sleep with your eyes open an hour after taking your post? An Asiatic dream that you shot to ribbons when you awoke from your unaccountable sleep?

We must work fast. And this time there shall be no jugglery of taking her away and returning her under our very eyes."

"What do you propose?"

"We will both stand watch in her room."

"After what happened last night," I objected, "They may get both of us with some devil's trick. Like that whiff of perfume."

"I have considered that," replied d'Artois. "And we will see. There was never a peacock hatched who can twice in the same way outwit Pierre d'Artois. Nor is it likely that the enemy would repeat that same device. They have too many tricks."

* * * *

Raoul admitted us. *"Monsieur,"* he began, "a visitor is waiting for you in the study."

"Magnifique! And is she handsome?"

"Mais, monsieur, he is a foreign dignitary. An emir."

"Then offer him a drink, and assure him that in but one moment I will have the honor of greeting him."

In Pierre's study we found the guest, a lean, wiry fellow with a predatory nose and the keen eye of a bird of prey. A broad, seamed scar ran from his right eye to the point of his chin; and another stretched diagonally across his forehead. Strangely familiar mustaches fringed his lip. And then I remembered that during the past few days I had fancied seeing foreign faces in Bayonne, where scarcely any face is foreign. Yet those were lean and swarthy in a different manner, and were set off with mustaches whose droop and cut were decidedly outlandish. And just this afternoon I intercepted a glance that was too casual to be convincingly casual.

There was nothing after all remarkably strange about those fellows. Only— well, they didn't wear coat and trousers with the manner of those born to our stupid costume.

"Your servant," began our visitor after a pause that was just long enough to be as impressive as his bow, "doubtless announced me as Nureddin Zenghi, an emir from Kurdistan."

He glanced sharply about him, stared at me for a moment, and found my presence acceptable: all this while d'Artois returned the emir's bow with one of equal profundity and rigidity.

"But in all fairness," he continued, picking his words with just the suggestion of an effort, "I must confess that I am somewhat more than an emir. The fact of it is that I am…"

He lowered his voice almost to a whisper. "I am the Keeper of the Sanctuary."

"Ah… *Monseigneur le*…" D'Artois paused to select a suitable title. Propriety above all else, was Pierre.

"Emir, if you must be formal, Monsieur d'Artois. Although I am incognito. Extremely so, in fact."

"A votre service, monsieur l'emir," acknowledged Pierre, and again bowed in his inimitable fashion, which I endeavored to duplicate as he presented me.

It is difficult to bow elegantly while seeking to keep a couple of fingers near the butt of a pistol in one's hip pocket.

"As I said," resumed our visitor, "I am Keeper of the Sanctuary at Djeb el Ahhmar, in Kurdistan, the center of the *Faith*. Viceroy, so to speak, of Malik Tawus."

Peacocks, I thought, were becoming monotonous. I thought of that dagger I had barely escaped last night, and that book in Diane's parlor.

"Moreover," continued the emir, "I am a friend of France."

The emir was impressive, but not excessively coherent, I thought. But Pierre was equal to waiting without committing himself.

"All of which I appreciate and respect. But pray continue, my Lord Keeper."

I wondered just what ax the emir wished to grind on the friendliness to France.

"Therefore," continued the emir, "I am here to seek your aid in doing France a signal service, and at the same time overthrow a malignant impostor."

"A pretender, I fancy, to the custody of the Sanctuary?" suggested Pierre, fencing like the master swordsman that he was, with word and steel alike.

"Precisely. And it will be very much to your interest to help me, Monsieur d'Artois. Indeed, the welfare of your *protégée*, Mademoiselle Diane Livaudais, is closely linked with my own success."

Pierre essayed a feint. "You mean, *monseigneur*, that you will lead me to the hidden vault where Mademoiselle Diane spends her nights seeking to enter the presence that asks her to open his grave?"

The emir's brows rose in saracenic arches. "That is interesting, of course, but most obscure," evaded the emir. "In fact, I am by no means certain that I understand what you have in mind.

"But," continued the emir, "this is what I have in mind: Abdul Malaak, who came from Kurdistan three years ago to seize the local sanctuary—yes, as you surely have learned from the events of the past few days, the servants of Malik Tawus gather in conclave here in Bayonne—Abdul Malaak has succeeded in using his occult science to gain control of the mind and will of your *protégée*, Mademoiselle Livaudais. And when his control is complete, he will use her as an outside agent to operate in his cause in France, as a spy, unearthing information from various prominent persons he will designate. She will to all intents and purposes be a charming, gifted woman, acceptable and accepted in the best circles; but in fact she will be no more than an automaton, her every thought and word dictated by Abdul Malaak, who sits in a *solitarium* behind the throne in the hall where the conclave meets."

"Ah…indeed…most interesting, *monsieur l'emir*," replied d'Artois. "And is it presumptuous to inquire as to the nature of Abdul Malaak's plans?"

"By no means," assured the emir. "I am a friend of France."

There was a stone. Now for the ax he wished to grind thereon.

"Abdul Malaak has assembled a circle of adepts in occult science," explained the emir. "Some from Hindustan. Others from Tibet and High Asia. Many from Kurdistan and Armenia, and Azerbaijan, the land of fire. And each a master in the science of fundamental vibration.

"To give you a crude example—though to a mind like yours, an example is scarcely needed—a company of troops on foot marching in cadence can wreck a bridge. The note of a violin string which is attuned to the fundamental vibration of a goblet will cause the goblet to shiver to fragments."

"Precisely," agreed d'Artois.

"And going from the physical to the mental, let one man in a theater rise and shout Fire! there will be a panic.

"Thus these adepts will concentrate in unison on whatever thought they wish to project: so that through the principle of resonance they will uncork the vast reservoir of hidden discontent with society, religion, and politics that exists in France as in every country, and in the end effect the overthrow of established rule."

"As in Russia," I interposed.

"Exactly," assented the emir. "You also are a person of rare comprehension. And, to bring us up to date, I was not amazed at what happened in Spain not long ago to the Bourbons. And being a friend of France, I am here to seek your aid in thwarting this powerful engine of destruction. Single-handed, I would be hopelessly outnumbered, for while I have friends in the circle, they have been corrupted by Abdul Malaak and turned against me."

"Very well, *monsieur l'emir*, I am with you, heart and soul. But tell me, is it true that the Marquis de la Tour de Maracq is dead?"

"Who says that he is dead?" countered the emir.

"It has been written," replied Pierre.

"What is written may be history, or prophecy. Who can say?"

Score one for the emir. He didn't know whether Pierre was for or against the marquis. He was sure of Pierre's interest in Diane, and in friends of France.

"May I ask—and I trust again that I do not presume," said Pierre, "—why it is that you are so anxious to thwart Abdul Mallak's plans? I mean, you comprehend, aside from your friendship for France."

"That is simple. Our cult is divided by a schism. There are those who seek temporal power, and those who care only for peaceful spreading of the cult of Malik Tawus, the Lord of the World. We believe that He has no need of or desire for political machinations in His behalf, and that in due course, the Lord of the Painted Fan will Himself assume the throne of the world, and exalt those who believe in Him—just as your early Christians said of the Nazarene.

"Now be pleased to give me a pencil and paper. I will make you a sketch."

The emir hitched his chair up to Pierre's desk.

This was a bit too good to be true. I remembered that saying about Greeks bearing gifts. The events of the past two days had likewise made me wary of altruistic Kurds. I loosened my pistol.

D'Artois caught the move from the side of his eye, and shrugged negligently.

"Start at Porte d'Espagne," began the emir, as he traced a line. "Then…"

But he spoke no further. Something flickered through the open window the emir faced. He pitched forward, clawing at his chest. I drew and fired, then leaped to the window, and fired again, not with any hope of hitting the figure that was disappearing around the first turn of the alley just as I pressed the trigger, but at least to give him my blessing.

"Give me a hand," said d'Artois.

The hilt of a dagger projected from the emir's chest. He shuddered, coughed blood which joined the stain on his shirtfront.

"Porte d'Espagne...to the left...great peril...take...many...armed...men..."

He clutched the hilt of the dagger, tore open the front of his shirt, and with a final effort, snatched from about his throat a thin golden chain from which depended a tiny amulet: a silver peacock with tail fanned out and jeweled with emeralds.

Neither d'Artois nor I could understand the utterance that was cut off by another gush of blood.

"Tout fini!" exclaimed Pierre. "He offered us this when he knew he couldn't give us even another scrap of information. This glittering fowl must be a token of admittance."

"Draw the shades!" commanded d'Artois. "And get away from that window. Likewise, stand guard until I return. On your life, admit no one. Not any one."

"The police?" I suggested. "I fired two shots."

"I will handle the police. No one must know that the Keeper of the Sanctuary is dead. As long as they are in doubt, we have a weapon against them: for they thought him important enough to kill him before he could tell his story."

As d'Artois dashed out, I barred the door after him.

I could hardly share Pierre's optimism about the police. Here we had a stranger in the house, neatly harpooned with a knife. And what a story we'd have to tell! Someone tossed a dagger through the open window just as the Keeper of the Sanctuary was to explain where Diane wandered every night to claw at the door of a vault whose occupant commanded her to open his grave. Even an American jury would choke at a tale like that!

I picked up one of the drab little things which in France pass as magazines, and came across an article on the prevalence of murder in the United States.

"This is good," I reflected. "Now here in law-abiding Bayonne, I sit peacefully at the door of a lady's bedroom, and some one tries to dissect me with a nicely decorated dagger. The next day, a visitor has his conversation punctuated by a knife thrown through the window by parties unknown..."

I shifted a bit more out of range of the window, and checked up on the cartridges in the Luger.

"To crown it, I'll get buck fever and let daylight through Raoul or Pierre when they enter. Or maybe they'll find me here, deftly disemboweled and marked, 'opened by mistake.'"

"Open my grave and see the smoke that curls about thy feet!..."

I was developing a marked dislike for Hafiz. That old Persian was distinctly macabre. Then this one:

"If the scent of her hair were to blow over the place where I had lain dead an hundred years, my bones would come dancing forth from their grave..."

Then I wondered how Diane's phantom lover tied into the psychic-vibration scheme of turning France upside down. Now that I'd mulled over the felonious assaults and successful assassination, I couldn't help but have several thoughts concerning this exceptionally lovely Diane.

The click-clack of the knocker startled me. *"Aui vive?"* I demanded.

"It is I. Pierre," came the reply.

"Enter with your hands in the air."

But I recognized the voice, and returned my pistol.

"*Eh bien*, she is fixed. *Monsieur le Prefet* was reasonable."

Do you mean that he swallowed that wild tale?"

"*Mais, certainement.* Though there was of course some talk of what in your charming country one calls a lunacy commission; but in the end I prevailed."

* * * *

That evening Pierre and I called on the lovely Livaudais.

"*Mademoiselle,*" began Pierre after acknowledging Diane's greeting, "you eluded us last night. But this time we will be more vigilant."

D'Artois deposited a large and very heavy suitcase on the floor.

"Oh, but you must be planning an extended visit, with all that luggage!" laughed Diane.

"And why not? Monsieur Landon and I keeping you under surveillance all the way around the clock, *n'est-ce pas*? But tell me, did we disturb you last night? Am I forgiven…"

"And so it was you that broke my cut-glass decanter and spilled wine all over the rug. But no, I didn't hear a sound."

"'Tis well!" exclaimed Pierre. "I would have been desolate had we awakened you. And I shall send you a new decanter, all filled with my own Oporto."

"Monsieur d'Artois, you're a darling. But how in the world am I to sleep tonight, with the both of you standing guard, staring at me as though I were a dodo come to life?"

"Simple enough. Take a bit of this sedative. It won't drug you so that you won't hear the voice."

"Well, why not give her a heavy shot of it," I suggested, "so that she won't hear the voice at all, and leave that devil behind his sepulcher door chanting in vain."

"Not at all!" objected Pierre. "She must find the way to open the door, and pass through and fulfill that which has been impressed upon her subconscious mind. Then, after she has done that, we shall land like a ton of those bricks. I, Pierre d'Artois, will land in person; and henceforth, *Mademoiselle* will see no tombs by night."

Then, to Diane: "It is now passably late. Suppose that when you have arrayed yourself in…should I most appropriately say, walking-costume?…take a bit of this sedative. And then we will stand guard, we two."

As the door of Diane's bedroom closed, I turned to d'Artois. "Why that suitcase? It's heavy as a locomotive."

"That you will understand before the evening is over. I have there various things which I may need on a moment's notice: though I can not say at what moment.

"We are fighting an organization that has infiltrated its members into every stratum of society. And by this time you have no doubt that you and I are marked and sentenced on account of our association with Diane."

51

"We are not only contending with enemies skilled in armed encounter, but equally gifted in psychic conflicts. Witness, for example, how this so lovely Mademoiselle Diane…"

"Taking my name in vain again?"

Diane opened the door and revealed herself in a negligee of blue silk curiously shot with gold. I wondered that Etienne hadn't bequeathed her his chateau as well as his house in Bayonne.

"But I assure you it was complimentary," replied Pierre. "And here is your potion."

She accepted the glass, sampled its contents, drained it, stood there, the smile slowly fading from her features. Then she shuddered. "These engagements with the dead… I'm so glad I won't be alone tonight… Goodnight, *Messieurs!*"

Vainly enough, we wished her a goodnight also, this incredible girl who could still, at times, smile.

Then d'Artois took from his suitcase a coil of flexible insulated wire, very much like the extension cord they use to increase the range of a vacuum cleaner. In addition to the lamp and reflector at one end, there was a small portable snapswitch, and a tiny globe scarcely larger than those used as Christmas tree decorations. This layout Pierre plugged in at a baseboard outlet, a convenience which is most unusual in Bayonne.

As Pierre uncoiled the wire and pulled it along the wall, I glanced again at the chair I had occupied the night before. Diane had accepted Pierre's myth about the shattered decanter, and hadn't noticed the scar in the back of the chair. But that one look was enough to bring out a sweat on me.

Then I thought of the hurled knife which had cut short the remarks of Nureddin.

"Mademoiselle from Bar le Duc, parlez vous…" I hummed as I fidgeted about.

"Tais-toi, imbecile!" snapped d'Artois. "Bawdy to the last."

Which of course was unjust in the extreme, as I'd spent hours trying to teach Pierre the rendition of that classic.

"Surely, she is asleep by now," he continued. "And like you, I likewise would whistle to keep up my courage. But give me your pistol," said d'Artois.

"How come?" I demanded as quietly as I could at that outrageous order.

"You are no less on edge than I am. And you shoot damnable straight. If by mistake you pointed that siege gun at me or Diane, you would have long regrets. And anyway, we want no disturbance or shooting. The enemy can't see us, though they must know we are here; and they must not hear us."

I surrendered the pistol. Pierre was right, of course, but with the start I made last night, I had begun to take an interest in that excellent gun.

"Eh bien, let us take our posts," directed Pierre.

I followed him into Diane's room, where he set up the reflector and lamp in a corner so that if the circuit were completed, the entire room would be illuminated.

"Take that chair and draw it up. Thus. Now mark well the position of mine."

Pierre stood at the wall switch.

"Should you catch a glimpse of a very faint bluish light, don't dive for it. It's just the pilot light of this lamp I've set up in the corner. As long as it glows, I'll know that the…what do you call her?…the juice is on, and that I can depend on light when I need it.

"Ready? Good!"

The wall switch clicked us into darkness. The sinister watch was on.

* * * *

Sitting in a lady's bedroom in Bayonne does not sound so terrifying. But when the lady is awaiting summons from the dead, and when the dead sends living envoys with keen knives, it is yet again something else.

I wondered whether I'd fall asleep with my eyes open, and whether d'Artois could resist that damnable influence, whatever it had been.

Have you ever been in Morocco and heard the drums thump-thumping in the hills, calling the tribesmen to revolt? My heart was giving a perfect imitation.

Diane's breathing was soft and quiet and normal.

Silence from Pierre's post. Once in a while I caught a passing glance of the bluish-green pilot light, as he noiselessly shifted in his chair. Lucky he told me about that light! And once I heard him draw a deep breath. Just a deep breath. But infinitely expressive!

It was getting d'Artois too. Not a comforting thought.

The clock in the cathedral chimed twelve. And then the quarter, ages later. Then the tension eased. It is born in us to place all diablerie at midnight: and that having passed uneventfully, I felt that nothing would happen until tomorrow night, when I'd be in a much better frame of mind. Thoughts would be so much more collected…

My relief was premature.

I felt rather than heard a vibration pulsing through the room. It was as though I watched some one beating a kettle-drum at great distance, getting the rhythm by seeing the drummer's body sway to the cadence instead of actually hearing it.

Then, finally, the pitch increased into the lower limits of audible vibration. I could hear it. *Tum-tumpa-tumtum-tumpa-tum*…low and massive thundering from across the wastes of space. The drumming of Abaddon of the Black Hands.

It filled the room. It was an earthquake set to a cadence.

I heard a soft, sulfurous cursing from Pierre's side of the room.

Then a hand on my shoulder.

"It is I. The pilot light is out. They have cut the house wires. We are watched. *And there will be someone sent for us.*"

The drumming was reaching a more resonant pitch, so that the walls of the room amplified it.

Diane stirred in her bed. The voice was calling her to the hidden tomb.

"When I am dead, open my grave and see…"

I could almost hear that sweet, rich Persian verse as an overtone of that sonorous drumming.

"They are here!" whispered d'Artois. "I can feel them."

"And we're in the dark."

"Here, take this flashlight." Pierre thrust it into my hand. "Quick, toward the window!"

The circle of light revealed a white-robed intruder armed with a drawn scimitar.

"Shoot him!" I whispered to Pierre.

"No. Hold the light! And stand clear!"

The intruder stared full and unblinking into the brilliant flashlight. His eyes were sightless and staring. He advanced with the fluent, slinking motion of a panther, straight toward us.

Then it all happened in an instant.

D'Artois with his chair parried the sweeping cut of his adversary's scimitar, and as he parried, he sank, squatting on his left heel and simultaneously kicking upward with his right foot.

Perfect, and deadly.

The enemy dropped in his tracks. His blade fell ringing to the floor, and in a flash d'Artois had the scimitar.

"Keep the light on the window!" cried Pierre.

The companion of the first invader dropped fully into the circle of light. After him came a second. Both were robed like the first, and armed with scimitars. And both stared sightlessly; yet as certainly as though they saw, they poised themselves like great cats, gathered for the final leap to overwhelm us.

Great God! Noise or no noise, why didn't d'Artois fire?

"Use your gun!" I croaked, trying to yell and whisper at the same time.

Facing those blades, empty-handed…

Christ! Was Pierre asleep with his eyes open, as I had been the night before?

Then a glittering streak from the darkness at my side, and the first one dropped, shorn half asunder by Pierre's scimitar stroke.

"Two!" grunted d'Artois, and drew back on his guard for an instant, just out of the beam of the light.

But before he could advance, the third leaped forward, covered in his charge by a circle of flaming, hissing steel…

Clack-clack-clack!

Pierre was parrying that blind assault, cut for cut. Parrying a desperate, reckless whirlwind of steel, stroke after stroke.

Then he slipped through the mill, and sank forward in a lunge.

I saw Pierre's blade projecting a foot beyond his opponent's back. The enemy was too close to use his scimitar. I picked up a blade and struck his weapon from his grasp, lest he maul Pierre to a pulp with it, since he couldn't slice him to pieces.

But that didn't stop him. He gripped Pierre's shoulder and drew himself forward, pulling Pierre's blade still further through his own body in order to close in.

I hacked again and again, in a frenzy lest that madman tear d'Artois to pieces with his bare hands.

"Tenez!" gasped d'Artois. *"C'est fini."*

He disentangled himself from the slashed, hacked body. As a surgeon or butcher, I'd never qualify, the way I mangle things when I hurry.

54

"Quick! That first one…"

D'Artois snatched the red blade from my hand, and with a single stroke decapitated the one who was rising to his knees and groping for his blade.

"Look!" exclaimed Pierre.

Diane, sitting on the edge of her bed, was slipping her feet into a pair of satin mules. It had seemed several lifetimes to me, from the time that d'Artois had advanced, armed with a chair, against the first intruder, until he had finished the third; but so swiftly had he worked that Diane had scarcely time to get out of bed, and find and don her robe and slippers.

"She's on the way."

"But where?"

"Idiot! She will leave the same way our three visitors entered. Look!"

We followed Diane with the beam of the flashlight.

She went straight toward the window, grasped the bars, and pulled herself to the sill.

"Follow her!" commanded Pierre. "Strip this one—his robe isn't bloody."

I stripped the one cleanly decapitated.

Those fellows didn't drop from the ceiling, but came down a shaft through the wall, whose opening was concealed by the window-casing.

"How about a turban?"

"This one will do. Wind it with the stained end in. Quick, now! Follow her. Put that damned turban on as you go. *Allez!*"

Diane had pulled herself up. A glimpse of her heels, and she was out of sight.

"Now my pistol."

"Take it. But hurry. I'll be busy here…"

"What?"

"Va-t-en!" commanded Pierre. "Have I ever failed? Go!"

I leaped to the window-sill, felt, and found a void over my head, grasped the edge, and pulled myself up. In spite of our knowledge of the thick walls of these old houses, the existence of such a shaft would never have been suspected. The flashlight revealed a narrow passage not over ten feet long. At its end was a shaft leading down. I ventured a flash down its depth, and saw a ladder leading to a level that was well below the first floor of the house. At the bottom I turned, and faced a low archway which opened into a passage lead-straight ahead.

Some twenty paces ahead of me was Diane. I slopped along as fast as I could in the loose red slippers of the enemy, and as I advanced, I wound my turban as well as I could on the march.

Diane was walking, with a slow, almost mechanical stride, or she would have been quite out of sight. As it was, I quickly overtook her, and then snapped out the flashlight. Diane, deep in her trance, was utterly unaware of my seizing her robe so that she could guide me through the darkness.

She was stepping to the cadence of those drums.

I could distinguish now that the sound was of many drums: the roll and purr and sputter of tiny tom-toms against a background of solemn booming that made the masonry quiver beneath my feet. Yet the source of the sound was still far away.

Although the incline was not steep, it was perceptibly downgrade. We were turning ever so slowly to the left. The air was becoming damp and musty and cool. Our descent must now be taking us far beneath the uttermost foundations of Bayonne. Somewhere, below and to the left, was the brazen door that guarded the one who chanted in Persian and invited Diane to a conclave of the dead that were lonely in their deep vaults.

Ahead of us was a faint glow. I halted to let Diane gain a few paces, and then, hugging the left wall so as to gain the maximum protection from the door-jamb in case there should be a reception committee waiting, I crept forward as silently as possible.

Then it occurred to me that unseeing automatons like those that Pierre had stopped only by hacking them to pieces would hardly be susceptible to surprise. And if more swordsmen, bound in a deep trance and directed by some master mind to overwhelm me, were waiting, I'd have my hands full. I wondered if a pistol would stop them…the Moro *jurmentados* down in Sulu, riddled with dum-dum bullets, continue their charge until they hack to fragments the enemy who hoped to stop them with rifle fire.

Well, at least those three swordsmen had been *alive*, and their blood was like any other blood when spilled.

I ventured a peep around the doorjamb. The passage opened into a small alcove which was illuminated by the red flames of a pair of tall black candles set one at each side of a brazen door. Diane was alone before the door.

She hesitated, half swaying on her feet for a moment, then knelt on the second of the three steps that led to the door. Where her fingers traced the arabesques and scrolls embossed on the bronze, the verdigris had been worn away.

How many hours had she spent in wearing the seasoned bronze to its original color? Or were there then others who sought the same doorway? And if there were, when might they appear?

Evidently she was seeking the hidden catch which would open the door; the gateway of the tomb.

Surely Diane needed no light to further her quest. Then why these lurid candles? Had they a ritualistic significance, or were they for sentries, or acolytes that served the Presence behind the panel? I knew not what cross-passages I had unknowingly passed in the dark, and what swordsmen might be marching from any of them. Swordsmen, or worse…

Then Diane spoke; not to me, but to the dead behind the door. "I'm trying, Etienne, but I can't find the spring."

She rose from her task and retreated, turning away. Her eyes stared sightlessly at me. Then she wavered, tottered, and retraced her steps. Some compelling power was forcing her to resume her task.

I followed her, and looking over her shoulder, studied the embossing her fingers traced. Each curve, each figure, each floral and foliate form that could conceal the hidden catch she tapped, fingered, dug with her nails: but there was one she did not touch. And that one of all others seemed the only one that could control the lock: the center of a lotus blossom, close to the left edge. Even in that dim red light I could clearly distinguish a line of demarcation that separated the substance of the lotus center from the surrounding metal. Then why didn't Diane press it? Why had she avoided it, night after night?

But had she avoided it?

It was smooth and polished. Someone had fingered and touched it.

Diane herself. It all came to me: door would not open until the Presence was ready for her arrival.

I watched her fingers working their way back and forth over the traceries of bronze, toward the center of the lotus blossom. She was touching it…

I took a hitch in my belt, slid the scimitar and its scabbard back toward my hip, shifted the Luger.

Click!

The door yielded, swinging inward on silent hinges. The drums boomed and roared and thundered. Their vibrations smote me in the face like the blast of a typhoon. An overwhelming perfume surged forth, stifling me with its heavy sweetness.

I leaped in ahead of Diane, advanced a pace toward the blank wall before me then wheeled to my right, and saw him who made a madness of Diane's nights.

He sat cross-legged on a pedestal of carven stone. His arms were crossed on his breast. He was nude, save for a yellow loin-cloth that flamed like golden fire in the purple light of the vault. His face was emaciated and his ribs were hideously prominent. If he breathed, it was not deeply enough to be perceptible.

The drumming thunder ceased abruptly: and the silence was more terrific than the savage roaring pulse that had halted.

Dead?

Dead, save for those fixed, glittering eyes that stared through and past me. But they lived, fiercely, with a smoldering, piercing intentness.

Then someone stepped in between me and the Presence.

Diane had followed me, and standing in front of me, faced him.

Like him, she crossed her arms on her breast. Then she advanced with slow steps, not halting until within a few paces of the Presence. She knelt on the tiles, and bowed. Then she spoke in the expressionless voice of one who recites by rote a speech in a foreign language he does not understand.

"Etienne, I am here. I heard you from across the Border, and I have obeyed. I have opened your grave."

I stood there like a wooden image, neither drawing my scimitar to cleave that living mummy asunder, nor my pistol to riddle him to ribbons. This couldn't be the Marquis de la Tour de Maracq; not this blasphemy from somewhere in High Asia, that might have followed the Golden Horde, ages ago. Yet she had called him Etienne. Then he spoke:

"Landon, it is not good that you have meddled and entered the *solitarium* behind the throne. Even the elect dare not enter here. But since you are here…"

He smiled a slow, sinister smile. His long lean arm extended like the undulant advance of a serpent. "Look!"

I followed his compelling gesture with my eyes, and saw the brazen door swing slowly shut. It closed with a click of ominous finality.

I stared for a moment too long, held by the voice and the gesture. Just a moment too long. There was someone behind me. But before I could move, strong hands, gripped my arms.

The Presence murmured a command. My scimitar and pistol and flashlight were taken from me. The hands released me: and all with such incredible swiftness that I turned just in time to see my four momentary captors filing into an exit that pierced the wall, carrying with them my blade and pistol. As the last one cleared the threshold, a panel slid silently into place.

I had been a splendid guardian of the lovely girl who knelt at the feet of that creature on the throne!

"That door," resumed the Presence, speaking so deliberately that the moment of my disarming was scarcely an interruption, "is easily opened from the *outside*, by those we wish to admit."

Again he smiled that slow, curved smile of menace.

He looked down at Diane, and spoke to her in purring syllables. She rose from the tiles, and stood there, vacantly regarding us, Diane's body devoid of Diane's spirit.

"This girl and I," said the Presence, "have a few things to discuss. You will therefore be pleased to excuse us…"

He inclined his head, and smiled his reptilian smile.

I saw his fingers caress the carvings near the top of the pedestal on which he sat. I leaped, but too late. The floor opened beneath me. As I dropped into the abysmal blacknesses below, I caught a glimpse of the purple light above being cut off by the trap-door lifting back into place.

I landed on my feet with force enough to give me fallen arches, and pitched forward on my face. The stones were cold and damp and slippery. I rose to my hands and knees, and crept cautiously along, feeling for openings in the floor, and hoping to locate a wall which I could follow to anywhere at all. A corner, or an angle, anywhere to get out of the heavy blackness and near something that would give me a sense of direction. Here there was only up and down, and neither north, south, east, nor west.

Caged in the sub-cellar of this subterranean vault; locked in the basement of hell's private office. And Diane in the hands of that animated mummy!

Finally I butted head-first into a wall. The stars unfortunately weren't of sufficient duration to let me see where I was. So I crept along, following the cold, moist stones.

My fingers touched a vertical bar: one member of a grillwork which blocked my advance. I reached forward with my other hand and grasped another bar, felt my way along, right and left. It was a gate, hinged to the masonry at one side, and chained shut at the other.

Something tangible at last. Something to grip and struggle with. The gate yielded protestingly for a few inches until the chain drew taut. I could feel the heavy scale of rust and corrosion on the links. I tugged and pulled and pushed, but in vain.

Then I removed my borrowed robe, folded it into a compact pad which I applied to my shoulder. I backed off, carefully measuring my retreat, gathered myself, and with a running leap, charged the gate. The chain snapped. The gate opened. I pitched headlong ahead of me, amid a clatter of links and the clang of the gate's crashing against the wall.

Before I could regain my feet, someone landed on me.

Clean, manly fighting may have its place in the prize ring, and possibly even the wrestling arena: but in hell's basement it is a needless grace. I shifted just in time to avoid the unknown's knee fouling me. Not to be outdone in courtesy, I closed in, and located his eyes, but before I could apply my thumbs to the best advantage, he broke my attack. Finally I back-heeled him, and we both crashed to the paving. Luckily, he absorbed the shock, but it didn't stop him. He lacked the simian strength and terrible arms of the assassin of the night before, but he made up for it in agility and devastating rage. We both were approaching exhaustion from the fury of attack, defense, and counter-attack.

I yielded suddenly, to throw him off his balance; but I tripped on the loose piece of chain, lost my own balance, and failed to nail him as he pitched forward.

And I couldn't locate him. My own heavy breathing kept me from hearing him. I was trembling violently, and my mouth was dry as cotton. And if my heart pounded any more heavily, I'd burst wide open. Well, he must be in the same shape. So I sank to the floor, hoping to catch him with a low tackle, or to thwart him in a similar maneuver on his part.

But I couldn't find him.

"Come here, damn your hide!" I frothed, finally getting enough breath to relieve my wrath.

"Thank God, a Christian!" panted a voice not far from me. "And by your speech, an American. Let us be allies, what is left of us."

"And who might you be?" I demanded.

"A prisoner like yourself. Let's declare a truce, and if we must fight, follow me to where there is enough light."

The fellow sounded convincing enough. His English was the meticulously correct speech of an educated foreigner.

"Done. Lead on."

"Then put your hand on my shoulder, and I will lead the way," he continued. "To show my good faith, I will let you follow. Keep your head down. The masonry here is low, and very hard."

My enemy chuckled.

"*Mordieu*! but I have been deceived about American sportsmanship. You would have gouged my eyes out. You bit a nice morsel from my throat—*apropos*, I'll show you the right way to do that some day, if we get out of here alive... Steady, now! On your hands and knees...here we are."

I followed him through a low, narrow opening that had been made by prying a few blocks of masonry out of place, and into a tiny cell illuminated with a slim taper. The ceiling was vaulted, and over a dozen feet above the floor.

"This has been my grave for some time." He indicated the brazen panel in the wall.

"There has been entirely too much talk of graves in the past few days," I replied. "Graves with living occupants."

He started at me curiously, almost replied. Then, seeing me eyeing the brazen panel: "*Mais non*! Even with your bulk and hard head, you couldn't budge that bronze. It doesn't corrode and waste away like the iron in this devil's nest."

"Well then," said I, "how do they feed you?"

"They let food down through a trap in the ceiling. Look!"

I looked up, and saw the outline of a trap-door.

"You look strangely familiar," I began. "I've never seen you, but somehow it is as though I had seen a portrait, or photograph, or heard you compared for likeness to some one I did once see, somewhere."

"No one has seen me for two years or more. But how did you run afoul of Abdul Malaak? Are you also an aspirant to the custody of the Sanctuary?"

He made a curious, fleeting gesture with his left hand.

"Hell's fire, *monsieur*," I replied, "how many custodians, aspirant and actual, does this devil-haunted town hold?"

Then, without pausing for an answer, I threw it at him:

"When I am dead, open my grave and see
The smoke that curls about thy feet."

"*Comment?*" he exclaimed.

A home run! I continued:

In my dead heart the fire still burns for thee,
Yea, the smoke rises from my winding-sheet."

He stared. I met his stare.

"*Que diable!*" he finally exclaimed. "Who or what you are, I don't know. But you know who I am: de la Tour de Maracq."

"And I am Davis Landon. This meeting with the gentleman who has chanted Mademoiselle Diane to the edge of madness is certainly a pleasure."

The marquis smiled wearily. "Chanted, and to what end? From your quotation of Hafiz, I know that she must have heard me, but she couldn't get my thought. Certainly not thus far, at least. So I am buried here, and awaiting the bowstring, or the fire, or the saw and plank: whatever Abdul Malaak in his kindness orders when he has sufficiently poisoned my friends against me. I thought a while ago that they had discovered my loophole and were trying to stop my private explorations. So I gave you a good fight..."

For just an instant a fierce light flamed in his eye; and then that thin, weary smile again.

"This is puzzling," I protested. "I happen to know that she did get your message which you 'willed' or projected, or whatever means you used. Every night she wanders in her sleep to obey a summons, and claws at a brazen panel..."

"What's that you say?" demanded the marquis. "Wanders in obedience to my summons? *Wanders?*"

"Yes. From your house which you willed to her on your deathbed in Marrakesh."

"But, *monsieur*, I never died in Marrakesh."

"That I can readily believe," I admitted. "But she showed me that letter from you, and a newspaper clipping announcing your death, and a note in Arabic from the companion of your last hours. And thus she accepted your legacy, the house on Remparts de Lachepaillet, where she was very conveniently situated to leave by a secret passageway to hell's front door."

Throughout my speech, the marquis stared at me, bewildered.

"I, dying in Marrakesh, willed her that house?..."

"Yes, damn it, and hoodooed her with strange dreams of graves to be opened, and voice chanting in Persian. And tonight I followed her through the gateway..."

"How's that? Followed her? Is she there?"

"Yes. And that devil touched a spring and dropped me into that dungeon before I could say aye, yes, or no. So you might tell me what started her wanderings."

"*Helas, monsieur*, what can I tell..."

"When I quoted Hafiz you seemed to hear familiar words."

"Certainly. I did chant them. I also am an adept. And I chanted the verse of Hafiz for the sake of the rhythm; not to give her a command to come and release me, which she couldn't possibly do, but to ask her to communicate with Nureddin Zenghi, in Kurdistan."

"Why the verse, did you say? What has it to do with Nureddin? That is dense to me."

"*Pardon*. You are not an adept. But to put it simply, it acted merely as a carrier wave, as your radio experts would put it. It gave me a rhythm on which to impress my thought. I can't explain it briefly. But go into Tibet, and High Asia; to Hindustan, among the *fakirs*. Study at the feet of one who might still be found sitting at the foot of a column in the vast ruins of incredible Ankor Wat. Speak with the priests of the Eightfold Path. Piece all your gleanings together; and you will finally be able to project your thoughts to one with whom you are *en rapport* —if you have the strength of will. The knowledge is jealously guarded. But I found it.

"Had I gone further with the art, I could have projected *myself* from my body, and spoken to her. But I couldn't. Can't yet. And shan't live long enough to learn how.

"When I was reported dead, I was actually in this cell. My enemy tricked me in a contest of occult arts, and here I am. Abdul Malaak... Servant of the Angel, as he calls himself. I see it all now. He forged that letter and clipping to get her into my house from which he could summon her to make the trip unobserved. And his concentrated thought aided by the circle of adepts in the great hall, overpowered my message."

"But Nureddin did come to town."

"*Magnifique*! Maybe she did send for him. And he will take the place by assault. He will not fail..."

"Nureddin has failed."

And I told what had happened in Pierre's study.

"Then we are doomed," said the marquis.

"Doomed, hell!" I said. "You suggested that we be allies. Now let me take command. Is it near your feeding-time?"

"Yes, So says my stomach," replied the marquis. And then, as he saw me glance once more at the trap-door in the crown of the vault: "Even if I leaped to your shoulders, I couldn't reach it."

"Who said you had to reach it?" I queried.

"How then?" demanded the marquis. "They don't get close enough for you to take the guard by surprise as he gives me my food. If they only passed it through that door there!"

"I have an idea. Stand close to the wall, out of sight. Better yet, back out through that hole in the wall..."

"But..."

"Be damned! Ask no questions, monsieur, or my inspiration will leave me. I have a hunch. Are you with me?"

"To the death and to the uttermost."

I accepted the hand he extended. "And there is another," I added: "Pierre D'Artois."

None better," admitted the marquis. "There is no love lost between us, but he will not begrudge me any help given you and Diane. But even that d'Artois risks his head if he dares enter."

"Never fear about d'Artois," I reassured the marquis, "but while we have time, tell me this: who has the hold over Diane's mind? Is it you, or that dried-up thing on the pedestal?"

"Both, it seems. Though he is aided by his circle of adepts. With them broken up, his power would be comparatively little."

"But would that release her, breaking them up, and him also?

"Yes. And I will die happy if I personally attend his breaking up. Into small bits, Monsieur Landon. If we get out of here alive, I will dismember him with my bare hands! And since she has obeyed the command, she can be awakened from the influence of the Power..."

"There they are now!"

The marquis beckoned me to be silent.

In my turn, I motioned him to crawl out of sight of trap, and followed him.

"Qu' est-cequec' est?" muttered the marquis, obedient, but puzzled.

"Wait and see."

* * * *

We heard the trap open. A basket was descending at the end of a slim cord.

"Pull that basket up and let down a rope. That isn't heavy enough," I directed in Arabic.

"Why not, *ya marqees*?" queried the voice, somewhat taken aback.

"This isn't *el marqees, ya bu*!"

I shouted. "Let down that rope and pull him up. He's still breathing, but he won't be when you come back with a rope."

From above I heard a mutter of voices.

"And who are you?" demanded the spokesman.

I heard the clank of arms. My unusual request had been passed along to the guard, doubtless. But as Pierre said, *toujours audace*!

"Come down and see, O heap of offal! One of the master's guests, O eater of pork! Would you argue with me?"

And then, aside to the marquis, "I've got 'em going."

The marquis grinned, and the fire returned to his eyes.

"Give me your rags," I continued, "and we'll fool 'em proper."

"Just a moment, *ya sidi*," resumed the voice, "while we get a strong rope."

"Make haste then, eater of un-clean food! I have much else to do than to butcher *Feringhi* swine, down here in the cellar."

"Patience, master," said the voice.

I dug up from my memory a few epithets collected in Mindanao, and growled them in return. They couldn't understand it, and were duly impressed with my importance. By the subdued and respectful murmurings, they must by that time have identified me as one of the master's pet assassins.

But the occasional tinkle of accoutrements and soft note of steel didn't reassure me. The death of the marquis and the lifting up of his body doubtless was of sufficient importance to detain a part of the guard.

A heavy rope, several centimeters in diameter, was let down.

"Give me more slack! Pigs and fathers of many little pigs, how can I tie this fellow's carcass with that little? And anchor it firmly up there. When you get him up, I'm coming after."

Then to the marquis: "I'll go first, and you follow."

"No, let them haul me up. I can't climb a rope," he whispered.

"You're a damned liar, but since you want the first crack at them, go ahead. But remember you're dead. Don't start the show until I get there."

I tied a running noose and drew it up beneath his arms.

"All right up there! Heave away! And wait for me. I'll tell you what to do with him."

They heaved away.

"Well," I reflected. "I'll be in a pretty jam if something goes haywire and that rope doesn't come down again. That hothead…"

By the time the marquis reached the trap, I was in a sweat and a fidget.

"Hurry up there!" I roared. "And let that rope down. Drop him anywhere. He won't hurt you."

"Shall we hoist you, *ya sahib*?"

"Let that rope down, and silence, *ya humar*!"

So far, so good. I had them buffaloed.

I leaped at the rope, and hand over hand, pulled myself up. As I approached the opening, I gripped its edge with one hand, heaved myself through, and sprawled face down on the floor.

"He still breathes, master," said one.

"I forgot my scimitar. Give me yours and I'll tend to that."

And as I was solicitously assisted to my knees, the hilt of a blade was thrust into my hand.

I leaped and slashed.

"Give 'em hell, Etienne!" I shouted.

And I laid about me, right and left.

The marquis closed in on the one nearest him, lifted him over his head, and dashed him head-first to the tiles. Then he snatched a blade from the floor, and came on guard.

The four survivors faced us, dazed by the swift turn. And then they charged. I hacked and slashed clumsily and desperately. Parried, and missed my *riposte*. Lashed out again, and had my blade dashed from my hand by a sweeping cut.

Etienne, crouched on guard behind his whirlwind, of steel, faced half to his right saw my peril, and with a dazzling snick of his blade, sliced my adversary's sword arm half off: and back again to his party.

As I booted my disabled enemy into insensibility, I marveled at the incredible skill with which he held those three fierce Kurds at bay.

I gave my opponent's head one farewell bounce against the paving, picked up his blade, and joined Etienne.

"Gardez-vous!" he snapped. "I have him!"

He slipped forward in a lunge, blade slicing upward to disembowel his adversary; and back on guard again, with but two to face him.

They were too dazzled by that terrific attack to be aware of my presence. Thus my neck-cut to the one on the right was most creditable.

"Tenez!" commanded Etienne, as he confronted the survivor. "I need him."

Standing as though his feet were spiked to the floor, he waved me aside, engaged his enemy, parrying cut after desperate cut as coolly and effortlessly as though fencing with a blunt foil instead of with blades that sheared from shoulder to hip with one stroke.

The Kurd fought with the savagery of one whose doom stares him in the face. But in vain. He could not crowd or break through the hedge of steel that Etienne built with his leaping, flashing scimitar.

Then the Kurd stood there, blinking and bewildered, staring at his empty hand. His blade clanged against the tiles a dozen feet away.

"Now, son of a disease, throw this refuse into the pit. And you, Landon, strip this fellow you kicked senseless. I need his clothes."

The survivor complied without a murmur, and one by one thrust the dead and dismembered down the trap-door.

"Tie that pig!" snapped the marquis.

I obeyed, using a coil of the rope with which we had been hoisted up.

"And now," said the marquis, "Tell us several things, or I will dismember you slice by slice."

The fellow growled.

"What! Tongue-tied? Well, then...but no, I will not slice you to pieces...

"Landon, pass me that torch."

I plucked the flaming torch from its socket in the wall. Etienne applied it to the Kurd's feet.

"Where is the girl, and what is the master doing?"

The Kurd writhed, and groaned.

"Speak up, dung heap, or I'll roast you alive!"

The smell of flesh roasted before it is dead is not pleasant.

"I will speak, *sahib*!"

"Very well. What is happening in the Throne Room, and what of the girl?"

"The master sits on the high throne. The girl is as one dead, awaiting the command to pass through the veils of fire to become the Bride of the Peacock. It is the night of power."

"The night of power...and here we are, two against a company. Landon, will you join me in dying like a man?"

"I don't relish this dying stuff any too damned much, Etienne," I confessed. "But I'll go any reasonable length with you. So lead on."

"*Magnifique*! Let us go…"

And then he turned. "This roasted pig here will spread no alarm," he growled as his blade descended.

We thrust this last body down the trap-door.

The marquis wiped his scimitar, and led the way. Torches illuminated the passage until the first turn, and thereafter it was lighted by an indirect glow, emanating from a molding along the arched ceiling.

"Your Arabic is acceptable. A lot of these fellows speak only Kurdish or dialects of Turki, but stick to your own, and all will be well. And very few will recognize me in that purple light. None, in fact. They've not seen me for better than two years, and my very existence has been forgotten except by a few jailers."

"There was one who evidently had not forgotten you."

I felt for the little peacock amulet, and found it still about my throat.

"Nureddin was speechless. Handed it to me, and coughed his life out. Since he was your friend, take it."

"Another vengeance to exact. But remember: on your life speak not the Arabic word Satan. Whoever inadvertently pronounces it must then and there be torn to pieces. Nor say any word resembling it. That would be fatal to you, and would draw attention to me."

"What is your plan?"

"I have none. Even as I had none but an urge to explore when I wandered into the darkness and found you. This labyrinth is not entirely known to me, Keeper of the Sanctuary before Abdul Malaak. But this part of it I know well enough, and our wits will do the rest."

The marquis led the way, down winding passages, up stairways, down others, curving and twisting, never once hesitating at a branch or cross passage. Sentries posted at intersections saluted us perfunctorily; and the marquis negligently returned their salutes.

As we advanced, I picked up the deep booming of the drums. Mingled with it was the wail of reed pipes, and the whines of single-stringed *kemenjahs*.

"Fight it," said the marquis. "Don't let it get a hold on you. Abdul Malaak sits nodding there on that tall throne, impressing his will on the circle of adepts. They receive and amplify it a thousandfold, and on that a thousandfold more, increasing in geometrical progression. They have but to attune their minds to the vibration frequency."

"Once I saw them project their thought to take material form."

"Juggler!" I scoffed.

"Jugglery if you will. But I saw what I saw: a material entity formed in the vortex of that resonating, countlessly amplified thought.

"But," continued the marquis, "if you resist it from the beginning, you may hold your own. We may break it up. Tonight's conclave deals with Diane, and thus our escape may not be noted."

As we turned a corner, crossed scimitars barred our progress.

Etienne made a curious, fleeting gesture with his left hand.

The sentries raised their blades in salute and advanced us. As we entered the arched doorway of the Throne Room, their blades clicked behind us.

A smoldering somber mist, red as the embers of a plundered city, hung in the air of that great domed hall. A heavy sweetness surged about us, wave on wave. Bearded adepts sat cross legged beneath three-decked, gilded parasols, and caressed with knuckles and finger tips and the heels of their hands the drums of varying sizes which they balanced on their knees. As they played, they swayed in cadence. Their eyes stared fixedly to the front. They were dead men driven by a terrific will.

Against the wall of the circular hall towered a pyramid terraced in steps of glistening black. Tongues of flame quivered up from orifices along the stairway that led to the dais at the apex. The dais was canopied with gold threaded damask, and crowned with the monstrous effigy of a peacock, tail fanned out, and enameled in natural colors.

On the dais sat the cadaverous Abdul Malaak, that animated mummy that was to smite all France with the devastating thought waves of his adepts. He sat there like a high god. He nodded to the colossal thunder of the drums, and the whirring strings, and the wind instruments that moaned of the blacknesses across the Border.

We took our places near the foot of the pyramid, so that we could see the entrance which faced Abdul Malaak. Through it filed a steady stream of devotees, all robed in white, with scarlet girdles from which hung scimitars. As they took their places on the cinnabar-powdered floor, they caught the cadence of the music and swayed to its rhythm. From their ranks row after row in a crescent facing the throne, came a hoarse whispering which grew to a solemn chant.

Acolytes marched up and down through the ranks of the communicants, swinging fuming censers. Others, robed in crimson, followed them, bearing copper trays laden with small, curiously shaped lozenges and wafers which they offered the followers of the Peacock.

The stones beneath us quivered. I could feel the world rocking on its foundations. That maddening music finally spoke in a wordless language of riot and pillage and chaos. And high above the adepts arms crossed on his breast, sat Abdul Malaak, directing the doom.

I thought of the violin note that would shiver a wine-glass; of the ram's-horn trumpets that leveled the walls of Jericho. It wasn't the sound. It was the thought that was in resonance, the mind of each individual hammering relentlessly in cadence, doubling and redoubling the sum whenever another of the circle put himself completely in tune. Resonance; perfect timing; until the hatred of one shriveled adept from High Asia would be magnified a millionfold and on that yet again as much more.

The air was tenanted with presences called from over the Border by that demon on his tall black terraced throne. Distinctly above that deep, world-shaking roll and thunder I began to hear twitterings and chirpings and murmurings. *They* were gathering, drawn by the master's resistless vortex of power. We were being hemmed in by a congress of evil infinitely greater than all humanity working with one thought could of itself devise.

The puny blasphemies and petty filthinesses of medieval devil-worship were childish against this monumental array of Satanism from Kurdistan.

"Fight it, Landon, fight it!" whispered the marquis. "Don't let it get you or you'll join them. Malik Tawus devised no such evil; not in Kurdistan and Armenia, where I learned the true faith to bring it to France."

An acolyte approached with a tray of wafers. The marquis and I both accepted.

"On your life, don't swallow it," he cautioned. "Palm it. With that music you couldn't stand the drug it contains.

"And to think that I brought all this into France," he continued. "Not *this*, tonight, but paved the way for that devil up there to get his hold. His death is more important than your life, or mine, or hers, even.

"If Nureddin were alive…"

And then, "Look!" exclaimed Etienne. "Over there!"

Diane, arrayed in wisps of scarlet and silver, and crowned with a strange, tall head-dress that flamed and smoldered with rubies and frosty diamonds, and glowed with great pearls lurid in that sultry light, was escorted by acolytes toward the steps of the pyramid.

Tongues of flame now spurted waist high along the dais and encircled it; and the jets of flame rose taller along the steps.

Pace by pace Diane approached the steep ascent of the pyramid.

"She is to pass through the veil of fire and become the Bride of the Peacock," whispered Etienne. "The flames will not hurt her body, but she will be enslaved beyond all redemption."

"Maybe we can make a fast break and charge up the steps and finish Abdul Malaak before these fellows come out of their trance," I suggested. "Do you know of any way of getting away after we've done that?"

"Yes. A door behind the throne opens into the *solitarium* where he sits, most of time, in meditation on his pedestal."

"Well, then…"

"The flames won't hurt her body," resumed the marquis. "But if one of us starts up there, all he has to do is to press a small catch, and the nature of the flame will change entirely. There are those who have passed through the veil unbidden, but they didn't live long."

Diane had begun the ascent.

Then Abdul Malaak spoke in a great voice, incongruously deep for that emaciated frame.

"Servants of Malik Tawus, I have summoned you to witness the Night of Power. Thus far we have failed because your lips served me while your hearts betrayed me. Some of you still think of *El Marques* who would not honor me and the message I carried from across the border.

"Others think of Nureddin, who would have kept you in Kurdistan, oppressed by the Moslem, and worshipping the Bright Angel as fugitives hidden in caverns.

"But Nureddin was slain in the act of betraying us to the *Ferringhi* so that he could liberate *El Marqees*. But I have devised a doom for *El Marqees*; I Abdul Malaak, have thwarted his power, and behold she is seeking me instead of him.

Behold; and believe, and give him freely to his doom, even as his comrade in treason was doomed."

"We see and we believe, and we give freely!" came the deep response!

Etienne clutched my arm.

"There is but one chance. I will go first, and settle with Abdul Malaak, and extinguish the flames. You follow, and when the flames subside, take Diane through the door behind the throne."

Etienne leaped to his feet, and three steps up the terrace.

I followed him, drawing my blade.

A murmur rose from the devotees.

Abdul Malaak stared, for once disconcerted. Then he shouted a command. The swordsmen stirred in their trance. Abdul Malaak smote a brazen gong at the side of the dais. Its deep clang touched them to life. They rose. Blades flashed.

Two against that host of madmen. Pierre had failed me. And I was glad that he had failed. Why should he also die in this butchery?

Abdul Malaak leaned forward in his throne. His fingers found and touched a knob: and the flames rose high about the dais, fierce, consuming fire.

"Hold them until I get Abdul Malaak. Then take her away while I cover your retreat!" shouted Etienne as he passed Diane on the stairs.

He leaped through that deadly, blinding flame and at Abdul Malaak on his throne.

Then came a voice loud and clear above the roar of the swordsmen: "Nureddin has returned! Nureddin with the assassin's knife in his chest!"

I turned, just two leaps from the flame-girt dais, where I had overtaken Diane and caught her in my free arm.

And Nureddin it was, drooping mustaches, scar-seamed cheek and forehead: a Kurd from Kurdistan. He flung aside his robe. A jeweled hilt gleamed from his chest: the very dagger I had seen impale him in Pierre's study!

"Who will exact blood indemnity for the death of Nureddin?"

He strode through the milling throng that parted wide for him.

"What? O dogs and sons of dogs, have you forgotten the bread and salt of Nureddin?"

And the wave of steel that was to overtake and overwhelm us subsided. There was an instant of silence. Then at the feet of the terrace the apparition halted, faced about, clutched at his chest, and wrenched the dagger free.

There came a low murmur from the crowd.

Nureddin hurled the dagger among the dazed swordsmen. "Take it and avenge Nureddin!"

"*Ya* Nureddin!" shouted one.

"He is our father and grandfather!"

"Nureddin has come from the dead!"

"Fraud and trickery!" shouted another.

"That's no dead man!"

"Kill the impostor!"

"It's Nureddin himself!"

The adherents of Nureddin were forming in a cluster. A scimitar rose and flashed swiftly down. Another, and another. The friends of Nureddin, shoulder to shoulder, were cutting their way into the company. Their number was growing every instant; but still they were outnumbered ten to one.

Nureddin was ascending the terrace, three steps at a time. He halted where I stood, scimitar in my sword hand, and my free arm supporting Diane.

The battle at the foot of the terrace was waxing hotter every moment. The friends of Nureddin were being forced back toward the wall. A dozen or twenty of the enemy were charging up the terrace to cut down the impostor, and me also.

Nureddin thrust at me a pair of Boukhara saddle-bags.

I dropped my blade, and took them.

Each of his hands emerged with an object a little larger than a goose egg. Then he tossed them one with each hand: grenades! They burst full among the enemy, halting the charge with their deadly, flaming phosphorous. Another grenade. And yet another. The assault broke and fled, howling and aflame.

And then Nureddin rained his grenades into the mob below.

Even in this damned place of madness, I knew now that this was no dead man.

"We're out of fire!" he growled in guttural Arabic. "Some high explosive!"

And that fierce Kurd, withdrawing the safety pins and holding the grenades to the last split second, hurled them so that they burst as they landed, rending and blasting the enemy.

The friends of Nureddin were now advancing, slaying-mad and frenzied by the fire and explosive that dead Nureddin had hurled at the enemy.

"*Ya* Nureddin!" they shouted. "Nureddin has returned with the fires of Jehannum! *Ya* Nureddin!"

I glanced at the throne. The terrific, searing heat had subsided; and flames were scarcely ankle-high. Etienne was clambering to his feet. He reeled, and tottered. Blood streamed from his mouth. His smile was terrible.

Then he stooped, picked an armful from the throne, and advanced down the terrace toward us.

"I told you I'd do it. Sorry you couldn't watch and take your lesson." He laughed as he wiped his lips. "Look!"

I saw from the torn throat of his burden that he had made good his boast.

Then Etienne with a supreme effort pitched the remains of Abdul Malaak headlong into the bedlam below.

The Kurd was hurling his last grenade.

One last detonation, muffled by the bodies it blasted and seared.

"Etienne," I demanded, "before we get into that butchery, release her so that her mind will be free."

"Tres bien!"

He turned to Diane, stroked her cheeks, whispered in her ear, shook her sharply, whispered again, tapped her here and there with his knuckles.

Her scream was piercingly natural and feminine. Diane the automaton had become a woman again.

"Oh, Etienne, I did find you! You weren't dead after all!"

"Found me, but not for long. Follow Landon out of here. Quick! I'm a dead man. Breathed too much of that flame. I'm following Nureddin."

He kissed her and broke away from her arms.

"Well, if you're following Nureddin, you're going in the wrong direction," said a calm voice at our side, not in guttural Arabic, but in French. "And here's your pistol, Landon."

Nureddin, nothing! Pierre d'Artois!

"Stand fast, fool!" he shouted, seizing Etienne's shoulder. "Nureddin's friends are winning. And dead Nureddin is avenged."

"Then," retorted Etienne, as he recognized Pierre, "take Diane out of here. This time I won't return to haunt her."

Etienne saluted us with his blade. "Swear not to follow me! The last will of the dead. I don't want to waste what little life is left…"

Pierre stared at him for a moment, and saw that Etienne spoke the truth. "You have my word."

Pierre's blade rose in salute; and then he turned the throne.

"Oh, Etienne!" cried Diane, at that moment realizing his intentions.

But Etienne did not hear her.

As I followed Pierre, I glanced over her shoulder and saw Etienne, blade flaming in a great arc, charge headlong into the melee. His scimitar rose and fell, shearing slashing. His voice rang exultant with slaughter. Then we heard his voice no more.

I half carried, half dragged Diane through the panel behind the throne into the *solitarium* of Abdul Malaak, and thence, finally, through the winding passages to Diane's apartment.

* * * *

"Tell me," I demanded of d'Artois the next day, "why you ordered me to follow Diane into the den of madness?"

"That was an error which I didn't recognize until after it was all over," admitted Pierre. "But since you acquitted yourself as you did, I claim a free pardon for having unwittingly sent you to face the Keeper of the Sanctuary instead of going myself.

"I had what you call the hunch," he continued. "It came to me in a flash that my idea of impersonating Nureddin would succeed. You understand, I had toyed with the notion from the day of his death. I knew that Nureddin would have enough of a following to divide the conclave if he suddenly appeared, risen from the grave.

"The disguise was easy. My nose is about right by nature. Those scars on the cheek and forehead, and the mustaches, and the eyebrows were simple. Just a few touches, and the essentials were there. And that dagger—well, that was one of those flexible-bladed weapons used on the stage, in sword-swallowing acts. But convincing, *bien*?"

"Finding my way into that den was not so difficult. Nureddin before his death mentioned Porte d'Espagne. I checked against Vauban's plans, and then made soundings with instruments such as prospectors use in your country to locate those oil domes. My men—you saw them, and remarked, that afternoon as we drove by—found considerable subterranean cavities where the plans showed none.

"And since I knew enough of the ritual of Malik Tawus, my detection as an impostor was very improbable."

"But what set you on the trail, originally?" I asked.

"Etienne's letter," replied Pierre. "I knew it for a forgery the moment I noticed that it had been written by someone who, being used to Arabic, which is written from *right to left*, forgot in his careful forging that Etienne would cross his t's from *left to right*.

"*Alors*, that sufficed. Then I telephoned Paris headquarters, where they have a file of every newspaper in the world. There was no such article in any paper printed in Morocco as the one Diane gave me.

"Thus I knew that someone was using Etienne's alleged death as a means of getting Diane into Etienne's house, where memories of him would make her an easy victim to the psychic influences that were directed toward her.

"And according to his remarks before you two escaped from his cell, the marquis had also been seeking to project a thought to her. And between the two forces…"

"Just a moment, "I interrupted. "Why did Abdul Malaak go to all the trouble of projecting his thought to Diane when a couple of his men could have seized and dragged her down there?

"Why bother to prepare the stage setting of Etienne's death? Just oriental indirectness?"

"Not at all! Don't you see," explained Pierre, "that they wanted not merely Diane in person; they wanted her as a slave of the will of Abdul Malaak. And when she had succumbed to his will sufficiently to begin her nocturnal wanderings and pick her way to the door, he would know that she was truly in his power, and ready for the next step, becoming an automaton whose activities as a spy could be controlled no matter where she went.

"But, *grace a Dieu*—with certain credit to Pierre d'Artois—Mademoiselle Diane's mind is freed, not only by the death of Etienne and Abdul Malaak, but also by having obeyed the command which had been impressed so firmly on her subconscious mind.

"And therefore, *mon vieux*," he continued, "since she is done for ever with opening graves in her sleep, you must during the remainder of your stay in Bayonne divert her mind from those gruesome memories. So out of my sight for the evening. I have work to attend to. *Allez!*" And thus on that, and on other evenings, I sought Diane with more confidence than I had any right to have.

* * * *

"Somehow," said Diane one night as we sat on the tall gray wall of Lachepaillet, watching the moon-silvered mists rise from the most and roll into the park, far below, "that moment's meeting with Etienne was so unreal. It was as if he'd appeared from the dead to put my mind at rest rather than that he was actually alive. In a way, he died two years ago, instead of on that made, terrible night… not a fresh grief, but the calming of an old sorrow…if you know what I mean…"

And then and there, as Pierre would put it, I had the hunch.

"You mean," said I, "that the Bride of the Peacock could be pleased with a much less colorful bird?"

Which was precisely what Diane had in mind.

THE RETURN OF BALKIS

Originally published in *Weird Tales*, April 1933.

"My friend," began Pierre d'Artois abruptly, one evening a few days after my arrival in Bayonne, "you have heard that two women can not occupy one house without discord, have you not?"

As he spoke, he thrust aside the untasted glass of *vieux armagnac* at which he had been staring.

"Eh, what's that?" I demanded. He had caught me off guard, and at loss for the proper response to what seemed the opening remarks of a discussion of wife versus mother-in-law: an odd topic, since, happily, it could at the best be only academic as far as either Pierre or I was concerned. "Well, now that you mention it, doubtless the situation has its trying features. But—"

"Alors," continued d'Artois, "what if two women are seeking to occupy the same body?"

"Good Lord, Pierre!" I began. "This is too thick. Two women *in the same body*?"

But I could not hurdle it, even with a running start.

"Yes. Exactly that," affirmed Pierre. "Madeleine's personality is splitting. An intruder from across the Border is taking possession of her."

D'Artois was referring to the daughter of his old friend, André Delorme. Her presence in Pierre's house had been a surprise to me, particularly since d'Artois in his letter of a week ago, inviting me from Bordeaux, had said nothing about his expecting a decidedly charming guest from the States to enliven my visit.

"An intruder from across the Border?" I said, groping for my wits.

The idea was hard to assimilate. But I had noticed something strange about Madeleine Delorme. She was colorfully charming, despite the swiftly changing moods that had baffled and disconcerted me; yet there was a suggestion of the uncanny.

"Now that you mention it," I continued, "it did seem as though some second personality was regarding me from her eyes. At times their expression was very old, and absolutely alien. Could that be what you mean?"

"For a fact, that is exactly what I mean," assured d'Artois. "'Someone is trying to crowd me out of myself,' she said to me a few days before your arrival. 'I dare not relax. Not for a moment. It is waiting and ready, lurking beside me. It is gaining in strength. At times I feel that I am some one else. I'm afraid to leave the house. It might take possession of me, and lead me—oh, good God, but where might it not lead me?'

"Alors, I had her leave the *pension* where she was staying, and move into my house, where I could observe her. I thought at first that it was a hysterical fancy. But one night I *saw*. Then I knew."

D'Artois paused. I wondered what it could have been that he had seen. There are vaults and passages far beneath the ancient city that for centuries have been lost to the memory of those who daily throng the arcades of rue Pont Neuf, and the narrow tortuous length of rue d'Espagne. Something archaic and malignant was whispering from the blacknesses of those unhallowed mazes. It had spoken to Madeleine, and she had heard.

Bayonne is ancient, somnolent, fantastic as a hasheesh dream, and as strangely beautiful when of a morning the gray walls and battlements of the citadel are afloat on the low-hanging river mists, and the cathedral spires reach into the early light like long slim lance-heads. But at night the blacknesses of the crypts far below the level of the moat that girdles the city begin their murmuring: and Madeleine had listened too long.

"But see for yourself," continued d'Artois. "We will watch in her room. It will return. It is growing strong in its success—"

"Who will return?" I demanded, as I followed him up the winding staircase. "What manner of thing, or presence, is haunting her?"

"See, and you will know," evaded Pierre, as he led the way down the hall.

D'Artois tapped gently at Madeleine's door.

"She is asleep," he said in a low voice, "But let us go in."

Madeleine lay under the canopy of a great four-poster bed. The moonlight filtering in through the bars of the window and between the heavy drapes caressed her faultless shoulders and graciously curved throat, and lost itself in the twining midnight of her hair. She was lovely, this Madeleine Delorme.

And something was crowding her out of her own body! The thought was outrageous. But I remembered other and equally incredible things that had taken place in Bayonne, and could not doubt Pierre's ominous words. And certainly I could not question his sincerity.

D'Artois nudged me, and gestured toward a chair.

"Seat yourself," he whispered. "Wait and you will see."

We sat there in the shadows. I wondered what specter from the dark background of that old city would appear to make good Pierre's ominous words. I heard the silvery chime of the cathedral clock striking eleven. I relaxed. It... whatever it would be...would not appear until midnight.

But I was wrong. I became aware of a subtle, poison sweetness that permeated the room. And in the darkness to the left of the moonbeams that marched slowly across the floor, I saw a shimmering phosphorescence that elongated, and spread, and took form. It was at first so tenuous that I could distinguish the mantelpiece looming out of the shadows behind it. The odor in the room was becoming more intense. It was like the aroma of embalming spices from some desecrated sarcophagus, but infinitely more pungent. The luminous haze was something from a tomb, or worse. Even as I watched, drugged by that spectral sweetness, the silvery mist became substantial. It assumed a definite form.

It was a woman of surpassingly gracious figure. She wore on her head a tall, curiously wrought diadem. As she turned to face us, I saw that her features were lovely with an evil beauty. Her smile was a curved sinister mockery. Her lips moved, but I could distinguish no sound.

Neither d'Artois nor I stirred. I doubt even that we breathed. We sat there, watching that shadowy, diabolical beauty return our stare. Then she noiselessly approached Madeleine's bed, moving with an undulant, serpentine grace. She bent over the sleeping girl, and made weaving passes with her slender hands.

Madeleine stirred, and murmured in her sleep, and made a gesture as if to repel the presence. She half rose and supported herself on her elbow. Then as she sank back among her pillows, her gesture became one of despair and weariness, and resignation. Her deep sigh was the only sound in the terrible, haunted silence of that room.

I saw a misty vapor rising from her half-parted lips. It floated, and spread like cigarette smoke in a room whose air is utterly still.

"Pardieu!" muttered d'Artois. "She defies us to our teeth!"

He rose from his chair, and advanced a pace.

"Balkis, Queen of the Morning, get you back to the shadows whence you came!" he commanded in a low, tense voice. "Back to the shadows, Balkis, and confuse him who disturbed your rest."

The presence ceased her gestures. She stood erect, and regarded Pierre with eyes burning with fury. She advanced a pace toward him. But instead of retreating, d'Artois took another stride toward that spectral presence. The air became tense from the silent conflict of Pierre's will and the resentment of that ghostly beauty. For an instant it seemed that she was becoming more substantial, and was poised, ready to claw him in her imperious, unspoken wrath.

D'Artois advanced another pace, almost within arm's reach, and confronted her, eye to eye. He feared neither man nor devil, that fierce old soldier.

Then he spoke solemnly in a sonorous language that reminded me of Arabic. His voice was low, but the syllables rolled like the surge of a distant surf. As he intoned, he extended his hand in a gesture of command. The presence became more and more tenuous, and retreated. It became a vague fleck of luminescence that paled in the slowly shifting moonlight; and in another moment it vanished.

I heard Pierre's sharply exhaled breath, and saw his shoulders droop wearily. The tension in the room eased abruptly. And then I noted that Madeleine no longer exhaled the misty vapor that had been passing between her lips.

He turned. Trembling violently, I followed him from the room. Under the light in the hall, I could see that his features were drawn and haggard, and that his eyes burned with a fierce light. He too was trembling; not from fright, but from the effort of will which he had exerted in defying the lovely, spectral presence.

"For God's sake, what was it?" I finally ventured to ask, speaking in a whisper. "Will it stay away?"

"That is what is seeking to take possession of her," replied d'Artois. "And it will not stay away, if he who sent it chooses to make it return."

"What is it?" I repeated. "A ghost?"

"In a way, yes," he said, "but no honest ghost walking of its own accord. It is a presence conjured up by some necromancer, and sent to possess her. And though I have driven her away tonight, she will return tomorrow night, and the one thereafter, until she has accomplished her end. I ordered her to leave. I used no formula other than that of solemn command. It was my will against that damnable shade from across the Border."

"But who is she?" I asked, still dazed by the apparition, and by the glare of deadly hatred she had turned on us.

"Balkis, Queen of the Morning," said d'Artois, "and having been aroused from her sleep, she is struggling eagerly to take the body that her damnable ally has sought for her to inhabit. And we can not stop her. True, I drove the presence away. But I must have a better weapon than my unaided will, or in the end, when I am exhausted, she will return, and finally take full possession."

"Good God, Pierre, that's terrible!" I exclaimed, horrified at the thought of a woman's soul being crowded out of her own body.

"But how do you know that this apparition is Balkis? And why did you call her Queen of the Morning?"

"I judged by her costume. And at times Madeleine in her speech gropes for words, as though she had forgotten the languages she speaks, or forgot what she intended to say. And then she drops a few foreign words, starts, corrects herself. And those foreign words were in that long-forgotten dialect spoken by the Sabeans. Judge for yourself. Balkis lurks in the body of Madeleine, and even during the day asserts herself.

"But that in itself proves nothing, you understand," d'Artois continued. "This, however, does: when I called her Balkis, Queen of the Morning, and addressed her in her own language, she obeyed me. That title is a play on the Arabic word that designated her ancient kingdom."

I pondered on this for a moment, then resumed my questions.

"But can't some one drive her away, and keep her away?" I demanded. "Haven't the clergy some ritual of exorcism, or has that been discarded in this day and age? I notice you didn't follow the old traditional sign-of-the-cross formula."

"There is nothing essentially evil about Balkis," explained Pierre. "She is only a woman whom some evil person has called from her grave. And a Christian exorcism would be as meaningless to her as it would be to a Hottentot. She never heard of such a thing. It would be utter vanity.

"An occult knowledge more profound than that possessed by any one in France is required," he continued. "I know of only one person who has it, and I have sent for him. He is a darwish, one of those eccentric mendicants who preserve the occult traditions of the Orient. He is an adept.

"With his assistance, we may succeed, if in the meanwhile Madeleine does not become entirely possessed. Sitting and watching her will be futile. To expel Balkis by the unaided will is a terrific task, and no sooner is it accomplished than she presently returns, and in no wise discouraged."

The mere announcement of the presence of our spectral guest would have been sufficiently disconcerting; but actually to have seen her was too much for my comfort. Yet I finally slept, thanks to a half-pint of Pierre's *vieux armagnac*. It burned like the everlasting fires, but it drugged my wrenched nerves. Dead royalty in the house, visible or invisible, is not an effective sedative.

* * * *

Madeleine spent most of the following day in her room. And charming as she was, I was glad that she remained out of sight. Her presence would have been disconcerting. I would have wondered whether Madeleine or her ghostly companion looked at me from those lustrous, almond-shaped eyes. The apparition of the previous night accounted for the indefinable foreign expression of her features. It was the spiritual intrusion of Balkis, leaving its imprint, bit by bit. And those successive visitations would be branded on her brain so that in the end, Madeleine Delorme would be thinking the thoughts and pondering on the age-old memories of dead Balkis.

We sat again in Pierre's study. The evening ritual of cigars and coffee and *liqueur* was somber and unrelieved by the scintillant d'Artois conversation and *esprit* that in the past had made him the perfect host. He was staring at the pattern of the Boukhara rug, and absently lifting a *demi-tasse* to his lips.

I heard the sharp crack of a pistol, the shattering of the cup, a tinkle of glass, and the solid *chunk* of something striking the woodwork behind him.

"The devil!" exclaimed d'Artois, diving to the floor. "We are under fire!"

I snatched the cord that drew the heavy damask drapes away from the windows, letting them close and mask the opening.

"Some one," said Pierre, "resents my expelling Balkis last night. Ah…there's where it landed."

With his penknife, d'Artois dug into the door-jamb and extracted a bullet.

"Probably a Luger," he muttered as he studied the jacketed missile. "And, thank God, a bungler fired the shot. My friend, they are hunting us. They see that we are keeping her, and that though they accomplish their devilish aims, it will avail them nothing. Resurrected queens may disturb one's mind, but they do not fire pistols and shoot a *demitasse* from one's lips."

Pierre seated himself, and pondered. His brow was cleft by a triple-furrowed frown, and he twisted his fierce gray mustache. Then, finally, he spoke.

"Some one has prepared Madeleine for this outrage, and has overcome her will, so that when she is asleep she can not any longer deny the ghostly intruder that would inhabit her body. And that one, *pardieu*, is the person we must find. Somewhere in this town is a necromancer whose terrible studies have led him to this outrage. Some one has called Balkis from the shadows of twenty-eight dusty centuries. She has not appeared of her own volition. This wasted bullet bears witness to her living sponsor."

He paused for a moment, regarded me intently, and continued in a low, tense voice, "Some necrophile is enamored of the Queen of the Morning, and wishes to give her a new body."

"Necrophile?" I shuddered at the hideous implication. "But that would signify —"

"That is hair-splitting," d'Artois interrupted. "Whether this one be in love with the very body of dead Balkis, or whether, as in the present case, it is her spirit for which he seeks a living body, he is still a necrophile. And this, while less horrible to contemplate than that which you had in mind, is really a greater outrage, since it is directed against a person who would much rather be herself than any number of departed queens. Mordieu! And rightly so!

"We know now that we have men as well as a phantom to combat. This wild shot has betrayed the nature of the enemy, and we shall track down this lover of dead Balkis. And then, when that old darwish appears—I cabled the consuls and

Residents of every port in whose hinterland he might be—he will expel Balkis and she will swallow her rage and go back to her disturbed sleep, to dream once more of Suleiman.

"Do you, therefore, watch by her room. Do not fear the presence if it appears. For it is constantly here, whether visible or not. If anything substantial enough to handle a pistol or knife appears, draw and fire. With the full moon, you may enjoy excellent shooting!"

Pierre's gray eyes had a steely glitter, and he spoke now with his old vivacity. That bullet which had picked the *demi-tasse* from his very lips had immeasurably encouraged him.

"We will hunt him down, *pardieu!*" he exclaimed. "And in the meanwhile, we will divide the watches of the night. Take your post, and your choice of pistols. I will relieve you at midnight. And until then, I will be busy with some deductions of my own. While we are awaiting the arrival of our excellent darwish, we may find that accursed lover of dead queens, and he will regret his poor marksmanship. *Salaud!* I will not miss!"

I selected a pistol from Pierre's arsenal, and took my post in the hallway, just outside Madeleine's door. I knew that her windows were barred, and that nothing larger than a cat could slip through. And being on the second floor, it would require exceptionally clever work for an intruder to steal in and make away with her. The sawing or forcing of the bars, moreover, would betray him, then and there.

This, however, did not lull me into a sense of false security. The knowledge that in the room beyond the door, Balkis might be bending over Madeleine, and with ceremonious gestures and passes be commanding her spirit to leave its body, was sufficient to keep me from becoming sleepy, or negligent in my watch. I paced up and down the carpeted hallway. Yet it was an eerie vigil, and I forced myself to cease visioning that sinister, shadowy presence that Pierre had confronted the night before. At times, I fancied that I could again smell the subtle sweetness that had heralded the materialization of dead Balkis.

There was a window at the end of the hallway. I glanced out, occasionally, and saw nothing but the light of a full moon. But the black shadows seemed alive with emanations filtering from the ancient, undisturbed soil of the citadel. A conclave of evil was abetting Balkis. This house had become a focal point of entities that the power of some necromancer had released in summoning Balkis from the dust. I entered the vacant room that adjoined Madeleine's. It was the one that her maid had occupied before leaving in terror one night after having seen the apparition. Like Madeleine's, it faced the tree-clustered parkway that extended from the gray walls and moat toward the highway that leads to ruined Château Maracq.

I looked down into the deserted street that ran along the city wall. Once I thought I could see a figure lurking in an angle of the parapet. And then it seemed after all to be only a wisp of river mist, or perhaps a whirling of wind-blown dust. But I started, stared for an instant, and shivered, for even the dust of this ancient town is alive and vibrant with that which it has received and assimilated since mediaeval sorcerers and alchemists crouched shuddering over their terribly charged alembics that bubbled and dripped strange distillates, and fumed in the red glare of charcoal furnaces.

But that dust cloud or fog wisp could not reach to the second story. So I returned again to the hall, to walk my post.

I heard Pierre stirring about in the study on the first floor. He commanded the entrance of the house. Then later, I heard him exclaim and mutter. Some late visitor, I thought, as the door opened. And then…

I heard a gasp, and a groan, and the thud of a falling body and the splintering of wood.

"Sacré nom d'un nom!" I heard Pierre exclaim.

That was enough. They were taking us by assault. As I bounded down the winding stairway, three steps at a time, I drew my pistol.

Another crash, and a splintering of glass, and the smack of a pistol.

"Hold 'em, Pierre!" I shouted. And an instant later, I landed with a leap in the vestibule. A man lay stretched out on the floor. Pierre was struggling with another, seeking to wrench from his hand a long, curved knife. A third, groaning and cursing, was reaching for a pistol that lay beyond his grasp. Just as d'Artois back-heeled his adversary and sent him crashing into a corner, I opened up with my pistol. The gentleman on the floor lost all interest in the weapon he sought.

"Back to your post, *imbécile*!" d'Artois yelled, as he turned to face me. "See if they are attacking the second floor."

"But the windows—"

"Back to your post! Immediately!"

As I turned to obey, I heard another crash, and saw d'Artois following me. The yard-long blade of a Moro kampilan flashed as he leaped after me, carrying the weapon at the port.

We burst into Madeleine's room.

Pierre's intuition had been right. In the moonlight we saw three intruders. Two of them were about to take Madeleine from her bed. The third with a gesture was indicating the window. I saw that the bars had been wrenched aside, and caught a glimpse of a rope ladder, apparently let down from the roof.

As we leaped into the room, the leader shouted a warning, and Madeleine's captors dropped her to the bed from which they were lifting her. A pistol cracked. I saw Pierre flinch from the impact, but the shot did not stop him. His blade flashed forward and up, ripping his enemy from waist to chin.

As I turned to let drive at the one who was leaping across Madeleine's bed, knife in hand, a fourth, emerging from a corner, struck my arm. My shot went wild; and then my pistol jammed as I whirled about to fire at the assailant from the side. A blade raked my ribs, and in another instant I was grappling hand to hand with the newcomer, striving to brain him with my clubbed pistol, and to avoid his curved knife.

We crashed to the floor. Luckily, it was his head and not mine that was dashed against the massive leg of Madeleine's bed. I rapped the useless pistol against his skull for good measure, and staggered to my feet.

D'Artois, blade in hand, was facing the two survivors. One was poised to leap and thrust with his knife. The other, pistol rising from his hip, was ready to drop d'Artois.

One of them would be sliced in half by that yard-long kampilan. One of them was a dead man. But the other would account for d'Artois as I hurdled the bed to close in, hand to hand. Neither thrust nor shot could miss at that range.

There was but one thing to do. I hurled my jammed pistol at the one about to fire. I missed. It crashed into a mirror. I had failed d'Artois.

Then, during that despairing instant in which I leaped, empty-handed and too late, it happened.

I saw an incredibly swift, fluent flash of steel, and a spurt of fire; heard a grunt, a shot, a yell of mortal terror, and once more the sound of steel biting home.

Pierre, poised and tense in his moment of extreme peril, had lunged as the shivering of the glass distracted the enemy's attention, and slashed asunder the one who fired, an instant too late. Then, cat-like, he whirled about to cut down the survivor.

All in a glance, I saw him, knife still clutched, sink to the floor. The kampilan, wedged in the bones of the hip, was pulled from Pierre's grasp.

D'Artois sighed, tottered, and leaned against the bed-post.

Of the two, I was the most shaken, as spectators usually are.

"Christ, Pierre!" I exclaimed. I had to say something. "You'd make a wonderful *jurmentado*! But did that first shot get you?"

"Only a scratch," he assured. "The second missed entirely."

He shook his head, and regarded the two at his feet.

"They should have died in good spirits," he muttered, "knowing how close they came to taking the hide of Pierre d'Artois. And that shot, earlier this evening—*mordieu*! Some one is cursing his poor marksmanship."

"That attack at the front door," he continued, "was undoubtedly a ruse to draw you from your post. As for the window—look!"

He indicated the bars that had been wrenched aside.

"Those were sawed in advance of the attempt. All of which confirms my suspicions. We are contending with more than ghosts. This necromancer has a well organized crew of cutthroats, who—"

"Good Lord," I interrupted, "she's not even awakened by all this rioting."

"No," replied d'Artois. "Nor is that strange. My guess—*tu comprends*, it is but a guess—is that Madeleine has been carefully prepared for this outrage. Some one has hypnotized her and impressed upon her mind certain commands which she executes without knowing why."

"But how could she be hypnotized, and not know it?" I wondered. "Did she mention—"

"That is simple," explained d'Artois. "He could order her to forget it, and all else but the commands he wants her to remember. But give me a hand, and we will heave this carrion into the courtyard."

One by one we dragged the intruders to the window and heard them drop to the paving below.

"In the morning," said Pierre, "I will have new bars set into the window. Better yet, we will move her into another room, although that will in all probability not fool them. And then I must report this skirmish to the police. It will be embarrassing, but I think that I can convince *Monsieur le Préfet*, without his having to listen to any talk about a queen loitering about the house."

Then, as I followed him down the stairway, "Those I left scattered about down below must also be disposed of."

But as we entered the vestibule, we saw not a sign of those that d'Artois had struck down.

He stared at me for an instant, and frowned.

"One would think from this, *mon vieux*, that we were indeed under close observation. Even as we fought up there, some one hauled the casualties away. Do you, therefore, sleep, and I will stand watch the rest of the night. While another attempt is not at all likely, it would be best to take no chances."

And though the events of the evening did not tend to promote sound sleep, I did better than the previous night. Nevertheless, I was up shortly after sunrise.

I found d'Artois sitting on the balcony overlooking the moat, and the rolling parkway below. Raoul was serving coffee.

"My friend," said d'Artois as I greeted him, "I will allow you no more than three of those guesses. What happened while you snored so melodiously to keep me awake on my post?"

"Good Lord, Pierre!" I exclaimed, fearing the worst. "Surely, they didn't return and—"

"They did indeed return, and—"

He laughed outright at my dismay, then continued, "And take away those we heaved into the court. Under my nose, *pardieu*, or while you and I surveyed the wreckage in my study. But they asked for no more steel!" he concluded with a grim smile, and a twist of his fierce gray mustache.

Then, as an afterthought, "But this enemy is no incompetent bungler, despite his poor marksmanship."

As I sipped my coffee, and digested Pierre's last remark, I glanced down rue Lachepaillet. The street extends from the citadel commandant's headquarters, along the city wall, to the guardhouse at the Porte d'Espagne drawbridge. An old man was striding jauntily up the grade. His white beard streamed in the morning breeze. He wore an Arab's burnoose, and headkerchief. The hilt of a scimitar peeped over his shoulder, and his belt bristled with daggers.

A frown wrinkled his scar-seamed forehead as he halted and regarded the number over the front door.

"Pierre," I said, "it seems we have a visitor."

D'Artois thrust aside his coffee, and glanced down from the balcony.

"*Holá!* Nureddin!" he hailed.

"*Ya* Pierre!" shouted the old fellow, as he looked up and recognized d'Artois.

The ensuing sputter of Arabic was too fast for my ear. And then d'Artois, after hesitating for a moment at the balcony railing, decided the leap was too great for his years, and dashed down the stairs to admit his visitor.

"*Ya sidi,*" said the old man, as Pierre seized his hand, "the British Resident at Aden sought me out in the desert and gave me your message. And behold, I am here, *el hamdu lilahi!*"

"And I also praise God, my good friend," exclaimed d'Artois devoutly. And then, "Raoul! Coffee!"

Turning to me, Pierre continued, "This is Nureddin, a holy darwish with whom I have had dealings in the past."

The old fellow grinned, nodded, and said, "By the bounty of Allah, I am indeed a pious recluse, but my friend Pierre summoned me from my meditations."

He made the last part of his declaration solemnly; but the twinkle in his keen old eyes convinced me that his holiness had been considerably diluted of late.

"There were no vessels, and I was in a hurry," he continued. "So in my despair, I approached the crew of a *zaroug* lying at anchor. I gave them various presents. We threw the *nakhoda* overboard, with the help of Allah, and set sail."

And then Raoul served coffee. Nureddin's piety did not keep him from relishing the brandy that Raoul had added.

This wrinkled old reprobate from the hinterland of Aden must be the ally that Pierre had summoned, relying on past friendship to bring him in such haste. Piracy, it seemed, was a new accomplishment, for as he sipped his coffee, he repeated with gusto how with the help of God they had thrown the captain overboard, and sailed up the Red Sea.

"We were not far from the shore, sidi," he added, "and the dog refused a fair offer I made him. My crew? *Wallah*, they will remain in the *zaroug*. Eight stout Dankalis. Wild men from behind Djibouti. The voyage kept them busy, but lying here in idleness, they will doubtless cut each other to pieces—"

"Say you so, my friend?" interrupted d'Artois. "I will give them cutting in good measure."

Nureddin's eyes brightened.

"Praise God!" he ejaculated devoutly, "But I saw no camels in the public square this morning, and I feared that there were no caravans to rob—"

"There are none," admitted Pierre. "But we have better game for you. And as for your Dankalis, let them make camp in the courtyard. I have work for the good fellows."

"In that case, my lord," replied the old darwish, "I will get them at once."

And Nureddin, striking light to a cigarette, strode briskly to the door, and thence down rue Lachepaillet.

Where," I demanded, "did you find him?"

"That is Nureddin, the darwish," said Pierre. "A pious and holy man—"

"Holy, hell!" I exclaimed. "Then I'm a cardinal."

"Despite his occasional trifling with caravans he is, according to his own standards, a pious and holy man," d'Artois insisted. "He robs only heretic Persians—"

"And dumps the *nakhoda* over the side, as his debut in piracy," I interrupted.

"Tiens!" scoffed Pierre. "He was in a hurry on my account. As I said, the good fellow is versed in occult sciences. He has even been in that lost city Madinat ash-Shams, far beyond the ruins of Mareb. He, if any one, can get to the bottom of this matter. Be of good cheer, my friend. This accursed pack of devil-mongers will have the crimp put in their style!"

D'Artois was enormously cheered by the arrival of his strange ally. I could see that he had shaken off the burden of despair that had weighed him down ever since my arrival in Bayonne.

In order to thwart a repetition of the previous night's raid, we decided to continue our watch. The power that was reaching forth to clutch Madeleine had become stronger. Her eyes had become strange in expression, and regarded us with curiosity mingled with resentment. Her slow, enigmatic smile made us shudder from its resemblance to the shadowy Balkis whom Pierre had commanded to leave, that night that we had seen the apparition. And then, once in a while, we caught flashes of Madeleine herself, bewildered, and dazed, and strange in her own body. Her gestures had become undulant and serpentine. It was terrifying to watch Madeleine being rapidly thrust into the background by the invader. She was lovelier, perhaps, than she had been, but it was a dismaying beauty that came from the grave of Balkis.

Happily, she was awake but little of the day. And shortly after sunset, she fell into a deep sleep.

"Watch her closely, my friend," said Pierre. "Do not relax from your vigilance even for a moment. Nureddin and I will divide the watches with you. Beware of any trickery to distract you. Call me if you should become drowsy—no matter how early it may be, call me at once."

* * * *

In view of the strategy employed by the enemy in the attack of the preceding night, I took my post in Madeleine's room. I examined the window-bars, and noted that they had not been tampered with. And regardless of whatever disturbance I might hear from below, I resolved not to quit my post. With Pierre, and the old Arab, Nureddin, and the crew of Dankalis from the *zaroug*, any handful of cutthroats that the unknown devil-monger might send would meet an adequate reception committee.

It was utterly inconceivable, a woman's being crowded out of her own body; yet Madeleine had actually become another person. When, during her waking moments, Nureddin had succeeded in cajoling her from her haughty silence, she had addressed him in what the darwish declared was the language of the ancient Sabeans.

The classic example of the illiterate servant-girl's reciting long passages of Hebraic which she had overheard her master, a philologist, declaiming did not apply to Madeleine. The servant in the delirium of fever *recited*, whereas Madeleine *conversed*. The distinction and the logical inference were painfully obvious.

Balkis the Queen remembered that her people, the Sabeans, were cousins of the Arabs, and she recognized the kinship between her and the darwish. She considered Pierre and me as aliens. She spoke in the present tense of the lost splendors of Madinat ash-Shams, that city whose ruins are in Arabia, far behind Mareb.

"By Allah!" the darwish had exclaimed at the end of one of those conversations, "I have seen those ruins. And I know that she speaks of that city as it was in the days of Suleiman, upon whom be the peace!

"She is verily Balkis, *Malikat as-Sabahh*!" he continued, lowering his voice in awe. "The Queen of the Morning. And look you, *sidi*, those are the eyes of a Sabean woman of the line of Iaraab, of pure race."

It was terrifying to think that a necromancer loved a dead queen, and could summon her from her grave, and plan so that his accursed lips might thrill to the caress of one who had smiled at Solomon.

Then what of the true Madeleine? Into what darkness was she banished? In what limbo, neither living nor dead, did she roam, desolate and become like a bird without feathers?

Hideous! Only in this hasheesh dream of a city could this infamy have occurred.

The moon was almost full. In another night, lean, wrinkled Nureddin would try his occult arts, whether or not the identity of the devil-monger was known. And in the meanwhile, he and d'Artois were taking counsel.

The night was warm and pleasant, yet suddenly I shivered. My thoughts were poor company. I knew that this room was alive with presences, and that the very silence masked the soundless murmuring of powers who were striving to make a final assault against that body whose soul they had banished.

I could not see them, but they were assembling.

The room had become a congress of evil, unseen shapes. Dead Balkis had been only an apparition, which should have been asleep rather than awake and wandering. But this which I now sensed approaching was malignant, and obscene in its own right.

The moonlight that had streamed in through the window was becoming dimmed.

"Only a cloud," I reassured myself. But I knew better.

Madeleine—Balkis—stirred uneasily, and murmured. Then her great dark eyes opened. They had the sightlessness of drugged sleep. I knew that something was commanding her silence.

The cloud that blotted the moon must now be very dense. The moon sought to hide her face from the evils of creation. The air was now vibrant with menace. Balkis, ghost that she was in a living body, was at least human. I wondered for a moment if I could awaken her, and let her dark eyes and strange tongue reprove me for my insolence, so that I would not be utterly alone in this whirlpool of evil. I wondered then if even Balkis was present. That darkened room had become appallingly empty, save for that malevolence that had become a concentrated fury.

I glanced at the window, and saw that which I had not heard. Then I wondered if, indeed, I saw. That which stared between the stout half-inch bars of steel was a thing which could not have any existence. It was a foulness and an abomination and an outrage, that slate-gray, amorphous presence, four of whose misshapen hands clutched the sill. It was that whose soundless approach, and not any cloud, had obscured the moon.

The reptilian stench of the creature choked me, and its baleful eyes paralyzed me. I gasped, and licked my dry lips, and sought to yell, but my throat was a dusty void through which my breath hissed and muttered futilely. I had a pistol, but as in a dreadful nightmare, my numb hands would not draw and fire. I knew that firing would be useless. I knew that it would be vain to alarm Pierre and the darwish, and the Dankali sailors.

Two of the hands gripped the bars, and strained against them, until they stretched and snapped. And then another pair gave way before the resistless force of that monster. It was translucent in the moonlight; and despite its prodigious strength, it was unsubstantial seeming, and formless. It was a foulness from those unhallowed vaults, coming to do the bidding of him who had resurrected and enslaved dead Balkis.

The window was now clear. That shapeless, monstrous thing flowed into the room with its ghastly confusion of limbs. The reptilian mustiness of serpent-infested subterranean caverns made the air dense and stifling and foul.

In that extreme of terror, I could no longer tremble. A lethargic resignation possessed me. And then I remembered that it had come at its diabolical master's command to seize Madeleine. My throat was still inarticulate, but with a mighty effort I regained command of my arms. I seized the chair on which I had been sitting and with the strength of frenzy, smote the creature on the head. I thought, at least, that it was its head, but I could not be sure, for the monstrosity transcended the anatomy of honest beasts.

The chair splintered, and yet bounded back as though I had smitten an inflated the. I lashed out again with what remained in my hand. It ignored me, and lumbered toward Madeleine's bed. It was as indifferent to position as it was to blows; for instead of rising from its dive to the floor, it waddled sidewise, crab-like. That formless foulness moved but with a single idea. It was devoid of perceptions. If it were cut to fragments, they would unite, and march on. Neither beast, nor reptile, nor plant, but a hideous blending of them.

It waddled, dragging its members with a scraping, hissing rustling. Nothing could stop that abysmal foulness.

It would take Madeleine to the den of the necromancer. Madeleine was doomed, and before my staring eyes. My paralyzed throat still sought to yell, but could not. A fragment of the heavy chair still hung in my grasp. Hopeless. Hopeless. What if the Dankalis drove their broad-bladed knives through it? What if Pierre sliced it with that two-handed Moro kampilan? Futile. Vain. The master demanded Madeleine. And it served. It advanced, deliberately.

"No, by God!" my mind said, though my lips were dumb. "There is a way."

I leaped past the terror, clutched Madeleine in my arms, and faced the monster. Madeleine—Balkis—was the beloved of that damnable necromancer. It would not hurt her.

I shuddered, and sickened as it embraced me and my still sleeping burden. I held her in a frenzied grip, so that it would seize us as one. My senses whirled and spun as the deadly vileness exhaled by the creature stifled me.

"Must...hold...tight."

Good God, what would not a breath...one breath...of pure air be worth! And that amorphous, textureless travesty on all creation was touching her. I wondered how her bare skin could endure that which made me shudder from the contamination that filtered through my heavier clothing.

That quintessence of all subterranean loathsomeness....

"Must...hold...tight...go with...her..."

My last conscious impression was that we were descending the masonry side of the building. Very vaguely, and as from a great distance, I heard yells of frantic men crying out in a strange language.

The Dankali sailors had seen it...

Then no more, until—I know not how much later—I opened my eyes, and saw that I was in a vast, high-ceiled room pervaded with a phosphorescent greenness that quivered and glowed and flickered maddeningly. The expanse of floor was so broad that the furniture, visible at the far side, seemed diminutive. I was lying near the wall. My hands and feet were tied with cords. My desperate strategy had worked, though to what end, I knew not. I had followed Madeleine into the house of the sorcerer, or into his subterranean den. I had no ideas on my location, whether above or below ground.

My clothing still reeked from the foulness of that which had brought us here, although the stench was rapidly becoming less intense. I shivered from the memory of that repugnant contact.

In the dim light of the room, I could distinguish hooded and robed figures. Some sat cross-legged, each on a bench scarcely larger than a coffee-table. Others, shadowy, ominous presences, conferred in low tones. A heavy haze of incense from several wrought-iron tripods clouded the room with its dizzying, breath-taking fumes. From another apartment, beyond the brocaded draperies, that concealed a doorway, I could hear the muttering of kettle-drums, and the whine of single-stringed *kemenjahs*, and the sobbing notes of pipes. The weird, minor harmony sent chills up my spine.

Then a man garbed in formal evening attire emerged from the shadows not far from me. He was tall and aquiline-featured; his eyes were glittering and phosphorescent, like those of a great cat.

This was the Master of the show, that necromancer who had defiled the very order of life in his attempt to gratify his ghastly whim; and those robed, hooded figures that moved through the spectral haze of the room were his acolytes, and his adepts in the devilish hierarchy which he had assembled.

One of the adepts strode across the tile floor and halted within a few paces of the Master. He was lean, and cadaverous, and his bald head was bulbous and dome-like. He carried in his hand a long, carven staff on which he leaned as he rendered his report in halting French.

"All is in readiness, Master," he said. "We are waiting for your command."

"Then wait no longer," replied the necromancer. "Bring her into the hall at once."

I had wondered for a moment as to my own fate. But as I heard the Master's instruction, and saw that corpse-like fellow with the staff hurrying from one group to the next, issuing orders in a low, hoarse voice, my thoughts reverted to Madeleine. Some final ritual, some uttermost outrage seemed to be necessary before Madeleine would be utterly expelled from her body, and everlastingly cast into the darkness from which dead Balkis had been summoned.

I heard the resonant clang of a brazen gong. A woodwind instrument breathed mellow, evil notes that bore a mocking semblance to the human voice. Then four litter-bearers, nude save for loincloths, strode across my field of vision. Despite my bonds, I contrived to wriggle to a sitting position, against the wall. I saw that it was Madeleine they were carrying to the dim shadows of the extremity of the hall. As they approached their destination, I saw a muffled figure flitting about, taper in hand, touching light to other tapers. Their glow was wan in that poisonous greenish phosphorescence; but the added illumination revealed an altar, and an arched shrine whose monstrous carvings leered horribly in the flickering, sickly flames.

The acolytes laid Madeleine on the altar. Then with ceremonious gestures and obeisance, they retreated and took their posts at the left of the shrine.

The Master, incongruous in his faultless *costume de rigueur*, then approached the shrine, and halting three paces distant, extended his arms.

At his gesture, the gongs clanged again, and as their brazen thunder subsided in a hissing, rustling shiver, he raised his voice in a terrific invocation.

"Balkis! Balkis! Balkis, Queen of Saba! I have descended into the shadows, and into the grave, and led you back to the morning! I have sifted the dust of forgotten centuries, and found for you a body lovelier than that before! Balkis, Queen of the Morning! Balkis, Queen of the Yaman! I will drive her into the shadows, Balkis, and you will rejoice in this body, and in this new life! I have faced the blacknesses of death, and the terror of the grave and the wrath beyond, for your sake, Balkis…"

It was somber and magnificent and terrible, that deep-throated chant. I shuddered with an ecstasy of horror as I heard that resonant rich voice declaim fullthroated above the wailing reeds and mocking mellow pipes. His words were a colossal blasphemy and a superhuman magnificence that echoed the voice of that arch-rebel, Lucifer, Son of the Morning, crying his defiance across the vastnesses of the gulf into which he had been hurled. And I knew that when he reached the climax of that awful invocation, Madeleine would be for ever damned to wander in unfathomable blacknesses; and resurrected Balkis would smile with new eyes and new lips at that mortal who had plunged into the shadows beyond the Border, and led her by the hand to greet once more the morning she had not seen for twenty-eight weary centuries of wasting her beauty among the cheerless dead.

Acolytes stood by, prepared to do that which the ritual prescribed, and waiting for the signal of the Master. The strange utensils and the uncouth objects that they held in readiness hinted at further blasphemies to come.

And then one from the farther shadows came running into the semicircular field of the tapers' glow. His oiled skin shone dully in the flickering light. He bowed his shaven skull to the tiles, and lifted his arms in supplication.

"Master, he is on the way! He knows!"

"What?" thundered the Master. "Who?"

"The enemy, Master!" replied the retainer. "And armed men are with him."

Pierre on the way! The necromancer's spies had come to warn him that the avenger had found the trail, and was on the road to end this toying with the dead, and affronting the living. Pierre had heard. It had not been my fancy, that terrified yell of the Dankalis in the courtyard. Pierre had in some way found a clue which would lead him to this den of uttermost damnation.

The Master stared at the white form on the altar before him, and at the acolytes ranged about him. He frowned, then clapped his hands. The bulbousheaded, cadaverous one advanced.

"What say you?" demanded the Master.

"Stop him at once," came the reply. "Send It out again. There is yet time. They can form the circle, and It will crush the enemy—"

"Set them to work!" commanded the Master; and then, perturbed, he strode up and down the expanse of tiles.

At a signal from the chief of the acolytes, an attendant smote a brazen gong. He shouted a command. Robed figures emerged from the shadows, each bringing with him his own bench. They arranged themselves in a crescent in the center of the hall. I heard the purr of drums; and then the adepts of the crescent began murmuring in cadence to the rhythm. Lips drawn to thin lines, jaws clenched, they hummed in a droning monotone, as they swayed from the hips, and made serpentine passes and gestures. Their eyes stared glassily in that awful greenish light and their bronzed features were expressionless. They had become automatons, moving to the cadence of those whining pipes and muttering drums. They were like the evil fantasies of Indian sculpture set to a devilish music. And then the music ceased, so that nothing was audible but that damnable droning, like the buzz of monstrous flies. Finally they broke the unison that had marked their start, and each carried on his own peculiar humming, so that it seemed as though articulate voices were chanting as from a great distance, pronouncing words that I could almost understand.

Then at the point on which their staring eyes were focused, I perceived a hazy, bluish vortex that spun, and expanded and contracted as it spiraled. It elongated, and began an axial spinning. That nebulous vapor expanded, and branched, growing in stature and becoming every instant more solid, until it evolved into a monstrous presence. It was neither human, nor reptile, nor beast, but a hideous travesty that was a blasphemy against created things. It was the counterpart of that which had seized Madeleine. It was even more horrible in that green luminescence than it had been in the moonlight of Madeleine's room. It was a horror and an outrage conceived by those six adepts; and projected by the concentrated force of their wills exerted in unison, it had assumed physical substance. It fed on their will-emanations, and waxed momentarily more and more substantial.

The Master contemplated the horror. He smiled thinly, as well he could, having marched into the grave and led Balkis by the hand to see the morning. He knew that it would waylay Pierre and his men, and crush them in its irresistible grasp, and sear their brains with the terror of its presence.

The droning of the adepts ceased and with it the mutter of drums and whine of strings. They swayed in cadence to the rhythm that had been established. They stared fixedly at the spot from whence the monstrosity had materialized, and gestured with the slow precision of an intricate machine.

The silence was absolute for a moment.

And then I heard the faint, sibilant hiss of the monster's limbs as it dragged them across the tiles. A choking, nauseous vapor exuded from its presence. As it advanced, it began to murmur, and flex its misshapen members as though to test their strength. It paused a moment, as if to receive its final instructions, and then it moved across the floor with a rapidity that belied its grotesquely deformed shape. I heard a door close behind it, and bolts slip into place as that foulness went out into the night to seek Pierre and waylay him. Nor could it miss, for it was guided by the fiendish intelligence of those entranced adepts, who were clairvoyant in that self-imposed hypnosis which enabled them to materialize their malignant thought-form. It would hunt him down. He could not by any chance avoid it; and he could not overcome it.

Madeleine was doomed. In my despair, I became resigned to my bonds. Balkis would smile from her new body, and be untroubled by any lingering vestige of that lovely girl's personality. The Master had but to resume his sonorous invocation, and weave again the spell, complete the ritual recitation of that which he had faced to woo her among the dead, then chant her back to the forgotten light of the morning.

Pierre was doomed, and with him, stout Nureddin who had come across the desert and sailed a frail *zaroug* coastwise from the Red Sea to France. It would annihilate them all, Pierre, the darwish, and the Dankalis with their broad-bladed knives.

A great rage then possessed me, and put to flight my resignation. I would burst my bonds, and bare-handed avenge as much of this infamy as I could until those adepts overwhelmed me. But as I strained at the cords that bound my ankles and wrists, I knew that even that was vanity.

And then a cigar-lighter fell from my vest pocket to the tiles. The Master had not even glanced in my direction. He still paced up and down before the altar, disturbed by the interruption of his ritual. He was waiting to learn of the destruction of Pierre and his party.

Arching my back like a measuring-worm, I placed myself over the cigar-lighter, and with the fingers of one hand, uncapped it, and whirled the milled wheel. The wick ignited. I could feel its tiny, fierce flame eating into my wrists; and above the fumes that rose from the tall wrought-iron tripod censers, I could smell the burning of the cord, and the singeing of hair and flesh. The pain was excruciating. I dared not move. The strain of keeping my body clear of the lighter, so that its flame would not be smothered, was intolerable. And then the cords yielded. Hands free! With my scorched fingers, I dug a penknife from my pocket and slashed the cords that bound me.

The Master stood before the altar, contemplating Madeleine's still body in the light of those flickering tapers. His hands were clasped behind his back, and his head bowed.

The shaven heads of the six adepts seated crescent-wise behind the Master were weaving and nodding in cadence.

And then I heard a shout, and cries of terror. Pierre's voice. He had avoided It until almost within striking distance of the enemy.

I leaped to my feet, and seized the wrought-iron tripod by its legs. I charged across the hall, scattering behind me a trail of incandescent coals. The Master heard me, and turned. He shouted a command. I saw emerging from the green shadows a file of short, muscular men, naked save for loin-cloths, and armed with short curved blades.

With my feet planted firmly on the tiles, I swung my fire-charged weapon—not at them, but crashing down on the shaven skull of the first of the six adepts and showering the others with fire.

That would break up their concentration!

Crash! Another found his brains oozing across the tiles.

They were almost upon me, those swordsmen. Their blades glittered as they advanced.

A pistol cracked, and the impact of the Master's shot whirled me back a pace. I recovered, and swung again as he fired a second time. And then I hurled the tripod full into the face of the leading swordsman. Their blades hacked and raked me as I stretched out in a lunge that carried me under their sweeping slashes. I clutched the second by the ankles and dragged him to the floor. They howled with pain as their bare feet trod on the live coals I had scattered.

The Master no longer dared fire, lest he strike his own men.

They were hacking and thrusting in that milling confusion of arms and legs and bodies, doing each other more harm than they did me. I salvaged a dagger, and stabbed blindly. But it was a hopeless melee. I was at the bottom of the heap.

Those few seconds of close-packed confusion seemed ages. No one could last long against such odds. Any instant would bring the finishing thrust...

I heard a splintering of glass, and shouts. The voice of Pierre! And Nureddin with his Dankalis!

In an instant, the milling tangle leaped clear, leaving me lying among the dead. I saw the darwish, white beard streaming, sword in hand, leading his copper-colored Dankalis toward the altar, slaying-mad and howling as they slashed with their broad-bladed knives.

One of them was about to cut down the Master.

"Stop!" cried Pierre.

The mad savage halted, and lowered his blade. I struggled to my feet, cut, blood-drenched, but not entirely dismembered.

The hall was a madhouse of slaughter. Nureddin's curved blade dripped bloodily. A Dankali lay on a heap of fallen swordsmen, still clutching his knife. Pierre's pistol, empty and fuming, was in his hand, at his side.

"Graf Istavan," he said to that tall, somber Master, "it seems that you are the only survivor. But I propose to remedy that in a moment."

"So the redoubtable d'Artois will attack an unarmed man?" he murmured disdainfully.

"By no means, *monsieur*," said Pierre, "but wait and see."

"My lord," said Nureddin, as he approached, "I will send Balkis back to the shadows."

And then he spoke to the Dankalis in their own language. They surrounded Graf Istavan with a circle of steel. The darwish picked from the floor a fragment of charcoal that had been spilled during the skirmish, and set about making good his promise to d'Artois. While he was marking upon the tiles the figure that was required, I turned to Pierre to inquire about the monstrosity that had been sent to waylay him.

"It met us as we drew up in the grove outside the château," he said. "*Mon Dieu*! A loathsome nightmare! The darwish slashed it with his scimitar. I fired at it, but the thing was invulnerable. The Dankalis were too frightened to run. So were we all, for that matter. It enveloped us in its limbs and was crushing us slowly but very surely, like some monstrous octopus, and stifling us with its poisonous exhalation."

D'Artois shuddered at the memory of the horror.

"And then," he resumed, "it suddenly became vague and shadowy. Now that I hear your side of it, it is all clear. You were right in bending that iron tripod over the heads of those adepts. The monster was their thought-form, projected into the physical plane, and when you so deftly addled the brains of two or three of them, the concentration was interrupted. As you describe the ritual, those adepts must have hypnotized themselves, each envisioning the same creature, bent on the same mission. The Yogis in Hindustan have a similar feat. The vortex of thought force became a physical entity with no motive but to annihilate us, just as the thing which took you and Madeleine had but one impulse, capturing her. Your device, my friend, in seizing her and being taken with her was shrewd strategy —"

"I was too scared to do anything else," I replied. "But where are we? How did you follow us? How—"

"Tenez!" exclaimed d'Artois. "I will enlighten you. One of the Dankalis howled as though Satan had prodded him with his red-hot trident. He had seen It leaving with you and Madeleine.

"Nureddin and I had been studying the case that evening. We carefully considered a list, as I told you, of all persons Madeleine had had any contact with while in Bayonne. I took the liberty of opening a letter addressed to her, from a friend in Marseilles, and there I found it. *'You didn't tell me about the séance at Graf Istavan's château,'* the young lady wrote to Madeleine.

"*Voilà.* There I had it. Why did she forget the handsome Graf Istavan, when she remembered all those shopkeepers and servants, and casual acquaintances? How could a girl reared in America, where a Hungarian count would be a sensation, forget an invitation to a *soirée* at his château? I inquired. It was simple. I knew then that she had forgotten *because she had been commanded to remember that she was Balkis, and to forget that she had ever heard of Graf Istavan.* It was obvious, simple, *n'est-ce pas*? And so when I found you two had vanished and heard of the *afreet*, as those excellent black fellows called the hideous thing, I set out on the trail. And the rest you know."

We glanced at the darwish. He had drawn a pentacle upon the tiled floor. In each of its five angles he was inscribing symbols, and characters in a script I did not recognize.

"Look!" muttered Pierre. "Madeleine's fate depends upon that darwish. When he arrived, he thought that it would be simple to expel Balkis. But she has taken such complete possession that it will be more than a simple exorcism. And the great danger is that Madeleine has been thrust so far into the shadows that there is no longer any bond between her and the body that once was hers.

"My friend, you think that the evening behind you has been one of perils and encounters. *À bas!* That has been nothing. The conflict is yet to come. That white-bearded nomad holds the destiny of two women in his hands. And, if I mistake not, perhaps another destiny."

At the corners of the pentacle, the darwish had placed glowing charcoal from the censers that had not been overturned. And on each heap he poured a handful of the same incense that they had been burning in the room. As the fumes rose in dense, stifling sweet clouds that almost obscured the darwish as he knelt in the center of the figure, we heard him chant.

"*Ya* Balkis! *Ya* Balkis, *malikat us-Sabahh*! Beloved of Suleiman! The thief and the spoiler has robbed the grave and called you from being queen among the quiet dead. The mocker and the defiler has disturbed your rest.

"*Ya* Balkis, come forth from the body which you have invaded!

"*Ya* Balkis, come forth of your own will, or I will pronounce your Hidden Name. I will pronounce your True Name. Hear me, Balkis, Queen of the Morning, for this I can and this I will do!"

Then he began solemnly intoning in that almost forgotten language. His voice rolled and thundered like drums beaten before a palace; and from time to time, during that sonorous invocation, we heard her name, and knew that he had not yet pronounced the True Name.

D'Artois shivered, and down my own spine there were chills leaping and dancing to the cadence of that great voice. A terrific tension was in the air, and a rustling and chirping, and a murmuring: and within the pentacle, beside the smoke-veiled kneeling form of the darwish, we saw another standing, who was slender and wore a tall, curiously wrought diadem.

The chanting ceased, and the muttering, rustling sounds that we had heard. And then the darwish pronounced a single phrase, and made a gesture.

There was a deep sigh, and a stifled wail of unutterable despair. The darwish was alone in the pentacle. His eyes stared and his face was drawn as he bowed to the five points of the pentacle, and stepped from its limits.

He addressed d'Artois.

"My lord, Balkis has returned to the shadows. Now let us see what tenant the stolen body has."

Madeleine lay motionless on the altar, in the wan light of the flickering tapers, and the green phosphorescence that pervaded the room.

"Look," whispered Pierre, "her expression is changed. *She* is indeed gone."

I saw then that while the features had not altered in any essential, there was an indefinable though certain difference. I wondered if Madeleine would look at us from those long-lashed eyes when she opened them.

"Awaken her at once!" commanded d'Artois, beckoning to Graf Istavan. He too had seen that presence in the pentacle with the darwish, and with her disappearance, his last hope had vanished. His haughty features were calm in despair: for Balkis, the beloved from the shadows, had died before his eyes.

Nureddin muttered a word to the Dankalis. As they advanced, their circle of steel urged Graf Istavan toward the altar. Then they halted, letting him approach the body of his victim. Their thirsty blades were poised, ready to cut him down at Nureddin's signal.

The necromancer turned toward d'Artois.

"Monsieur," he said, "this has gone too far. I can not awaken her."

"Try it!" demanded d'Artois. "It is worth trying. If you fail, these black fellows will tear you to pieces and eat your raw flesh. Awaken her!"

Graf Istavan knew that d'Artois had used no figure of Speech when he made his threat. He saw the darwish thoughtfully fingering the edge of his sword. Then he faced the altar, and made stroking passes and gestures. He addressed the sleeping girl in sharp syllables of command. Perspiration cropped out on his forehead. His hands began to tremble as he exerted his will to its utmost, trying one device after another to awaken Madeleine. He was fighting for his life, and he knew it. But in vain.

His arms dropped to his side. He turned to Pierre with a despairing gesture.

"It is useless, *monsieur*," he said. "She has escaped. She is beyond my reach. She—"

"Is she dead?" I demanded. "Pierre—"

"No," said d'Artois. "Her body is alive. It has suffered no violence. But her spiritual essence, her intelligence, her soul, call it what you will, had been forced so far into the shadows that it wanders, lost and confused, and can not find its way back. Try again, Graf Istavan, or by the living God, these fellows will tear you limb from limb, and I am not jesting!"

The necromancer shrugged his shoulders resignedly, and shook his head.

"What I can not do, I can not. Do your worst. I am beaten, and I do not complain. That white-bearded juggler of yours, that wild darwish from the desert, has driven Balkis beyond my reach. I heard him command her by her True Name, and she obeyed. She is gone—"

Again that gesture, and that haunted look of despair.

"So it makes little difference what happens to me. Let them strike. Perhaps I can find her somewhere across the Border, where she is with the untroubled dead. Strike, *monsieur*. I am unarmed."

And the eager steel that touched him, waiting to drive home, did not make him flinch. I saw that he welcomed it. I sensed that we were but saving him from seeking his own life. It was I, rather than Graf Istavan, who felt the supreme despair of that tense moment when the steel would blossom red again and complete the evening's vain butchery. For vain it was, with Madeleine lying there, a thing of exquisite beauty: living, yet dead. Madeleine's *self* was wandering blindly in a limbo whose dim mazes confused her groping search for her body. I saw the fierce light in Pierre's eyes and the passionless, serene gaze of the darwish, and the grimness of the Dankalis poised to strike: and saw but futile vengeance whose bitter fruit would be a lovely, soulless body.

Nureddin's gesture beckoned the savages away from Graf Istavan, whose life they wanted as blood indemnity for their fallen comrades.

"Nureddin," said d'Artois, "is there no way? Are we too late?"

His voice was unsteady, and his features were tense. For a moment I wondered if he would with his own hands kill an unarmed man.

"*Sidi*, there is a way," replied the darwish. He spoke very slowly and solemnly. "Do you remember that night? We were in Kuh-i-Atesh?"

D'Artois' tanned cheeks paled at the mention of the Mountain of Fire, in Kurdistan. "Good God! you don't mean that you'll try *that* ritual?"

"If it please Allah, I will," affirmed the darwish.

D'Artois bowed his head for a moment. He glanced at the sleeping loveliness on the altar. His eyes were somber and despairing.

"I can't let him do that," he muttered. "And she's the daughter of my old friend. I can't refuse…"

Pierre's features quivered with emotion. He paced back and forth, head bowed, and eyes staring at the tiles. Pierre was playing the heart-breaking role of destiny. His choice would decide the day. Madeleine would remain a lovely, lifeless thing—or old Nureddin would face some awful peril. I had sensed that from the moment I had heard the name of that mountain in Kurdistan. Now I knew it.

"My friend," said the darwish, "I will make the venture, *inshallah*! Do not seek to dissuade me. You have no choice. I will not fail!"

The darwish turned to the Dankalis and spoke a few words in a low voice. They stared, and made gestures of protest. Nureddin hushed their murmurings with a sharp command. Then they escorted Graf Istavan away from the altar. I had not understood a word of that Somali Coast jargon, but I saw from their faces that the words of Nureddin had instilled fear, and consternation, and grief.

"Mordieu!" exclaimed Pierre as he faced me. "He has taken the initiative so as to absolve me of all blame. He knew that I could neither consent nor deny."

In a low, hoarse voice he continued, "To stand here and watch, helplessly—it is terrible!"

The darwish in the meanwhile had been scratching a circle on the tiles with the point of his blade. Then he wiped it clean and forced it between the tiles so that it stood upright before him. The steel glistened frostily in that weird green light.

Nureddin knelt and crossed his arms on his breast. He bowed thrice, touching his forehead to the tiles just in front of the sword. We heard him muttering words that he pronounced so rapidly that we made no attempt to understand or even recognize the language. Then his voice became a faint murmur as he stared fixedly at the glittering steel. Finally it subsided to an indistinct whisper, then to silence. His body swayed ever so slightly, like a reed in a gentle breeze.

Nureddin's features were transfigured with an awful solemnity. His eyes had become fixed in an intent stare. I held my breath, and quivered from a growing tension. Neither fuming censers nor chanting acolytes: only an old man kneeling before an upright blade, and staring fixedly; yet it was more awesome and compelling than any of the thaumaturgy and sonorous rituals I had witnessed that night, and more terribly thrilling than Graf Istavan's mighty recital.

I knew that this darwish who knelt in the circle was indeed a pious and holy man; that such peccadilloes as the robbing of caravans were trifles not to be charged to his account.

The room was a brooding silence such as precedes the relentless stroke of doom. I glanced at Pierre, and was glad that I did not know what to expect.

We stood poised on the very border of—

A great cry wrenched our tense nerves. Then we heard a gasp, and the scream of a startled woman.

Madeleine sat upright on the altar. She was bewildered, and her eyes were wide with terror. Then she recognized d'Artois.

"Oh, Uncle Pierre!" she exclaimed, as she slid from the altar that had come so perilously close to being her bier. "What in the world—where—an old white-bearded man was leading me through an awful fog where I'd been lost so hopelessly—"

She laughed hysterically, and clung to her Uncle Pierre.

"He took me…by the hand…and led me… Oh, it was terrible, but his face was so kind…"

"My dear," said d'Artois, making an effort to control his conflicting emotions, "let us go home. We have—here, take her!" he commanded in a voice whose gruffness nearly cracked for an instant. "The car is not far from the château, in front."

As Madeleine clung to my arm, I caught a glimpse of Nureddin lying face down on the tiles. His arms stretched out before him. Only a glance: but I knew now why d'Artois had paled at the mention of Kuh-i-Atesh.

The exit from the room was through the window. As I helped Madeleine through the shattered sash, I heard Pierre's voice, very stern, and too well controlled. He spoke to the Dankalis in Arabic.

"One of you help me with your master's body. He is dead."

"Monsieur d'Artois," said Graf Istavan, "death is nothing to me. But would you leave me to be mutilated by these savages?"

"Their master," replied d'Artois sternly, "went across the Border to lead your victim back to her body before it died. But he himself could not return. Before he left, I fancy that he instructed his men. Who am I to ask them to disobey?"

I leaped to the ground. As Madeleine dropped to my arms, one of the Dankalis followed her. After him came d'Artois, who let down the body of the darwish.

Pierre, however, carried Nureddin single-handed to the car, for the Dankali was in great haste to rejoin his comrades...

* * * *

We drove back to Pierre's house as fast as the powerful car would carry us. Madeleine, still unstrung from her sudden awakening, was startled at the sight of Nureddin.

"Oh, that's the same old man that I saw in my dream!" she exclaimed. "He led me back through the fog and the darkness. It's been the most miserable nightmare! Most of the time I thought I was some one else."

Later, as we three sat in his study, I said, "Pierre, what really did happen, now that it's all over?"

"That old darwish," said d'Artois, "knew that there was but one way of bringing Madeleine back to her body. He knew that that would be a feat that even an adept can perform but once. Yet, knowing that it would be fatal, he persisted.

"My dear," he continued, turning to Madeleine, "although your body was still alive, *you* were dead. And had Nureddin not acted so quickly, you would have joined Balkis in the shadows, for there would have been no living body to await your return."

For a few moments we were without words. Death had taken the darwish, but the living girl was testimony that Death himself had been robbed by that strange old man.

"But why didn't he use the True Name—whatever that may be?" I finally asked d'Artois.

"Nureddin's occult studies could scarcely have included Madeleine's True Name," replied d'Artois. "He did not know it, and thus could not call her back to her body. But an adept from the Orient would know the True Name of Balkis.

"That principle," d'Artois continued, "is one of the oldest in the study of magic and the occult. The ancient Hebraic cabala made much of the holy and awful mystery of the True Name of Javeh. Egyptian sorcerers claimed that they would work miracles by threatening Osiris with the public revelation of his True Name if he did not lend them his power.

"Everything, in fact, is supposed to have a secret name by which it can be commanded," concluded Pierre. "But few have that knowledge."

"And to think," said Madeleine, "that that old man deliberately gave his life for a strange woman." Her eyes sparkled with tears as she continued, "That took greater courage than facing—oh, but I shouldn't say that, after what you and Uncle Pierre did. What I mean—if I could only express—"

"Don't try to, my dear," said Pierre. "We know how you feel about that heroic old fellow." And then, solemnly, "You can best express your appreciation by never regretting that you are not a queen."

D'Artois, deeply moved as he was by the sacrifice of the darwish, smiled, and twisted his mustache. "You might," he suggested, "remember him, and some day name your first son Nureddin!

"And now I must busy myself with certain arrangements with *Monsieur* the Prefect of Police, on account of the messy condition of the château of the late Graf Istavan. His title, by the way, is as fictitious as your claim to the throne of Balkis. Those good Dankalis would do well to leave Bayonne quietly and quickly. And while I arrange—"

D'Artois winked at me, and grinned, making an unconvincing attempt to conceal his emotions.

"See if you can console this young lady for her sudden loss of a crown," he said.

"That," murmured Madeleine, as the door closed behind Pierre, "should be easy enough, unless you take after Graf Istavan and insist upon royalty."

But she was wrong: for my thoughts as well as hers, that evening, were of an old man who had gone empty-handed on a raid to rob Death, instead of a caravan of Persian heretics.

LORD OF THE FOURTH AXIS

Originally published in *Weird Tales*, November 1933.

"My friend," began Pierre d'Artois, "what would you say if I told you that one man could have halted the terrific march of Genghis Khan's Golden Horde, or stopped the relentless sweep of Tamerlane's power?"

"I would say," I replied, certain that d'Artois was proposing one of those paradoxes with which he loves to garnish his speech, "that Jake had mixed too many Sazerac cocktails."

"And you would be wrong!" retorted d'Artois. He struck light to a *Bastos*, several hundred of which villainous cigarettes he had left of the supply that he had brought with him from France. "But I grant that it could not have been accomplished unless that one man had acted in time."

"Certainly," I conceded. "If either of those conquerors had been assassinated at an early age."

"Perhaps," suggested Pierre, "if that excellent servitor of yours would mix you another one of those cocktails, your stunted imagination might be equal to what I am about to explain. Listen then!

"There is another conqueror stirring in Central Asia. And he will make what you call the monkey of Genghis Khan, and lame Timur who limped his way over half the earth, destroying and building as pleased his fancy. And I, Pierre d'Artois, am here to stop him!"

D'Artois, who had arrived in New Orleans not more than an hour before, is the most sane and practical man I have ever known. I had been delighted when I received his unexpected telegram, announcing his proposed arrival on the Crescent Limited, Wednesday; and surprised when he arrived a full day ahead of time, having travelled via air from New York. He had smiled cryptically at my demands for explanation of his haste, and had changed the subject; but now, apparently, he was in his dramatic way startling me into full attention.

I could see from his grim expression as he pronounced the last words of his speech, that he was in earnest, and that the Sazerac cocktails which Jake, my negro handyman, had mixed, were in no wise responsible for Pierre's staggering remarks. Nevertheless, I regarded him with a stare that finally made him smile at my bewilderment.

"But no! It is not that I propose to stop an army, single-handed," he continued. "It is rather that I am here to thwart a psychic menace which is to pave the way for a conqueror who will be more devastating than Genghis Khan, whom they rightly called the Mighty Manslayer. I said psychic; yet perhaps I should have said cosmic, or possibly ultra-cosmic. But decide the word for yourself."

He exhaled a cloud of acrid smoke from his vile cigarette. Pierre would have none of our widely advertised American brands. And then he resumed what already promised to be as strange a discourse as that which had preceded his fight against the Lord Peacock in Bayonne, that devil-haunted, charming city in the foothills of the Pyrenees.

"History has commented on the super-human genius of Genghis Khan. History offers no comparable figure. Alexander the Great—Iskander Dhoulkarnayn, they call him even to this day in the Asiatic lands he invaded—was what in your idiom is termed a boy wonder, a flash in the pan, which soon burned out, and left an empire that disintegrated before the dead of his last battle. And our Napoleon, that Corsican made his fame by wasting the manhood of France, and to what end? Consider, he abandoned an army in Egypt, lost a larger army in Russia, rode to the fiasco of Waterloo, and died in exile, leaving his infant son heir to a fictitious crown. That sweeps the field clear, except for Genghis Khan, and his successor, Tamerlane. They came from the nowhere of High Asia, and they ravaged the world from end to end. The successors of the Great Khan amused themselves building empires of the fragments of that vast heritage left by an obscure nomad chieftain from the Gobi Desert. History has been baffled at the colossal force of him they called, and rightly, the Master of Thrones and Crowns, the Perfect Warrior, the Mighty Manslayer, the Scourge of God, that Genghis Khan whose line and whose conquest persisted for generations, cropping out in that brooding, terrible Tamerlane, and Baber, that empire-builder.

"Mark this well: Central Asia is a vortex and a reservoir of power. There was in the old days, *and there is today*, a fountain of energy which at irregular intervals surges forth and sweeps the world with fire and devastating slaughter."

* * * *

Pierre sipped from the glass which Jake had filled. I followed suit, but scarcely noted that Jake had poured wine instead of another cocktail. The history that d'Artois had summarized was familiar territory to me; but the voice with which he had recited his epitome gave it a terrible significance that had heretofore escaped me.

"Central Asia is a vortex and a reservoir of power!"

That, and his previous remark about the impending appearance of another invasion which he, Pierre d'Artois, was to halt, left me dazed.

Then he produced a sheaf of papers from his inside coat pocket. They were official documents. Two bore the seals of European powers; and one, I noted, had the spread eagle of the United States to give it authority. I saw how Pierre was accredited, and wondered at the eminence he had attained. And if I had any doubts as to his sanity or sobriety, they were dispelled by the evidence he presented. I knew then that Pierre was actually in New Orleans to halt the impending apparition of some terrific menace, for those whose signatures followed the embossed seals would scarcely accredit one suffering from hallucinations, or delusions of grandeur.

"As you know," he resumed, "before you made my acquaintance in Bayonne, I spent a number of years in High Asia, and in Kurdistan, the land where they worship Satan as Malik Tawus, the Lord Peacock; and in the mighty ruins of Bora Bador, in Java; and in Ankor Wat. I was admitted to the secret circles of adepts in thaumaturgy and occultism of a nature that makes the astonishing feats of Hindoo magic and telepathy seem puerile. And in Tibet I saw things of which I do not care to speak in detail, except to mention that I know that men have the means of becoming gods. Literally, not figuratively.

"Yet beneath this diversity I sensed a unity of effort and purpose: the opening of the Gateway through which the Lord of the Fourth Axis can march to our plane of existence."

"What do you mean, Fourth Axis?" I ventured, as he paused to light another cigarette. "That suggests fourth dimension, and the like."

"You are not entirely out of order," admitted Pierre. "But more of that, shortly. Now, as I hinted, there was an underlying oneness of purpose in all the obscure places I visited, and the rituals I witnessed. And once, I took part in them."

He shuddered just perceptibly as he paused to re-vision the scene that he had mentioned in passing. And then he continued.

"As a result of those studies, I unearthed certain evidence to show that the superhuman power of Genghis Khan arose from his having reached across the Border and made contact with the Fourth Plane. He tapped a reservoir of forces that enabled him to overrun the world, overthrow the finest armies of Europe, not by force of numbers as is commonly supposed, but by a terrific genius that valor and steel could not resist. In their terror, Europeans—your ancestors and mine— called him the Scourge of God, but they were wrong. He was the neophyte, the insignificant servant of Him who is beyond the scope of our God who rules a universe of three dimensions."

"Good Lord, Pierre, that's almost blasphemy!" I protested.

"Blasphemy lies in intent, not in expression," retorted Pierre, solemnly. "If I could explain the thing as a whole, you would see that there is nothing irreverent in that statement.

"But Genghis Khan did not make complete contact, else the very features of the earth would have been everlastingly altered. And his successors retained but a fraction of his inspiration from across the Border. Yet they were gigantic in their way. Consider Tamerlane, sitting at chess while his troops hacked to pieces the army of Bajazet, reputed the greatest captain of his time. Is that the doing of any *man?* I mean, man in the sense that other commanders were men.

"The credentials that you examined show that I am not the only one who holds that opinion. A certain Captain Rankin, of the British Secret Service, years ago, rendered a report of his investigations in High Asia, and among the Yezidees of Kurdistan. Captain Rankin was politely but firmly placed in a sanitarium for observation and treatment. But the successors of his short-sighted superiors were wiser. They know, now, that if the impending disturbance is not halted, all Asia will burst into a mad flame of destruction which will end by sweeping an empire from its already unsteady feet."

"But where does New Orleans come into this picture?" I demanded.

"You suggested, a moment ago, that I had hinted at something mathematical in my expression, Lord of the Fourth Axis. There was more truth in that than you realized. There is a mathematical relation of this earth to our space, and to the ultra-space of more than three dimensions. That relation demands that the Enemy start his operations in the neighborhood of New Orleans.

"New Orleans is but a mathematical point in this colossal scheme. *Point d'ap-pui*, if you comprehend my idiom; taking-off point, I might say…occult, rather than geographical.

"And thus you see the reason for the documents which I carry. And finally, the credentials from those United States, they are but the courtesy rendered to other governments. With all respect to your government, they are strangely blind. Their doubts as to our sanity are concealed more politely than effectively.

"'Most obscure, Mr. d'Artois,' said that one whose signature you see here. 'How can the ghost of Genghis Khan, and forty or fifty Chinese spiritualists, upset the world?' he remarked as he set his hand opposite the seal with its eagle. And vainly I explained that it was not the ghost of the Mighty Manslayer that we fought, and that those were not the Chinese laundrymen he knew, but Mongol adepts from High Asia that we were to thwart—not by force of arms, but by weapons like their own. *À bas!* That one, I fancy, thinks Genghis Khan a cousin of Otto Kahn!"

D'Artois paused, drew a farewell draft of his foul fuming cigarette, and extinguished it against the side of the ashtray.

"Specifically, we will combat them by gaining possession of a certain piece of ritual equipment they require; or failing that, by upsetting the vibration-resonance they must develop in order to break down the barriers, and establish contact with super-space. And this is what I propose to do in order to thwart the successor of Genghis Khan! And now may I look at your telephone directory?"

I handed him the book, which he consulted.

"Ah, here she is," he remarked, after a moment's glance down the page. "Mademoiselle Louise Marigny. Note the address, and drive me there at once, if you please. Immediately, in fact!"

* * * *

"But how does this Miss Marigny come into your plans?" I wondered, as we drove up St. Charles Avenue.

"She has unwittingly come into possession of a unit of that ritual equipment I mentioned," he replied, "a rug of unique design. It is one of three which first appeared in Central Asia. Panopoulos, a Greek, brought the first one into the country. As a courtesy to one of the governments to which I am accredited, he was detained for questioning, but not for long. He was stabbed, and the rug was quite inexplicably stolen from the officials who held it pending further investigation, made at the instigation, let us say, of other governments. Nazar Shekerjian, an Armenian, bringing into the United States what was reputed to be the second of the three rugs, met a like fate when detained for questioning. The officials in whose custody the rug was were placed in an embarrassing position, I assure you. And thus, finally, I was detailed to trace the third rug, which secret agents of a power interested in Asiatic tranquility knew was on its way to Stamboul, and thence to the United States."

"That accounts for your unexpected arrival, ahead of schedule?" I suggested. "To get ahead of those who are seeking to take the rug?"

"Precisely," admitted Pierre, as we turned down one of the cross-streets not far from Lee Circle, and drew up at one of those old-fashioned houses with tall white pillars that supported a broad gallery on the second story.

The Marigny's were an old Creole family; *vieille noblesse*, you might say. I had never met the Miss Marigny we sought, but I remembered her as queen of the Mardi Gras several years previous.

An old negro servant took our cards and ushered us into a high-ceiled living-room to await Miss Marigny.

"How do you do, Mr. d'Artois? And you, Mr. Landon? This is an unexpected pleasure."

Her manner was cordial, albeit reserved. But she contrived to convey, in spite of her gracious air, that she was at a loss to know just why she was thus favored.

"I am sure," began d'Artois, with that inimitable bow which always assures him of a favorable reception, "that you will pardon the liberty we take in calling uninvited. Would you be kind enough to show us that rug which you bought in Stamboul, in the course of that Mediterranean cruise from which you have just returned?"

"Why, certainly," assented Louise Marigny. "But how did you know—"

"That I will explain presently," replied d'Artois. "In the meanwhile, I would appreciate your great kindness." And then, a few moments later, as a servant un-rolled the rug and spread its lustrous folds across a table: "*Regardez donc*! It is magnificent, yes?"

It was more than magnificent. It was utterly outlandish. Those rich colors had not come from the dye-pots of Persia or Turkistan; and its pattern was as unique as its dyes. The interlaced and interwoven curves of Moorish architectural adorn-ment were expressed in a textile, giving an effect utterly different from the floral richness of Persian, or the straight-line geometric motifs of Caucasian weaves. The longer I looked at it, the more compelling it became; and in spite of the closeness of the design, there was an effect of sweeping curves of inexpressible breadth and vigor.

The rug was about four feet wide, and hardly more than seven feet in length. Its upper corners had been clipped, giving it a form similar to the inner panel of a Turkish prayer rug; but the cut had run along the line of a corner piece, so that the unity of the remaining pattern was unmarred.

"Look at it!" Pierre repeated. "It is vibrant and alive, like a beast of prey lying asleep and dreaming of stalking resistlessly to its next slaying."

There was something breath-taking about these incredible arabesques, with their dynamic, fluent curves; and something ominous. I glanced at Louise Marigny, and saw that she was regarding d'Artois curiously as he made his com-ments on that satanically lovely piece of weaving.

"It seems that we agree on its personality," she said, "except that you per-ceived its sinister beauty at a glance, whereas it took me several days to get the effect."

"For once, *mademoiselle*," replied d'Artois, "advance knowledge is superior to feminine intuition. You sensed, in a few days, what I know as the result of years of study, and a definite warning."

"Why, Mr. d'Artois!" she exclaimed. "That sounds alarming! It did make me uneasy, the longer I looked at it, but I didn't suspect that there is anything dan-gerous about it."

During their exchange of remarks, I noted that it had not been mutilated, as I had at first thought. The remaining vestiges of finishing web and fringe, such as Oriental rugs have at their ends, were present. This added to the utter oddity of the piece, for in my several years of dabbling in rugs, I had never encountered one in the form of a rectangle with the upper corners shaped by the weaver as though they had been clipped.

"It is a sinister thing," I remarked. "It looks as though some master weaver went mad, and played monstrous tricks with all known color schemes, yet achieved beauty in the end."

"But how in the world did you know I had this rug?" wondered Louise Marigny.

Pierre offered her the document with the seal of the United States.

"This will introduce me, although I am not permitted to go into detail," he replied. "Secret agents of various powers learned that it came from an obscure spot in Central Asia, and found its way to Stamboul. And while I do not know, I have my suspicions as to how you acquired it. Did the person who sold it to you know that you were bound for New Orleans?"

"You're nothing less than a mind-reader, Mr. d'Artois! Or else you are very well informed," she answered. "I was shopping in the bazaars of Stamboul, with the intention of selecting something as a souvenir of my cruise. The merchant, an old, white-bearded fellow with unusually keen eyes, was asking the most exorbitant prices for perfectly wretched rugs. But I sat there, drinking tiny cups of coffee, which they serve prospective customers. And in the course of the bargaining, I mentioned being on my way to New Orleans. He then and there dug into a pile, and brought out this rug. At a glance, I knew I couldn't possibly afford such a magnificent thing. It fascinated me at once. But to my great surprise he offered it at a perfectly ridiculous price. I naturally took it at once.

"But on the remainder of the trip I had a feeling of being followed, kept under close surveillance; though to be truthful about it, I can't even remember any one's actually spying on me, or even staring obviously. And when I landed in New Orleans, and had the rug unpacked, it began to grate on my nerves. I hung it on the wall of my room, and in the early morning light the sweeping bands of color in the pattern seemed to writhe, and twist, and change in hue. I knew it must be the illusion caused by the angle of the light striking the rug, but I couldn't stand seeing it when I awoke in the morning; so I put it on the floor.

"But that was no better. To use your own words, it suggested a beast of prey, sleeping, but ready to awaken and leap."

She shuddered; but before she could continue her remarks, d'Artois began, "That rug was given to you for a purpose, Miss Marigny. You were the unwitting means of getting it into this country. And I venture to state that you will not keep it long."

"Why, what do you mean?" she demanded, arching her brows in amazement.

"I am not permitted to go into detail," replied Pierre. "But glance at this report."

He handed her the report I had seen.

"You will note," he remarked, as she regarded the paper intently, her alarmed expression becoming more intense as she read further, "that Panopoulos, a

Greek, and Shekerjian, an Armenian, both encountered serious difficulties. Fatal, as you observe."

"But they were detained at the customs. I passed this rug lawfully," she protested.

"So did they. They were detained for other reasons. And they died because some one did not want them to answer what they would have been asked. The reason that you were allowed to pass the customs without questioning is that after two failures, those I represent decided upon different tactics. I am here to pay any price you care to name. And to assure you that this is bona fide, you may confer with the Federal officials in New Orleans. They do not yet know that I am here, but they will recognize my credentials."

Louise Marigny reflected for a moment before replying. She glanced at the sinister, satanic beauty before us, and shivered.

"Mr. d'Artois, I'll take your offer. That rug has worried me ever since I unpacked it."

Pierre took from his pocket a thick roll of bills.

"Tell me when to stop," he remarked, as he stripped them off, one by one, laying them fan wise on the rug. "It is your property by purchase. I do not want you to feel that I am forcing a deal."

"Oh, Mr. d'Artois!" she gasped, as she noted the denomination of the bills. "One of them would more than pay what it cost me."

"*Tenez*! Never let it be said that Pierre d'Artois drove a sharp bargain," he said as he added another bill to the pile. "The pleasure is mine, Miss Marigny."

We then took leave of Louise Marigny, who, despite her more than moderate circumstances, had reason to feel that it was a fortunate stroke of business to have her casual purchase in Stamboul pay several times over for the entire cruise. And Pierre on his part had made progress in his mysterious mission.

"They planned to relieve her of this rug at their convenience," said d'Artois. "But now they have me to rob, which will not be so simple. But from now on, you and I are in danger of assassination and robbery. This is a dangerous article.

"But now, let us get to work on this devilish rug; although first I must call the excellent Father Martin, of the Society of Jesuits."

"Help yourself," I said, handing him the directory. "And by the way, what has this priest to do with your mission? I would hardly think him to be an adept at the devil-mongering you suggest."

"Father Martin," replied d'Artois, as he thumbed the directory, "is an outstanding mathematician, and a prominent member of that most learned society. I met him in France, where he served as a chaplain with an artillery regiment during the late war. While our problem is occult, there are mathematical relations to consider. Modern science is finally realizing that chemistry, physics, and the meta-physical sciences are interlinked, and that every manifestation of matter is finally re-solved into ultimate force, which has a mathematical expression. We are reverting to alchemy, devoid of its trickery and charlatanism, in a way. But more later. I must ask Father Martin to call on us, at once."

* * * *

While d'Artois was at the telephone, I turned again to the oddly shaped rug. The workmanship was exquisite, and the knotting was exceptionally close, surpassing that of any museum piece from the looms of Ispahan.

"Pierre," I said, as he returned from the telephone, "how does this thing fit into the picture? It is all scrambled to me."

"Listen, and let me make the un-scramblement, so to speak," he replied. "It is thus. Watch!"

He took three slips of paper from a pocket memorandum, clipped the upper corners with a pair of shears, and then set the cut edges together, so that a three-branched figure was formed by the slips of paper, with an equilateral triangle in the center.

"Very much like three prayer rugs placed so as to get their upper edges as close as possible to a common central point," I remarked.

"Precisely. And as I said, there are two similarly shaped rugs," he replied. "They are to be arranged as I have indicated. Then three adepts will take their posts. The figure at the center, formed by the junction of the rugs, is what they call the Triangle of Power, and in that space will be the Gateway that opens into the Marches beyond the Border."

"Interesting, but obscure," I remarked, more puzzled than ever. "What is the point of this ceremony, and what has it to do with the successor to Genghis Khan, whom, by the way, you are to stop in his tracks?"

"Concealed in the intricate arabesques of this rug," explained d'Artois, "are curves which represent mathematical equations relating to ultra-dimensional space. This rug and its companion pieces contain the key to a complex system of vibration harmonies, psychic and physical, which if set in motion will open the Gateway."

The door-bell interrupted his further remarks. Pierre accompanied me to the door.

"Good evening, Father Martin," he said, after I had greeted the priest and invited him in. "My good friend here finds my explanations somewhat difficult. Be pleased to join us, and cast light on the matter."

I led the way to the living-room.

"And this is the rug concerning which you and I have corresponded for some time," said d'Artois, as the priest seated himself at the table. "You doubted its existence, *n'est-ce pas, mon père*? But there she is. And where my elementary mathematics leave off, your learning shall pick up the trail."

"And so this is what you have called Satan's Prayer Rug, eh, Pierre?" remarked Father Martin, as he scrutinized the exquisite border. Then he frowned, and indicated a certain figure in the design.

"This," he said, as he glanced up at d'Artois, "leads me to believe that there is something in what you hinted. Our missionaries have encountered Asiatic cults that make that symbol the object of mysteries whose outward manifestations—"

Father Martin stopped short, apparently unwilling to start any discussion of that ominous device.

"Suppose," he resumed, "that you let me hear your views. Just to refresh my memory concerning your letters, and to add any new features you have discovered."

I hitched my chair up closer to the table.

D'Artois began by repeating his earlier remarks about the vortex of power that existed in Central Asia, and its historical manifestations in the unbelievable conquests of Genghis Khan and his successors.

"The assault," he concluded, "will probably begin by the enemy's establishing contact with the Fourth Plane. The first move will be made as soon as this one of the three rugs falls into their hands."

"Well, why not destroy it, here and now?" I asked.

"Because until we have studied the rug, we can not be certain whether its presence is vitally necessary, or whether the space equations represented by its curves would suffice the enemy. In a word, we must be prepared to fight them with their own weapons. Thus we delay in order to study. Perhaps its destruction will suffice; perhaps we must in the end track them to their rendezvous and use our knowledge to overthrow them. We know only that they are here, in New Orleans, to make a permanent connection with the Fourth Plane.

"And now, Father Martin, let us get to work on our calculations," said d'Artois as he turned to my desk and took from it paper, pencils, and colored crayons. "And you, *mon ami*, stand guard while we study this accursed thing. We have no right to invite the fate that overtook Panopoulos and Shekerjian."

I loaded my Colt automatic, slipped it into my pocket, and made the rounds of the house, locking doors and windows. Then I posted myself where I could watch both the street, and, from an inside window, the courtyard of the house.

Sitting there and listening to the muttered remarks and occasional exclamations of d'Artois as he and Father Martin paused in their calculations to confer on some intricate bit of integration would have been the height of monotony: but this was no dry discussion of theory. The room was a battlefield. It was pervaded with the tension of actual physical combat. The priest's strong features were set grimly as he hunched over the table; and d'Artois peered fiercely from beneath his shaggy brows at the many sheets of cross-ruled paper before him. They were fighting the master from High Asia: and that magnificent silken rug was mocking them as they sought to tear from its intricate mazes the secret of the Fourth Plane.

I glanced at my watch. Scarcely three hours had passed since we had left the Marigny house. Then I realized that the tense atmosphere of the room had made the time seem much longer.

* * * *

The crackle of the radio at the farther end of the room startled me. I leaped to my feet to cut off the power. Then I remembered that I had last set it to tune in on the local police calls, and paused.

"Attention all cars," it began, after the station call. "Three men impersonating Federal Revenue Agents. Driving Packard, Louisiana License number 43376." The number was twice repeated, then: "Number one: six feet, weight about 180. Very white skin. Brown eyes. Scar on forehead. Black hair. Age about 40. Broad features. Eyes slightly slanted.

"Number two: at wheel. No description.

"Number three: sat beside driver. No description.

"Last seen in 1400 block Louisiana Avenue heading toward Saint Charles. Wanted at headquarters for questioning. Detain at all costs. Report at once. McGowan."

"Ha! We were just in time!" exclaimed d'Artois as he leaped to his feet. "They were trying to get the rug from la Marigny! And she reported them to the police. The slanted eyes betrayed him!"

"Shall I phone her for particulars?" I asked.

"*Mordieu*! Of all things, not that!" exclaimed d'Artois. "*Imbécile*! Will they not be watching her? Tapping her telephone? Tracing calls?"

He glanced at the dial setting of the short wave set, then continued, "Leave it as it is. Its occasional chatter will not disturb us. We know now that they will be making their next move. *Eh bien*, back to your post, and keep that siege-gun ready for visitors!"

Pierre and Father Martin resumed their calculations. Time and again I forced myself to relax from the unconscious tension of my muscles as I watched them in their desperate struggle with the mystery from High Asia. The enemy's setback at the Marigny house had revealed our hand in the counter-attack: and the master would not remain idle. It was urgent that we solve the riddle, and destroy that satanic rug. A doom was even now seeking us. Two men armed with pencils, and one with a .45, striving to halt the march of the Golden Horde! Fantastic, and terrible.

It was dark now. I had drawn the shades. We had moved the table into a corner not commanded by any of the windows. We dared not chance a shot from the outside. We remembered Shekerjian and Panopoulos. The courtyard was a dangerously weak point in our defense. The enemy could approach from the roofs of the buildings whose walls enclosed the patio, and advance through the shadows.

Our hope was that Pierre's movements had been so swift and secret that the enemy would not be able to track him down in time. And once d'Artois succeeded in closing for ever the Gateway that they sought to open wide, that fierce old soldier would take the attack and hunt them down to the last man. The Master, if he but knew it, was himself in peril.

The outcome depended upon strokes of a pencil. Had it but been sword thrusts!

Midnight was approaching.

* * * *

Father Martin sighed wearily as he pushed his chair away from the table. Pierre shook his head, and ground a cigarette butt into the floor with his heel. I did not wonder at the gesture of disgust and baffled rage. For the past hour the room had been vibrant with intense concentration. I had begun glancing nervously about me, at times sensing a personal opposition to d'Artois and the priest. I had dismissed it as the result of a highly keyed imagination, until Pierre spoke.

"*Mon père*," said d'Artois, "did you notice it also?"

The priest started and regarded d'Artois intently for a moment.

"Yes," he admitted. "For the past half-hour *something*—I would almost say, some one, has been fighting me." He stabbed with a red crayon at the paper before him. "And it was not that equation, either. A personal presence in the room has been opposing my efforts to reason this thing out."

"Mordieu!" growled Pierre. "Then it was not my imagination. We outwitted them, and they do not know where we are. That is, their physical bodies do not know," he amended. "So they are projecting themselves, or their mental force, into this very room. For the past hour my mind has been all awry. While the enemy is seeking the rug, and us, he is striving to prevent our learning the secret. Just how much have you deduced? Before this projected force addled our brains?"

"I was very close to the solution," replied Father Martin. He then explained very briefly the mathematical relations he had deduced from the curves. His voice was hurried. He sensed that it would not be long before we would be overwhelmed either in body or mind.

"Magnifique!" exclaimed d'Artois. "Then with what I have done, we are almost through. Forward! Let us hurry before they completely paralyze us!"

His voice rang like a bugle sounding a charge.

They hunched forward once more over the table to renew the fight.

The fate of the world depended upon pencil strokes and integration symbols, and on the significance of strangely spiraling curves that marched across the sheets of paper.

The priest's high forehead was now beaded with sweat. Pierre's lean dark features were drawn. He muttered to himself as he calculated. The tension was heightening. At first I thought that it was the suppressed excitement of realizing that victory was around the corner. I sat clutching the arms of my chair, just as one watching men heaving at a heavy weight will contract his muscles in sympathy. Then I saw my error, and realized that it was not impending victory but the redoubled efforts of the Master that made the room vibrant with energy.

A mist was gathering and thickening the air. It swirled in eddies, and wraithlike wisps emerged from the corners. They were closing slowly in on the table. The lights were dimming. I could now look at the hundred-watt bulb and see its filament very clearly, so much was its incandescence obscured by the density of the air. Along the walls and in the shadows were shapes of spectral gray: vague blots whose quivering and twitching suggested monstrous forms seeking to assume substance.

We were walled in. The table was now an island in a fog-shrouded sea. The forms that lurked in the shadows were becoming more distinct. I could distinguish tall, bearded men with solemn faces. They regarded us menacingly, and rhythmically gestured toward us.

D'Artois, despairing but grim, thrust his chair aside as he rose.

"Look at them!" he cried, as with a sweep of his arm he indicated the ever-shifting, weaving fog wisps and the silent presences that they but half obscured. "They have projected their selves into space to seek us, and their thought-force to beat us! We know all but the ultimate secret. And that we can not get. We are lost, unless—"

"Light the gas grate!" he yelled. "Quickly! Destroy this accursed rug. We have waited too long!"

The one-hundred-watt globe over the table was now a sickly, half-hearted glow. The air was so dense that the features of d'Artois and Father Martin seemed to peer at me through veils. I struck a match and could barely see its wan flicker.

"Quick! The grate!" shouted d'Artois. "When their *selves* return to their bodies, they will know and will come to overpower us!"

But where was the gas grate with its imitation logs heaped on andirons? The mist had grown immeasurably denser even during those few moments of dismay. The mist about us was viscous as oil. A writhing impenetrable grayness walled us in.

I seized the rug and turned to plunge into the gray horror that surrounded us. But d'Artois seized me by the shoulder.

"*Tenez!*" he cried. "They may be in the shadows waiting for it. They may be materialized enough to grasp it!"

The filament of the bulb was now a dull reddish ember. Breathing was difficult. The density of the atmosphere hampered our movements even as waist-deep water impedes one's wading ashore through the surf.

D'Artois cursed fiercely in a low voice as he paced back and forth, clenching his fists, striving to grasp at some thought that would save us. Father Martin's lips moved soundlessly.

Then we became aware of something that was imperiously demanding our attention. As I glanced up, I saw that both Pierre and Father Martin were staring at the grayness that encircled us.

The presences that hemmed us in were slowly fading into their background. As they lost their identities a vortex of spiraling mist was momentarily becoming more and more dense.

"*Mordieu!*" exclaimed d'Artois. His lean, tanned features had become paper-white. "Did you see the center of that whirlpool?"

The priest nodded, and shuddered.

The vast sweeping spiral was dizzying. Its involute curve extended immeasurably beyond the confines of the room. My senses reeled, and I saw d'Artois and Father Martin clutching the edge of the table for support.

"Good God, Pierre, what is it?" I whispered.

"The bottom of that whirlpool extends beyond space as we know it," replied d'Artois. "It is just as our calculations led us to expect. It is sucking the light out of this room as a centrifugal pump would empty it of water. We are marooned in space."

He shivered. I noted that it was becoming colder in the room.

"*Regardez,*" he continued, "we are now in an island of dimness surrounded by a sea of absolute cold blackness. The rug is safe. We can not destroy it. The master has indeed found us."

"Well, let's *try* to get out!" I yelled. And before d'Artois could restrain me, I leaped toward the encircling grayness, but in vain. That twitching vibrant mistiness was an adamantine wall, I dropped half senseless to the floor, bruised by the shock as though I had dashed myself against the door of a safe.

"The master has found us, and we must await his pleasure," said d'Artois resignedly, as I picked myself from the floor. "There is no power—"

"There is indeed a power!" declared Father Martin solemnly, with a gesture of invocation.

D'Artois nodded, and bowed his head.

"I beg your pardon, Father," he muttered. But I saw that his reply testified to his unfailing courtesy rather than to his faith. I recalled his remarks about the three-dimensional god of a three-dimensional universe, and wondered how that calm priest could still hold to his belief.

The vortex was reversing its spiraling. Even as we watched, it became a vast evolute curve. We instinctively shrank, for its appearance was now as if a water-spout were to emerge from what had been a maelstrom in space. But the mists instead of jetting forth were coalescing. They became denser. We heard a whirring and humming as of monstrous flies buzzing and droning.

Then we saw him.

He was there, the Master.

His head and shoulders filled the room: a solemn presence, but shrouded with mists so that we could get only the impression of awful majesty and brooding omniscience that mortal eyes could not bear to scrutinize without a protecting veil.

"Pierre d'Artois," said the Presence, "you might have thwarted us had you denied your childish curiosity and destroyed the rug. But now that you know, your knowledge will avail you nothing. Neither you nor your two acolytes may use that forbidden knowledge.

"An occultist, a scientist, and a soldier: we will use all three if you will serve us. If not, we will utterly destroy you and your assistants. We remember you from old times when you sought us in High Asia. Now that we have found you, you may profit by your knowledge as no man has ever before, or else you will be annihilated as no mortal has ever been reduced to non-existence."

The voice paused. The mists shrouded the awful features and almost hid them. The room still reverberated with the surging thunder of that declaration, that threat combined with a promise.

D'Artois stared full into the shadows that marked where those all-seeing eyes had burned. His face was strangely exalted: and I knew that he shared with me the compelling charm of that mighty voice and that august, mist-shrouded face.

"Beware, my son," said the priest at his side, "the spoiler and the outlaw is tempting you. The Rebel himself is speaking."

That quiet voice cracked the spell. My exaltation at being included as one of the servants of such a Master was dispelled, and I trembled with fear.

"I will go," said d'Artois. "But my acolytes are not suited—" The veiling mists thinned, and the features of the Presence became more sharply limned than before. The prodigious voice thundered again, "Your acolytes will go or we will destroy them. You have no present choice. You will choose when you are in our holy of holies, where you will see in full that which we have tonight hinted. We do not request. We command."

We were animalculisms before that lordly head whose tall, many-terraced miter towered in the weaving, dancing grayness. The satanic rug glowed and smoldered and twinkled in the dim light. It mocked us for having spared it.

The Presence was fading. The grayness was now a multitude of fine, wavering tongues that wove an impassable barrier. The awful personality had departed.

I turned to d'Artois. He sensed my question before I spoke.

"The Master and all his adepts were concentrating. That face was either the Master, or a composite of all his hierarchy of adepts. They will be here in physical presence at any moment, now that their projected minds know where we are. They know the secret of this mist they have created, and can penetrate it.

"Think, while you can yet think," he concluded with a gesture of despair, "and picture an enemy who can surround us with a wall of thought-concentration as infrangible as granite!"

The mists were closing in and engulfing us. The doom was settling.

"Good God!" I gasped, as a hand clutched my arm, and another seized my pistol.

D'Artois nodded. I could barely see him.

"They are here," he murmured. "Resistance is vain."

I wondered at the gleam in his eye, and the glance he shot at Father Martin. The priest saw, and nodded almost imperceptibly.

We were drawn into the impenetrable blackness of everlasting night. But the hands that clutched us were human: and that in a degree relieved the horror.

I felt the paving of the courtyard beneath my feet.

"Not a word!" growled a harsh voice at my side. The muzzle of a pistol prodded my ribs.

We were on Saint Peter Street, in front of my house. Our captors were thrusting us into a sedan. The Master, it seemed, had not thus far developed enough power to whisk us through space and into his sanctum. The awful grayness ended at the door leading to the court.

As we seated ourselves, with two of our captors facing us, pistols leveled, we saw that they were stalwart fellows with grim, Mongoloid features. Resistance would be futile. And the rug was in the hands of the one who sat next to the driver, commanding the party.

"I wonder why they don't blindfold us?" I asked d'Artois.

His smile was grim and despairing.

"They do not intend for us to leave our next stopping-point," he replied. "What harm if we see?"

Then he slumped back against the upholstery.

* * * *

Pierre seemed resigned, but I felt that he had not yet abandoned hope. Father Martin's face was white and stern. Nothing but his faith remained after that terrific demonstration by the Master. As for me, I was numbed by the enormity of it all. The mighty utterance of that awful Presence, the fearful weaving grayness that had overwhelmed us, the throbbing, surging hammer-blows of psychic force that had shattered the concerted attack of d'Artois and Father Martin: these were but preliminaries to what would happen when the Master unleashed the full armory of his powers, rent the veil, and loosed into the world those monsters from beyond the Border, those ultra-dimensional horrors whose existence Pierre had but suggested.

"The neophyte, the insignificant servant of Him who is beyond the scope of our God who rules a universe of three dimensions."

And if this dreadful master were the neophyte, then what would emerge from the Gateway that led from the Fourth Plane?

In the meanwhile, the police were looking for three men who had impersonated Federal Agents! They were seeking to arrest the servants of the Last Scourge for impersonating customs officials: and the Golden Horde was about to swarm over the earth again, slaying and pillaging and spreading ruin as even the Grand Khan had never dreamed when he heaped 70,000 heads into one ghastly pyramid.

The envoys of the Last Conqueror, liable to arrest!

I laughed. The laugh was too terrible and mocking for the despair that one expresses in the face of disasters that men have heretofore faced.

Pierre started, then understood: not my words, for I had not spoken, but rather my mood.

"Mon ami," he whispered, "you are right. Even with what I once saw in High Asia, I am at a loss to predict what will come next, except that we have seen but a vague glimpse of the terror to come. This fog was but a trifle."

We were driving out toward the Chef Menteur Pass that connects Lake Pontchartrain with the Gulf of Mexico. Somewhere in those marshes was the rendezvous of the Master. Somewhere in that maze of swamps and bayous was the *sanctum* of the Last Conqueror. He would rise triumphant from the mud and sweep dazzlingly across the earth, followed by his acolytes and those forces from across the Border.

Our captors left the highway as we approached the bridge that spans the Chef, and drew up on the elevated ground near the abandoned fort that years ago commanded this one of the two approaches to New Orleans from the Gulf via Lake Pontchartrain. In the moonlight we could see the brick bastions with their gunports that commanded the surrounding marshes. Dismantled cannon lay on the crumbling gun emplacements.

From the parapet we could look down into the area. It was all overgrown with weeds and shrubbery. Trees had taken root and forced the masonry apart in spots.

"Where are we?" whispered d'Artois.

"Chef Menteur fort," I replied in a low voice, although, as far as I could see, it made little difference where we were.

"Silence!" snapped our escort.

The commander of the party led the way. The two who had faced us in the car fell in behind us. Their pistols were still drawn and ready.

We heard the car starting. The Master, it seemed, had other errands requiring attention.

* * * *

We descended from the parapet into the area, and thence to the entrance that opened into a casemate. Our footsteps rang hollowly in the vaulted passageway. Through the embrasures of the casemate I caught glimpses of the surrounding moat. As we advanced, I saw that we were on the side nearest the Chef.

Sentries at intervals challenged us. Our escort muttered a password, and continued the march. Finally we halted at the end of the casemate.

The leader advanced and tapped. What had seemed in the light of his flash-lamp to be a blank wall of seasoned brick swung silently out, revealing a wall of concrete and a door of steel plates.

He beat a tattoo on that barrier. We heard the whine of an electric motor picking up speed, and a muffled humming of gears. The massive, armored door slid slowly aside. Our captors thrust us forward into a passageway pervaded with a diffused, rosy glow.

From a guard room at the left of the entrance a dignitary in yellow robes and a tall miter emerged to take charge of us. He addressed d' Artois in a language unfamiliar to me. Pierre answered in the same tongue, and without hesitation. Then he turned to me.

"I hope to see you and Father Martin later," he said. "The Master wishes to confer with me. Acolytes, it seems, are not entitled to interview him. In case I do not see you again—" Instead of completing his speech, he bowed gravely.

Two others in yellow robes escorted Pierre into the guard room. The leader of our captors, carrying the rug in his arms, followed. We were for the moment left alone in the pulsing rosy glow of the passage.

The massive sliding door was firmly sealed behind us.

As I looked about and saw that we were surrounded by walls and a ceiling of reinforced concrete, I began to realize the resourcefulness of the enemy. Most, if not all, of the rendezvous must be underground; and in this marshy country caissons would have to be sunk before excavations could be made. With what infinite patience they must have worked, setting the first course of a caisson, then digging, and moving the excavated earth by night through the casemate embrasures and into fishermen's skiffs, thence to be dumped far out into the lake, lest mounds of earth about the fort betray their presence.

And what of the laborers? Why had not some one of them mentioned the mysterious excavations?

The solution had a dreadful simplicity.

Drifters had been engaged, brought out by night, imprisoned until the job was completed, and then—the waters of the Chef were deep, and the current was swift. There would be none to betray the Master's digging.

All surmise: yet how else could this system of passages have been sunk so secretly?

"Father Martin," I finally said, "do you think that the Master seeks us as allies? Or is this just to give us a secret graveyard?"

"God alone can say," replied the priest, "although it seems that Pierre is known to them, by reputation at least. He seems to have commanded their respect to such a degree that they believe he can be of service. Much of his past is a riddle to me. I know only that he is a very learned and profound student of things which the Church has forbidden."

He paused a moment, then hastened to add, "Understand, I do not personally criticize. His attempt to thwart this menace is indeed worthy. Only—" I understood his uncompromisingly orthodox view. Mathematical research as such was one thing; the actual dabbling in forbidden mysteries was another.

As we speculated on the outcome of Pierre's conference with the Master, I heard the faint, high-pitched whine of a dynamo picking up its load. Then I heard the humming of transformers being energized.

"We'll soon know," I remarked to Father Martin. "Something is about to happen."

* * * *

My opinion was soon justified. Scarcely half an hour elapsed when a squad of our captors, arrayed in saffron-colored robes and tall cylindrical miters, approached from the guard room.

The leader, a Mongol like his men, addressed us.

"Be pleased to accompany us," he ordered in the impersonal tone of a soldier.

They formed in a hollow square in whose center we were to be escorted. We marched to the end of the long passageway. Its floor sloped at a steeper pitch than we had realized from glancing down its length.

The detachment halted at the end of the long passageway. The steel door that barred further progress slid open in response to the leader's command.

"Let them enter," said a voice.

The Master was speaking. We, Pierre's supposed acolytes, were about to enter the Presence.

The front rank of the square side stepped to the left. The rear rank advanced, so that Father Martin and I were thrust ahead of them and into the blackness beyond the doorway. Then the massive door slipped silently into place, leaving us in a darkness so dense that my first thought was that no natural exclusion of light could possibly result in such an absence of even the faintest suggestion of visibility.

"You are now in the presence of the Last Conqueror," announced that same voice, speaking with the majesty of inexorable doom. "You will witness the opening of the Gateway and see the Lord of the Outer Marches. Then you will serve Him whole-heartedly or else be destroyed in a way inconceivable to your human minds."

Silence. Then from a great distance I could distinguish a scarcely perceptible pin-point of light. It began to expand into a glowing disk of phosphorescence that pulsed like a living thing.

"You have opposed us out of incomplete understanding," resumed the voice. "Therefore see, hear, learn."

The disk of light became nebulous, then coalesced to form the head and shoulders of a man whose Mongol features were the very majesty of fate itself : a sage whose contemplation of the vastnesses of space had sublimated every trace of humanity. We saw clearly outlined the awful Presence we had seen limned in weaving mists and spectral grayness. The Master had revealed the august splendor of his presence so that there could remain no lingering doubt that it had indeed been he who had projected his *self* to thwart our meddling with his monstrous plans.

The slightly slanted eyes were profound and inscrutable as those brooding colossi that hold eternal watch over the wastes of Egypt: without pity, without passion, and without prejudice.

And d'Artois, the only man who could contend with this master of doom, was a prisoner somewhere in this vortex of madness, to elect either service with the enemy, or destruction.

Blackness blotted out the Presence.

Then I noted that the darkness was rolling away like a wind-driven mist. Light advanced pace by pace until it occupied the entire vast, vaulted chamber into which we were looking. We were standing in an entrance passageway from which to witness the ritual that would prepare for the apparition of the Lord of the Fourth Axis.

The hemispherical dome of the chamber was supported on walls buttressed with severely straight columns, and recessed with arched niches—entrances, presumably, like the one in which we stood.

Along the wall sat the enemy's dignitaries, each on a throne shaded by a gilded parasol. The thrones of those adepts were arranged according to height, the tallest ones being nearest the lofty dais of the Master, whose position was exactly opposite our niche.

I saw now that some of the arched niches in the wall contained intricate networks of cables, helices, and bulbous glass tubes; a part of the ray and vibration generating devices that Pierre's explanation had led me to expect.

We tiptoed forward, halting in the archway of our niche.

"I wonder where Pierre is," I finally ventured to whisper to Father Martin. He did not answer. A human voice was outlawed in the presence of those impassive faces along the wall. They were devoid of emotion. They were passionless brazen sphinxes crouching in wait, the masters and not the slaves of time. They sat like old gods brooding over the destinies of worlds not yet created. Hatred, fanaticism, thirst for blood; anything would have been a relief from this terrific emotional vacuum.

The first sound other than our whispered remarks was a single note of exquisite sweetness. As its vibrant richness died, the Master on the central throne made a gesture with his left hand. From one of the arched entrances emerged three figures, gray-robed and wearing cylindrical miters. Each held before him, by the fringe, a rug: Satan's Prayer Rug, and its two companion pieces.

As they stalked statuesquely toward the center of the hall, I noted for the first time their obvious objective: three panels so placed that they joined, leaving a triangular space in the center. Each panel was shaped like the rugs: a rectangle with clipped corners. They were advancing as if in cadence to a rhythm; then, halting, each before his appointed panel, they spread their rugs with ceremonious gestures and genuflections. This done, each stood erect at his post behind his rug.

There was a moment of silence as heavy as that which broods in the lost gulfs between the uttermost stars, and the farthest frontiers of space; and then the resonant, majestic note of a brazen gong rang through the hall, mighty as the greeting to a god stepping from world to world across the vastnesses of unlimited space. It rolled and thundered, and died to a whisper like the rustling of silk, and the hissing of serpents, then swelled full-throated and triumphant in a peal of colossal splendor, its surge and sweep shaking that cyclopean vault and reaching the unplumbed depths of creation.

Then the ultimate note of that tremendous brazen roar blended into a piping, wailing harmony that sighed and moaned and whispered against a background of muttering drums purring in a rhythm that started chills dancing up and down my spine. It was the complex, maddening cadence of elemental spirits chanting sinister invocations as they plucked stars one by one from the face of heaven and mirthfully discarded them.

"That music is a greater blasphemy than the tongue of any man could utter!" exclaimed Father Martin, speaking into my ear. "Resist it, or you will join them!"

He was right. And I clenched my fists, and set my teeth, seeking to fight the compelling wizardry of that diabolical music.

In the niches along the wall I caught the flare and sputter and glow of the bulbous glass tubes. Beams of many-colored lights swept the vault. Some interlaced in dizzying networks; others were deflected into swirling vortices at the center. Tiny tongues and flashes of bluish flame played and leaped along the thrones of the adepts, and hovered in halos about their miters, and glorified their solemn features. The vault was a concentration of vibrant energy, visible and invisible forces that wove, and writhed, and twisted in accord with the harmonies of a law beyond our conception.

Thus far, ours had been the only human voices since the blackness had rolled out of the hall. But as the sweeping bands of light interwove, the transfigured adepts on their thrones began a chanting that rose and fell, sinking to a whisper, and rising full-throated and sonorous in an infinitely rich, obscure tongue. It was with such resonant syllables that Lucifer sang to the morning star, and Shaddad enticed the gardens of Irem to rise from the sands of Arabia.

Above the rolling thunder of the chanting, and the whine and sob of those soul-searing pipes, and the savage clang of mighty gongs, I could hear the three at their posts by the rugs, each in his turn pronouncing a sentence, each syllable as crystal-dear and clean-cut as it was utterly foreign. They were enunciating the inscriptions on the borders of their rugs; reading the poisonous runes woven into those oriflammes of darkness that lay shimmering in sinister beauty before them.

The Master on his dais was nodding, now, and with a tiny baton beating the cadence of his intricate symphony of sound and, color and invisible radiations. And sound and color were blending into one! I could now *see* the color of that terrific brazen roar of the gong, and I could *hear* the vibration of those surging waves of light. Every conception of matter and force was running amuck, maddened by the concentration of force directed toward the central point where those solemn hierophants in regular order read their archaic runes, and shook the foundations of all creation with their portentous utterances.

In that weird weaving of heretofore incompatible elements into a harmonious pattern, every belief and certainty was melting away and blending with madness. If those inscrutable squatting figures beneath their parasols had shown only a trace of human emotion! Some shadow of lingering humanity, some vestige of kinship with flesh-and-blood men! But they sat there, holding in reserve some power as yet unsuggested and unhinted, some awful force yet to be unleashed. And the fear that there could and would be a further rending asunder of all logic and reason froze and terrified me.

I was trembling violently, shivering from the immeasurable cold of interplanetary space; but my brain was a glowing ball of incandescence that threatened to burst forth and mingle with the terrific splendor before me.

"Steady, my son," came the voice of Father Martin from the other end of a succession of infinities, "this too is illusion and mockery. We are in the presence of more than seemed possible to this master of unmentionable blasphemies. But High God is witnessing this infamy. And He will speak."

Strange, hearing mention of God in that diabolical mockery of every rational fact and foundation of the universe. I remembered Pierre's solemnly irreverent-seeming words, and believed that we were indeed before the servant of Him who is beyond the scope of our God and His three-dimensional divinity.

The harmonies became even more outrageously baffling. They were now interfering, and the interference beats were weaving even stranger patterns of vibration. This colossal engine of frequency-blending was pouring together not only light and sound, but the higher rays from the bulbous glass tubes, all into one heterodyne whose beats were now upsetting the very geometry of creation.

The circle of the vault was no longer a circle, but a curve that my mind could not name, or even conceive. It is madness to speak of a hemisphere with angles, but angles it had, and they were neither right, nor obtuse, nor acute. There were parallel lines crossing before my very eyes. The insane geometry of that vault was now a defiance of every principle of engineering and architecture. I knew that the dome would have to collapse, and bury us beneath its mass. No substance aggregated into that shape could cohere. I shrank instinctively, to avoid the crash of that impossible structure.

"Hold to your sanity!" shouted Father Martin. "If it must fall, it will fall!"

Sanity! When even he was resigned to the madness of it, and the absence of his God from this maelstrom of perverted space!

Bands of light rang with infinite sweetness in my ears. I could see hyperbolas and parabolas from their origin to their extremities that extended to infinity, and mighty spirals that reached beyond. And there were sounds whose curves swept with inexpressible grace. There was neither forward, backward, sidewise, neither up nor down in that vortex of vibration. I began finally to understand the words of that obscene chanting!

Then came the supreme terror, the uttermost blasphemy; I became aware of a column of greenish haze in the space between the rugs. In that space was the final outrage: the three dimensions of our cosmos, and a fourth axis of direction at right angles to each of the three we know. In that zone of fourth dimension, I could perceive a pathway along which I could walk to escape from the heart of a steel globe without penetrating its walls. And whoever could march along that Fourth Axis could master this and all other worlds with the forces that would follow him from across the Border of our tridimensional universe of height and breadth and length.

There was the Gateway, and there were its keepers, reading the equations that defined the pathway, pronouncing tremendous syllables of the master vibration.

"They are doing it!" groaned Father Martin. "The door is open. And lock— great God, look!"

I looked. And even in that horror of visible sound and audible color I could still recognize the destruction of the last hope, and the severance of the last link to sanity.

Our world was but the intersection of a plane that cut a fourth-dimensional cosmos. In the incredible geometry of that section of super-space, the small triangular base between the rugs contained enough room to deploy armies and engulf worlds. In our world that triangle covered but a few square feet, but in that diabolical perversion of all sense, it was an abyss that cleft the uttermost depths and frontiers of the universe. The Golden Horde of Genghis Khan, the uncounted hosts of High Asia could march and countermarch, lost in that vastness; Antares and Aldebaran could roam about, lost, hopeless sparks in that terrific gulf. In that green, shimmering haze was a Presence, the Lord of the Fourth Axis marching at right angles to our three dimensions; and in his trace were monstrous entities that transcended all experience and conception. I closed my eyes to the terror, but in vain; for our eyes looked along the Fourth Axis, and through our eyelids!

The edges of the green zone were rolling toward us, engulfing the master hierophants, and reaching toward those on the outer fringe. The Master on his throne saw, and terror swept his god-like features, and the adepts crouched back toward the wall, shrinking from the march of the Lord of the Fourth Axis and his followers. They, the evokers, were stunned by the apparition of that which they had evoked.

At that instant of immeasurable terror, a figure leaped from the niche at our left. Pierre d'Artois! He charged across that anteroom of hell to confront the Presence from across the Border. In his left hand he held, extended, a roughly fashioned *crux ansata* of copper. As he advanced, he chanted, full and clear against the terrible weaving of harmonies of rays and sounds and colors.

Green, crackling flames leaped about the thrones and parasols. We heard the tremendous wrathful murmur of outraged space; and above it, new, strange whisperings and rustlings and chirpings. Pierre's great voice and prodigious utterance was rending and slashing the web of sorcery, and shattering its exquisitely attuned harmonies. The uncannily distorted angles and monstrous spirals and terrifying, nameless involute curves were assuming rationality as the perverted geometry of the vault began to correct itself. And the zone of greenish haze in the center grew vague and unstable; and the clear vistas of spatial vastness grew dim and obscure.

"Look!" I yelled, clutching Father Martin's arm. "He's breaking it up!"

With a howl of rage, the dazed adepts emerged from their stupor, and poured from their thrones and their posts. Father Martin and I charged through the dim twilight that remained of the wrenched symphony of blended vibrations, joining Pierre, and seizing the staves of parasols from the vacant thrones. The enemy, still dulled by the rending of their mesh of vibrant power, of which they themselves had for the time been an actual part, could not collect their wits soon enough to prevent d'Artois and the priest and me from forming, back to back, for our hopeless stand.

We were lost, and the world with us. For having seen, we now *knew*, rather than surmised. They would overwhelm us, and re-establish that awful vortex of power at their leisure, the next time stopping short of the full evocation which had terrified even those bronzed lords of doom. Pierre had for the moment saved the world, but he had surely saved its destroyers also.

We used the parasol staves as quarterstaff or pike. We salvaged blades from those disarmed by Pierre's uncanny adaptation of any arm, however hopeless, to the cunning play of a skilled swordsman trained in the *salles d'armes* of those old French masters among whom he was eminent. It all happened in a moment; and then, steel in hand, we sought to resist the wave that rolled toward us as the adepts got their wits back to the third dimension.

"Here's to a finish!" I shouted to Father Martin above the howling rage of the enemy.

"A good finish!" he roared in return, swinging his salvaged ceremonial blade with unskilled but vigorous strokes.

"*Tenez*! Hang on! Sock them!" bellowed Pierre, as with deadly skill he wove harmonies of steel as amazing as those vibration harmonies he had just shattered. His blade bit and slashed, lengthwise and athwart, compensating for our cruder, heavier efforts. He was slaying with a dazzling swiftness that was so precise and finely timed as to seem deliberate. "We can hold them!"

Luckily the enemy had only their broad, curved ritual swords. One pistol in the crowd would have wiped us out. The priest had turned into a fighting-man, sturdy but awkward, leaving himself open with every stroke he made. And Pierre, dancing in and out with his flickering steel, found time once and again in that mill of slaughter to deflect with his own blade the cut that would have shorn Father Martin in half. As for me, I held my own; but my arm was becoming numb, and my parries were slower, and my returns less effective.

"We can hold them!" Pierre had shouted, confident in his mastery of steel. But the priest and I were wearing out. It was Pierre's indomitable spirit that spoke, rather than his reason.

The cuts and batterings of the raid were telling. And soon Pierre was favoring me with the protection of his blade. The enemy, wary from our first whirlwind of slashing, was now more subtle. With a great cry, one of them hurdled the wall of slain behind which, we resisted their advance, and impaled himself on Father Martin's sword-point; and at the same instant, his companion slashed clear through the priest's lowered guard.

Two of us now. Stout Pierre, and I, on my last legs. Another rush of Mongol swordsmen, and then—

A terrific detonation shook the floor beneath our feet. Then a second and sharper explosion, and a rush of smoke from the passageway leading into the vault.

"*Tenez!*" roared Pierre. "Hang on! They are here!"

Even as he spoke, I heard the crackle of pistols and the roar of a riot gun. I saw men charging in through the acrid clouds of smoke.

My distracted attention cost me a grazing sweep that parted my hair. But I emerged from my crouch with an upward stroke, felt my blade rip home, and free again. Then through eyes half blinded by blood, I saw the sheriff's posse driving in and closing, hand to hand.

"Those excellent deputies!" exulted d'Artois. "*Imbécile! En garde!* We are not through!"

I followed behind the shelter of his blade as he hacked his way toward the posse.

* * * *

It was soon over. In another instant the surviving adepts had been swept back and slugged into submission. We found Father Martin where he had fallen athwart the three satanic rugs. He clutched the fringe of one, as though to guard it as long as life remained.

Pierre knelt at his side.

"Carry on where I left off," he contrived to say between gasps, and coughing of blood. "On your life, destroy those rugs…"

Pierre's fingers closed about the grip of a sword. But as he rose, the priest's hand detained him.

"Those who live by the sword—"

Father Martin could not complete his speech.

"Very well, Father," replied d'Artois as he laid down his blade. And then, with more reverence than I had ever before heard in his voice, "*Grâce à Dieu*, he lived long enough to know that he did not take up the sword in vain. And if I recollect rightly, it was a well-established precedent that he followed."

The posse was returning from the corner where the enemy lay in a heap about the throne of the Master.

"Ho, there, *Monsieur le Shérif*!" he hailed, "Be so good as to have several of your deputies lend us a hand." He indicated with a gesture the body of Father Martin. The sheriff started in amazement at seeing a priest lying in the tangle of fallen adepts. He lifted his hat, and inclined his head for a moment.

"You do well, *monsieur*," said d'Artois as he saw that gesture of respect to the cloth. "And you know not how well. That is more than a priest. He is—"

Words failed d'Artois for an instant. Then, to me, and speaking with a hoarse, strained voice, "And do you give me a hand with these accursed rugs before Satan himself snatches them from our grasp. They have cost us too much already!"

* * * *

We followed the posse to the cars in which they had come to our rescue.

Our adversaries, like most Asiatics, had used the cutting edge instead of the point; and though they had just fallen short of slashing us to bits, they had not vitally damaged us. One good thrust is worth a dozen of all but perfectly directed cuts. And then, they had been occultists and not masters of the sword, else they had hewn us to pieces before the rescuers arrived. Nevertheless, it might be said that when we returned from the emergency hospital, we were so bandaged that we had to be stacked into chairs in the courtyard of that house on Saint Peter Street, which I had not expected to see again.

"Now that we're back in the third dimension," I began, "suppose that you tell me how it happened."

"Skipping details," replied Pierre, "I learned, shortly after I left you and Father Martin in the hallway, that they had a radio sending-set for communication with their other units about the country. They were so sure of themselves that they did not watch me as closely as they might have. They were certain that they would make an ally of me, doubtless. At all events, I bent a wrench over the head of the radio operator and took advantage of the opportunity to put in a few words which most fortunately were picked up by the New Orleans police sets. You see, I remembered the proper wave length from having seen the dial of your set when we heard the general alarm and orders to pick up those agents of the Master who were impersonating Federal men.

"Those explosions?" Pierre grinned. "*Mordieu*! I was too busy to inquire! But judging from the smell of the fumes, I should say they used a good quantity of 80 percent blasting gelatin. Whatever it was, it tore the steel door from its housing. And incidentally, the shock for a moment halted the charge that would have overwhelmed us."

"Whether it was blasting gelatin or TNT," I said, "the sheriff didn't get in a second too soon! But what I wanted to know was what happened just as you popped into the scene. When the Last Conqueror looked flabbergasted, right when space and geometry and time and light and sound were so hopelessly scrambled, and that damnable Thing came marching down—it seems like a pipe-dream, but for a moment I could see It approaching at right angles to height, length, and width, all at the same time. *Four mutually perpendicular axes!*"

D'Artois smiled and shook his head.

"*Cochon*! He overstepped himself, that one! First, of course, in assuming that I would be tempted by power unheard of, and join him. But as your American aviators put it, he over-controlled, and the Gateway became too wide. It admitted too much. That is a crude expression, but it must suffice. There are no exact words, you comprehend. We were closer to the fourth dimension than I ever wish to be, myself!

"He was momentarily disconcerted at having done more than he had intended, perhaps more than he dreamed possible. I don't know what would have happened if I had not interposed."

"Neither, for that matter, does *he*!" Pierre smiled grimly, then continued, "And he'll never find out, that would-be successor to Genghis Khan, who was a schoolboy compared to what today's enemy would have been had he achieved his purpose."

Then he resumed his explanation.

"At that instant, I ran to the center of the vortex of force and upset the complex harmony, destroying that devil's resonance of light, rays, and sound vibrations which he had created. It was so terrific, yet at the same time so delicately synchronized and balanced that it could be shattered more readily than you would think.

"I pronounced the equations of super-dimensional space that I had with Father Martin's aid deduced from studying the rug; although to be frank about it, I'm not sure that it made any difference what I said. For right in the heart of the vortex, even a discordant *thought* might conceivably cause that diabolical heterodyne to skip a beat or ring a false note in its higher harmonies of interfering waves.

"That piece of copper cable I had twisted into the shape of a crude *crux ansata* was to—how do you say it?—buck up my own courage, for I carried with me the moral backing of what it symbolized.

"And you, my friend, were not out of your mind when you thought that you heard colors, and saw sounds, and observed angular circles. That vortex of vibrations all attuned to the conditions demanded by the equations woven into those rug patterns literally upset a portion of what we call space of three dimensions, and did outrageous things to it.

"And that reminds me." D'Artois paused a moment, then resumed in a low, solemn voice, "I made Father Martin a promise. And had it not been for his profound learning—"Jake, build for us a fire! *Immédiatement!* At once! Here, in the courtyard."

Then, as Jake heaped kindling and touched a match to it, d'Artois resumed, "And God forbid that we delay another moment in carrying out the last wish of that brave priest. Those damnable rugs are unique in containing the secret of opening the Gateway to the Fourth Plane, of Super-space of which our world may be but a cross-section.

"Jake, throw them into the fire!"

"No, suh, Mistah Peer, no suh! Ah ain't gonna tech *none* of them!" he declared, rolling his eyes and edging away.

"*Mordieu*, and I do not blame the boy," said d'Artois as he painfully emerged from his chair. He flung the rich folds into the hungry flames. Instead of the stench of burning fabric there came a sweetish, pungent odor, and clouds of violet smoke.

"No honest rug would bum that way," I remarked.

"That flame," replied Pierre, "does seem to confirm some statements made by the Master. The *late* Master, I could more accurately put it," he amended. "He claimed that the dyes and yarn came from beyond our three-dimensional cosmos. Whether that was in good faith, or to impress me so that I would join them, I can not say. But you were in that vault, and you saw."

"Which makes it all the more unreal," I answered, "to be sitting here in my own courtyard, looking at the coals that contain all of that vast scheme."

THE DEVIL'S CRYPT

(Also published as "Gray Sphinx")

Originally published in *Strange Detective Stories*, January 1934.

CHAPTER 1

Satan's Footprints

Guidebook tourists to Southern France concentrate on Biarritz; but those who love unspoiled antiquity prefer Bayonne, that gray-walled city that basks in the warmth of the Pyrenees and guards the road to Spain. The moat that girdles the citadel is dry, and the drawbridges are no longer serviceable; but at sunrise, when the Lachepaillet Wall and the cathedral spires seem floating on banks of low-lying river mists from the Nive and the Adour, Bayonne is a hasheesh dream rather than a city.

France and Spain, England and Navarre, have contended for possession of that fortress, and before them, the Moors occupied that old city which was once the encampment of Roman legions; but it is only at night that one remembers the crypts and passages that undermine the citadel, and senses that soil which for centuries has drunk the blood of defender and invader alike is still thirsty.

Bayonne is an old gray sphinx, somnolently smiling through the veils of her mystery.

Two men emerged from the Lachepaillet Gate as the cathedral clock struck eleven. They were bareheaded, and in full evening dress. Davis Barrett, the younger, was tall, bronzed, and rugged as the massive masonry of the walls. The elder was grizzled, with fine, stern features and bristling, close cropped hair that gleamed white in the moonlight. It was no promenade to continue a private discussion that would have been disturbed by the laughter and music and tingling glasses in José Guevara Millamediana's luxurious apartment; they walked with expectant, searching alertness; and the elder was perturbed, as though he feared to find what they sought.

"Why," demanded Barrett, "do you think you'll find Louise here, of all places?"

"Her apartment, just a block from Don José's, must have been her destination, but she's not there. And since she left without her cloak, she must have intended to return in a few minutes. As it is—"

D'Artois shrugged, regarded his friend. Barrett glanced up toward the parapet along which ran rue Lachepaillet.

"She could have slipped," he admitted.

"Precisely, my friend," replied Pierre d'Artois. "With a bit too much of Don José's wine—a moment of dizziness, a misstep in the mist—there's no guard rail up there."

Barrett agreed. It was logical; yet he sensed that his companion had withheld more than he had expressed. He shivered in anticipation of the end of what had started as a casual courtesy to allay the misgivings of Yvonne Marigny concerning the unduly prolonged absence of her sister, Louise.

They rounded the swelling curve of the bastion that marks the turn of the wall toward the Gate of Spain. Barrett's heart and breath for a moment stopped as he abruptly halted, frozen by the horror that confronted them.

The gray sphinx had lifted her veil, and revealed not her seduction, but her terror and darkness.

A woman lay on the sandy bottom of the dry moat. Fright had so hideously transfigured her face that it was her scarlet gown and blue-black hair and silver *lamé* slippers rather than the olive tinted features which Barrett recognized. He saw how Louise Marigny had died, and tried to convince himself that it was illusion, and the fantasy of a moon-haunted night.

"Pierre—look at her throat! Look at—"

His voice cracked, and for a moment failed. Louise Marigny's throat had been terribly mangled, as by a beast of prey. Barrett resolutely denied the thoughts that followed his first impression.

D'Artois, his seamed features pale and drawn, nodded.

"My friend, look again. You have seen but half of it."

Barrett wondered what further horror there could be; but his gray eyes followed the old man's commanding gesture and saw the footprints of that which had roamed by moonlight.

Man, beast, or devil, its feet were webbed; yet for all the resemblance of the tracks to those of some monstrous aquatic fowl of aeons past, there was that which suggested a hybrid combining the feet of an anthropoid with those of a web-footed bird, or bird-like reptile.

"And the prints end after a few paces," muttered d'Artois.

"It might have jumped to the bank," countered Barrett, making a final effort to lend a touch of sanity to the outrageous implications of the suddenly ending trail.

D'Artois shook his head.

"Impossible. Facing the way its tracks indicate, it would have had to clear the moat by leaping crabwise. It must have flown away."

"Good Lord! A bird with feet that large! Or a winged reptile—couldn't possibly be!" Barrett was thinking of the *pterodactyl*, that flying, reptilian slayer which has been extinct for uncounted thousands of years.

D'Artois for a moment studied the uncanny trail.

"Something worse than any honest reptile," he muttered somberly. Then, to Barrett: "Let's notify the *Sûreté*. At once."

Barrett was glad to leave that sinister spot; but as d'Artois turned: "Pierre, one of us should watch here until the police arrive."

"There is no time to waste in courtesies to the dead," he countered. "And I may need your assistance. *Allons!*"

And presently, passing the Lachepaillet Gate, they ascended the slope, skirted the parapet, then turned down rue Tour de Sault, near whose end was the 13th Century ruin which d'Artois had restored and modernized, making of it a town house wherein he was not only comfortable, but content in being in the heart of the old city he loved so well.

D'Artois led the way to his study on the second floor, stepped to the telephone, and called the Prefect of Police. The machine gun sputter of d'Artois' French was too much for Barrett, but he caught a phrase from time to time, and the incredulous horror of the Prefect's voice as it filtered faintly from the receiver.

"He will make plaster casts of the footprints; he will measure the stride; he will look for bits of hair, thread, lint," d'Artois enumerated as he replaced the instrument. Then, with an expansive gesture, "but he will find nothing!"

Barrett set down the decanter of *Vieux Armagnac*, whose level he had appreciably pulled down while listening to d'Artois' remarks. The fiery liquor burned out the chills that had raced up and down his spine.

"You haven't much respect for the Prefect," he said with something approaching a smile. D'Artois' extensive studies in criminology and psychology at times made him critical of the *Sûreté*.

"This is something which transcends scientific crime detection," the old man countered. "It is not a case of an assassin disguising his feet with something which will leave an outlandish footprint. Yet that is what *Monsieur le Préfet* will attempt to prove, and he will fail."

"But I will approach from another angle."

As he spoke, d'Artois, with swift gesture, swept his desk clear of its accumulated debris. Then he laid out a sheet of paper and with a compass drew a circle which he divided into twelve equal sectors. That done, he took from a bookcase a thin volume whose pages were divided into columns. It was an ephemeris.

"Mon ami," explained d'Artois in response to Barrett's exclamation, "astronomical tables are not exclusively used for navigation. An ephemeris, you recollect, is also used by astrologers."

"I am inquiring into the planetary aspects. In the meantime, do you swill the rest of my brandy. Your stomach doubtless needs settling."

Barrett selected a cigar from d'Artois' humidor; then, his curiosity overcoming him, he peered over the old man's shoulder, watching him enter astrological symbols in the twelve sectors of the circle. The cigar had accumulated less than an inch of ash when d'Artois thrust back his chair.

"I see more than murder and mutilation," he declared. "I see a sinister configuration that cries out of an old and malignant magic. Neptune, in the Eighth House, indicates death by *strange spiritual causes*. And look at the position of Saturn, the lord of those who follow *subterranean pursuits*; Uranus, the sovereign of thaumaturgists and black magicians; and over all is the evil aspect of the moon, the mother of sorcery."

"Still and all, Pierre," interjected Barrett, perplexed by the astrological jargon, "you've only repeated what we already know. We saw it was uncanny and horrible. Anyway, this astrology business—"

"Has been degraded by charlatans, I grant," snapped d'Artois. "But it is none the less a true science, and only limited by the intelligence of the investigator.

"I am looking into the background of this monstrous crime. And the first move is to seek *underground*, a black magician working in some of the hidden vaults beneath the city. Check up on all those known or suspected of having occult connections. Thus we have already eliminated all common criminals, *n'est-ce pas?*"

Barrett, impressed by his friend's solemnity, conceded the point, outrageous as it was to hear a sane, hard-bitten old soldier and scholar to speak of black magic as an actual menace; but d'Artois' ensuing assertion left Barrett too astonished even to protest.

"And the first of these devil mongers and dabblers in the occult that I will investigate is our charming host of the evening, Don José. He is the head of a clique that has gathered in Bayonne. On the surface, they seem to be harmless cranks who babble of telepathy, mysticism, and the like; but tonight's tragedy confirms my contention that modern Bayonne is living up to its ancient reputation for being a nest of malignant occultists and necromancers!"

"Good God, Pierre!" Barrett finally stammered. "Why—that's utterly impossible—"

"So was the gruesome tragedy in the moat," retorted d'Artois, his blue eyes cold and glittering as sword points by moonlight. "And wait till I tell you the rest: Yvonne and Louise are twins. If there is one iota of truth in astrology, Yvonne will succumb, or at the best, narrowly escape the doom that overtook her sister.

"Their horoscopes, while, of course, not identical, would be so similar that both would be susceptible to the occult evil that is stalking tonight. The stars have warned us. You watch the living while I set out to trip up the monster responsible for that ghastly crime. Hurry—before it's too late!"

Barrett's last remnant of skepticism melted before his friend's unwavering conviction. He followed d'Artois to the street, and through the river mists that billowed from the Nive and marched up rue Tour de Sault like a phantom army.

CHAPTER 2

The Beast From the Crypt

D'Artois' car was parked near Don José's house.

"I will not only need it tonight," explained d'Artois as they hurried along rue Lachepaillet, "but we must also get Mademoiselle Yvonne—get her away from that party. That Spaniard—"

"But I don't see how he could be connected with it," contended Barrett. "He was there, all the time, among his guests. Yvonne just stepped out for a moment for a breath of air, or—"

"Imbécile!" snorted d'Artois. "That's just the point: Don José being always in sight of his guests gives him a perfect but deceptive alibi."

"But that doesn't prove—"

"Of course it proves nothing. But if you'd read that fellow's book on Tibetan magic, and heard the rumors of his doings near the roof of the world, you would think twice, *pardieu!*

"Alone, I am handicapped. But fortunately there is in Bayonne an occultist who can help me. A profound scholar whose researches can perhaps save the day: Sidi Abdurrahman, an Oriental mystic and *Chêla*, a disciple of an occult Adept."

Barrett shuddered as they passed the bastion of the Lachepaillet wall and heard the detectives, already on the case, and the crisp, incisive voice of the Prefect who had appeared to take charge in person. And then, presently, they heard music, and laughter, the mirth of Don José's guests. Barrett nerved himself tc ascend the stairs and enter the glow of lights and the mocking presence of gaiety.

Yvonne, they learned, had left Don José's house only a few minutes after d'Artois and Barrett had gone in search of Louise.

"Por Dios, Señor," said the courtly Spaniard, "she fancied her sister was ill and went home to join her. I trust that you will present my compliments and regrets to the lovely Louise. I am indeed sorry that she had to leave so early. Is it possible that she may return for her wrap?"

Don José was mocking them; and Barrett, remembering d'Artois' dreadful surmises, sought to deny the thought that Yvonne, like her sister, had gone out into the mist and the moonlight to meet a horrible death; nor was he reassured by the fierce glitter in d'Artois' eyes and the twitch of his waxed moustache as he paused a moment before replying, "I will take her wrap, and leave it on my way past their apartment."

D'Artois and the Spaniard regarded each other as though they had crossed swords instead of glances; and during the exchange Barrett sensed a sudden tension, a current of deadly animosity, like a dagger biting through a shroud of silk. He saw Don José's cheeks for an instant lose their olive tint; and the dark eyes, troubled by the frosty, unwavering stare of d'Artois, seemed eager to shift.

"Sacré salaud!" hissed d'Artois, "you know she will never need her wrap. I am busy this evening—*and you know why*. But I will meet you, with sword or pistol. Soon."

Don José recoiled before the insult and the vague accusation. Then he shrugged, smiled blandly, twisted his black moustache.

"Señor, I have not the least idea why you insult me, or what you are implying. Neither am I interested. But if you live long enough, and your courage is equal to the occasion, I will be happy to meet you with any weapons you may prefer."

The stilted, formal speech would have seemed absurd to Barrett had he not sensed the deadly, blazing hatred that flashed for an instant from Don José's eyes.

"Mordieu, cordieu, pardieu!" retorted d'Artois, advancing a pace. "If anything happens to Mademoiselle Yvonne, I will not meet you with weapons—I will dismember you by hand."

They exchanged bows with punctilious formality; and then d'Artois turned and led the way to the Mercedes.

"I am more than ever convinced that in some way he's responsible. He, or one of his devil mongering clique," declared d'Artois as he took the wheel.

"But how could he? It's utterly incredible—"

"Science scoffs at sorcery, glibly explains its manifestations as hysterical hypnosis," countered d'Artois. "But that does not make it any the less magic. Remember what you saw in the moat and how the horoscope confirmed our first impressions. Certainly I am at loss, but Sidi Abdurrahman's years of study will solve the riddle."

"Maybe," conceded Barrett, "you're right. Oddly enough, your remarks didn't puzzle him as they should have."

"By no means strange," retorted d'Artois as they drew up before the apartment of the two sisters. "He knew that I knew."

A sturdy, white-haired Basque maid admitted them. Yvonne Marigny received them in the living room. Her olive skin was deadly pale, and her dark eyes burned with an unnatural light.

"Yes. The *Sûreté* notified me, just a few minutes after I arrived," she said with a calmness that was more devastating than any outburst of grief. "I had a premonition of evil when Louise slipped out for a breath of air. And when I sent you to look for her—*mon Dieu*! It was too late."

"But why did you leave before we returned?"

Yvonne shook her head.

"I don't know. Just an irresistible urge to get away. To go home. Like the instinct that urges an animal to creep off to its den and die."

She shuddered, made a perplexed, despairing gesture.

"So...you were almost driven from there," said d'Artois, speaking very slowly, and glancing meaningfully at Barrett. Then his eyes flashed toward the windows and their closely spaced wrought-iron bars. He nodded approvingly; and Barrett caught the unspoken thought.

"*Mon vieux*, do you stay here with Mademoiselle Yvonne. I am going to get Sidi Abdurrahman. He lives out beyond the Mousserole Wall, not far off the river road." Then, as Barrett accompanied him to the door, he continued in a whisper, "The same strange, unreasoning compulsion that sent Louise to her death may send Yvonne wandering by moonlight. Don't let her out of the house. Hold her. Tie her, if necessary!"

The door clicked closed behind d'Artois; and a moment later they heard the soft whirr of gears.

The proximity of tragedy depressed Barrett. He resolutely directed his eyes away from the barred window, and the moon drenched mists beyond, and sought to banish the memory of what he had seen in the moat; but a strange fascination forced him to gaze into the ghastly glamour of the night. Barrett shivered, rose from his chair, intending to draw the shades to screen that ill-omened view. Yvonne nodded, sensing his motive, and smiled wanly through the tears that glistened in her dark eyes.

"Monsieur Barrett," said Yvonne, "this is all so terribly unreal...it is like an awful nightmare. It seems as though all the evil that has ever existed is concentrating about us."

Thus she described the feeling that Barrett had vainly sought to dispel. He had assured himself that it was but natural for Yvonne, grief-stricken and horrified as she was, to infect him with her own emotions; and yet, that reassurance by no means convinced him.

He noted that the lights were dimming. He frowned perplexedly, and resumed his seat, instead of drawing the shade.

"Bum voltage regulation," he insisted; but Barrett's intuition told him that the trouble was not electrical. Then he saw that wisps of mist were swirling and drifting in through the window.

Yvonne stared into the coals of the grate, whose ardent glow had suddenly cooled. The girl herself had become lethargic, as though her spirit had left her. For a moment Barrett felt utterly alone. It was as though Yvonne were a lovely simulacrum and not a woman who shrank shuddering into the depths of her spacious chair.

Gray vapors swirled and surged through the room. A chilling breeze urged the mist whorl into sweeping spirals; mists that came neither from the Nive nor the Adour, nor any earthly river. Barrett thought again of d'Artois' solemn declaration, *"Saturn, the lord of subterranean places, Neptune, who governs strange spiritual enemies, and malignant Uranus, rule this night."*

Barrett stepped to the center of the room, where he could see the double windows that overlooked the Lachepaillet Wall. He saw a monstrous shape peering at him as, perched on the sill, it clutched the window-bars and slowly wrenched them apart.

The walls had become obscured with dense, vibrant mist banks, so that only in the center of the room was any light left. The incandescent lamps were now a dull, sombre red that vainly sought to filter through the surging haze.

The creature's feet identified it as the monster of the moat.

Barrett saw now what had torn Louise's throat and drunk her blood, then taken three long strides and—

It had spread its membranous bat-wings and soared into the moonlight, and thence to whatever unknown hell had sent it forth. The face was anthropoid, but malignant, beyond the bestial wrath of any honest ape. The body was hybrid, neither reptilian nor simian: a blasphemy and an outrage whose hideously confused anatomy was all the more abhorrent in its mingling of hair and scales.

The feet were almost human at the heel, but branched into three claw-like toes, joined by webs. Beast it was, yet bird, and reptile. The hands were similarly formed, with arms long enough to accommodate the broad sweep of the membranous wings.

Barrett knew that the creature had no thought for him. He knew that he could then and there stride safe and harmless through the ever-thickening mist banks, past the sombre, vengeful forms that leered out of the haze, and pass on, unmolested. The beast ignored him. It advanced with a slow, fluent, serpentine motion that was entirely out of accord with its grotesque, awkward bulk. It paused, ready to spring forward and rend Yvonne's throat, mutilate her as it had her sister.

The Basque maid, alarmed by Yvonne's single shriek of mortal terror, came running in, stared in incredulous horror. Then she screamed and collapsed on the threshold.

As the monster lunged toward Yvonne, who was paralyzed by the apparition, Barrett seized a heavy chair and lashed out, shattering it across the simian skull. The beast recoiled, sank back to its haunches, shook its head as though bewildered.

Barrett stood for an instant regarding the fragments that remained in his grasp. Then in a flare of rage born of terror and outraged reason, he charged, driving the splintered stumps full into the monster's face.

The assault was vain. He had disconcerted the beast more than he had shaken it. It lashed out with arms that reached almost to its ankles, and enfolded Barrett with its shroud of membranous wings. It screeched and hissed in inarticulate fury. Its long carnivorous teeth sought his throat, even as Barrett, beyond terror or reason, evaded the fangs and sought to throttle the beast, and tear it to pieces with his bare hands.

It was a mad dream of combat in a steaming, prehistoric jungle. The reptilian exhalation of the monster, its squeaking, gibbering wrath and the stifling embrace of its wings, drove Barrett to an insane rage. The thing was strong, but not beyond the strength of human wrath spurred to frenzy; and the very horror of its presence stirred up reserves of destructive fury whose force was dimly echoed in Barrett's ears as he heard the splintering of furniture that crashed and fell into fragments as he and the monster rolled and leaped, broke, and closed in again, seeking each other's throat.

And yet for all his rage-inspired strength and agility, Barrett vainly sought to rend that tough, scaly body which yielded instead of tearing or breaking as he applied in succession, one after another savage trick of wrestling, and murderous holds practiced by Japanese experts. Though it could not quite overcome Barrett, it resisted the full flame of his fury. Its endurance was unflagging, and its counter attacks fresh and vigorous as from the start. It seemed to gain strength from Barrett's blood, which streamed from a score of cuts and scratches and long, ragged furrows gouged by its teeth.

Barrett's strength at last was consumed by the futility of his rage. As in a confused dream, his mind began double-tracking: one half still a vortex of flaming wrath, the other impersonally pondering on d'Artois' astrological observations. He knew that this division of consciousness heralded the end of his resistance; and exerting an ultimate, despairing effort, sought to sink his teeth into the monster's throat. But the mists blackened, and the enemy evaded him. His arms clutched a void of abysmal coldness shot with burning flashes of scarlet and orange and dazzling, metallic blue. Then it seemed that he was falling swiftly through unbounded space...and as from a great distance he heard a long drawn wail of uttermost terror.

CHAPTER 3

The Savor of Blood

When Barrett finally regained consciousness he saw that the lights were bright again. D'Artois, kneeling at his side, was sponging his wounds.

"...all in the approach," a calm, deep voice was saying. "Your friend—though God alone knows how—withstood the beast by pure force of will to slay. But that was misguided effort."

Barrett with a sudden effort propped himself up on his elbow to confront the person who so lightly disposed of that nightmare battle with that monster from an unknown hell; but his strength was unequal to his curiosity, and he sank back to the floor.

D'Artois helped him to his feet. Barrett, still dazed, for a moment had assumed that d'Artois' presence left victory to be taken for granted; but a second glance at his friend's grim features and despair haunted eyes told him the truth.

"Where is she?" he demanded, stubbornly resisting his fears. "Good Lord, did it—"

And then Barrett saw d'Artois' companion, Sidi Abdurrahman. Despite the freshness of the occultist's bronzed skin, he seemed incredibly ancient. Barrett's first impression was that some solemn Assyrian colossus had come to life. The neatly trimmed, square cut beard added to the resemblance; only the tall mitre was lacking. For an instant Barrett's despair subsided; and then he remembered that d'Artois had failed.

"Where is she?" he repeated. "We can't stand here, idle."

"We do not know—yet," replied the *Chêla*, unperturbed by Barrett's impatient outburst. "But there are ways of finding out. First, be so good as to clear the floor."

Barrett shot a dubious glance at d'Artois. His friend's answering nod was reassuring. And while they cleared away the wreckage of the furniture, Sidi Abdurrahman laid off a circle which he subdivided into seven sectors, and about which he drew a concentric circle.

"As I was saying a few moments ago," resumed the occultist, "fighting that monster was misdirected effort. We must find its master; for even though we destroyed the beast, body and soul, he would create—"

"Soul?" exclaimed Barrett. "That—"

"Yes. We are confronted by the recrudescence of an ancient evil that began among the Black Magicians of Atlantis. It is written in the occult records: *The Atlanteans had become magicians who created monsters with the strength of the brute and the cunning of the savage; and these they ensouled with the most malignant of elementals, who became guards and messengers, the terrible symbols of the power of the Kings of Darkness.*

"To bind these dread beings more closely to their service, they offered them sacrifices of slain animals and slain men. Fifty thousand years passed: and then the Dragons of Wisdom sent a doom forth from Holy Shamballah."

"Is that creature fifty thousand years old?" wondered Barrett.

The *Chêla* smiled and shook his head.

"That is only the time during which the Black Masters were at the height of their power. They were destroyed something like 850,000 years ago when the word went forth from Shamballah. And as it was done then, so must we do now: make the slave betray the master," continued Sidi Abdurrahman as he drew a seven-pointed star in the innermost circle.

"We will bribe and drug that monster with blood. It shall find its doom in the very evil by which it has lived all these ages; it can not resist the bait; and instead of warning its master, it will lead us to him."

"For a Mohammedan," whispered Barrett as the *Chêla* reached for a small copper bowl which he had brought with him, "he certainly is unorthodox."

"*Mordieu!* Who said he was a Moslem?" countered d'Artois. "His name signifies nothing. He gets his knowledge from study of occult records which are the fountain-head of learning, and transcend race and religion."

Sidi Abdurrahman set the bowl at the center of the circles; then he cast into it the contents of a small packet: a fine, bluish powder.

That done, he drew a dagger, saying, "This will be its last drink of blood! And it cannot refuse the bait; for such is the law of its kind."

But before the keen blade touched the vein of the *Chêla's* forearm, Barrett interposed.

"Let me in on this," he said, thrusting forward his own arm.

"No. I have an old debt to pay. One contracted in a former life, by a former failure. Just is the Wheel and unswerving, and this is my debt."

With the evening's earlier madness, Barrett found the occultist's reference to a previous incarnation entirely rational. He stepped back as the blade bit, and the old man's blood spurted redly into the copper bowl.

When the bowl was filled to the brim, d'Artois stepped forward and with a handkerchief and lead pencil devised a tourniquet to check the flow.

They watched the occultist bow ceremonially to the cardinal points of the compass, and make ritual gestures. They heard him intone, *"The hour has struck, and the black night is ready... let their destiny be accomplished..."*

And then Barrett could no longer understand the *Chêla's* utterance. The sonorous, majestic intonation was in a tongue so foreign and archaic that it seemed not even remotely related to any speech of mankind.

They stood, poised and expectant, watching the copper bowl and the blood that glowed like a monstrous carbuncle. They became aware of another presence in the room. A grayish vapor finally coalesced above the red surface; and then as Sidi Abdurrahman's great voice thundered the ultimate, triumphant syllables of that age-old occult chant, the materialization became complete.

Barrett started in sudden alarm as he recognized at the center of the circle the same beast which had so nearly overcome him; but it was now translucent and unsubstantial, a phantom replica of the living horror. It knelt submissively, wings folded over its back as though it were a bird of prey subdued and garbed in the mockery of human form; and as with bestial eagerness it lapped up the bowl of blood, its body seemed to become more dense. A musty, reptilian stench pervaded the room.

When the bowl was empty, Sidi Abdurrahman's arm flashed out in a commanding gesture. The monster shrank as from the touch of red hot iron, then stepped from the circle.

D'Artois slipped an automatic pistol into Barrett's hand. The cold metal reminded him that at least a shred of reality remained.

"There will be men, later," d'Artois explained. Then, anticipating Barrett's question: "When this is over, I will tell you the answer—if we survive."

The grotesque procession filed down the hall and to the deserted rue Lachepaillet. The monster shambled down the street and at the end of some fifty yards, crossed toward the parapet, then stepped into a narrow doorway. They followed it down a steep, rubbish littered stairway that led to a vaulted chamber which, by the beam of d'Artois' flashlight, Barrett recognized as a long untenanted dungeon; and then, on its hands and knees, the apparition crept through a low archway. It emerged on the bottom of the moat.

"Ah…this is not entirely a surprise," muttered d'Artois as he noted the direction taken by their spectral guide. "And we'll soon see whether Don José is its master."

After passing Porte d'Espagne, they ascended the steep bank of the moat, and thence toward the sombre grove at the Spring of St. Leon, where their spectral guide turned toward a casemate which was barely visible in the shadow of a solitary, gigantic tree.

Sidi Abdurrahman halted at the entrance of the casemate. His majestic features were tense; and the fixity of his gaze betokened the concentration whereby he maintained his control of the monster. The occultist gestured toward the passageway which led straight into the heart of the knoll that rose from the level of the clearing.

"Part of Vauban's fortifications?" wondered Barrett, as by the beam of d'Artois' flashlight they stepped into the darkness.

"For a distance, yes," agreed d'Artois. "But before we are through, we will enter a place which neither Vauban nor any other honest engineer ever built."

Although the apparition was faintly luminous in the darkness, Barrett was certain that the *Chêla* followed it by some sense other than the five which normal humanity has.

"How did he call that thing out of thin air?" whispered Barrett, to whom the entire uncanny proceeding seemed like the fantasy of a nightmare.

"He provided it with a body, very much as a spiritualistic medium furnishes the substance for a materialization," explained d'Artois. "Its visible form is made up of part of the etheric double which every living creature has. And in order to maintain the form that the creature is using, Sidi Abdurrahman is exerting a tremendous effort, and drawing on an incredible reserve of psychic and physical energy. Few can endure the strain of lending too much vital force: which accounts for the eventual collapse of most spiritualist mediums.

"The force that animates this materialization of the monster is the elemental spirit that ensoulled the body of the beast that killed Louise. This which we now see is not its physical body; and thus, being bound in an artificially created etheric form, the elemental cannot warn its master of our approach—ah…we're getting somewhere!"

The passageway had opened into what seemed to be a squad room for that portion of the outer defenses of the citadel. Sidi Abdurrahman and his guide had passed through an opening which pierced the further wall of the chamber.

"This is where Vauban's work ends," muttered d'Artois. "Beyond—God alone knows!"

The opening had been roughly cut through the masonry. Beyond it was a low tunnel whose spade-marked walls showed that it had been recently dug. At the end of a dozen paces it terminated at the upper landing of a staircase which was not the work of any military engineer. It had been relieved of the earth which had buried it for uncounted ages—brought to light again by the black master who had sent death stalking in the moonlight.

An aura of incalculable antiquity oppressed them as they stepped to the threshold of the blackness below.

Flight succeeded flight, until they arrived in a vaulted passage whose walls were buttressed with pilasters of masonry whose prodigious bulk dwarfed the mighty columns of Karnak.

"Good Lord!" whispered Barrett, awed by the monumental architecture. "It looks as though we've gone beyond time and reason and—"

"*Mon ami*," countered d'Artois grimly, "the evening is young. Listen—"

Far ahead of them, out of the age-old darkness, came the muttering of drums and the wailing of pipes. Sidi Abdurrahman halted, gestured.

"He will stay here to hold the messenger," explained d'Artois. *"Allons!"*

As they advanced along the passage they heard chanting, and the antiphonal responses of a ritual. And finally, as they rounded a turn, the corridor opened into a vault which was pervaded by a vibrant bluish glow.

The dome, supported by colossal pillars, swelled high above those who flitted to and fro in the satanic twilight of great glowing orbs whose quivering radiance was beclouded by fumes that rose stiflingly sweet from tall censer-tripods. They were warped and gnarled, those subterranean dwellers, long-armed, hairy survivors of a race that had vanished aeons before man in his present form appeared.

One among them, however, was tall and towering, and resplendent in a robe that flamed and coruscated as though woven of gems; and on his head he wore a conical mitre of beaten silver. At his gesture the drumming and piping subsided and the acolytes ranged themselves on each side of an arch that pierced the further extremity of the vault. The arch was veiled by a heavy damask drape of crimson shot with gold.

"The master of the show," whispered d'Artois. And then, as the tall, resplendent leader turned: "And I was right—*Don José*!"

The dabbler in forbidden arts had finally descended to become high priest of those subterranean beastmen. Barrett shuddered as he thought of what their food might be, since they did not appear by daylight to eat of what grew beneath the sun. He wondered whether they had always lived in those archaic vaults, or whether they had but recently been revived from suspended animation—

And then the crimson drapes parted like flames torn by the breath of some nether hell. Barrett knew then that Sidi Abdurrahman had guided them well.

In the niche exposed by the parting of the gold-shot curtains was a lotus blossom carved of rock that glistened with the glassy lustre of lacquer-ware. In the heart of the black lotus sat Yvonne, eyes veiled by her long lashes, arms crossed on her breast, head slightly inclined. Her fine features had the tranquility of the drugged, or of the quiet dead.

Barrett's hand flashed to his pistol butt as he gathered himself to spring from the concealing shadows; but d'Artois restrained him.

"They will cut us to pieces with their knives," whiskered the old man. "This calls for strategy."

The odds were twenty to one. Though they emptied their pistols and extra clips, the survivors could still overwhelm them; and the enemy had to be exterminated if Yvonne were to be taken from that satanic vault.

"Then let's go back and get reinforcements," suggested Barrett.

D'Artois shook his head.

"Maybe, maybe not. Better see what this show signifies. We might not be able to return in time to—"

"What's that—over there?" demanded Barrett. "Good Lord! Did it get away from Sidi Abdurrahman?"

He indicated something that stirred in the shadow of a pillar at the right of the altar; and then he saw that despite its similarity to the beast which had overcome him, it was distinctly another creature.

"A new monster about to be ensouled by an elemental, to be a companion to the one that killed Louise," explained d'Artois. "And Yvonne is here to provide the blood offering—remember Sidi Abdurrahman's remarks?"

"Let's go out blazing!" growled Barrett; but again d'Artois restrained him.

"Not yet," murmured d'Artois. "We have to get her out of here."

But despite the calmness of his voice, his features were pale, and perspiration cropped out on his forehead as in desperation he searched his brain for some device to accomplish the impossible. Sidi Abdurrahman, holding the first monster helpless, was out of the question as an ally; but now, if ever, they needed that great occultist's aid.

"He won't fail us," d'Artois said. "And we'll see our moment..."

Two acolytes were advancing toward the altar. One had a bowl of burnished copper, the other, a long-bladed knife. And as they took their posts, Don José began chanting.

"Bal-Taratan, come forth! Bal-Karadîn, come forth! From the blackness and from Avichi, Dark Lords, come forth!"

The braying and bellowing of strange wind instruments and the savage thunder of drums was bestial as the sluggish shape that crouched whimpering by the altar, awaiting the elemental that was to emerge from Avichi, the eighth and nethermost hell.

"God...that's awful," muttered Barrett as he watched the weaving gestures of Don José and his acolytes.

Brass clanged. The deep, hoarse, booming blasts of horns shook the vault. Mists were writhing like phantom serpents basking in the rays of a phantom sun that revived them from the chill of night.

"Bal-Taratan! Bal-Karadîn! I open the Gateway! I mark the Path!" intoned Don José, his voice rich and clear above that lustful bellowing and the sharp *clack-clack* of pebbles rattled in a yellowed skull. The acolytes, gesturing now like automatons, stared glassily, unaware of the shapes that were becoming visible.

Bal-Taratan! Bring him forth! Bal-Karadîn! Bring him forth! I have a house for him! And for him I have food! Ia Bal-Taratan! Ia Bal-Karadîn!"

And as Don José paused at the enunciation of the names of the Lords of the Eighth Hell, the acolytes hissed a phrase that was a dying, evil echo of those dread words.

"A feast of blood! A drink of blood!"

The acolytes responded, "Yea, the fumes of blood! The fumes, and the savor!"

The mist was now thicker, and its coldness had become folds of reptilian foulness. D'Artois and Barrett crouched in the angle of the pilaster, stricken by the sorcery of that evil chant. The terrific blasting of that awful rhythm had numbed and paralyzed body and mind.

"Yea, the fume of blood, and its savor!" thundered the chorus.

They were weaving a red symphony. Blood…blood…red mists shot with streaks of blackness that coruscated, and blackness that flamed! There was a stirring and chirping and twittering, and the flapping as of monstrous wings beating the upper air of the vault.

D'Artois' cheeks were gray, and Barrett's face was distorted from the acute physical misery induced by that terrific reiteration and weaving of words. His teeth were clenched, and sweat poured from his brow.

The words of the chant now became strange syllables whose fusion and blending gave a meaning that transcended language, striking into the very souls of the two who crouched in the shadows, binding them with a hideous fascination.

The bowl was ready. And the knife was rising…

CHAPTER 4
The Lords of Fire

A solemn command came from the chaos of sound: "Bring him forth, Bal-Taratan! Bal-Karadîn!"

Don José's voice was the final assault to pierce the veil, and open the Gateway for the elemental that was to possess that hideous body; but it served still another purpose. D'Artois flinched from the anguish of the impact; the shock wrenched into life his numbed muscles, his stupefied brain; and his wrath, suddenly released, sent his hand flashing to his holster—

Smack smack smack! The acolyte with the knife pitched forward. The one who held the bowl dropped to the flags.

"Gardez-vous!" shouted d'Artois, with his left hand jerking Barrett to his feet. "Pick them off! Steady, now!"

The ranks of the acolytes wavered before the deadly fire, broke in panic.

"Missed him!" growled Barrett, as Don José flattened behind a pedestal and a bullet ricocheted, whining into the shadows.

The enemy re-formed and charged, knives advanced. They flashed forward like serpents, darting and zigzagging, hunched forward in a crouch. Some jerked suddenly upward as a slug pitched them end for end. Others, riddled, charged on to collapse within a pace of their mark. But many lived.

"Give me a clip!"

"Fini!" snapped d'Artois. "Take a knife—*voilá*!"

His pistol for another instant chattered like a machine gun; then came a sudden silence. The enemy paused, wondering; then they understood, and closed in.

Hoarse breathing, and the *slip-slip* of bare feet that wove in and out, devildancers darting back and forth with flickering blades.

"Too many," gasped Barrett, during a breathing space when the fury of their concerted assault drove the enemy back in momentary panic. "Get us—yet—get that—get José—"

D'Artois, master swordsman, might with his uncanny skill bore through the press and close in with the high priest. No other resource remained.

But the voice of Don José urged his beast-men to the attack, and the overwhelming wave surged resistlessly forward.

"Back!" yelled d'Artois. "Before they surround us. Into the niche, Ça!"

Even as he spoke, he flashed forward—then back, and on guard again, blade dripping afresh, hand ready to strike again, slash through some weak spot in the dense line.

Another command from Don José. The attack withdrew, and he advanced to parley.

"Ah...d'Artois," he said, "since steel will not dislodge you, let us try—"

Suddenly his dark eyes became fixed, and his hands made rhythmic gestures. D'Artois and Barrett, caught off guard by the unaccountable action of their empty-handed enemy, faltered for an instant, perplexed. Despite the wrath of battle, their instincts for a moment restrained their attack on an unarmed man.

D'Artois was the first to recover.

"Rush him!" he cried, leaping forward. But he had waited too long.

Flames began lapping up from the paving in a crescent that imprisoned d'Artois and Barrett in its semicircle. The fires slowly converged, inch by inch, hungry blue flame relentlessly advancing.

"Hold your breath and dive through!"

"No!" shouted d'Artois, seizing Barrett by the shoulder. "It'll burn us to cinders. *Elemental fires*!"

Barrett did not understand; but he read the desperation in d'Artois' eyes.

"Resist his will. Fight his thought! If you fear, you are lost!"

"What do you mean—"

"Do as I say or you're lost—she's lost!"

Barrett was dismayed by that uncanny, marching flame above whose wavering crest burned the fixed, malignant eyes of Don José. The madness of that awful night had reached its climax when blue flames were exhaled by solid flagging. But when he saw that d'Artois' gaze was fixed, and his features composed, he gained courage.

"I defy your will and your power with my will and my force!" he heard d'Artois tensely whispering. The low murmur became rhythmic as drum-beats, and inexorable as fate. And Barrett began to repeat d'Artois' words, halfheartedly at first, then confidently.

"I defy your will with my will, your power with my power!" he repeated.

Suddenly he felt a strange thrill of triumph surge up from within him; and for an instant the psychic concussion of the liberated force shook him, and his dry eyes blinded as he blinked, caught a sobbing breath, and repeated, "I defy you, my will against your will..."

He saw that the flames no longer advanced. The intolerable heat scorched and singed, but no longer increased.

The flames retreated—only by the breadth of a finger—but they retreated, beaten back by will that fought will.

And then Barrett faltered, cracking under the terrific strain.

"Can't make... I'm done in!"

They heard a cry of triumph from beyond the wall of flame. Don José knew that his victims were helpless, and stood waiting for the fires to close in. D'Artois and Barrett exchanged despairing glances.

"Try it!" muttered Barrett. "It'll roast us anyway—"

D'Artois nodded, and his fingers closed on the haft of his red knife, but his occult knowledge assured him that the blade would fuse from the terrific heat.

Don José's exultation, however, was checked as a mighty voice thundered from the passageway, *"My will against your will, and my power against your power!"*

It was awful in its richness and volume. Sidi Abdurrahman was chanting as he advanced, solemn, prodigious-seeming as a descending doom—a colossus of power stalking across the Border.

"I have returned to accomplish where once I failed. You escaped me, ages ago, when the Dragons of Wisdom proclaimed the black night of doom for lost Atlantis. I failed, but in the many lives I have lived since then, I have gained *power against your power, and will against your will*!"

Don José made a gesture. Then he found his voice, and uttered a command. The flames wavered as he spoke, then surged high as his followers clustered about him. They resisted the *Chêla's* awful will—but in vain. The tips of the crescent of fire drew from the wall. Don José had lost command of the weapon he had devised; it lived on by the force that the *Chêla* concentrated. Flight was futile; space is nonexistent in occult combat. And the beast-men and their chief made their last desperate resistance as the flaming crescent reversed its curvature, enfolding them in its terrific embrace.

There was no outcry—only a hissing and crackling that endured but an instant. Then came the dreadful stench of searing flesh as flame, hungrier than any earthly fire, lapped with deadly swiftness, roaring as winds lashing monstrous cliffs. A column of awful radiance burned for a moment with adamantine brilliance.

When their dazzled eyes had become accustomed to the ensuing dimness, d'Artois and Barrett emerged from their niche and strode over the blistering tiles. They were careful not to look at the spot where the flames had centered.

Sidi Abdurrahman's august features were still transfigured, but the power was leaving him. It was only with an effort that he kept his feet as, smiling wanly, he made a gesture of benediction.

"This is the end of an old feud that started many lives ago. I was not ready for this meeting—but to save her—and you—I spoke. The Occult Masters sought to help—did help—"

He gasped, caught his breath, and with difficulty resumed, "They warned me —I could not endure the test—since I could not—receive all the force they were sending. But I could not decline—"

D'Artois caught the *Chêla* as he collapsed. The silence for a moment was unbroken save for the bestial whimperings of the wounded who had dropped short of the vortex of flame.

"We can do nothing for Sidi Abdurrahman," said d'Artois. "Get Yvonne— quick! Before we all go mad!"

* * * *

As the sun rose, Yvonne, revived from the drugs of the Satanic ritual and quite unharmed, heard d'Artois' narrative. Barrett, bandaged and smarting from his wounds, answered her weary smile, then turned to his friend:

"Pierre, I'm still stumped by a few things."

"Only a few?" countered the old man with a flash of good-humored irony that for a moment struggled through the sombre memory of death's double thrust at a lovely girl and a great-hearted occultist.

"Where did he get that awful body for the elemental spirit?"

"The crypts beneath the city," said d'Artois, "have spawned strange broods. Monstrous hybrids, perhaps archaic survivals of lost Shâlmali, revived from suspended animation by Don José. But that is an occult rather than a scientific problem."

"After all," said Barrett, "the final riddle is, why did anyone with Don José's talents dabble in such ghastly studies? What motive—"

"He was following the tradition of the Black Brotherhood," replied d'Artois. "He was moved by the lust for power given by the services of elementals. He needed familiar spirits to help him further his pursuit of dark arts. Blood alone would bind them to his will; and you know to what lengths he went."

Yvonne shuddered at the evening's memories, then interposed, "But why did your friend's heroism end fatally?"

"At the best, I can only guess," admitted d'Artois. "Despite his great learning, he was only a *Chêla*, not a full initiate. Thus he could not endure the forces which he called forth, and he knew that he could not. Yet he accepted the challenge.

"He created a psychic explosion whose repercussion literally blasted him to pieces. Not his physical body, but his vital forces, which were unable to withstand the strain of mastering that elemental fire."

D'Artois paused. The silence was acute; and for a moment it seemed that they felt the presence of Sidi Abdurrahman. Finally Barrett spoke.

"He mentioned other lives—"

"According to the traditions of his order," resumed d'Artois, "he believes in reincarnation. And it seems that in some former existence he failed in his duty, so that in the lives that followed, he sought to redeem himself.

"He stood there in the vault, holding the captured elemental a prisoner. He was oblivious to his surroundings; but when Don José called the fires down on us, the psychic impact aroused Sidi Abdurrahman and brought to his consciousness the presence of an age-old enemy of all mankind.

"But whatever the reason and however science may try to explain it, we owe our survival to Sidi Abdurrahman."

D'Artois cleared his throat, rose, stepped to the door.

"I am an old man," he said, "and vengeance leaves me weary. Let me therefore leave you in good hands while I rout out *Monsieur le Préfet*. I will have him dynamite the entrance of that accursed vault, so that no matter how ominous the stars may be, there will be no more archaic survivals coming forth in search of victims."

And Barrett, regarding Yvonne Marigny, knew that when grief had received its due, untroubled moonlight on the Lachepaillet Wall would make the Gray

Sphinx of the Pyrenees more alluring than before.

SATAN'S GARDEN

Originally published in *Weird Tales*, April 1934.

CHAPTER 1

Invisible Scourge

It was long past the hour of tinkling glass, and song to the guitar, and crowded tables at the Café du Théâtre. The gray-walled city of Bayonne slept in the moonlight like an odalisque overcome with wine and lying bejeweled in a garden whence the musicians had departed. It is thus that Bayonne has slept each night of the full moon for more than nineteen centuries at the junction of the Nive and the Adour, guarding the road to Spain.

There were two who sat in a room on the second floor of a house that faced the street running along the city wall. One was old and leathery, with fierce, up-turned gray mustaches, and eyes that smoldered beneath shaggy brows; the other was not more than half his age, a lean, broad-shouldered man whose bronzed features were rugged as the masonry of the fortress, and seamed with a saber slash that ran from his cheek-bone almost to the chin.

The younger emerged from the depths of his chair like a panther leaving his cage. He paced the length of the room and paused at the window to stare out into the dazzling moon-brightness that slowly marched from the rolling, tree-clustered parkway and invaded the shadows cast by the city wall across the dry moat that skirted it. Then, as he retraced his steps, he glanced at his watch.

"Later than usual tonight, Pierre," he observed. His voice was weary from baffled wrath. "Do you suppose that It may skip a night?"

Pierre d'Artois shook his gray head and sighed.

"Why should It fail to torment her? We sit here like dummies, you and I. And to what purpose? Look!" He indicated the seals on the door at his left. "It could get through neither door nor window without breaking those seals—"

"But It did, by heaven!" exclaimed the younger. And Glenn Farrell resumed his pacing the length of the Boukhara rug that carpeted the room. He made a gesture of futile rage, then resumed, "But how, Pierre—and why?"

Pierre d'Artois twisted his mustache, shook his head again, and struck light to a cigarette. Farrell sank into the depths of his chair and retrieved the cigar butt he had laid on its arm.

"We couldn't have slept on post without one of us being aware of it," resumed Farrell. His voice was monotonous from repetition of a statement so often made that he himself had begun to doubt it. "And if we had—"

He regarded the waxen seals on the door.

"Those seals couldn't have been duplicated, with your die locked in a bank vault each night. And she couldn't have escaped."

"No, she could not," agreed d'Artois. "But some one—some *thing*—got in."

"A weasel, a cat, a snake," enumerated Farrell, "might slip through those bars. Nothing larger. Certainly nothing large enough to—good God! *Listen!*"

Grim and trembling they stood at the sealed door. They heard a moaning and a sobbing, then the screams of a woman seeking to stifle her outcry.

"Give me that key!" demanded Farrell.

He unlocked the door and flung it open, shattering the seals and breaking the cord that ran from panel to jamb. D'Artois followed him. They halted a few paces past the threshold.

"Look, damn it, look!"

As Farrell switched on the lights, he pointed at the woman who lay face down on the broad, canopied bed. She was writhing and moaning. At regular intervals she flinched as from a blow, then shuddered, and relaxed.

"Lord! I can almost hear the whip," muttered Farrell. He leaped forward and thrust out his arm as if to ward off blows that flailed the girl's bare shoulders. Then he retreated, shaking his head.

"If we can't see it, how can we stop it?" he muttered despairingly.

They stood, fascinated and horrified, watching a lovely girl being flayed by an invisible scourge. They saw the red welts rising, crossing and recrossing her shoulders, and cropping up under the filmy silken folds of her nightgown.

"Look at it! Her gown didn't move a hair's breadth, but the whip raised another welt! Pierre, it's impossible! That gown ought to be cut to pieces by that flogging. Or else nothing's really hitting her. Or else"—Farrell shook his head in bewildered despair—"or else we're both crazy as hoot-owls!"

"Tenez donc," said the old Frenchman, taking his friend by the arm. Though he himself shrank in sympathy with the girl who writhed under the invisible lash, his voice was calmer than Farrell's. "Let us study this thing. And man or devil, in the end we will have his hide!"

"You take the devils, Pierre, and give me a handful of whatever men you think are messed up in it! I'll—eh, what's that?"

He knelt beside the bed, gestured to d'Artois.

"Listen to that, Pierre!" he said in a tense whisper.

"Junayn' ash-Shaytan..." they heard her say.

"Holy smoke!" gasped Farrell. "*Junayn' ash-Shaytan*...and did you get what she said after that?" Then, before d'Artois could reply, "It's over now." The sleeping girl had ceased writhing and tossing. Her cries had subsided to a drowsy murmuring. The two watchers stared at each other for a moment.

"But yes," said d'Artois finally. "I heard it, though it has been several years since I heard any one use such villainous language. It would do credit to one of the dancing-girls in Abu Aswad's dive in Cairo. But this *junayn' ash-Shaytan*, that puzzles me."

"Simple!" said Farrell. "Satan's garden."

"Mais oui!" agreed d'Artois with a touch of impatience. "Only, what is the point?"

He frowned fiercely and twisted his mustache.

"Mon vieux," he said after a moment's reflection, "in this first articulate speech in her sleep we may find a clue to the invisible scourge that leaves her

141

back crossed with welts."

Farrell shook his head.

"Crazier and crazier," he muttered. "We're all nutty. I am, you are, she is—all of us! Now she's talking Arabic! I'm beginning to wonder whether her back is really beaten or whether we're both suffering the same delusion she is."

D'Artois led the way to the door. Farrell followed.

"I have been expecting that," he said as he reached for a brief-case lying on the table. He opened it and withdrew a photograph. "Look."

Farrell scrutinized the glossy print.

"That proves your point," he admitted. "The camera isn't subject to hallucinations or delusions of persecution. Antoinette has been beaten. Severely. The old black-and-blue marks photographed darker than the new, red welts. No argument. I'm not, she isn't, you're not bughouse. That is, *not yet*. But if this doesn't stop soon—"

He bit the tip off a fresh cigar, chewed it for a moment, struck light.

"Let us be impersonal about it for a moment," suggested d'Artois, "and consider what we have.

"First, she tells us that her dreams have become so real that she is confused and wonders during the day which is dream, and which is reality. She dreams that she is in an outlandishly beautiful garden, dim as by moonlight, yet warm as the glow of morning sun. The plants are strange, and the flowers have an unnatural, poison sweetness.

"And strangest of all, she herself has a different body, brown-skinned, with blue-black hair, and very large, dark eyes. The other girls, her companions, are also dark," summarized d'Artois. "Now do you see how her first speech in this troubled sleep begins to lend a touch of rationality?"

Farrell pondered for a moment, then replied.

"Yes. Those few words she spoke in Arabic tonight suggest a dual personality, give us a bit more background. But on the other hand, didn't she tell us that she couldn't understand the language of the other girls, and of the guests: lean, swarthy fellows with staring, dilated eyes? If she couldn't understand them, how the devil is she talking the fluent, unsavory Arabic of a dancing-girl in a Port Said dive?"

"That sudden gift of tongues can be resolved," said d'Artois. "There is something else, which is perhaps more relevant: the veiled Master, whom the guests of the garden regard with great reverence. Does that suggest anything?"

"It does, and it doesn't," replied Farrell. "'Way back in my mind it's there, but I can't express it. And you, I fancy, are in about the same fix?"

"I am," admitted d'Artois. "But before many days pass, we will pick up the trail. We will have this invisible wielder of an unseen scourge. Him, or his hide. But now get yourself some sleep, *mon ami*."

Farrell glanced at the door at his left.

"She'll be all right," assured d'Artois. "The ordeal is over. And what purpose did we serve, after all?"

"Guess you're right, Pierre," assented Farrell. "Let's go."

CHAPTER 2

142

La Dorada

Glenn Farrell was up at dawn. His carefully tiptoeing down the winding stairway of Pierre d'Artois' house, however, was wasted consideration. He found that gray-haired *ferrailleur* hunched over the littered desk of his study, fuming and muttering in a thick, foul cloud of smoke that momentarily became more dense as the cigarette between d'Artois' fingers added its stench of burning rags. The shining brass pot of Syrian workmanship, and half a dozen tiny cups, each with a thick residue of pulverized coffee grounds and cigarette stumps, indicated that the old man had been at work ever since they had left Antoinette Delatour some six hours ago.

In the clear space in front of d'Artois was an open book whose pages were in illuminated Arabic script. Beside it were a pad of note-paper and a half-dozen loose sheets closely scribbled.

"Pierre, why didn't you tell me you were going to carry on?" reproached Farrell as he drew up a chair. "This is really more my funeral than yours, getting Antoinette out of this terrible mess."

"Mordieu!" exclaimed d'Artois. "This is work for a scholar, not a towering blockhead like yourself."

"Oh, all right, all right," said Farrell with a smile that for a moment cleared his features of the dismay and wrath of the preceding night. "Only, I can read that stuff myself, almost as well as you can." He scrutinized the book for a moment; then, indicating the title, he said, "*Siret al Haken*—how's that for a blockhead?"

"Very good," approved d'Artois. Then, with a wink and a grin, "And after all, perhaps I should not call you a blockhead, even though I do exceed you in intelligence and in skill with the sword."

He paused a moment after that time-honored raillery in which each reviled the other's talents, then continued, "But seriously, I have been pursuing some exceedingly roundabout speculations, and before I inflicted them on you, I wanted to study them out myself."

"Oh, all right, then," agreed Farrell as he found a clean *demitasse* and poured some of the lukewarm, syrupy Turkish coffee with which d'Artois drugged himself during his midnight studies. "But I see no connection with the *Memoirs of Haken* and Antoinette's terrible predicament."

"Listen then, I will enlighten you!" began d'Artois. "Mademoiselle Antoinette has been dreaming of a garden rich with roses, and lilies, and jasmine. It is alive with strangely colored birds. In fact, she described the very garden"—d'Artois indicated the page of Arabic script before him—"that Haken has so glowingly described: lovely girls playing the *sitar* and the *oudh*, and entertaining the guests of paradise with song and wine. And a veiled master who ruled the garden."

"But what," demanded Farrell, "has that to do with those unmerciful beatings? How about it?"

"Did I not say that I was working indirectly?" countered d'Artois. "The scourgings, you understand, did not come until later, after the dreams had recurred for some time. Therefore they must be but an indication of the gradual increase—"

"Of the undoubted insanity of all three of us!" interpolated Farrell.

"Mademoiselle Antoinette," declared d'Artois, ignoring his friend's outburst, "is not dreaming. She actually spends her nights in that devil's paradise. She awakes and tells us that she had another body; but her *self* retained its identity. I conclude then that her personality, her spiritual essence, whatever you will, is wandering, driven by some damnable compulsion to inhabit that garden, and a strange body."

Farrell sighed wearily and shook his head.

"This scrambling of selves and personalities is enough to drive one nutty. It doesn't make any sense."

"Ah, say you so?" murmured d'Artois as he reached for another cigarette. "My logic is scrambled, in that I have not attempted to show *how* this can be; but by assuming that it is, I get to the next point.

"Listen somewhat further, yes? We have but to find that place which Antoinette's physical body, speaking like a Syrian dancing-girl, so graphically damned and called *junayn' ash-Shaytan*, Satan's garden.

"There is such a garden at this moment in physical existence; or else there is one which, reaching out of the dimness of nine hundred departed years, is *en rapport* with Antoinette."

"Hell's fire!" muttered Farrell. "The ghost of a garden haunting a woman in Bayonne, in 1933!"

D'Artois tapped the cover of *Siret al Haken*.

"The author," he said, "tells of Hassan al Sabbah. Shaykh al Djibal, the Chief of the Mountains. The lord of the Hashisheen—"

"I get it!" exclaimed Farrell. "The garden paradise into which hasheesh-drugged devotees were tossed while unconscious, so that when they awoke they would believe themselves to be in the Moslem heaven of cool water, beautiful women, and forbidden wine?"

"Precisely, my excellent blockhead! I drink to your wit!" said d'Artois with a smile that flashed over the edge of his cup of cold coffee. "And your Antoinette is bedeviled in some way by a garden like that of Hassan al Sabbah, the master of those assassins who terrorized all Syria and Persia, centuries ago."

Farrell grimaced.

"Worse and worse yet! Hasn't this old city of Bayonne got enough ghosts and devils in its own right, lurking under the blood-soaked foundations of the citadel, without importing them from Asia?" His eyes shifted to the clustered scimitars and yataghans, kreeses and kampilans, darts and assegais that adorned the walls of the study. "Now if they were men, we might do something about it!"

"Have no fear on that score," assured d'Artois. "We find that every phantom as malignantly directed as this ghostly garden has a man pulling the strings—a flesh-and-blood man you can neatly riddle with bullets, or slice asunder with some of those toys up there on the wall."

Farrell smiled grimly and took heart.

"Reasonable, at that. And now, suppose that we drop in and see what Antoinette has to say about her newly acquired gift of Arabic speech. It took me several years to learn that fluently."

"Barbarian!" scoffed d'Artois. "It is too early. You with your military hours —"

144

"And you're another," countered Farrell. "Working the clock around. But see if you can persuade Félice to scramble some eggs, at least a pound of bacon, and perhaps a stack of waffles."

"*Magnifique!*" agreed d'Artois. "Some of those barbarous American customs of yours are not utterly vile. And since you so kindly sent me an electric waffle-iron, *à l'Américain*—but as a lover, you are most unconvincing! At six of the morning, you howl for food—utterly out of keeping! Romance is dead, slain by such as you."

"Ghosts," submitted Farrell, "can not be fought on an empty stomach."

Breakfast stemmed Farrell's impatience for a while; but as they lingered over the brandy-laden coffee, he proposed again that they set out at once to call on Antoinette Delatour.

"Or at least, let's stretch our legs and get the air. I'll be turning flip-flops if I don't get going."

"The air, then," agreed d'Artois. "Look! It is but little past eight."

So saying, d'Artois selected one of his collection of canes and led the way down the stairs of the restored ruin which served as his town house. The circular donjon dated back to the Thirteenth Century; the remainder, though not so ancient, was old when Columbus set sail; and the narrow street on which it faced was in accord with those far-off days, crooked, dingy, and paved with cobblestones. Yet, being in the heart of that colorful city which he loved so well, d'Artois was content, and with the modernization of the interior, he contrived to be comfortable.

They strolled along the *quai* that follows the Nive to its junction with the Adour, then turned to the left toward Place du Théâtre. Before crossing the street that skirted the plaza, d'Artois paused a moment at the curbing to give the right of way to the glittering, costly Italian car which was approaching, presumably from the Biarritz road. The chauffeur and footman were in livery; and the crest on the door was one that d'Artois recognized as that of the Marquis des Islots. Farrell, however, being ignorant of heraldry, had eyes only for the passenger in the back seat: a dazzlingly beautiful girl whose costly furs and sparkling jewels betokened a background as golden as her hair. Her lovely features were drawn and weary, and her eyes haggard and blue-ringed.

"Good Lord, Pierre!" he exclaimed as he clutched his friend by the arm. "Did you see—for a moment I thought—"

He blinked, passed his hand over his eyes, then sought to catch another glimpse of the beauty in the back seat.

"And what did you for a moment think?" wondered d'Artois, as the car rolled majestically toward the Mayou bridge. His voice was grave, but his blue eyes twinkled.

"I thought it was Antoinette," said Farrell, still perplexed. "Or else I'm seeing things!"

"My friend," said d'Artois reprovingly, as they crossed the street, "let Antoinette ever hear that you mistook La Dorada for her!" He shook his head in solemn warning. "Blasphemy, you understand. *Lèse majesté.*"

"But doesn't she—" began Farrell, his gray eyes still narrowed with perplexity.

"Truly! She does just that," admitted d'Artois. "Antoinette has often been accosted at Biarritz and Santander by admirers of La Dorada. But on second glance, their error becomes apparent, unless they are strangers. A similarity of coloring, perhaps a likeness of posture or mannerism that would deceive one only for a moment, if one knew either woman well. Had you been able to look again—anyway, La Dorada is the current playmate of *Monsieur* the Marquis des Islots. She was in his car, and on her way to his château where she is spending the season. Doubtless she is returning from a night of baccarat or roulette at Biarritz."

"Returning? At this hour?" wondered Farrell.

D'Artois smiled and nodded.

"You do not know La Dorada. She got the name in Madrid, where she was discovered by a café proprietor and sponsored by a grandee of Spain. La Dorada, the gilded, the golden."

As they passed along the broad plaza, then to the left and up the slope of rue Port Neuf, d'Artois held forth at length concerning the colorful career of La Dorada who at first glance so strikingly resembled Antoinette Delatour.

At the head of rue Port Neuf they turned to the left, past the old cathedral whose tall spires tower like silver lanceheads into the morning light, and ascended the incline to the broad drive that follows the parapet of the Lachepaillet wall.

Despite the barbarity of the hour, they found that Antoinette had disposed of her morning chocolate and rolls. She wore a negligée of jade chiffon whose curled ostrich trimming fluffed up about her ears and caressed the copper-golden hair that enhanced her resemblance to La Dorada. Her lips smiled, but her dark blue eyes were sombre and haunted as she greeted Farrell and d'Artois.

"*Hélas*! It was worse than ever, last night," she replied, with a despairing gesture, to Farrell's solicitous inquiry. "But be seated, and I will tell you."

She shifted her feet to make room for Farrell at the foot of the chaise-longue on which she reclined; then, as d'Artois drew up a chair, Antoinette continued, "It was terribly clear! Just fancy: my hair was jet-black, and so were my eyes. And my skin was as dark as an Arab's! They beat me most unmercifully...as usual."

She shuddered at the memory of the dream. D'Artois stared at the dainty feet and their turquoise and silver mules. As Antoinette was about to resume her remarks, he said abruptly, "In your dream, what have you been wearing? On your ankles, I mean."

Antoinette closed her eyes for a moment to visualize her dream.

"Heavy golden anklets set with massive uncut stones," she replied. "Emeralds, I think. But why?"

"Were they *very* heavy?" persisted d'Artois.

Farrell regarded him curiously, wondering how adornments could be relevant to the case.

"Terribly so!" assured Antoinette. Then, with a wan smile, "Only, I've become used to them."

"Look!" commanded d'Artois, indicating the girl's ankles.

146

"Well I'll be damned!" exclaimed Farrell, and frowned perplexedly. Then he glanced at his left hand and shifted the heavy signet on his finger. "Her ankles are marked just as my finger is by this heavy slug of a ring!"

"*Voilà*! That further indicates an interchange of bodies during the night!" declared d'Artois. "As a Syrian dancing-girl you are beaten, and the welts appear on the body of Antoinette Delatour. And the heavy anklets of the Syrian girl mark your daytime body just as they leave prints on her.

"Now what else do you remember, ma petite? Your impressions become more distinct each time, *n'est-ce pas*? Your recollections—"

"Exactly," she assented. "And last night—oh, I know I'm becoming utterly mad!—the veiled Master was accompanied by a man who walked through the garden with him."

"And how," wondered d'Artois, "is that more peculiar than the rest of the dream?"

"The Master's companion," replied Antoinette, "is the Marquis des Islots. *Mon Dieu*, is the whole city of Bayonne bound for this devil's garden?"

"What?" D'Artois started and glanced sharply at Antoinette, then at Farrell. "*Monsieur le Marquis* has been added to her dream. Do you see any connection?"

"I don't," confessed Farrell. "After all this madhouse she's been through might it not be a fancied recognition? Pure imagination?"

"*Cordieu*! exclaimed d'Artois. "Would she not sooner imagine that she saw ibn Saoud, or Saladin? That would be more in keeping. *Diable*! Her seeing *Monsieur le Marquis* is so wide of any fancy that I am now convinced that she is not dreaming."

"Eh, what's that?" demanded Farrell, aghast at the wildness of d'Artois' implication. "That it wasn't a dream? Good Lord, man—"

The recurrent nightmare had driven Antoinette Delatour to the verge of distraction, so that d'Artois' contention did not amaze her as much as it did Farrell.

"*Mon Dieu,*" she sighed wearily, and took Farrell's hand. "It's all become such a terrific confusion… I don't know who I am. Oh, how my poor back aches from that beating!"

"Courage, my dear!" reassured d'Artois. "The enemy has slipped." Then, to Farrell, "*Allons*! Let us get to work at once. I have several of those hunches."

"The quicker the better, Pierre," agreed Farrell. And as Antoinette's slender arms released him, he followed d'Artois down the stairs to the street.

CHAPTER 3

The Hand of Hassan

"Your task, my friend," began d'Artois as, back again at his house, they sat down to plan their campaign against the phantom garden, "will be to watch at the plaza. You will loaf, and drink an occasional *apéritif*, and smoke your way into the day. You may see nothing; but with time and patience your watch will have results. All of Bayonne passes the plaza, sooner or later."

"But what," wondered Farrell, "am I to look for?"

"People who show signs of hasheesh intoxication, particularly Arabs or other Orientals," answered d'Artois. "You know the symptoms. You have seen enough *hasheeshin* in Egypt and Syria. I need not describe their manner, or peculiar stare. We are in search of addicts who in addition are fanatic Moslems. A slender clue at best, but while you pursue that, something else may happen.

"And I, in the meanwhile, will be doing some private snooping of my own. This *Monsieur* the Marquis des Islots is due for an investigation. That one has an open reputation for dabbling in obscure arts, and not such a savory reputation either."

"But," protested Farrell, "how do hasheesh addicts come into this?"

"Listen, I will enlighten you," began d'Artois. "We mentioned the Assassins, the followers of Hassan al Sabbah, the terrible Chief of the Mountains, *n'est-ce pas*? Those Assassins were of the fanatic Ismailian sect of Moslems. Those guests of the garden mentioned in this book"—d'Artois indicated *Siret al Haken*, lying open on the desk—"actually believed that their master had the power of admitting them to paradise for brief visits, at the end of which they were drugged, and dragged forth to awaken once more on earth, and ready for any infamy that might be demanded as the price of returning to the garden."

"I have all that," admitted Farrell. "All right, then?"

"The sect of the Ismailians," continued d'Artois, "was more than religious. It was political. Its members did not content themselves with theory. And if, as Antoinette's strange dreams indicate, we have a nest of Ismailians—that is, *hasheeshin*—to contend with, sooner or later one or more of them will be noted about town.

"As for Antoinette, it is quite possible that she is, without being aware of it, *clairvoyante*. And thus *Monsieur le Marquis* will bear investigation. Do you therefore stand watch as I directed, while I pursue some private snooping. *A bientôt!*"

Whereat d'Artois turned to his desk, leaving Farrell to go to the plaza and seek a table under the striped awning of the café.

* * * *

Farrell was none too optimistic, but upon his arrival at Café du Théâtre he assumed an indolence that in any place but southern France would have seemed a pose. But in Bayonne the enjoyment of placid idleness is an ancient art: and thus it was eminently suitable for him to sit and watch the smoke spiraling from the cigarette that smoldered between his fingers.

All of the Bayonnais, and all visitors, eventually pass the plaza: Portuguese and Spanish and Italian sailors, Arabs from Algiers and Morocco, Basques from the hills; English tourists on their way to the arcades of rue Port Neuf, where they found the only *épiceries* in Bayonne where they could buy Scotch whisky; peasants, loafers, soldiers on leave; quietly dressed and unpainted girls who had left behind them, in their rooms beyond the Nive, all the gauds and garniture of their profession. Costly imported cars flashed by, to cross Pont Mayou and Pont de Saint Esprit; ox-carts lumbered past, the drivers, arrayed in dingy smocks, trudging along and reviling their placid beasts. Bayonne marched by in review; and Farrell watched the parade.

But despite his apparent idleness, Farrell's gray eyes were occupied with more than wisps of smoke, and the tall glass of *anis del oso* that sat on the marble-topped table before him. Without in the least shifting his slightly bowed head, he was peering between his drooping eye-lashes at the passers-by, and at the boule-vardiers who like himself sat sipping the meridional *apéritif*.

He was particularly interested in the trio that sat two tables to his right, where they could command a view of rue Port Neuf as well as the street that led to the Mayou bridge. They were swarthy and aquiline-featured. Two were Syrian Arabs; but the third, despite his dark skin and foreign air, was no Semite, but an Aryan: a Kurd from Kurdistan, one of those fierce mountaineers who in their na-tive land are the terror of Turk and Persian alike. Yet the trio had kinship in at least one feature: the dilated pupils and the staring glassiness of their eyes.

As Farrell raised his glass and sniffed the odor of the cloudy drink, he smelled trouble as well as *anis del oso*. D'Artois' sombre hints were having substantial realization. Farrell's first reaction was to loosen the pistol in his shoulder holster. The peculiar stare of their eyes convinced Farrell that he had picked up the trail of that which d'Artois felt would lead to the source of the bedevilment of An-toinette's nights.

Farrell continued his apparent enjoyment of idleness. His broad shoulders slumped. He languidly passed his fingers through his sandy hair; but for all his efforts to maintain his poise, his long, lean frame was tense, and chills raced up and down his spine, despite the warmth of the day.

He summoned the waiter and called for brandy.

Then he noted that an exotic, imported car was coming to a smooth halt at the curbing. A footman in livery opened the door and stood at attention as a woman emerged from the rich upholstery and silver and cut glass of the town car that bore the crest of the Marquis des Islots.

Farrell recognized the woman as La Dorada. He wondered, as he saw her step to the curbing, why a carpet had not been unrolled to keep her feet from the con-tamination of the paving. The scarcely perceptible breeze wafted a breath of per-fume whose cost rumor had for once fallen short of exaggerating.

La Dorada was passing the table of the trio from Asia. The one facing the Mayou bridge made a gesture. His lips moved. At that distance, Farrell could not hear what he said. La Dorada apparently paid no attention to the murmur. She was accustomed to whispered admiration.

Farrell ignored the warning of his intuition: it was too unbelievable and outra-geous.

Then it happened. The Kurd, who faced Farrell, leaped cat-like to his feet. A knife flashed in his hand. La Dorada started at Farrell's warning cry, and added her own note of dismay as she saw his hand with an incredibly swift gesture seek his armpit.

Smack-smack-smack! roared the heavy automatic.

The Kurd pitched backward to the paving, groaning and clutching his stom-ach.

But even as Farrell drew and fired, the Syrian whose back had been turned to Farrell leaped from his place. And the knife he held found its mark, full in the breast of La Dorada.

The pistol spoke, but too late. Even as the impact of the heavy slug bowled the Syrian over in a heap, his blade sank home.

La Dorada screamed, reeled, and collapsed, clutching the dagger whose hilt projected beyond the blood-splashed fur collar of her coat.

As he leaped forward, pistol in hand, Farrell knew that she would be beyond assistance. A shot at the survivor of the trio was impossible, and pursuit was futile. Waiters, patrons of the café, and passers-by clustered about the dying beauty. In the confusion Farrell heard the clash of gears and caught a glimpse of a car tearing madly down toward the road leading to Maracq.

La Dorada moaned, and shuddered.

"Hassan—" she articulated with an effort. Then she coughed, and gasped.

A red foam flecked her red lips.

The arrival of a pair of gendarmes, and, a few minutes later, a passing doctor, scattered the dense cluster of frantically gesticulating citizens.

"Monsieur," said one of the gendarmes, who had seen Farrell holster his automatic, "be pleased to accompany us. Purely as a matter of form, you understand. It is plainly evident that that one—"

He indicated the second of the assassins that Farrell's pistol fire had bowled over.

Farrell shrugged. It would be awkward for a stranger in town to be dragged into the formalities of a police investigation; and doubly annoying in view of his having a serious problem of his own to handle.

"Very well, *monsieur*," agreed Farrell with a wry grimace.

Then he saw d'Artois emerge from the fringe of the crowd that still persisted, at a distance of several paces. He whispered in the ear of the gendarme—only a few words, but they sufficed.

The gendarme turned from d'Artois to Farrell.

"Your pardon, *monsieur*. You may call on us at your leisure. It was routine, you comprehend."

Farrell in his turn bowed, and followed d'Artois to his car, eager to be clear of the plaza. And as they drove past the parkway that lies between the road to Maracq and the wall of Lachepaillet, Farrell gave his companion an account of the assassination.

"Sacré nom d'un nom!" swore d'Artois at the conclusion of the narrative. "That is the technique of the Fifth Order of the Ismailians. They worked in threes, so that if the first and second were cut down, the third would nevertheless slay the victim.

"They hunted Saladin seven hundred years ago. They slew Nizam ul Mulk. The Sultan of Cairo, Baibars the Panther, barely escaped them. They terrorized the Near East until Tamerlane in his wrath took by assault their almost impregnable castle of Alamut, tore it down stone by stone, and put to the sword 12,000 Ismailians. But the order persisted, though its power has been broken for these past five centuries, thanks to the savage efficiency of Tamerlane.

"And I am thoroughly convinced," continued d'Artois, "that you witnessed a recrudescence of that plague which ate at the heart of the Moslem world for several centuries. They seem to be branching out again. Even as during the Crusades they assassinated Conrad of Montferrat, so are they again carrying secret war against the infidel."

"But why," demanded Farrell, "did they strike La Dorada in the public square? They could have killed her stealthily. Even though they could not foresee that I would shoot two of them down in their tracks, the other spectators or the police might have killed or captured them."

"You miss the point," declared d'Artois, "which is pardonable, since even your extensive travels in the Orient would not of necessity bring you into contact with the Ismailians. They killed her in public as an example to instill terror in others. It is a matter of history that Ismailian assassins were often ordered to slay a dignitary and to make no attempt at escape. In one case the slayer struck, then sat down and began eating his travel rations of bread and dates, calmly awaiting the guard that would drag him to the executioner and impalement on a sharpened stake. The besotted *hasheeshin* faced a horrible doom for the sake of re-entrance to the paradise with which their master duped them. The utter fearlessness and indifference to death and torture aroused more terror than the assassinations they perpetrated.

"So much for the *fedawi*, or Devoted Ones, Ismailians of the Fifth Order. The first four orders were the Grand Master, the Grand Priors, and simple priors, or initiates; and then a grade known as *rafiqs*, or associates. These upper grades were intelligent persons who after sufficient study in the free-thinking, heretical doctrines of the Ismailians would be eligible for the highest offices in the Order.

"The Ismailians became a state within a state; they undermined Persia and Syria, and for several centuries exacted tribute from sultans and emirs, with summary vengeance as the penalty of non-payment, very much," concluded d'Artois, with a malicious grin, "like those racketeers they have in your United States. That should make it clear!"

"But how," wondered Farrell, "does Antoinette fit into all this?"

"The companions and initiates of the Ismailians," replied d'Artois, "were adepts in alchemy, magic, conjuring, and occult arts. They used Islam as a mask for all manner of forbidden heresies and as bait to attract the pious oafs and religious fanatics who did the actual slaying and—how does one say it, *à l'Américain*?—and took the rap!

"Maymun the Persian founded the order. A free-thinker, heretic, and magician, he fled from the wrath of the Khalif Mansur, with his son Abdallah, to whom he imparted all his vast knowledge of medicine, conjuring, and occultism. And Abdallah built up on this start by promising the return of the vanished Seventh Imam, who had never died, but who was waiting for the day to return and rule all Islam. They still wait for the return of Ismail, the Seventh Imam. And in the meanwhile, behold the deviltry with which they amuse themselves, bewitching Antoinette, slaying La Dorada—*le bon Dieu* can only say what will come next."

They drew up at d'Artois' house as he concluded his refreshing of Farrell's memory on the origin of the menace that had taken root in Bayonne.

"How about my watching the plaza?" wondered Farrell as Raoul admitted them.

"You have watched enough," declared d'Artois. "In fact, you have made yourself so painfully conspicuous that from now on I will have to watch you more closely than Mademoiselle Antoinette, or you will be found full of daggers yourself."

"Nuts, Pierre!" protested Farrell. "I've been away from home before, and I'm used to being hunted."

"Nevertheless, be on your guard," cautioned the old man.

CHAPTER 4
Shirkuh Makes Magic

That evening, after dinner, d'Artois' man, Raoul, entered the study with a large envelope that had just been delivered by a messenger.

D'Artois glanced at the large waxen seal that secured the flap.

"The crest of *Monsieur le Marquis*," he observed. Then, with a wink and a grin at Farrell, he continued, "Like Satan in the first lines of the Book of Job, I wandered up and down the world, and in it, particularly at Biarritz, and somewhat about the estate of our good Marquis. But need I assure you that if my presence was noted, it was also amply accounted for? *Mais oui*, of a verity!"

He slit the envelope and withdrew an engraved invitation.

"Hmmm... *Monsieur le Marquis* requests the honor of my presence at a *soirée* at his château. The Thaumaturgical Order of Thoth is meeting in open conclave."

"Wait a minute," interrupted Farrell. "There's something fishy about this. La Dorada, his sweetheart, is murdered around noon. And now he sends you an invitation to—what was it?—some kind of juggler's convention. Anyway, it's utterly out of keeping. Not only inhumanly callous, but damned poor form; no matter what his private morals may be, a man of his station would have better manners!"

"Granted," acquiesced d'Artois. "But consider: this thaumaturgical society may be depending upon the meeting-place designated, and can not postpone it for the sake of one man's grief. That there is such an order has been for some time an open secret. Then, he himself may be absent from the conclave, even though it assembled in his name. Or again," continued d'Artois, "it is even possible that Monsieur the Marquis does not know of La Dorada's death."

"Absurd!" objected Farrell. "In a town this small—"

"Wait!" interrupted d'Artois. "Remember Antoinette's dream: the Marquis walked through the garden with the veiled Master. He may still be in that garden, not to emerge until the hour of the soirée."

"By the rod, that's possible," agreed Farrell. "Since La Dorada was presumably killed by the Ismailians, the Marquis may be in their hands, dead, or a prisoner."

"Now, as to this invitation," continued d'Artois, "it may be a device to exact vengeance for your excellent pistol practice. Their espionage would inform them that you, my friend and guest, would surely accompany me to the *soirée*.

"But mark you this: they can scarcely know that your Antoinette could tell you of seeing the Marquis in the garden. That, you comprehend, is the information that ties the scattered ends together, and makes their otherwise subtle trap seem obvious to us.

"My friend, do we go and defy them, or shall we stay at home?"

Farrell laughed.

"Pierre, you're comical at times! We'll go, and be damned to them and their trap. We can shoot our way out of any handful of knife-artists they throw at us, what?"

"Ha! Is it that you are informing me?" scoffed d'Artois with a fierce gleam in his steel-blue eyes. "*Voilà*—have your choice of my arsenal," he said, gesturing at his collection of pistols, ranging from flintlocks and cap-and-ball antiques to heavy Colt revolvers and automatics. "And perhaps, since we shall be outnumbered, we might slip into those shirts of Persian chain-mail. They are not much heavier than a sweater, and so exquisitely forged as to be proof against knives and any but the heaviest pistols. *Parbleu*, we will attend that conclave!"

After arraying themselves as d'Artois had suggested, they dressed for a formal evening affair.

"Thaumaturgy…thaumaturgy…" muttered Farrell as they stepped into the Renault and d'Artois took the wheel. "Wonder, or miracle workers, what?"

"Precisely," agreed d'Artois. "Jugglery, sleight of hand, trickery, but withal, an underlying substratum of fact that can not be dismissed. I myself have seen unbelievable things done by the adepts of Tibet. A corpse, *par exemple*, animated and made to dance by some devilish magic. The fact of my having been admitted to their inner circles in Tibet has in time leaked out; and it is to this that they would expect us to attribute my receiving tonight's invitation."

The chateau of the Marquis was out in the hills beyond the Mousserole Gate. It was perched on a knoll that commanded the surrounding country. Several cars were parked in a level space near the entrance.

"It seems," observed Farrell, "that there are other guests, although that may or may not mean anything."

D'Artois presented his invitation to the butler.

"*Monsieur le Chevalier* Pierre d'Artois," he intoned in impressive but oddly accented French. Then he glanced at Farrell.

D'Artois interposed and instructed the butler, who then announced Farrell.

They advanced through the vestibule and thence into the salon, a vast, high-ceiled chamber illuminated by a pulsing bluish glow. The walls were hung with black arras embroidered in silver to depict with unsavory realism the grotesque imagery of Asian mysteries. At the far end of the salon was a dais flanked by tall tripod-censers whose pungent, resinous fumes made the air thick.

The assembled guests were in formal evening dress. There were Spaniards with black mustaches, and Frenchmen with spade-shaped beards; and here and there Farrell saw lean, hawk-faced Arabs, and several distinctly Mongolian faces.

"More guests than the number of cars would indicate," muttered Farrell, nudging d'Artois. "This is all very flossy, but I smell trouble."

"And no Marquis," added d'Artois with a quick glance about the salon. Then he advanced to meet the man who seemed to be acting as host. After the exchange of a few words, d'Artois presented Farrell.

In the course of the conventional courtesies, Farrell appraised the master of the show. He was lean as a beast of prey, and as sleek. His moves and gestures had a cat-like grace, and his speech had the indefinable blur of accent that marks one who speaks many languages with equal ease.

"And thus I have the honor," concluded the host, "of offering in the name of *Monsieur le Marquis* his regrets and the hospitality of his house."

He paused for a moment, regarding them with his intent, deep-set eyes; then with a gesture toward a row of chairs arranged before the dais, "Be pleased to seat yourselves, *messieurs*."

Farrell watched the broad shoulders and tall figure pass among the guests like a cat stalking through a jungle.

"Shirkuh of the clan of Shadi," muttered Farrell. "Ought to be an honest fighting-man, but—"

"'But' is correct," interrupted d'Artois. "There is nothing honest about that playmate of Satan. Mark my words, we shall see more of that gentleman, if we live long enough."

As they seated themselves there was a clang of bronze, and the faint, muffled wailing of pipes and the whine of single-stringed *kemenjahs* from an alcove behind the arras. As the guests took seats, an attendant passed up and down the rows of chairs, offering small glasses of wine, and triangular pastries iced in curious designs.

"On your life, don't eat it!" muttered d'Artois as he palmed a confection he had selected from the tray. "Drugged, there is no telling what may happen to your good sense. This is all damnably familiar."

Another peal of bronze; then, as Shirkuh sprang effortlessly to the dais, the music dimmed to a sighing whisper, a sinister murmuring from outer darkness.

Six lean, brown men, nude save for loin-cloths that glowed like golden flames in the spectral bluish light, emerged from an entrance concealed by the silver-embroidered arras, and filed across the hall toward the dais. Following them came four others, likewise arrayed, but blacker than any negroes Farrell had ever seen. They bore a litter on which lay a form whose gracious feminine curves were not entirely concealed by the silken, metallically glistening shroud.

"Good Lord!" muttered Farrell. "A woman!"

The brown-skinned sextet ascended the dais. The blacks followed with their burden. As they halted, two others emerged from the back-drapes of the dais, bringing with them wrought bronze trestles on which the litter was placed.

Shirkuh took his post behind the litter as the sextet of adepts from High Asia seated themselves cross-legged in front of it.

"Fellow thaumaturges," he began, "I, the least of your servants, beg leave to present a feat that has never been accomplished save in far-off Lhasa."

He paused, smiled, and stroked his mustache. Then he gestured toward the shrouded form on the litter. An attendant gathered the silken folds and drew them aside.

Farrell barely suppressed a gasp of horrified amazement.

The woman on the bier was La Dorada. Her copper-golden hair flamed like living fire in the bluish-purple, pulsing light of the room. The hands, folded across her breast, sparkled with jewels. She had no other adornment or dress. La

154

Dorada, the Golden, dead not over ten hours, and stripped of all but her exquisite beauty, lay exposed to the gaze of that assemblage of devil-mongers. For one terrible instant Farrell had thought that Antoinette lay on that bier; then he remembered her resemblance to the dead actress, and assured himself that Antoinette was and must be in her apartment on rue Lachepaillet, awaiting another night of fantastic dreams of an assassin's paradise, and the lashing of an invisible scourge.

"Monsieur le Marquis," continued Shirkuh with a smile that flashed satanic mockery, "is unable to be with us. But I trust that that which I offer will be worthy of your presence."

"Lord!" muttered Farrell. "I don't know the Marquis, but exhibiting her dead body here in his house—I've half a notion to start the show right here!"

D'Artois' fingers closed about Farrell's right wrist.

"*Imbécile*! This infamy is none of your business. Tend to your own sheep."

Shirkuh nodded and made a gesture. The faint, whimpering music became louder. Among the plucked strings of *sitar* and *oudh* Farrell could distinguish the notes of a wind instrument that was a mockery of a woman's voice. The drums muttered and purred in complex rhythm.

The adepts were swaying from their hips, and making statuesque passes and gestures that resembled an animation of the figures of Egyptian sculpture. Their glassily staring eyes shifted in regular cadence to follow their darting finger tips. They were as revivified corpses that had not yet gained full control of their bodies.

Then they lifted their voices in a chant like the wailing of ghouls imprisoned in a looted tomb: dead brazen faces chanting to the dead. And Shirkuh, arms extended, made antiphonal responses in a voice that surged and thundered like a distant surf.

The notes of that diabolical wind instrument behind the arras became more and more like the voice of a woman: a mellow sweetness against a background of sepulchral wailing and the solemn intonation of Shirkuh.

"Good Lord, Pierre, that's awful!" muttered Farrell.

"Wait until it fairly starts," countered d'Artois in a whisper. "This is primitive magic. Very primitive, but deadly. They are imitating that which they design to accomplish.

"*Pardieu*, hear that damnable pipe—*her* very voice, now. They imitate in music and symbolize in their chant the triumph of the dead as they return from Beyond."

That satanically sweet voice was now almost articulate. Farrell strained his ears as he leaned forward, clutching the arms of his chair. He sought to distinguish the words that it spoke. And then another instrument came into play: a hoarse, reverberant roaring like the lustful bellowing of pre-Adamite monsters. The hall trembled with that terrific bestial blast.

The fumes of the censers were swirling and twining like fantasmal serpents in the ghastly blueness, weaving arabesques, spiraling in vortices, gathering about that hellish sextet and its leader like shapes from beyond the border clamoring at the periphery of a necromancer's pentacle.

A luminous haze was gathering and drawing to itself the censer fumes. The nebulous iridescence pulsed and quivered like a sentient thing. It throbbed with the slow, persistent beat of a turtle's heart after it has been removed from the body. It elongated; then as it slowly settled, that amorphous luminescence took shape: the graceful form of La Dorada.

The pipe that mimicked a woman's voice was articulating now in unison, joining the necromancer's antiphonal answer to the chanting adepts and the minotaurean bellowing of that monstrous horn.

The master had called her, and she was there.

The phantom presence slowly merged with the nacreous body of La Dorada. The dead woman shivered for a moment, extended her shapely arms, sat erect on the bier. Her cry was a mingling of exultation and bewilderment; then she accepted the hand that Shirkuh offered her, and splendid in her unclad beauty, sprang gracefully to the dais.

The music and the chanting and the bestial roaring of that terrific horn had ceased. The assembled thaumaturges sat fixed and staring as though their life and their spiritual essence had been torn from them and given to the dead who saluted them with a gesture and a bow.

Shirkuh smiled triumphantly.

"You have seen, Brethren. I called her and she came. And I am but Shirkuh, the least of the slaves. See, she is alive, with the warmth and beauty that at noon of this very day was a coldness, and a sister of the dust."

The red-gold head inclined in affirmation, and her smile was a slow, curved sorcery.

"Good God, that's the awfulest blasphemy!" muttered Farrell. "Or is it an illusion?"

"It is all too real," whispered d'Artois.

And then she spoke: "I have come back from the shadows and from the blackness of death. I have come to greet you and to say that there is a Garden to which I must soon return. And those who meet me there need not ever think of farewell.

"I came from across the narrow bridge, and back across it I must go. Yet not this time to any blackness, but to the Garden, to be the Bride and the reward and the welcome of those who believe. Oh, *Fedawi*... Devoted Ones..."

La Dorada, lovely in death, and more alluring than ever in life: yet a cold horror clutched Farrell as he heard that dead woman's caressing voice entrance the thaumaturges with promises that no human woman could fulfill or even imagine. Her voice was a poison sweetness, a full-throated richness that pronounced the beguilements of Lilith chanting to the Morning Star.

"Death so loved me that he has allowed me to leave," she said in that wondrous voice that had made her the darling of Paris. And then her exultant tones became a poignant sorrow as she continued, "But the beloved of death must return..."

"*Cordieu*! That is a foulness beyond mention!" growled d'Artois. Then:

"Let's go! Before we go utterly mad—" He leaped to his feet and thrust back his chair. And as Farrell followed, he expected at any instant a fanatical outburst, the flash of blades, the crackle of pistols. But the thaumaturges sat like the ancient dead awaiting the newly died.

La Dorada was ascending the bier. Her motions were graceful, but very slow, as though the animation was being drained from her body. She was dying a second time.

This as they paused at the threshold for a backward glance; then, advancing, Farrell and d'Artois sighed deeply, and strode to the Renault. The hideous life-like unreality had dazed them.

"Dieu de Dieu!" muttered d'Artois as he glanced at Farrell's lean, drawn features, and shoulders drooping as though from the weight of the Persian mail they had so needlessly worn. "What did that blasphemous monster want with us? Did he hope to drive us to madness?"

"No," said Farrell wearily. "He was mocking us. Certainly he didn't withhold his cutthroats because he was afraid to try."

The long beam of the headlights swept the château, then picked up the winding road as the car headed back toward the city. D'Artois sat hunched behind the wheel. Farrell shivered at the memory of that ghastly loveliness that had greeted them from the grave.

"I know she was dead," reiterated Farrell. "She couldn't have been alive. Not with that dagger I saw jammed into her breast this afternoon. But why did he invite you? What everlastingly damned mummery—there's something behind all this—she's going to greet them in the Garden and there will be no farewell—was that all illusion, or—"

Farrell slumped back against the cushions and made a gesture of bewilderment and futility.

They left the river road, passed through the Mousserole Gate, and threaded their way through the unsavory quarters between there and the Nive. As they crossed the first of the seven bridges that span the river, d'Artois suddenly jerked back from his crouch behind the wheel.

"Nom de Dieu!" he exclaimed.

Farrell, aroused by the note of alarm, glanced at his companion and saw that the horror on his face was in keeping with the consternation in his voice.

The car leaped forward as d'Artois stepped on the accelerator.

"Death and damnation!" he shouted above the full-throated roar of the motor. "We sat there like dummies. *That* is what he wanted!"

"What?" demanded Farrell, tense, and alarmed by d'Artois' contagious excitement. A sudden fear seized him.

"A trap. Not for your worthless head nor mine, but for her! Thaumaturgy! If there is but one greater damn fool than Glenn Farrell, it is Pierre d'Artois!"

They passed the plaza, and with a screech of brakes slowed down enough to make the turn at rue Port Neuf. Then up rue d'Espagne, around the hairpin turn, and thence down the street along the city wall. Again the brake linings smoked their wrath and squealed their protest. Fuming and cursing in a high rage, d'Artois leaped to the curbing, dashed up the steps, and pounded Antoinette Delatour's door with the butt of his pistol.

"Qu'est-ce qu'il y a?" cried the terrified, bewildered maid.

"Flames and damnation! Open quick!" demanded d'Artois. *"C'est moi!"*

"But she is sleeping," protested the maid, still half asleep.

"Hasten, then. If she sleeps, wake her—is she indeed—"

And as the door yielded, d'Artois, pistol in hand, charged up the stairs, taking them three at a time. Farrell was but a jump behind him.

They pounded on Antoinette's door. No response.

"The key—" began d'Artois.

But Farrell stepped back, gathered himself, and charged the door. It resisted the shock; but a second assault burst it open, tearing the lock from its socket.

The floor of Antoinette's room was covered with fallen plaster. Her bed was empty. A hole two feet square yawned in the ceiling. The turquoise and silver slippers mocked them.

"Gone!" muttered Farrell.

"While we sat there ready for an ambush that didn't materialize," added d'Artois.

Farrell turned to the door. D'Artois seized him by the arm.

"*Tenez*! If you are going to tear the château to pieces," he said, "spare yourself the trouble. They have taken her elsewhere. No effort was made to detain us when we left because none was necessary. And they will not be at the château, not any of them."

Farrell's eyes were cold as sword-points as they flashed back again to the empty, canopied bed. Then the slaying rage left him.

"Right, Pierre," he admitted. "It's your move. With some head-work."

"Head-work, indeed!" retorted d'Artois with a bitter, mordant laugh. "It was my headwork that led to this. We should have watched her."

CHAPTER 5

Ibrahim Khan

"Now, where do we start?" demanded Farrell the following morning, as he tasted the strong coffee that was to banish the remains of the nightmarish sleep from which sunrise had awakened them. "You've got the *Sûreté* on the trail. But there's a lot of this that no honest policeman could swallow."

"It is indeed a madhouse," admitted d'Artois. "But let us sum up for a moment: Antoinette is evidently *en rapport* with some one in that Garden; some one with whom she identifies herself, and whose savage beatings in some way leave marks on Antoinette's body.

"By means of clairvoyance or other unusual perception, she recognized the Marquis in her dream garden, her description of which tallies closely with the traditional paradise devised by the higher Ismailians for the deluding of their fanatical assassins.

"Assassins operating very much like the *fedawi* of five centuries ago murdered La Dorada, the sweetheart of the Marquis. La Dorada bears a marked resemblance to Antoinette, though far from enough to make her a double, except under the most favorable conditions.

"The terribly resurrected La Dorada last night spoke of a Garden. And the dying La Dorada pronounced the name Hassan just before she expired in the plaza. Through the whole chain of horror and deviltry, we see a continuous linkage of the Ismailians and the *hasheeshin* of accursed memory.

"Antoinette," continued d'Artois, "must in some way be involved in a mesh of necromancy and murder that hinges on her resemblance to La Dorada. It is not impossible that she was kidnapped to double for La Dorada in that accursed Garden.

"And finally," concluded d'Artois, "this society of thaumaturges, which has made such overgrown fools of us, is obviously allied to or even an integral part of the society of Ismailians and its higher orders, adepts, occultists, necromancers, and devil-mongers of all degrees."

"Now that you've summed it up, what are we going to do?" reiterated Farrell.

"You will take the trail at once," replied d'Artois.

Farrell brightened perceptibly at the hint of direct action.

"Shoot," he said bruskly.

"Mais non," countered d'Artois, "it is you who will shoot if my plan is right. You are deft at disguise, and you speak several Oriental languages like a native."

D'Artois paused, intently studied the lean, bronzed features of his friend, and his cold gray eyes.

"An Arab," he muttered. "Possible, but not so good. A Kurd...yes, that would be better."

"Wrong!" contradicted Farrell. "There were some Kurds at the château last night, notably that hell-hound of a Shirkuh. And the first of the assassins I shot down in the plaza was a Kurd. Too many of them in the picture. I might be tripped on their dialect."

"An Afghan, then," compromised d'Artois. "They are Aryans, and our blood brothers, those Afghans. You will loiter around the waterfront. I will warn the *Sûreté* to arrest you at times, but to release you for lack of evidence; so be careful not to be too brazen in building up a local background of feuds and slayings to substantiate your supposed reason for having left your native hills.

"It is a slim chance; but it is possible that you will stumble across some Ismailian who will favorably mark your possibilities. In the meanwhile, I will keep in touch with you as much as possible.

"But remember, one false move will betray your mission. And the first warning you will receive will be a dagger jammed very deeply into your back. You are flirting with sudden death the moment you leave this house."

* * * *

That afternoon Farrell lurched from a doorway that the most vivid imagination could not have associated with the house of Pierre d'Artois. The shape of his eyebrows had been changed by judicious plucking. His hair had been dyed, and the cut of his mustaches altered. Tenacious, finely powdered pigments had been rubbed into his eyelids and about his eyes so as to change their expression: all trifles, yet the total effect, aided by the drunken swagger, the gestures, the reek of *'araki* and foreign tobacco, was that Glenn Farrell had disappeared, and that a hard, haggard, quarrelsome Afghan sobering up from a spree strode muttering down rue Saint Augustin, and thence toward the *quai* along the Adour.

He found fishing-vessels, tramps from Algiers, and a *zaroug* that had sailed all the way from the Red Sea with its crew of stout Danakils. Husayn, its *nakhoda*, was a lean, grizzled Arab whose manner suggested pearl-poaching, smuggling, or slave-running from the Somali Coast to Arabia, with piracy thrown in for good measure... Husayn spoke of his health, which forbade further traffic on the Red Sea...

There was a Levantin, oily and cringing, who peddled narcotics...

There were brawls along the waterfront. No true Afghan would or could abstain. A fight was a fight.

Very soon the waterfront boasted a new character, a quarrelsome Afghan, drunken, bawdy, stranded, swearing loudly by the honor of the Durani clan, and ready for any skullduggery. Ibrahim Khan, they called him.

Once in a while some whining cadger of drinks would mutter as Ibrahim Khan reviled him and tossed him a franc. That was a member of the *Sûreté* giving, and receiving, the lack of news that is falsely said to be good news. Sometimes it was warning, but never encouragement.

The quarter of the city that lies between the Nive and the Mousserole Wall is so disreputable that during the war it was out of bounds for soldiers. It is a district of narrow, dingy streets, dirty cafés, bawdy-houses of the lowest order; it abounds in cheap wine, cheaper women, and all the scum and riffraff of a polyglot border-and-seaport town.

While the upper stratum of the enemy was doubtless of high degree, the foundation layer would be in the mire. The underworld of France would furnish its quota for the lower order of assassins. The master mind needed dirty tools for dirty work; and here, among the thieves, pimps, cutthroats of beyond the river, the trail might be picked up.

Ibrahim Khan sat in one of the dingiest of those unsavory resorts, muttering in Pushtu and Arabic and broken French, alternately gross and poetic as he courted the attention of Marcelle, the barmaid whose coarse, buxom loveliness drew trade for all departments of the house.

Tie your husband to a rope, Bimbar,
Tie the rope to a tree;
Throw the tree in the river, Bimbar,
And come to your lover.

Thus he chanted in amorous, wine-muddled accents, the whole stanza in one breath, and, in the Afghan fashion, ending in a high-pitched, gasping cry, a full octave higher.

The girl did not understand the words; but there was one sitting in the corner who did.

"Oh, my brother," he murmured, and spat contemptuously, "are such as that sister of pigs fit for the pride of the Durani clan?"

Ibrahim Khan's hand flashed to the hilt of one of the knives that bristled in his belt. But before he could draw, the thin-faced man smiled.

"Put that knife away, brother," he said. "I have news for you."

"Well?" interrogated Ibrahim Khan a little less belligerently. "Out with it."

"Softly, softly," murmured the stranger. Ibrahim Khan had never seen him along the waterfront, or in the Mousserole quarter. "I am Nureddin. I have been interested in your handiness in certain matters...and Husayn, the nakhoda, speaks well of you—"

"He should, Allah blacken him!" admitted Ibrahim Khan, who under his layer of grime was Glenn Farrell, trembling with eagerness to follow up what he sensed was the first open move to take the bait he had so patiently and thus far vainly offered the enemy.

"There are women," continued Nureddin, "lovelier than the brides of paradise."

Farrell laughed contemptuously, and made an insulting remark that left little doubt as to his opinion of Nureddin's profession: but that was to play his part as a truculent Afghan.

"Nay, by Allah!" protested Nureddin with a good-humored laugh. "It is not what you think. Follow me, if you have courage."

Farrell scrutinized Nureddin for an instant. Whatever game Nureddin might be playing, it would certainly not be for small counters. Then Farrell, still feigning skepticism, drew from the pocket of his grimy, ill-fitting suit a small pouch, hefted it so that the gold it contained clinked softly. He tossed the money to Marcelle.

"*Ya* Nureddin, I will fight as eagerly for my naked hide as for a pouch of gold. Now if you still want me to meet your friends, I will entertain them royally, *inshallah*!"

Nureddin smiled and stroked his chin.

"By Allah, O Afghan, you are suspicious. Follow me."

"Lead on," agreed Farrell.

He followed Nureddin to the street and thence to an alley so narrow that with his outstretched arms he could at the same time touch the buildings on both sides: and the narrowness was exceeded only by the stench. Nureddin halted at the end of the alley. A heavy, iron-bound door barred further progress. "From here you must go blindfolded," said Nureddin.

"By your beard!" mocked Farrell as his hand flashed into view with a pistol whose cavernous muzzle gaped ominously. "Perhaps you would like to bind my hands also? Now, forward! Or I will blow thy teeth right and left…if it so please Allah," he concluded piously.

"Fire!" retorted Nureddin. "The Master would give me a less pleasant death for disobeying his orders."

In the moonlight Farrell could see the perspiration that glittered on Nureddin's forehead; but he did not flinch.

"Ya billahi!" ejaculated Farrell after a moment. "Were there a blood feud between us, I would. But as it is—"

He shrugged, holstered his pistol, and turned, to stalk down the narrow alley.

Farrell was certain, now, that he was on the right trail. But since spies are notoriously eager to agree to anything and everything to gain admittance to forbidden doors, Farrell had to play the blustering, alternately suspicious and foolhardy Afghan. He swaggered away in his lordly fashion, presenting his back as a fair target for hurled knife, or pistol fire.

"*Ya* Ibrahim!" protested Nureddin. "Be reasonable. He ordered. It is on my head—"

"He, whoever he is," retorted Farrell, "may then seek me himself and I will induce him to change his rules. *Wallah!* And your head, that is no more than a ball to play with!"

"Oh, well, have it your own way," agreed Nureddin resignedly as Farrell again turned. Then he clapped his hands sharply.

Farrell sensed his danger; but before he could whirl and draw, something soft and clinging enveloped him. It was a net whose fine, stout silken cords bound his limbs and entangled him.

"God, by the Very God, by the One True God!" he swore, struggling with the soft, relentless thing that enmeshed him like a monstrous spider-web, and seeking to draw a knife. "Pig and father of pigs!"

Something emerged from the shadow of the pilaster that buttressed the wall. Farrell dropped flat, still striving to extricate himself and tackle his enemy. He secured a footing and leaped up, butting his shoulder with a terrific jolt into his enemy's stomach.

A grunt and a gasped curse. A warning cry from Nureddin. The knife in Farrell's hand slashed a dozen meshes in the net. Then, before he could follow up and extricate himself, a form dropped from a window directly above, driving him flat against the paving. His knife dug vainly between the cobblestones. He recovered, thrust upward...

Smack! Something hard and heavy and swiftly moving swept his senses away as he felt his blade bite home.

CHAPTER 6
Satan's Garden

The slow, steady drip-drip-drip of water dropping against stones crept into Farrell's consciousness and finally became an impression distinct from the triphammer throbbing of his battered head. He stirred, and found that he was not bound. The holster under his left arm was empty. One of his knives, however. remained.

"If they wanted my hide, they could have taken it in the alley," he reflected as he pieced together his recollections of the encounter. "So far, it looks as if I've got 'em fooled."

Then, in Arabic, "*Aie*...my head! O dogs and sons of dogs, come out and fight! *Ya* Nureddin, thou son of a strumpet, thou uncle of camels! Thou eater of unclean food!"

The cell echoed with his bellowing. As he paused for breath, he reeled, clutched at the wall from whose base he had arisen, and supported himself. A torch flared smokily in the distance, from its sconce in the wall of the passage that opened into his cell.

"Father of many pigs!" he stormed as he kicked the iron grillwork that barred his advance, and rattled the chain and lock that secured the door.

The clattering and jangling finally drew a protest from beyond Farrell's field of vision. Then a fat, white-bearded fellow with bleary eyes and a bloated, sottish face emerged from a cross passage.

"Silence a moment!" he croaked as he took the torch from its sconce and advanced toward the grille.

"Bring me that dog of a Nureddin!" raged Farrell.

"One thing at a time," replied the warden. "Calm down and I'll promise you action."

"Oh, very well, then," agreed Farrell. "Lead on, Uncle."

Uncle drew a pistol and, keeping Farrell covered, unlocked the door.

"Now, wild man, forward!" he ordered. "And no false moves."

The slimy, glistening sides of the passage indicated that they were far beneath the surface of the city; perhaps in that labyrinth of vaults and connecting tunnels of which local tradition has murmured darkly and vaguely. Although his head ached from contact with material weapons wielded by physical enemies, Farrell shuddered at the evil that brooded about that archaic masonry and muttered of that which had emerged to defile the dead with obscene necromancies, and torment the living with monstrous hallucinations that came in the guise of dreams. The aura of age-old menace overpowered the terror of the Ismailian assassins.

"To your left," commanded the warden.

As Farrell rounded the turn, he saw ahead of him a glow of light and smelled the heavy, lingering fumes of incense. An Arab, and a bearded man whose race he could not determine, stood watch at the farther archway. Their hands rested on their belts, ready to draw knife or pistol. Their eyes stared fixedly from immobile features. They were drugged, or entranced: and Farrell shivered at the necessity of convincing himself that they were not dead.

"Pass on," commanded the warden as Farrell hesitated at the threshold. "The Master, our lord Hassan, will receive you."

The lord Hassan—the one whose name the dying La Dorada had with her last breath pronounced. She had known who had ordered her death.

A thrill of exultation was mingled with the flash of dread that assailed Farrell as he stepped into the reception hall of Hassan, that slayer of women and master of necromancers.

The room was long and narrow, and sweltering in a red glow of light. A Persian carpet ran down the center toward the divan in an arched alcove at the farther end. A man wearing a silken kaftan sat cross-legged among heaped cushions. His face was veiled, but his fierce eyes, smoldering in their deep sockets, were more menacing for being all that was visible.

Farrell halted midway between the alcove and the entrance. From the corner of his eye he saw a row of men, dressed in European clothes, sitting cross-legged along the wall on either side of him. Their arms were crossed on their breasts, and their eyes stared as glassily as those of the guards at the entrance. They were drugged, or deep in a hypnotic trance.

Farrell offered the peace.

"No peace and no protection, *ya* Ibrahim," responded Hassan, "until we have made a test of you."

"Tawil ul 'Umr," demanded Farrell with a touch of respect such as even a blustering Afghan would concede an old man; "Prolonged of Life, how am I to be tested?"

The old man reflected for a moment. His glittering eyes narrowed to slits.

"Tell me, can you obey as well as slay?"

"How should I know, Prolonged of Life?" proposed Farrell. "By your beard, I have never tried obedience. I am of the Durani clan."

"You will learn," said Hassan. "I will set you an example." He glanced to his left and clapped his hands. "Asad!" he called sharply.

One of the staring figures rose from his place along the wall. He moved as one receiving will and animation from some external source.

"Harkening and obedience, *ya sidi*!" he acknowledged as he halted before the dais.

"Your canjiar," murmured Hassan.

The curved blade flashed from its sheath.

"That knife is your gate to Paradise, *ya* Asad," said Hassan in his gentle, purring voice. Yet beneath its suggestion Farrell sensed a relentless command.

Asad inclined his head as he touched his fingertips to his forehead, his lips, and his breast. A pause—the blade flashed again as Asad thrust it full into his own chest. He stood for a moment fingering the hilt; then he tottered and sank to the tiles, to relax and lie sprawled face down in the dark pool that slowly spread across the paving.

Farrell knew that beneath his grimy skin his cheeks were bloodless. It was horrible to see even a *hasheeshin* spill his life carelessly as a glass of wine to humor that old man who peered over the edge of his veil.

"There, *ya* Ibrahim, is obedience."

Farrell collected his courage and demanded boldly, "And why should any man yield such obedience?"

"Because," came the reply, "I am the keeper of the gateway. He is even now in Paradise, and exempt from any recall."

Farrell grimaced.

"No more than any true believer gains for slaying an infidel," he retorted.

"You will enter the Garden, *ya* Ibrahim," murmured Hassan, "and see for yourself. Then you may accept or reject."

To the Garden! There, unless all d'Artois' deductions were wrong, he would find Antoinette. But Farrell restrained his eagerness, and pondered a moment, as became the role he played.

"I am ready, Prolonged of Life," he finally replied, as he advanced a pace.

"Softly, softly," said Hassan. "Are you armed?"

"Ay, wallah!" replied Farrell, drawing his remaining knife.

Hassan again clapped his hands.

"*Ya* Suleiman! Yusuf!"

Two rose from the ranks and approached.

"Harkening and obedience, my lord," they said as they bowed.

"This one claims to be a man of valor, O Devoted Ones!" said Hassan. "Draw!"

Their blades were drawn as one. The slayers stood like panthers poised and ready to close in on their prey. Their eyes glowed in the red glare like beasts lurking in the shadows beyond a fire. Slaves to the mesmeric power of Hassan, and to the hypnotic hasheesh, they were men in form only.

Hassan glanced at Farrell.

"You may decline without penalty or dishonor," said the old man. "You are free, and owe us no obedience."

"They are your men, *ya sidi*," replied Farrell with a shrug. "If you can spare them."

The old man chuckled, and his eyes for a moment smiled.

"Strike!" he commanded.

They paused for an instant before closing in. One of them, Farrell was certain, would go down before his first thrust, but the other would slay him. Farrell's success depended upon finesse. He shifted his feet as if to test the footing. He glanced over his shoulder as if to assure himself that he had room to retreat. All in a flash: and then they sprang, blades thirsty and a-glitter.

Farrell's leap took him to the left instead of to the rear. He dropped his knife and snatched the wrist of the nearest enemy, who, missing his quarry, plunged forward abreast of his comrade.

His own momentum was his ruin. There was the snap of a breaking bone, and Yusuf pitched in a heap before the dais. And Farrell, picking his knife from the tiles, confronted Suleiman, who despite his fanatic frenzy was profiting by Yusuf's mishap.

They circled, feinting and thrusting, seeking to shake each other's guard. Suleiman avoided Farrell's efforts to close in to make it a test of strength. Nor would rushing in to exchange thrusts suffice: for if they slew each other, the Master would still not have the test he ordered. They wove in and out, shifting and side-stepping, each seeking an opening in the other's defense.

Then Farrell made a desperate feint at his enemy's throat. As Suleiman's blade rose to parry, Farrell evaded, and stretched out in a full lunge, point forward and arm extended as with a rapier. The unexpected play caught Suleiman off guard. His downward thrust came an instant too late: Farrell's knife sank to the hilt in the enemy's stomach, ripping upward.

Farrell, bleeding from the cut on his shoulder, emerged from the engagement empty-handed as Suleiman collapsed.

"Well done, *ya* Ibrahim!" approved Hassan. Then he smote a gong beside the dais.

"*Ya* Musa! Abbas! Khalil!" he shouted.

A panel opened at right of the dais, and three tall negroes entered. They made no expressions of obedience; only the inarticulate gurglings of those whose tongues have been removed.

Hassan indicated the two dead, and the one whose arm was snapped.

"To the black pool with them. All three!" Then, as two stepped forward to execute the command, Hassan spoke to the third: "Take our new aspirant, Ibrahim, to the Garden."

Musa bowed, and at the Master's gesture of dismissal, led Farrell into a dimly lighted room which was arranged after the fashion of a *majlis*, or reception hall of an Arabian house.

A narrow divan extended the full length of the wall. At the end farthest from the entrance were the customary coffee hearth and polished brass pots. And save for those, and the cushions and rugs with which the divan was covered, there were no furnishings.

Farrell noted that he was not alone. Those who lay sprawled on the divan were, apparently, likewise to visit the Garden.

"Dead-drunk…drugged…or spies to watch me," reflected Farrell.

Musa, who after indicating that Farrell was to seat himself, had left, presently returned with a tray on which was a goblet and flagon. These he set on a small tabouret, bowed, and left Farrell to refresh himself.

The proof of hand-to-hand fighting had been severe enough; but the flagon of wine, fragrant but reeking of hasheesh, represented a more subtle and dangerous test. If under the influence of the drug Farrell made one remark or gesture that would betray his imposture, the awakening would be death, either swift, or else by torture administered to find out how much the outside world knew of the Is- mailians. Nevertheless, Farrell dared not abstain from the drugged wine. He knew not what eyes might be regarding him through loopholes in the wall.

"Bismillahi!" he ejaculated, and seized the flagon, draining it at a draft. He hoped that despite the insidious drug, his years of wandering in the forbidden places of Asia had impressed upon him enough of his assumed character to in- sure him against a fatal slip.

Farrell wondered at the suicide ordered by Hassan. The value of Ibrahim Khan as a *fedawi* could scarcely balance the self-slain and the two killed in ac- tion. He reconciled this point, however, when he considered the probability of the slain being offenders against the discipline of the order…

The intoxication of hasheesh was gripping him. Then an artifice occurred to Farrell. He might still save the day and avoid complete intoxication.

"*Ya* Musa! *Shewayya' khamr!*" he bawled drunkenly. "More wine!"

The slave came hurrying with a full flagon. Farrell's chance was to drink so much of the drugged liquor that his stomach would rebel, and expel it; and such sottishness would be quite in character. He seized the flagon with unfeigned ea- gerness.

But the saving thought had come too late.

His heart-beat became terrifyingly slow. His arm seemed so long that the weight of the flagon, already the size of a cask, and momentarily becoming larger, would exert a leverage that would upset him. The room was expanding to allow for the abnormal length of the arm that sought to raise the wine to his lips.

Farrell became aware of a duality of identity. Half of him was struggling fiercely to assert itself and overcome the confusion of his senses; the other half was yielding to a languorous drowsiness, and a soporific humming which per- vaded the room.

There came finally a rustling of wings, and a piping, haunting music that sighed amorously. All sense of time had ceased. Farrell did not know whether he was being carried through an archway into a vast domed vault, or whether he had floated in on clouds of overwhelming sweetness.

A fountain was bubbling, and splashing him with its spray. He stared up at the ceiling. Its luminous blue was dusted with stars that were arranged in unfamiliar constellations.

Drums muttered somewhere in the shifting, warm fragrance. He heard the sil- very clink-clinking of anklets. He rolled over on his side, and as he glanced along the rose-hued tiles, he saw dainty feet with hennaed nails stepping in ca- dence to the whining notes of a *kemenjah*, and the moan of pipes.

166

As he made an effort to sit erect, a warm, soft arm supported his head, and slender, golden-brown hands offered him a bowl of cold, aromatic liquid. He drank it, and found that his reeling senses became more stable. The girl who smiled at him had great dark eyes with kohl-blackened lids.

Another heaped cushions behind him.

Paradise indeed; *al jannat*, temporarily offered as the reward of whatever infamy the lord Hassan demanded, and promised for all eternity to the fanatic *fedawi* who died executing his commands.

There were other guests scattered about the jasmine and rose clustered garden, and the brides of *al jannat* were reviving them with flagons, cold drinks, and warm caresses.

Farrell made an effort to fight the illusion of distorted time and distance, and the sensuous allure of the music and hasheesh. He rose, and ignoring his amorous companions, set about exploring the garden. Strange birds flitted about among the orange and pomegranate trees and mocked him with their almost articulate cries. A parrot mimicked in a loud voice the endearments that a Malay girl murmured in the ear of one of the Devoted Ones.

"Where is the Golden One?" he heard a swarthy Kurd demand as he thrust aside his slant-eyed Eurasian companion.

The last of Farrell's intoxication left him. The Golden One—Antoinette!

The girl laughed.

"She'll scratch your eyes out! Let her alone!"

"But the Master, our Lord Hassan, promised she'd greet us in Paradise," protested the Kurd.

Farrell knew now beyond any doubt that Antoinette had been kidnapped to double in this satanic garden for the murdered La Dorada, to prove to the *hasheeshin* that the Lord Hassan indeed held the keys to the garden of resurrection.

"*Al Asfarani*, the Golden One—"

Farrell seconded the Kurd's inquiry.

"Snarling and spitting in her alcove, O Strong Man!" smiled the girl.

Farrell left her to entertain the Kurd, and wandered past the rows of potted trees that paralleled the walls of the garden. The walls were pierced with deep niches that formed small rooms whose arched entrances were scarcely shoulder-high. As he glanced into each in succession, he noted the trinkets and cosmetics and perfumes, and articles of feminine apparel. Each bride of *al jannat* seemed to have her own lupanar; but they apparently preferred to lounge among the fountains and arbors.

Finally, however, Farrell found an occupied alcove. A woman lay face down among a heap of cushions. Her hair was copper-golden, and her bare shoulders were latticed with long, bluish stripes.

Farrell knelt at her side.

"Antoinette!" he whispered.

At the touch of his fingers on her shoulder, she started and with a quick motion drew away. Her hand emerged from the cushions clutching a long sharp steel skewer used in Syria for grilling meat.

167

It was Antoinette, wide-eyed with terror. She cried out, and stabbed at Farrell with the skewer. The point raked his cheek as he seized her wrist.

"'Toinette! Don't you recognize me?" he whispered hoarsely.

She regarded him for a moment, puzzled and incredulous. The skewer dropped from her fingers. But before she could cry out in amazement, Farrell continued, "Not a word! If any one passes by, start raising the devil! Don't seem to recognize me…understand?"

She nodded, but he saw that she did not grasp the point that might make the difference between life and death. She was still bewildered.

"Oh, Glenn…" She stroked his cheek and regarded him, still incredulously. "Are you—isn't this—my dear, this is that awful garden I dreamed of. Only, now I have my own body, and I don't wake up—"

"Pipe down!" he commanded in a low, tense voice. "I'm supposed to be one of these devils! You're not dreaming. Pull yourself together—"

He heard footsteps approaching. They were steady, not the jerky lurchings of wine and hasheesh intoxication. Whoever it was, was for Farrell a death sentence if Antoinette in her hysteria spoke one false word.

"Scream! Claw me! As you treated the others!"

Then he seized her in his arms and murmured drunken endearments in her ear.

But Antoinette was too dazed by the meeting to play her part. She clung to Farrell as the one fragment of reality in all that unending nightmare of hasheesh-drugged assassins who courted her favor, and pawed her, and abandoned their advances only at the suggestion of more amiable brides of *al jannat*. Instead of clawing and defying Farrell, she clung to him, sobbing hysterically.

That deliberate tread of doom, soft slipper shod, drew nearer, paused.

Farrell trembled like a trapped animal. He sought with his own feigned drunken, amorous approaches to drown her betraying sobs and murmurs.

The swish-slap of slippers…another halt. Farrell felt the intentness of the gaze at his back.

He broke from Antoinette's embrace and turned. Standing just within the entrance of the tiny room was Shirkuh the necromancer. He had seen Farrell at the château, face to face. And he had heard. He knew.

"Ah… La Dorada has lured you to the Garden?" he murmured with deadly emphasis on the dead woman's name.

The smile was slow and mocking; the relentless eyes burned with a fanatical hatred. For a moment Farrell was paralyzed with terror, and horror at the doom from which Antoinette had no further chance of escape.

Shirkuh relished the encounter, and gloated—but just an instant too long.

Farrell sprang from his crouched position in one swift, fluent motion. Shirkuh, taken cold-footed, could not draw his knife. They crashed to the floor. But once Shirkuh recovered from the surprise of the assault, he was more than a match for Farrell, who was battered, weary from combat, and shaken by the drugged wine. The iron fingers of the Kurd sank into his throat and throttled him. Shirkuh whipped his lithe body aside, avoiding Farrell's frenzied efforts to drive home with his knee. As Farrell's struggles subsided to a futile gasping for breath, the Kurd's hand flashed to his belt and drew a knife—

But before the stroke descended, there was a crash and a splintering of glass. Shirkuh toppled over, felled by a decanter that Antoinette had broken across his head. Farrell gasped, and caught his breath, then slowly dragged himself clear of his enemy.

Antoinette, still clutching the neck of the broken decanter, regarded him with terror-widened eyes. Then she gestured toward Shirkuh, who muttered and stirred.

Farrell's fingers closed about the hilt of the knife the Kurd had dropped.

"Me or him," muttered Farrell. "If you don't want to see it, look the other way."

The blade flashed thrice.

Farrell wiped the red steel and slipped it into his empty scabbard. Then he sighed wearily and despairingly.

"Finish anyway…they'll miss him…and no place we can hide him." Antoinette stared at the dark pool that spread across the silken rug.

"Can't cut my way out," muttered Farrell. "But you have a chance. Pierre and the *Sûreté* are on the job—is there any place we could hide that fellow?" Antoinette shook her head.

"Nowhere. The pool of the fountain isn't deep enough—"

"Never mind the fountain!" interrupted Farrell, as he leaped to his feet. "I have a hunch. We're not quite ready to hang old man Farrell's youngest son!"

At the entrance Farrell turned, reassured Antoinette with a gesture, then stalked out into the Garden, chanting a bawdy song in Turki.

Beside the fountain he found the object of his search: a bemuddled Kurd, and the Eurasian girl who had finally convinced him that the Golden One was best left to the blustering Afghan.

"Get us more wine, O Moon of Loveliness," said Farrell with his most engaging smile. He nudged the Kurd.

The girl laughed softly.

"You look as though she gave you your fill of clawing!"

"Ay, wallah!" agreed Farrell with a broad grin. Then, as the girl picked up an empty flagon, he said in a low voice to the Kurd, "Brother, you fellows didn't approach *Al Asfarani* the right way."

He winked and beckoned.

The Kurd clambered to his feet and followed Farrell. They paused at the arched entrance of Antoinette's alcove.

"She's in there now," whispered Farrell. "She'll not claw you."

Thus encouraged, the Kurd stepped in, Farrell following.

"Ya sitti," he began, addressing Antoinette. Then he started, seeing the body of Shirkuh.

Farrell slipped past, and toward Antoinette's divan.

"Out of my way, O shamelessly Besotted!" growled the Kurd, pausing to nudge the body with his toe.

During that instant Farrell found what he sought; and as the Kurd decided to ignore the supposed sot, the steel skewer drove home, its point projecting beyond his shoulders.

"Sorry, old man," muttered Farrell as he regarded the Kurd twitching and coughing his life out in a bloody foam. Then he rapidly searched the body.

He found no weapons.

"Disarm 'em when they come in here...leaves me handicapped..."

He thrust Shirkuh's knife into the hand of the dying Kurd and closed the fingers about it. Then he guided the hand of Shirkuh and clenched it about the blunt end of the skewer.

"This may save the day," he explained to Antoinette. "Remember, they fought and killed each other. That may give me a long enough lease on life to come back and get you out of this hell's hole, or get word to Pierre. Now I've got to go out into the Garden and do some quick thinking. Something else may turn up...no, I can't stay here with you...and I've got to leave the bodies where they are."

Then, as he kissed her, "Hang on. There's still a chance for you. Maybe for us."

He strode out into the Garden, and washed his blood-stained hands at the fountain. The Eurasian girl had not yet returned with the replenished flagon. And as Farrell glanced about, looking for her, and preparing to divert her from any thought of her former companion, Musa the mute negro approached with a jar on his shoulder and a cup in his hand.

This, Farrell surmised, would be the end of the visit to Paradise. The negro would administer a sleeping-potion; the devoted ones would drink, and upon awakening would find themselves lying in the *majlis*, mysteriously translated from the empyrean realm of the Lord Hassan, and ready for whatever butcheries he could assign them.

As Musa offered him the cup, Farrell extended his own flagon, saying, "Fill this one, Father of Blackness. That cup of yours is too small."

The negro grinned, emptied the cup into the larger vessel, and went his way to minister to the other guests.

The Eurasian beauty, who returned at that moment, was easily diverted, so that Farrell contrived to spill most of the drugged wine over his shirt-front and into the fountain. Then, as he saw the *fedawi* succumb to the effects of the drug, he himself lurched forward, feigning unconsciousness.

"No chance to look around...no chance of cutting my way out," he reflected as he thought of Antoinette and her ghastly companions. "And maybe the Shirkuh versus drunken Kurd formation will hold water long enough to give me time to qualify as an assassin and be sent out to do a bit of slaying!"

The negro was making the rounds, taking the *fedawi* one by one from the Garden. He picked Farrell from the paving as though he were a bag of meal, shouldered him, and deposited him on the divan in the anteroom, beside his drugged companions.

And from sheer weariness and the futility of further thought, Farrell fell asleep.

CHAPTER 7

A Left-Handed Kurd

When a cold sponge on his forehead and the rim of a copper bowl pressed to his lips awoke Farrell, he had no idea as to the length of his sleep.

Musa helped him to his feet and led the way down a narrow passage whose floor sloped perceptibly upward. The negro halted before a panel and tapped thrice. As the panel slid aside, he gestured and flattened himself against the wall so that Farrell could pass him and enter the chamber ahead.

Farrell stepped into a circular vault fully twenty yards in diameter. In its center was a pool, likewise circular, and surrounded by a coping about a foot high. A dark splash on the tiles near the pool convinced Farrell that this must be the place into which the bodies of the victims of his test before Hassan had been tossed.

Farrell wondered if as a matter of convenience he had been conducted to the vault before the master cut him down. One slip would suffice...

Directly opposite Farrell was an arched niche in which sat an old man whose head was bowed in contemplation. Suspended from the crown of the arch was a cluster of crystalline prisms that slowly rotated, giving the effect of a glowing, coruscating ball of light.

As Farrell advanced, the door behind him slid silently into place. He skirted the edge of the pool in the center, and wondered from what abyss its black, untroubled waters emerged; what creatures lurked in its darkness to devour the bodies tossed into their pit. Then, leaving the pool, Farrell continued toward the bearded sage who still ignored his approach.

"At thy command, *ya shaykh*!" said Farrell as he halted some five paces from the Presence.

"Step forward," directed the ancient one, looking up and indicating a small hearth-rug that lay at the foot of the steps that ascended to the niche. "Look, *ya* Ibrahim: hast thou seen me before?"

As the smoldering eyes narrowed, Farrell recognized Hassan, now unveiled. He returned the old man's unblinking stare, and strove to remain unperturbed by its intent concentration; but his effort was vain. He felt a sense of futility and weakness creeping over him.

The rotating cluster of prisms now flamed and flashed with an adamantine fire that expanded and contracted and pulsed like a living thing. It seemed now to be glowing between the eyes of Hassan. An overwhelming weariness assailed Farrell.

The old man's voice intoned sonorously, and as from a great distance.

"I am the keeper of the gateway...even in the hollow of my hand I hold *al jannat* and its coolness to the eyes... Yea, behold my hand..."

Farrell regarded the outstretched hand of Hassan.

"In the hollow of my hand, even in this hand I hold *al jannat*..."

A mistiness was gathering about Hassan, and his features became obscured so that only his glittering eyes peered through. The outstretched hand was expanding; and strangely enough, it seemed fitting to Farrell that this should be so, and that there should be hazy figures, and clots of greenness appearing in the blankness above the hand. Trees were taking root. Their outlines were hazy, and through their immaterial substance he could just distinguish the jambs of the niche, and the swirling mists that veiled Hassan.

The voice was now murmuring softly and compellingly.

"Even in this hand I hold the Garden... I am the keeper and the warden... I accept and I reject..."

Then that which in the back of his brain had kept Farrell from utterly succumbing to the sorcery of that murmuring voice and those burning eyes asserted itself, and he knew that it was illusion. As he sought to resist and deny, he felt a terrific impact as of a physical substance. A mighty, implacable will bludgeoned him as with hammer blows. He knew that if he continued assenting he would be for ever enslaved.

"There is no Garden. It is illusion," he asserted to himself, and forced his lips to move and silently enunciate the negation. He trembled with an all-compelling fear, the awful fear of losing his very identity. That devastating will behind the cloud-veil was crushing him. How easy to assent, and end the agony!

Great beads of sweat glistened on his forehead. His face was drawn and haggard with the torment of his battered will. But to surrender would betray Antoinette into the hands of the enemy.

"There is no Garden," he persisted. "His hand is *empty*. EMPTY. EMPTY!"

He forced his last vestige of strength into that final declaration. The trees dwindled to pin-heads of green, and with them vanished the gray mists. The hand *was* empty!

Farrell sighed from mortal weariness and relief. Then he smiled triumphantly. He had withstood the terrific psychic assault that would have made him a slave, and a vassal of that old man and the murderous heritage of Asia.

Hassan smiled as at an ancient jest.

"You have withstood my will as no man before you," he said. "There was one who resisted to the uttermost, but he dropped dead."

Hassan, the heir of Maymun the magician, the sorcerer, the heretic, took his defeat gracefully. Then his smile became ominous and mocking.

"Who but you would have had the wit to slay Shirkuh, the chief of my servants, then so arrange the body of another you slew, that it would seem that they had died quarrelling over *Al Asfarani*? Subtle serpent, you erred in putting the dagger in the right hand. That Kurd was left-handed."

As those words hammered home, Farrell wondered if his heart would ever again start beating. He was lost, and with him, Antoinette. Doomed by his own cunning.

But thus far, no word about his imposture; therefore Farrell laughed full in Hassan's face, as became the honor of the Durani clan.

"*Wallah*, you put a premium on slayers! Now what award do you give me, seeing that I was unarmed when I slew Shirkuh?"

Hassan regarded him admiringly for a moment.

"*Billahi*, but you do belong to us! Not as a hasheesh-besotted fool to slay and be slain, but as an Associate, and finally, an Initiate. It is such as you that we seek, and seek in vain."

A fierce light flamed in Hassan's eyes.

"Yet your victory over my will is your doom. In the fullness of your effort to deny the illusion, you finally spoke your negation aloud. *And you spoke in English!*"

For an instant Farrell was dazed by the horror that had been heaped on the soul-racking triumph he had just won. Doom was at hand—doom inescapable, else that old man would not dare confront him alone.

With a cry of rage, Farrell sprang to throttle Hassan despite what unseen allies he might have. But the floor sank beneath his feet as Hassan, smiling and unmoved, fingered a knob near the jamb of the arch. Farrell clutched at the edge of the opening through which he was dropping. His fingers sustained him for a moment, but the momentum of his body swinging free into vacancy broke his slender hold. He fell into the impenetrable blackness below.

CHAPTER 8

Monsters of the Pool

Instead of an interminable drop to the bottom of an abyss, Farrell landed in less than a second, and feet foremost, on slippery flags. He noted that the air was not as stagnant as one would expect in an oubliette.

"Plenty of circulation…just put me in temporary storage until they get around to organizing a committee to finish me with pomp and ceremony," he muttered as he struck a match.

Farrell saw that the walls of the dungeon were curved. He strode toward the center, and by the light of a second match saw a massive column of masonry which rose from floor to ceiling. He remembered the pool he had seen on the floor above, and concluded that the pillar before him was a hollow shaft which led to some subterranean spring in the heart of the knoll on which Bayonne was built.

"All in one piece, unhurt, and no enemy in sight—yet!" he reflected as he skirted the column.

Among the inevitable rubbish with which the dungeon would be littered Farrell hoped to find some fragment of rock, scrap of wood, anything, in fact, which would give him the means of meeting the enemy with more than bare hands. But before he could strike his next match, Farrell saw a glow of light at a considerable distance to his right. It faintly outlined a low archway, and suggested possible escape from the dungeon into which he had been dropped by Hassan. That same light, however, betokened the immediate presence of the enemy, and perhaps an armed sentry. Farrell therefore crept on in darkness until he was well out of line with the source of light, then left the column and progressed toward the wall.

His knee came into contact with something hard and metallic. He struck a match, and saw that he had found a chain, one end of which was attached to a massive leg-iron, and the other secured to an eye-bolt sunk into the wall. The shank of the eye-bolt was badly corroded where it entered the masonry. A few minutes of wrenching and tugging sufficed to separate the chain from its anchorage. The result was a crude flail which in a strong hand could shatter whatever skull it struck.

Farrell was armed again, and his spirits rose accordingly.

He retraced his course and crept down the passageway toward the light. As he halted in the shelter of a jamb he saw that the vault ahead of him was illuminated

173

by a glowing brazier; and the scene gave him a foretaste of what his own fate might be.

The black, oily form of a muscular negro crouched beside the brazier. The bellows in his hands wheezed from his vigorous efforts to fan the charcoal fire to a white heat. Tongs or other long-handled implements projected from the incandescent mass.

Limned in harsh highlight and black shadows Farrell saw two white-robed Ismailians whose predatory, Semitic features were stern from the contemplation of their task. Both were armed with scimitars and pistols. The object of their scrutiny was a man who sat crouched by a pilaster. Farrell could distinguish no features beyond the aquiline curve of his nose, and the black, spade-shaped beard. The hands, clasped about the knees, were fettered at the wrists.

"God!" muttered Farrell as the red glow became a dazzling whiteness. "That lad sitting there looks for all the world like an innocent bystander. Either that party isn't for him, or he has more guts than any ten men I've ever seen... I've not been here long enough for that to be my reception committee..."

Farrell appraised the situation, and gauged the distance between his lurking-place and the group at the brazier.

"Too far! They'd get wise before I got within striking distance...now if this piece of chain were only a solid bar so that I could slug, swat, and parry instead of having to use it like a whip...now what?"

The taller of the Ismailians glanced up, and with a gesture indicated the ceiling. Farrell could not distinguish his words, but it was evident that he had addressed the negro, who set aside his bellows, picked up a length of thin rope, and rose.

Then Farrell understood. They were going to slip the cord through a ring in the low ceiling, lash the prisoner's ankles, and suspend him so that the white-hot irons could be applied without interference from the victim's agonized writhing.

"Missed my chance!" growled Farrell. "They were all off guard, and I could have cold-calked them! Too late, now."

The Ismailian on the right addressed the prisoner; but the other was looking in Farrell's direction, though not directly at his lurking-place. The negro was shifting the implements that projected from the bed of coals.

Then Farrell tested the idea that came to him an instant after his expression of disgust. He reached into his pocket and found a large silver coin the size of an American dollar. He sent it spinning across the vault. It struck the opposite wall and tinkled to the floor.

As the Ismailian at the left of the group started, caught the gleam of silver, and stooped to pick it up, Farrell, whirling his flail, leaped from cover and charged.

The startled cry of the crouching negro was simultaneous with the impact of the swinging fetter against the skull of the stooping enemy. The massive circlet of iron crunched home as the other white-robed enemy whirled from confronting his prisoner and drew a pistol. Farrell knew that he could not lash out with a second blow of his flail. He ducked as the pistol flashed, gripped the Ismailian's wrist as the pistol cracked again, and back-heeled him. They crashed to the flags, Farrell striving to keep the pistol out of effective action and to disable his enemy before the giant negro recovered his wits enough to overwhelm him.

174

With a fierce wrench, Farrell disarmed the Ismailian and sent the pistol flying against the wall. And then the negro took a hand. They pounded and crushed Farrell as they sought to drive home with knife-thrusts which he evaded in his struggles to drive in with boot or knee. He finally, thrashing about, seized the shackle end of his flail; and as the Ismailian's knife darted in, Farrell jabbed the ponderous iron to the enemy's jaw with a crushing blow.

Then the negro crushed Farrell to the paving. Farrell's struggles were futile; the cumulative effect of previous combats was telling. In another moment his breath would be completely cut off by those relentless black hands...

Then an agonized yell, and the stench of burning hair and flesh. The pressure relaxed as a shower of white-hot charcoal rained from the frenzied enemy and seared Farrell's hands and face. But the respite, though brief, sufficed. Farrell's boot laid the enemy out flat.

Then he rose, recovered the pistol that lay against the wall, and turned to confront the fettered prisoner.

"Fortunately," said the prisoner, "I was able to reach the tongs and flip that brazier into the party."

The mutual benefactors regarded each other a moment.

"Monsieur," began Farrell, recognizing the prisoner as a Frenchman, "I am more interested in getting out of here than exchanging compliments. Judging from the preparations I interrupted, you were in for a pleasant evening, morning, or whatever it may be."

"Unfortunately," came the reply, "these fetters are riveted, and none of the tools they brought—"

"I'll tend to that," assured Farrell. He turned and set the brazier right side up, then with the tongs collected the still glowing charcoal, and fanned it once more to a white heat. "Get your chains hot enough," he explained, "and we can break them by hand."

"Magnifique!" Then, regarding Farrell more intently, "But I don't recognize you as any of the Brethren who might be kindly disposed—though those fellows lying on the floor prove the case."

"I'm not quite what I seem," admitted Farrell as he arranged the chains so that they could get the full heat of the brazier. Then, staring for an instant at the prisoner and at the device engraved on the emerald set in his massive ring, Farrell hazarded a guess that seemed warranted by the absence of the host who had issued the invitations to the *soirée* at the château.

"Are you by any chance the Marquis—"

"C'est moi! Des Islots, and everlastingly at your service!" The saturnine features brightened for a moment.

As Farrell pumped the bellows, he wondered at the fortuitous meeting.

"Did Hassan put you in here?"

"No. Shirkuh, his second in command, arranged this. Hassan is too busy to bother with details—"

"He had plenty of time for me," countered Farrell.

"Hmmm...then Shirkuh must be occupied with some important mission," began the Marquis.

"The *late* Shirkuh," corrected Farrell with a grim smile.

"Sacré bleu!" ejaculated the Marquis. "Did you—"

"I have the honor—and pleasure," admitted Farrell.

"Thank God! He was my evil genius. Years ago, in Syria, I joined the Ismailians as an Associate. I was a student of the occult, you understand. Their aim at the time was harmless enough: the overthrow of Islam, and the pursuit of mystic speculations. For centuries the order has had no secular significance, you comprehend.

"I advanced to the rank of Initiate, then returned to France and organized a thaumaturgical society which was to carry on with the researches I had made in Syria, and in High Asia. And this was all well until fellow Ismailians came to Bayonne, one by one, and ended by converting the thaumaturgical society into a chapter of Ismailians.

"Shirkuh was the chief of these, a prior. And then they reverted to the tactics of the Twelfth Century. To augment the *hasheeshin* that they sent over, they recruited cutthroats from the underworld of Paris. Various actresses and women of the *demi-monde* were led to believe that they had been admitted as Associates, and were set to work as spies.

"There is a plot even now under way which, if successful, will upset the French colonial empire and end in a *jihad* that will stir up the entire Moslem world.

"Another chapter has been organized in Lyons, with a prior in charge: and Hassan is Grand Prior of France, acknowledging only the supreme chief in Damascus.

"At all events, when I saw the political aspect of the Ismailians who had gained their foothold through my thaumaturgical society, I protested to Shirkuh —and here I am. Hot irons and other pleasant devices were to make my end most colorful."

"Where," wondered Farrell, "does La Dorada fit into the picture?"

"Eh? La Dorada? Why, a sort of chief female spy—she is friendly with many high officers and civilian dignitaries, you comprehend. She is—"

"Was," interrupted Farrell. "Three assassins finished her."

"Diable!" exclaimed the Marquis. He was amazed rather than grieved.

"You take it calmly, for a lover," remarked Farrell.

"Lover?" The Marquis laughed sourly. "I, her lover? Camouflage, to account for her presence down here, and along the Riviera. As to her being assassinated, that is easily explained: her mission must have been completed. So she was killed to insure her continued secrecy, and also to warn her dupes that they would follow suit if they relented or weakened in the course dictated by Hassan. And that move makes it all the more conclusive that France is due for an explosion."

The confusion was being untangled. Farrell wondered at Antoinette Delatour's connection, and the source of the dreams that had haunted her; but the chains that bound the Marquis were white-hot and ready to break, so that conversation would have to wait.

"All right, heave!" directed Farrell.

The chains parted.

They stripped the bodies of the white-robed Ismailians, and armed themselves with their scimitars and pistols, as well as taking the extra cartridges that studded one of the belts. And the keys that had admitted the executioners completed the equipment. As the hot ends of the chain cooled, the Marquis bound them to his limbs so that they would not clank.

"I wonder," said Farrell as they turned toward the iron-bound door, "if those lads are completely out."

"*Cordieu*! But I am absent-minded!" growled the Marquis. He drew the scimitar at his side.

As Farrell unlocked the door, he heard the sword-strokes that assured beyond all doubt that three more had entered *al janat*.

"Wait a minute!" exclaimed Farrell as the door closed behind them. "We may run into a detachment on the way down here to finish me. Do you know of any other way except the passage used by your executioners?"

The Marquis reflected for a moment as he wiped and sheathed his blade.

"I do," he replied. "But we'd stand a good chance of getting lost and perishing in a labyrinth. This network is older than the Roman occupation. We have reclaimed but a fraction of it. It is the sanctuary of some awful, prehistoric past. And there were living proofs…" The Marquis shuddered at the recollection of what he had seen. "We killed most of them. But—as for me, I prefer to face men like ourselves! Anyway, if Shirkuh is dead, Hassan will be busy until another Prior is appointed. Shirkuh was an adept who studied in Tibet. A necromancer —"

Farrell shivered, and as they advanced up the passageway, told the Marquis what he had seen at the château.

"*Canaille!*" muttered the Marquis. "The night I was imprisoned! Just like him. And as you suspect, enough assassins in the crowd to spread the rumor of his miracle.

"Our best chance," he resumed, "is to go to the vault where you saw Hassan unveiled, thence to the assembly hall of the assassins. Then cut our way out—if we can! The chances are slender—"

"How about passing by the Garden?" wondered Farrell.

"Out of our way," protested the Marquis. "But why?"

"A…friend," replied Farrell. "Mademoiselle Delatour—"

"What?" exclaimed the Marquis with a start. "*Dieu de Dieu*! How—"

Then he controlled his agitation, beckoned for silence.

They emerged from the darkness and turned into an upward-sloping branch passage illuminated by torches thrust into sconces on the wall. Ahead of them they heard the measured tread of a sentry walking his post.

"Hang back," whispered the Marquis as he fingered the hilt of the broad-bladed knife that kept his scimitar company. "I know the passwords. And he may not know I'm a prisoner—but be ready for trouble if he does!"

The sentry challenged the Marquis. There was an exchange of sign and countersign. Then as the sentry saluted, the Marquis' right hand flashed to the right; his body jerked forward. As Farrell advanced, he saw the sentry collapse and sprawl across the tiles in a grotesque heap.

"So far, so good," muttered the Marquis as he wiped his blade, and led the way.

A barred door yielded to the Marquis' touch on a concealed lever. They continued on their upward march. They halted finally before a door whose panels were of heavy and elaborately carved woodwork.

"Diable!" growled the Marquis as he tried the door. "Barred from the other side. The release this side does not help us."

The mutter of drums and the plucked strings of a *sitar* were plainly audible. "Better wait until the place is vacant," whispered the Marquis. "And in the meanwhile, let's cut a loophole and see what's happening."

They drew their knives and set to work.

Peering through the loophole, Farrell could see the arched niche from whose foot he had been precipitated into the dungeon below. Hassan was again, or perhaps still, at his post. He was veiled, but there was no mistaking the posture and the expression of the eyes.

Sitting cross-legged along the curved wall of the vault were a score of Ismailians in white ceremonial robes. They wore white turbans, scarlet slippers, and belts of the same color: and all were armed with the richly adorned scimitars suitable to a formal assembly.

A group of musicians squatted on the floor, along the coping of the circular pool, whose dark water reflected the spectral glow that pervaded the vault. The wind instruments joined the music with a demoniac sobbing and moaning, and a brazen gong clanged.

Four litter-bearers emerged from an entrance. Attendants followed them, bearing tripods of bronze. Farrell shuddered at the similarity of that scene to the horrible beauty of the resurrection of La Dorada. Then he noted that the figure on the litter was that of a man.

As the shroud was lifted, he recognized Shirkuh of the clan of Shadi. The Prior of the Ismailians was to receive the final homage of his subordinates. The pipes wailed mournfully in honor of that desecrator of the dead. Farrell sighed with relief, and glanced at the Marquis.

He peered once more through the loophole.

"Good God!" he gasped in dismay.

Four more litter-bearers were filing into the vault, and after them came attendants with tripods. The tiny feet and the feminine curves that the shroud revealed unmistakably betokened a woman's body.

Farrell's cheeks whitened beneath their stain as he caught the glint of red-gold hair.

An attendant stripped the brocaded shroud from the body.

Antoinette Delatour, sleeping—or dead.

With an inarticulate growl of rage, Farrell gathered himself to charge the door with his shoulder. But the hand of the Marquis gripping his arm restrained him.

"Wait!" whispered the Marquis. "It is hopeless, now. But later—stand fast. I will tell you—you see, I am acquainted—"

Farrell stared somberly at his companion. He saw that the Marquis' face was white and that his eyes flamed with wrath. The hand on Farrell's arm trembled.

"All right," he conceded. He wondered at the Marquis' incoherence and agitation in excess of what he would expect of a right-minded gentleman. He gained assurance from the Marquis' apparent knowledge of what was to be; but with it came the dread of some new peak of horror.

"Great God!" muttered Farrell, remembering once more the necromantic ritual at the château. "Is she—"

Then, in a flare of rage and grief, "I'm going through!"

"Restrain yourself!" commanded the Marquis. "I know."

Farrell shook his head, and turned to the loophole.

The attendants and the litter-bearers were filing out of the vault.

The Grand Prior, Hassan, rose from his cushions.

"Brethren and servants of the Seventh Imam," he began, "your Prior, the learned Shirkuh, has crossed the Border. He who could raise the dead can not resurrect himself. But we, *inshallah*, can send a courier to lead him back to us."

As his upraised hand dropped to his side, a monstrous peal of bronze echoed and reverberated through the vault. The assembled Ismailians stirred, and corrected their posture, so that their feet and hands were placed with ritual precision. Even their features assumed a oneness of expression: an intent, solemn stare. The silence became absolute. The musicians sat motionless, awaiting the signal to sound off.

The Grand Prior nodded.

The single-stringed violins, the moaning pipes and the purring drums wove a harmony that sighed and sobbed like a fallen angel bewailing his lost estate. The great gong pealed with mighty, brazen reverberations. Acolytes filed into the vault, and paced in cadence to the music, and rhythmically swung fuming censers as they passed thrice in procession about the dead, and the exquisite unclad beauty of the living woman. And as the acolytes retreated, Hassan descended from his dais.

He drew on the floor with a piece of chalk a circle several paces in diameter, and within it a pentacle. Each of the five points he marked with cabalistic symbols. Then with a ceremonious gesture he summoned three Initiates from among those who sat waiting beside the dais. Each Initiate took his post at his assigned station; then all four bowed to the fifth vertex and the Presence that was to be summoned.

Hassan intoned a sentence; and the Initiates, beginning at his left, each in turn chanted a line of the invocation. Those without the circle solemnly pronounced a fifth sonorous phrase.

"For the vacant corner," whispered the Marquis to Farrell. "They are representing the One they are calling to occupy the fifth angle."

And thus they continued their prodigious utterances, four verses riming in succession, with the surge and thunder of the unrimed, antiphonal response from without. Each time the circle was completed, the riming syllable changed; and from the Arabic with which they had started, they shifted to Himyaric, and then to obscure, antique tongues whose sound was an elemental roar of deep gutturals. Then finally came a primal, bestial murmuring and muttering, a chirping and clucking of the tongues that were spoken by those who wandered through the Void before the first man walked the earth. And recurring through the entire progression was a portentous name that is seldom pronounced above a whisper.

The very features of the Initiates changed as they pronounced those rustling, shivering syllables. They were achieving a unity with that which crept and crawled and loathsomely slunk through chaos and reviled the unborn stars, and mocked the light that was to be...

Farrell, staring now with a dread that obliterated every other emotion, saw that a Presence was materializing at the fifth vertex. A vibrant glow like the luminous vapor of a mercury arc was momentarily becoming more dense and substantial. Lambent flames played about the brows of the Initiates in the pentacle. A terrific tension pervaded the vault. The bluish glow became deeper, and was shot with flashes of crimson and yellowish green. Each drawn face was now a ghastly slate-gray: the Presence at the fifth vertex was drawing the living essence from the swaying, gesturing bodies of Hassan and his trio of Initiates.

The Presence took human form: a lordly, satanic visage and a magnificently muscled body that quivered and throbbed to the droning chant. Then, rich and clear as a god calling across the wastes of space, the Presence began declaiming:

"*Al Asfarani*! *Al Asfarani*! *Al Asfarani*! I come from the realm of fire to command you! I have come out of the depths! Harken! Harken! Harken! *Al Asfarani*! Golden One! Step forth from your body and walk into the darkness among those whose bread is dust! Walk among the lonely dead and seek Shirkuh! Call him by his name and take him by the hand! Guide him from the shadows and into the morning!"

The unconscious woman shuddered at the sound of that mighty voice. She made a despairing gesture as if to resist the command that came from the fifth vertex. Then she relaxed.

The Presence continued his prodigious chant. Even the brazen reverberation of the gongs was drowned by his awful utterance.

A thin streamer, like the thread of smoke rising from an almost-quenched altar flame, rose from Antoinette Delatour's half-parted lips.

"Cordieu!" shouted the Marquis in Farrell's ear. "They're doing it!"

His gestures rather than his voice stirred Farrell to action. They retreated, then charged crashing against the door. It resisted the shock. Farrell drew his scimitar and hacked at the tropical hardwood. A carven panel splintered.

"Good God! Look!" he yelled in despair.

The Presence was now towering toward the ceiling. It was bending over like a monstrous serpent in human form, arching and writhing, reaching as though over some invisible wall, making passes and gestures over the silver-white body of Antoinette.

The Initiates in the pentacle were paper-white. They swayed to the cadence of that great voice whose concussion was now making the very vault tremble.

The train of smoke-like vapor that emerged from Antoinette's lips was becoming more dense, and hovered over her body like a veil.

"Quick!" shouted the Marquis, as they frantically hacked the stout wood. "Hold them, while I exorcise the Presence!"

The door was reinforced with iron rods that bound it together. Their blades were nicked and saw-toothed from the fierce assault.

"Again!" cried the Marquis as his scimitar flashed home.

A chunk of the hardwood tore loose from its severed reinforcement. They shouldered through, torn and cut by the splinters and the ragged ends of the rods they had hacked.

A musician cried out and sprang to his feet. And then one of the Initiates who sat beside the dais saw Farrell and the Marquis as they dashed across the circular vault. He aroused his comrades from their fascinated contemplation of the invocation of which they were now accessories rather than principals. They started as from a deep sleep, stared for an instant, then drew their scimitars and charged to meet the intruders, and to protect the left flank of the pentacle, from which the Presence still leaned over the unconscious girl, intoning the mighty commands that would send her across the Border.

Shoulder to shoulder, Farrell and the Marquis met the assault with deliberate, deadly pistol fire. The attack was checked; but the enemy stood fast and firm, protecting the pentacle. And despite the hail of lead they had poured into the ranks of the Ismailians, Farrell and his ally were still outnumbered ten to one.

The musicians were salvaging weapons.

There was not enough time to reload the pistols. The Ismailians had recovered from the shock of their murderous reception, and seeing their advantage, leaped forward, blades ready.

Then a clash of steel, and a red mill of slaughter. The Marquis fought with vengeful desperation. He wove in and out, sidestepping and parrying, shearing and slaying. And Farrell, keeping at his side, carved a gory path into the enemy. He fought with a blind, unreasoning fury, seeking to hack his way through the press and clear a road for the Marquis who could cope with that monstrous Presence that was in thunderous tones chanting the life and vital essence from Antoinette.

The enemy, sensing that the Marquis was the keystone of the arch, concentrated their attack on him; and despite his exquisite swordsmanship, he was being slashed to pieces by a desperation and force that discounted his skill.

He sank once beneath a whirlwind of blades, and recovered under the shelter of Farrell's blade; but he was coughing blood from a deep wound.

And Hassan and his trio had left the pentacle. The Presence, now endowed with the power borrowed from all that the Initiates had conjured from across the Border, was self-sustaining and no longer needed its portion of human vitality.

Hassan, behind the line of the assault, directed his Initiates in the attack.

"Cut him down, O sons of flat-nosed mothers!" he cried, as he saw the Marquis recover and press forward.

But that magnificent last effort burned out. With a cry of mortal rage, the Marquis lashed out with a final, devastating stroke, then collapsed on a heap of slain.

"Finish!" despaired Farrell. He was doomed, and Antoinette also—even though he could cut his way out. An adept was required to exorcise that terrific Presence that was drawing her from her body.

But the enemy, instead of closing in to hew him to pieces, gaped stupidly, then yelled in terror. They were staring at something at his right, and to the rear. He glanced over his shoulder, compelled by the consternation that stopped them where they stood.

Farrell lowered his own point, himself struck with awe. He recalled what the Marquis had said about the denizens of that labyrinth of passages.

A monstrous, amorphous thing had emerged from the circular pool into which Hassan had ordered the dead *fedawi* to be flung. It was misshapen, and grotesque in its vague semblance to humanity. Its bulbous head had a single, circular eye the size of a saucer. It glittered glassily in the bluish, spectral light. The limbs were shapeless and ponderous, and it lumbered, dripping wet, across the tiles. Its feet fell with a metallic clank, and its breath hissed and wheezed.

A second and similar creature was emerging from the water, even as the first advanced with slow, laborious pace. The hand clutched a short iron bar.

The bar rose in a sweeping arc and crunched down on the skull of an Ismailian, spattering blood and brain in a shower. The second monster clambered over the coping, unlimbered a bludgeon, and with gruesome deliberation picked a victim and struck.

There was a moment of silence unbroken save for the wheezing breath of the creatures from the pit. Then the Ismailians yelled in mortal terror. They forgot Farrell with his dripping blade and bewildered eyes; they forgot the Marquis, who stirred, and strove to lash out once more with his red scimitar; they forgot the golden-haired girl, and the malevolent Presence that, now silent, throbbed and pulsed, an aggregate of quivering, electric-bluish cold fire.

They broke and fled toward the splintered door.

At the height of their panic, Farrell understood. The monsters were men in diving-suits.

The Marquis was down. Farrell could not himself thwart that monster that was drinking Antoinette's vital essence and taking her across the Border beyond recall; but he could slay until he dropped from wounds, or from weariness of slaughter. He hurdled the hedge of fallen Ismailians and with a cry of rage and grief joined his allies to exact vengeance.

A third diver was at that moment emerging from the pool and joining the assault against the frenzied enemy, striking them down with remorseless precision as they struggled to crowd through the splintered panel of the door that had given Farrell admittance.

Farrell, however, was not the only one whose wits had recovered from the terror inspired by the apparitions from the black pool.

"Back and face them, *ya mumineen!*" shouted Hassan. "They are men like ourselves!"

But his attempt to rally his men was vain. Those who abandoned their efforts to crowd through the jammed door, and circled around to escape by way of the opposite entrance, were blocked by the arrival of a file of *fedawi* who, knives drawn, had come running from the assembly hall.

The dripping revolvers that the divers drew as they discarded their grappling-irons crackled and flamed, pouring a deadly fire into the new center of action.

Then Farrell conceived the desperate device of capturing Hassan and forcing him to recall the elemental monster that was drinking Antoinette's life. He leaped forward, cutting and slashing his way through the few who interposed.

"We meet in Paradise, *ya mumineen!*" Hassan shouted, seeing that the day was lost. And before Farrell could seize him, Hassan released the trap-door before the dais and dropped into the vault below.

The last hope was gone. Pursuit through those subterranean mazes would be futile. As Farrell turned from the yawning trap that had allowed the arch-enemy to escape, the rage of slaughter left him. The crackle of pistols died out. He saw that the circular chamber was cleared of all but the dead and wounded Ismailians. The divers, handicapped by their heavy suits, could not carry out an effective pursuit of the survivors of their deadly fire.

Weary and despairing, Farrell nerved himself to confront the diabolical creature that was drawing Antoinette across the Border. He turned—

The Marquis des Islots was raising his hacked, bleeding body from a heap of slain. He tottered, swayed, then advanced toward the lambent flame-presence. Farrell stared in fascination as that gory wreck of a man advanced, making ritual gestures with his faltering hands, and muttering in a low voice.

The Presence was shrinking and dimming, and that shimmering exhalation from Antoinette's lips was being retracted. The Marquis sustained himself with will alone. He staggered, sank—Farrell's heart sank with him—he recovered, stepped forward again, still gesticulating and murmuring. The Presence leaned forward to confront him, and menaced him with its remaining energy, seeking to outlive the dying adept.

The Marquis' bleeding, gashed face was drawn and white; his eyes were fixed and staring. He achieved another pass; then he collected himself, paused, and instead of murmuring, thundered a final phrase of command.

The Presence vanished; and the last vestige of grayish, luminous haze disappeared between Antoinette's lips.

Farrell leaped forward in time to catch the Marquis as he collapsed.

The divers, returning from the farther entrance at which the Ismailians had made their last stand, lifted one another's domed helmets. Then, grimy and exultant, Pierre d'Artois and the two members of the *Sûreté* gathered about Farrell and the Marquis, who was regaining a little of his strength.

"Messieurs," he said, as he gestured toward Antoinette, "she is safe. She will presently awaken. It can not return. *Jamais!*... It was my fault...in the beginning...but this infamy was not my intent... I loved her, but she rejected me...persistently. And for revenge...and to break her spirit... I administered without her knowledge a compound...of hypnotic drugs...so that she and that Syrian girl would each night exchange bodies...then Hassan took a hand..."

He regarded d'Artois for a moment.

"You, *monsieur*, doubtless understand—" Then, to Farrell, "But this last infamy...was not mine—Shirkuh and Hassan—I tried to make...amends—"

For an instant Farrell regarded the dying man with revulsion. Then he saw the remorse on the drawn, blood-splashed features, and thought of the Marquis' last gallant stand, confronting and exorcising that diabolical presence from beyond the Border.

"Stout fellow," he muttered, as he grasped the Marquis' hand.

"C'est fini," murmured d'Artois a moment later. "Magnificent in his death as he was misguided in his life...dying on his feet, he had the will to conquer, and make restitution."

Then d'Artois rose and glanced about him.

"Do you know the way out of here?"

"Through that door," directed Farrell. "He told me, before we made our rush."

"Messieurs," suggested d'Artois, "be ready with your pistols, should any of these assassins be lingering. I will take charge of the young lady, and you, my friend, lead the way. *Monsieur le Marquis* perhaps deserves greater courtesy, but we can not carry his body and take the risk of being caught without weapons drawn and ready."

Farrell led the way. Without much difficulty, he found the passage that opened into the vault where he had lain while regaining his consciousness preliminary to submitting to Hassan's tests. And from there they finally emerged in the heart of the citadel. A few moments later Farrell and d'Artois, carrying Antoinette, met Raoul where he was waiting at the wheel of the Renault.

CHAPTER 9

D'Artois Is Envious

Antoinette, an hour later, was entirely herself.

"Oh, it's wonderful to be out of that awful garden," she said, and curled herself up in the depth of a large, upholstered chair. "And now that *Monsieur le Médicin* admits that I'm as good as new, you might satisfy my curiosity on a few points. How did you ever—"

She glanced up at Farrell, who had seated himself on the arm of her chair. He was not yet through convincing himself that Satan's Garden was a thing of the past, and insisted on keeping Antoinette within arm's reach.

"Suppose you ask Pierre," he said.

D'Artois laughed.

"After all, *mon vieux*, you were responsible. We found two bodies floating down the Nive. One of them wore—oh, very becomingly, I assure you!—a knife in his stomach. The *Sûreté* informed me. I identified the knife. It was one of mine, which you had taken from my collection to wear while disguised as Ibrahim the Afghan ruffian.

"'*Alors*,' said I, 'Ibrahim Khan has given good account of himself. Perhaps, but God forbid, his own body will follow.' I assure you that we watched with anxiety. But no further signs. At low tide, however—you know, the Nive rises and falls with the tide, since we're so close to the sea—we found another body, mainly as the result of our continued close watch for yours. This one was wedged near the central of the seven bridges. We investigated, and found an uncharted drain of considerable diameter.

"'*Mon dieu*,' said I to *Monsieur* the Prefect, 'if bodies came out, bodies can also go in.' We got diving-suits. The tide in the meanwhile rose, but we had the location well marked. We advanced up the drain until we came to a dead end.

"Even before we left the water we heard the clash and crackle of your skirmish —"

"Massacre, you mean," interpolated Farrell, grinning as much as his bandages permitted. "Not a second too soon."

"*Eh bien*, we shut our exhaust air-valves and thus rose to the surface. Our grappling-irons snagged to the coping helped us unaided over the top. Then we sliced our airlines and lifelines, opened our exhausts and—"

"Scared them out of a week's growth!" added Farrell as d'Artois paused to light a cigarette. "But that damnable thing all of quivering fire—good Lord!"

"That," submitted d'Artois, "is something that I can explain but vaguely, if at all. I called it some more mummery, and decided, rather hastily, perhaps, that you and the Marquis needed help first of all. On reflection, and in view of some of your remarks since we left, I am of the opinion that it was either an elemental conjured up by those devil-mongering adepts, or else a wandering and malignant astral that was energized by the vital essence of the adepts, or perhaps by the vibration concentration of their ritual. *Monsieur le Marquis*, God rest his erring soul, could doubtless explain what it was, since he used his last spark of will to combat it and thwart its attempt to convert Mademoiselle Antoinette into—what did you tell me?—a courier to call Shirkuh from the hell in which he now must be roasting.

"I would very much relish," continued d'Artois, "questioning Hassan, who devised all that deviltry. But alas! he escaped. And while you, both of you, were causing the good doctor a certain amount of concern, I heard that the *Sûreté* and a handful of *gendarmes* cleaned out the entire nest. Unhappily, two were taken alive of that crew of assassins. And of course, those lovely ladies of the garden."

Farrell sighed from weariness and contentment, then grimaced from the ache of his wounds.

"The Marquis," he observed, "didn't have time to explain how that hypnotic drug enabled him to project Antoinette's *self* into the body of the Syrian bride of the garden—Lord, it's impossible to imagine how a brave fellow like him could have let his resentment and disappointment carry him to such lengths! Having her scourged by proxy, so to speak."

"Too much occultism and devil-mongering upset his brilliant mind," replied d'Artois. "Sombre, gloomy, and drunk with his talents. And translating Antoinette into the body of a bride of the garden, whom he could flog at will, was his warped expression of denied affection. As to just how he accomplished it, we can but surmise. Strange drugs are compounded in the Orient. When I complete the analysis of the pastries they offered us that night at the château, I may further enlighten you."

"But the stripes and welts that appeared on Antoinette's body?" wondered Farrell.

"For once you ask me something simple," retorted d'Artois. "Did you know that if a hypnotic is touched with a pencil, for example, and offered the suggestion that it is a red-hot iron, he will develop a blister, and all the symptoms of a burn at the spot touched? Moll and others concede that point with very little argument. It has often been experimentally demonstrated.

"*Alors*, the body of the Syrian girl was scourged. Antoinette's *self*, though in a borrowed body, retained what we can roughly call an astral connection with her own body; otherwise she could not have returned to it at the end of each ordeal. And through this connection, the body of Antoinette developed the same welts that were raised on the skin of the Syrian girl; just as, by rough analogy, the hypnotic subject through suggestion shows all outward signs of a burn. And the marks of the heavy anklets the Syrian bride of the garden wore were similarly branded on Antoinette's ankles.

"The Marquis during his unsuccessful courtship of Antoinette had ample opportunities to administer the hypnotic drug at which he hinted, so that his influence could have been gained without her knowledge. This, together with the objective symptoms, convinces me that if it was not the conventional hypnosis we know, it was at least a quasi-hypnosis. And as you know, there are vegetable compounds which, if properly administered, will effect a partial release of the astral counterpart of a body, or its spiritual essence. To pursue it to its origin would lead you to a study of Egyptian magic, and the nine traditional elements of every living human body.

"I will leave all this to you, *mon vieux*, to study, this matter of stigmata resulting from suggestion and other psychic influences. Me, I am no lecturer.

"And as to Antoinette's Arabic remarks in her sleep: the bride of the garden, dispossessed of her body for the time, sought Antoinette's. And by that astral connection which she retained with her own, she felt the scourgings administered in the garden, and expressed herself, through Antoinette's lips, as you heard."

D'Artois emerged from his chair and bowed with formal precision.

"I will therefore leave you here, my blundering Afghan, to have your wounds properly nursed while I go about doing all that an old man can do under the circumstances: envy you, and write a monograph on *Messieurs les Assassins*, and Satan's Garden, from which you so happily emerged."

With a peremptory gesture, he cut short Antoinette's insistence upon his pausing for at least a moment. Then, halting at the door, he concluded as he glanced at Farrell, "*Mordieu*, and to think that you enjoyed all that fine swordplay, while I, Pierre d'Artois, had to wear a diving-suit to find a fight, and then had to use a crowbar! In *several* ways I envy you."

186

QUEEN OF THE LILIN

Originally published in *Weird Tales*, November 1934.

CHAPTER 1

The Lurking Menace

"First a slater's hammer slides from a roof and comes within a hair of braining me. The next day a bust of Napoleon falls from its pedestal and narrowly misses me—and then one of my brother's collection of swords joins the conspiracy of inanimate things and—*mon Dieu*! It's only a miracle that I wasn't beheaded!"

Diane Livaudais sighed wearily and made a despairing gesture. Glenn Farrell's bronzed, rugged features contracted in a frown, and his gray eyes narrowed as he pondered on the sequence of accidents that had made Diane's past few days a nightmare. He turned to his old friend and host, Pierre d'Artois, a retired soldier whose scholarly pursuits had not obliterated his military bearing.

"That does seem to wrench the long arm of coincidence entirely out of joint," Farrell admitted. He no longer marveled that Diane's dark eyes were haunted, and that her gestures were abrupt and nervous; but her next remark was too much for Farrell's practical mind to digest.

"And the worst of it is," d'Artois' lovely visitor continued, "I'm certain that those weren't accidents—"

"Eh, comment?" demanded d'Artois, leaning forward and twisting his fierce gray mustache. "If I'm not mistaken, you just said—"

"I've sensed a malicious presence lurking about me for the past week," Diane resumed. Then, noting Farrell's silent but unconcealed amazement, "Oh, I know it sounds insane! But I caught a glimpse of a shadowy figure which faded almost the instant I turned to confront it—and I know she's responsible."

Diane paused, regarded them with a touch of defiance, challenging Farrell and his host to dispute her sanity. Farrell stroked his square chin and said nothing. He could not very well declare that Diane Livaudais was the victim of delusions and hallucinations; but such was his conviction, and he thus disposed, somewhat regretfully, of the most attractive girl he had met during his few weeks in southern France. D'Artois' reply, however, caught Farrell like a hammer stroke.

"And so there's an apparition following you around, making heavy objects fall in your direction...hmmm...very well—I will summon this pestilential specter here and now!"

"Good Lord!" was Farrell's unspoken comment as he saw that d'Artois was serious. "He's as bad as she is!"

They were sitting in d'Artois' study on the second floor of a Thirteenth Century tower that commanded the foot of rue Tour de Sault in the old city of Bayonne. The afternoon was young; but artificial illumination was needed to aug-

187

ment the sunlight that filtered feebly through the narrow casements that deft the yard-thick masonry walls of the restored and modernized ruin in which d'Artois lived.

The old scholar snapped the switch of the tall Damascus brass floor-lamp, leaving the circular room a sombre depth of gloom unbroken save for the patch of sunlight that played on the wine-red Boukhara rug.

"We will see what manner of phantom is following you around," he continued. "Sit back in your chair, *Mademoiselle*...relax...forget your fear and your worry...do not fight it...it can not harm you... I am watching..."

Diane's dark eyes became fixed and staring as she relaxed in response to that soporific murmuring. Farrell noted with wonder that though but a moment ago Diane had been not only wide awake but with nerves keyed to the snapping-point, she was now almost asleep. She was breathing very slowly and regularly; her long lashes drooped, masking the lower eyelids.

Such long lashes... Farrell himself felt the spell of that solemn, droning voice. He realized in a vague way that d'Artois was hypnotizing his distracted caller. Then Farrell frowned, shook his head perplexedly, glanced at d'Artois, and marveled...but only for a moment—and then Farrell perceived something which made him start violently, catch his breath with a gasp, and sit rigidly erect, hands clutching the arms of his chair.

In the shadows of that ancient tower-room he saw what seemed to be a tenuous, wavering streak which despite its semblance to a wisp of smoke was throbbing and pulsing as though it were alive. Moment by moment it became more dense. Farrell knew that a fourth personality had entered the room; a newcomer whose presence he could feel more distinctly than he could see. A cold thrill raced up his spine, and he shivered as though an icy wind had displaced the blood in his veins.

D'Artois' eyes were fixed, and his brow was furrowed with a frown of intense concentration. His lips moved inaudibly, and his lean hands gestured as to a slow, unheard rhythm.

The presence was becoming a transparent, clearly defined feminine form of exquisite proportion. On her head was a tall diadem of archaic workmanship; and her smile was a curved menace as evilly alluring as the loveliness of her delicate, haughty features. She was colorless, a mere luminous form; yet Farrell sensed that her hair should be black, with bluish highlights, and that the slightly aquiline face and graciously curved shoulders and slender arms should be a warm, olive hue.

Yet for all her loveliness, the presence was an evil brooding in the shadows. The tension in that sombre circular room moment by moment became more acute. Farrell felt perspiration trickling down his cheeks, and wondered how much longer he could endure the uncanny menace that had taken form before his eyes. But d'Artois broke the spell. He sharply clapped his hands.

"Wake up!" he commanded bruskly.

Diane started, regarded them both with eyes wide open and amazed. And when Farrell's glance, for an instant distracted from the darkness behind Diane, shifted back toward the spot where the presence had appeared, he saw but a thin thread of silver mist which vanished even as he stared.

"Oh! Did I fall asleep? I'm sorry—"

Diane's bewilderment was obvious. Farrell knew that she had been utterly unaware of the strange shadow-figure at her shoulder.

"Now I remember," she continued, collecting her wits. "We were discussing an apparition, and—"

"It was here, and it left," replied d'Artois. "But let us talk about something else. Tell me about those objects that came so near to killing you. What's their history?"

Diane closed her eyes for a moment, and frowned.

"Well...really, I don't know," she said, speaking very slowly, "except that Graf Erich gave me the bust of Napoleon not long ago, and gave my brother that Moro kampilan. But—"

"Graf Erich?" interrupted d'Artois. "*Mordieu*! Your choice of playmates!"

"Why, what's wrong with him?" wondered Diane. "He's perfectly fascinating, and he's been ever so attentive."

D'Artois nodded, and pondered for a moment. Farrell saw that while his friend had apparently gathered another loose end, the riddle had at the same time become more complex.

"Suppose," suggested d'Artois, "that you ask Graf Erich to invite me and Monsieur Farrell to his château this evening at almost any convenient hour after dinner. Offer him any plausible pretext. And you will of course accompany us."

"Why...but yes, certainly," Diane agreed, although she was as puzzled as Farrell. "But did you really see—do tell me—"

D'Artois smiled and shook his head.

"Before I commit myself, I prefer to see Graf Erich. And now run along and leave me to my studies. In the meanwhile, do be careful of falling objects. We don't want a tile or coping-stone to drop and kill you before I can get to the bottom of this riddle."

Diane knew the futility of persistence. Acknowledging Farrell's bow with a smile, she allowed d'Artois to escort her to the door at the ground floor.

Farrell perforce restrained his curiosity until d'Artois returned.

"How did you predict the appearance of that phantom?" he demanded.

D'Artois chuckled as he seated himself and struck light to a cigarette.

"I didn't predict it—and neither did I conjure it up. It follows Diane around—"

"Good Lord!" exclaimed Farrell. "Why—that's worse than if you'd actually evoked it. Do you mean that the girl is actually haunted?"

"In a way, yes," replied the old man. "And the evidence of our eyes is corroborated by those unusual accidents. Some personal, directed intelligence is working against Diane.

"By hypnotizing Diane, I subdued her conscious resistance and thus allowed the spectral companion to materialize by appropriating some of Diane's etheric double. A glance at any work on occultism will explain that to you."

Farrell shuddered, then resumed, "But where does Graf What's-His-Name come in?"

"I don't know, exactly," admitted d'Artois. "But consider for a moment: Graf Erich gave her the bronze bust. He gave her brother, who is a collector of arms, a

Moro kampilan. And every object which has featured in these uncanny accidents —excepting the slater's hammer—has passed through Graf Erich's hands. Simple, *n'est-ce pas?*"

"Yes, certainly—very simple indeed!" admitted Farrell with elaborate irony. "And so, very logically, a heathenish, Queen of Sheba sort of female ghost follows Diane around and makes a personal appearance when you do your hocus-pocus. Exceedingly clear, Pierre. I get it perfectly."

"Let it go at that," chuckled d'Artois. "I already begin to see a light; and tonight we may learn why all inanimate creation is conspiring to kill Diane."

CHAPTER 2

A Twisted Wire

Graf Erich's château was not much more than two kilometers beyond the Mousserole Gate. It crowned one of the knolls that were the advance guard of the Pyrenees. The salon, with its tapestried walls, its beamed ceiling and its ornate, massive chandeliers, reminded Farrell of a miniature of the dining-room of Henri IV at Pau.

Graf Erich received his guests in person. He made no reference to the lack of servants, and left it to his callers to decide whether poverty or eccentricity accounted for the absence of the servitors that should second the sombre richness of the appointments.

"A fighting man," was Farrell's first thought as he grasped the Count's extended hand and met the unwavering regard of his dark eyes. And then Farrell shifted his gaze. He was disconcerted as at an unintentional eavesdropping or spying. Graf Erich's eyes were too expressive for Farrell's entire comfort. In them he saw misery and regret, and an iron will that was equal to the terrific struggle that was branded in deep lines on his lean cheeks, and the droop of his mouth.

"He spends his time in the shadow of the ax," was Farrell's thought.

"Good God, what has he on his mind?…"

Diane, the first to acknowledge Graf Erich's greeting, had insisted that she would be quite content to leave her hat and coat in the Count's study, which was at the end of a low, vaulted passage that led from the salon.

"The light is just as good, and I have my own mirror," she assured him, as she declined his offer to escort her to a dressing-room. "And it's a day's journey from any one to any other part of this house."

Diane was in higher spirits than she had been that afternoon. Her laugh was light, and her eyes sparkled as she went on with her comments concerning architects who design a château that is a place of magnificent distances. Then she turned to step toward the study.

Farrell saw that a cluster of heavy Persian maces and battle-axes adorned the crown of the archway through which she proposed passing, and knew that Diane was stepping into line with peril from overhead. An instant later he caught her eye.

The mirth was gone. She also had seen. Farrell, while replying to Graf Erich's courtesies, shook his head. Diane's change of expression showed how plainly she had read his thought. She paused for an instant, then advanced.

"Going to fight it, eh? That's the spirit!" was his unspoken thought; but Farrell could barely resist his impulse to detain her.

"Er…beg your pardon, Count," he said, seeking to palm off his moment of inattention as a lapse in his actually excellent understanding of French. "My ear's a shade thick, you know—just landed on this side a week ago…"

Even as he spoke, his eyes shifted to follow Diane's advance. Then he saw it happening, and could no longer doubt.

Nervous tension brings an abnormal sharpness of the senses, and an accompanying illusion of the cessation of time.

The flexible picture-wire that bound the cluster of heavy weapons together had parted. He plainly saw that the ends of the stranded wire were separating, knew that their deadly burden was about to fall. But there was plenty of time. Those heavy, skull-crushing weapons had to drop three feet before they struck her…and they had not yet started falling…but they would, soon—now, they were dropping…and faster…

Farrell's fingers closed about Diane's shoulder and yanked her backward just a split instant before the burnished steel flashed down and rang crashing against the tiles.

"Oh-h-h! *Mon Dieu*, again!" cried Diane.

Graf Erich's dark face had become paper-white as he and d'Artois leaped forward.

"Look, *Monsieur*!" commanded d'Artois. His finger pointed accusingly at the ends of the stranded wire.

Graf Erich started violently. *"Was für Teufelei!"* he exclaimed in wrathful dismay. "That wire has been broken!"

"Broken? Are you sure it wasn't *cut*?" demanded Farrell.

"Mais non!" exclaimed d'Artois as he drew forward a chair and leaped to the seat. "Look! You can see how each strand has a sharp bend. *That wire was broken by repeated twisting, not by cutting.*"

"Oh, good Lord!" interposed Diane, who now trembled violently from the reaction of the shock. "Did you say someone broke the wires that secured those weapons to the wall? How—but what do you—it just couldn't—"

"Someone, or something," said d'Artois, regarding Graf Erich with stern, unwavering eyes.

The Count started. His swarthy features darkened.

"Just what do you mean by saying *someone*?"

"That wire," countered d'Artois, "could not have kinked itself. My meaning should be quite obvious."

Wrath and dismay struggled for the supremacy of Graf Erich's features.

"Impossible! How could any person have timed the breaking of that wire?—who, for that matter, knew that she would pass through that door, instead of going to the rear of the building, and up a flight? How—"

"Do not misunderstand me," interrupted d'Artois. "This is not a personal accusation. Nevertheless, *Monsieur le Compte*," he continued with a hard glitter in his blue eyes, "be pleased to correct me if I am wrong in saying that you might, with careful study, account for this fourth member of a series of coincidences."

Farrell saw Graf Erich's eyes suddenly drop before d'Artois' cold, unblinking gaze.

"Oh, what ever can you be hinting?" exclaimed Diane.

"Do not misunderstand me," repeated d'Artois. "I do not mean that you are *consciously* concealing anything. But ponder on this succession of busts, and kampilans and Persian maces and battle-axes that have dropped for no reason at all. And now, *Monsieur*, with your permission, I will escort Mademoiselle Diane back to the city. Later, perhaps, we can discuss this at greater length."

Graf Erich regarded d'Artois for an interval that was becoming perilously close to a painful silence. Then he bent over Diane's hand, and bowed formally to d'Artois and Farrell.

They drove in silence from the château. Farrell was communing with a growing conviction that Graf Erich could have explained why that heavy ax and heavier mace had dropped from their support; yet he was equally certain that Graf Erich was on the verge of desperation.

"Naturally, he'd be shaken," reasoned Farrell as they approached the Mousserole Gate. "Sure. But he looked as if he'd seen a ghost *that he was expecting to see.*"

D'Artois presently brought the Daimler to a smooth halt at the door of Diane's apartment on rue Lachepaillet.

Diane waved farewell as d'Artois headed the long car down the incline toward the old guardhouse at the Gate of Spain. Then, passing rue d'Espagne on the left, he skirted the city wall and drove toward the Nive and the little, square courtyard on which the d'Artois tower faced.

D'Artois pounded the massive brazen knocker that adorned the iron-bound and iron-studded oaken door to summon his man Raoul, who admitted them, then took the wheel of the Daimler and drove it to the garage.

"Now that we can speak our minds freely," began d'Artois as he led the way to the study, "what do you make of this last accident?"

"Someone twisted that wire and broke it," replied Farrell. "But how could anyone time the trap so that it would spring at the very instant? Why, it just doesn't make any sense!"

"I am not so sure of that," maintained d'Artois. "You heard Graf Erich's exclamation—*was für Teufelei!* That may have been nothing but an expression of wrath; but I believe he meant it literally. Deviltry. Graf Erich has been up to something that is now kicking back at him. That harassed look of his could not have been so deeply branded in a week.

"And just to give you food for thought," continued d'Artois, "I will now mention something which I withheld to avoid prematurely influencing you. Graf Erich is and has for several years been noted as a dabbler in thaumaturgy."

"Thaumaturgy...thaumaturgy..." muttered Farrell. "Miracle or wonder worker, eh? Or is that just an impressive word for fakery?"

"Your first definition is correct," said d'Artois. "Although thaumaturgy at times descends well into the last named, surprising results often flash forth from the quackery that clouds occult research. Graf Erich has started something he's lost control of. But, *mordieu*, what is it that he has started? To wipe out that interrogation is our present problem. And in the meanwhile, I am certain that our charming young friend, Diane, is in much graver peril than she realizes."

CHAPTER 3
Lilith

Graf Erich, immediately upon the departure of his guests, stalked toward the great fireplace at the far end of the salon. He halted at the hearthstone, glanced sharply about him—an instinctive precaution that had not yet given way to the security resulting from the absence of servants—and then knelt just clear of its edge. He fingered a tile which was nearest the foot of the andiron he faced. The hearth-slab swung silently on pivots, exposing a narrow flight of stairs that led into cavernous depths far below.

Graf Erich took from his pocket a small flashlamp and by its slender pencil of light illuminated his descent into the subterranean blackness. At the foot of the stairs he pressed a button. The click of the wall switch was followed by a glow of bluish-violet, wavering light.

He was standing in an alcove in the wall of a circular vault not more than five yards in diameter. Seated cross-legged about the curved wall were five men, each with his arms crossed on his breast; and the head of each was inclined as in sleep, or profound meditation. Their eyes were open, but they stared as though fixed in the contemplation of something that was beyond the sight of normal, human eyes. The posture and the drape of their robes suggested adepts from High Asia.

They sat at the vertices of a pentacle inscribed in cinnabar, whose orange streak glowed fiery-golden in the violet light. Each squatted in a small circle whose center coincided with the vertex which he commanded; and in the center of the pentacle was another circle, this one scarcely more than a yard in diameter.

"It's there…always there, now," muttered Graf Erich, as he stared somberly at the phosphorescent haze that throbbed and pulsed with rhythmical beat in the center of the cabalistic pentacle. "I'll never get rid of her. It's too late…"

He shook his head wearily, and sighed. Then he stepped from the alcove into which the staircase opened, and passed along the wall until he came to a station marked on the periphery that was circumscribed about the interlaced triangles of the pentacle. He halted there, facing the prime vertex; then, extending his arms, he bowed his head for a moment.

At first he spoke in low, hurried syllables, his voice scarcely more than a murmur, but as he warmed up to his recital, he assumed a more commanding tone until at last he was intoning a resonant mantra that rolled and thundered as though, besides reverberating through the vault, it also surged through caverns and passages that reached into the uttermost depths of the earth.

In response to Graf Erich's chanting came the low, sweet voice of a woman who basks in a perfumed garden and purrs contentedly as a cat before the luxury of a fire. It was an amorous, caressing voice in whose suave, mellow murmur was the quintessential sweetness of all women who had ever been, and who ever would be: it was the voice of not any one woman, but rather a hierarchy of women, from dusky slave-girls to diademed queens.

"Baali," said that sighing, luminous mist, "Lord and Master, I warned you, but you would not heed. I have failed four times, now, but the Power is increasing. *Baali*—"

The voice addressed Graf Erich by that Semitic word which signified *lord* and implied *husband.*

"Abandon your attempts!" interrupted Graf Erich in a low, hoarse voice. "And from now on—from this very moment—I will never see her. I promise that as the price of her life."

The laughter of that shimmering, sentient haze was bitter and mocking and poison-sweet; and a breath of perfume heavier than jasmine and the roses of Shiraz was exhaled through the crypt.

"Too late," murmured the voice as the laughter subsided. "With your dark magic, and your knowledge of the True Name, and your command of Powers and Presences, you called me from the forgotten blacknesses of Time's beginning. You lured me from oblivion. And ears that for uncounted centuries had not heard the voice of adoration again thrilled to those solemn words which mocked Time and the higher gods and the laws that were ordained.

"*Baali*, I rose from the perished memories of uncounted lovers. From the dust of their dead brains and from the lingering traces of their time-bleached souls— bleached gray in the home of the cheerless dead—there came once more a memory of me, and I lived.

"You chanted like Lucifer singing to the Morning Star on the crest of Zagros. You sang like Lucifer crying his defiance across the vast gulf. And now that I am here, you are seeking her in preference to me…"

She laughed, that woman's voice, with ominous sweetness.

"I am here. Even I, Lilith—Daughter of the Dancer, the Queen of the *Lilin*— and you thought that I would stand aside for any earth-woman? Whoever summons me must have thought for no other."

"You devil! I'll send you back—" Graf Erich choked with wrath.

The phosphorescent presence in the center of the mist column laughed again: low, musical, and withal, a bitter laugh.

"You can not send me back, *Baali.*" The voice enunciated that appellation of respect with a finely modulated note of defiance.

Graf Erich's dark eyes flashed somberly, and shifted from the shadow presence to the bronzed, inscrutable faces of the five who, squatting at the vertices of the pentacle, stared with their fixed gaze beyond the Border.

"You dare not," murmured the voice of the iridescent mist. "You know that you dare not use that weapon against me," reiterated the softly speaking doom. "Even you would stop short of such infamy. They are your disciples in dark magic. Even to save *her*, you would lack the courage to attempt that hideous treason. And you know that!"

The mist presence was becoming momentarily more substantial, until finally at the middle of the pentacle a woman of incredible loveliness stood in the place of the luminous haze-column. And from the half-parted lips of the solemn-faced hierophants came faint wisps of vapor that were drawn toward the center, even as cigarette smoke is drawn to an air-vent by the draft of an exhaust fan. The Presence—Queen of the Lilin—was now transparent…now translucent…finally opaque, solid, and despite her fantasmal origin, seemingly of flesh and blood. Her exquisite, exotic features were lovely with a beauty that the world has not dreamed or fancied for uncounted years. Lilith who smiled from the pentacle was a loveliness too long forgotten even to exist as a remote memory; Lilith, the everlasting Queen of all moonlit nights, the Queen of the Lilin, who danced before Suleiman, upon whom be prayer, and the peace!

She smiled a slow, carmine sorcery. The dark, long-lashed eyes were without fear. Her slender arms gestured like twin serpents of nacre as she patted the midnight of her elaborately dressed, long hair.

"You prefer me to all earthly women, *Baali*... And even though you did not... you could not kill those five acolytes...could not buy her safety at the cost of such infamy... *Baali*, am I not lovely?..."

CHAPTER 4

Two Long-Haired Women

Farrell and d'Artois in the meanwhile had been pondering on the events of the evening, and seeking to devise a wedge to split the solid front of contradictions that opposed them.

"The fact that in three cases the falling object which almost struck Diane," said d'Artois, "came from the house of Graf Erich is certainly significant. But on the other hand, I can scarcely imagine his wishing to harm Diane."

"Yet it must track back to him," persisted Farrell. "Consider, the strongest manifestation: that of flexing a wire until it snapped and released its deadly burden."

"*Pardieu*, you have right," admitted d'Artois. "Graf Erich's château must be the focal point where maximum intensity is developed."

Farrell stared somberly into the glowing coals of the grate. D'Artois paced slowly back and forth, each trip marking the length of the wine-colored Boukhara rug that filled the center of the study. Suddenly he halted, and flung open the casement.

"Look!" he commanded, making a sweeping gesture of his arm.

Farrell gazed across the moon-drenched wilderness of roofs. It seemed for a moment that he stood in the tower of some mediaeval necromancer, looking into a vista of freshly opened hyper-space and across the roofs of a dead city of enchantment.

Wraith-like mists were slowly marching from the Nive, and along the dry moat that girdled the walls, and up into the citadel, to clamor at the heavily armored door at the ground level. Farrell felt a sudden chill flash down his spine, despite the warmth of the study.

"Like a Chinese dream," he muttered. "Old, and evil, and beautiful...like some pearl-gray sphinx smiling through her veils of mystery... Lord, but it's old —I never realized, till just now—"

"Old? Old indeed, mon ami," said d'Artois solemnly; "old when the Moslem conquerors took the city by assault; old when the Roman legions drove the stakes of their first encampment on the banks of the Nive. And beneath this citadel there are passages and crypts..."

Farrell sharply regarded his friend and noted the stern, hard lines about his mouth and the glitter of his eyes.

"Do you mean to say," demanded Farrell in a low, hoarse whisper, "that you think that some elemental has emerged from the everlasting midnight of the vaults beneath this city to destroy Diane?"

D'Artois shrugged, slowly shook his head, and smiled somberly. Then his eyes shifted for a moment toward the open casement. He ceased smiling.

"Pierre," Farrell abruptly resumed. "I've got a whim, and I'm going to humor it whether you think I'm goofy or not. I'm going for a walk, along rue Lachepaillet—to see the moonlight advance across the parkway, down below."

D'Artois' eyes narrowed as he scrutinized his friend.

"Me, I will go with you," he announced, "Unless—"

"Glad to have you," assured Farrell. Then, as he picked up his hat and jammed it well down on his head, "I've had the creeps for the past hour. And it's been getting worse ever since we left Diane. Now, if you must laugh—"

"But no, I refuse to find anything humorous about the thought," protested d'Artois. "Your interest in the young lady, while a trifle sudden, is certainly warranted."

"You've got me all wrong. She doesn't interest me. It's just that I've got a hunch. That ever increasing force! Just as we were saying—"

"Precisely," agreed d'Artois. "In fact, no one was contradicting you." Then, with a malicious grin, "Which contentions on your part prove indubitably that you are not one damned bit interested in Mademoiselle Diane."

D'Artois selected a Malacca stick from his collection, then led the way to the door; but he had scarcely crossed the threshold when the telephone rang.

"*C'est moi*, d'Artois," he assured the speaker. Then, "But yes—we will see you at once. With pleasure. *À bientôt*!"

"Diane?" wondered Farrell.

"Certainly none other," said d'Artois. "No, there is nothing wrong, yet. She sought to explain, but I gave her no chance, lest she end by explaining herself into a state of mind. You two, it seems, have had a hunch, yes? Dignifying it by the name of telepathy or intuition is hardly necessary."

D'Artois paused at his desk and took from a compartment a small device in the shape of a Greek letter *tau* with a circular handle where the cross-bar joined the stem. He shook his head in response to Farrell's query, and thrust the silver symbol into his pocket.

"A *crux ansata*," he said. "Later, perhaps, I will explain."

They walked briskly up rue Tour de Sault toward the head of rue d'Espagne, where the latter reaches out toward the breach in the fortification. From there they turned to their right and followed the Lachepaillet wall for two short blocks to Diane's door.

"I've been so terribly uneasy," Diane explained as she admitted Farrell and d'Artois. "Ever since Graf Erich phoned—"

"Eh, what's that?" demanded Farrell. Mention of the Count abruptly jarred him from his preliminary survey of the exquisite effect of apricot-hued negligee and coral lamé mules worn by a girl of Diane's coloring. "When was that?"

"A little over half an hour ago," said Diane as she ushered them into the living-room. "He seemed terribly agitated, and hinted that I might expect a repetition of the accident at the château. But I couldn't get him to be explicit about it; and that's what alarmed me. I fancied it must have been because he was worried about those accidents, and particularly the one of tonight. So—"

She made a quick, nervous gesture of her hand.

"So, as you see, I've taken down the pictures and bric-a-brac and everything that could possibly fall. But that's not why I called you. It was something Graf Erich said tonight: before he hung up, he insisted that I should cut my hair."

"Comment?" demanded d'Artois. *"Cut your hair?"*

"Yes," replied Diane. "He hinted to that effect shortly after that bust fell down and nearly struck me as I lay on the chaise-longue, over there in the corner. At the time I fancied that he was teasing me about my whim of wearing long hair. But his mentioning it again tonight, and insisting on it, despite his agitation about the possibility of something falling—"

She stopped short, shook her head, and made a gesture of perplexity.

"It seems to me that our friend Graf Erich is plumb loco!" declared Farrell. "Good egg and all that, but just off his chump! Worried about a succession of uncanny accidents, and then kicking about the way Diane wears her hair." D'Artois shook his head.

"Au contraire," he said, "I fear that Graf Erich is only too well balanced. Tell me, did you say that you would cut your hair?"

"But yes," replied Diane. "Anything to please him, he sounded so upset. And as soon as I agreed, he hung up."

"My dear," said d'Artois, "suppose that you get a pair of scissors."

Diane and Farrell regarded him with amazement.

"Good Lord!" exclaimed Farrell, "Now *you've* got it!"

D'Artois stifled the retort that was on his lips. He considered for a moment the sleek, blue-black coiffure, then smiled mirthlessly.

"Perhaps it would be hasty to sacrifice such exceptionally lovely long hair in this day and age—still—but suppose that I call Graf Erich and see if I can get some sense out of his incoherence. That one is far from irrational. There is something in what he says; and right now I will find out!"

He glanced about him, seeking the telephone. Farrell stroked his chin and regarded d'Artois with wonder and a tinge of alarm. Diane indicated the adjoining room. But as d'Artois rose, a bell rang.

"Perhaps," he said, stopping short, "it is Graf Erich calling back."

Diane shook her head.

"That's the door-bell, not the telephone. Excuse me—just a moment, please." As Diane left the living-room, d'Artois caught Farrell's eye.

"Mon vieux, I am not demented," he protested.

"But why cut her hair?" persisted Farrell, scrutinizing d'Artois as though he expected to find symptoms of delirium.

D'Artois shrugged. "To be frank, I don't know—*yet*. But I do know Graf—"

A scream at the front door cut d'Artois' remarks short. Then another: an agonized shriek that betokened an outraged mind rather than a wounded body.

"Good Lord!" exclaimed Farrell, as he sprang toward the door, and started down the hallway. "Diane!"

"*Mordieu*! It's after her!" And d'Artois followed.

The front door was wide open. They saw Diane on the sidewalk, struggling hand to hand with a slender, sinuous woman who sought to drive home a long, frostily glittering dagger. Diane, straining and gasping, strove to wrench back and break the grip of the woman who relentlessly menaced her with that deadly slip of steel.

Farrell halted for an instant in utter amazement. Like Diane, the other woman was dark and long-haired and exceedingly lovely; and like her, arrayed in a shimmering, silky fabric which, conspiring with river mists and moonlight, lent an unreal, almost terrible beauty to the swaying, lithe forms that struggled for the icy splinter of a blade.

The enemy's features were branded with a venomous smile that made her crimson lips seem like a fresh wound.

All in a glance; all in one fleeting instant which can be longer than a lifetime.

Farrell leaped forward and seized the enemy's wrist.

He gasped in dismayed horror as his fingers closed about the exquisite, nacreously gleaming arm. She was serpent-cold; yet an electric thrill numbed his arm all the way to the shoulder.

"Oh, Glenn!" panted Diane as she caught her breath and renewed her efforts.

"*Tenez!*" snapped the voice of d'Artois as Farrell extended his arm again. He clapped his hands sharply, then continued in a brusque, dominant tone, "*Lilîtu! Agrat bat Mahhat!*"

The smile vanished from the crimson lips as d'Artois pronounced those strange words. The dagger wavered in her grasp. She suddenly wrenched her wrist free from Diane's grip, but instead of striking, she turned to confront d'Artois. The lovely features were menacing, but they were also clouded with apprehension.

Farrell, his arm still tingling from the uncanny contact, supported Diane, who shrank away from the diabolically lovely enemy.

D'Artois again addressed the stranger. He stood firm and erect, and looked her full in the eye. His right hand flashed from his coat pocket. He grasped the silver *crux ansata*.

Once more he pronounced, "*Lilîtu!*"

Then he began intoning in a language that Farrell dimly recognized as an archaic Semitic tongue. His voice rolled and thundered like a distant surf; it crackled and snapped sulfurously, and his fierce old eyes were frosty cold as he intently regarded that evil beauty whose luminous loveliness seemed to be a concentration of solidified moonbeams rather than any aggregation of flesh and blood.

"Who is that woman?" muttered Farrell as Diane clung to him. "A human snake? Look!"

Then, before Diane could turn her head from his shoulder, "*No, don't look!*"

The nacreous gleaming arms and shoulders and the imperious features were becoming diffused and misty. Farrell heard a low, wrathful cry, and the tinkle of steel against masonry.

"Where is she?" he demanded, seeking to collect his outraged senses. "Where —" As d'Artois turned, Farrell saw that the lean, leathery features were drawn and haggard, and that the old man's brow glistened with sweat. The outstretched arms dropped wearily back to his sides. One hand still clutched the silver *crux ansata*.

"Back in whatever unknown hell hatched her," said d'Artois.

Farrell started at Diane's half-articulate cry.

"I'm all right," she said. "Only...m*on Dieu*!...where did she—"

Farrell shook his head. "I thought—"

But Farrell's thought had been too wild for expression. So he abruptly cut his speech; and then, seeing a glitter on the paving, stooped to pick up a dagger whose jeweled hilt glowed and flamed in the moonlight.

"It seems so ghastly and unreal, now that I look back at it...as though it happened years instead of just seconds ago," said Diane as she led the way back to the living-room. "I greeted her, and then she said something in a language I couldn't understand. Instead of asking her in, I leaned forward and asked her to repeat. And before I knew it, she had seized me by the shoulder, pulled me off my balance—she was terribly strong, in spite of her slight figure—"

D'Artois and Farrell had exchanged glances during Diane's remarks; and from long association, they understood each other's moods without the aid of spoken words. Farrell yielded the floor to d'Artois.

"The strength of madness," said d'Artois as his eyes shifted from Farrell to Diane. "If you'd seen how she slipped clear of me! Too bad that anyone so beautiful would be so utterly insane."

D'Artois paused to note the effect of his bit of fiction, and saw that Diane was accepting his story at its face value; which, in view of her fright, and distracted attention, was reasonable enough.

"Now run along to bed, *chère petite*," continued d'Artois. "I'm certain she won't be back tonight."

Diane rose from her chair, and would have protested.

D'Artois shook his head.

"We must go. I will explain later. Wake Félice and have her sit up with you. She'll grumble, but pay no attention to that."

"I will—" began Farrell.

"Of verity, I know that you would," replied d'Artois. "But you and I have to find that poor demented girl. And in the meanwhile," he continued, again addressing Diane, "do not admit anyone. When we return, we will ring two long and two short; but before you open the door, first peep out the window and identify us."

Diane made no further effort to detain them.

D'Artois turned to Farrell as they reached the paving.

"Monstrous blockhead!" he exclaimed. "I was wondering just when you would declare that that accursed creature vanished in a wisp of fog—and then you insisted on remaining to guard the roost!"

"But," protested Farrell, "it seems that leaving Diane there with old Félice, the cook—"

"Would I have left her alone if there were reason to fear danger? This creature lured Diane to the door because she could not bring a material thing like a dagger into the house in the same manner in which she herself could have appeared therein. Had she materialized in the house, she could not have injured Diane with her bare hands. Do you understand?"

"Perfectly," assured Farrell with elaborate irony. "Among other things, who was she, and what happened to her? I'd have sworn that she vanished in a puff of mist. Can you—"

"She did indeed so vanish," said d'Artois. "And let me see that dagger which you picked up."

They were close to the old guardhouse now, and about to turn down rue Tour de Sault.

"Ah…just as I expected," muttered d'Artois as he examined the dagger and its sapphire-sparkling hilt. "I suspected it from Graf Erich's warning Diane."

"How does he fit into it?" demanded Farrell impatiently.

"This," declared d'Artois, "is a dagger from his collection. I know it well indeed. A rare and distinctive piece."

"Good Lord!" gasped Farrell. "And we thought he wasn't mixed up—at least, not—"

"We'll soon know!" interrupted d'Artois.

"But I'd still like to know what happened to that girl," persisted Farrell. "That was an illusion, or else—"

"You were so certain that it was an illusion that you suddenly checked your speech so as to avoid alarming Diane, yes?" D'Artois chuckled mirthlessly.

"Graf Erich's devil-mongering?" hazarded Farrell.

D'Artois nodded.

"Well, what was she—it—that creature?" demanded Farrell. "And did you or didn't you begin talking to her in what sounded something like the Arabic you hear in Nejd?"

"I did," replied d'Artois. "I solemnly commanded her to leave. I presented the *crux ansata*, a very ancient symbol of power. And she left. My will against hers. None of what you call hocus-pocus. I called her by her proper designation; at least, by one of her names. That is an essential in any ritual of exorcism. I guessed, but not blindly, when I called her *Agrat bat Mahhat*, the Daughter of the Dancer."

Farrell perplexedly shook his head.

"How did you know—where did you ever meet—"

"She had exceptionally long, heavy hair, if one were to judge by her curious coiffure. So had Diane. Then she is Agrat bat Mahhat, said I. Very simple."

"Pierre, this is getting to be a madhouse!" despaired Farrell. "Even a bit of common sense would help—"

"Wait till we see Graf Erich," countered d'Artois grimly. "Then you'll understand."

CHAPTER 5

The Vengeance of Lilith

They found Graf Erich sitting at a table in the circle of illumination cast by the single chandelier that burned in the salon. As he rose to greet them, they saw that his dark features were wan, and his eyes haggard and feverish. Farrell and d'Artois sensed that Graf Erich was on the verge of making a monstrous confession, and was nerving himself for the plunge.

His half-coherent hints, his jerky and meaningless gestures, his nervous glances about him as he sought to anticipate and, at times, evade d'Artois' questions made it plain that Graf Erich was indeed being driven to death by some terror of his own evocation.

"You, *Monsieur*," he finally said, jabbing his forefinger like a sword-thrust at d'Artois, "doubtless know already what I have sought to hint. Look at this."

He reached into a drawer and produced a sheet of paper on which were drawn astrological charts and cabalistic figures.

"An experiment in an ancient magic," continued Graf Erich. "I need not name those symbols. You understand them. And you"—he glanced at Farrell—"would do well *not* to understand."

Farrell nodded his whole-hearted agreement, and shivered as he caught the full force of Graf Erich's glance.

"In a word, I evoked her. Lilith, the Demon Queen of Zemargad."

"Diable!" exclaimed d'Artois. "But why did she attempt to assassinate Mademoiselle Diane? *And with this dagger!* Yours, Graf Erich!"

The Count turned paper-white at d'Artois' accusing words and gesture.

"Jealousy," he replied in a low voice. "Insane jealousy of Diane, to whom I recently began paying my respects.

"As to the method of evocation? I assembled five adepts, and caused them to put themselves into a state of catalepsy induced by auto-hypnosis. You understand the principle and purpose?"

"Quite," assured d'Artois.

"She is their thought-image," continued Graf Erich. "Thought is in the last analysis electrical energy. And all matter is, ultimately, electrical energy. They— the Five—concentrated, all on the same image and same concept, and achieved what you might call resonance.

"You know what resonance will do in electrical circuits. Further comment on my part would be insulting to your intelligence; not so?"

D'Artois nodded his agreement. Farrell felt that his intelligence would be none the worse for a bit of additional insult, but he held his peace.

"At all events, she materialized. And at first, she subsisted only on their vital force. She told me of those ancient days when bearded kings built monstrous *ziggurâts* on the plains of Babil. She spoke of Naram-sin of Agade. She spoke—"

Graf Erich shivered as though an icy blast had been deflected into his marrow, and made a despairing gesture.

"Herr Gott! And she spoke of other things. I listened...too long...and finally believed her outrageous claims. No living woman—"

"I know," muttered d'Artois. "Beautiful as no human woman ever could be. Like that one they still speak of as Bint el Kafir...others call her Agrat bat Mahhat. Many titles, but the same entity."

Farrell's eyes widened at the ominous, half-understood names d'Artois and the dark Count pronounced in awed whispers, like the mutterings exchanged when a pair of necromancers encounter each other.

"And then Diane entered the picture," resumed Graf Erich. "You know the rest. Lilith—or a thought-image resembling that which Lilith was supposed to be—became wildly jealous of Diane. I tried to induce Diane to cut her long hair. But I dared not tell her why; and she laughed merrily and ignored my whim."

"Her hair?" wondered Farrell.

But d'Artois, nodding, silenced him with a glance.

"I knew, tonight, that that ax—"

Graf Erich's voice failed. He muttered inarticulately, then raised his head from his hands and regarded d'Artois with a sombre, smoldering glare.

"And now—yes, I knew, even before you showed me that dagger. *She* told me how you had beaten her, flayed her with words of power, driven her into the night—"

The Count paused and looked at d'Artois with wonder and respect.

"But she defied me and challenged me to use the sole way that remains to send her back into the shadows."

"And that is?" wondered d'Artois.

"Killing those adepts. Fellow students and disciples who trust me to the uttermost."

"Why not awaken them?" asked Farrell.

Graf Erich shook his head.

"At first she existed but as a figment of their imaginations; but their concentration became so intense that even when they are awakened from their trance, she will continue to exist. She is now not only their materialized thought-form, but also an accretion of disembodied energy and matter that has been attracted by the terrific vortex of power we have set up."

"Good God!" muttered Farrell in dismay as he caught the full import of Graf Erich's statement, and its implication of independent life created by thought-concentration.

"Something," said d'Artois in a low, solemn tone, "must be done. And at once." He slid the dagger slowly across the table toward Graf Erich. "You are responsible for the existence of this terrible creature from the shadows who not many minutes ago sought to murder Diane, and who would even now be repeating the attempt if her meeting with me had not sapped most of her energy. You must send her back to that nethermost hell where she belongs. And quickly!"

"But how?—*Herr Gott!*—how?" despaired Graf Erich. He leaped to his feet, thrusting back his chair. For a moment he regarded d'Artois steadily; then he paled, losing the color he had somewhat regained. His eyes stared vacantly, through and past the old man.

"I can not command you to kill your disciples," said d'Artois slowly. "Neither can I permit you to hold your hand…"

The evening was becoming a vortex of horror, whose center was the tense face of Graf Erich. His deep-set eyes shifted, and stared at the sparkling pommel of the dagger that lay on the table.

Finally he spoke. His face was grim with a terrible determination.

"I will settle it. Here and now."

He strode across the salon, knelt at the great fireplace, and fingered for an instant an embossed tile in the hearth. As the slab sank out of sight, Graf Erich descended the stairs that it had concealed.

Farrell regarded d'Artois intently for a moment.

"Is he crazy, or are we? Are there really—"

He gestured, indicating the floor, and the foundations of the château. "Is he going to—"

D'Artois nodded.

"Yes. All five of them," he affirmed, slowly shaking his head. "It is horrible, damnably so...his acolytes...his friends...but if he doesn't—"

D'Artois' voice and gesture were remorseless, without pity, or passion, or prejudice. Farrell, now whiter than his shift-front, sat poised on the edge of his chair.

"Isn't there any other way?" Farrell muttered. He leaped to his feet.

"Idiot!" snapped d'Artois, as he seized him by the arm. "If you stopped him, you would condemn her to death. If this horrifies you, remember that before you are many hours older—many minutes, perhaps—this will seem a pleasure excursion..."

Farrell resumed his chair.

They heard Graf Erich's footsteps ring hollowly in some subterranean vault at the foot of the stairs. They heard a faint, metallic tinkle...then no sound at all— only the breathing of an awful silence, and the presence of fivefold death.

Then at last came a familiar *swish*, and the impact of steel driven home. A heavier, likewise familiar sound.

"*Un...deux...*" d'Artois counted; "*trois...* steady, there! *quatre...*"

"Good Lord," muttered Farrell, wondering whether the fifth stroke would ever fall.

"*Dieu de Dieu*! He is collecting his courage, poor devil...they were his friends...*cinq*!"

With a deep, weary sigh d'Artois sank back into his chair. They exchanged glances; and each saw the pallor of the other's tanned features. Then d'Artois rose.

"Five men have died so that Diane may live," he said solemnly, and bowed his gray head for a moment, then added, "*Grâce à Dieu!*"

But before Farrell could second the older man's words of gratitude, there came from that subterranean slaughter-vault a voice whose amorous sweetness was an outrage and a blasphemy to ears that had heard the impact of steel on flesh, and the sound of bodies as they toppled one by one across the flags. That woman's voice was the ultimate mockery. It told d'Artois and Farrell that Graf Erich's terrible decision had been in vain.

"*Baali,*" she was saying, "I know now beyond any doubt that you planned to drive me back again into unending darkness—me, Lilith, Queen of Zemargad."

Her laughter was crystal-clear and poison-sweet.

"*Cordieu,*" muttered d'Artois, speaking as one stunned by a severe cudgeling, "even *that* failed... And now that female fiend is free and unhampered."

"Is she out of control?" demanded Farrell.

D'Artois nodded. "Yes. She is living in her own right. Malignant, vengeful, satanically jealous. Human malice, and superhuman power—you saw her an hour ago."

The voice was speaking again:

"Look at them, *Baali*! Lying in their blood. Sprawled across that pentacle at whose center I appeared when their old magic evoked me from the shadows of time and from the ghosts of memory. And now I shall go on with my plan."

D'Artois started violently as he caught the sinister implication.

"Quick!" he snapped. "Before it's too late."

And Farrell, crossing the room in three great bounds, charged after d'Artois, and into the violet glow of the circular vault that was at the foot of the steep staircase.

He stared in horrified bewilderment as he sought to convince himself that his first glance had not been a hideous illusion.

Graf Erich, red-handed, shrank against the curved wall of the vault. He stared at the luminescent figure of a woman whose long, ornately dressed dark hair sparkled with bluish highlights, and whose imperiously carried head was crowned with a tall, curiously wrought diadem. Her jewels and her costume and her dark eyes suggested an antiquity that no living creature could have; and in that insane, purple light, she seemed even more unreal than in the moonlight and mists on the Lachepaillet wall as she sought Diane with a dagger.

At Graf Erich's feet lay the sword that had done its vain, red work.

D'Artois was advancing across the floor, seeking to avoid touching those whose heads and blood had become so terribly intermingled. As he stepped forward, he gestured with his hands, and chanted.

That dark, imperious woman for an instant shrank before the fierce eyes of d'Artois; and then she smiled as if in sudden remembrance.

"Meddler," she murmured in low, clean-cut syllables, "that will not work a second time. I have gained too much strength for you, as well as for him."

Her laugh was mocking as she became a shimmering haze that thinned and spread, dividing like the tentacles of an octopus. D'Artois, seeing the enemy flowing away in a five-branched mist, halted, lowered his arms, and ceased his chant. He was bewildered by the defiance and mockery that had accompanied the apparent surrender of the apparition.

As the last trace of luminous vapor flattened out, and writhed serpent-like among those who lay on the floor, the evening's horror reached its apex. There was a rustling and a sighing, and an unbelievable stirring among those dead forms sprawled across the dark, slippery tiles.

D'Artois turned to Graf Erich.

"What kind of deviltry is this?" he demanded. "Quick! Tell me, before it's too late!"

Graf Erich's reply was an inarticulate groan, and a despairing gesture. Farrell, as he saw those dead forms stir and twitch, wondered if his own face was as stricken as that of the Count.

The vault had become a swamp of dark blood and darker things which paddled about in it. Then, as their motion became more directed and more terribly distinct, Farrell saw the pattern of the devilish manifestation: they were closing in on Graf Erich to exact their vengeance.

Farrell stooped and snatched the curved sword from the floor. In the extremity of his terror he scarcely realized what he did.

They were on their feet now, tottering, but momentarily becoming more steady. Horrible, blood-drenched headless trunks, guided by some omniscience toward their slayer, were closing in on him. Their hands were flexing, opening and closing as if to test their newly gained strength. A faint, luminous cloud of mist enveloped the monstrously animated dead, and supported them when they faltered, guided their steps, directed those lifeless hands.

Yet Farrell's terror did not reach its climax until he heard Graf Erich's outcry as they closed in, seeking remorselessly to tear him limb from limb. Then he heard no more. He lashed out with his blade, hacking, hewing, slashing with a blind, outraged frenzy. The curved scimitar bit and sheared through flesh and bone; but Farrell saw that his sweeping cuts were vain. The portions that he had shorn off persisted in their awful advance, twitching, crawling, squirming with diabolical animation as though Farrell's devastating cuts had been puffs of wind; and then they closed in and joined those that had escaped the shearing steel.

The time of the ghastly melee could scarcely have been more than a few seconds; but each of those seconds was a lingering lifetime of red horror to Farrell, whose blade rose and fell with no result other than to multiply the grotesque, sanguinary morsels that were clutching at Graf Erich.

"Stand clear!" d'Artois cried. And as the red blade sank again, d'Artois leaped in from the rear, pinioned the sword-arm, and dragged Farrell from his futile task. "You can't save him."

Farrell stared at that which had overwhelmed Graf Erich.

"Look! *They* are dying now."

A hand relaxed its death-grip, and dropped. Other fragments one by one subsided from their unnatural motion.

"Let's get out of here," added Farrell.

"Tais-toi," replied d'Artois, shortly. "There is something worse in the wind. She dematerialized in order to destroy Graf Erich. Now the next move—"

"Lord! Look at that!" interrupted Farrell.

A misty exhalation was creeping from the gory butchery that concealed the hapless Count. It was as though the ghosts of serpents were writhing and twining, seeking in the farthest dim nooks of the vault a refuge from the violet glow.

"Quick! Do you drive as though the devil were after you!" exclaimed d'Artois as he saw the eerie manifestation. "Arouse Diane, and bring her here, at once!"

"But why—"

"Because she—it—that fiend will be seeking Diane in her apartment. By taking Diane away, you will gain time, since materialization is not instantaneous— but hurry! I'll wait here."

D'Artois led the way upstairs to the salon.

"He has books and charts here," explained d'Artois as he took the steps three at a bound. "I will study this thing out. It fooled him. But I know now that the death of those five adepts has nothing to do with her. Thus one fatal side-issue is eliminated—hurry, *mon ami!* I have the hunch!"

D'Artois, softly cursing, tore out one drawer after another of the tables and cabinets in the salon.

"Grâce à Dieu!" he muttered as he heard the Daimler crunch down the driveway and start thundering down the river road. Then he proceeded with his search, leaving the salon, and working his way into the study of Graf Erich.

A bed of coals glowed sullenly in the grate at the farther end. By the red glare d'Artois saw that the walls of the study were hung with black arras embroidered in silver to depict the monstrous and unhallowed images of obscure Asian myths. One medallion represented a woman mounted on a lion, and receiving the adoration of three bearded kings. Another depicted a woman who drove a chariot drawn by a quadriga of grotesque monsters that no sane artist could have limned; and on the mantel was a chrysoprase statuette of *Agrat bat Mahhat* in all her evil loveliness.

All at a glance: then d'Artois found the wall switch, snapped on the lights, and continued his search for the saving clue that might yet thwart that vengeful demon-beauty before she found and killed Diane.

CHAPTER 6

The Chrysoprase Statuette

Some fifteen minutes later d'Artois heard the Daimler drawing up in front of the château. He went to the door to meet Farrell and Diane.

"Do tell me what this is all about! As if I've not had my fill of mystery for tonight, with that nightmare of a woman!"

Diane had quite recovered from the shock of her encounter with what she supposed was a madwoman who waylaid her on her front steps. Then, as they stepped into the study, "Where's Graf Erich?"

"He has been detained," said d'Artois, "and presents his regrets. You were right. Those seeming accidents were the work of a malignant entity bent on your destruction."

"Aren't you consoling!" exclaimed Diane. Her laugh, however, was forced. "And was she—oh, where did he get *that?* The very image of her!"

"Where?" wondered Farrell.

"That little green statuette," replied Diane. "Why, it's an absolute likeness of that girl that tried to stab me!"

"Coincidence, my dear," declared d'Artois. "And now let's get to work."

He indicated with a gesture the heap of diagrams and manuscripts he had been studying during Farrell's absence, then thrust aside the table at the center of the room and rolled up several small Persian rugs that masked the tiled floor. He took a lump of chalk and laid out a circle, which he divided into quadrants. Each quadrant was then marked with cabalistic symbols, some drawn from memory, others from consultation of the scrolls and heavily bound vellum books he had selected from their cases and laid out for reference.

"What in the world is he doing?" whispered Diane, after having watched d'Artois in silent wonder.

Farrell, still horrified by the memory of what he had seen, and the older man's hints about what might be seen before the evening was over, shook his head.

A bowl of beaten copper served as an improvised censer, which d'Artois filled with coals from the grate. He added a handful of incense which he had found in a compartment of one of the cabinets; and as the fumes rose in thick, bluish clouds, pervading the room with a stifling, resinous sweetness, d'Artois said, "Step into those quadrants. That's right. Number two, and number four. I'll occupy number one, and then command her to materialize in the remaining sector, and, *pardieu*, I'll cook her to a turn!"

A low, soft laugh interrupted d'Artois' remarks.

"Ah…but I prefer to elect my own time, *Baali*," said a voice, "when I will not be bound by any conditions of yours."

In a dim corner of the room a spot of misty luminescence was elongating to a spindle of quivering light. Then it expanded, and solidified. The materialization was more rapid than before.

"Getting stronger," muttered d'Artois. "She has absorbed additional energy." Then, to the presence, "Lilith, back to the darkness of forgotten midnight! All those who evoked you from the ghosts of memories and from the shadows of ancient prayers are dust and less than the dust of those who loved you long ago!"

From his waistcoat pocket d'Artois drew the silver *crux ansata*, which he advanced at arm's length as he paced deliberately toward the Presence, stepping to the cadence of the adjuration which he pronounced.

"Go therefore in peace; *Ardat Lilî*!

"Go in peace, Queen of the Lilin!

"Go in peace, and trouble no longer the living. For he is dead, and so also are his friends, and for you there is neither vengeance nor hope, Queen of Zemargad! Go therefore to the shadows and the early dawn of time, and to the dust of those whose fancy gave you life anew!"

Diane and Farrell, standing in their quadrants, thrilled as they heard d'Artois' sonorous voice intoning as he advanced toward that malignant beauty whose wondrous body had become firm and substantial in the dim glow, and half shrouded in a diaphanous mist that served her as a gown.

Again that poison-sweet, evil laugh; but instead of shrinking or retreating as she had done earlier in the evening, she stepped forward to meet d'Artois. Her smile mocked him, but her phosphorescent eyes regarded Diane from beneath their long lashes with a cold, deadly stare.

D'Artois halted. He was baffled. His solemn command had failed. For an instant his shoulders slumped hopelessly. Then he reasserted his will. His teeth clicked grimly together, and he extended his arms. But the diabolically lovely enemy evaded his grasp as though she were a wisp of haze drifting in the wind. Farrell, seeing d'Artois' futile gesture, leaped clear of his quadrant and sought to intercept the demoniac beauty who slipped forward like a panther to seize Diane. She evaded Farrell's grasp, and closed in.

An instant later, d'Artois and Farrell vainly sought to break her deadly hold on Diane's throat. The phantom woman's strength was great, and her limbs, seemingly solid flesh and blood, were flexible and yielding and elusive as writhing serpents.

Diane's desperately won gasps of breath told how those relentless, slender fingers sank home, mocking the strong hands that tried to break her fierce grip. The phantom snarled in bestial fury, and thwarted the efforts of the two men striving with her as vainly as though they were wrestling with eels.

Farrell snatched a knife.

"God!" he gasped in despair. "She's not human—"

Even in that extremity, he instinctively paused to justify the use of force against such a radiant, feminine beauty, evil though it was.

"Tenez!" cried d'Artois, seizing his wrist. "The blade will go through her and stab Diane."

D'Artois stepped clear. He was baffled and beaten. She—Lilith—Queen of the Lilin—had stolen the energy of five adepts whose mangled bodies lay in the vault below; she had summoned from out of space bit after bit of disembodied force; her strength had become superhuman.

Diane had ceased to struggle. The slender, deadly fingers were sinking remorselessly home. The scarlet lips were twisted in a sneer that was made all the more terrible by the beauty of Lilith.

D'Artois flung the silver *crux ansata* into a corner with a wrathful, despairing gesture. Then with a triumphant cry, he saw and recognized his last hope: the image of green chrysoprase. He snatched it from the mantel.

His lips moved soundlessly as he smote the image against an andiron, fracturing the lovely throat, so that the head rolled across the floor. He struck again, cracking the faultless body.

Farrell stared for an instant; then, "Bust it again, Pierre! Look!" he shouted.

He shrieked the last word in a frenzy of exultation.

The phantom woman was becoming misty…almost transparent.

Smash! Another spattering of fragments as they glanced off the column that buttressed the fireplace.

Farrell turned just in time to catch Diane, who, no longer supported by the spectral slayer, was about to collapse.

"A last-minute guess. And it worked," muttered d'Artois. He glanced about for a moment as if to reassure himself that vengeful Lilith had indeed vanished. Then he continued, "Let me give you a hand. Get Diane out of here—quickly!"

* * * *

When Diane regained consciousness, the grayness of early dawn was making the electric lights of her apartment a sickly, yellowish glow. She sat up among the cushions of the chaise-longue, smiled wearily, and declined the glass of brandy d'Artois offered her.

"My throat's terribly bruised, but otherwise I'm all right," she said. "And now tell me what it was all about."

Farrell and d'Artois exchanged glances. They remembered all too well the horrors of the night just past. Diane sensed their thought.

"I wasn't so nearly unconscious as you supposed," she resumed, "and I heard what you two said. So tell me the rest—I mean, the reasons."

"All of our memories, our thoughts, our emotions," began d'Artois, "are vibrations in the ether, similar, perhaps, to radio waves. And the occultists agree that a thought vibration, however attenuated it may become, never actually dies out. And just as by amplification a radio wave can be increased a millionfold, so also by harmonious mental concentration can a thought be infinitely strengthened.

"Graf Erich's five adepts by their contemplation of the chrysoprase statuette summoned from the vast limbo of undying thought forms an entity that had once been associated with the green image. That entity was Lilith—*Ardat Lilî*—*Agrat bat Mahhat*—whatever name you wish. They all imply a female demon.

"She should have vanished with the death of Graf Erich and his adepts; but the accretions of countless disembodied entities, human and otherwise, that were attracted by the thought vortex created by the intense concentration, were all assimilated by the personality whose materialization became strong enough to strangle Diane.

"That chrysoprase statuette was the focal point of the concentration; it was the model for the visualization of the adepts, so that they would have an absolute unity that could not have been gained from verbal description. I noted this fact from the records I studied, but did not get its full significance until the very last and almost fatal moment.

"My plan was to force the demon to materialize in the circle, and then command her to depart for ever—but she thwarted me by materializing of her own volition, thus evading the compulsion I intended to exercise.

"And the last, and perhaps the strangest feature of this grotesque tragedy, is the apparition herself—"

"You've confused us," interposed Farrell, "by using so many names in addressing her and speaking of her."

D'Artois laughed and struck light to a cigarette.

"Different designations for the same entity. Most of the terms I used are not proper names but class designations. According to Assyrian tradition, Lilith is the head of a hierarchy of female demons or *lilin*. She is Queen of Zemargad, *Agrat bat Mahhat*, Daughter of the Dancer, who roams about at night with myriads of *lilin*, whom Solomon is said to have summoned to appear and dance before him.

"Graf Erich, poor devil, tried to perform a similar feat, and fell afoul of the vengeance of Lilith."

"But how about cutting my hair?" wondered Diane. "What in the world—"

"The old tradition," said d'Artois, "describes Lilith as 'a seductive woman with long hair.' To use an awkward expression, long-hairedness is an essential of the Lilith-image or concept.

"Graf Erich, therefore, wanted you to cut your hair so as to destroy that which you had in common with her. In other words, divested of your exceptionally long hair, you would be degraded in the eyes of Lilith and thus beneath her jealousy. Again, you might have lost your identity as Diane, the rival."

"But why didn't you get scissors instead of drawing that circle and making the other preparations?" wondered Diane.

"Lilith had become too strong," explained d'Artois. "First, you recollect, she had but enough power to cause a hammer to slide from a steep roof. Later, she appeared in person to stab you; and finally, she gathered enough strength to throttle you with her bare hands, and to resist our efforts to overpower her. And, anticipating such an increase, I recognized the need for more desperate measures than the sacrifice of your hair."

"A terrible sacrifice," interposed Farrell, as he admiringly regarded Diane. Then, seating himself at the foot of the chaise-longue, "And now that you're through diverting us with demonology, I'm going to quote a modern author, on an old theme: 'Diane is a seductive woman with—'"

"Pardieu!" interrupted d'Artois, "if that is what you call the lay of the land, there is nothing for an old man but to go home and get some much-needed sleep, and leave you to the mercy of this seductive, long-haired woman!"

"I think," said Diane with a smile and a gesture toward her blue-black hair, "that I'll ask the coiffeur to take the biggest, sharpest scissors the first thing in the morning, and—"

"Over my dead body!" protested Farrell.

D'Artois paused at the entrance of the hallway, twisted his mustache, and grinned broadly.

"By the rod, *Monsieur*, if you do not this afternoon return with worthwhile amendments to an ancient Assyrian tradition, you are an oaf, a mouse, and an uncouth fellow! *Cordieu*! Were I but your age!"

ONE ARABIAN NIGHT

(Also published as "Makeda's Cousin")
Originally published in *Spicy-Adventure Stories*, November 1934.

The breeze that swept out from the Arabian Desert wafted a whiff of even hotter fumes from the now silent engines of the great tri-motored plane and assured Glenn Farrell that it was not a dream. Petrol and hot lube and exhaust gases were never that vivid in any mirage.

Farrell was lean, broad of shoulder, craggy jawed, and at home from Surabaya to Timbuktu; yet his gray eyes were wide and the stern lines of his rugged face had dissolved in wonder. He had landed in a lost city whose very existence had for some twenty-eight dusty centuries been no more than a legend: the capital from which Balkis, Queen of Sheba, had set out to visit King Solomon.

And it was inhabited. Bronzed, bearded men were emerging from the purple shadows of colossal palaces and terraced *ziggurats* that rose dizzily up and into the red glow of the setting sun. Slender, shapely women with olive hued bodies peered through transparent veils that were not intended to conceal their scarlet lips and *kohl* darkened eyelids.

The natives halted. Their guttural murmuring subsided; but Glenn Farrell had heard enough to know that the language which they spoke was similar to Arabic in the way that the English of Chaucer's time resembles the language of our day. Without turning to his two companions, he said, in a low voice that was unsteady with wonder, "Talk to their leader, Ismeddin."

The old, white bearded Arab who had followed Farrell from Mekinez to Boukhara advanced and greeted the stern faced *amir* who had stepped from the silent but ever thickening throng of natives. They were armed with curved scimitars; but a few carried silver mounted, long barreled *jezails*, and flintlock pistols —weapons which they must have bought from wandering Bedouins who had ventured into the terrific Rub' al-Khali.

Farrell knew that Ismeddin's parley would decide the fate of the party. He turned to his friend, Colonel Pierre d'Artois, on leave from the French Air Service to pilot Farrell's plane to Africa.

"If we have to take it on the run, do you think you can lift her out of this plaza and clear of the walls?"

The grim faced old soldier shrugged, twisted his waxed moustache to a finer point and said, "*Mondieu*! Trying is the only way to find out. Though if that girl near the chief doesn't quit eyeing you that way, *mon ami*, there will be some of that hell popping."

Farrell followed d'Artois' glance. Her faintly aquiline face was delicate as a Persian miniature, and his pulse quickened as he caught the inviting gaze of dark eyes that smouldered behind the transparent veil which was held in place by disc-headed pins thrust like monstrous marigolds into her black hair. Farrell no longer tried to follow Ismeddin's sonorous Arabic. He caught his breath, and his gray eyes narrowed as he returned the intent appraisal of the slender Sabean girl whose graciously curved body and shapely legs gleamed golden-ivory through her sun-pierced gown. And then the corners of her amorous mouth lifted in the shadow of a smile.

"Let her look, Pierre," whispered Farrell. "You can pilot that crate the rest of the way to Djibuti and then sell the damn thing for scrap. I'm staying here to learn the language a bit better."

"Some of those nuts, mon ami!" growled the Frenchman. "You young fool, you'll probably end up by being flayed alive and crucified. Anybody that's done as much exploring as you have ought to know better than to look at native women—"

"Nuts yourself, Pierre!" countered Farrell. "When anybody that's done as much exploring as I have gets cold-calked by an eyeful like that, something's got to be done about it. That girl's going with us to Djibuti."

"*Imbécile!*" grumbled the Frenchman. "Talk Arabic to match your clothes. That's our only hope of getting out of here with whole hides. Particularly with your damned romantic stupidity!"

And then Ismeddin returned from the parley and announced, "The *Amir* welcomes you. These people worship the sun and stars, like they did in the days of Queen Balkis; so I told him that you came to pray at the shrine of the moon goddess, and that beside being able to fly like a bird, you can raise the dead, and—"

"You would!" growled Farrell. "And now there will be the devil to pay—if anyone dies here—"

"No wonder she looked at you that way," interpolated d'Artois. "But when do we eat and where do we camp?"

"As I was about to say, *ya Bimbashi*," resumed the old Arab, "we will be quartered in one of these ruined palaces. And tonight we will witness the ceremonies at the temple of the moon. This way, *sidi*. That tall fellow will show us to our quarters. And we will leave, *inshallah*, before there is any occasion to raise the dead."

"Like hell we will," muttered Farrell as he followed his guide. "You couldn't have doped out a better way of crabbing the act!" Then catching a parting glimpse of the large-eyed girl with the golden hair pins and noting the amorous curves of her slender body silhouetted by horizontal rays that glared through an archway, he added, "But miracles seem to be in order in this man's town."

Grilled lamb, flat cakes of bread, and water from the spring that made Madinat-ash-Shams a verdant spot in the blistering southern desert was presently served to Farrell and his companions as they were breaking out their kits in the vast ruin which darkness had suddenly enveloped. The menace and lurking mystery of antiquity oppressed Farrell; and the camel dung fire over which Ismeddin was brewing coffee cast a glow that seemed to animate the gigantic, solemn faces sculptured on the masonry. He shivered, and not from the evening chill that had followed sunset. Then he pictured again the subtle invitation that had lurked on the lips of that Sabean girl and heard in his fancy the tinkle of her golden anklets.

D'Artois' face became grave as he sensed the significance of Farrell's sudden change of expression.

"I'll watch here," he said, "so I'll be on hand to warm up the motor at the first sign of rioting."

"Hell, Pierre," chuckled Farrell. "I won't look for her tonight. They don't allow ladies at the prayer meeting."

He gathered his flowing *djellab* about him and followed Ismeddin up the broad avenue to the loftiest of the *ziggurats*, or tower-temples erected centuries ago by the worshippers of the heavenly bodies. He heard the mutter of drums and the insinuating whine of stringed instruments, and the heart shaking clang of great brazen gongs.

"It is insane…this idea of making a date with the granddaughter of the Queen of Sheba…"

Smoking torches illuminated the broad stairs that led to the *ziggurat* on the first terrace of which thronged the last of the Sabeans who had once ruled all of Arabia. Farrell felt cold chills race up and down his spine as the chanting and drumming hammered into his very soul; and something told him that the Sabeans were a cruel and lustful race to make drums and cymbals whisper such things to a man's heart.

Farrell saw curtains slowly parting to reveal the shrine, and forgot all but the sinister spectacle before him. He barely understood the words of the clean shaven, chanting priests ranged beside the altar, a great square block of carved basalt; but the knife that gleamed in the hand of one who whetted the frosty steel needed no interpretation. They were about to offer a sacrifice. The victim was a young, dark haired girl who had been stripped of all but her dazzling beauty, and a broad, sapphire encrusted girdle about her slender waist. Her eyes were closed, and her head was inclined. She sat cross-legged, and with her arms crossed on her breast. For an instant Farrell tried to assure himself that that was no living woman, but a tinted statue, the goddess of the shrine. He relaxed, exhaled a sighing breath, then froze anew as he noted that she was breathing. She was unbound; and Farrell knew that she must have been drugged so that neither struggle nor change of expression would detract from her ceremonial posture.

The gongs now clanged deafeningly, drowning the chant of the priests and the chilling *snick-snick* of the sacrificial knife. Farrell glanced about, and saw row upon row of fanatic faces, wolfishly gleaming eyes, tall, muscular men enthralled by the blood lust that made the very atmosphere a corrosive poison. To interfere would be suicide. He would be torn to pieces by the frenzied worshippers. Those amiable Sabeans were drunk with the sadistic thrill of waiting for bare steel to sink into warm flesh…

The silver-mitred priest had now taken the knife. Farrell's drawn face was pale. His brain exploded in a blaze of wrath. He reached for his pistol.

A hand snatched his wrist just as his groping fingers told him that his holster was empty; and then Ismeddin's voice hissed in his ear, "I took it—stand fast—this is no business of yours—"

Ismeddin's grip restrained Farrell and restored his sanity. But before he could lower his eyes, or turn his head, he caught the flicker of steel, saw the red tide gush in the wake of the retracted knife, and horribly redden the still crossed hands, drench that shapely golden body and mask the sapphires of the girdle at her waist. His brain reeled, his stomach revolted; and his wrath died in the sickeningly lurching pit of his stomach.

Ismeddin whispered, "There will be no more this evening. The other two will follow—one tomorrow night—and the night after—"

"The other two!" Farrell's horrified glance swept the shrine. In alcoves at either side of the altar he saw what he had not previously observed; two girls arrayed like the one whose blood the priests were collecting in golden bowls and sprinkling on the howling, frenzied worshippers who had surged toward the altar. By the torch glow he recognized the one at the left; it was she whose amorous lips had smiled at him through her transparent veil only a few hours earlier.

"Get out before the accursed of Allah see you and read your mind," urged Ismeddin. "She is safe enough tonight."

Farrell staggered down the broad steps of the *ziggurat* and into the darkness; but that cool gloom was hideous with the image that mocked him from every shadow. And as he strode down the wide avenue toward the plaza, he heard Ismeddin say, "One tonight, one tomorrow night, and the third just as the new moon rises above the lip of the valley. And here is your pistol. Haste is of Satan. You could not save the first. But you may yet have a chance to find the—the one you were seeking."

They were chanting again in the *ziggurat*. The cries of blood lust had become a hymn of praise to the Sabean goddess of the moon.

D'Artois said nothing when he saw Farrell's tense, pale face and the murderous light in his eyes.

"Better sleep," said Ismeddin, indicating the rugs spread out on the paved floor. "I will take the first watch of the night."

Even after silence had crept over that accursed city, the mutter of bloodthirsty drums still rang in Farrell's ears, and that red tide still flowed before his eyes; but finally his senses were dulled by a troubled drowsiness that was more tiring than wakefulness.

He awoke with a start. Someone was kneeling at his side, and plucking him by the shoulder. A woman whispered in that language which was first cousin to Arabic. The hand that gripped him was withered as the voice that said, "She is waiting for you. She dies tomorrow night if you do not save her."

Farrell was on his feet in an instant. Ready for trouble, he had slept full pack, and thus lost no time in dressing. As he followed the stooped, shrivelled old woman, he caught a glimpse of Ismeddin's tall figure lurking in the shadow of the silvery fuselage of the plane.

The old woman led the way down a narrow alley between two of the smaller buildings that faced the plaza; and presently Farrell was lost in the ribbon of blackness that wound in and out among houses that were old when Queen Balkis, young and beautiful as the one they had sacrificed to the lunar goddess, had confounded King Solomon with her riddles and had herself been ensnared by a shrewd bargain that could only be kept by giving herself for a night to that wily monarch whose wisdom she admired more than his patriarchal beard. Lucky Solomon...

Farrell sensed that this guide was a servant of the girl whose eyes had invited him at sunset. He wondered why she was taking him past the *ziggurat*; but he followed until she finally halted at a low doorway that pierced a massive wall of masonry. There, beckoning for silence, she caught his hand and drew him into the blackness of a narrow, tortuous passageway, at the end of which she pushed him ahead of her and across the threshold of an open door. Before he could turn, the door closed against him and he heard the soft, ominous metallic sound of a bolt sliding home.

"What a sap!" he muttered. "Trapped by an old hag."

Farrell drew his pistol as he cleared the pilaster that buttressed the wall. Then he returned the weapon. He was looking through a low archway into a brown, dismal vault which was illuminated by a single taper. A girl was lying face down on a couch of rugs and cushions spread on the mosaic floor. Her dark hair was unbound, and its blue black length enveloped her to her hips. Her face was buried in her arms, and she was softly sobbing to the silence. Her slender ankles were fettered, and her chains were attached to heavy eye-bolts anchored in the masonry of the wall; but her arms were free.

Though Farrell could not see her face, the gracious contour of her waist and the luxurious curve of her slender hips and shapely legs identified her beyond question. She sensed his presence, and sat erect. The misery faded from her dark, wide eyes. Her pomegranate-hued lips smiled; and then she remembered that she was unclad except for the broad, jeweled cincture about her waist. One hand drew her rippling hair about her, but thick as it was, it could scarcely conceal from Farrell's beauty-dazzled eyes the magnolia blossom contour of her firm, ivory-smooth breasts and the lovely roundness of her thighs.

"Don't bother," said Farrell in Arabic, as he finally found his voice. "I won't look lower than your shoulders..."

"I'm sure you've not skipped anything—so another glimpse—" She laughed softly and brushed away a tear that glistened on her long lashes; and then the smouldering darkness of her eyes again became troubled pools of misery. As Farrell knelt on the tiles, her arm twined about him and drew him to the couch of silken rugs. He felt the clinging curves of her warm body and inhaled the dizzying sweetness of the attar which perfumed her lustrous hair; and for a moment Farrell forgot the deadly peril of the situation, and the menace that lurked in that lost city. But before he could find her lips, she shuddered, and whispered as though she feared that the very walls might hear, "Were you there—did you see —"

"God, yes!" Farrell shivered from the chill that even her intoxicating presence could not dispel. He snatched the chain that secured her, wrathfully tugged against its stubborn, hand forged links, then shook his head. "If I'd only brought a chisel from the tool kit—"

As he turned to rise, she caught his arm and drew him back, saying, "No. You can't cut that chain. It would make too much noise. And if you went and returned, someone might see you. And then—oh, there'd not be a chance..."

Her arms twined about him, and fresh tears moistened the folds of his *djellab*.

"Damn it! Then how will I get you away—"

"You can't," she sobbed. "It's impossible. They're watching. I don't know how my old nurse ever slipped you in here... You must leave tonight before they —"

"Wait a minute!" interrupted Farrell. "Did you send for me to tell me to leave before the natives mobbed us?"

She drew her head from his shoulder and for a long moment regarded him. Her smouldering eyes and half parted, amorous lips told him why he had been summoned; and the deep, sighing inhalation of breath, raising her faultless breasts through her streaming hair left no doubt. Terror had departed from her eyes, and passion burned in their dark depths as she sank back among the cushions and with outreaching, inviting arms drew Farrell toward her...

Her pomegranate blossom lips were sultry as breath of the desert, and her quivering, supple young body was a multitude of questing, devouring flames that seemed to envelope Farrell as her arms closed on him with a possessive fierceness that forced from him the breath that she drank from his lips...and neither heard the ironic, mocking note of the ankle chains that tinkled with every movement...

Time had been lost in that perfumed darkness that was broken only by the now faintly flickering taper...but her inarticulate murmur at last found words as she caught her breath.

"God...who are you anyway..." Farrell hoarsely muttered, stirring as he finally became aware once more of the silken rugs beneath him. He understood, now, why in the face of death she had sent her faithful slave to bring him to her arms, and perhaps to a savage doom. And though slaked passion made way for the lurking of peril, Farrell understood, and was glad; for if she must die, she would now die a woman, and not a girl who had never lived...

"I'm Makeda," she murmured. Desire had for the moment left her eyes, yet her smile was a caress. But Farrell was perplexed by the triumph that glowed from her lovely face. He leaped to his feet, cursing his folly in having succumbed to his desire and thus robbed him of a chance to go to the plane and get tools that might sever her chains. But Makeda drew him back.

"You don't understand," she continued. "Now I won't die on the altar. *Only virgins are eligible for sacrifice to the moon goddess*."

She sighed luxuriously and shrugged aside a long black tress that twined over her left breast. Farrell's brain was again a whirling confusion. He frowned, seeking to collect his thoughts; but his eyes persistently strayed to that perfect left breast—perfection heightened by a star shaped, black mole.

"But how," he finally demanded, "will the priests know you're no longer a virgin? If you told them, they'd just think it a trick to escape—"

Her eyes clouded, and then Makeda answered, "Why...the same way anyone else would. That's part of the ritual. But now they'll merely keep me locked up in the temple. They won't throw my blood to the crowd."

Farrell's eyes blazed wrathfully. To think of that incredible girl going from his arms to one of those blood drinking priests seemed worse than watching her face the sacrificial knife. He tore and tugged and struggled with her chains until his

216

hands were raw; and then, abandoning his vain fight, he said, "I'm going to cut you loose. I'm coming right back—"

He ignored her protests. He shouldered the door before he remembered that it had been barred. But it yielded to his touch; and presently Farrell was slinking through a maze of bewildering passageways. The stars, however, gave him his general direction; and then as he emerged in a wider alley, he noted the familiar bulk of the ruined palace that overshadowed the plaza. He hastened toward his landmark, and in a few moments he saw the glistening wings of the trimotored plane.

Ismeddin, appearing suddenly from behind the colossal stump of a shattered column, recognized Farrell and turned to walk his post; but when he saw him enter the plane, and presently emerge with a hammer and chisel, he seized his arm and said, "Don't go back. It's—"

"Hell!" snapped Farrell, jerking clear. "I know what I'm doing."

But the old Arab shook his head. "I talked to that old woman. Do you suppose she sneaked by without my seeing her? She told me all about it. You can't get back into the house. You're lucky to have gone as far as you did. Listen—"

Farrell cocked a sharp ear at the silence. He heard muffled hoofbeats, and the subdued ring of steel. Then he noted that the false dawn was breaking, and that the true dawn would soon follow. In the deceptive grayish murk of the street from which he had entered the plaza he saw the spectral bulk of a tall man on horse; and a second followed him into a side street.

"Can't make it, *sidi*," said Ismeddin as a curse of exasperation rumbled deep in Farrell's throat. "Without a guide, how could you pick the right doorway, or find her room?"

Ismeddin was right. Farrell turned and without a word entered the hall where d'Artois was sleeping; but when the sun flamed up over the sombre walls of Madinat-ash-Shams, he was still groping for some device to extricate Makeda from the grip of the priests.

* * * *

The old Arab, seeing Farrell gloomily engrossed with the morning coffee, read his thought, and said, "It is not absolutely impossible. Get out the medicine chest and sit here in the plaza to bandage the wounded and give pills to the sick. That will make you popular here. And that is what you need, until—"

And then Ismeddin began talking about the weather; nor could Farrell's insistence make the old fellow reveal his plan.

And thus from necessity he followed Ismeddin to the further edge of the plaza, where he laid out his first aid kit and the simple drugs he had taken from the medicine chest of the plane. Then, as the Sabeans clustered about, the old darwish proved himself a master juggler. He picked small trinkets and coins from the air, and from crevices in the paving, flinging them to the fascinated spectators; and all the while he chanted his patter:

"The learned doctor! The healer of the sick! The mender of the broken! He sets aright whom the gods have afflicted!"

As Farrell painted his patients with iodine, gave them powerful purgatives, and packed decayed teeth with oil of cloves, the old darwish vanished as though he himself had been palmed by a juggler. And late that afternoon, while Farrell was lancing and cauterizing a snake bite, Ismeddin was engaged in a way that would have made his chief's eyes widen perceptibly.

At sunset Farrell was accompanied to his quarters by three porters loaded down with gifts presented by grateful patients. Ismeddin was awaiting his return; and as he noted the display of food, trinkets, and clothing heaped on the floor, he grinned and said, "This will get you a place of honor at the ritual of sacrifice tonight."

"Why the hell should I attend that butchery?" growled Farrell. "Makeda told me—"

The darwish grinned and stroked his beard.

"*Wallah*! And so did the old woman, this afternoon. For reasons best known yourself, Makeda is not eligible to die on the altar. But you miss the point. You must attend the ceremonies. You are chief of the party, and your absence would not only be discourteous, but would arouse suspicion.

"In the meanwhile, I will be arranging things. Perhaps I can get Makeda out of her cell while everyone's attention is occupied with the orgy at the temple."

"Nothing doing!" snapped Farrell. "I'm going with you."

But the darwish shook his head.

"Better do as I say. I can work more quietly alone. Take your pistols with you, so if that blood drunken crowd should get wild, you can hold your own. And don't forget to wear a scimitar. But keep your head, and on your life, don't interfere with the butchery—it is none of your affair.

"And you, my lord *bimbashi*," he concluded, turning to d'Artois, "be ready to leave in a hurry."

So saying, Ismeddin stalked to the archway, and vanished in the shadows before Farrell could detain him.

"I smell trouble," muttered Farrell. "I don't like this being split up."

He grasped d'Artois' hand, then strode to the plaza.

The savage drums were rumbling, and as he walked up the broad avenue toward the *ziggurat*, the shivering clang of brazen gongs chilled Farrell's blood. He scarcely felt the paving beneath his feet. He shuddered at the thought of being forced to witness a repetition of the past night's savagery; and then his pulse raced maddeningly as he remembered Makeda's loveliness shrouded only by her twining black hair. If his presence would lull suspicion, and give Ismeddin a free hand in liberating Makeda from the priests who were going to keep her as a temple slave, Farrell could swallow his qualms.

He descended the broad stairs and found the terrace ablaze with smoking torches. He saluted the *Amir* who sat at the right, surrounded by his guard. Then Farrell worked his way to the front of the group at the left, close to the curtains of the shrine. As he waited for the parting of the veil, he glanced about, and up to the second stage of the terraced tower. There he saw a vague, whitish splotch in the darkness; and as he wondered at that lurking figure, it vanished behind the parapet that guarded the dizzy drop to the lower terrace. That shrouded shape might be Ismeddin, still seeking Makeda. Then the pipes and stringed instruments tore Farrell's nerves to shreds. He steeled himself to endure the impending orgy.

A warning clang of bronze told Farrell that the curtains of the shrine would part; and despite himself, his gaze was drawn to the altar. As before, a girl sat on the sacrificial block: nude, save for the jeweled girdle, arms crossed on her breast, and her head inclined. She awaited doom in drugged tranquility, and the tall priest stood by to receive the fatal knife from the hands of the acolyte who was whetting it with deliberate, ceremonial gestures.

The chanting ceased. The silence was broken only by a restless stirring, and the gasp of sharply drawn breath. Farrell's blood froze in his veins, and horror paralyzed him. *It was Makeda who was awaiting the knife*. Makeda, whose sultry kisses still tingled on his lips. Makeda, whose amorous frenzy had left his throat scarred and bruised. She had failed to save herself from the altar. Someone had misled Ismeddin.

"God..." he muttered. The paving beneath his feet seemed to surge and billow, and his brain had become a blazing frenzy of blind despair. The knife was ready, gleaming in the high priest's hand.

Like the blood drunken Sabeans, Farrell's eyes stared in fascination at the glistening steel. The priest's sonorous voice rolled like the rumble of doom. Yet none knew whose doom it foretold; not even Farrell, for though he moved with panther swiftness, it was as in a hideous, incredible dream.

As the great gong thundered, Farrell's revolver cleared its holster. The brazen clang muffled the blast of the .45. The priest pitched backward in a heap beside the altar; and for a frozen instant no one but Farrell moved. The hypnotic spell of the interrupted blood ritual was not broken until the bewildered participants saw him bound forward, revolver in hand.

The priests fled before Farrell's insane charge; but the amazed Sabeans sensed his purpose. They surged forward in a yelling, steel armed wave.

Farrell whirled at the altar. For a moment the deadly chatter of his revolvers held the blood maddened mob at bay. They recoiled, riddled by the murderous hail of lead. And then the hammers clicked on empty chambers.

All in a crowded instant. Then he seized the drugged beauty and bounded forward, his ceremonial scimitar flashing in whistling arcs as the first of the mob closed in. Steel struck sparks from steel, and Farrell's blade dripped red; but as he cleared the threshold of the shrine, a crescent of swords had him hemmed in. Encumbered by his lovely burden, Farrell had not been able to move fast enough to reach the stairs before his retreat was cut off. He backed into an angle to make his final stand. They saw no need for haste; and they knew the peril of crowding a man who had no chance. He would kill a dozen of them before they overwhelmed him, and no one wanted to be first.

An angry voice from the rear urged them forward, but the charge was checked before it started. Something dropped from the parapet overhead, and burst into searing, blue white radiance that overwhelmed the wan torchlight, and dazzled the eyes that were fixed on Farrell.

The distraction was no more than momentary; but in the face of a hedge of swords, that moment seemed a lifetime. Though blinded by that blistering glare, Farrell had the advantage. Slashing blindly, he bounded along the balustrade and to the head of the stairs. He knew that the choking, dense white fumes enveloped the mob and would for another instant screen his flight. And as he took the stairs three at a leap, he knew what had given him his chance: a landing flare Ismeddin had taken from the plane.

Savage yells and deep voiced commands roared behind him; steel clanged, and the brazen gong thundered to urge the Sabeans to the pursuit as their eyes recovered from the incandescent blaze; but Farrell, as he dashed down the avenue, heard the drumming of the motors, and knew d'Artois was warming up. Farrell was now tearing across the plaza. He heard the clatter of hoofs, the roar of *jezails* and flint lock pistols, and the whistle of lead.

One final effort. The horsemen were on his heels. Farrell tossed his burden ahead of him and plunged headlong into the cabin after her. And then the roar of the motors drowned the clamor. The plane rushed headlong across the great square and straight at the dizzily towering walls. Then it zoomed upward at a ruinous angle; but the powerful engines made it, and in another moment, d'Artois flattened out.

"Holy smoke!" sighed Farrell. And then, raising his voice: "Ismeddin! Break out some brandy."

But Ismeddin had stepped into the pilot's compartment. Farrell turned toward the girl he had stolen from the sacrificial altar. She was still unconscious, and beautiful as a sleeping goddess, despite the blood that had dripped on her slender body from a dozen grazing cuts which seamed Farrell's head and ribs.

And then Farrell's blood froze. He now saw what he had not noted in the hell glare of smoking torches: *it was not Makeda he had carried through a wall of blades.*

"Good God!" he muttered. There was no more than a mocking similarity. He swept aside the long strand of dark hair that curled over her shoulder and caressed her left breast. He knew then that she could not be Makeda, for there was no star shaped mole on the magnolia blossom perfection.

It was too late to return. Triumph was bitter as the dust and blood on his lips. The girl on the lounge was stirring. The effect of the drug was wearing off. She sat up and regarded him with wonder widened, dark eyes...

Farrell heard a click behind him. And for the second time within a few moments he stood dazed and gaping. A smiling girl stood framed in the doorway that opened into the pilot's compartment, and behind her was white-bearded Ismeddin.

"Well, for the love of Mike!" Farrell finally blurted out. "How—why—what the devil—"

The girl was Makeda—Makeda as she had been that mad, amorous hour in that sombre vault, except that the splendor of her body smiled warmly through a gown of transparent gauze.

Her arms closed about Farrell, and her lips stopped his queries. Finally she said, "Forgive me. But I had to do it. It was my cousin who was to die on the altar tonight. We resemble each other, and I didn't think you'd notice the difference by night. So I put on those chains and sent for you—to—well, give you a reason for saving me—I mean, her."

"You mean you slipped into the plane while I was being damn near chopped to little pieces—for a total stranger?"

Makeda smiled and shrugged. "I'm awfully fond of my cousin. And that old fellow said you could raise the dead, so I knew that saving her would be simple enough…"

"Billahi!" interposed Ismeddin, "I didn't know that until the old slave woman told me, the last minute. And I thought the flare would be better than—"

"It was. And now you and Makeda's cousin go forward and talk to Pierre. And break out something or other she can use to cover the points of interest. I don't want Pierre to get eye strain and crack us up in the middle of this desert.

"Now, get the hell out, the both of you. I'm going to be busy studying astronomy for some time to come."

"Astronomy?" wondered the old Arab as he wrapped a blanket around Makeda's cousin. Then he winked, grinned, and added, "*Sidi*, that's a new name for—"

"Get out or I'll break your head!" threatened Farrell as he snapped out the cabin lights. "I was referring to a star-shaped mole, which is something you'd not understand."

And then Makeda's arms closed about Farrell and her questing lips sought his in the darkness.

"And so you did notice that mole?" she finally murmured, as she sighed contentedly and untwined her arms. "I was rather worried…you see, I thought you'd be terribly angry, and I just dreaded coming in here to face you…but I was afraid you might make a perfectly *terrible* mistake—she looks so much like me…"

SILVER PEACOCK

Originally published in *All Detective Magazine*, May 1933.

As the clock in the living room of Glenn Farrell's summer home at Pass Christian struck five, old Isaac, the negro handyman, punctual to the minute, emerged from the kitchen and placed on the tabouret beside Farrell's chair a large copper tray. On the tray was a tall, mint-garnished glass, and a stack of mail that Isaac had brought from the post office.

Judged by the post marks and return addresses, the lot would be uninteresting. While waiting for the glass to blossom out with a white frost, Farrell opened the first of the stack.

As he read the brief, typed message, he sat bolt upright in his chair. His gray eyes narrowed, and a frown furrowed his forehead as he re-read the note. A dozen years of hunting men, minerals, and beasts had accustomed Farrell to surprises, pleasant and otherwise; but Isaac had brought in a masterpiece.

Isaac, hearing Farrell's exclamation of wrath and incredulity, started, stared for a moment, then retired to witness the storm from cover.

Bring one hundred thousand dollars in new, unmarked hundred dollar bills to the L.&N. Railroad bridge at midnight of the twentieth. A boat will be waiting for you. Do not fail, and do not attempt any trickery or resistance. The penalty will be death.

In lieu of a signature there was a spot of red wax stamped with a peacock. The seal was obviously the impression of a signet ring.

"Well, I'll be everlastingly double-damned!" exploded Farrell as he emerged from his chair with a fluent motion that made the tawny, striped tiger's skin on the hearth seem like evidence of fratricide. Then he frowned, and stroked the long white scar that seamed his right cheek; a claw mark of the great cat that had almost succeeded. For a moment Farrell's eyes peered through, and past the note in his hand.

"Peacock...hmmm..." he muttered, as the symbol stamped on the seal recalled memories of the fanatic Yezidees of Kurdistan, who worship Satan, and represent him as a peacock. "One hundred thousand, or else—! And they'll be waiting with a boat to pick it up?"

He paced the length of the Boukhara rug, and back again. Then his frown relaxed into an amiable grin that contradicted the steel-gray glitter of his eyes.

"I'll be waiting with a boat myself. Oh, there, Isaac! Lay out my clothes! Right away!"

Farrell's voice rang through the drowsy, afternoon silence like a bugle.

"Yassuh, Mistah Glenn, yassuh!"

Farrell stepped into his bedroom, inspected and loaded a Colt .45.

"Now roll out the wagon, Isaac," he directed as he stripped off his lounging pajamas and put on a suit of tropicals. Then (as he thrust the pistol into his shoulder holster) "Damn it, he would lay out this of all ties!"

He corrected Isaac's selection of neckwear. And a few minutes later, Farrell's Hispano was a glittering flash and a high-pitched scream that streaked across the bridge toward Bay Saint Louis, and thence down the highway toward New Orleans.

Farrell realized that there was no need for haste. The enemy had given him three days in which to prepare a counter-attack—or, as they doubtless thought, to raise a hundred thousand dollars; but Farrell's swift trip to New Orleans was expressive of impatience to take the initiative, rather than any need to hurry the simple preparations he had in mind.

An hour and a quarter later, the Hispano drew up before police head-quarters in New Orleans. Farrell strode into the smoke clouded office of the chief of the Detective Bureau.

"Evening, Baker," he greeted, then glanced about. "Where's the chief?"

"Out now, Mr. Farrell," replied the sergeant. "Anything I can do for you?"

Farrell slid the extortion letter and a long cigar across the desk.

"Stuff that in your face, and give Healy that love-letter, if you don't mind." Then, as Baker reached for the cigar and bit off the tip, "Tell the chief I'm staying at the Union Club tonight, in case he wants to get in touch with me. And if not, I'll see him in the morning. If you want to, you can take a peep at that letter yourself. You'll hear plenty before we're through."

Without waiting for Baker's comment, Farrell left the office and drove to the club.

* * * *

Although he dined alone that evening, Farrell's thoughts were sufficient company. Even a perfectly grilled guinea hen and a bottle of Chablis did not suffice to divert him from his plan of campaign. While equipping his speedboat with a pair of machine guns, and bolting boiler plate to the cabin would be a simple procedure, Farrell did not underestimate the enemy's possibilities. The exultation of the warpath was diluted by flashes of misgiving, such as assail all but the foolhardy when in the face of peril.

He finally decided that his plans would be none the worse for a fresh start in the morning. As he thrust aside his *demitasse*, and wondered as to the best disposition of the evening, the waiter approached with a portable telephone, set it on his table and plugged it in.

"Farrell speaking... Hi, there, Burnham... How'd you know I was in town?... Sorry, but I can hardly understand you. Bum connection... Better now... Uh-huh... Sure, I'll meet you in the lobby of the Plaza, right after the show. But better than that—"

A sharp click. Farrell jiggled the instrument. The line was dead.

"Want to call back, sir?" wondered the waiter.

Farrell shook his head.

"Take it away—just a minute, I'll sign my check, too." Then, as he took his hat, "Guess Burnham was in a hurry and was satisfied when he heard me say I'd be there; but he might have asked me to join him. Funny egg, Burnham. Never could dope him out. And why meet me in the lobby instead of here at the club?"

Whereupon Farrell dismissed the query, paused at the desk to leave word as to his destination, and strode down Canal Street, toward the Plaza.

The theatre, however, did not prove to be the diversion that Farrell had anticipated. The peacock was not to be dismissed so lightly. After burning his way through the better part of a pack of cigarettes, Farrell left the smoking room, and stepped out into the lobby a few minutes before the conclusion of the performance.

The usher who opened the door regarded him for a moment, then said, "Mr. Farrell? Mr. Burnham will be looking for you at the box office."

Before Farrell could question the usher, the latter vanished in the darkness of a side aisle.

"What in the hell's eating Burnham?" muttered Farrell as he took his post. He loosened the pistol in his shoulder holster, then reflected, "I'm jumpy, that's all. No point in anyone putting me on the spot. It's money they want, not my hide."

* * * *

A moment later, the show was over. Farrell, standing at the box-office, surveyed the crowd that was advancing down the long, narrow, sloping floor. And just as the head of the chattering procession reached the sidewalk, Farrell saw Burnham in the middle of the lobby. He was lifting his leghorn hat, and mopping his bald head with a handkerchief. Burnham, it seemed, had enjoyed the performance no more than Farrell. His pale, heavy face was worried and haggard. Two men were accompanying him. One edged closer and whispered a word into Burnham's ear. Farrell recognized them; plainclothes men. He frowned perplexedly.

"Wonder if he's in a jam, and they caught up with him. Maybe he's short in his accounts..."

Just behind Burnham were two men who wore colored glasses of the kind favored by those susceptible to eyestrain caused by the semi-tropical glare of New Orleans: a detail that Farrell later recalled.

Burnham was now but a few paces distant.

"Looks like the devil on horseback," was Farrell's thought. "Hi, Burnham!"

Burnham's companions, catching Farrell's voice clearly above the chatter of the crowd, regarded Farrell intently. Burnham started. Farrell wondered at his expression of *surprised recognition*.

Farrell repeated his hail and stepped forward from the box office. At that same instant an arm shot up out of the crowd midway between Burnham and Farrell, and his voice was drowned in a surging, gusty roar that was accompanied by a blinding flash which blazed from the upward reaching arm. A wave of blistering heat singed Farrell's eyelashes and scorched his cheeks. Two splotches of bluish-white flame danced before his dazzled eyes as the chatter of the crowd roared into gasps of dismay and bewilderment, and shrill screams of fright, and—Farrell caught it distinctly—a single cry of mortal anguish.

"Steady, there! Quit shovin'!— Just a flashlight! Man hurt—stop him! Grab him!"

The lobby was a bawling, milling confusion.

Farrell plunged headlong toward that point where, a split instant ago, he had seen an arm rise in a gesture that ended in a sheet of flame. He heard a grunt, and a metallic clatter. His arms, reaching out instinctively, closed about someone who eluded his grasp before he could get a firm hold. A knife raked his ribs lightly; and he heard a low, guttural exclamation in a language he had not heard for years.

"The Peacock!" flashed through his mind.

"Get back and stay back!" roared a commanding voice. "Sam, don't let anyone out of this lobby!"

The panic subsided almost as suddenly as it began. Above the bedlam of protests and inquiries, Farrell heard the scream of a siren. The alarm had reached police headquarters. And then Farrell's eyes, more severely dazzled than those who had not looked directly at the flash, began to function. He saw one of the detectives who had accompanied Burnham kneeling beside a man who lay sprawled on the tiled floor. A stream of blood trickled redly across the white tiles. The hilts of two daggers, driven home to the guards, projected from his back. It was Burnham.

The plainclothes man looked up and shook his head.

"Finished," he declared.

And then the massive bulk of John Healy, chief of the Detective Bureau, plunged through the crowd that was detained by the police cordon.

"I might have known I'd find you right in the midst of the mess!" he exclaimed as he recognized Farrell. Then, seeing that Farrell's coat was slashed, and that blood was staining the light tropical cloth, "Hell's fire, did they get you, too?"

"Just an accident. I grabbed someone. That damned flashlight powder blinded me, and—but what makes you think—"

"Plenty! Burnham got the same kind of letter you left on my desk. He didn't pay off last night, like they told him to. And here he is—knifed right under our noses! Of all the slick tricks. What are you going to do? Payoff?"

Farrell's laugh was mirthless. His eyes answered Healy before he spoke.

"I came to town to declare open season on peacocks, John. And I'm paying Burnham's account along with my own. By the way, did they shake him down for the same amount?"

Healy nodded.

"Then," declared Farrell, after a moment's thought, "this whole show was a plant to show me what'll happen if I don't pay off. Burnham could no more raise a hundred thousand cash than a hundred million. I know. I was in on a couple of deals with him. And if that doesn't convince you—" Farrell outlined the telephone strategy whereby he had been induced to wait for Burnham in the lobby; then, as he turned to leave, "If you want me tonight, or in the morning, I'll be at the club. Night, John."

CHAPTER II

Lydia and the Silver Peacock

The following afternoon Farrell returned to Pass Christian with his borrowed machine guns. Up to the time of his departure, the police had made no progress in solving the case. The assassins had escaped during that moment when everyone, that is, everyone but two men wearing colored glasses, was blinded by the blast of photographer's flashlight powder. The clues were more colorful than helpful: two antique daggers, so the evening papers stated, of Persian workmanship; and the peacock seal which had taken the place of a signature on the extortion letter mailed to Burnham several days previous. As an afterthought, and by way of incongruous contrast, a battered flashlight gun, and two pairs of colored spectacles were listed.

That night Farrell's sleep was interrupted by the persistent ringing of the doorbell.

"If anyone's waking me up to offer me a drink I'll kick him into the Gulf," he muttered sleepily. He heard the purr of a powerful motor idling in the drive in front of the house. "Hmmm...that engine sounds like class. Maybe a distinguished visitor."

The doorbell rang again, a long, persistent ring, followed by several staccato jerks. Someone was impatient and eager.

"Keep your shirt on, brother," Farrell shouted as he found his slippers. Then through his sleepiness came the recollection of his being hunted. He picked his Colt .45 from the dresser.

Farrell strode silently across the thick carpet, yanked the door suddenly. As he leaped clear, he covered the entrance with his pistol. Then he stared for a moment, and lowered his automatic. His caller was an uncommonly pretty girl. As Farrell snapped on the gallery light, he noted with approval the costly simplicity of her sports costume.

"Oh, Mr. Farrell!" she exclaimed, her greenish eyes widening in dismay. "Don't shoot!"

She laughed softly at Farrell's embarrassment, but despite her amusement, she was agitated. She was nervously fingering the handle of a circular hat box that she had picked up and was holding in her arms as though guarding something fragile and precious.

"I beg your pardon," said Farrell. "I wasn't expecting a lady at this hour. And —" He glanced at the pistol in his hand. "I'm awfully nervous, you know, alone in a big house like this."

"You look it," the girl retorted. She laughed and glanced over her shoulder. The green eyes shifted to the tightly clutched hat box. "They're on my trail, and I can't shake them. I hate to ask you to take—"

"Step in and tell me about it, Miss—"

"Lydia Wilson," she said as she entered.

"Wonder what's eating her?" was Farrell's thought as he saw her start violently as the door clicked closed behind her. "She's got 'em, and got 'em bad!"

As he gestured toward a chair, Farrell regarded the long lashed eyes and copper tinged hair.

"I'll tell you all about it," Lydia answered as she opened the hat box.

"Good Lord!" exclaimed Farrell as she removed the silver image of a peacock with outspread fan. The body of the bird was scarcely larger than a spring chicken. "Are you by any chance calling to remind me of that hundred thousand? Now, if they'd sent you in the first place," he continued, dividing his glance between the exquisite Persian workmanship of the peacock, and the loveliness of the girl, "I'd have coughed up in a minute."

"Why—I'm sure I don't know what you mean," countered Lydia, obviously puzzled.

"Oh, well, never mind. I've just got a private grudge against peacocks. But what's it all about? And how come you're picking on me?"

"It's for Hillman Parr, in New Orleans. They've been after me ever since I left Pensacola. I hate to ask you to take such a terrible risk—"

"I take risks for fun, money, or marbles," assured Farrell. "But why elect me?"

"Heard of you—spent a summer on the Gulf Coast, once. But call me at the Cortez tomorrow morning. I simply can't stop to explain. You will, won't you?" she pleaded, then thrust the peacock into his hands as though she feared that he might refuse. "Hillman Parr, the collector. Everyone knows him. And do be on your guard!"

She fairly ran to the door as she uttered her warning.

"Hey, wait a minute—" protested Farrell as he turned and set the peacock on the table, then started after her. The door clicked in his face. As he fumbled with the latch, he heard the door of her car slam. "Steady, there!" he called, as he opened the house door and cleared the gallery with a bound, "Hold on a minute!"

But Lydia stepped on the accelerator. Farrell caught a glimpse of a New York license plate, and her hand waving him farewell as she cleared the gatepost by a hair.

"Afraid I'd turn her down and make her carry her own jewelry—" Then, as he heard the roar of the motor, "Going like the hammers of hell! But if she was so scared, why didn't she stay here?" he wondered as he retraced his steps and entered the living room.

Farrell grinned at his reflection in the mirror.

"Did my map scare her out, or was she afraid of compromising me?"

He picked up the silver peacock which had been forced on him for delivery to Hillman Parr. On the breast was a medallion engraved in obsolete, angular Arabic script.

The work of the Servant of the Angel, Abdannar, Emir of the Faithful, may our Lord be well pleased with him.

"Pretty thick; the Peacock assassinates Burnham just to serve as a good example to me, and does it right before my eyes! And now this nice looking red-head comes charging up in a high flurry. Where does she fit into this, or does she? Persian daggers jammed into Burnham, and now this hoodoo all bespattered with inscriptions—"

He glared at the bird for a moment.

"And where does Hillman Parr come in on this? Probably stolen property and he knows it. Never saw a collector yet that'd turn down a hot work of art."

Farrell grinned knowingly and glanced at some of his own collection; rich old rugs from Persian palaces, scimitars, kreeses, kampilans; bits of jade, and Japanese lacquer. But all of the arms that were grouped on the wall in clusters were not antiques. Some of them were mementos of their owners, indiscreet fellows who had hunted Farrell.

Farrell opened his wall safe and made room for the silver peacock. As he spun the dial, he heard a car thundering past, throttle wide open. He heard the savage scream of brakes as it slowed down to make the sharp turn in the road that crossed the L.&N. tracks and led to the highway bridge. For a moment he thought that he was listening to another example of more speed than brains.

"That bird's in more of a hurry than she was."

And with that thought, Farrell's march to his bedroom halted abruptly.

"By God, that might be someone chasing her! Naturally they'd keep on her trail, not knowing she'd stopped here and left the peacock with me. And if they overtake her and find she's not got it, they'll take it out of her hide—"

Farrell slipped trousers over his pajamas.

"Let's go! Trouble always follows these red-headed women."

He slipped a pistol into his hip pocket, dashed to the garage, and in another moment the Hispano was justifying Farrell's affectionate boasting.

"Gangway!" he cried above the roar of the motor as he charged up the grade to the two-mile highway bridge and jammed the accelerator home. He crossed the bridge in a shade more than ninety seconds. The Hispano was a blur and a high-pitched whine as it flashed through Bay Saint Louis toward Waveland and another sharp turn.

"That jane has more nerve than sense," reflected Farrell as he slowed down out of deference to the loose gravel leading out of Waveland. "Leading the pursuit away from the peacock. Or else," Farrell smiled sourly. "Or she's playing me for a sap. She knew entirely too much about my weaknesses and meddlesome habits, even allowing for the rotogravure section and press notices. Wouldn't take such a gigantic intellect to dope it out that I'd take a tumble and follow her, to see her safe to New Orleans. Rather nice, the way she checked out without giving me a chance to say aye, yes, or no.

"And now all they've got to do is to yank a decrepit flivver across the road, some place where I won't be able to pull up in time, knock my bus end for appetite, pick me out of the wreckage, and haul me to a boat waiting at the Rigolets Pass. Then they can keep me filed for reference, and be sure I'll pay off the money Mr. Peacock wants. Borrowing those machine guns probably tipped them off. Probably been watching me all day. Such a nice looking girl, too..."

And having the ambush plotted out in advance, Glenn Farrell played true to form; he crowded the Hispano to the limit. Until the pursuit reached the road fork at Slidell, there was but one route suitable for fast travel to New Orleans.

As Farrell passed the Pearl River Bridge, he saw that he had made a surprisingly accurate guess. A car, hall athwart the road, was waiting, ready to halt or wreck him. He jammed on the brakes and came to a smoking halt.

"Didn't figure my bus would stop that quick," he muttered. "That crabs their game. And if they try to rush me—"

Farrell drew his .45.

"Clear moonlight, and damned nice shooting!"

He waited for a moment to see if the assault would materialize. But instead of a rush of dark figures and the crackle of pistols, there was a curse of exasperation, and a woman's scream. Two men emerged from the swampy depression that flanked the road. They half carried, half dragged a struggling, sobbing woman toward the car that was partly headed into the highway.

One of the woman's captors shouted. Someone in the car replied. The engine raced as the driver stepped on the gas, preparing for a fast getaway.

Farrell leaped to the road.

"What's this monkey work?" he demanded as his pistol rose into line.

No answer. One of the men took complete charge of the woman. Farrell saw his fist smack home. The other as he released his hold on the captive drew and fired at Farrell. The bullet smashed through the windshield of the Hispano as Farrell's .45 roared. The enemy staggered, recovered, fired again.

Then, pistol flaming, Farrell charged the rear guard, fearing to risk a shot at the woman's captor. But as his second shot drove the gunman into a heap on the running board, an arm from within dragged him into the car as it took off with a bound and soared down the road. A farewell bullet from the fugitives gipped harmlessly overhead. It was a gesture of derision to which Farrell did not reply.

"Damn his hide," Farrell growled as he noted the blood splashes on the paved road, "his wild shooting kept me dodging enough to give the other guy a chance to make the bus. Well, we'll ride some more!"

As Farrell turned toward his own car he saw the wreck from which the girl had been carried. The New York license plate identified it as Lydia's machine. He saw at a glance that the gas tank had been ripped open, and the upholstery slashed. They had looked for something, presumably the peacock, in every conceivable place of concealment; and now they were taking her away to be sweated until she told them what she had done with the silver image.

In another moment Farrell was on his way down the highway.

"Come on, sister, we've not started yet!" he declared as he opened the Hispano wide. "If we can't overtake 'em, we'll make their arrival in town conspicuous."

At all events, Farrell reflected, as mile after mile of darkness slipped past, Lydia's story had been bona fide, even though the whole affair was decidedly shady. Something, he decided, was absolutely off-color: else, why had the peacock been shipped by messenger, instead of by express?

Farrell flashed through Slidell unchallenged by highway patrolmen. If any were on duty, they would be in pursuit of the car ahead. At the road fork just beyond Slidell, Farrell turned to the left, reasoning that the fugitives would avoid the Pontchartrain Bridge in order to keep from being observed by the toll keeper.

Several miles beyond Slidell, the guess seemed justified. Far ahead of him, Farrell caught a glimpse of a tail light. Farrell was slowly gaining.

"Shake it up, sister, we got to catch 'em!"

But the car ahead was no sluggard, and the start from the Pearl River Bridge was more than could be overcome in a few miles. Farrell, however, persisted in the chase instead of halting to telephone ahead to New Orleans. He finally observed that he had gained appreciably on the tail light ahead.

They were approaching the railroad crossing near Gentilly. Farrell heard the scream of the limited, and caught the long beam of its headlight.

The enemy was slowing down to make the sharp turn just before the road crossed the tracks. Farrell unlimbered his pistol. Four shots left, but enough.

"Should have brought an extra clip!" he muttered in disgust. "One bum play after another…"

The limited was bearing down on the crossing.

"Got 'em sewed up!" he exulted. "Can't slow down to make the turn, and then pick up enough to beat the train—crazy if they even think of it—"

Farrell held his breath for an instant, swallowed his heart, and jammed his own brakes. He expected to see the car smashed to fragments by the onrushing locomotive.

Then he slumped back against the cushions.

"Made it—Good Lord!"

He sighed wearily, and became aware of the violent trembling that shook him, and made him try a second time to holster his pistol.

"Red Head, you sure came near getting yours…"

After a seemingly interminable delay the crossing was clear. As he let in the clutch and crossed the tracks in the wake of the train, Farrell realized that further pursuit was useless. The enemy would by now be well into the suburbs, driving at a moderate pace, and secure against all but the most remote chance of being overtaken or recognized.

* * * *

Farrell halted at the first filling station to telephone police headquarters.

"Glenn Farrell speaking…trace black Cadillac sedan…no, couldn't get the number…three men, one of them with at least two bullet holes in him. One girl, red hair, green eyes, beige sports costume…looks exactly what the well dressed woman will wear…yeah, that's the type!… Hell, I'm no good at weights or dimensions, but I'd say she must be about twenty four-five… And tell John Healy I've got a hunch this job ties in with the knifing of Burnham…no, can't explain it, but you tell him. And I'll see him later in the day."

Farrell hung up and paused to consider his next move.

He could continue on into New Orleans and spend the remainder of the night at the Union Club, or else he could return to Pass Christian and get the peacock.

While Farrell was not acutely concerned about the disposition of Hillman Parr's property, the last move was obviously the best, since the silver image would give him an immediate opportunity of investigating the possibility that Hillman Parr was in some way connected with the death of Burnham. Therefore, after having his tank refilled, Farrell set out for Pass Christian, albeit at a more moderate pace than he had taken during the vain pursuit of Lydia.

CHAPTER III
Mr. Parr is Embarrassed

It was close to sunrise when Farrell arrived at his estate, which fronted the highway that follows the Gulf Coast from Bay Saint Louis to Biloxi. He summoned old Isaac and called for coffee. Then, while awaiting the brewing of the black, chicory-tinctured eye-opener, Farrell opened the wall safe. The silver peacock awaited his inspection.

In order to be prepared for his call on Parr, Farrell felt that he should be fairly conversant with the inscription whose translation he had not completed. He therefore renewed his study of the engraved medallion. He had read the first line at sight; but on closer scrutiny he saw that those which followed were made up of characters worked into an intricate arabesque pattern whose deciphering would require considerable study: several days, perhaps.

"Hell with that!" he exclaimed, and set about making several pencil and paper rubbings of the medallion, to be studied at his leisure. "I'll sink Parr with a good bluff on the lines I do know."

Then, as Isaac served his coffee, "Lay out my gray checkered suit. And stuff this bird into a cardboard box. I'm damned sick of peacocks, and I want it out of my sight before it spoils my breakfast."

"Yassuh, Mistah Glenn," agreed the negro as he carefully set aside the penciled note and secured them with a paper weight, "peacocks is bad luck."

"And that's only half of it," muttered Farrell glumly, thinking again of Burnham, his own prospects, and the kidnapping of the charming Lydia.

But with a coffee, a shave, and a fresh suit of tropicals, Farrell's spirits revived. And thus, after issuing a few instructions to Isaac, Farrell reloaded his .45, stuffed a handful of cigars into his breast pocket, and resumed the wheel of the Hispano.

An hour and a half later, Farrell drew up at Parr's house on Saint Charles Avenue. He presented his card, and without delay was ushered into the dusky solitude of the high ceiled library. Parr's desk was an island in a broad expanse of hardwood floor. The dark visaged bronzes that rose, here and there, from their marble pedestals, were lonely as lighthouses. Farrell resisted the temptation to hang his hat on a bust of Napoleon, and gravely set the cardboard box on the scholar's desk.

"Pray be seated, Mr. Farrell," began Parr in his oratorical manner which always left the listener wondering whether Parr addressed an individual or a historical society. "This is indeed a pleasure."

He paused impressively for a moment, then resumed, "A rare pleasure, Mr. Farrell. At times I fancy that the solitude of my study tends to repel visitors."

He carefully fitted his fingers tip to tip, beamed at Farrell with a trace of condescending cordiality, and permitted himself a glance at the none too neatly wrapped parcel that marred the orderly desk top.

Farrell cut the string and pulled the silver peacock from its newspaper swaddling.

"A young lady asked me to deliver this," remarked Farrell casually as though being drafted as a messenger were part of his daily routine.

"Er-r, most unusual, Mr. Farrell," declaimed the scholar. His eyes widened perceptibly. Parr was plainly at loss.

Farrell wondered if Parr realized how truly extraordinary the transaction had been. The morning papers of course had not contained a word concerning the kidnapping. Farrell knew that despite Parr's evident discomfort, that bland, pompous little man, whose bachelor of oratory diploma held a place of honor among his collection of framed dignities and degrees, would be a slippery customer. And seeing that Parr was itching to be alone with the peacock, Farrell lost no time in making himself a nuisance.

"Mr. Parr," he began, giving an acceptable rendition of the orator's formality, "I took the liberty of closely scrutinizing that unusual example of the silversmith's art. *Very closely* scrutinizing it, I might say."

He paused impressively, noted the increasing concern on his host's pale features, he resumed, "And while I certainly can not lay claim to learning even remotely approaching your own, I was nevertheless convinced—"

The pauses were driving Parr's consternation to the surface; therefore he indulged in an elaborate gesture, smiled engagingly.

"Convinced that this effigy has an unusual history. The inscription, 'The work of the Slave of the Angel, Abdannar, emir of the faithful, may our Lord be well pleased with him,' reminds me of a certain episode a number of years ago, while I was in Kurdistan. However, that which follows—"

Parr, having reached the end of his endurance, interrupted.

"Might I suggest, if you grasp my meaning, but what I intended to convey was that that inscription is figurative? One of those obscure Oriental plays on words. Exceedingly ambiguous, you understand—"

As Parr paused, not for dramatic effect, but to collect his wits, Farrell, convinced beyond all doubt that he was on the right trail, drove home.

"Right you are!" he declared in his usual decisive tone. "And a solution does tax one's ingenuity. Otherwise, I would have delivered it last night. And now that I'm here, I want to know where you got this, and why it was necessary to have it carried to New Orleans by special courier. And why did it leave Mount Lalesh, in the Sinjar Hills?"

"I'm sure I don't quite know what you mean," replied Parr. His hand trembled, and his fingers played nervously with the severed cords of the cardboard box.

"I mean," explained Farrell, "why did you smuggle it into the United States?"

Parr's perceptibly protruding eyes evaded Farrell's intent gaze.

"Where did you get it, and what's behind it?" demanded Farrell as he planted his hands on Parr's desk and leaned forward to fire his questions directly at the disconcerted scholar. "It's none of my business, but I don't think that you're in any position to tell me so!"

"I bought it in Paris," replied Parr. "From a dealer who insisted—"

"I understand," countered Farrell with significant emphasis, and a nod of his head. "I've bought things myself from dealers who wanted the transaction kept confidential, only I took better precautions than you did. All right?"

"I picked up a XVI Century Persian manuscript," continued Parr. "A most unusual document which referred to this very image. And by a happy chance I found the image itself, a week or so later—"

"Uh-huh. I got it," said Farrell with an amiable smile.

"And in view of the unusual circumstances, I assure you, the dealer did not fully explain—it was necessary—"

"To smuggle it into this country and have it delivered by courier. Now open up and tell me the rest of it." Farrell paused, then essayed a shot in the dark: "Or would you rather talk to Federal agents?"

Parr started. His pale face became white.

"There is absolutely nothing more to say, Mr. Farrell. I assure you nothing at all," he replied in a low voice. "But may I ask what your interest might be?"

"You may. And if you remember something, later on, you might phone me and tell me about it, particularly when I tell you that this silver peacock ties you up with the murder of William Burnham!"

"Oh, I say, Mr. Farrell—" gasped Parr, and then stopped short.

But Farrell did not pause to await Parr's regaining the power of speech.

"Let him simmer," reflected Farrell as the door closed behind him. "Longer he thinks, the more he'll cough up when I hear from him. And if he is messed up with the killing—well, we'll see."

He drove down Saint Charles Avenue.

"Better stop at the bank and ask Goodman to round up a hundred thousand in new bills, according to the peacock's prescription. Humor 'em till I can open up with that pair of Brownings and let 'em smell hell!"

Farrell's conference with a friend who occupied an inside desk at the First Trust was brief, and involved no more than a request to have the desired quantity and denomination at Farrell's disposal. This done, he resumed his drive down town, toward police headquarters.

"Hi, there, Glenn," greeted Healy as Farrell stepped into the office of the Chief of Detectives. "Been trying to get you all day. Now give me an earful about the red-headed girl. How'd you happen to get in on that job, and what's it got to do with Burnham's death? We've not found as much as a tire track of the car they kidnapped her in."

Farrell briefly outlined the entry of the silver peacock.

"She checked out," he concluded, "before I could make her stay. She was too rattle brained to think that the gang would chase her, as they'd naturally not know she'd left the peacock with me. And when I heard a car roaring by like the hammers of hell, just a few minutes later, and the brakes squealing like a locomotive whistle as they made the turn toward the L.&N., I knew business was picking up, so I started out. Could have been a bunch of merry drunks, but I had a hunch."

"A hunch," admitted Healy, "is better'n a lot of good sense. But where does the bird fit in? All I know so far is that she was *some* girl, or you'd told her to chase herself and her peacock. Musta been the kind you buy fur coats for—"

"Nuts!" countered Farrell. "Not that kind at all. Nice girl, and I'll tell—"

"Pipe down, pipe down," grumbled Healy. "I know she musta been a knockout, making you forget your hide and a hundred grand. I'm interested in peacocks, now."

"All right," agreed Farrell, "here you go: first, there are too many peacocks in the picture *all at once*. Second, the engraving on the peacock."

He quoted the first line of the inscription.

"Without going into details, that peacock and as much of the inscription as I could translate, convinces me there is a crew of devil worshippers—"

"Eh, what's that?" demanded Healy, removing his feet from his desk.

"Devil worshippers, John," repeated Farrell. "A tribe called Yezidees. Hang out in Kurdistan, a district in Western Persia. They worship Satan, represent him as a peacock, and call him *Malik Tawus*."

"Holy smoke!" exclaimed Healy. "Do you mean there's a bunch of heathen rats of that kind runnin' around town, worshippin' Satan? And—" he added as an afterthought, "killing and blackmailing."

"Looks a lot like it," replied Farrell. "Understand this is just a hunch, and the case isn't *proved*. But I've been in Kurdistan and I know 'em. They have a temple in the Sinjar Hills. They let me into it, although I couldn't go beyond a certain point."

Healy regarded Farrell askance.

"I've a notion to run you in as a dangerous and suspicious character," he muttered, still trying to reconcile the fact that a rational man had associated with devil worshippers.

Farrell laughed.

"Don't worry, John, I didn't spend any time worshipping Old Nick, but I did learn a few things. For instance, that it's even forbidden to pronounce the name of Satan—*Shaytan*—in their dialect. The penalty is death, then and there, for using the holy name. So they say *Malik Tawus* instead."

"Well, where does Parr come in?" wondered Healy.

"Don't know, exactly," admitted Farrell. "He went straight up in the air when I blatted right out that I knew he'd smuggled the bird into the country, and that he was tying in pretty close with the murder of Burnham. The learned doctor is worried and plenty."

"Hell!" scoffed Healy. "He may have smuggled some antiques, but he can't be mixed up in murder." Then as Farrell rose to leave, "And in the meanwhile, be watching your own hide."

"That," countered Farrell, pausing at the door, "is something I'm giving an uncommon amount of thought. I'll be at the Howard Memorial this afternoon, getting a bit of dope on puzzling out the rest of that peacock inscription. And this evening you can get me at the Union Club, if anything turns up. Be seeing you!"

CHAPTER IV
Nuri Plays a Stack

That evening, not more than an hour after dinner, Farrell received a telephone call from Healy. In response to the urgent summons, Farrell went immediately to headquarters, where he found the chief of detectives impatiently awaiting his arrival.

"Take a ride with me," he began as Farrell entered the office. "We're going to make a pinch, right away!"

"The devil you say!" exclaimed Farrell, as he turned back toward the door, to follow Healy and two plainclothes men to the police department car that was waiting at the curbing. "Where do I come in on this show?"

"You seem pretty well posted on peacocks," replied Healy as then, headed toward Canal Street. "And this kinda checks in with what you told me this afternoon."

"Parr, you mean?" wondered Farrell. "Or—"

"Wait and see," evaded Healy. "I know you're all eaten up about that redheaded girl, but we've not got a thing in that quarter, so far."

They left Canal Street and drove several blocks into the French Quarter, where they parked. Then they proceeded on foot toward Decatur Street, crossed, and picked their way through a series of alleys. They finally halted in the shadow of a warehouse which faced the River Café, a speak-easy that masqueraded as a soft drink parlor and lunch counter.

Several minutes later a laborer, drunken and mumbling, lurched past their point of observation.

"That's Bronson," whispered Healy. "That boy can stage a drunk in anything, starting with coveralls and working up to soup and fish, with a gold headed cane. He'll cover the joint from the inside."

The drunken Bronson had successfully passed the side door of the speak-easy. The doors were still swinging, although not as violently as at first, when a cab drew up at the main entrance.

"Look! By God, it's working!" exclaimed Healy. "A Liberty cab! Just like they said."

A small, slightly stooped man emerged from the cab. He carried a square cardboard box nestled in the crook of his left arm. After pausing a moment to peer nervously about him, he entered the speak-easy.

"Hillman Parr!" whispered Farrell.

"Right," assented Healy. Then, to the plainclothes men, "Alcide, you and Johnson cover the side door. Farrell, you follow me. All right, get set."

They shifted their holsters, and loosened their pistols. The two plain-clothes men were tense, and ready to charge. Healy's broad red face was set and scowling. He lifted his hat, wiped his forehead, jammed his hat firmly down to his ears.

"Look out you don't pop old man Parr," cautioned Healy. "But don't take any chances on anyone else. Pour it to 'em first and question—"

A crash of glass and a yell interrupted his remark. The quartet leaped from concealment and dashed across the narrow street. As they crashed through the swinging doors, they saw the no longer drunken Bronson covering three men with a pistol that wavered no more than the muzzle of a siege gun.

"Don't shoot!" quavered Parr. But when Healy flashed his shield, Parr regained his courage.

"Gentlemen, this is an outrage," he protested.

"Take those two birds away!" directed Healy, indicating Parr's companions. And then, "Mr. Parr, I'd like to have you accompany us."

"But I protest against this outrage!" exclaimed Parr. "These two men and I were meeting here on purely private business. I assure you—"

"Sorry. Mr. Parr," replied Healy with courteous deference to the learned man's substantial position in the city, "but we'll need you as a material witness. Farrell, you and Mr. Parr take a cab and meet us at headquarters."

"Okay," assented Farrell. And before the collector could begin an address: "Mr. Parr, as far as I know, no Federal men are interested."

Farrell smiled at Parr's sigh of relief.

* * * *

The detectives had departed with their prisoners and were escorting them toward Chartres Street, where the squad car was parked. Farrell and Parr were waiting at the curbing near the side door of the speakeasy.

"Come to think of it," remarked Farrell as he looked down the dark, narrow street, "there aren't many cabs cruising along here. Maybe I'd better phone for one."

Farrell stepped back into the speak-easy and glanced about him.

"That little guy left his package lying here in the mix-up," said the proprietor, as Farrell stepped toward the phone booth.

Farrell picked up the parcel and tucked it under his arm.

"Parr must be up in the air, forgetting that precious bird," he said to himself as he dropped a nickel into the coin box. "Main 7400—"

But the call was not completed. Farrell heard a suddenly stifled cry of alarm, then an agonized groan, and gasping. He drew his pistol, and dashed from the telephone booth toward the side entrance. Parr lay on the paving, groaning and clutching at his chest.

"Call an ambulance!" Farrell shouted as the proprietor, following him, stopped short as he saw the body lying on the paving. Farrell fired at the figure he saw disappearing into an entrance several doors down the dark side street.

As Farrell reached the entrance into which the fugitive had vanished, he heard a door slam and a latch click in the darkness. The assassin had blocked pursuit. Moreover. Parr's remarks, if he could make any, would be worth more than anything that could be expected of blundering into the darkness. Farrell accordingly retraced his steps.

Parr's pale face was grayish, and the bland, suave features were drawn with pain. A red foam flecked his lips.

"Do you know who stabbed you?" began Farrell as he knelt beside the dying man.

"Nuri...that peacock..."

The rest of his speech was unintelligible.

"Nuri?" repeated Farrell. "That his name? Nuri?"

Parr was incapable of speech; but he made a successful effort to nod.

"And curtains!" said Farrell a moment later. "Dead as Julius Caesar."

Farrell stepped back into the speak-easy. The cardboard box was still lying where he had dropped it in his haste to run to the attack on the sidewalk. He seized the box, hefted it and noted that it was not empty.

"Phone police headquarters," Farrell directed.

The proprietor complied. Farrell, pistol drawn, stood guard by the body, wondering when or if a hit and run assassin would emerge from the shadows to make a clean sweep.

* * * *

A squad car arrived before the ambulance. Two patrolmen were left to watch the body. Farrell accompanied the corporal back to headquarters, and went directly to Healy's office.

"Give me the low-down," began Healy as they took seats at his desk. "Every detail as closely as you can remember." Farrell complied.

"And now," resumed Healy, at the end of the recital, "give me your guesses. All of 'em. I don't care how wild they are. Now what was the name Parr pronounced before he croaked?"

"Nuri."

"Huh! Don't make much sense," remarked Healy.

"Man's name in Arabic," countered Farrell.

"More of those damned Turks!" interpolated Healy. "All right?"

"Parr was stabbed in the chest, so he had a chance to recognize his assailant. And he named him," continued Farrell. "The box contained the peacock. I peeped on my way up here; and here's the bird, on your desk.

"Either Nuri struck before he noticed that Parr didn't have the box, or else he didn't want the box. If it was just the box he wanted, he could have nailed Parr later, instead of striking right under our noses.

"We do know that two men did want the peacock, and met Parr to pick it up. You've got them. Somebody else—Nuri—wanted Parr's hide, and he got it. Now dope it out."

Healy glared at the silver bird on his desk.

"That damned hoodoo! I thought your line about devil worshippers was pure hooey, but if the devil isn't messed up in this, I'm a monkey's uncle!"

"Who tipped you off to make that raid?" asked Farrell.

"Anonymous. Couldn't trace it. Said Parr was being shaken down by the same outfit that got Burnham. And—"

The entrance of a clerk cut further discussion of the call.

"Look at what we found in Parr's inside coat pocket," he said as he laid a sheet of paper on the desk.

"Hell's bells!" exclaimed Healy, as he recognized the familiar red wax and its sinister signet. "That anonymous caller sure knew what he was talking about." It was a short note:

Take the peacock to the River Café on Decatur Street at 8:30 and give it to Gordon and Rubenstein. Do not go in your own car but call a Liberty cab. Do not notify the police. Obey orders or follow Burnham.

"Boy, this is hot! We got 'em now—Rubenstein and Gordon are the guys we pinched. Nothin' to do but hang 'em for knifing Burnham!" Healy shifted his cigar stump, leaned back in his chair, and beamed with satisfaction. Farrell, however, did not share his enthusiasm.

"Maybe, and maybe not," he objected. "There's still something fishy about this."

"Fishy, hell!" exclaimed Healy. "And I'm going to put 'em over the hurdles myself and find out what all this peacock stuff is about!"

"See you in the morning, John," said Farrell as he stepped to the door. "And never mind having me tailed. No one's going to pop me off until after pay day!"

CHAPTER V

Inside the Peacock

Dubois, the clerk at the desk, greeted Farrell as he stepped from the elevator to the main floor of the Union Club, the morning following the death of Parr.

"A gentleman left a message for you about half an hour ago."

"Thanks, Dubois," acknowledged Farrell. He opened the envelope.

Good work, making arrangements to raise that money. Remember Burnham and Parr, and forget this nonsense about chasing us with machine guns.

The peacock-seal authenticated the message beyond any doubt. The brazen assurance of the enemy was shaking Farrell, despite his determination to fight it to a finish. The assassination of Burnham and Parr had savored of executions rather than murders. And this was the morning of the twenty-first. One hundred thousand by midnight or else—!

Before leaving New Orleans, Farrell stopped at police headquarters to get the overnight developments that had resulted from the arrest of Gordon and Rubenstein.

"Another souvenir for you," Farrell replied to Healy's greeting, and presented the morning's reminder from the peacock.

"Hell's hinges!" exclaimed Healy, as he read the note. "They are watching you closely. Are you paying off, or will you smoke 'em out?"

"So far, I'm still for shooting it out," declared Farrell, "even though they're wise to my plan. But what's really eating at me is what's happened to Lydia Wilson. She knows too much and they're going to cut her throat, just on general principles."

Farrell shook his head, bit the tip off a cigar, and sank into a chair.

"What did Gordon and Rubenstein have to say about Nuri?"

"A page full," affirmed Healy. "But they've got the guts to claim they don't know anything about those peacock notes! And that's only half the rich story. They handed us a hot one about the peacock being stuffed full of pearls smuggled in from the other side. Said they were trying to get the pearls, and later, return the peacock to Parr. I ask you, ain't that a hot one?"

"The devil you say!" exclaimed Farrell, sitting bolt upright and regarding Healy intently. "That ties in with my hunch on Parr, right from the start. Did you open the bird?"

"They opened it," answered Healy. "Funny hocus-pocus work, twisting its neck, and feeling around for hidden catches and the like, and click! It split right in half—though looking at it, you couldn't have seen a sign of a seam anywhere —"

"But the pearls?" persisted Farrell.

"Empty!" grunted Healy. "What did you expect?"

"Wait a minute!" countered Farrell. "Maybe there *was* something in it. Parr was squirming like he had worms, the minute I got him believing I read the inscription. You see, it may be the combination for opening the peacock. Get it?"

"Uh-uh…maybe," admitted Healy. "But where'n hell's the pearls? They couldn't have been taken at any time after Parr stepped out of the taxi, in front of the River Cafe, and you didn't snitch them on your way to headquarters."

Farrell smiled.

"I might have, if I'd known how to open the damned bird. But that the pearls weren't in it when Gordon & Company opened it doesn't prove there never were any.

"It's a cinch Gordon and Rubinstein didn't keep that engagement just for their health. They believed it contained something they wanted. And then the unknown Mr. Nuri kills Parr the minute my back is turned. If he had wanted the peacock, he could have waylaid Parr on his way home, but Nuri didn't want the peacock, because he knew it was empty. Parr was killed to keep him from talking to the police."

"Yeah, that's reasonable," agreed Healy. "But what of it? What's that got to do with killing Burnham, and shaking you down for a hundred grand?"

"That," declared Farrell, "means that Nuri is higher up in this crew than Rubenstein and Gordon. Nuri is the guy that pulled the strings. Get him and you'll know something. By the way, where did Gordon and his buddy say Nuri hung out?"

"They didn't know for sure," replied Healy. "But they suspected it was at a Syrian restaurant on Decatur Street, not far from the River Café. Aswad's place, they called it, whatever kind of name that is."

"Better and better!" exulted Farrell. "Did you raid the joint?"

"Yeah, and drew a blank. All blanks!" growled Healy from the right of his cigar. Then he gave a detailed account of Aswad's restaurant, patronized by Syrians and Armenians, for the sake of its native cooking, served on the ground floor, and the highly alcoholic *'araki* served upstairs.

"These winding passages in back of the main room wouldn't fool anyone. We just had to break down a few doors, and even at that, the poor saps didn't get all their liquor ditched."

Farrell pondered for a moment, and regarded his cigar ash.

"That peacock gang," he finally remarked, "know all about me arming my boat. And with what you've just told me, I'm going to spring a surprise they won't have time to dope out."

"I'll go to Pass Christian tonight, to establish my presence. After dark, I'll run my boat into the Gulf and come ashore at Waveland in a canoe. You pick me up there and drive me back to New Orleans, and I'll start the show."

Healy frowned, and scratched his head.

"Where's the surprise?" he demanded.

"I'm going to Aswad's disguised as a native," replied Farrell, "and while they are hunting me all over New Orleans or Pass Christian to knife me for not paying off, I'll be in the safest place in the world: right in their own hangout. You pick me up half an hour after sunset, right where the road leaves the seawall."

CHAPTER VI
Yezidee Den

Shortly before sunset, Farrell cruised about in the neighborhood of Cat Island. After tossing empty oil cans overboard, he turned the wheel over to old Isaac, then with bursts of machine gun fire riddled them. But as the sun approached the horizon, Farrell abandoned his target practice and set to work with a razor. A few strokes removed his moustache. With tweezers he began shaping his eyebrows until they rose from a thin line to decided points at the middle.

As they headed out toward Waveland, Farrell stained his entire body.

"Not bad, not half bad," he commented, as he regarded his make-up in the mirror. "Now for the last touch."

Farrell's four front teeth matched their mates perfectly. His dentist had been a master of his profession, and had fashioned a removable bridge that was a work of art. Farrell plucked the platinum anchors between thumb and forefingers, removed the bridge, and for a moment considered the craftsmanship which so neatly camouflaged a gap left by a pistol butt in the course of a heated argument in Mexico.

"Isaac," he pronounced painstakingly, "take these teeth and put 'em in my dresser. And now unlash that canoe. I'm going over the side. You'd better leave the house and spend the next few days with friends. Lay low until I come back. Understand?"

"Yassah. Mistah Glenn. Yo'all's takin' a trip fo' yo' health an' ain't nobody s'posed to know," replied the old negro with a knowing grin.

Whereupon Farrell went over the side and into the canoe. As he paddled toward Waveland, Isaac started up the motors and headed back toward the pier at Pass Christian.

Farrell, when he came within wading depth of the breakwater that lines the coast for miles, set the canoe adrift and started ashore. A glance at his watch assured him that he had timed his maneuvers so that Healy, if he was on time, would pass within a few minutes.

His machine gun practice, Farrell reflected as he seated himself on the breakwater, should have given any observers the impression that he was determined to shoot it out. At all events, they would scarcely expect to find him in their midst, and disguise, being a matter of gesture and mannerism rather than striking external changes, did not particularly worry Farrell.

A car was approaching the turn in the road that leads at right angles away from the breakwater.

"Hi, buddy, give me a lift!" Farrell hailed, jerking his thumb.

"I'm stopping at Waveland," said the man at the wheel as he slowed down and glanced about him. The driver was John Healy.

"That's all right," countered Farrell. "Gimme a lift that far. Been hiking all day. Ain't et since yester-day."

Healy tossed him a quarter.

"Get yourself some grub and beat it!" he growled.

"Thanks, John, but I'd rather ride," insisted Farrell.

"Well, I'll be damned!" exclaimed Healy. "That ought to fool them."

"It'd better," said Farrell as he stepped into the car. "My hide if it doesn't."

* * * *

As they cleared Waveland, Farrell continued, "Aswad's has to be the right place. That raid of yours was too easy. They serve liquor on the ground floor. Why bother with that back room? There's a chance that your raid last night carried you through a maze of passages and into the building next door."

"That's possible!" admitted Healy.

As they drove toward New Orleans, Farrell continued his argument.

240

"Another thing I checked up with the Public Service, just before I left town this afternoon. I found out there's been a sudden increase in the amount of power they use at Aswad's—something behind the scenes. Meter spinning like a top, and hardly any lights burning in front. Get it?

"And finally, Aswad's is the only low class Syrian joint in town. In other words, the only place a gang like that could use as a front. Any place else they'd be too conspicuous, coming and going."

As they drove into New Orleans, and drew up along the curbing of upper Magazine Street, Farrell concluded the outline of his plans.

"You cover the joint from the outside, but don't try to crash it until I start the circus. They're likely to cut that girl's throat at the first sign of trouble. She knows too much. Camp on the job. I may be in there a couple of days."

"Hell's fire, you may be there a lot longer," was Healy's pessimistic farewell as he grasped Farrell's hand. "But here's luck."

Farrell watched the tail light of Healy's car disappear around the corner. Then he inspected his pistol, and shifted into a handier position the sheaths of the pair of long bladed knives at his belt. They were similar in design to those that had stabbed Burnham.

Half an hour's brisk walk brought Farrell to Canal Street, beyond whose bright lights lay the black shadows of Decatur Street, and the French Quarter.

Aswad's place, less than half a block from the River Café, was in the blackest of shadows cast by the warehouses across the street. It was on the ground floor of an old, dilapidated stone building. The one on its right had been recently razed.

Farrell entered and took his place at a vacant table.

The air was dense with the fumes of half a dozen gurgling, bubbling water-pipes the Syrian hangers-on were smoking. Backgammon and pinochle games were in progress. The players chattered and gesticulated with an enthusiasm entirely in contradiction of home-grown ideas on Oriental poise.

Farrell called for coffee and a water-pipe, slouched back in his chair, and gazed about. At the rear of the dining room were two doors. One led to the lavatory. The other, presumably led to the back room which Healy's men had vainly raided.

Half an hour passed.

Aswad's place was grimy, dingy, greasy—but so far, it showed no sign of the sinister *habitués* that Farrell expected to encounter. His arrival had been scarcely noticed, just another stranger seeking a pipe and coffee, and an evening of idleness.

"Ya Aswad! Shewayya 'araki!" roared a burly, ruddy faced fellow at Farrell's right, indicating with a gesture that all at his table were to be served with more of the fiery liquor whose milky dregs still clouded their glasses.

"Sell liquor openly enough," reflected Farrell. "That supposed drinking room on the second floor must be a plant to side-track raiding parties looking for something else—peacocks, for instance. And sooner or later, someone will go in or out of that door to the right of the lavatory."

Farrell settled down to maintain a close watch on the unused door. He ordered more coffee, and called for fresh charcoal to complete the burning of the tobacco that was still in his pipe. He picked up and glanced at an Arabic newspaper lying on a vacant table.

The sudden lull in the chatter of the natives startled Farrell. He glanced about and saw a newcomer stalk majestically across the room, and pause to greet the proprietor, oily, hook-nosed Aswad.

"Business is picking up!" was Farrell's thought. "That lad's no Syrian merchant or Armenian pedlar. Looks like a Kurd and talks like one."

The proprietor paid his respectful compliments. The Kurd bowed, acknowledged the salutations of several of the patrons, then stalked toward *the* door.

Farrell forced himself to continue drawing languidly at the mouthpiece of his pipe. He called for more coffee. As it was being served, he remarked, "I am a Kurd, and a stranger."

Then he paused and made a quick gesture with his left hand, and a sign with his fingers.

"Do you know if any of the brethren will recognize me?"

The proprietor's eyebrows rose.

"Allah alone is wise, all-knowing," he evaded as his eyes shifted for a passing glance at the door.

Farrell realized that his conclusions were far from certainty. In the last analysis he would have to trust to American bluff with Oriental trimmings. And entering whatever rooms lay beyond the door might be very much easier than leaving them.

Farrell drank his coffee, rose, and approached the door. He tapped. He felt that every eye in the dining room was regarding him. The chattering of the players ceased, and the pipes no longer bubbled and gurgled. The door opened. As Farrell stepped into the dimly illuminated cubicle, a figure emerged from the shadows and challenged him.

"A slave of the peacock and a servant of the fire," he replied in Arabic.

The guardian, whose features Farrell could barely distinguish, muttered a phrase of assent. The door behind Farrell closed; bolts clicked into place; and before he could gain a clear picture of the cubicle, the lights flashed out, leaving him in absolute darkness. A hand urged him to his left. Farrell heard a grating, sliding sound as of panels moving.

Then a switch clicked, and Farrell saw that he was in a passageway of brick. There was no sign of the maze that Healy had described. Farrell's guide led the way up a flight of stairs.

The door at the head of the stairs opened to admit them. His guide stepped aside, leaving Farrell to confront a bulky, pock-marked man who sat at a desk which commanded the entrance to what seemed to be an anteroom. Again Farrell heard a lock click, and a bolt slide home behind him, but he returned the unwavering scrutiny of the swarthy, unpleasant features of the inner guardian.

Finally the man at the desk addressed Farrell in Arabic.

"Whom do you seek?"

"The Master, and the keeper of the Silver Peacock," replied Farrell as he repeated the gesture with which he had accosted Aswad, the proprietor of the restaurant. Then he continued, quoting, "God created of fire seven bright spirits, even as a man lights seven tapers one after another; and the chief of these was *Malik Tawus*, to whom—"

"No good!" snapped the man at the desk, interrupting with a peremptory gesture Farrell's quotation from the Yezidee's *Al Yalvah*. "You're in the wrong place."

The speech was equivocal: it might either signify that Farrell had not yet satisfactorily established his identity as a servant of the Peacock, or, what increased his peril, that he was not in a rendezvous of Yezidees.

Retreat was impossible, unless Farrell leaped to the doorkeeper's desk and plunged through the fanlight in the wall behind it. Farrell advanced a pace. He heard the whirr of a buzzer. After an interval of a few seconds came an answering buzzer-note.

"Tell Hassan about it," directed the man at the desk, indicating with a gesture the opening that was revealed by the sliding aside of a panel.

Farrell stepped across the threshold and into the sultry glare of a great bronze lamp that hung from the ceiling. He glanced about him and saw along the walls a dozen men sitting cross legged on the floor. Their features were as devoid of animation as though they were in a trance. They were dressed in the tropical worsteds worn at that season in New Orleans, which, with their alien features and posture was an incongruity that was heightened by the white turban and *kaftan* worn by the old man who sat on a cushioned platform at the further end of the room. Farrell advanced along the narrow carpet that led from the entrance to the dais of Hassan, the master of the show.

"I heard your recital to Zayd," began the old man with disconcerting abruptness as Farrell halted. "You have made a serious error in coming here. Our interest in peacocks is not what you think. We are not Yezidees."

Hassan's eyes regarded Farrell with feline fierceness.

Farrell knew then that his peril was acute. An impostor who ventures into a sanctuary of the Yezidees does so at the risk of his life; but it is equally dangerous for a Yezidee to mingle with fanatic Moslems. Hassan's smile as he stroked his beard was no omen of a happy ending.

"Prolonged of Life," said Farrell with a nonchalance that he achieved with considerable effort, "Since I am intruding, give me your blessing and I will leave."

But Hassan gave neither his blessing nor his consent, which according to Oriental etiquette Farrell required before he might leave. Instead, Hassan spoke a single word, a fatal word that Farrell as a Yezidee could not ignore: *Shaytan*, the forbidden true name of *Malik Tawus*, the Lord Peacock, which no Yezidee might hear pronounced in his presence, and permit the speaker to live.

If Farrell did not strike, he would be branding himself as an impostor; and if he struck, those along the wall would overwhelm him. Farrell was neatly trapped by his own cleverness.

There was no retreat. He drew his knife. Hassan smiled. Despite his age, he radiated a consuming energy and fierceness.

"Steady!" he warned in a low, mocking voice, "they will kill you before you reach me."

"No matter," retorted Farrell, "you have pronounced the Forbidden Name."

Farrell sensed that if he retreated from his stand, the end would be more disastrous than if he drove through to a finish. Those who sat along the wall had risen to their feet and drawn long, curved knives.

Hassan's smile was whimsical, and sinister.

Farrell lunged full to the chest. Hassan chuckled as he recoiled before the impact. The blade snapped and tinkled to the floor. Hassan, it seemed, very prudently wore a shirt of chain mail beneath his white *kaftan*.

"And now that you've made a very fair attempt," he purred, "can you let well enough alone, or must you attempt to tear me to pieces with your bare hands?" He gestured to his henchmen, who retreated. Then he resumed, "Suppose you forget your Lord Peacock. You have courage, although your wits are rather dull. You might have known that every silver peacock is not attended by priests from the Sinjar Hills."

Hassan's voice was now gently mocking, as though he were with exceptional broadmindedness letting a pagan peacock-worshipper live instead of having him cut to pieces.

"Now tell me what you're doing here, blustering into this rather private place and quoting from a book whose very mention is enough to tempt any true Moslem to cut your throat?"

"The peacock," improvised Farrell, "was stolen from Mount Lalesh. I heard, in one way and another, that it is here. And to assure my friends that it is in good hands—"

Farrell shrugged, and gestured. Hassan nodded and smiled.

"In this city," he counseled, "the less you know of peacocks, the better. It is not here, and never was. Now, since you were so ready to stab an unarmed old man who had pronounced a forbidden word, I think that if we can settle our religious difference we might come to an understanding. *Ay, wallah!* Stab an unarmed old man—and in the face of a dozen armed retainers... Hmmmm...not bad...

"Who are you?"

Farrell started at the abrupt question that had popped at him from the old man's musing.

"Ayyub the son of Yusuf," he replied promptly, assuming a name that he had used, years ago, in his wanderings as a native.

"Very well, Ayyub bin Yusuf," said Hassan, again stroking his white beard. "In spite of your outrageous beliefs, there is a place prepared for you in Paradise."

Hassan's smile was as ambiguous as his speech. Farrell's glance shifted at the armed retainers along the wall. A dozen thirsty blades—place in Paradise, indeed!

Then a familiar memory began clamoring for recognition. Those staring eyes with their dilated pupils—

Hassan's smile widened.

"La, billah!" he reassured as he noted Farrell's side glance. "That's not the road I had in mind. You still think that because you stabbed an unarmed old man, I am resentful. By no means, *ya* Ayyub! To the contrary."

He extended his hand, palm up, toward Farrell.

"I hold Paradise in the hollow of my hand," he said in his rich, sonorous Arabic. "Yea, even *al-jannat*. I am the keeper of the gateway. You have but to believe, and abandon your infidel heresies."

An old familiar exhortation, and Farrell recollected those he had seen in Syria and Egypt who had dilated eyes that stared at sights and wonders that were not perceptible to the un-drugged. Hasheesh! The riddle was being resolved.

Farrell stared at the inscrutable eyes of Hassan, but could not guess whether the old man was leading up to some monstrous, fatal jest, or whether in his extravagant Oriental figures of speech he was seeking a recruit to his entourage of hasheesh addicts.

"And to convince you, you shall see the place that is prepared for true believers. A glimpse of its coolness and its fountains. I, even I, Hassan, am keeper of the gateway, and I will let you see for yourself."

Farrell's increasing interest was unfeigned. He concealed, however, his determination to plunge through to the end, and instead pretended to have doubts.

"While we believe in Muhammed, upon whom be the Peace, and in the One True God—whose name be exalted—it is not well to slight *Malik Tawus*, Lord of the World and all its evils! But, nevertheless..." Farrell paused, perplexed and indecisive.

Hassan's smile became more assuring.

"Try and see, *ya* Ayyub...rich wine and the lovely brides of the garden, and coolness to the eyes. And if you still refuse, why, then, you refuse."

"Done!" agreed Farrell. "Provided that no one pronounces the Forbidden Name in my presence, until—"

"I understand," said Hassan. "That will be arranged. These stubborn Yezidees!"

Hassan clapped his hands.

"*Ya* Abbas!" he shouted.

A panel at the left of the dais opened and a tall negro entered.

"Ayyub is our new brother. Take him to the Gateway!"

* * * *

The negro led Farrell to a narrow, high ceiled reception hall along whose walls extended a low platform, about two feet wide and covered with rugs and cushions, on which half a dozen Syrian Arabs lay stretched out in a drugged stupor.

Abbas, the negro, returned presently with a tray of sweetmeats and a pitcher of wine. History was repeating itself: the fanatic Ismailian sect of Islam was blossoming out in New Orleans under the guidance of a master criminal. Farrell knew that he was expected to drink himself into a stupor; then, overcome by the hasheesh drugged wine, he would be carried into a synthetic paradise which to the distorted perceptions of an addict would seem real. After an interval in paradise, he would again be drugged, and upon awakening would find himself in the ante-room again, having supposedly returned from what might be called a week-end excursion to the Moslem paradise.

Then Hassan, if he had not in the meantime learned Farrell's true identity, would give him a knife, and name a victim whose death would be the price of a return to the delights of the garden. For several centuries, during the Crusades, the Ismailians, or Assassins, as they were called, were the plague of Syria, Egypt, and Persia; and now, in modern guise, they were invading New Orleans to practice extortion from wealthy business men instead of from emirs and sultans as they had in the old days.

Farrell tasted the wine. It reeked with hasheesh. He knew not what eyes might be regarding him. Hassan's ready acceptance might have been to submit him to the test of wits upset by drugs, and a will conquered by the hypnotic power of the infusion of hasheesh. Yet such a trap could not be evaded. Farrell therefore drained the pitcher without taking it from his lips; and as he gulped the drugged wine, he contemplated a trick that might in a measure counter-act the full effect of its insidious poison.

"*Ya* Abbas!" he yelled drunkenly as he set down the empty pitcher. "*Shewayya khamr!* More wine!"

He lurched and reeled about the room. Then he began singing bawdy songs in Turki. He tossed sweetmeats at his unconscious comrades, and finally sent the serving tray sailing against the wall.

Abbas came running.

"More wine!" demanded Farrell.

And more wine he received. He had already taken enough to drug two men, but he had drunk so rapidly that its effect had not enough time to develop.

"Hold on," he muttered to himself as he gritted his teeth. "Can't pass out! Got to stay safe and sane; one boner, and it's lights out! And if she's alive, she's in that hell's hole of a garden."

Farrell shuddered at the possibility—worse, probability, that Lydia was in Hassan's synthetic paradise, and at the mercy of Hassan's drugged assassins.

He drank more. He reeled, staggered, and dropped into a corner. His actions would establish him as a Kurd gone mad with wine to which he was not accustomed.

"A bit of mustard and warm water would help," he reflected. "And I'd give a thousand bucks for ten cents worth of syrup of ipecac...oh, hell, or even a feather..."

But Farrell's improvised emetic worked famously. Neither his companions, even if their unconsciousness was feigned, nor watcher from the outside could have suspected the trick. He rose, relieved of his excessive draughts of wine, then, consistently, howled for more. He seized the pitcher that Abbas brought, tripped, fell flat, spilling the drugged wine over himself, the couch, and the floor.

"Good camouflage," he said to himself. "Now fake passing out...damn it, hope I've not soaked up enough of the stuff to make it real."

Farrell was alarmed; for he did feel the effect of the drug. His heart beat seemed very slow and heavy, with incredible pauses when it seemed to have stopped entirely. In the dim light he regarded his outstretched hand, still clutching at the pitcher. He marveled at the monstrous fingers. The room alternately contracted to the size of a match-box, and expanded to rival the dome of the Capitol. But despite these and other disturbing illusions, Farrell knew that he had established himself without having become soddenly drugged. And he understood how an ignorant, fanatical Moslem, passing from hasheesh illusions into

246

sleep, and thence to an awakening in a synthetic paradise, could scarcely do other than believe that he had by special dispensation been translated alive to a true paradise.

CHAPTER VII
The Garden of Evil

While Farrell retained consciousness, his perception of time became as distorted as the fixtures of the room. Thus he did not have any idea of how much time had elapsed before someone turned a light full on his face, seized him, and carried him away. For a moment Farrell wondered if the sudden transition from the New Orleans humidity to the dim coolness into which he had been dropped was not, like the distortions of time and space, another illusion. He heard faint, sobbing music as from a great distance. He sensed that others were being carried into the coolness after him.

At times Farrell's senses left him. He knew not whether the blank intervals had been five second or five hours, yet it seemed that his unconscious moments were fleeting. Someone was supporting his head and offering him a cold, sour drink that refreshed him and cleared his rambling wits and reeling senses. His head sank back upon a cushion before he could catch more than a glimpse of a gracious, feminine form disappearing around a cluster of broad leafed plantains.

Then Farrell saw stars twinkling in a blue vault above him. His mind was now clear enough to realize that the paradise into which he had been translated had an artificial dome and an efficient cooling system; but to Hassan's thoroughly drugged followers the miniature celestial vault and the "coolness to the eyes" would be miraculous.

A fountain sprayed mistily in the neon-bluish twilight. The air was fragrant with the heavy sweetness of cape jasmine and the fumes of burning myrrh. Faint, wailing music and the purr of a tom-tom came from somewhere in the shadows. This fantastic reality, blending into the wild illusions of hasheesh intoxication would indeed seem to be an awakening in the Prophet's paradise, *al-jannat*. Hassan had devised well.

Half a dozen or more Syrian girls with great languorous eyes emerged from the further end of the garden to greet Hassan's guests. They approached with tinkling anklets and undulant, swaying pace as they sought their hasheesh muddled companions to revive them with chilled drinks and warm caresses.

Farrell seized the flagon a slender, black haired girl offered him, drained its pungent draft, then thrust her aside. He had not seen Lydia's red-gold hair; he hoped, and he feared to find her in the den of illusion. Farrell clambered to his knees, rose, then splashed heavily into the fountain. She laughed and passed on to the next guest. He reeled dizzily about the dim court and past the rows of shrubbery that screened the further end of the garden. There he saw that the walls were pierced with low archways that led to small alcoves carpeted with rugs and strewn with cushions.

One alcove had an occupant. She lay on a silken rug. Her face was buried in a heap of cushions. Farrell's heart stopped for a moment as he perceived that her hair was reddish, and that her arms were white. He shook her gently by the shoulder.

247

"Ya sitti," he began in Arabic, for he dared not risk a word in English until he knew who she was.

She shivered and emerged from her cushions. Her laugh terrified Farrell more than the thirsty blades of the assassins. It was Lydia, exotically arrayed for the entertainment of the hasheesh drugged guests of the garden. Her fingers closed about the stem of a heavy goblet at her side. Farrell jerked his head aside but the glass struck him a glancing blow. He recovered and seized her in his arms.

"I'm Glenn Farrell," he whispered into her ear. "Pull yourself together."

She laughed hysterically.

"Glenn—"

He stopped her further utterance by laying his hand across her lips. The mention of his name would be fatal to them both, if pronounced audibly.

"Glenn Farrell," he whispered. "Don't you remember me?"

She regarded him, wide eyed and incredulous, then recognized him.

"Oh, they'll kill you, those devils!"

"Not a word!" he exclaimed hoarsely. "Pull yourself together."

He heard the approaching footsteps of someone who paused from time to time as he advanced, apparently seeking someone or something. It was the firm tread of a sober man, not a hasheesh drugged assassin.

Hassan, perhaps, inspecting his synthetic paradise; death seeking an impostor.

"Kiss me!" he whispered. "Play it up, or we're finished!"

And as her arms encircled him, he murmured extravagant endearments to her in Arabic, thankful that she could not understand the Oriental frankness.

Desperate love-making, indeed! Farrell had to ignore the approach of the visitor and carry on in his role of a recruit having his first glimpse of the luxury of the garden. But when the footsteps halted at the entrance of the alcove, Lydia screamed. Her mock embrace closed on Farrell in terror.

"Ah, you have finally accepted the attentions of the Brethren?" murmured a suave voice in English almost free of accent. "That is excellent—and prudent."

Farrell extricated himself from Lydia's arms and confronted the intruder.

The speaker continued his stare for a moment, smiled thinly, and passed on.

Farrell's first glance had sufficed to identify Hassan's second in command as the Kurd whose entrance into Aswad's dining room had been greeted with such marked respect. A door closed, and a lock clicked as the Kurd left the garden.

"Who's that bird?" whispered Farrell.

"Nuri," replied Lydia.

"What?" gasped Farrell, though he had understood clearly. He had been right; perhaps fatally right.

"Nuri," she repeated. "Oh, this terrible place. I don't know what you must be thinking after I left you that night—"

"I know," interrupted Farrell. "I exchanged a few shots and then chased them to the L.&N. crossing. Good Lord, I thought that train would smack you into the middle of next week!

"But who are Gordon and Rubenstein?"

"Oh, then you know—well, they were the agents I worked for in New York. They asked me to carry the peacock to New Orleans. Their story was plausible, and I asked no questions. I was badly in need of money and they paid well. They spoke of their partner, Nuri. And here I am in this terrible den. And those drunken beasts… Good Lord!"

Farrell began to see how the disjointed fragments would fit together. Nuri, Gordon, and Rubenstein, smuggling the peacock to Parr; and Nuri, one of Hassan's assassins, had double crossed his partners.

"Tell me about this dump," Farrell demanded, abandoning his speculations in favor of action. "How long do I stay here in this hop-head's paradise?"

"They'll bring in some drugged wine that lays the visitors out cold. And then that big negro drags them out. But what kind of an awful place is this?"

Farrell explained very briefly about the Ismailians of the time of the Crusades, and of the terror they had spread throughout the Near East with their extortion and assassination.

"And here we are," he concluded with a wry smile, "in a modern version of the original *hasheeshin* heaven. This place must be artificially cooled. There must be air ducts leading from a refrigeration unit, and an exhaust line for stale air. We might work our way through the exhaust. Let's go!"

Farrell took her by the hand.

"Pretend you're looking for something," he whispered.

He led the way, searching the garden and muttering in Arabic about a bracelet. He stopped at times to shake one of the brethren and demand the adornment. But they were too far gone in intoxication and too interested in their companions to pay any attention. Farrell continued his mutterings and went on, making a circuit of the wall.

"Look!" he finally exclaimed as he found the outlet and indicated a sheet metal lined shaft that pierced the wall of the garden. "I can crawl through! Just barely make it. You can go through easily. Go back to your alcove and see if you can find anything we can use to make a rope. Hurry, it's our only chance!"

Farrell crawled into the ventilating shaft. Ahead of him, as he cleared a turn, he saw a barred window, and across the street, a light. He was on the third floor of the building. Below, on the second, was an iron railed balcony.

Farrell drew his remaining knife and set to work picking at the mortar of the bricks in which the bars were embedded. For a moment he thought of firing a shot to attract the patrol of detectives that Healy should have posted. But he would not be able to fight his way back through Hassan's audience hall, through the ante room, and finally, through the barred doors that opened into the restaurant. With a rope, however, they could drop from the air shaft to the balcony, even though the latter was somewhat out of line.

A brick yielded to his attack.

Then he heard Lydia's voice, low but anxious, calling him.

He backed out of the air shaft.

"Got a rope ready?" he demanded.

"You've got to leave," she replied. "The negro is passing the knock-out drops. If you're missing they'll suspect."

Farrell handed her the knife.

"Talk about breaks!" he growled, "Well, take this. If anyone recognizes me, I'm finished. So you get busy and work on the bars. Let yourself down the rope, and swing until you pass the balcony railing, then drop."

He seized her in his arms and resumed his endearments in Arabic. The negro filled the glass that Farrell had picked up. Then, as the cupbearer made his way among the guests, Farrell poured the wine into the fountain. He watched his comrades so as to time his feigned unconsciousness to accord with their real stupor.

One lone survivor was still chanting drowsily. It was a bawdy song about the forty daughter of the sultan. And then he slumped in a heap.

Abbas dragged Farrell out of the garden. One by one he laid the brethren on the floor of the waiting room. Though feigning unconsciousness, Farrell finally fell into a troubled, nightmarish sleep.

* * * *

His drugged companions were stirring. He heard a murmur of voices from beyond the door that led into Hassan's hall of audience. Then Nuri walked down the line, helping to their feet those who had freshly returned from Paradise. They steadied themselves and then filed after him into the audience hall, where Hassan sat on his dais, under the glare of the one great red lamp that glowed like a satanic moon in that firmament of hell.

One of the brethren stood before the dais, reporting to Hassan.

"We searched his house but he was not there."

In spite of his peril, Farrell relished the irony of the situation indicated by this obvious discussion of him.

"What proof have you?" demanded Hassan as those returned from Paradise took their seats along the wall.

"Nothing important. Except—"

The speaker fumbled in his pocket.

"Except four teeth, mounted in gold, with hooks of silver."

"Wallahi!" exclaimed Hassan. "When we hunt him, we'll have to remember that his front teeth are missing."

"He may have another set," suggested Nuri. "According to the custom of some of these wealthy infidels. These may have been left to fool us."

"True," admitted Hassan. "But nevertheless he may have discarded his teeth as part of a disguise. We'll hunt him right away! Habib! Suleiman! Musa!"

Three assassins advanced from the wall as their names were called. They would seek Farrell with daggers, as they had sought Burnham and Parr.

Farrell saw his chance. The grim humor of it appealed to him. He leaped to his feet.

"Ya sidi," he exclaimed, "let me hunt the infidel!"

Hassan smiled.

"Well said, Ayyub. Your zeal does you credit. Take Habib's place."

It was too perfect to be true, walking out, cracking his two companions across the head with a pistol butt, then calling Healy and raiding the place. But before Farrell could derive much satisfaction from his fortunate stroke, Nuri interposed. Catlike, cunning, sinister Nuri, the predatory Kurd from the mountains.

"Master," he said, "Ayyub is a recruit, and this is a perilous mission. He'd better wait for further training." He paused. His smile was ominous and his eyes gleamed with menace as he continued, "Ayyub's toothless smile seemed to please that red-haired wench who wouldn't look at the rest of the boys. How much more he could please her if he had those splendid teeth, gold mounted and fit for a toothless king!"

Farrell saw at a glance that though he dropped a man with each shot of his automatic, the survivors would still suffice to overwhelm him and cut him to pieces. Then he heard Hassan's voice of doom.

"Meestair Farrell, in spite of your stupid moments, you are clever. *Mashallah!* That was magnificent, seeking our hospitality, where you would be least of all expected, and then volunteering to be your own executioner. What a *hasheeshin* you would make," he concluded with ungrudging admiration.

Then he clapped his hands. The impact sounded like a crash of thunder in the silence that had suddenly fallen over the assembly.

"*Ya* Abbas! Pen and ink!" Then, to Farrell, "I am sorry that we must accept such a low ransom. I would really prefer your services. If I could only convert you!

"But be pleased to sign an order for the sum we demanded."

CHAPTER VIII
Gleaming Blades

Out of the corner of his eye Farrell saw the assassins gathering in a half circle that gleamed with blades. One word of command would send them forward, stabbing as they leaped. But Farrell knew that they would not strike until he had signed; perhaps not until the check had been cashed.

"Oh, very well," said Farrell. "Doubtless I will sign. And I will pay as much again if you release the red-headed girl. The second payment to be made when she is safe and free. Fair, is it not?"

"Praise God for the red-headed girl," said Hassan piously. "And I regret that we can't let you live." Farrell seated himself on the edge of the dais and began writing a check. He handed it to Hassan.

"Read, and see that I have not written a trap for your men."

"You won't trifle. Not when she is our security," replied Hassan as he took the paper and beckoned to Nuri.

The security that the assassin gained from their numbers, and the recollection that Farrell had drawn a knife to punish Hassan's use of the forbidden word, *Shaytan*, made them discount any possibility that he had other weapons.

As the two leaders glanced at the ransom check, Farrell drew his pistol and fired, not at the enemy, but at the great red globe that illuminated the room.

Nuri, though taken by surprise, drew and returned the fire. Farrell whirled and shot at the flash. He heard the Kurd drop. Hassan yelled an order. There was a click, and a grating, sliding sound.

In the darkness Farrell could just distinguish the white turban and white *kaftan* of the Master as he turned toward the panel that had opened in back of the dais. Hassan was retiring to give a clear field for the ring of blades that was closing in from all sides.

Farrell knew that he could not shoot his way out. But there was one resource left. He holstered his pistol and lunged toward Hassan, clutching him in his arms and halting his departure. Then he seized the chief assassin and pitched him headlong into the midst of his own killers, whose blades flickered in the trace of illumination that leaked in from the ante-room.

Despite the old man's shirt of mail, his hasheesh crazed butchers would slash his throat or finally hack him to pieces in the darkness unless he dispersed them.

"Back, fools!" Hassan shrieked. "Back! It is I, the Master!"

And as they retreated in bewilderment, Farrell dashed straight ahead toward the thread of light that came in from the doorkeeper's room.

But before Farrell had half reached his goal, the door of the outer room opened, admitting a flood of light. He saw that the assassins, obedient to Hassan's yell of dismay as he landed in their midst, were retreating toward the walls. They stared, for a moment confused. Then Hassan's cry urged them to the attack.

Zayd the doorkeeper barred Farrell's exit. He leveled a pistol and fired. Farrell dropped flat as the weapon flashed, and from the floor returned the fire, catching Zayd full in the chest. But as Farrell regained his feet the assassins were closing in.

He emptied his pistol into the advance. The enemy fell back, riddled by the well directed fire. During that moment's respite, Farrell saw that the fanlight in Zayd's guardroom was not barred. He leaped to the desk, seized a chair, and swept the window clean a stroke. And as the assassins re-formed and charged, he cleared the window, dropping into the foundations and rubbish of a recently razed building.

Farrell picked himself up from the refuse, wondering by what fortune he was able to move. He saw a file of men with drawn pistols entering the ground floor of Aswad's place. Healy was leading the raid.

"Hey, John!" he yelled. "Give me a gun and I'll show you the way."

Hobbling as best he could with his twisted ankle, he joined the attack.

By sheer weight they took the first two floors by assault. Then they charged into the audience hall. Foot by foot they fought their way down the room, clubbing and shooting. A squad of patrolmen joined the skirmish.

Farrell recognized Hassan, pistol in hand, rallying his assassins.

"Get that guy with the beard!" he shouted as he fired and missed.

Farrell's pistol jammed before he could make good the error. But Healy's .38 cracked as Hassan turned toward his private exit.

"Got him, by God!" grunted Healy "Now give 'em hell!"

The police drove through. The survivors were clubbed into submission. They found the garden empty of all save its dark eyed, richly adorned girls who due to the insulation of the walls, had not heard the disturbance.

"Be Jaysus!" muttered Healy as Farrell led the way into the dim coolness. "if this ain't the flossiest dive I've ever seen!"

Farrell went directly to the air outlet.

"Lydia," he called. "Come out. All clear."

"Thank God," they heard her say. Healy eyed the red-haired girl in her bedraggled costume, and wondered at the dagger in her hand.

"I pried enough bricks loose to clear two more bars," she explained. "And I found enough odds and ends to make a rope." Then, as she saw Healy lift his hat and rub his head. "Oh, did some of that mortar hit you?"

"It sure did," said Healy with a grin. "So that was you, wig-wagging at me with a scarf after you beaned me. That wasn't mortar, that was a brick!"

"Oh, I'm so sorry!" exclaimed Lydia. Then she laughed as she saw the twinkle in Healy's blue eyes.

"So that's how come you started the raid, eh, John?" asked Farrell.

"Yeah. No woman can toss bricks at me from the third floor and get away with it!"

"Well, I'll take her into custody myself," said Farrell as he took Lydia by the hand. "I'm the worse for wear, and my teeth are somewhere out in the battlefield."

As Farrell and Lydia entered the audience hall, they heard a patrolman exclaim, "Jeez, what ritzy teeth!"

"Officer," said Farrell, "let me try them on. If they're not mine, they're close enough a match to have nearly cost me my hide a few minutes ago."

"Yeah, with all your monkey work," interpolated Healy, who had returned from the garden, "it took a red-headed girl heaving bricks to start the fireworks. Now where's this fellow Nuri?"

"Here he is," said Farrell. "Right where I plugged him."

Healy stooped to examine the body that lay beside the dais.

"Peacock ring on his finger! That cinches it. We'll hang every last man alive in this dump. Accessory before the fact."

"And that lets Gordon and Rubenstein out of it, after all," continued Healy. "Here's the line-up. The day you gave Parr the peacock, Nuri told Gordon and Rubenstein to meet Parr at the River Café, saying he'd persuaded Parr to give it up. The seal this bozo's wearing shows that he must have sent Parr that threatening note. And of course, he must have tipped us off to make the pinch.

"We went through Parr's papers and found lots of dope on that holy peacock. That, and the story Gordon and Rubenstein put out cleared up most of the loose ends," continued Healy. "Nuri called on Parr and removed the pearls before Parr could take the peacock to the River Café. The way he worked it was simple.

"Remember, that note ordered Pars to ride in a Liberty cab? That's a new company that just opened up, so he had to ask information for the number. And the telephone is in back of the library, which gave Nuri plenty of time to pinch the pearls, and then snap the peacock closed again. He sent the shakedown note by messenger, and timed his own arrival so everything would click.

"Looks like Parr was the goat all around. The peacock was planted and so was the old manuscript. The idea was to sting Parr with the holy relic and later blackmail him for smuggling it into the country. He never knew anything about the pearls.

"Then when Nuri framed his partners he had to kill Parr, so he couldn't squawk when Gordon and Rubenstein spilled their story after they were pinched. Naturally enough, nobody'd believe they weren't mixed up in the Burnham killing, and so of course they'd take the rap.

"But now that I've spoken my piece," concluded Healy, "supposing you open up with some of your monumental learning and tell me what kind of a dive this is."

"I'll tell you later," countered Farrell. "As I said, I'm taking this young lady into custody for heaving a brick at you. Let's go, Lydia."

Then, as Farrell led the way to the street: "You'd better let me take you to the Delano, and wait until I can find you some suitable clothes. They have a private entrance there, and you'll not have to pass through the lobby. Though that costume is becoming!"

"Oh, but you think of everything," murmured Lydia. "Now do tell me what you were saying to me in Arabic, when Nuri came in."

Farrell regarded the smiling green eyes for a moment, then nodded.

"I'll do that—and you'd better like the translation!"

THE KING'S PEACOCK

Originally published in *Clues Magazine*, December 1933.

Glenn Farrell, lean, rugged, and tanned by the searing breath of the Asiatic deserts from which he had recently returned, had not yet accustomed himself to the Latin gayety of New Orleans. The music and tinkle of glasses and the laughter in Lorraine Cartwright's apartment in the French Quarter jarred brazenly on ears that had been attuned to the whispering silence and murmuring menace of nights in Arabia.

He shook his head and disgustedly flicked a cigarette butt into the basin of the fountain that sprayed mistily in the center of the plantain-clustered courtyard of the old building.

"The French Quarter," he reflected as he crossed the court and strode toward the vaulted passageway which opened on Orleans Alley, "would be charming, if it weren't for studio parties."

"Sour and savage as ever!" mocked a laughing voice at his right. "After doing my best in the way of festive riot, here I catch you slinking into the dark corners."

Farrell turned and recognized his hostess, who was emerging from the shadows of the arcade that flanked the patio.

"The change is a bit too sudden," he said with a vague gesture that was half apologetic. "Let's go to the French Market for a bit of coffee."

"Well, why not?" agreed Lorraine, eager to humor his whim. "They've elected a bartender. The party's out of my hands already, and they'll never miss me. Just a minute till I powder my nose."

Farrell lingered for a moment at the entrance, then strolled slowly toward the corner of the building, which faced the tree-clustered expanse of lawn behind the abside of Saint Louis Cathedral. Several paces brought him to the intersection of Pirate's Alley. There he paused to wait for his hostess, and strike light to a cigarette; but as he fumbled for a match, Farrell started and recoiled a pace.

Death was stalking in the French Quarter.

A man lay in the half-lighted shadows. His low, agonized groan was just perceptible above the music that sifted through the casements that pierced the two-foot walls of the building. Farrell saw a dark pool spreading across the paving slabs, and a lean, muscular hand, outstretched and reaching for something beyond its grasp. The man stirred, shuddered, made an effort to worm his way across the alley. Farrell sensed the iron will that still defied death. He knelt beside the wounded man, and leaned forward to hear the low guttural murmur which was his final effort to explain a gesture toward the doorway two paces beyond.

And then Farrell's hostess arrived. Her scream of dismay kept him from catching the scarcely articulate words.

"Call a doctor, quick!" Farrell commanded brusquely. "And the police."

In the dim light he recognized the aquiline features and swarthy skin of an Arab.

"Try it again, brother," said Farrell, speaking in Arabic. The ornate, silver hilt of a Persian dagger projected from the side of the wounded man. Farrell wondered that he could still stir or murmur.

"Malik—" The Arab pointed again toward the doorway across the alley, then slumped back against Farrell's supporting arm. He tried to pronounce a second word, but the effort ended in a cough, a gasp, and a rattling in the throat.

"Dead, the poor devil." Farrell knew that *malik* meant 'king.' "But king of what? What was he trying to tell me?"

As he pondered, Farrell suddenly sensed that he was not alone with the dead. A whiff of a heavy, exotic perfume told him that some woman as foreign as the dead was near, or had but a moment ago passed by. He turned—and in time to get a glimpse of a feminine form that in another instant blended with the deeper gloom at the farther end of Orleans Alley. She must have emerged from the shadow of the buttresses of the cathedral.

"Knifed him, and now she's making a get-away," was Farrell's first thought. But before he could dash down the alley to detain the woman, he heard the racing of an engine and a clash of gears. "And that's that! Gone, clean!"

Farrell again regarded the swarthy, black-mustached features of the dead, then glanced in the direction of the Arab's last gesture. Something glittered in the obscurity. Farrell picked it up.

It was half of the image of a peacock with its tail fanned out. Complete, it would have been only a trifle too large to be an acceptable watch charm. Farrell was certain that there must be another portion. The sawed surface had been vertically grooved to form a dove-tail joint so that a correspondingly mortised half would fit and thus complete the image.

Farrell's features lengthened, and he stroked the long white scar that seamed his cheek. He recognized that sinister token from far-off Asia; and he knew now what king the dying man had tried to name.

"Malik Tawus!"

Farrell's steel-gray eyes narrowed as he pronounced the words aloud. Though his posture did not perceptibly change, he seemed for a moment as alert as a tiger stalking through the jungle.

His glance flashed searchingly into the dimness of Pirate's Alley.

Malik Tawus—Lord Peacock—was the name by which Satan is worshiped in the Sinjar Hills of Kurdistan. Malik Tawus was the devil-god of the Yezidees, whose true name, *Shaytan*, no man may pronounce in the presence of his followers and live.

More than death lurked in the French Quarter. The music from the studio party had become an overture of doom. The Lord Peacock had invaded New Orleans; and the testimony of his presence was half of his golden image, and an Arab lying in a pool of blood.

The shrilling siren of a patrol car coming down Chartres Street told Farrell that his hostess had notified the authorities. He thought for a moment that a radio car might still intercept the mysterious woman who had vanished save for a lingering trace of her perfume. Then he realized that few indeed would recognize it.

The scent was one in a thousand. Farrell had once sampled its fragrance in the bazaar of perfumers in Damascus; and this was the first time in a dozen years that he had encountered that costly essence. And to find it here!

"But even so, we *might* trace her that way," he reflected, thinking of his old friend, John Healy, chief of detectives. Then, adding to the slender thread of evidence: "The peacock belongs to the Arab. Some one stabbed him, fumbled it, and was frightened away before he could recover it. I popped out of the doorway just in time to alarm that girl. She stuck around until she saw me approach the body."

He scrutinized the golden amulet, held it to his nose.

The strange, heavy sweetness clung to it. Farrell could no longer doubt that the fleeting figure which had eluded him was involved in the death of the unknown Arab. That was certain.

Farrell slipped the peacock into his vest pocket, then knelt to scratch a cross on the paving where it had lain.

"Against the rules," he admitted as he closed his penknife. "But I think I can do more with this than the police."

He smiled in grim reminiscence as he thought of his encounter with the followers of the peacock god in Kurdistan. Farrell's vigilance for a moment relaxed. The approach of the police had lulled his momentary alarm. Only for an instant —but that was too long.

He whirled, sensing peril anew, and saw the cold flash of steel in the hand of a man who was leaping from the doorway but two paces distant. Yet, though taken off guard, Farrell's panther-swiftness saved him from instant death. Instead of sinking into his back, the curved knife raked his side from shoulder to hip as he turned. But before he could collect himself to repel the attack, he was thrown off balance by the frenzied rush of the assassin, and crashed heavily to the paving, jarring the wind from him.

Farrell was dazed by the impact against the slate flags. He was conscious, but without any command of his strength. As from a great distance came a siren note. The dark features and feral eyes of the enemy were grim and relentless during that instant before the long, curved blade began its downward drive.

Farrell knew that with but a split second of respite he could snatch the enemy's wrist, and deflect the thrust. He knew that at any moment he would hear the gritting of brakes and the heavy tread of the police; but he also knew that they would arrive too late, and that the slayer would escape through the door from which he had emerged. That could not be avoided.

But the blade did not flash down. The enemy, sensing Farrell's helplessness, seemed to remember a more important mission. The keen, deadly Persian dagger tinkled to the tiles and long, eager fingers probed Farrell's pockets.

All in an instant! Farrell felt the searching, nervous touch of the assassin who crouched astride of him; and he realized that it was the peacock rather than his life which the enemy sought in the few moments that remained.

Farrell had gained the respite that he needed. He mustered all his force, lashed out with his fist, and writhed clear of the overconfident assailant who, realizing his error, snatched frantically at his abandoned dagger. Farrell, crouched and waiting, seized the steel-armed wrist that darted toward him, deflected its deadly sweep, and drove home with a blow that sent the assassin crashing senseless against the door jamb.

But before Farrell could follow up his advantage, he heard a familiar voice.

"What the hell you guys think you're doing?"

"All done, Duval," gasped Farrell as he recognized John Healy's right-hand man. "I got him—just in time."

He gestured toward the man who lay sprawled across the threshold. The squad of detectives slowed down to a walk. Farrell advanced to meet them.

"Where's that stiff the lady phoned about?" began Duval. "Looks like there's a field day in the quarter—*for cripes' sake, grab him!*"

As he cried out, the detective's hand flashed toward his holster. The service .38 crackled. A bullet ricocheted from the masonry. Farrell whirled.

"Damn it!" he exclaimed in exasperation, and plunged headlong toward the doorway. Two men, reaching from the entrance, were dragging their unconscious comrade to cover. Even as Farrell grabbed at the ankles of his assailant, a final yank from within thwarted his effort. The door closed with well-oiled smoothness, and a latch clicked.

For an instant Farrell and the detectives regarded each other with disgust.

"Right under our noses!" growled Duval. "And I couldn't risk a second shot."

He turned to his assistants.

"Surround the building. Bust down the door and get those birds!"

Duval's whistle shrilled the alarm. The detectives charged the stout barrier. Its heavy, iron-studded panels resisted the attack, but the latch tore loose from its seat, and then it was short work.

Duval detained Farrell as he advanced to join the rush.

"Nothing stirring. You keep out of there—we don't want any civilians croaked in that mess."

"Aw, nuts!" protested Farrell.

"It's not your hide so much," amended Duval. "But Healy'd raise hell if you didn't live long enough to tell us about this jam."

"Guess you're right," agreed Farrell. Then, listening to the advance of the detectives: "Damn little you'll get out of there."

There were no shots, no outcries, no sounds of combat. Farrell and the detective regarded each other for a moment, nodded, and grinned sourly.

"Slick customers, Duval," said Farrell finally. "I'd like to hear what Healy says when you report that they made a clean get-away."

CHAPTER II

Farrell, disheveled and battered by his vain struggle with his assailant, made his apologies to his hostess and explained that he would have to confer with the chief of detectives. On his way to his car, he paused for a word with the patrolman on guard at the door through which the detectives had charged in their hot pursuit of the assassin.

"What luck?" he inquired.

"Devil a bit. Not a sign of 'em. And you had better keep an eye open."

"I'll be looking," countered Farrell as he took the wheel of the big Hispano and headed it uptown.

Farrell would have considered the affair in Pirate's Alley fantasy from beginning to end, had it not been for the ache of his battered head, the long grazing cut that seamed his ribs, and the golden amulet in his vest pocket. The Oriental colony of New Orleans is a quiet, law-abiding handful of Syrians and Armenians; traders, tobacconists, and restaurant keepers catering to their countrymen and to tourists. The symbol of the peacock god, however, lent a sinister touch to the death of the unknown Arab, and betokened the presence of a crew of fanatics in the cosmopolitan French Quarter. Farrell knew that the police would efficiently cover the routine of homicide investigation; but he realized that they might well miss the point of evidence significant only to one who had spent years in the Orient. He therefore persisted in his impulse to study the fatal amulet instead of immediately surrendering it to John Healy.

Farrell knew well the peril of his course. He knew beyond all doubt that he was marked.

"That girl probably didn't kill the Arab," he reasoned, thinking again of the rare, exotic fragrance that had lingered about the scene of the crime. "But she knows something about it!"

A short, wiry, leather-faced man admitted Farrell to the colonial house which he was occupying for the first time in seven or eight years or more.

"Business is picking up, Bronson," said Farrell to his salaried comrade at arms. "Shake up a drink, and I'll tell you about it."

Bronson was Farrell's former first sergeant. In the years following the War they had covered the so-called uncivilized continents in search of trouble. And in view of Farrell's welcome to New Orleans, he had already begun to think that the domestic crop was easily equal to the imported variety.

He followed Bronson to the library in the left wing, settled into his favorite chair, then took the golden amulet from his pocket. Farrell marveled anew at its exquisite workmanship, and turned it over to scrutinize the inscription on the bottom of the half of the six-sided pedestal on which the bird's right foot rested. The characters, which were finely engraved in elaborate Persian script, were all done exactly in reverse.

"When both halves of the image are joined," he decided, "it's a signet."

He took from his desk a stick of sealing wax and with a match melted enough to make a pool the size of a fifty-cent piece on a sheet of paper. Even though the imprint of the engraved base would form but half of the inscription, it might nevertheless afford some hint as to the origin of the image.

"Holy smoke!" exclaimed Farrell as he read the fragmentary inscription. It was beyond doubt the symbol of the peacock god. He sniffed again the perfume that lingered about the golden amulet, and shook his head.

"And Satan's little sister just missed getting it."

One avenue of investigation was already open. He could prowl around in the French Quarter, go to Aswad's Syrian restaurant as a native, sip uncounted cups of sticky-sweet Turkish coffee, and bit by bit accumulate morsels of gossip and rumor that no detective could hope to get.

Bronson, entering with a frosted shaker, regarded Farrell with narrowed eyes as he poured a Sazerac into a stemmed glass.

"We're in for it," concluded Farrell, after summing up the evening's events. "Whoever wants this wants it bad."

Bronson nodded and slid a Colt .45 across the teak table.

"And I think we might as well lock Mr. Peacock in the wall safe until I can hand it to Healy."

"Got something doped out?"

"Nothing definite, yet. To-morrow I'll work on the boys at Aswad's."

The ringing of the doorbell halted Bronson before he reached the safe. He glanced inquiringly at Farrell.

"Leave it here, and see who's giving us a buzz."

Farrell's fingers closed about the butt of the .45 as Bronson left the room to answer the insistent summons of the bell.

A moment later, however, his hand retracted from the weapon, which he had instinctively grasped. He heard the soft, modulated voice of a woman who almost succeeded in suppressing the anxiety that prompted her late visit. She was apologizing for her intrusion. Farrell noted the faint, indefinable blur of accent that betokened one who spoke several languages with equal fluency. And then, wafted in on the draft that followed the opening of the front door, Farrell caught a breath of the perfume whose heavy sweetness had lingered in the alley.

"Fast work," was his thought as he hunched forward in his chair.

"Miss Matar," Bronson announced as he admitted the visitor.

She was uncommonly lovely, and her long-lashed eyes were an untroubled blackness. But her nervous fingering of the clasps of her hand bag belied her otherwise faultless poise and calm. Farrell rose, bowed, and indicated a chair.

"Ah—this is a pleasure, Miss Matar. Bronson, how about some coffee?"

He marveled at her audacity, and wondered what prompted her visit. With that damning aura of foreign sweetness, no second thought was necessary to link her with the net of doom which the peacock god had cast over the French Quarter

"Azizah Matar," she supplemented as with serpentine grace she settled back into the chair which Farrell had indicated. Her smile was a slow, crimson sorcery that revealed nothing but her fascination.

Farrell eyed her narrowly, seeking to look through and beyond the poise that served her as a mask. He saw the appeal that lurked in her dark eyes, and sensed the tension that pervaded her supple, graciously curved figure.

"Azizah," he repeated. "Appropriate. Though appearances are deceptive."

Farrell's play on her name, which in Arabic signifies "beloved," told her that she was dealing with one who was not an entire stranger to the Orient, where a pun is the highest form of wit. She came to the point at once.

"I came for the peacock of Najd."

Farrell was taken aback by frankness where he had expected evasion and trickery to take the place of force.

"You're certainly not wasting words," he countered. "Though Najd seems to me to be an odd place for it to come from."

Azizah's eyes narrowed as though she had from that last observation received a new light on Farrell. She made as if to speak, but smiled cryptically instead.

"Damn it, I've spilled the beans now!" was his unspoken exclamation. To the girl he said: "You might at least tell me about it."

But Farrell knew that he had betrayed his ignorance, and that Azizah would not relinquish her advantage. He saw the flash of confidence in her smile as she resumed: "Let's not go into that, please. I saw you pick it up."

The dark eyes flashed a glance of recognition at the seal impressed on the sheet of paper that lay on his desk. Farrell grinned and shook his head.

"Oh, all right, I have it. But I'm keeping it."

"Surely you wouldn't do that, Mr. Farrell. Not if you know what it means to me. Do let me have it, please."

"Not until you tell me why one of your playmates came within an ace of killing me for it," he countered grimly. Fascinating as she was, Azizah was nevertheless an enemy; and Farrell settled down to match his wits against the messenger of the peacock god.

"*You*, killed?" Her surprise was genuine. Azizah glanced over her shoulder, then settled back against the Shemaka cushions as Bronson entered the room with a tray of hammered brass and a bell-mouthed Syrian coffeepot of similar workmanship.

"Stand by, Bronson," directed Farrell as he poured the foam-topped Turkish coffee into tiny cups. "Now, Miss Matar, suppose you tell me a few things. I came uncomfortably close to being knifed, which naturally makes me suspicious of any one interested in peacocks."

Azizah regarded him somberly. Her dark eyes were brooding, and her lovely features were thoughtful. She spoke, finally, as though she were thinking aloud rather than addressing Farrell.

"Maybe I can get there in time. But if he escaped, they'll be waiting."

"What's it all about?" Farrell reiterated.

"You must know," she countered, "or else you'd not have kept it from the police. And that's what puzzles me. Who are you, anyway?"

Farrell regarded her fixedly. He dared not risk a word, lest he betray further ignorance and defeat his design to unravel the tangle. She avoided his hard gaze and twisted the heavy emerald-set ring that sparkled on her finger.

"Are you a friend of Hussayn? He had friends in this country," she began, in a tone that expressed her hope of an affirmative answer.

Farrell's face was set in a poker mask. He had learned his lesson.

"But you must be!" she exclaimed vehemently. "Or else you'd not have taken the peacock and then fought *them*."

"You'd be surprised if you knew who I am," evaded Farrell, taking his cue from her bewilderment. "And I'll give you the peacock if you'll prove your good faith."

"And how must I do that?"

"Very easy," assured Farrell as he reached for the telephone. "I'll call the detective bureau and we'll go into this scenario."

"Oh, no!" cried Azizah, laying a detaining hand on Farrell's arm. "That would be—"

"I thought so," interrupted Farrell grimly. "It would be embarrassing."

She met his stern gaze unflinchingly, shook her head.

"No, it's not what you think," she protested. "If a word of this leaks out, the entire Moslem world will be shaken from end to end. I hate to think what might happen." Farrell knew that her contention was plausible. All of India had once burst into a flame of red revolt because cartridges were greased with suet. And that golden symbol of the peacock god might set half of Asia into an uproar.

"It might be political," he admitted, eying her narrowly. "But we're not interested in that. We are—"

"We?"

"Yes. The chief of detectives and I."

She regarded him with alarm.

"Oh, good Lord!" she gasped, glancing about her as though seeking some way of escape. "I didn't—you must believe me—Hussayn is not—"

"Yes?" Farrell prompted after a moment of silence. "You didn't kill Hussayn, of course."

"I'm so glad that you believe me," she said with obvious relief.

"Only, I don't!" declared Farrell. "And I would like to know why you dusted down Orleans Alley and stepped into a car that was waiting there for you, if you didn't kill that fellow I found lying in the cross alley."

"That's why I left," she said. "I knew that I'd be accused of killing Hussayn. And when you sent for the police, I was sure the peacock would be safe."

"You'd have had to claim it from them, instead of me," said Farrell.

"I could have arranged that, as a close relative. But now that you've identified me as a witness, I'm put in a terrible position. I'll be questioned. I'll have to show Hussayn's papers. And that would cause international complications—revolts—uprisings—"

Farrell intently regarded her for a moment. He knew that her story was plausible.

"I'm not trying to hang a murder on you," he finally said. "I'm not officially connected with the police, and I can—and will—get you all the breaks I can."

She sighed with relief at his amiable assurance and the twinkle in his gray eyes. Farrell reached into the desk drawer into which he had swept the golden peacock and set it on the blotting pad.

"Now open up," he demanded. "If you're not messed up in that killing, I'll see that you get the peacock without embarrassing questions. Tell me the story, and if it makes sense, I'll put it across to the police and keep you in the clear."

"Oh, you can't imagine how grateful I am," she exclaimed as she eagerly reached for the glittering amulet.

"Just a moment," murmured Farrell, on guard against sleight of hand. "Suppose you prove your point before—"

But Farrell did not complete his suggestion that she establish claims before taking possession of the token. Azizah's terrified scream startled Farrell as he reached forward to stay her eager hand. Leaping from his chair, he whirled in the direction of her wide-eyed stare. Bronson, at the end of the desk, drew his pistol as he turned.

Farrell caught a glimpse of a broad, sallow face and the muzzle of an exceptionally heavy pistol emerging from the window drapes. The flame and stinging blast of Bronson's automatic for an instant blinded Farrell. There was an answering crackle, then a peculiar, coughing report, and Azizah's high-pitched shriek.

Farrell snatched the butt of his .45; but even as his fingers closed about the checkered walnut stock, he choked, gasped for breath, reeled dazedly—

The lights became dim and murky and the sounds of struggle and the Syrian girl's outcry trickled into his consciousness as though he were miles away. He could just distinguish Bronson at his right front, and the jet of flame from his automatic. A swarthy face with high cheek bones parted in a flicker of white teeth as the marine pitched headlong to the floor, and vague, shadowy forms darted into the ever-thickening darkness that was closing in on Farrell.

The pistol in his hand became intolerably heavy. He forced himself to press the trigger. He felt the jerk of the weapon, heard a bullet splinter a windowpane —

And then, as he plunged headlong into impenetrable blackness, he heard a triumphant laugh above the roaring and drumming and droning in his ears. He knew that the long arm of Malik Tawus, the peacock god of the Yezidees, had reached into his very house and drugged him with a puff of narcotic gas shot from a pistol with an exceptionally large bore.

CHAPTER III

When Farrell recovered his senses, his first impression was that his throbbing head must at least extend from wall to wall. There was a rank, metallic taste in his mouth. The room still reeked with the acrid tang of smokeless powder blended with the sickeningly sweetish fumes that had overwhelmed him as he leveled his .45 at the first of the invaders.

"Damn that girl!" he muttered thickly as he rolled over and laboriously struggled to his feet. Farrell tottered crazily for a moment, clutched the edge of the desk, and regained his balance. He saw Bronson, bleeding from a scalp wound, sprawled face-down on the floor. Near him, at the edge of the Feraghan carpet, was a black-haired man whose swarthy hand still clutched a pistol.

Farrell saw at a glance that the intruder was dead. He turned to Bronson, who was muttering and stirring. Farrell took a decanter of brandy and poured a draft between his comrade's teeth. The marine coughed, blinked, clambered to his knees.

"That'd raise the dead!" he exclaimed as he reached for the source of supply and lowered its level a full inch. "Just as I folded one of 'em, something socked me; but that's not what put me out."

"Gas," replied Farrell. "And we might as well call the police, now that our foreign friends have made a couple of monkeys of us."

He grinned sourly and leaned across his desk to pick up the telephone. A siren blast interrupted the gesture.

"Neighbors beat us to it." He glanced about him, noted the plaster that stray bullets had knocked from the walls.

"Anyway, the coroner can't claim this bird met his death at the hands of person or persons unknown."

But before Farrell could continue his survey of the room, he was interrupted by the ringing of the doorbell. Bronson admitted John Healy, who was leading a squad of detectives.

"First it's Turks in the French Quarter, and then you go home for more street fighting!" he exclaimed as he surveyed the disorder. "And who the hell's this fellow you've laid out?"

Farrell summarized the evening's events and omitted nothing.

"They sent that jane after the peacock I picked up, and to be sure I'd not hold out on her, they raided us while she was flim-flamming me," he concluded. "And she looked like a perfect lady."

Healy snorted something pungent and unintelligible about ladies, then once more examined the imprint of the seal, which still lay on Farrell's desk.

"Do you mean to say this whole mess is hinging on half of a peacock?" he demanded.

Farrell nodded.

"Right on the face of it, it certainly does look as though a gang of Yezidee devil worshipers—"

"What's that?" demanded Healy with an incredulous stare. The detectives accompanying him, who had already begun their routine, turned to second their chief's amazement. *"Devil worshipers?"*

"Right, John. They worship Satan in the form of a peacock. And this inscription—" He translated the broken lines. "It checks closely. The first chapter of *Al Yalvah*, the Yezidee sacred book, opens up:

"'The Lord God created of Fire seven shining spirits, even as a man lighteth seven tapers one after another: and the chief of these was Malik Tawus, Lord of Evil.'"

Healy glanced from Farrell to the grim features of the dead intruder.

"Devil worshiper, eh? But how come you know so much about them?"

"I've been around them, in the Sinjar Hills."

"I always thought there was something wrong with you," snorted Healy, outraged at the thought of any friend of his having dealings with the followers of Satan. "It's damn good judgment you showed in leavin' home at an early age."

"Aw, cheer up, John," interpolated Farrell. "What I want to know is something about that Arab that was killed in Pirate's Alley."

"Oh, you mean Abdul?"

"Abdul?" Farrell frowned. "The girl said his name was Hussayn. I don't think she—"

"Hussayn, is it?" Healy chuckled. "Oh, all right. Only I always call these Turks Abdul when we can't identify them. There wasn't a sign of identification on him. Not even a laundry mark. Looks like he'd made a careful effort to conceal his identity.

"But he had a roll of hundred-dollar bills on him as big as a bolt of calico."

"That," said Farrell, "just goes to prove that the peacock is the point of it all. They weren't after money. It was the bird they wanted. I picked it up, and they went for my hide."

"That's what you get for meddling," growled Healy, pretending to censure Farrell's turn at investigation. "Anyway, it doesn't make any sense, all this peacock stuff."

"I knew you'd say that," countered Farrell. "That's why I held it out and started studying it—"

"Lot of studying you did," interrupted Healy from the right of his cigar stump. "But it must have been fun going to school with you."

"Oh, have it your own way, John. But you're going to hear more of this peacock. The other half is likely to crop out."

He penciled a sketch to show how the vertically dove-tailed groove indicated that there must be two halves which would fit together.

"And if you can't take the peacock god theory," Farrell added, "just remember that religion and politics are closely allied in the Orient. It may be a token of identification of some secret clique that's planning a holy war—a *jihad*.

"Arabia is one boiling mess to-day. There's Ahmad, King of Najd—the King of Iraq—and the King of the Hejaz, all at each other's throats, and all trying to gang up on the European powers that are edging in. International politics—"

"Then where does the devil come in? Those A-rab fellows are Mohammedans."

"Right," admitted Farrell. "But the golden bird may be camouflage. Nobody would suspect the symbol of a gang of mountaineers they all consider as low-down heathens."

"Which is what the whole crew of 'em is!" And delivered of that opinion, Healy pondered for a moment. It was entirely beyond the class of criminal investigation which he handled with relentless efficiency. Racketeers left town faster than they entered—that is, those that could leave under their own power. And local talent was jerked up with dizzying abruptness. But this outrageous foreign slant left Healy at loss; and though outwardly skeptical, he was glad enough to profit by Farrell's years of adventure in the Orient.

Healy's thought were interrupted by the ringing of the telephone.

"For you, John," said Farrell as he handed the instrument to the chief of detectives. "And it sounds like hell to pay somewhere."

The crackling of the diaphragm seconded Farrell's opinion.

"What's that?" barked Healy, his face suddenly grim and wrathful. "Who? Gimme that address. O. K., Duval! I'll look into it myself."

He slammed the hand-set back to its yoke, glared at Farrell for a moment.

"That makes you a prophet!" he exploded. "Martin Wentworth just beaned a burglar!"

"Was it—"

But Farrell knew the answer even before Healy interrupted.

"Another one of them damn Turks!"

Farrell chuckled.

"If you call my unidentified guest Abdul, how about the fellow Wentworth knocked off? It's a cinch he'll have no more identification than the others."

"I'll call the both of 'em Abdul!" Healy declared. "O'Hara! Dobson! Carry on with your routine! Let's go, Glenn."

Farrell followed Healy to the department car. They drove down St. Charles Avenue, and turned into the Garden District, that mellowed stronghold of ancient mansions, old families, inherited wealth, and departed riches concealed by the subterfuge of paying guests.

As they drove, Farrell wondered how Martin Wentworth, chairman of the board of the Asiatic-American Oil Corporation, had become embroiled with the outcropping of Oriental criminals. This, to Farrell, was the most fantastic note of the evening.

Even though there is scarcely a day when ships from India, the Persian Gulf, or the Malay States, are not anchored along the river front, with their foreign crews squatting on deck, grinding curry powder or preparing *pilau* over charcoal fires, a burglary by an Oriental, and so far uptown, was unusual enough to border on incredibility.

Farrell eliminated coincidence, and concluded that Martin Wentworth must be involved with the servants of the Golden Peacock.

Wentworth's mansion, square and massive as a fortress, was ablaze with lights that were visible despite the surrounding magnolias, bamboos, and clustered plantains of the estate. A police car which had come directly from headquarters was already at the curbing. A patrolman at the entrance of the grounds saluted as Healy and Farrell approached.

Wentworth personally admitted them. His heavy features were still flushed with wrath, rather than excitement and alarm. Farrell wondered whether Healy had noted that slight but striking discrepancy.

"Damned outrage!" Wentworth exploded by way of greeting. "Town's a hotbed of crime!"

Then, recognizing Farrell, whom he met at the Union Club at rare intervals: "Hi, Farrell—what are you doing here?"

"I've just enjoyed a bit of an outrage myself," Farrell explained. "We're keeping Healy out late these nights. Looks like some one has declared open season."

Wentworth regarded him curiously for a moment. He seemed on the verge of inquiring as to the outrage, then changed his mind and led the way to his study.

The room was a confusion of overturned furniture and book cases. A black marble pedestal was athwart the threshold, and a white marble bust of Napoleon lay in fragments on the broad hearth. The door of a wall safe yawned mockingly.

Sprawled across the carpet before the safe lay a man whose head was a gory pulp in a scattering of pottery fragments.

"When I woke up," Wentworth explained, "there was a fellow trying to chloroform me. Lucky I sleep light. So I took a shot at him with my pistol, chased him downstairs, and found this lad in front of the safe. He was so intent on his work that the racket hadn't aroused him. Guess he depended on his buddy to settle me. Just as he got on his feet, I pitched that jardinière at him."

Wentworth paused for breath, glanced about him, scowled fiercely, then laughed. "Always was a bum shot, so I had to throw something."

Farrell grinned appreciatively. Healy nodded, shifted his cigar stump, and scrutinized the prostrate intruder.

"Looks like Mr. Abdul must have been pretty intent on his looting if you fired a shot and then came downstairs in time to catch him at it." As he spoke, Healy sharply regarded the oil millionaire.

"Well, that's the way it happened," Wentworth declared, with just a shade more of acrimony than the situation seemed to warrant. "And—"

"What did he take?" interrupted Healy as he reached for his notebook.

"Not a thing," replied Wentworth promptly. "I'd not even have called you, if —"

He gestured toward the intruder.

"Uh-uh. Of course."

Healy lifted his derby, scratched his almost bald head, glanced inquiringly at the detectives, who were painstakingly going over the room.

"Finger print everything in the safe," Healy directed. "And we'll find out just what this fellow was pawing over in his search."

This seemed to Farrell to be logical enough, until it occurred to him that Healy's approach was far fetched. Whatever the intruder had been seeking, he would have to handle every paper and packet of documents, go through every one of the drawers and pigeonholes—and then Farrell suppressed an exclamation. Wentworth's sudden change of expression indicated that Healy had scored a bull's-eye.

"Er—Mr. Healy, I don't see what that would tell you," countered Wentworth. The objection was vehement, yet at the same time hesitant, as though, while he wished to protest vigorously, Wentworth nevertheless wanted to avoid the appearance of objecting. For some reason, Wentworth did not want any one to know what had and what had not been handled by the battered fellow who lay sprawled in front of the safe.

Farrell's glance flashed from Wentworth to Healy. He caught a momentary flicker of the detective's right eyelid and a passing gleam in his frosty blue eyes. Wentworth had become decidedly uneasy as he watched Healy's probing gaze deliberately cover the room and its somber, magnificent appointments.

"Too much burglary in this man's town," Healy finally remarked as he turned again to Wentworth. "First they gang up on Farrell, then they clean you out. What have you fellows been up to? Hoarding gold?"

Wentworth's heavy, florid features relaxed.

"Gold!" He snorted, and grimaced jovially. He was apparently relieved. "With the oil business all shot to hell!"

"And a gang of Turks pulling both jobs."

Farrell knew that Healy had timed the remark to jar Wentworth's sudden relief, and sharply regarded the millionaire to note its effect.

"Turks?" echoed Wentworth, his glance shifting to the body. "Oh, that fellow."

"Uh-uh. Farrell just conked a saddle-faced gentleman that pulled a raid on him about half an hour before you turned in an alarm. What the hell you two birds been messed up in, anyway?"

"Stumps me," was Wentworth's ready reply. He chuckled and shrugged. "Now Farrell, with all his adventuring around in the Orient the past dozen years, might be expected to make a few enemies."

He paused, struck light to a cigar, then as an afterthought gestured invitingly toward the humidor. As they declined the Havanas, Farrell pondered on the obvious implication of the oil man's remark: that in contrast to Farrell's fame for blundering into foreign perils, he, Wentworth, was in an entirely different class.

Healy apparently accepted the comparison as it had been intended. He glanced about once more, issued routine instructions to the men on duty, and led the way to his car.

"What do you make of that guy?" he demanded as he stepped on the starter.

Farrell caught the unmistakable glint of Healy's eyes and knew that the detective had missed nothing.

"I've got a hunch," declared Farrell, "that that is one of the queerest burglaries you've met in a long time."

"Right," affirmed Healy. "Fishy as kippered herring."

"But how?"

"Says there wasn't a damn thing taken. Only, he didn't have time to check up."

Farrell had missed that point.

"And that's only a start," continued Healy. "That battle scene was phony. If he cold-calked the Turk with a flower pot, why did the bust of Napoleon get all cracked up? And no matter how interested the burglar was, wouldn't he have heard the pistol shot?"

"The fellow might have heard it, but thought his buddy was doing the gunning," suggested Farrell. "And if they were after big game, they'd stick to the last second."

"That's all right," admitted Healy. "But why didn't Wentworth want the stuff in the safe finger-printed? Because the Turk hadn't touched a thing that was in it! And I dropped the matter then and there just to let him think he got away with something."

"You mean Wentworth sapped that fellow in the course of a quarrel, then when he realized he was dead, opened the safe and faked the breaking and entering?"

"That's my hunch. And I want to know what's eating at Martin Joseph Wentworth, Esquire. Right now, we've got no case, even if we *knew* he did just what I'm sure he did. So I'm giving him plenty of rope."

Farrell caught the point. Unless murder could be directly *proved*, Louisiana law favored a householder supposedly defending himself, or ejecting an intruder. Lacking witnesses, the law could scarcely question the millionaire.

Farrell frowned thoughtfully as they turned into the midnight traffic of St. Charles Avenue.

"John," he said, "I'm beginning to build up a bit on that slant. Wentworth, according to gossip around the Union Club, returned from Al Hasa not many months ago. That's the seacoast province of Najd, on the Persian Gulf. And that Syrian jane, Azizah, cracked off about peacocks of Najd. Pure baloney, but she had that district on the brain, so she mentioned it instead of some Persian locality where peacocks would be more in keeping."

Healy recollected Farrell's account and interposed "But the King of Naj-ud— how the hell ever you say it—could have peacocks in his back yard, couldn't he?"

"Sure he could. But the place isn't famous for anything but sand, camels, and vermin." Farrell squirmed uneasily in recollection of his last visit to Arabia. "And right here and now I'm going to take a hand in this case. Pull up!"

"Huh!" snorted Healy. "With the start you got since eleven P.M.!"

"I got a hunch," persisted Farrell as Healy eased up to the curbing. "That jane was a slick customer, but I'll trip her at her own game. You phone Wentworth's house and jerk the boys out of there as quickly as you can without making it seem phony. You can call it justifiable homicide and nothing more to be said—*for the time*. And I'm going back to look around while Wentworth is grinning about what dumb clucks you and your playmates are. I want to see what I can see. And don't crab the game. Actually pull your men, so his suspicions won't be aroused if he checks up and learns they're hanging around. I'll handle this jam."

"And get socked on the nut again."

"My nut," was Farrell's contention. "And whoever gassed and beaned me is due for another inning. This mess is so crooked that even the devil-worship slant is getting cockeyed."

"Devil worship!" muttered Healy. "These blank-blank millionaires!"

Farrell knew that he had gained his point. He stepped to the curbing, watched the tail light of Healy's car flicker to a red pin point as it approached Lee Circle, then crossed the street to an apartment hotel, from whose phone booth he called Bronson.

"If the cops aren't through yet," he said, "tell 'em to close the door when they leave. You meet me near Martin Wentworth's house, but keep strictly out of sight. If I leave there, you trail me. And if I don't leave, bust in and collect me and the peacocks."

CHAPTER IV

Farrell dismissed his cab a few blocks from Wentworth's mansion and proceeded on foot.

As he approached, he saw that all the lights except those in the right wing and in the entrance vestibule had been turned off. The dim glow struggled feebly through the magnolias and sycamores that were clustered thickly about the extensive grounds. For a moment Farrell wondered whether he would have to scale the tall, glass-guarded wall that surrounded the estate; but before making the attempt, he tried the gate. It yielded to his touch. A wad of paper dropped from the socket in which the latch should have seated. Healy had paved the way.

Farrell stepped from the winding walk, and vanished in the dense shadows of the broad-leaved plantains and bamboos that dotted the luxuriant garden.

If Bronson was lurking about, Farrell had noted not a trace of him. This, however, was as he had expected. Bronson was a seasoned campaigner and a master of the art of taking cover.

Farrell approached the house and, circling it warily, sought to find a position from which he could command not only the front door, but also the wing which housed Wentworth's study. In view of Healy's suspicions, Farrell was certain that Wentworth, as soon as the police departed with the body of the intruder, would busy himself with destroying any evidence that had supposedly escaped the notice of the detectives. He stealthily climbed the trunk of a magnolia near the bay window of the library and settled down to watch from the shelter of its dark, waxen leaves.

Wentworth, as Farrell had anticipated, was clearing up some of the disorder instead of leaving it for his servants. This, while not entirely out of keeping, was nevertheless significant. The man rearranged a few pieces of furniture, shut the wall safe, then seated himself before the empty grate and struck light to a fresh cigar.

"It's a cinch he didn't blunder into this mess," was Farrell's thought as he watched Wentworth. "It would stretch coincidence all out of joint if we both *accidentally* got mixed up with the peacock, and on the very same night."

But for this conviction, Farrell would have abandoned his vigil, for perching on the limb of a magnolia and watching Wentworth staring at the gathering ash on the tip of his cigar did not savor of progress. Farrell's patience, however, was finally rewarded.

The window through which he was looking was open. Farrell heard the faint whirring of a buzzer.

Wentworth looked up, frowned with annoyance at the interruption of his pondering on a weighty problem, and stepped out of the room.

A moment later there was a click as the gate at the entrance of the estate opened.

"Rang for admittance, then found it wasn't locked." As he heard the *click-click* of heels on the concrete walk, Farrell added to his observations: "I should have latched that gate. Now Wentworth knows it wasn't locked, which isn't so good."

In the darkness, Farrell could just distinguish the slender form of a woman, who a moment later was swallowed up by the deeper shadows about the house. He heard the front door opening, and then the murmur of greetings. Though he caught the note of surprise in Wentworth's voice, he could not understand the remarks of either. The adverse breeze, and the heavy sweetness of the magnolias surrounding him, deprived Farrell of any chance of noting whether the millionaire's visitor wore the exotic scent that had heralded the presence of Azizah.

"Even so, it *might* be the girl of my dreams," he muttered grimly as the persistent ache of his head reminded him of his defeat by the peacock.

A moment later his suspicion was verified. He saw Azizah Matar preceding Wentworth into the study.

Her dark eyes burned with a smoldering, somber fire. Farrell wondered whether she might not be the advance guard of vengeance to be wreaked in reprisal for Wentworth's killing of the unknown foreigner. He loosened his pistol in its holster. Regardless of Wentworth's doings, Farrell was determined to thwart any crew of cutthroats that might be using the lovely Syrian girl as a decoy.

As she seated herself facing Wentworth, Azizah resumed the conversation which apparently had begun at the door.

"I'm representing the King of Najd," she declared. "And I can prove it."

She took from her hand bag a document which she offered Wentworth.

"That doesn't mean a thing!" snapped Wentworth, waving the papers aside. "Where's the peacock?"

"Look at this and then you'll believe me!" she flared as she unfolded and thrust before Wentworth's eyes the document he had declined.

Farrell, even though not confronting that wrathful, high-spirited girl, nevertheless felt the compelling force of her voice and gesture, and he understood why Wentworth, brusque and violent as he was, accepted and began reading without protest or argument.

"And now it's coming! She's got his attention!" was Farrell's thought. He glanced sharply about him, seeking to probe the surrounding gloom and detect the shadowy, avenging forms that he felt must be closing in on Wentworth's house. But his momentary alarm seemed vain. He heard not a sound other than the faint rustle of leaves in the breeze.

Azizah's dark eyes were desperate and eager. Her slender hands were clenched, and her full, crimson lips had thinned to a hard line. Farrell felt the increasing tension, and wondered from what quarter to expect an explosion.

Wentworth finally glanced up from the paper he had read line by line. He was more perplexed than ever, and nodded abstractedly as he balanced against each other the contradictions that his scrutiny seemed to have brought out.

"And now what do you think of it?" demanded Azizah. "Phone the police and they'll tell you that Hussayn was killed and robbed down in the French Quarter this very evening."

Some of Wentworth's assurance had cracked in the face of the evidence he had just received. He glanced again at the document and then shook his head.

"This does sound right, I admit—but there's been too much monkey work already. So I'm calling for a new deal," continued Wentworth. "Direct from the King of Najd."

He thrust the document into his pocket.

"Wait a minute!" the girl demanded, detaining his hand. "That's Hussayn's! Let me have it!"

"Nothing doing!" Wentworth shook off her grasp. "I need it myself to show the king what a mess this has become. *This and the phony papers.* You say the peacock was stolen from Hussayn. How do I know you didn't steal this document from him?"

"You don't need to know."

Azizah's voice was low and purring and unnaturally soft, and her features were tense with wrath that was about to flame forth. Suddenly her hand flashed toward her hand bag, and emerged with an automatic pistol.

"Now give me that paper," she demanded. "And both halves of the peacock."

"Be damned to you! Go ahead and shoot!" the oil man challenged.

Farrell admired Wentworth's courage more than his judgment. Wentworth was not close enough to snatch the automatic whose black muzzle was leveled at his stomach. The slender Syrian beauty was deadly as a cobra and reckless with Oriental fatalism. Farrell knew that she was on the verge of firing.

"Something's got to happen—quick!" was Farrell's thought. He had little sympathy for either party to the desperate tableau; but Wentworth's foolhardiness was inviting death.

There was but one chance. Farrell prepared to take it.

"Give me that paper—*and the peacock*," reiterated Azizah.

Wentworth defiantly faced her. Her body was swaying imperceptibly forward. Any instant now—

Farrell's hand shot forward. His shoe, hurled through the open window, knocked a decanter from a lacquer cabinet and crashed through the framed picture at which it had been aimed. Azizah was distracted for only an instant, but that sufficed.

Farrell had not misjudged his man. Wentworth, alert and surprisingly agile for his portliness, lunged forward and seized her wrist.

Farrell, springing from the limb of the magnolia, caught the window still and swung himself into the room.

"I'll take that gun," he said, as he confronted Wentworth. Farrell's swift gesture toward his holster was needless. The millionaire relinquished the pisto. he had jerked from Azizah's grasp. Farrell laid on the lacquer cabinet.

"I hope you'll pardon the intrusion. But it looked as though arbitration were in order," he continued.

"Of all the everlasting nerve!" exploded Wentworth. "What are you doing here?"

"Hunting peacocks," explained Farrell with an amiable grin. He recovered his shoe, seated himself on Wentworth's desk, and gestured toward chairs. "Since I've dodged assassination a couple of times in the past three-four hours on account of that bird of ill omen, I'm looking for a new deal myself, regardless of what the King of Najd does."

Azizah, still paper-white, was trembling violently. Wentworth, though relieved by the turn in his favor, groped for words as he sought to assimilate Farrell's remarks.

"Now, after having me gassed and slugged," continued Farrell, turning to Azizah, "you're making pretty good time in trying to get the other section."

"But I'm not! Those thugs were working against me, not with me," protested Azizah.

"Possibly," he admitted. "But what is it all about? Both of you are in something up to your chins and not a rope in sight. Suppose you open up, and I'll see that the police respect your personal whims—unless you're both messed up in the murder of Hussayn, to say nothing of sundry climbings of my frame."

Azizah and Wentworth exchanged glances, which in an instant changed from mutual inquiry to understanding.

"Tell me, *unofficially*," urged Farrell. "It'll be easier than letting this get to a point when you can't stall off an indictment. Right?"

Farrell's voice was crisp, but his smile seconded the amiable twinkle of his eyes.

"Fair enough," agreed Wentworth. The Syrian girl nodded.

"All right; spill it."

"The fellow I beaned this evening brought me the right half of that peacock to identify himself as the envoy of the King of Najd. But the papers he handed me were all screwy, and I told him to get the hell out of the house. He insisted on taking both halves with him. I needed them myself to convince the King of Najd that something went haywire, or prove that his agent tried to gouge me!

"So I reached for the faker. He ducked and pulled a knife, and I beaned him."

"Why the devil didn't you tell Healy?"

Wentworth grunted.

"If that story got out, my deal with the King of Najd is shot! And I'm out plenty dough. Nothing stirring. So—"

"That ees verree interesting," murmured a voice from the hallway. "But will all of you please lift the hands?"

CHAPTER V

Farrell, turning to face the arched entrance, saw that the evening's work had but started. A tall, well-dressed man was covering them with an automatic. His crafty eyes and air of complacent superiority would have been enraging under any circumstances. At his left and slightly to the rear stood three swarthy ruffians whose drawn pistols spoke for themselves.

"Who the hell are you?" demanded Wentworth, rising from his chair.

Azizah stifled a cry of alarm. Farrell saw the color suddenly leave her cheeks. Her dark eyes were wide with terror and recognition.

"I am Demetrios Pappadopoulos," said the leader, with the air of a herald announcing royalty. "It is indeed a pleasure to meet you all assembled in one room."

Farrell knew that an attempt to draw his own pistol would be fatal. He would have risked shooting it out with one man; but with four covering him, the odds were hopeless. Reaching for Azizah's pistol might catch them off guard—but the distance was too great.

"And an added pleasure, I assure you," continued Pappadopoulos with a thin, sallow smile, "is this meeting the distinguished Federal agent with the rest of my ever dear friends."

His bow seconded the irony of his voice. Farrell appraised the master of the situation as one of those international hybrids whose names afford not the least clue to their mixture of breeds. The Greek name could camouflage Slav, Latin, and Semite, with none of the virtues of any of the components, and packed with the villainies of all four at their worst. Pappadopoulos was a well-groomed and well-barbered cutthroat, in contrast to his henchmen, who were saddle-colored ruffians from the Near East. The entire quartet was a composite portrait of iniquity.

"All right, out with it!" snapped Wentworth angrily. "What's the game?"

Pappadopoulos smiled again. He did it charmingly. It saved words and maddened the spectator.

"The peacock," he said as his eyes shifted from face to face. "Where is it?"

"I'll see you in hell first!" retorted Wentworth.

Farrell, who had been scrutinizing the sinister features of the three who accompanied Pappadopoulos, recognized a familiar face. The tallest was the one who had grappled with Farrell in Pirate's Alley. His jaw was still swollen where Farrell's fist had landed; and the ferocity of his eyes confirmed the recognition.

"Tie them, Habeeb," murmured the Greek adventurer. "Suleiman! Ali! Watch closely—you have seen Meestair Farrell in action before. And search them all.

"One move," he continued, "and I will—"

His gesture and the muzzle of his pistol completed the needless warning.

They had come prepared with two hanks of clothesline.

Wentworth, confronted by odds that subdued even his blustering, stubborn belligerence, muttered in inarticulate wrath. Azizah, regaining her poise after the initial shock of the encounter, gazed fixedly ahead of her, and ignored the quartet.

"Father of many little pigs," murmured Habeeb as he lashed Farrell's ankles. "You escaped me a few hours ago—but you won't get away this time—neither you, nor that *Feringhi* dog."

He spoke in Arabic, his native tongue. Wentworth of course did not understand; but Farrell, glancing at Azizah from the corner of his eye, knew that the Syrian girl had heard, and that she had no hope of escaping the fate that confronted her late adversaries.

Habeeb deftly and effectively bound the trio hand and foot. Farrell, realizing from the beginning that resistance would be futile, had hoped for some moment of distraction during which he could precipitate a free for all. But Pappadopoulos's businesslike methods had taken even that slender hope.

"Stack them on the floor," the Greek directed. "Yes. By the floor lamp is room enough. No, leave Meestair Wentworth where he is. We will have a word with him, immediately. Habeeb, you know the arrangement of the house. Somewhere in the basement must be a furnace."

"You can't get away with this!" flared Wentworth, catching the savage implication. A furnace, in New Orleans, is a clay pot with perforated bottom to afford a good draft for the charcoal fire which many of the old-time Negro domestics find more to their liking than gas. Whether for laundry, or cooking a mess of crawfish, or broiling game, the furnace still holds its own against modern devices.

"Ah, but I have already gotten away with it," was the Greek's amiable retort. "The clever Meestair Farrell has pulled the police from the investigation of your highhanded killing of my excellent assistant this evening. Which facilitates this little—ah, study in roasting. Yes.

"And your house. Thick walls, and buried in a city block of tall trees. It will nicely muffle any sounds. Thus I do not have to gag you. I leave you free to tell me where you have concealed that quaint little peacock."

"You low-down rat, do you think I'll tell you?"

Pappadopoulos chuckled, and shrugged.

"You are a stubborn man. And my assistant, poor fellow, learned that you are hard to deal with. Still, now that I am here in person, I think it can be arranged. Suleiman, see if that stupid Habeeb has found the charcoal."

"Good Lord!" muttered Farrell to Azizah. "All my fault. If the police had stuck around—"

"That would only have delayed him," she whispered. "And they would have caught up with me, sooner or later. But probably sooner. Save your regrets for yourself. You blundered into this out of sympathy for dead Hussayn. I knew the risk I took."

She paused for a moment, and wormed her way closer to Farrell. She had heard the wheezing of bellows, and the muttered consultation of Pappadopoulos and his cutthroats as they took tongs from the hearth and thrust them into the fire pot, whose lurid glow now was plainly perceptible in spite of the lights of the library.

"But they won't kill you," Farrell reassured.

"Surely they will," she said. "So that I will not carry back any reports to the King of Najd. I am doomed even as you are, and Wentworth. For one of us to live will cost Pappadopoulos the loss of a large reward. We all know too much."

Despite his bonds, Farrell contrived to roll over to face the group gathered about the fire pot. The satanic redness of the charcoal now dominated the mellow lights of the library. Habeeb, pumping at the bellows, was perspiring from the fierce heat. Beaded sweat glistened on his forehead like tiny rubies. His two companions stood by, stoically regarding the preparations. At times they exchanged a muttered word. Pappadopoulos sat back in a chair, stroked his mustache, and smiled thinly.

Wentworth, his heavy features defiantly set, glared at the Greek as though by sheer force of wrath to shake him from his impersonal calm.

"If I ever get my hands on you, I'll—"

"Ah, but you won't live that long. Meestair Wentworth," murmured the Greek. "Where is the peacock, pliss? Your stubbornness is causing my men much delay—although fortunately we have plenty of time. It is still early."

Farrell wondered how long Wentworth would persist in his obstinacy, how long the millionaire's nerves could stand the menace of those evil faces, that diabolical red glow, and the appraising glances of Habeeb as he critically inspected the tongs, then thrust them back into their bed of incandescent coals.

"We'll live as long as Wentworth holds out," he heard Azizah whisper. "Once he cracks, they'll have time for us. But the peacock is most important."

"It must be," Farrell agreed somberly. Even in this crisis, his mind cut back to the inexplicable three-cornered contest for the possession of that golden symbol of the Yezidee devil worshipers. Azizah's interview with Wentworth had convinced Farrell that the token had no occult or religious significance. It seemed rather to be political, with a baffling jargon of agreements, documents, and the King of Najd.

"But I'd a damn sight rather be dealing with Yezidees," he concluded.

They were now thrusting the glowing tongs forward for Wentworth's inspection, evilly chuckling, and reminding him of the wrath to come; and as they paused, the silky voice of the Greek renegade repeated his query: "Meestair Wentworth, where is the peacock?"

Wentworth's reply was a snarl, a curse, and a flat refusal.

"But he can't hold out. Guts aplenty—but they'll crack him," was Farrell's opinion. "I'd have coughed up long ago—"

Something razor-sharp jabbed Farrell's wrists, which were bound tightly behind him. Then a warning hiss from Azizah. He felt the toe of her cobra-skin shoes graze his forearm. Again something lacerated his wrists.

Then he understood. Though her ankles were tied, she had nevertheless managed to work a fragment of the broken decanter against his bonds. It would tear his wrists to ribbons. But it *might* liberate his hands.

"You will not tell us where is the peacock?" Pappadopoulos's soft voice was now a venomous murmur. "Ah—a little closer, Habeeb—"

Azizah gasped. Farrell's stomach was on the verge of revolt. He carefully avoided looking. But he smelled an odor that made his flesh creep, and heard a low, stifled groan from Wentworth.

"He can't hold out!" Farrell muttered between his clenched teeth. Then, aloud: "For God's sake, Wentworth, tell them!"

"That is wise counsel," seconded Pappadopoulos.

"Damn you!" snarled Wentworth. "I'll take it! You've not got guts enough to hang around here! The police will return—"

Farrell, tense from the horror of Wentworth's torment, scarcely felt the vicious cutting and jabbing as the glass slashed and gouged his wrists. Each cut should have severed the cord—would have, had it been directed by hands instead of feet —but instead, it only drenched his wrists with blood. And a severed artery would thwart even this slim chance—

Again that odor of scorching. They were not forcing the issue. They knew better than to torment their victim to unconsciousness. Very cleverly they kept the agony of branded flesh just short of unbearable. They were working on his courage rather than on his body, and working cunningly.

Another—and final excruciating slash of glass; and Farrell's wrists were free. But his ankles were bound. Azizah's automatic was on the lacquer cabinet, still unnoticed by the invaders, but beyond Farrell's reach. Despite his marksmanship, he needed more than a gun in his hands. He needed fast footwork to duck and twist and lunge as he shot it out with those four assassins—if he could get a weapon.

Then his numbed hands closed on the blood-dripping fragment of glass. There might be a chance of applying it to the cord about his ankles, undetected by the enemy. Farrell could not understand Azizah's whisper as she noted his gesture. He wondered what she was trying to tell him.

"Where is the peacock, Meestair Wentworth?" the Greek persisted.

Wentworth had reached the end of his endurance. His reply was an inarticulate snarl, then a hysterical chuckle as he answered: "I'll tell you where it is—take that iron away!"

Wentworth had spoken at the worst possible moment. Habeeb and Suleiman, rising from the furnace, looked directly toward Farrell and Azizah. Though their eyes were dazzled by the glare of the fire, they could not fail to note any move Farrell might make to free his ankles. And time was passing; Wentworth had cracked—and the doom would descend.

"It's in the safe," Wentworth was saying. "Right where you wouldn't expect to find it."

Pappadopoulos crossed the room and knelt before the nickeled door.

"The combination, pliss."

"Right five times to forty-five—"

Pappadopoulos spun the dial, glanced over his shoulder at Wentworth to receive the next turn. Each whirl of the glistening disk was bringing death closer; and one move to use the piece of glass would draw a spray of lead.

"Left four and stop at ten," Wentworth muttered brokenly.

The Greek's long fingers turned the knob. But before he completed the fourth revolution, the room was suddenly plunged into darkness unbroken save by the now dying, sultry glow of the unfanned charcoal.

A curse of exasperation. Then: "Habeeb, give me a match—no, bring that fire pot—"

Farrell slashed home, freeing his ankles at a single stroke. And though unsteady on his numbed legs, he leaped to his feet, and snatched Azizah's pistol from the lacquer cabinet.

All in an instant. As a match flared before the safe, the pistol in Farrell's hand dropped into line.

Crack—crack!

Pappadopoulos toppled from his knees face-down on the Persian carpet. But before Farrell could whirl to his right to fire at the three remaining ruffians, he knew that his weapon was empty. He flattened to the floor as a hail of lead from their heavy automatics crashed into the plaster above him. That move saved him from quick death.

During the instant's respite that followed the volley, Farrell took cover behind the lacquer cabinet. His move told the enemy that their shots had missed. They dropped to the floor to avoid being silhouetted against the dying glow of the furnace.

"Give 'em hell!" cried Wentworth with a hysterical laugh.

Farrell knew that his first move across the room would draw a hail of lead that would cut him down. The cabinet was a flimsy shield. But he might distract them for an instant. He thrust his shoulder against a book case and lurched to his left. It crashed to the floor. And as the enemy's pistols stabbed the darkness, Farrell seized the lacquer cabinet, thrust it before him, and plunged headlong into a flank attack that splintered the pride of Wentworth's collection across the heads of the assassins before they could shift their line of fire.

It was now hand to hand, and too close for firearms.

A pistol clattered to the hearth. A knife raked Farrell as, in the heart of the combat, he drove home with a jab that doubled one of the enemy and sent him smashing into the andirons.

"Two to go," Farrell gasped as he struggled to his knees, writhed free of a knife thrust, and wiped away the blood that was trickling into his eyes. A yell of pain told him that in the confusion one of the combatants had stabbed his ally. Farrell wrenched free of the tangle to salvage a weapon.

Habeeb, sensing his play, dropped his knife and snatched the discarded pistol from the floor. But quick as he was, he was not in time to dodge the clay furnace and its charge of glowing coals that Farrell hurled at the pair with all the strength of his wiry muscles.

A howl of terror—a splintering of glass—they were diving through an unopened window. Farrell reeled, stooped to pick up a pistol and pursue. He tripped, measured his length on the floor, battered and weakened from loss of blood. But even as his senses were taking leave of him, he heard the crackle of pistol fire, and sharp commands. Healy was on the job.

* * * *

"Before you pour me into an ambulance," protested Farrell when, thanks to a stiff drink of Wentworth's brandy, he was able to move about under his own power, "I want to see the end of this peacock mess. Did you get those two—"

"Your man Bronson fixed them up," interrupted Healy. "This gang slipped in through the tradesman's entrance, and he didn't get wise until you started the show. But when he did—"

Healy shook his head admiringly, and added: "Though they cut him up a bit, he'll be O. K."

"All right! Now that that's cleared up, I want the dope on this devil's mess." He glanced at Azizah. "Those lights going out was one lucky accident—"

"Only it wasn't an accident," the Syrian girl explained. "I noticed that the cord of that floor lamp was badly frayed. While my wrists were tied, my fingers were free. And this ring across the bare wires did the trick."

"Made a short circuit and blew the fuses. But I still want to know about this peacock. I'll vouch for Healy's discretion, and I'm sure Wentworth won't kick— not after your made-to-order eclipse."

"Oh, very well," agreed Azizah, catching the affirmative nod of the oil man and the detective. "This evening—oh, Lord, but it seems years ago—I sensed that Hussayn was walking into a trap. I didn't follow him closely enough, though I got a shot at the man that stabbed him. A second later you stepped into the alley, and I had to get out quickly, as I couldn't afford to be held as a witness."

"That would have exposed the deal between Ahmad, King of Najd, and Mr. Wentworth, who were secretly negotiating for an oil concession in the Al Hasa province."

"The point is," supplemented Wentworth, who had received first aid for burns that were more painful than serious, "King Ahmad wanted to raise upward of two million dollars to finance an uprising of a fellow prince against the—well, let's say some European power.

"I wanted the oil concession. I saw him several months ago, secretly. The European power of course didn't want him to release newly discovered oil territory to American interests, but having trouble in Africa as well as all over Asia—they didn't dare give him an ultimatum. So they commissioned this Pappadopoulos fellow to impersonate King Ahmad's personal messenger and make me an offer they knew I wouldn't accept. Make me think the king was trying to gouge me.

"The messenger was to identify himself by presenting half of the golden peacock to match the half the king gave me. But they overplayed their hand, and I got wise."

"But it's still a puzzle," interposed Farrell. "The deal was off—you made that clear when you beaned that impostor that tried to knife you. Why all this excitement afterward?"

"Simple," explained Azizah. "Mr. Wentworth explained why he wanted to keep both halves. Pappadopoulos also wanted both halves to prove to his employers, the—er—European power, that he had seen Wentworth and spiked the deal. Lacking that as proof of successful imposture, Pappadopoulos and his assassins could not get their pay. Do you see?

"I followed you as soon as I learned your identity. I hoped to close the deal with Mr. Wentworth on Hussayn's behalf. But the assassins had similar plans. Then they—"

Farrell rubbed his head reminiscently.

"But why didn't they kill you—and me—then and there?"

"No need, then. They underestimated me, until I practically emptied my pistol into the thug who was guarding me while Pappadopoulos's assistant called on Mr. Wentworth. They did not figure you as a secret-service agent until they found you here. When they finally realized that Mr. Wentworth was fully aware of the trick and would at once get in touch with King Ahmad by cable, we all had to die; otherwise, they wouldn't receive their fee."

"But what the devil did *you* want with the peacock?" Healy demanded.

"Speaking of that bird of bad luck," interposed Farrell, "let's see it, here and now, eh, Wentworth?"

"You're entitled to, you two," the oil man admitted, as he opened a secret compartment in his desk. Then, with a nod and a wink: "Damn right it wasn't in the safe. I figured that bum steer would gain us a minute or two."

He slid the tiny image toward the center of the desk. A scarcely perceptible line marked the junction of the halves.

"But what do you want with it?" he asked Azizah. "Bad enough to shoot me down in my tracks?"

Azizah's smile was amiable, and her eyes brightened at the sight of the golden symbol.

"I wanted it to convince the King of Najd that Hussayn had executed his mission, and that he wasn't killed until after he'd seen you. I thought you'd sign up, lie like a gentleman, and save Hussayn's reputation as an infallible agent."

Her dark eyes gleamed with tears.

"Wentworth, give her the peacock," said Farrell. "She's proved her case."

"I'll do just that! Healy, let me take your pen."

Wentworth took the agreement from his pocket.

"Hussayn's a lucky guy," said Farrell thoughtfully, as he regarded the lovely Syrian girl. "Even if he is dead."

TRIANGLE BY ARRANGEMENT

(Also published under the title "Desert Girl")
Originally published in *Spicy-Adventure Stories*, May 1936.

Hodeidah is a section of hell enclosed by a crescent-shaped stone wall whose both ends reach to the shallow harbor. The lousiest spot in Hodeidah is the *samsarah*; a flop house for itinerant merchants, thieves, men who prey on women, and Red Sea riffraff.

The two men who squatted on the pounded earth floor of a second story cubby hole opening to the gallery that overhung the compound of the *samsarah* blended admirably into their surroundings. One was broad-shouldered, wiry, and had a lean, aquiline face. The other was iron hard, body and face alike, and was built like a box car. Though both were tanned to the color of old leather; neither were Arabs.

The lean man was Glenn Farrell, and like his companion, he wore a compact turban and a loin cloth. The other was Red O'Hara whose flaming beard was the envy of the Somali Coast.

Farrell, leader of the duet, passed as an Arab; O'Hara's blue eyes, and bold, rugged face and henna-colored beard automatically made him an Afghan. Their names varied according to circumstance.

They dared not risk even a whisper of English. Their speech was Arabic, but in effect Farrell said, "Red, something is screwy. Why in hell did that gun boat blast our *sambuk* out of the water? And why did they hose us with a machine gun when we went over the side?"

"Because, like a couple of saps," countered O'Hara, "we left Tajura in a boat loaded with nigger slaves, and the British patrol was tipped off."

"But that," declared Farrell, lowering his voice, "doesn't account for the persistent search of the whole damn' town. How do they know *who* to look for?" O'Hara's face lengthened.

"By God! That's right."

Farrell ceased his coffee-making and probed his loin cloth. He dug out a packet of oiled silk. The papers it contained were faked credentials to enable him to go north to Sanaa, the capital of the fanatic Imam of al Yemen. He tossed the documents in the fire.

"Someone in Cairo got wise that Ibn Saoud is sending us to spy on his friend the Imam. If we're caught with this evidence, our number is up."

O'Hara glared at the coals.

"We can't make it without papers," he muttered. "But in case we're jammed up trying to get out of this louse-bound corner of hell, we'd better separate. Chances are better for at least one of us to get through."

"Right," agreed Farrell. "Be seeing you in Sanaa."

The two American soldiers of fortune were making their final coup before resigning from the service of King Ibn Saoud. Their mission was to enter the guarded capital of the king's enemy, the Imam of al Yemen and find out what strangle hold that sour-faced prince had on a powerful desert tribe whose allegiance Ibn Saoud had thus far not secured. That done, the pay-off; then back to the states, and to hell with Arabia.

Farrell turned again to his coffee-making, but before the contents of the burnished brass pot foamed up to the bell mouth, the door burst open. A squad of the governor's *askaris* filed in, bayonets lowered.

"In the name of His Excellency—"

"Nuts for His Excellency," rasped Farrell, and as he spoke his hand flashed forward, splashing the now foaming, sticky coffee into the sergeant's face. O'Hara flung himself aside as a ragged volley raked the room. Farrell, kicking over the taper that illuminated the cubicle, hurled a newly purchased duffle bag at two bayonets closing in on him. As it entangled the blades, he tackled low, bowling over one of the *askaris*.

O'Hara's lunge from the flank carried him through the doorway and down the gallery.

Farrell snatched a rifle. Plying butt and bayonet, pounded his way to the gallery. The pack wheeled, but he cleared the railing.

A blast of rifle fire spattered slugs about him as he dropped to a tower of baled merchandise stacked in the compound. The group of merchants at its foot scattered in every direction. Farrell, rolling down the heap of bales, dashed for the entrance of the compound.

It was blocked. A squad of *askaris* guarded it.

"Hell on the sea shore!" gasped Farrell. "Which way did Red go?"

No time to think. But the merchant's evening meal gave him a hint. Snatching a pot of *pilau* from the fire, he hurled it at a bearded Arab who was scrambling to his feet. The kettle connected, catching the merchant squarely between the shoulders. He pitched headlong, covered from head to foot with rice and gravy.

"I've got him!" roared Farrell diving from the shelter of the bales and toward the prostrate Arab. "Help, O true believers! I've got a robber."

The guard at the entrance charged.

As the law pounced down on the gravy covered merchant, Farrell skirted the wall and dashed toward the exit.

It worked for about three split seconds. Then the sergeant learned what was beneath the *pilau.* The pursuit wheeled. A ragged volley followed Farrell into the street.

A donkey with a heavily laden pack saddle blocked the narrow street. Farrell stretched long legs, hurdling the obstacle. The pursuit, however, was seriously disorganized. Farrell gained; and to improve the lead, he tried looping and doubling. Each turn stole a yard from the foremost pursuer; but his grin faded as he reached the end of a blind alley. The maze had tricked him.

A blank wall faced him, and not the archway he had expected. Shouts and the pounding of feet around the corner became louder every moment The wall was too high to scale.

An *askari* rounded the corner. Farrell froze into the shadow of a pilaster, but he was an instant too slow. A whoop, a rifle blast, and a slug flattened against the masonry.

"This way, *ya naik*!"

The *askari* paused to gesture to the detachment that followed him. As they answered, he bounded down the alley, bayonet lowered.

Farrell wrenched savagely at a loose block in the face of the pilaster, hoping to brain the *askari* with a well placed missile. It was slipping. Another tug—

And that was much too good. The sudden yielding threw Farrell off balance, and empty-handed. But during that heart-stopping instant in which he was wondering whether to pray or curse—the only two things left to do—he not only crashed backward against the wall, but through it. A door, un-perceived in the shadows, had flung open, precipitating him into a dark passageway.

Farrell gained his feet with an instant to spare. He slammed the door and shot the bolt home. The alley was now a confusion of voices. And as he crossed the courtyard, the *askaris* attacked the door with rifle butts.

The house had the musty odor of vacancy.

Farrell dashed up three flights of stairs and to the roof. The bolt of the street door was still holding, but it was time to travel.

He was too far up to dive down into the street in the rear of his pursuers. He dashed to the further coping. From its edge he looked down to the adjoining roof, a story lower.

A plump, full-breasted woman was reclining among heaped cushions, seeking the sea breeze that filtered in from beyond the city wall. She was unveiled. Her broad, sensuous mouth was a crimson splash against the whiteness of her face. Hennaed curls crept from the confinement of a head dress spangled with golden coins. She wore voluminous trousers of scarlet silk, gathered at the waist by a girdle embroidered with gold thread.

A Circassian, judging from her white skin and reddish hair. The number one wife of some dignitary. One yeep from her, and half a dozen eunuchs would make short work of an intruder.

And in the meanwhile, the *askaris* were pounding the door to splinters. If Farrell dropped to the adjoining roof, and thence to the street, the Circassian woman would betray his direction of flight.

"Might throttle her before she yelps!"

He gathered himself to clear the parapet; but he checked himself as a slender, shapely Syrian girl with swaying hips and long lashed, dark eyes emerged from the stairway and handed the henna-haired Circassian a note. He certainly could not nail both at one swoop.

And then the door yielded. The pursuit surged into the house.

He had to risk an alarm set up by two women.

Luck, however, turned his way. The Syrian maid, dismissed by her mistress, turned to the stairway and faded into its sombre depths.

Farrell lowered himself over the side. He was barefooted. His landing would be soundless. And while the hennaed Circassian's attention was distracted by the letter she was trying to read by the failing light, he could slip to the shadow of the western parapet without being observed.

282

Only, it did not work out that way.

Farrell had scarcely landed when he heard a crumpling of paper and an exclamation of annoyance. The Circassian woman was looking directly at him. The discarded note lay at her feet.

"Ayyub!" she exclaimed. "Why—I just got your letter—"

And then she saw it wasn't Ayyub. Her eyes widened.

Farrell gathered himself to lunge; but she smiled and regarded him with friendly interest.

"Let's say no more about Ayyub," she said, beckoning. "It may be just as well that he is conferring with the governor tonight."

Whoever Ayyub was, his breaking two dates in succession was giving the Circassian beauty vengeful ideas.

Beauty?

Well—a few years ago, yes. Her hips were as generous as her full blown breasts, and nothing shorter than Farrell's long arms could hold her tight enough to do either party much good; but she had nice features, and tiny feet.

Her appraisal of Farrell's aquiline face and bare, bronzed chest put an eager look in her splendid eyes.

"With that terrible riot going on next door," she said, catching him by the hand, "I think we'd better go downstairs. We'd be conspicuous here."

Before they reached the lower floor, he learned she was Djénane Hanoum, whose husband was in Zanzibar; but though that was a long way off, Zayda, her maid, had arranged to open the vacant house so that Ayyub could follow the route which had saved Farrell.

"Because I simply couldn't have him come in my front door," she explained. "I have to be awfully discreet. The governor's wife is a very dear friend of mine."

The room into which she ushered Farrell was a grotesque blend of Arabic architecture and European furniture of the gilt-rococo period; but Djénane gave him little time to survey his surroundings.

From a cabinet she took glasses and a flask of *arrak*, downed a slug of the blistering stuff, and then draped herself around Farrell's neck. The enthusiastic embrace toppled him over in a heap of cushions. He began to envy the missing lover; but before he could regain his balance, the torrid softness of her body made the problem of leaving Hodeidah less and less important.

Somehow she managed to wriggle out of her pearl-embroidered jacket, leaving nothing but a silk slip between Farrell and that simmering double armful of amorously scented flesh. And when he finally caught his breath, he saw less and less reason for objecting to the match; though he was outweighed by thirty odd pounds, they were well placed...

By dint of straining one arm, he drew her close enough to wake up to the advantages of Circassian upholstery. There was lots of Djénane, and she was alluringly soft and resilient and clinging.

Her lashes shaded her misty eyes, and in the wavering light of a pair of tapers she was becoming lovelier every moment. Her breath murmuring in his ear sent thrills racing down Farrell's spine...and when one arm uncoiled from his neck to loosen still further her clinging, pearl-embroidered garments, Farrell didn't know whether to lend a hand or hold her tighter—

But both alternatives were out of order.

The door flung open. Djénane gasped and broke away. Zayda, the Syrian maid, was at the threshold.

"Sitti," she apologized, "I thought—I'm sorry—"

"Get out, you idiot!" flared Djénane.

But Zayda persisted, *"Sitti,* the governor's wife—I didn't know—"

A chatter of feminine voices and a tinkle of anklets came from the hall. Djénane's expression changed thrice in as many instants. Then she lifted the lid of a teak chest. Farrell needed no directions. He made it just as the ladies entered the room.

"Darling," the governor's wife greeted, "your maid said you were bored to tears, and that you'd like to go to the *hammam* with us."

"Awfully sweet of you," purred Djénane, assembling scattered odds and ends, and doing some swift retouching before her gilt-framed mirror.

In a few moments Zayda had her dressed for the street, and with her mistress was following the invasion out of the house.

Farrell emerged from the chest. He wrathfully cursed the governor's wife, then decided that it might have been for the better. Find some of the absent husband's clothes and check out.

His search, however, was interrupted. A hinge creaked. The teak chest was too far away. He snuffed the taper and darted to the shelter of a pilaster. The door slowly opened. He could just distinguish a shadowy, shapeless figure silhouetted against the sky glow filtering in through a barred window.

Farrell poised himself. The robed figure advanced into the gloom. He lunged. They piled headlong across the room and into the cushioned alcove.

But those feminine curves certainly did not belong to any *askari!* Farrell struck light.

It was Zayda. The gauzy veil could not conceal the crimson loveliness of her lips and the delicate olive oval of her face. And her legs, exposed by the disarray of her gown, were amber-tinted fascinations in the taper glow.

"Ya Allah!" she gasped, recognizing him as she regained her breath. "I thought you'd still be in that chest."

"Allah be praised, I wasn't!" countered Farrell, still tingling from the pleasant contact.

"The governor's car," explained Zayda, "is the only one in town, and his wife's friends are so crazy to ride in it there wasn't enough room for their maids, so I had to come back."

All of which gave Farrell time to decide that his antics with Djénane had been a bit foolish. A deadly waste of talent.

Her next remark hinted that Zayda had a like opinion on what she had witnessed.

"Are you awfully wild about her?"

"Yes—if she stays at the *hammam* long enough," he countered; and to make the point clear, he reached for an armful of Zayda.

The shapeless native robes tricked the eye but not his sense of touch. He simultaneously learned that she was high-breasted, that the inward curve of her waist had been designed for his left arm, and that another instant's delay in kissing her would have left her smoking. Djénane's unintentional demonstration apparently had left Zayda a bit upset!

The Syrian girl finally had to break away to catch her breath, and shed her *habara* and a few other encumbering odds and ends. Farrell saw that his caressing explorations had given him scarcely a suspicion of the ivory-tinted loveliness that now smiled at him through a single layer of gauze. But before he was fairly cross-eyed from trying to cover all her fascinations in one glance, Zayda cut short the sightseeing by drawing him to her torrid lips.

And that was better than any amount of looking...

"Maybe," she finally suggested, "we could do with a bit of that *arrak* Djénane Hanoum always keeps locked up."

The first few gulps of the blistering stuff were hard to take, but as they reached the bottom of the flask, Zayda remembered a quaint Turkish song. Then they hunted and found more *arrak*. Farrell became very despondent.

"Allah blacken his face!" he cursed, referring to the governor. "I've got to get out of town before sunrise."

Between planning on making the flight a duet, *arrak* and Farrell contrived to give Zayda a few hints about the governor's unaccountable grudge against him and Red O'Hara.

In the meanwhile, the taper was guttering to extinction. They both were passably dizzy. Zayda was warm and clinging; and they forgot that the governor's wife would not stay at the *hammam* forever...

* * * *

They made a charming picture, some hours later, but not to Djénane Hanoum, who had spent an entire evening wondering when she could break away from the Hodeidah center of gossip.

Farrell, breaking away from a closely fitted armful of Zayda, thought for an instant he was back in the states listening to a police siren.

"Ya mumineen! O true believers! Help!"

Djénane was calling for the guard, and the tiles shuddered. Farrell was the first to reach his feet, but his dash toward the street was hampered by Zayda, who clutched for support and caught him about the ankles. He pitched headlong to the floor.

But it wasn't the guard that floored Farrell a second time. It was a vase Djénane smashed across his head. And when the city watch arrived, scooping Farrell from the deck was simple enough.

They hustled Farrell down the deserted streets, and through the side door of a pretentious building. A long corridor opened into an audience room at the further end of which was a dais occupied by a hook-nosed, white-bearded Arab who radiated garlic, attar of roses, and wrath in equal proportions: Shaykh Yussuf, the governor of the city.

"The peace upon you, *ya shaykh*!" Farrell saluted.

"No peace to you, O son of disease!" countered Shaykh Yussuf. He addressed Farrell by his most recently acquired alias: "Abu Faris, we know that you are a spy sent by the enemy of our Lord, the Imam."

That deflated Farrell's last chance of bluff. One stroke of a sword would take the place of evidence and a trial.

Then the governor uncorked his second surprise. He smiled amiably and said, "You may buy your head by serving me instead of Ibn Saoud. My Lord the Imam is holding my cousin as a hostage in Sanaa. You will go there and release him from captivity."

The wily Imam had secured the fidelity of this official by imprisoning some relative whose head would guarantee good faith. Shaykh Yussuf's demand hinted that he was preparing to revolt against his overlord, the Imam; but, how could that white-bearded schemer trust Farrell?

Shaykh Yussuf anticipated the query.

"I have a hostage to compel your fidelity," he explained.

Farrell froze. That must mean that Zayda had been denounced by her jealous Circassian mistress. Her head would answer.

The governor clapped his hands. An orderly left the audience hall. In a moment he returned, followed by a squad of *askaris*. They had a prisoner: Red O'Hara.

"Abu Faris," said the white-bearded intriguer, "if my cousin is not in Hodeidah within thirty days, this man's head will be spiked to the city gate. And I may first have the hide peeled from his carcass."

Then, to a steward, "Daoud, get Abu Faris some clothing and a mule. See that he gets clear of the guards. And happy journeying to you, Abu Faris!"

"Satan rip you open!" countered Farrell as they marched him away. But as he passed O'Hara, he said, "Hang on, Red. I'll make it."

* * * *

A week later, Farrell reached the end of his march to Sanaa, a pearl grey city whose shimmering spires and minarets towered above the verdant Arabian plateau.

In the old days when the Turks misruled Sanaa, it was a red hot spot; but since the conquering Imam had taken charge, there was neither music nor mirth, neither bawdy houses, liquor, nor hasheesh. Sanaa had become an unpleasantly moral town where the executioner's sword cured people of amiable vices.

Farrell glumly eyed the foreboding fortress in which Habeeb Ali, the governor's cousin, was imprisoned.

"Be damned if this isn't the first time I ever had to break *into* jail!"

For a week Farrell prowled about town, getting the lay of the land.

The women of Sanaa were fascinating, with their Himyar veils, that concealed nothing; but the sword of the Imam kept the ladies looking straight to the front.

At sunset of the eighth evening, Farrell wandered into the leading and lousiest *samsarah* in the city. No travelers had any gossip from Hodeidah. Farrell was about to go his way when he heard a stifled, plaintive sobbing from a room on the second floor.

Farrell investigated. Anything to escape his own hopeless problem.

"Destour!" he rumbled, tapping at the door.

A woman answered. She did not raise her veil in time to cheat Farrell of a dazzling eyeful. A lovely little creature, with long lashed dark eyes that reminded him of Zayda's. She was younger than Zayda—but not too young.

Her name was Ayesha, and her room at the *samsarah* had been stripped clean by sneak thieves. She was stranded in Sanaa. Walking to the coast would be tough on bare feet.

"My father," she concluded, "came to Sanaa to be a hostage in the Imam's prison. I accompanied him, and was to go on to Hodeidah to stay with my aunt. And now—"

A fresh supply of tears impended.

Farrell had spent over a week trying to get into the Imam's prison, and here Ayesha was in a tough spot because her father had succeeded! He was thinking fast. By pleading Ayesha's case with the Imam, he might get a chance to play his own cards.

"By Allah!" he declared. "I will go to the Imam. I will demand an escort and money for you—I will tell that white-bearded goat—"

A brave voice and a face to match; but Ayesha had every reason to fear the stern Imam and his many spies.

"Oh—do be careful!" she warned, interrupting the tirade. "If anyone hears—"

She was quite close now, and her dark eyes were wide with mingled fear and admiration. Her soft fingers closed on his wrist, ripe, warm curves whispered to Farrell through her shapeless outer robe. Ayesha was marvelously well equipped, and as she drew closer, Farrell became less and less concerned with immediately defying the pious Imam.

His plans were becoming slightly incoherent, but Ayesha was not critical. That might have been because only one of Farrell's hands now gestured. The other was shaping itself to the latest discovery.

Ayesha's eyes were becoming misty and her breath came in short gasps that made Farrell's ears simmer, and when he found her lips, she eagerly clung to him.

Luckily, the thieves hadn't stolen the prayer rug...

But unluckily, Farrell hadn't barred the door. It slammed open. Ayesha's scream lifted the tiles, but fright froze her arms about him. Before he could break clear, he did not need a guide book to tell him that someone was jabbing a pistol against his back.

"Don't!" shrieked Ayesha, her shrill voice piercing the oaths that rumbled like a cavalry charge. "Would you kill your own daughter?"

She doubtless overestimated the penetration of the pistol; but the blast was delayed.

If the man behind the gun was Ayesha's father, he had a remarkably wide range of action for a hostage! If this wasn't a frame up, nothing was.

"No, by Allah!" raged the irate parent. "But I will call the guard! I will have him impaled in the public square!" Farrell was up to his neck. This sort of thing wasn't being done in Sanaa any more. Not by anyone who wanted to keep his head.

"And you—cutting up this way before I even get to my cell!" raged the old man. *"Ya Allah—!"*

"Wait a minute!" interposed Farrell, desperately snatching at the last words. *"Haven't you been there yet?"*

The Arab gasped, taken back by the irrelevant, insistent question.

"Nay."

"Then I will take your place," said Farrell.

"There is no God but Allah!" exclaimed the astonished Arab.

The pistol sagged. Farrell whirled.

Sock! Arms and the man crashed into separate corners. That calmed everyone ; and explanations were forthcoming.

"Wallah, I am Shareef Nuri," said Ayesha's father. "And before reporting to the warden, I remembered my prayer rug. So I returned—"

"Does the Imam inspect his hostages very often?" Farrell interposed.

"What difference?" countered Shareef Nuri. "He has never seen me. He knows only my uncle, whose fidelity my head guarantees."

That made it a bargain. Farrell took the Shareef's credentials, gave him half of his cash, and paused only long enough to exchange a regretful glance with Ayesha.

"Too bad," he muttered as he strode across the *maidan,* "this would have worked just as well an hour or so later..."

Presently Farrell presented credentials to the warden.

The food was good, and the vermin not excessive. Only one move remained: find the governor's cousin, and make good use of the hack saw blade which had eluded the search of the sentries.

A few moderate bribes, and Farrell found his man. Habeeb Ali was in a tower at the end of a corridor, and overlooking the city wall.

That night he hailed the jailer: "Take me to the cell of Habeeb Ali. Get some tapers, so we can play chess."

Plausible enough, and three Maria Theresa dollars clinched it. Farrell ceremoniously saluted Habeed Ali. As the jailer's footsteps receded down the passageway, he whispered to the wizened, sharp-featured little man, "Keep up a lusty argument about this game, O brother, and Allah will reward thee."

Habeed Ali was perplexed, but as Farrell set to work with his hack-saw blade, he caught the point and staged a good act. It muffled the rasp of the saw, and though the blade was giving Farrell more blisters than a rowing match, it was biting into the soft, hand-wrought iron window bar.

An hour passed, and a second yielded. Farrell bounded to the sill, gripped the free ends, and slowly wrenched them upward.

"Go first, *ya* Habeeb, and may Allah prosper thee," Farrell invited; but the Arab drew back.

"Nay," he protested. "Go your way. I stay where I am."

He meant it. It occurred to Farrell that perhaps Habeeb Ali suspected a snare.

"Your cousin, the governor of Hodeidah, sent me to liberate you."

"I stay here, regardless," declared Habeeb Ali.

Farrell was convinced that he was dealing with a madman.

288

"You idiot," warned Farrell. "Supposing your cousin is planning a revolt. You know what would happen to you."

"My cousin wants me released to have me assassinated," declared Habeeb. "So that he can inherit my estate. Now rub your head, or by Allah, I will call the jailer."

"Listen, fellow!" growled Farrell. "You're going to be rescued, whether or not!"

He lunged; but he landed only after Habeeb's yell had echoed down the corridor. An earthenware jar crashed to shards. Then Farrell caught up with Habeeb. *Pop!* The Arab froze in his tracks.

Farrell unwound his prisoner's turban, spliced it to his own, and looped the free end under Habeeb's arms. Then, shouldering his captive, he bounded to the sill as the jailer and the guard came pounding down the corridor.

It was touch and go. Farrell lowered Habeeb to the city wall. He leaped clear of the sill as the guard surged into the vacated cell.

Seizing his unconscious prisoner, he cleared the crest, beating a hail of slugs by a split second. He crashed heavily to the ground; but badly shaken as he was, there was one advantage; the nearest of the city's gates was half a mile to the north. Shouldering the wizened Habeeb, Farrell charged across the plain.

If he could reach the pass that cleft the encircling mountains, there was a chance. But Farrell's heart was pounding; his legs were stiffening, and the veins at his temples stood out like fire hose. He had to detour to dodge a walled estate.

Habeeb was showing signs of life. Farrell dumped him to his feet.

"Gallop! Or I'll blow your head off!" he bluffed.

Habeeb tottered half a dozen steps, then caught his stride. The damned little runt was swift as a horse! And he headed for the highway instead of the open darkness.

Farrell's desperate sprint closed the gap, but the drumming of hoofs became louder as that accursed Habeeb reached the Hodeidah highway.

The captive tripped and sprawled headlong across the road.

"Head for the hills or I'll bust your head against the rocks, you—!" growled Farrell as he closed in. "Son of a flat-nosed mother—"

His blood froze. He heard the padding of camel's feet and the muffled sound of arms just ahead of him. They were almost upon him, and the Imam's soldiers were closing in from the rear. He seized a rock and crouched by the roadside. There were only three camels, and one lacked a rider. He hurled the missile at the leader's chest.

Chunk! He reeled in the saddle, cursed wrathfully, and recovered. Only one such voice in Arabia, and only one man who could digest such a blow: Red O'Hara.

"Hold it, Red!" shouted Farrell, ducking the answering pistol blast.

"Pile on!" said O'Hara, wheeling his beast.

"Just a second—"

The Imam's cavalry was perilously near, but Farrell had urgent business. He turned, booted Habeeb headlong into the gloom, then swung to the saddle.

"Sure, and I got the breaks," explained O'Hara, as they raced southward. "She was a fine figure of a woman, and she slipped a knife into my cell. So we stole some camels and I came to get you."

It was only then that Farrell noted that O'Hara's companion was a woman.

"You have all the luck, Red," concluded Farrell, as he told how he had almost escaped the governor of Hodeidah.

"And what do you say her name was?" demanded O'Hara. "Not the fat one, but her maid."

"Zayda."

"Zayda, eh?"

There was something odd about O'Hara's voice; but what confirmed Farrell's suspicions was the soft laugh of their companion, and the lowering of her veil.

Zayda herself! For a long moment the silence was broken only by the padding of feet of the camels. The sudden chill was not from the desert night.

"And so you got me out of jail just to do him a favor?" growled O'Hara.

"You big louse, as if you had any kick coming!" retorted Farrell. "After a week across the desert with her!"

Then Zayda interposed: and her solution of the tangle was simple.

A long, three-cornered exchange of glances in the moonlight, and grimness expanded into grins.

"Be good, now, and ain't *our* girl got the answer!" admitted O'Hara. Then he frowned, and demanded: "But what's this polyandry stuff she's talking about?"

"Oh, that?" Farrell chuckled. "That's the great ambition of every Arab woman. But now that that's settled, let's dope out some alibi to hand Ibn Saoud for the way we muffed that job of spying."

O'Hara snorted.

"To hell with Ibn Saoud and the rest o' them kings until we find out how our girl's idea works out!"

SCARLET RENDEZVOUS

Originally published in *Spicy-Adventure Stories*, April, 1936, under the pseudonym "Clark Nelson."

The crags of Tanjong Merah jutted out into the savagely pounding China Sea. A red sunset was following the typhoon that had just subsided; and red jets of rifle fire poured from the parapet of the half ruined fortress that crowned the long, narrow cape.

Tsang Wu, the Chinese pirate was bottled up; and Glenn Farrell, the American beach-comber who had become commander of Sultan Iskander's vest pocket army, could not pull the cork.

The short, stocky Malay *askaris* could digest just so much lead from Tsang Wu's rifles. Farrell, grimy and tattered, his rugged face raked by splinters of flying rock and his long, lean body creased with scorching slugs, scrambled to his feet. His blue eyes blazed wrathfully, but he had only one move.

"Datu Hamid," he shouted to the second in command, as he deliberately turned his back to the blistering fire of the enemy, "keep those yellow devils ducking for cover while our right retreats to the barricade! Throw dust in their eyes!"

The wiry, squint-eyed *datu* in the green *sarong* relayed the order. A volley rippled down the left of the skirmish line, chewing chips from the parapet and blinding the Chinese snipers as the right drew back.

And by repeating the maneuver, the American soldier of fortune withdrew his forces with little loss.

The Malay troops were muttering wrathfully. Datu Hamid, whom Farrell had displaced as commander of the sultan's army, made no move to quiet them. Their resentment ignored the fact that to continue the charge would have wiped out two-thirds of the attackers.

Farrell's binoculars swept the foothills far to the west. He cursed.

If the two field guns the sultan had borrowed from a neighboring prince didn't arrive soon, the water would calm down enough to let Tsang Wu return to the armored yacht which lay aground on a sand bar, far off shore. By some freak of the typhoon, the pirate's miniature warship had not been battered to pieces. All he had to do was put out in the launch in which he'd escaped, and tow the yacht into deeper water.

If Tsang Wu escaped, Farrell would be discredited. Worse than that, he hated to fall down on the job. Sultan Iskander had given him a lift when the whites of Malaya had kicked him on the chin.

Too many gin *pahits* one night, and an unfortunate tangle with a woman notorious from Singapore to Siam, the news spread like wild fire, and lovely Irma Stanley gave him the air. Then more gin *pahits* and Farrell landed on the beach.

For a moment Irma's ivory and golden beauty, and the kisses they had exchanged by moonlight were a painful, mocking memory. Damn that gin-inspired bit of playfulness, just when Irma's reserve was at the melting point! He grimaced wryly, scanned the horizon, and resumed methodically cursing the artillery.

And then, just before the swift fall of night, he saw a gun carriage drawn across the distant crest by a pair of water buffaloes. A caisson lumbered after it.

Farrell turned to his tent to wolf the pot of curry his orderly had prepared. As he ate, he cast about for ways of salving Datu Hamid's grouch. He didn't blame the old fellow for getting his nose out of joint at the sultan's favor to a foreigner.

But before he devised an approach, Pa'dullah, his orderly, stepped into the kerosene lantern glow of the tent.

"*Tûan*, a messenger from Tsang Wu," he announced, thrusting ahead of him a slender Chinese girl.

And what a girl! Her vermillion tunic and black silk pajamas were tattered, and her sleek black hair was disordered, but her exotic loveliness left him scarcely aware of her disarray. Small, firm breasts modeled in amber-shadowed ivory peeped coyly from the rents in the high necked tunic, and its severe lines could not quite hide the suave flare of her hips. And the gracious curve sweeping upward from her left knee was a charming hint at the fascinations she still kept in reserve.

Her dark, slanted eyes, reflecting her crimson smile, made him think of several things he'd like to do when the siege was over.

"If you're a sample of what pirates carry around, I'm getting in that business myself—but what's up now?"

"I'm Chan Li. One of Tsang Wu's prisoners," she said in Mandarin. "Just before the typhoon he captured the *Semiramis*, bound from Hong Kong to Singapore."

"What's all that to me?" His smile faded. She might be a spy.

"Tsang Wu," she explained, "demands that you let him escape to his stranded yacht. He saw your artillery coming up. To save your face, you can take the fuses out of the shells so they will not do any great damage."

The effrontery of it was almost as striking as Chan Li's alluring loveliness.

"And if you do not," she resumed, "Tsang Wu will—"

She paused, and a slender hand probed her tattered silks. Whatever she was hunting, it'd be uncommonly pleasant helping her. Then she found it: a silver vanity case.

The initials engraved on it were I. S. Farrell's expression changed. He opened the case. Inside the cover was a snapshot, somewhat frayed and stained: his own face, and next to it, the smiling sweetness of Irma Stanley. Taken that day at Tanjong Rhu, when Irma almost forgot she was a nice girl...

The sudden rumbling in his ears was not artillery fire.

Irma was Tsang Wu's prisoner. The pirate, recognizing the familiar face of Sultan Iskander's field marshal, was making the most of it.

"He will release her unharmed if you let him escape. Otherwise," explained Chan Li, "Tsang Wu and his lieutenants will make their doom a bit more pleasant. The yellow-haired girl will not like it.

"She came to Singapore to find you. But when the siege is over, you won't want to see her. Not after having refused to save her."

Farrell's shoulders slumped and his face became gray. He planted himself in a folding chair. He could now hear the curses and shouts of the Malays, and the grunts of the water buffalos dragging the three inch field guns to blast Tsang Wu into dripping shreds. But first there was plenty of time for Tsang Wu's Mongolian vengeance.

Farrell racked his blazing brain for some saving device. Let Tsang Wu escape. Suppose the British did depose the Sultan for not maintaining order? They were looking for some pretext against that gray-haired man of iron. If they missed this one, they'd find another.

But that wouldn't go down straight. To hell with Irma and her narrow-mindedness! Sultan Iskander had picked him from the beach.

And then desperation whispered an answer.

"Go back and tell Tsang Wu he wins!" he said.

For a long moment those black, inscrutable eyes regarded him from a cream-colored mask. Then Chan Li's fingers closed on his wrist and a slow, sorrowful little smile took the sting from her words: "It is hard to be a traitor, isn't it?"

"Go and tell Tsang Wu!" he rasped.

She had scarcely slipped into the shadows between the tent and the guard fires when brisk footsteps and a tinkle of steel startled Farrell. He turned and saw that Sultan Iskander had come from the capital to watch the finish. He wore a white turban that accented the leathery color of his stern face; and his eyes were grim as sword points for just an instant before he greeted his protégé.

During that moment of deadly uncertainty Farrell wondered if his chief had overheard the bargain; and then old Datu Hamid broke in, salaamed to the sultan, and dashed on ahead to the halted artillery.

Farrell's strategy was blown up by his patron's arrival. He had planned to delay the bombardment, slip single-handed to the fortress, and liberate Irma before blasting the pirate off the map. One man could make it where a detachment could not. But to misdirect the artillery fire, right under the shrewd old sultan's nose, was impossible. The troops would miss the trick; but he would not.

Shells, unpacked and fused, were waiting. Men were filling sandbags to make a protective wing a dozen feet from each gun. Shrapnel is safe enough, but if a high explosive shell in spite of its safety fuse-lock prematurely burst in the gun barrel, an unsheltered crew would be blotted out.

Sultan Iskander watched the *askaris* awkwardly going about their unfamiliar business. A fused shell was slipped home. The breech swung shut. Farrell laid the gun. Make every shot count—keep Tsang Wu busy—if possible! The lanyard was attached. The crew took cover; but Sultan Iskander stood his ground.

"Better take cover, your highness!" Farrell warned. His face was drawn.

"At my age?" snorted the grim old fellow.

You couldn't argue with him. The gunner was watching Farrell's upraised hand, waiting for it to drop. He shivered, and not from thinking of Irma Stanley. He felt the presence of something dark and deadly. A blind hunch warned him of peril.

His right hand shot out. As he jerked the sultan sprawling behind the breast-works, the gunner yanked the lanyard.

A vast blot of flame enveloped the gloom. A terrific blast smote the gun crew like a hammer. The impact tore the sandbags to shreds. Metal screeched far into the night. And as blinded eyes finally recovered from the deadly glare, they saw what remained of a three inch gun; a warped, grotesque tangle of steel.

When they finally regained their feet, Sultan Iskander and Datu Hamid and Farrell exchanged long glances unbroken by words. Somehow, Farrell felt those iron eye-thrusts. Odd...though he had not expected that gruff old sultan to thank him for a saving hunch.

"Try number two!" commanded Sultan Iskander.

This time he did not have to be jerked behind the sand bags.

Farrell signaled.

The lanyard yank destroyed a second gun. *Two muzzle bursts in succession!* Though obsolete, the guns were in good condition. Farrell's head was ringing; and then he realized that Irma was saved. There would be no bombardment. Tsang Wu could escape to his boat.

He felt limp but happy—for an instant. Then the world smashed to fragments across his head.

"So this is the way you ransom Tsang Wu's prisoners, is it?" The sultan's voice was iron. "I heard just enough. But I could not believe. So I refused to take cover. You knew, so you acted to save me.

"And since you would not let me blow up with the plugged gun, I will spare you your life. But not if I ever see you again!"

"The gun was not plugged!" declared Farrell. "You saw me inspect it when the tompion was removed!"

Sultan Iskander did not argue. He plucked Farrell's pistol from its holster, flung it to the ground, drew Farrell's curved sword, dashed it against the smoking stump of a gun barrel. Then his outflung arm pointed to the farther darkness.

"And on your life, do not return!"

Farrell stalked like a walking corpse toward the mainland. But as he stumbled across a wagon trail leading eastward, his numbed brain began to ache.

He was hoodooed. First Irma and his own people had disowned him...now the sultan whose life he had saved. Suddenly he straightened, and his laugh was a sword caressing a whetstone.

Go empty-handed to Tsang Wu's fortress and go out in a big blaze. Let Irma see what kind of man she'd rejected. Following his original plan, and moved by the courage of a man who amounts to something, he might have saved her. But now—!

He turned to head for the narrow beach and toward the jutting headland, unseen either by the pirates or his former troops; but a stirring at the edge of a clump of causarina trees checked him.

In the dimness of the half risen moon he saw a slender spindle of silken luster, and the blurred whiteness of a woman's face; but it was the voice he recognized.

I heard," said Chen Li. "So I waited. Naturally I'd not return to Tsang Wu, and lingering around your former camp would have been as bad."

They eyed each other in the half light. She sensed the purpose that made his face a gray, grim mask; and his direction had told her the rest.

"Don't be a fool. You're unarmed. That's not valor. It's insanity. You can't save her."

"Well, what the hell am I to do?" he demanded. In weariness he yielded the initiative.

Chan Li's smile became a crimson blossom.

"You are a man among men. Even though some traitor has ruined you. Come with me to Penang. Though Tsang Wu does not know it, my father is a wealthy trader, with ships and plantations, and—"

"Nuts for your father!" he growled, rebelling at Chan Li's honeyed bribe.

"He will be grateful." She drew closer and murmured in his ear: "And so will I—if you help me back to Penang. Alone, I have no chance."

She was soft and lovely and silken. Prowling outlaws would grab her. That was none of Farrell's affair; but it restored some of his courage to know that this woman could still regard him as one to be sought in the face of peril.

Her plea whipped to life his wavering self-esteem and beaten pride. She was very close now, fragrant and clinging. The cream-colored flesh that smiled through the torn tunic and pajamas became golden in the rising moon, and Farrell's pulse responded to the strange lure of that exotic creature. Those piquant glimpses of sleek, slender loveliness were just enough to remind him that so much more was concealed. This was no sing-song girl whose supple curves clung insistently to him, whose caressing hands seconded the supplication of her voice.

Irma had condemned him with the rest. She'd forgotten to discard that snapshot. Down in his heart he knew now that she hadn't, but Chan Li's silken sweetness made anything plausible.

Someone had told him that the Chinese know nothing about kissing, but Chan Li's torrid lips disproved that slander. Her eyes had become black opals mysteriously veiled by long drooping lashes. Her breath quickened, and the ripples of desire that pulsed through that slim, cream-colored body were pointed by roundnesses Farrell had thus far unsuspected.

"Even if we should fall into the hands of bandits before we get to Penang," whispered Chan Li, "I'll have at least this to remember. I'd rather you were first…"

That struck his weak spot: regardless of what was ahead of him, he would have at least a short memory of one person who believed in him.

"This little hour will cheat death." But as her arms closed about him, her voice became inarticulate and her lips an insistent, consuming fire…

* * * *

Finally the moonglow invaded the clearing and silvered Chan Li's languid loveliness. She stirred drowsily, snuggled closer, but Farrell withdrew from her possessive arm.

Her seeking him had dispelled the blank uselessness that had oppressed him; and with its departure came the renewal of responsibility.

"I can't leave her there. Tsang Wu is still waiting. Both guns were destroyed. Sultan Iskander can't carry on the bombardment."

Chan Li knew that her caresses had put iron into his soul; but she smiled at his defiant anticipation of her outburst.

"I lose," she said. "You'll surely be killed. But I might have expected this of a man among men. If you'd been less than what you are, my hour would have been a mockery."

"I'll be damned," he muttered as he noted the misty softness of her eyes.

"I'll show you a way," Chan Li continued, "to slip past a sentry. If that succeeds, you'll have a chance."

Did she mean it, or was this subtle Chinese vengeance in the bud? Steel blue glance clashed with black. And then, as he always did when things were at the worst, Farrell decided to shoot the works.

"Let's go." He did not add that if they succeeded, he'd put Irma on a train to Singapore and accompany Chan Li to Penang.

They crept along the beach. When they reached the shadow of the ruin, they scaled the crags of Tanjong Merah. Just before they cleared the crest, he listened to Chan Li's description of the fortress, and watched her lengthening the rents in her rumpled tunic and pajamas. The display was as dazzling as it was frank.

Farrell, flattened to the ground, now watched Chan Li advance. From a narrow gateway came a challenge in Chinese.

"Tell Tsang Wu I have returned," she answered. "The white captain has agreed."

The sentry hailed the guard. The commander emerged from the ruin. Chan Li went to meet him. The sentry craned his neck to refresh his eyes with another glimpse of her moon-kissed flesh as she glided toward the commander of the guard.

Chan Li's rear elevation was worth anyone's eye; but the sentry's vision was blotted out by a blaze of shooting lights. He never knew that Farrell, silently slipping up from the rear, had cracked him across the head with a rock the size of a coconut.

Farrell dressed himself in the sentry's salt-caked jacket and trousers. He rolled him into outer shadows, and took his rifle and dagger.

He strode boldly into the court and toward a blot of light that marked a barred window in an angle of the wall. Peeping over the sill, he saw a short, square-shouldered Chinese with long, trailing moustaches and a grim, handsome face: Tsang Wu, the terror of the south China Sea.

Chan Li stood facing him; and at her side was a burly Manchu nearly as tall as Farrell. Judging from his richly brocaded jacket and embroidered felt boots, this must be the pirate's lieutenant.

"Wang Ho," said Tsang Wu at the completion of the girl's report, "how soon will you be able to pull the ship off the sandbar?"

"The sea will calm down enough in three or four hours, honorable captain," answered the Manchu. "But as soon as we return the yellow-haired girl, the troops will bombard us. And if we don't return her, they'll do the same. Our bargain is useless."

"You are stupid, Wang Ho!" snapped the chief. "Leave her on the sand bar. He'll know enough then not to shell our boat. We'll be able to pick her off with a rifle until we're out of range of his guns, way back there on the mainland."

"The sun of wisdom sets behind your head," admitted Wang Ho. "Now, about this Chan Li? She is going to waste, and that would be a shame."

"Don't touch her!" warned Tsang Wu. "I'm saving her for a customer in Java. He'll pay enough to buy us girls all around."

Then, to one of his crew: "Lock her up!"

Farrell followed Chan Li and her captor down a gloomy tunnel leading toward the northern wall of the fort. As they approached the entrance of a casemate illuminated by moonlight filtering in through a gun port, he drove home with the salvaged rifle. The butt splintered, crushing the Chinaman's skull.

Just ahead of Farrell, ankle shackled to a ring-bolt sunk in the masonry, was Irma Stanley. One glimpse of her lovely face and the shapely whiteness of breasts that half evaded the remnants of her tattered bodice justified his recklessness; but he had not counted on iron fetters.

"Get out!" he said, catching Chan Li's arm. "I'll tend to this. It's going to take time."

"I'll take my chances with you," she persisted, following him into the cell.

Irma recognized him, despite his disguise.

"Glenn—my God—are they gone—?"

"Pipe down!" he warned, breaking clear of her arms. "Get out of my way so I can dig into this mortar."

As he set to work, Chan Li joined him. She was armed with a knife taken from her late guard. Together they gouged and chipped, but the task seemed hopeless.

"Shear off the shackle!" As that thought cropped up, Farrell picked up a loose block of stone and struck the back of the knife against the soft iron pin.

Sping! The blade snapped half way between point and guard. Still gripping the useless weapon, he reached for Chan Li's knife.

"Now get out! You can't help!"

He did not hear her answer, or get the knife. A thunderous rumbling had drowned the angry roar of the lashing waves far below. An unseen hand flung him backward; and as he recovered, he saw a sullen glow, far out on the water. It rose, a column of flame reaching skyward.

Tsang Wu's armored yacht had been destroyed. Somehow, Sultan Iskander had managed to strike. And Tsang Wu, thinking that Farrell had mocked him, would pause for Chinese vengeance that would endure after the pirate's head was grinning from a lance head.

To liberate Irma was now impossible. Regardless of how the yacht had been destroyed, the troops could not take the place by assault—not until long after Tsang Wu's vengeance.

One slim chance, however, remained. Slip up in the confusion, knife Tsang Wu and his lieutenant. Break for the sultan's camp, risk his wrath, lead his troops up the slope while the pirates were demoralized. Insane, but it might work.

The court was already crowded with raging pirates. Darkness and excitement protected Farrell as he followed the wave to Tsang Wu's quarters. There he saw the chief, grim but cool, curbing the panic.

"We can hold out," he roared. "His guns blew up, I told you! Those two explosions. He can't attack. Wang Ho, take the launch and go to Pulau Gajah for a boat big enough—"

A shout drowned his instructions. The jabbering crowd parted. Someone was leading a prisoner: Datu Hamid!

But a moment later, Farrell knew that his rival was a traitor.

"I have the answer for you, Tsang Wu," said the datu. "I will go back and dispose of the sultan. Then you attack in force and scatter his men before they recover from their panic. That done, we all march back to the capital. I will be the sultan—I have powerful friends—you will be rewarded—"

"How did he blow up our boat if he had no guns?" interrupted Tsang Wu.

"He sent out two *prahus*. One was loaded with shells. The crew of the other touched off a time fuse. Simple. Now will you follow my plan?"

"Very well," agreed Tsang Wu. "And to be sure it is not a trap—"

"Make sure any way you want!" snapped Hamid. "Do you think I'd have come here if I couldn't stand any test?"

"We'll see," said Tsang Wu. A crafty light gleamed in his eyes, and he beckoned to Wang Ho. A whispered exchange, then he again addressed the traitor: "Go, and hurry. We will wait."

Farrell now had time to release Irma; but the life of Sultan Iskander was at stake. That stern old man who had spared Farrell even though convinced of his treason was still the American's benefactor.

Whatever might happen to Irma, it wouldn't kill her!

The crowd parted to make way as Datu Hamid strode swiftly to the gate.

Farrell wormed his way among the pirates. He had to hug the wall, move with the crowd, avoid detection at all cost.

When he finally reached the exit, Datu Hamid was far below in the darkness. No chance of overtaking him, short of the camp.

Farrell now knew why the two guns had exploded. Datu Hamid's treachery explained it. The trick was easy. A high explosive shell fuse has a safety lock that is flung off by the rotation of the flying projectile. Its purpose is to prevent accidental discharge during the handling of the shell. Its removal would permit the fuse plunger to strike home the instant the gun was fired, causing the shell to burst before it left the muzzle.

Farrell lost precious minutes worming his way past the sentries. With infinite caution he worked his way toward a cluster of shrubbery that commanded a view of the sultan's pavilion. He heard Hamid's voice. They were conferring. A sound from the rear distracted Farrell. Another section of artillery was on the way. The sultan was receiving reinforcements.

That would goad Hamid to faster action. The traitor had to strike before the bombardment robbed him of his Chinese ally; yet Farrell, discredited, dared not reveal himself.

The sultan and Hamid emerged from the pavilion.

"Your Highness, those guns should be placed at the north—"

"No, by Allah!" snapped Sultan Iskander. "I said—"

"But be pleased to look over the ground," persisted the traitor. He gestured toward the spot where he proposed placing the artillery.

Farrell flanked them as they paralleled the camp. Bit by bit Hamid drew the sultan out of earshot of his troops.

And then it happened, swift as a striking serpent. As the conspirator gestured, his hand flashed to his belt. Steel now gleamed.

Farrell's warning yell startled the sultan. He whirled, still unsuspecting. The blade raked him. For an instant he was dazed by the unexpected attack by his trusted follower. Then as he leaped aside, jerking his pistol, Hamid lunged. He snatched the weapon before it rose into line. A premature alarm would be fatal.

They grappled, crashed to the ground, flailed and threshed about, both stabbing and slashing.

Farrell's last leap carried him home. His half-blade slashed as they rolled into the shrubbery. Spurting blood drenched him. The ragged steel ripped flesh. But as he struggled to his feet, a man in Chinese brocade came ploughing through the underbrush. He caught Farrell off balance. His knife flashed down. Though Farrell writhed clear, his arm was wrenched and numb. He drove up with his knee, but missed—

And then a muffled pistol blast sent a backlash of blinding flame across his face. The enemy collapsed, the top of his head blasted away.

Farrell kicked clear. He saw the wounded sultan, smoking pistol still in hand, struggle to his feet. Hamid's ally was Wang Ho, sent to check up on the conspirator.

"This has been an instructive moment," said Sultan Iskander, eyeing Hamid's Mongolian ally.

The sultan's jacket was slashed and red, but he kept his feet. And then an officer, followed by a squad of *askaris*, came charging from camp.

"They came to take your head and toss it into camp to demoralize your men," explained Farrell. "Wang Ho followed Hamid to be sure of his good faith.

"They expect him to return. And I'm taking his place. Surprise is our only chance. You can't get the artillery into action in time. I'll put on Wang Ho's coat. That will fool the sentry. Once a few of us get in, the rest can charge up the slope, the quick way."

He dashed to the beach. His heart pounded like a riveting hammer. Tsang Wu having arranged for a counter attack against the murdered sultan's camp, would seek Irma to celebrate in anticipation.

As he scaled the ragged cliff, he heard the singsong chatter of the exultant pirates. And then, as he reached the crest, a woman cried out from the northern casemate. It was clear through the gun port, and the confusion of voices in the courtyard did not drown that scream.

Irma's voice. Tsang Wu's savage laugh. A curse, a slap. Her nails were raking deep, but her agonized gasp all too plainly marked the end of her resistance...

Farrell's blood froze—but he did not dare to hurry. He popped out into the open moonlight. His face was shadowed, and he wore Wang Ho's brocaded silks.

"Quick, pig!" he growled in Cantonese, mimicking the Manchu's curt voice. "Where's the chief? Tell him—"

The startled sentry, listening to the sounds that made him envy Tsang Wu, whirled as that commanding voice broke in. A short flash of steel blotted out his second-hand thrills.

Farrell snatched the sentry's rifle. And as his handful of Malays cleared the narrow, unguarded gate, he bounded into the court.

A swift glance. A cluster of pirates squatted in front of Tsang Wu's empty quarters.

Farrell's rifle, suddenly jerked to his hip, poured fire and lead into them as they clambered to their feet, off balance and without a chance to act.

A ripping volley from his right and left seconded his surprise attack. The Malays mowed them down, but reinforcements came from the further end of the court. Yet for a moment Farrell and his handful had the advantage. Hot lead and cold *krisses* swept the enemy back in confusion.

He could no longer hear the voice from the casemate. They were pocketed now, and the angle of the wall became a red nightmare.

Tsang Wu was not leading the counter-attack...

Three of Farrell's men were down, bullet-riddled and slashed, but they still crawled on, stabbing upward with their red blades, as though hoping to drown in enemy blood before they died of their wounds.

And then a familiar voice rang above the mad confusion: Sultan Iskander. Farrell caught a glimpse of him from the corner of his eye as he discarded his rifle and snatched a curved sword.

A wrathful howl, a savage ripple of musketry, and the Malays charged.

Farrell pressed on, and as the battle surged past the entrance of the passageway, he bounded toward the casemate.

What he saw confirmed the outcry he had heard. Irma, still shackled by one ankle, lay sprawled on the floor. She stirred feebly. One arm was still bent in a repulsing gesture. Only a few shreds of her gown were left. Tsang Wu concealed most of her bare body. His head was a gory pulp, and his blood spattered Inna's drawn face and her breasts. Near him lay the block of stone that had crushed the back of his head.

Farrell had arrived too late even for vengeance. Something silken crouched in a corner. A woman—

"Chan Li! What the devil—!"

She recognized his voice, and explained, "I tried to use my knife, but he knocked me against the wall. And later, I picked up that rock."

Farrell dragged Tsang Wu aside. Irma stirred feebly, cried out, then recognized him.

"God..." Her voice was low and trembling. "Why didn't you stay away altogether?...you're lucky...they didn't get around to your yellow sweetheart—"

She was hysterical, but Farrell's nerves were wire-edged.

"Listen, damn it!" he snapped. "I went back to save a Malay who took me from the beach when you and the white colony threw rocks at me.

"And what's happened tonight'd be nothing to what would have happened if Chan Li hadn't showed me the way to slip in here. Your having kept that picture all these months sort of made me hope I might stage a comeback—"

Her defiance cracked.

"I'm sorry, Glenn…" She questioningly eyed him through her tears, saw the grimness leave his face. Then her glance shifted to Chan Li. "Do you really care for her—"

"Of course he doesn't," said Chan Li. "He was betrayed and beaten. I had my hour and I helped him. Send me to Penang, and we will forget this, the three of us. He was mad enough to try to release you single-handed. I knew from the beginning that I couldn't have him."

Farrell and Irma eyed each other. Then he said, "It'd been a lot worse if you'd been killed, darling. You and I both have a lot to forget. So we can start out even."

TREASURE FROM KURDISTAN

Originally published in *Spicy-Adventure Stories*, August 1936, under the title "No Questions Asked" under the pseudonym "Ralph Carle."

Bagdad was in evening dress. The squish of bare feet sinking ankle-deep in the rubbish-laden street competed with the racking cough of a hasheesh smoker, and the high-pitched cursing of a native woman, getting very much the best of an argument.

A drum muttered, and the whimper of a lute invited passersby into Abou Kassim's café. A girl tapped on the shutters and whispered the Arabic equivalent of, "Show you a good time, Baby…"

Some accepted, but the tallest of the turbaned specters sifting through the gloom stalked straight on, though he grinned and answered, "Not a chance, little one!"

He was lean and rangy, with a face the color of a cordovan boot. He called himself Shir Khan, and prayed five times a day—which was more than he did when at home, and wearing his own name.

Glenn Farrell was on the prowl again.

As usual, he was broke, but the collector who had sent him to Bagdad had everything but the nerve to track down the fabulous prayer rug, woven five centuries ago for Khalil Sultan, Tamerlane's drunken grandson. It was a sea-green witchery of silk and threads of gold, with pious texts embroidered in pearls.

A month in the native quarter of Bagdad verified the rumor. It was all over but the payoff, and to hell with girls tapping at shutters! Later—well, that was something else…

A block past the Merdjan Mosque Farrell knocked at a barred door. A tall negro led him from the high odors of the street into a storeroom heaped to the ceiling with baled Persian carpets.

A white-bearded man with sharp eyes and a beak of a nose saluted him. They seated themselves on an upholstered bench in an alcove. The old man clapped his hands and whispered an order to the negro. He left, and presently reappeared with Khalil Sultan's fabulous rug. There was no doubting its authenticity; yet to remain in character, Farrell continued his haggling.

"Twenty-five hundred pounds, *Inglesi*, and my blessing," demanded old Abbas. "Were I not sorely in debt, I would not sell at any price."

"Two thousand, and may Allah reward the generous!" pleaded Farrell. "I am poor, and I buy only to keep it in the family."

"In the family?" echoed the Arab.

"Ay wallah!" swore Farrell. "The grandfather of my great grandfather took this at the looting of Kabul. Some thief stole it from my father, may Allah be pleased with him!"

The bargaining was finally interrupted by the negro.

"Nurredin Shirkuh," he announced; and then the visitor, stalking in at the negro's heels, spoke for himself: "*Ay wallah!* Nurredin Shirkuh, a Kurd from Kurdistan."

He was tall, rawboned; a mountaineer richly dressed, and bristling with weapons. His eyes, like Farrell's, were the color of frost-bitten steel. Whether he was a prince or a bandit, Farrell could not guess. But he knew that Nurredin was one to be reckoned with.

"That rug," continued the Kurd. "I heard you offer it for twenty-five hundred pounds!"

"I should have said three thousand," countered the old Arab. "It belonged to the grandson of Tamerlane."

"My illustrious ancestor," Shirkuh modestly admitted. "For his sake, I will pay what you ask."

Farrell leaped to his feet.

"*Ya* Abbas," he sternly demanded, "what fraud is this? A confederate to raise the price?"

Shirkuh's retort was a heavy wallet that tinkled as it dropped to the floor.

"Count it," challenged the Kurd.

Trick or not, Farrell had to work fast. He thrust a sheaf of bank of England notes at the Arab merchant.

"Here is as much as he has offered. I have a first claim. Hold it until I come back with as much again. They say you are honest. You cannot deny me this right."

"Thou hast spoken," assented the Arab, ignoring Shirkuh's wrathful protests. "One full day to raise the money, and may Allah prosper thee."

Shirkuh's hand slipped to his arsenal. For a moment their glances crossed; then Farrell deliberately turned his back and stalked toward the door.

"Something," he pondered as he strode down the narrow street, "is screwy. Old Abbas is honest according to his lights. But if it isn't a set-up, what in hell is it anyhow?"

Half an hour later, at the Alwayeh Club, Farrell presented his credentials to a man who could raise five hundred pounds sterling at any hour of the day or night.

"Good luck, Farrell," said the official as he handed him a packet of bank notes, "but be careful. The way this Kurdish chap popped up is a bit off color."

"It is," admitted Farrell. "But old Abbas is on the level."

"No doubt," answered the other. "I wasn't thinking of him. You'd better take an escort," Farrell shook his head. "Once old Abbas suspected that a European was on the trail, he would deny he ever heard of such a rug."

He turned back to the native city; but as he approached the mosque, a pair of heavily-laden camels blocked his way. Farrell turned left down a narrow alley. Too late, he realized that was a mistake, and that an escort would have come in handy.

A fisherman's net, flung from between two buildings, settled down about his shoulders. As he sought to disentangle himself, half a dozen dark figures bounded from a doorway, belaboring him with clubs as they bore him to the earth. Farrell drew his heavy bladed *jambia* and thrust upward into the pack.

There was a howl, a scrambling and a threshing of arms and legs.

As the pack shifted, Farrell slashed the slimy net. Though still entangled, he gained freedom for one arm. His fist shot forward, driving the heavy pomme. of his knife smashing full into an acre of ivory. A kick in the stomach doubled him, but did not check his resistance.

Farrell shook two active assailants from his shoulders; before he could get clear, they discarded their clubs, and dragged him into the side alley. A lucky kick drove one of his captors smashing against a wall. Farrell, still clutching his knife, slashed out—

But it was not his blade that broke the riot. A woman screamed. Pottery spattered to fragments and a flood of scalding water drenched the top layer of the writhing tangle. They scattered. Farrell plunged toward the door that had opened at the right. But as he crossed the threshold, the lady shrieked, "Out of my house, O father of a pig! Out—"

She meant out. Farrell stumbled, still trying to dodge the earthenware pot. It caught him a glancing blow, flattening him to the floor. Only his compact turban saved his skull. His wits went out in a red haze; but his assailants, having their fill of hot water, were dashing down the alley. And they had the police to reckon with.

* * * *

Farrell, as he came out of the fog, sensed that he was not a prisoner. The stench of the side street still clung to his clothing; but the mud had been wiped from his face. He was in a small, clean room of a native house, stretched out on a bench that paralleled the mud wall. A young woman was kneeling beside him.

"I thought you were one of them," she explained. "I didn't realize my mistake until you dropped."

"Say no more about that," Farrell grinned.

He hastily felt for his wallet. It was intact. Then he found time to appraise his hostess.

Her dress was striking—what there was of it! Her blue-black hair was heavily laden with gold coins linked together. Beneath her brown woolen cloak she was quite bare, except for the hammered silver disks that cupped her breasts, and the broad girdle of silver and turquoise gleaming against her walnut-colored skin. She was an entertainer of one of the native cafes. That explained her costume, but did not account for her failure to go through Farrell's wallet.

The girl, sensing his unspoken query, began, "I am Zobeide. Just like the great Khalif's wife." She reeked with attar of roses, and her eyelids were heavily blackened. She was plump, full-breasted, but shapely. A substantial armful of a girl.

"What's the idea, Zobeide. Taking an evening off?"

"No. There was a quarrel with the son of the proprietor, Allah curse his grandfather! So I brained him with a *narghilah*. When I heard the riot at my door, I thought he had sent some of his bouncers to take me to the police."

He drew a new bank of England note from his wallet and slipped it into her hands, then stepped toward the door; but Zobeide caught his arm.

"Don't go!" she implored, fairly dragging him back.

"I won't be gone long," he said, smiling grimly. "I've got a bit of business to attend to…"

"Then let me go along," she begged, "if that brother of a dog doesn't have me arrested, he will dump me in the river."

Zobeide was alarmed, and her persuasion was as vigorous as her hurling of pots. She fairly overwhelmed Farrell with her strong, supple arms, and a stifling gust of attar of roses.

After all, old Abbas had given him a twenty-four hour option. Farrell, moreover, was still groggy, and Zobeide's vigorous embrace offered several reasons for humoring her whim. He couldn't see her legs, at the moment, but she was supple as a serpent, and made the most of her talent for clinging tight…

"Maybe there's something in your idea, after all," gasped Farrell, finally getting his mouth dear of her sultry lips, "but we'd get along better if you took off some of that jewelry!"

Zobeide's silver brassiere was gouging into Farrell's knife-creased chest; and he was wondering whether she really needed any such adornments.

As he seated himself beside her on the upholstered *mastaba*, Zobeide admitted that they weren't appropriate except at the cafe…

For a badly battered rug collector, Farrell did well enough by the girl who had been named after Haroun el Rashid's favorite wife… In fact, about all the original Zobeide could show her would be a face perhaps a trifle more aristocratic…

The rising moon was gilding this domes of the great Kadamain Mosque when Farrell and Zobeide declared a truce.

"Something tells me that I'd better see Abbas right now," Farrell decided. "And don't sap me when I come back."

"I'll go with you, so you can protect me against that father of many pigs."

She fumbled beneath the upholstery of the *mastaba*, and produced a Webley automatic which she thrust into his hand, explaining, "I stole this from a soldier the other night. It may come handy."

* * * *

Old Abbas received Farrell in his reception room. His face was grim and his eyes were bleak. He declined the packet of bills that Farrell offered him.

"Nurredin Shirkuh's servants saw you receive this money from the infidel officials, and heard him greet you as one of them. So I would not favor you against a True Believer. He has the rug."

And that finished Farrell's case.

"So that explains my being waylaid! Your pious friend tried to rob me. Allah blacken him!"

Old Abbas made no personal issue of Farrell's having impersonated a true believer.

"Wallah, sahib," he admitted, "it was not right to have you waylaid."

He reached into a cabinet for the deposit Farrell had left with him.

"This is yours. Perhaps if you seek Nurredin in his native town, you might bargain with him."

"Is he really descended from Khalil Sultan?" wondered Farrell.

"He must be, or he would not be fool enough to want that ragged rug," answered Abbas. "Only pride of race could make him so extravagant."

Nurredin Shirkuh, knowing that his men had attacked an infidel, would hastily leave Bagdad; but on such a long pursuit, a fresh start, rather than a quick one would be best for Farrell.

Two days later, Farrell and Zobeide followed the Tigris upstream. Being accompanied by a native woman enabled him to avoid undue association with fellow travelers halting at village taverns. Zobeide in more ways than one, was a priceless acquisition…

* * * *

Weeks later, they reached the last leg of the trip. Nurredin Shirkuh, Farrell learned, was an emir. That made him easy to find; but getting into his house, or even venturing into the village at the foot of the hill which it crowned, was like tickling a tiger's tonsils.

In a grimy, verminous *serai*, Farrell and Zobeide plotted the approach.

"By Allah, *sahib*," she explained as she grilled bits of mutton over a charcoal fire, "each day when I go to the market, I will look for Nurredin's servants. The rest will be easy…"

"You're priceless," interrupted Farrell, affectionately eyeing the plump, pleasant-faced girl who had adopted him as a protector. "I don't know how I'd get along without you."

They were far from the arm of British or any other law, and surrounded by Kurdish tribesmen who cherished age-old feuds, plotted assassinations for pleasure or profit, and raided in the lowlands for food or sport.

"And you will always love me, Shir Khan?" she would whisper of an evening when the glow of the charcoal fire on the packed earth floor barely peeped through the film of gathering ashes.

"Always, Zobeide," he would answer, half meaning it.

The end of his quest was far away. Looting the house of Nurredin Shirkuh was fantastic beyond reckoning.

Then came Ramadan, when for a month every Moslem fasts from sunrise to sunset, and spends the night in gluttony. The local dignitaries held open house, feasting until the sunrise gun announced the beginning of the day's long fast.

The upsetting of all routine was Farrell's opportunity.

* * * *

Late that night he scaled the wall of Nurredin's courtyard. The horses in the stable on the ground floor were restive, but the grooms were noisily making away with a roasted lamb.

Farrell ascended the stairs to the reception room. It was dark. Nurredin was out, as Zobeide had predicted. The sky glow filtering in through barred windows coaxed reflections from brazen tea pots, and silver mounted blades. He risked using his pocket flash he had hoarded ever since leaving Bagdad.

Long narrow rugs ran along the stone benches that skirted the wall, and an oblong carpet was in the center. They were all ancient and mellow and precious, but the antique he sought was not at the master's seat of honor, near the hearth, where he had expected to find it displayed.

He would have to search the entire house. It might even be in some secret treasure vault. No one except the master and perhaps some trusted steward would know where the crypt was: and in that case his quest was hopeless.

Then he heard the tinkling notes of a *sitar*, and the voices of women on the floor above. One was singing, and the sound was like a draught of old wine. But while their presence was an added peril, it suggested the next move: they would be gathered about to listen to her, and thus might not notice Farrell's prowling.

He crept up the narrow stairway. It opened into an arched passage that had cross branches which penetrated the murky depths of that massive heap. He heard the tinkle of anklets, feminine laughter, then again that girl's heart stirring voice.

> "...sabiyat il unsi ilaya
> Badri quabl al fawat
> Wunshéri tibun sakiyun
> Mun 'ashan fi el-hyat..."

"Come to me, Gazelle, before I die..." He wondered where she had learned that one, and in Arabic, up here in the wrong end of Kurdistan. He grimaced wryly, muttered, "Stay where you are, Gazelle, or *I* die!"

But as he headed in the opposite direction, he wished that he could have one glimpse of her. If she looked like she sounded...!

Farrell was now in the quarters reserved to the master and his immediate family. Even the emir's closest male friends would not dare go that far.

Finally he reached a room where boots and holstered pistols and curved swords in gilded scabbards took the place of cosmetics and massive jewelry.

Slowly the pencil of light picked out one barbaric detail after another, but not the prayer rug of an emperor's grandson. Yet there was still time; the women in the other wing were still chattering...

Farrell's first warning was a faint rustling behind him. A breath of sweetness invaded the scent of tobacco and leather and horses. He whirled to silence the person whose outcry was to be his death-warrant. One scream, and the house would be in an uproar. The grooms in the stable would be aroused...

A girl was in the doorway. She held a taper whose flickering glow was reflected from the uncounted jewels of her ornate headdress. Her eyes were dark and long, slightly widened with amazement. They glistened, and tears beaded her lashes.

She was startled, but her lovely face betrayed not a trace of fear. Though standing fast, she was poised like a young tigress. The sudden rise of her breasts betrayed the momentary catching of her breath; but she was utterly unafraid. That suggested a better play than trying to throttle an outcry.

Even one *yeep* would bring the house down on his neck. Peril and tension sharpened his wits.

"What's the trouble?" he asked. The steadiness of his voice surprised him. "Didn't you like their singing?"

She blinked away her tears, narrowly regarded him, and smiled somberly.

"No. I came here to my father's rooms to get away from them. And if you are poor, go abroad tonight, where men are giving alms. Allah will provide." Having been tripped up at the start, Farrell's quest was over. Henceforth the house would be guarded. Bitterness made him reckless.

"Then it was you that I heard singing," he said, as if he had not noted her gesture.

"Yes. And they mocked me. My father's new wife. She hates me because my own mother was the daughter of a prince in Gurjestan."

That explained her indifference to the presence of a harmless looter. She had troubles of her own. And that gave Farrell his next play…

"The sweetness lingered in my ears, and from listening for the next verse I did not hear your approach."

"You don't look like a thief." She smiled, and the imperiously gesturing arm dropped to her side. "Who are you?"

"No friend of your father's," he answered. "He robbed me, but I am Shir Khan and I do not forget."

A feud is a debt of honor which any Kurd could understand.

"I'm Djenane." The smile became dazzling. "I prefer my father's enemies to his wives. Let us wait for him," she mocked. "I know he will receive you well."

Djenane knew that she was in no danger from an honest assassin. Her invitation gave him choice of immediate flight or staying and facing murderous odds.

The challenge was too good to decline. Not even her loose garments could hide the shapeliness of her body. If she listened long enough, let him help her damn her stepmother…the evening was rich with possibilities.

"I will wait," he said, seating himself beside her. "But not too long."

"You're much wiser than my father's usual choice of enemies, Shir Khan. Most of them would have snubbed me by taking to their heels at once."

Farrell's thoughts were no longer concerned with prayer rugs. He could not misunderstand Djenane's scrutiny. He had interested her, and in Kurdistan, to lie in wait to assassinate one's enemy is one of the traits of a man of honor.

"Malika," resumed Farrell, "if your father were my friend, I could oftener hear you sing…what was that last one about the gazelle?"

She hummed a line, cast an anxious glance at the door, and silently closed it. The gleam of the taper light on her lustrous dark hair, the shimmer of brocaded silk that clung to her slender body, and the sweetness she exhaled made Farrell's brain a whirling madness.

He caught her in his arms, and though she drew back, she did not raise her voice. Her dark eyes flashed a haughty reproof, but after a long moment, she yielded, drawing closer into his embrace. Her warmth was intoxicating, and the touch of her clinging silk was maddening.

Farrell kissed her full on the mouth. She gasped and protested…but not as vigorously as she might have. She broke away, then smiled and curled up in his arms like a silken kitten.

308

"I rather like you, Shir Khan," she sighed, "though I'm sure you'll die an early death..."

"But a happy one," he answered; and this time his embrace squeezed her breathless, and his mouth crushed her eager lips.

Farrell meant it. She was unlike any native woman he had ever seen. She was an intoxicating fragrance, and an armful of heart-stabbing beauty.

Djenane Hanoun was lonely, and though Shir Khan was her father's enemy, he had kissed away her tears. She no longer repulsed him as he pressed her closer...

* * * *

The taper had sputtered down to a bit of wick floating in a pool of wax when Djenane at last extricated herself from his embrace and whispered, "He'll soon be returning from the feast. I'll show you a way out. The next night he is gone, come back again. But promise not to try to slay him..."

"Let him live for another day," Farrell generously conceded. He followed her down a maze of passages that finally opened in a secret exit in a cluster of trees just outside the palace.

Farrell floated on air back to the village at the foot of the hill.

If was not until he was almost at the *serai* that it occurred to him that he had made absolutely no progress in finding Khalil Sultan's prayer rug. But he was on the right track, and this was more than squaring up with Nurredin Shirkuh!

Then his face lengthened. Zobeide had an overload of intuition...

He shook his head, grimaced, and picked his way among the grumbling camels and sleeping jackasses in the courtyard. Maybe Zobeide was asleep...

Ramadan was wearing on. Farrell and Djenane were flirting with sudden death but neither any longer cared for anything except the kisses exchanged in the shadow of the sword. He forgot himself so far as to tell Djenane that he had come to loot and not to slay; and Djenane reciprocated by telling him of the secret vault in which the emir had stored the plunder of generations.

"Loot enough to break the back of a dozen camels," she whispered as Farrell again left her at the secret door. "In another day or two I will have the secret. I will watch him when he digs out some gold for Ramadan alms-giving. It will be easy. And you will take me away from this place."

Farrell's heart was heavy as he went to the *serai*. The rug might not be missed at once, but with Djenane also gone, the lid would blow off. They'd have to ride hard. Nor did he want to leave her. Sooner or later she would be connected with the looting...he'd have to take her.

"It'll be great when she and Zobeide tangle up," he muttered.

Zobeide had followed his account of exploring Shirkuh's house, and without the least trace of suspicion. But one lingering trace of Djenane's perfume could betray him; and until it was all over, he would be as uneasy as a cat with wet feet.

* * * *

Farrell spent the following day selecting fast horses, and picking up information as to the mountain passes he would have to clear.

Zobeide was honey and sweetness that night as they awaited the time for the raid.

"I almost had it," he told her, "but one of the servants broke in, just as Nurredin was returning. I barely slipped out. But I found the treasure vault."

"Who else could be as clever?" marveled Zobeide.

And presently Farrell was prowling through the village to assure himself against upsets, such as the chance that the emir would be entertaining at home.

As he circled towards the north of the village, he heard the *click-click* of hoofs, and the jingle of arms. Two horsemen were entering the village. Farrell slipped behind a buttress. But as they emerged from the shadow of an overhanging rock, a crackle of musketry and the savage screech of ricochet bullets told Farrell that this was no Ramadan celebration.

The first of the two riders pitched from his saddle. His horse screamed and reared, and toppled over in a kicking heap. The other, drawing a pistol and firing as he wheeled his beast, suddenly slumped, wobbled crazily, and slid to the ground, jerking a wild shot as his horse bolted into the darkness.

Another feud, and no business of Farrell's. A clean sweep...so he thought for a split second, and then pistol fire spurted from the further darkness. Black figures were ducking from rock to rock, firing as they ran. Steel gleamed, and the cleft in the cliff echoed with yells and curses. The town would be in an uproar in another moment.

The man firing from behind the body of his fallen horse was wounded, but evidently far from dead. At the first sign of peril, he must have taken a dive from his beast. But while the horse had caught the slugs intended for its rider, the carcass had pinned him to the rocks.

The further side of the cleft blossomed into a crop of curved blades and flaming pistols as the raiders closed in to finish their victim and get away before help came from the village.

It was none of Farrell's business, but something urged him to take the part of the man pinned down by his horse. Moreover, he might come in handy. His good will would spare Farrell embarrassing questions; and flight would make him dangerously conspicuous.

Revolver in hand, he bounded from cover as the dismounted slayers charged, and hosed them with lead. The leader pitched headlong across the fallen horse.

Another staggered and shifted his weapon toward the new attack; and then Farrell was in the midst of it. Two more shots and his revolver was empty; but the odds were whittled down and he gained the shelter of the dead horse. He snatched a pistol from the belt of the last fallen. The attack overwhelmed him and his unknown protégé.

It was over before it was fairly started. The two survivors bolted to their horses. There was a clattering of hoofs and a shower of sparks as they charged forth to safety. Their retreat was hastened by the farewell chatter of Farrell's salvaged revolver.

He was creased and slashed and half a dozen slugs had seared him, but he managed to jerk the horseman clear of his riddled beast.

"Allah requite you," grimly chuckled the man whose life but a few seconds ago had not been worth one of the cartridges used against him. "Who are you and why...?"

Farrell laughed bitterly. Face to face, he recognized Nurredin Shirkuh; and it was mutual.

"Father of a thief," said Farrell, "I should have helped your assailants."

"It is not yet too late, infidel," retorted the Kurd, his steel gray eyes gleaming in the moonlight. "There is still a weapon in your hands."

For a long moment they stared each other in the face. Then Farrell handed Shirkuh the red blade he still gripped.

"Take this so that you can defend yourself on your way," he said. "Our blood is mixed in the ground. I will have my reckoning with you later."

A swarm of natives came charging up from the village. Half of them were the emir's retainers.

"You may tell then that I am an infidel," Farrell remarked in a careless tone, "but your enemies left a spare horse behind…"

"Then ride in peace," said Shirkuh, turning toward his friends. "Your life is now on my head…but whatever your business, infidel, you would do better not to linger."

Farrell caught the bridle of a beast belonging to one of the fallen, vaulted to the saddle, and headed north. Shirkuh, thinking him either a spy or a trader, had given him a break by way of gratitude. It would never occur to him that Farrell was planning to loot his house.

And since Farrell had in error saved his life, the Kurd considered that the score was even. Which it would be, when Farrell had the rug. Half an hour later, he was backtracking toward the palace.

* * * *

Djenane was waiting. He followed her to her father's apartment. There she fingered a block of stone that in no way varied from its fellows except that it had been worn somewhat smoother by the probing fingers of many generations. It swung upward revealing the treasure vault.

He watched her reaching into the shadowy crypt. His hand was trembling as he took the time-worn, frayed prayer rug and shoved it under his arm.

"Never mind the rest," he said, drawing her from the niche. "Let's get going… quick…"

But a tinkle of anklets and a murmur of voices warned them. They lost precious moments waiting for the other women of the household to clear the hall. And when they finally dared move, he fairly dragged Djenane toward the secret staircase. They crossed the garden. Farrell froze at the sound that came in from the direction of the village: the muffled tinkle of steel, a muttered oath, a whispered warning.

Shirkuh's enemies were attempting a stealthy raid, hoping to elude the vigilance of the guards at the palace gate, or else someone had seen him tracking back and had turned out a scouting party to investigate. In any case, there would be hell to pay. There was only one thing to do. He thrust the rug into her hands.

"Put it back. No matter what's going on outside, two of us wouldn't have a chance. Alone, I'll be able to sneak through and get to my horse. And I can't stay here, particularly if there is a raid on the house."

"But take the rug," she urged.

"No. It would hamper my getaway. I'd have to move fast. Anyway, if he missed it after this disturbance, there'd be no more chance for anyone either to get in or out. Play it my way, and we can make it tomorrow night."

That settled it. Djenane slipped from his arms and back into the house, leaving him to skirt the shadow of the wall until he reached the secret exit.

Lucky that she had not come with him, that he had no prayer rug to hinder his moves. He had scarcely left the thicket when half a dozen lurkers bounded toward him. He evaded the rush, but the shadows became a blaze of yellow and purple flame as he flung himself to the saddle and headed for the hills: but in pausing to fire, they lost their chance to mount up and pursue.

When he finally reined in his winded horse, he had only to return to the village. He could not have been recognized in the treacherous alternation of moonlight and blackness. He still had a chance at Khalil Sultan's rug.

* * * *

When Farrell reentered the village, the disturbance had subsided. He ascended to the cubicle in the *serai*.

It was empty. Zobeide's sleeping rug was unoccupied. That was unaccountable. He wondered where she was at that hour.

Gruff voices, and a heavy tramping rumbled from the courtyard. He stepped to the gallery. The darkness was broken by the yellowish flare of torches.

The men were armed. Shirkuh was leading them. He was advancing up the stairway. His face was long and grim. Something was wrong! There had been some upset.

Not a chance for flight. Brazen it out. Farrell met the emir at the doorway. He came alone, except for the two followers who carried a large, bulky bundle.

An exchange of salutations; but Farrell could not believe what followed...

Shirkuh was handing him the prayer rug of Khalil Sultan!

"You came to get this, after outwitting the men I sent to waylay you in Bagdad. Tonight you put me in debt to you. Therefore take this, and my men will escort you to the limits of my territory. Your life is on my head...*provided that you never return*."

Farrell fingered the silken fabric, that hung over his arm, but he was thinking of Djenane, who would vainly await him.

"Your courtesy leaves me without words," said Farrell.

"I trust," countered the emir, "that there is no reason why you cannot leave at once?"

"Yes," said Farrell, "there is Zobeide, who should go with me."

"I have done well by Zobeide," said the emir, then clapped his hands.

His two retainers set their bulky bundle upright, full in the glow of the smoldering charcoal.

Farrell's numbed brain was now beyond all comprehension.

"Zobeide," continued Shirkuh, "told me tonight that my daughter interested you more than Khalil Sultan's prayer rug. This was not until after you saved my life. So I told my men to take you alive...which explains their poor marksmanship. In trying to square you, they missed the horse as well."

312

He stripped the wrappings from the tall bundle, revealing a great glass urn which glowed in the firelight like a monstrous bead of amber.

"A jar of honey," said Shirkuh, speaking very slowly. "Honey to sweeten your trip. A final gift to remove the last trace of dishonor on my house."

It was a jar of honey, yet it was more like an amber bead, and like a mass of amber, something was embalmed in its pale golden depths.

Djenane Hanoun, lovely in death as she had been in life, seemed to smile from the golden depths. About her throat was a fine, silken cord. Shirkuh had blotted out the dishonor of his house: an old custom in the Orient.

"Go," he said, his voice like a whetstone kissing a blade. "I give you the daughter of an emir in exchange for Zobeide, whose suspicions you should have anticipated." And that night Farrell rode from the hills with his treasures from Kurdistan…and as he rode, he no longer pondered on Shirkuh's honor, but on the wisdom which had told him how death could be sweeter than life.

CHASTE GODDESS

Originally published in *Spicy-Adventure Stories*, October 1936.

From their window, they could see the blue hills of Keddah, and below them, the myriad masts and lateen sails of Malay *prahus* and Chinese junks; but Glenn Farrell and Nadja were not interested in scenery.

Though they occupied the costliest suite in the Pacific and Oriental Hotel, they were not welcome in the best clubs of Penang: which did not break their hearts. The four thousand mile honeymoon was over, and perilous adventure was ahead.

Nadja's black hair swept sleekly back from a low, broad forehead to a lustrous knot at the nape of her neck. Her skin was tawny, and the disarrayed folds of a severely tailored dressing gown revealed glimpses of contours whose feminine sleekness could not quite mask the cat-like ripple of muscles.

Nadja, for all her Slavic loveliness, was no toy. Her long, shapely legs, and her supple arms that moved with the languor of sleepy serpents, were designed to match her full, firm breasts and the red curve of wanton lips.

Once they nailed Draupadi's ruby—

But first, they had to find the pear-shaped gem that was the subject of the sheaf of newspaper clippings, covering the past three months, which they were scrutinizing.

"Street fighting in Singapore, where it was stolen," summarized Farrell. "Rioting in Moulmein. Disturbances in Malacca. But not a whisper as to the thief."

"It's pleasant here." Nadja's mockery was in her greenish eyes rather than her purring voice. "Maybe the thief will come up to offer it to you."

Farrell's aquiline, sun-bronzed face crinkled in an amiable grin. Then he explained, "Hong Li will attend to that. He is Grand Master of the Sa Tiam, a society of thieves. There's nothing you can steal in this country without giving him a cut—"

Farrell resumed, "You stay here. I'm digging in at a native section where a white woman would be too conspicuous. Hong Li already knows I'm in Penang, but he won't make contact until I get out of this silk hat hotel."

"Then why come here in the first place?" wondered Nadja.

"To gain face. Front, we call it in America. My reputation as a connoisseur is greater than my financial standing."

"And these frills you bought me—six trunks full—are advance advertising?"

"Exactly, darling." said Farrell. "And while I'm gone, don't join any indoor exploration societies…"

She probably would play around, but she was discreet. Nadja's shrewdness in Batum had helped him with a dangerous but profitable deal in jewels that had once belonged to the former Sultan Abdul Hamid.

* * * *

That evening Farrell called on Hong Li, a shriveled little Chinese whose gilt and vermillion palace occupied half a block on Leith Street.

Farrell presented an antique fan on whose face the Emperor Kang Hsi had with his own hands inscribed a verse.

"This humble person," he said, "offers a trifling gift to the Honorable Hong, whose taste for art is known even in my country."

"My poor house," countered Hong Li, "is unworthy of this treasure. It is plain that my Elder Brother has a notable appreciation of costly rarities."

He was right. The fan had cost a trifle over six hundred U.S. dollars.

Farrell, questioned about his age, income, and the rest of the things that we call prying and a Chinese includes in courteous interest, mentioned that he had been in Mogôk, looking for rubies.

Hong Li knew that that meant gems bootlegged from the mines. He beamed. Farrell reached for his tea, and the interview was over.

Nothing to do but wait for Hong Li to return the call. The odds were that he would mention Draupadi, the Hindu goddess of chastity, who had been robbed of everything but her virtue.

"And that," grinned Farrell, taking a short cut down a street where the fronts of the houses were open to the public, "is a drug on the market."

Night life in Penang would be fun, if one didn't have a ruby on the brain.

But for his preoccupation, Farrell might have sensed that he was being followed.

Once, glancing back, he saw a slinking shadow duck into the space between two houses. He decided that some member of the Sa Tiam was already checking up on him. Which was great.

He hailed a rickshaw and headed westward along the water front. Great place. Penang. Colorful and foreign, but a clean little island where a man didn't get his throat cut unless he insisted. Not a bit like northern Kurdistan, or the Red Sea Coast.

Or so he thought, until he rounded the turn just before reaching the outskirts of the Malay settlement at Bagan Jermal.

Half a dozen natives were closing in on an eastbound rickshaw. The coolie, screeching and chattering, fled down a cross road. His deserted passenger cried out, but more in wrath than terror.

By the bright moonlight, Farrell caught the ivory blur of her face. She was white, and her fingernails were giving them hell. He halted his own coolie, leaped to the road, and joined the fracas as the girl was overwhelmed by her assailants.

He caught glimpses of silken legs, and pale skin revealed by a dress ripped to the waist. The thugs did not sense his arrival until his cane smacked down on a Malay skullcap.

A chatter of oaths and dismayed outcries, a gleam of steel, then the splintering of Farrell's stick across an acre of white teeth. He felt a blade graze his ribs. He sidestepped. His fist dynamited a little brown brother.

Farrell's coolie joined in with a club. The approach of a Sikh policeman from the Pulau Tikus station ended the party. The Malays fled.

"See, I ran for help," declared the girl's rickshaw coolie, emerging from hiding.

She answered in Chinese. The fellow looked foolish but remained. Then she thanked Farrell and the policeman, gave the latter her name: Antonia Valles.

Farrell handed her into the rickshaw, and offered to accompany her to her destination.

"You're very kind, but I'm far from presentable now," Antonia declined. "I'll be returning."

She did not live far from Farrell's bungalow. His further appraisal of the amber-shadowed curve of pert little breasts that reminded him of matched lotus buds, made her address uncommonly interesting.

Antonia was Eurasian: her name and coloring and the faint slant of her dark eyes indicated Chinese and Spanish blood. She was pretty and sweet-faced, despite the inevitable bitterness that marked the corners of her luscious mouth. Eurasians, scorned by European and pure Asiatic alike, reach for life and find it a porcupine.

"I haven't any address," she said, as their coolies jogged along, neck and neck.

Farrell's shaggy brows rose incredulously.

"I lost my office job," Antonia explained. "It was sweet of you to give me a lift. If you're alone—"

Then, bitterly: "This is the last night I'm entirely my own. If you were a woman, you might understand why I'd like to share it with—well, a friend."

"Maybe I do, anyway," answered Farrell. No wonder she didn't want to waste her last morsel of freedom.

* * * *

Ling Foo, the number one boy, took Antonia's suitcase and then approached with brandy and soda.

"No *stenghas* for me," she said, "and no soda."

Farrell matched her order. The treacherously mellow brandy burned out some of her sombre mood. Farrell, noting the instinctive reserve with which she guarded the slender, cream-tinted loveliness beneath her kimono, began to feel that it would be foolish for her to spend her last night in prayer and fasting. He was sorry for her.

She was slight, almost frail, but exquisitely formed. Her long, slanted eyes were a smouldering blackness that became misty as hungry lips returned Farrell's kiss. She clung to him with a desperation born of a desire to draw the utmost of this last night of freedom from those who prowled in that glaring, hideous street along the water front...

* * * *

"Better stay a while," he said the next day. "You remind me...of a statue of Draupadi I saw in Moulmein."

But before she could unravel that subtlety, Ling Foo announced the Honorable Hong Li. Antonia slipped into her room. Not for secrecy, but because the presence of a woman at a meeting of gentlemen was unseemly.

316

Farrell and the master of thieves spent forty minutes in exchanging bows and inquiries about each other's health.

"Your house is a jewel," remarked Hong Li.

"It is unworthy of your presence," deprecated Farrell. Then, noting the odd accent on the old fellow's last word, he added, "The friendship of the Honorable Hong is like a pear-shaped ruby."

"Alas, it is less than mud," he deplored. "But my Elder Brother loves rubies?"

From then on they got along much better than brothers... When Ling Foo served tea, Farrell had an engagement to inspect an unworthy gem which sentimental reasons alone gave to it the trifling value of two hundred thousand dollars, Straits currency.

Another session of bowing, and Hong Li's gilded sedan chair carried him back to Leith Street.

A brother of Hong Li had a pear-shaped ruby. That meant, a member of the Sa Tiam, who steal anything from a pound of rice to a war elephant in full regalia.

The goddess of chastity had not once been mentioned, but it could not be any other gem. Enough time had elapsed for it to come from the original thief to the Sa Tiam...

Antonia was becoming a problem. Sending her away was unthinkable; but paying off her debts would be a sucker trick. Farrell had once fallen for that one, and loudly mocked a friend who had bailed out the same girl, several days later.

He heard Ling Foo tell someone that the master was not in, and was scarcely annoyed. But when the number one boy's screech was followed by a resonant slap, a spattering of pottery, and a familiar feminine voice husky with wrath, the memory factory became a tangle of cushions and legs.

They broke as Nadja proved that a woman can move like a leopard. Shapely Nadja was substantial, slavic and savage. She ignored Farrell, except for a smack that popped like a pistol shot, and tore into Antonia.

The Eurasian girl, though slight, was no slouch with her long nails. When Farrell finally separated them, neither was fit for the public gaze—not until the Scottish plaid pattern of scratches and bites healed up enough to convince a man that she was a woman and not a sieve.

Farrell told Nadja that Antonia was a present from Hong Li, knowing that she would not believe it. She didn't, and she said so with dirty-sounding Russian and Turkish words. Then she pulled together the most revealing gaps in her dress and headed back for town.

"I've caused you so much trouble," deplored Antonia.

"Better stay," said Farrell, wryly.

But Nadja would get over it. His alibi had been plausible. He couldn't have insulted Hong Li by declining a shapely temporary slave. Once Nadja found some suitable vengeance to salve her pride, the corporation would carry on.

That night Farrell had a sedan chair haul him to the house of the Honorable Hong. He hated such a conveyance, but "face" demanded it. He was important; he had to be, to dicker for Draupadi's ruby. There was no danger in calling at the house of the Honorable Hong.

A street urchin might hand him the ruby in a twist of tobacco, later that night. If the Chinaman collected in advance, well; if he preferred payment after delivery, likewise well. The honor of the Sa Tiam, and its swift vengeance on an island from which no white man could slip away unseen guaranteed good faith on both sides.

Farrell was quite carefree. One really can't rob a goddess...they told one in Sunday school that a goddess is a heathen fancy... No one but the British law and the priests of Draupadi could consider it dealing in stolen goods; and a lot they'd know about it!

He saw nothing amiss when the gatekeeper admitted him into the tortuously landscaped garden of the rich estate. He did not know that the block was infested with bearded Sikh policemen.

A servant bowed him into the house. The Honorable Hong was happy to receive his Elder Brother—

But he had scarcely taken half a dozen steps when he heard an old man screech wrathfully and curse in Cantonese. A girl shrieked. Woodwork groaned and snapped.

Farrell dashed to the disturbance, the servant at his heels.

A lean, turbaned Arab was grappling with the Honorable Hong. A girl in a peach-colored tunic was belaboring him with a small lacquered screen. A curved *khanjar* bit into the old man's dove-gray tunic.

The bearded Arab, poised like a hawk, swooped clear as Farrell bounded across the threshold. He hurled a vase at the American. Farrell caught it on his shoulder. The effort broke his stride. While his flying tackle brought the Arab crashing to the floor, Farrell overreached himself.

The knife raked his clutching hand. The invader feinted toward the rush of servants, doubled back, plunged through a window, and into the ground. Farrell, leading the pursuit, had a flash of Hong Li, coughing blood, the slender girl trying to staunch his wound. She was his daughter.

The Arab cleared the wall as a leopard might have; but Farrell was on his heels.

They were neck and neck in the mud of the side street. The shadows seemed to disgorge every policeman in Malaya: tall, broad men with grim faces, curled beards, booming voices. Good God! If that Arab had the ruby—he had snatched something from the floor—

Another sliver of time. The madness became a nightmare. Four tall Hindus in massive turbans and Brahmin robes and plump, oily faces cleared the wall and splashed down beside Farrell. Priests!

If Farrell could only nail that Arab, get the ruby, jam it deep into the mud—

The slayer's red blade whistled into the darkness. He had flung it away to soften his capture. The Hindus parted to let him pass. They blocked the charging Sikhs, cried out and pointed at Farrell, plunged after him.

The law overwhelmed him; and the Hindus seemed to fade like mists.

* * * *

It was a tough half hour in the Chinaman's palace. Hong Li was dead. His daughter cleared Farrell, and cursed the Sikhs for blocking the man who had pursued her father's slayer.

318

"But we were told that this man came to buy stolen goods!" growled a policeman. "Here is the Inspector *Sahib*."

The weather-beaten Englishman with the drooping mustache did not arrest Farrell, but the American was taken to headquarters and all but X-rayed. Then the inspector apologized, but his eyes were wrathful.

"Who the hell told your men that rot?" stormed Farrell. "About stolen goods?"

"My dear man," smiled the inspector, "those Sikh chaps take the oddest notions."

He turned to the Sikh and reproved him in Hindustani. Farrell pretended he couldn't understand. But it had been a tip-off, as he had guessed, and the policeman caught hell for the break.

* * * *

He went back to Hong Li's house. The police were turning it inside out. They could not deny him a word with the slender Chinese girl. Her fine, pale yellow face was like a mask, but her eyes blazed as she said, "There is more to this than the eye sees. My honorable father told me before he died that this was not your work."

"But a pear-shaped ruby?" Farrell cut in, his voice iron.

She pointed at a ball of gum opium. It had been cut in half. In its heart was a faceted, pear-shaped depression. Hong Li had removed Draupadi's jewel from its hiding place in anticipation of his visit.

"The Honorable Hong kept his promise," said Farrell, bowing very low. "I will recover it. But that Arab?"

She did not know. Nor had any of the servants ever before seen him.

Farrell, going back to his bungalow, regretted his rash promise. If he failed, he would lose face, which is more precious than rubies when dealing with Orientals; and Farrell's fortunes lay in the east.

Those damned Hindus! Deliberately giving the Arab a break; a man plainly an Arab and an enemy of their faith. Why?

And half the police force of Penang waiting to nail him on a tip off? Again, why?

Nadja?

When he reached the house, it was darkened. Antonia was gone. A chair was overturned. A decanter was smashed, its shards reddened. Blood flecked the floor, and there was a ragged wisp of silk from her kimono snagged on the latch tongue.

She had been kidnapped, but not injured. The blood splotches coincided with the prints of men's bare feet in the compound. She had sapped someone.

It became more puzzling and more dangerous every moment. But Farrell was certain that the ruby of Draupadi was behind it.

He slumped into a chair, smoking for a long time and drinking numerous slugs of straight brandy. He did not need the profit in the ruby, but failure and Nadja's treachery bruised his pride.

Damn her Slavic temper.

The brandy only made him wrathful. His rage blazed in his eyes as at the sound of feminine footsteps on the verandah he stalked to the door. He recognized that swaying, panther gait.

Nadja, green eyes glittering, smile over-sweet. He slapped her into a corner before she could dodge, but she came up purring. He did not dare hit her again, or he would kill her. Or she, him.

I'm awfully sorry, darling," she murmured. "Now listen. I went up in the air and told the police. When I changed my mind, it was too late to warn you. So I came out to face the music.

"I heard Antonia phoning someone named Selim. They're playing for the ruby."

"They *played*, and it was good!" he growled.

"I know where Selim is," she purred. "Be a good boy, and I'll tell you. Also, four Hindus kidnapped Antonia. I didn't interfere. I didn't care where they took her.

"She made a jackass of you. So I'll forgive you. You do need a guardian, don't you?"

Her gorgeous effrontery dazed him. Then she kissed him, and he liked it.

He returned the kiss, and Nadja, gasped, her eyelids drooped, and her hips drew closer—then she slipped from his arms and reminded him of Selim.

"And here's a pistol," she said. "I'd better wait here. The police would wonder, if they saw us together."

A hired car carried Farrell to a house near the mosque on Acheen Street.

He made the last block on foot. He hugged the shadow of a wall as he noted four tall Hindus at Selim's door. A voice from within was ladling out choice obscenities in Arabic.

"Come in and get me, father of many pigs!"

The door opened, but there were no takers. Farrell crept forward. His head was whirling, and not from brandy or Nadja's kiss of forgiveness.

The Hindus were of the priestly caste. Then why had they helped Selim escape the police when their very presence here proved their knowledge of his possessing the ruby of Draupadi?

Why, if they had been so close to Hong Li's house, had they not exposed or attacked the old fellow. They must have been lurking in the grounds, watching Farrell from cover.

The only thing that was plain was that that hawk of an Arab could and would kill the quartet without exerting himself.

"We come in peace," soothed the chief.

"You are wise," mocked Selim, opening the door wider.

Farrell, pistol ready, was about to take charge; but instead, he hung back. As the door closed, he skirted the house, scaled a wall, and dropped into the courtyard. He crept through darkness and odors. A door blocked him but he could hear, and from an angle catch a glimpse of Selim's hawk face.

"We have your accomplice, Antonia," said the Brahmin spokesman. "She dies if you do not surrender the ruby of Draupadi."

The Arab laughed; but his mouth tightened and his eyes became bleak when he saw the proof. A plump hand held Antonia's ear pendants that Farrell recognized as well as Selim.

Seconds flatfooted by. For a moment Farrell waited for Selim to cut them to ribbons. Then the Arab made a sign of assent. The fellow must care for Antonia, even though he had with a fake hold-up planted her as a spy in Farrell's house, to pave the way for his sale of the ruby, once it was stolen from Hong Li.

The plump hand was again extended, this time to receive the ransom.

"Dogs," snarled Selim. "How do I know that you will release her?"

"Then bring the ruby," said the priest. "The police now know that you killed Hong Li, that only you could have taken the stone. So you dare not bring them when you come to get her."

They gave Selim the address.

"Now go, son of many fathers," snarled the Arab. "I will have to move in stealth."

They went. Farrell cautiously pulled himself up the sloping face of a pilaster, clutched a second floor balcony railing, and drew himself over the side.

He crept through deadly darkness in which he found stairs leading to the ground floor. Halfway down, he paused and watched Selim poking a knife blade into the crevice between two blocks of masonry.

Farrell edged down into the wavering shadows cast by a peanut oil lamp. A weak tread sank underfoot. He lashed out at the balluster. It yielded, pitching him down four steps.

Selim's surprise and Farrell's heavy landing for an instant leveled the odds. The Arab dropped something that gleamed like a monstrous gout of blood, snatched his *khanjar*, flung himself across the room.

Farrell was numbed by the shock. Though he instinctively drew his pistol, he did not want to shoot. He parried the knife with the barrel. The Arab's shoulder slammed him against the wall. Farrell's muscular contraction jerked the trigger.

The blast shook the room. The slug ricocheted from a window bar and went screaming into the street. Farrell dropped the weapon, caught Selim's arm, wrenched his second stab out of line. He flung his opponent half way across the room. He had to work fast, before the police arrived.

Farrell took a power dive at the ruby, but the Arab rebounded, blade point on. The American swayed on his knees, evading the thrust. They sank in a struggling tangle. Though outweighed, Selim was iron hard, and elusive as a snake.

The door crashed in under the impact of heavy shoulders. Silhouetted against the opening was a pair of Sikh policemen. Payday in Penang!

Farrell's fist crashed home, knocking Selim end for end. He blotted the peanut oil lamp with a kick as his hand closed on the ruby.

The Sikhs, charging home with clubs, tangled with Selim. The wick guttered out. Darkness covered Farrell's flight. But he read the sounds: a hoarse bellowing, a cry of rage, the smack of a baton.

Farrell's escape was good. But as he cooled, from the melee, he laughed bitterly. He now understood Nadja's sweetness!

She had anticipated the reason for kidnapping Antonia. Selim, deprived of the ruby, could not ransom her. Vengeful Slavic wit had seen a chance to doom the Eurasian girl.

Antonia had tricked him—but that was one of the rules of the great game of adventure. Her exquisite loveliness had left him with memories. He could keep Draupadi's ruby, and condemn her to death, or—

Damn Nadja and her cat's intuition!

But she had not anticipated that he would have the address of Antonia's captors. There was a chance to release her, and keep the ruby. Perilous, but the laugh would be on Nadja.

Farrell hastened to an all-night bazaar, bought a turban and robe. They would take his absence of beard to be the disguise of a fugitive slayer.

Presently he was knocking for admittance. He kept his face half muffled, and cursed them in Arabic.

A Hindu admitted him. Farrell's foul language made scrutiny of his face needless. He followed his guide down a dark passageway. In the dimly lighted room beyond, he saw three Hindus whose foreheads were branded with Brahmin caste marks.

Lying bound and gagged on an upholstered bench was a slender, amber-hued girl whose bare legs and half concealed breasts identified her: Antonia.

The light, and six sharp eyes detected the imposture. Farrell was unarmed, but he had expected recognition: they had not. He drove in with smashing fists, ducked a hurled crock, jammed his shoulder into a flabby stomach. A prostrate but conscious kidnaper snagged his ankles. Farrell crashed headlong.

Two Hindus not yet casualties pounced on him with hands and feet. Farrell kicked upward, but too high. A knife raked him. He jerked clear of another.

A third, bleeding at the mouth, recovered and leaped into action. They crushed Farrell to the floor. He clung to the haft of a dagger he had wrenched out of the tangle.

Hands were clawing and tearing at him. He shouted to Antonia. Though bound, she wriggled clear of the bench, thudded to the floor. His blade darted out of the melee.

A slash, and her hands were free.

Farrell erupted from the heap, but was tripped. His knife skated across the floor. Antonia reached and seized it. Her ankles free, she dashed to the door, shrieking until the tiles shivered.

She had recognized Farrell. She did not know that he had the ruby. Her cries for the police carried at least to headquarters!

A squad of Sikhs ploughed in.

Worse yet, the sardonic inspector appeared as they laid out the five combatants. Worst of all, among the blood splashes on the floor was a gout that gleamed: a ruby.

The inspector picked it up, eyed Farrell and Antonia, and observed, "I'd just heard rumors of a woman having been carried into this place. And this stone seems to explain why a handful of Hindus picked on you at Hong Li's."

"I was looking for the girl," said Farrell. "They took her from my shack."

"Singular, what?" resumed the inspector. "Finding Draupadi's ruby in the possession of four of her priests? Y'know, I do believe they must have gotten it from Hong Li."

"My word!" exclaimed Farrell, so burned with wrath that he was cool. "But that Arab fellow—how does he fit?"

"He didn't live long enough to say. He was arrested at his house. On the way to the station, he broke away. He was killed while escaping."

Farrell thrust Antonia into a *ghari*. God, wouldn't Nadja have a laugh: *Glenn Farrell helps recover Draupadi's ruby!*

"Let's go to Selim's house," said Antonia. "There's some things I want to get."

"His death doesn't bother you," he observed.

"He made me trick you. I'm glad he's dead." Her voice was venomous; then it softened, and she murmured endearments that ended in a breath-draining kiss.

And Selim, the fool, had given a ruby and his life in a vain effort to save her!

The *ghari* halted. She entered the deserted house. In a moment she returned. She thrust something cold and hard into his hand, saying, "You lost a ruby to save me. This pays for all but your love."

In his palm blazed a matchless flare of red: a pear-shaped ruby.

"This is the true ruby of Draupadi," she explained, "which Selim took when he went to kill Hong Li so that the Chinaman could not sell it to you.

"He did not expect to get it; only to kill him. Selim had a ruby smuggled from Mogôk. He had a lapidary cut it to the exact shape of Draupadi's world famed jewel *before the theft*, intending to palm it off on an unwary collector as an antique. He planned to bribe the priests into falsely announcing that their stone was stolen, so as to fool the victim. But before this was arranged, Draupadi's jewel was stolen.

"You are more widely known than you realize. So, with the much advertised theft, and genuine disturbances, we counted on your buying this duplicate. We did not at first know that the original would be offered you."

"But damn it—those priests—they were priests—"

"They robbed their own goddess," explained Antonia. "It was a flawed stone, but being *stolen* from a temple it would bring a greater price than if merely sold by the temple. That's why they didn't want the police to recover it. Hong Li was their sales manager! They dared not sell it—the people would call it a sacrilege."

Her words cleared the confusion; and her voice told him more. The death of Selim, lover and accomplice, had left her alone in the world: and a jewel that size could be sold only by a master at the game. She had seen Nadja's wrath, and she knew that Farrell would be lonely.

All this from her endearments and gratitude: though maybe she did in her way care for him.

* * * *

When they arrived at the bungalow, Nadja was waiting, and with a smile for two.

The sudden freezing of Antonia's face and the deadly blackness of her eyes confirmed Farrell's suspicion, told him that the Eurasian girl had lost a bet.

"Darling, maybe you don't need a guardian," Nadja admitted, when she heard the story. "It's a clear profit, now—better than buying as we planned."

323

"My dear," said Farrell, "I made Hong Li's daughter a promise. I'm paying her for the ruby. She will give a slice of it to Antonia. Or to you, if you're staying in Penang."

"Take him!" flared Antonia. "He's an easy mark!"

"That's why I like him," yawned Nadja. "And that's why I'm getting him out of Penang. Hong Li's daughter must be nice, or he'd not have made such a stupid promise."

DOUBLE CATSPAW

Originally published in *Spicy-Detective Stories*, December 1936.

"Mr. Farrell, I do hope I'll see more of you," was what Madeleine said as she watched the porter stow her hand luggage into the *ghari* at the Tanjong Pagar station in Singapore, but her crimson lips and dark eyes said a great deal more—though most eloquent of all was her supple, sensuous body and its aura of radiant vitality.

"That," smiled the tanned, broad-shouldered American, handing her into the *ghari*, "is something you can't dodge. I'm going to be busier than a Chinaman eating soup with chopsticks, but somehow, we'll find a chance to dance out at Tanjong Katong, and—"

"Don't forget—the Wellington," she cut in as the coolie smacked the shaggy Shan pony across the rump and the *ghari* rolled into the traffic.

Forget? Well, rather not. The good-humored gray eyes that peered from the shadow of the American's pith helmet narrowed acquisitively. Madeleine Fortesque had lots of it where there should be lots, and little where she should be slim. Only thing wrong with Madeleine was her way of saying no.

"If we'd only missed the express and stayed another day in Penang," he told himself, remembering how the soft white curves smiling from Madeleine's negligee had left him cross-eyed.

Farrell's urgent business, however, had not permitted him to miss the Singapore express. Millwood Industries, Incorporated, wanted to find out what was wrong in northern Malaya, why the Raja of Batu Gaja could not keep banditry, sabotage, and assorted assassination from playing the devil with the mines and plantations controlled by the estate of the late James Millwood.

Farrell, like many others, knew the answer: a sinister master of intrigue who for want of a more accurate name was called the Claw of Iblis. Murder in Malacca—revolt in Acheen—gun-running to Borneo—all manufactured in Singapore, but find the maker.

If Claw of Iblis—the Hand of Satan—was not precise enough, then dope out his real name.

It wasn't like a guessing contest in the states. This was *á L'orientale*: if you are wrong, you wake up wondering who laid your head between your ankles.

Farrell drove out Orchard Road to a furnished bungalow he had engaged by wire. Hotels might be safer, but also more conspicuous. And not as handy if he had to leave town in a hurry…

Leaving towns was his specialty. Someone once said that all he left in Moulmein was a pagoda and an oil barge, but that was unjust. He left a Chinese merchant's daughter with pleasant memories.

An hour later, Hop Wing, the number one boy, was stowing the luggage while Farrell donned fresh drills, a newly whitened helmet, and a .450 Webley.

A rickshaw took him through the sunset glow to an estate well out on Balestier Road. A black Tamil as thin as a bamboo rod admitted him to the house of Wallace Crosby, the resident manager of the East Indies Trading Corporation.

They traded, all right; but while they came back from Borneo with nuts—coco and palm—they left Singapore loaded with trouble. Farrell's hunch was that Wallace Crosby must be connected with the hidden trouble-maker of South East Asia, the venomous industrial spy who blackmailed native princes, organized revolts, upset thrones for whoever could pay off.

A stocky, bald-headed man with shrewd blue eyes and a wolf-trap mouth rose from behind a rosewood desk as red as his face and extended a hard hand.

"I've been looking for you," he said, ringing for brandy and soda. "You've been doing things out here."

"I figured we ought to get together," was the response; but he knew that using Wallace Crosby as a stepping stone would be foot-blistering work. "A couple of up and at-'em Americans can turn the East Indies inside out. Look at this—"

He handed Crosby a sheaf of bills of lading and warehouse receipts.

"Ummm…" Crosby's eyes narrowed, then his head cocked quizzically. He demanded, "Does this stuff have to go to Sandakan? I could use it up north."

That was as good as a confession. Munitions and guns to be used—well, in Batu Gaja. But that was penny ante stuff. He wanted the man behind Crosby, the Claw of Iblis. His gray steel glance shifted about the room. He was noting details; filing cabinets, book cases, windows, doorways. A tree outside…

"It's tied up," temporized Farrell. "I'd get in a jam canceling that consignment. If I had more drag here—suppose I see you tomorrow?"

"Hmmm…" Crosby stroked his jaw and nodded. "Do that."

Farrell headed back toward his bungalow. The papers that had built him up as a rising young smuggler were phony. Scrutiny would spill the beans.

The trader's reaction had confirmed the hunch: there was someone behind the scenes. Looting the files in the bungalow might reveal the master mind. The strictly legal records, in the company's offices in the Hong Kong & Shanghai Bank building, would be uninteresting.

In the meanwhile—just to keep from becoming jittery while awaiting the hour of the raid, he told himself—why not see more of Madeleine? As much more as he could; she had plenty worth seeing!

He drove to the nearest telephone station. There had been delay in installing one in the bungalow. He presently learned that Madeleine was not at the Wellington.

Damn it! She had lost little time in finding someone to show her the town.

Farrell returned to the bungalow. From the compound gate he saw lights in the living room. That was odd.

And why was the Number One boy beaming so expansively?

* * * *

The reason was a lovely surprise.

Madeleine was smiling from the chaise longue. The soft lights coaxed warm reflections from her silken legs, and her dark eyes were a promise. Her voice was a heart-stirring murmur that was like a whisper of love. Somehow, that suggestion flashed through his mind as his glance shifted from the sleek curve of her hip to the ivory line of her throat as it swept down to meet the fascinations that rounded out the upper reaches of her bodice.

"It was so lonesome at the Wellington," she explained. "So I had the *ghari* driver go back to the station and find where your checked baggage was going to be delivered."

As if Farrell gave a happy hoot how she'd found her way!

"Take an evening off, Hop Wing!"—which was what the Number One boy had been expecting.

The Chinese servant lost little time, and Farrell lost less. The display of dimpled knees was driving him mad.

She tried to keep him at a distance, but he had profited by experience. The repulsing hand, instead of blocking his chin, failed to connect. Madeleine got the soundest kissing of her score plus four or five years. Since she couldn't effectively slap him, she decided to like it.

Madeleine, however, went beyond her intentions. She returned the caress with interest, and her arms drew him closer. When the clinch finally broke, she was gasping for breath. She had some difficulty in regaining it. She tried to say something, but her remark was inarticulate...

She couldn't be strictly coherent, with someone kissing the hollow of her throat. Farrell felt the sudden rise of her breast and knew he was making a job of it. The luxurious little sigh, and the way she hitched herself back among the cushions confirmed his suspicions.

This wasn't tracking down the trouble-maker of Malaya—but after all, the raid would be safer if delayed until quite late that night.

"I didn't bring my overnight case or anything," she deplored, although Farrell hadn't had a chance to complain on that score.

"What you did bring is plenty," he said, dismissing that irrelevancy as he tried a one arm squeeze that would leave his other hand free for—well, what would anyone do with an unoccupied lunch hook?

"Darling," she finally whispered, "I'd be ever so much more comfortable if I had a lounge robe or something to—You're terribly rough!..."

She proved that by wriggling out of his arms. The gleam in her misty eyes hinted that she might like being kissed some more.

"There's a mandarin robe in that trunk in the other room—I picked it up for my sister, but I'm sure she'd not mind—"

"Oh, delightful!" Then, with a malicious little smile, "Bet the frills on it make a liar of you—about the sister, I mean."

Whoever it was intended for, the dragon-embroidered garment saved the ensemble from a thorough mauling...and the whirring of uncounted tropical insects without drowned whatever protests Madeleine had...she wasn't raising her voice...presently she agreed with Farrell's program for the evening...it really was too late to go anywhere...

But somehow, Madeleine did cast a few furtive glances at her wrist watch.

Just a trifling distraction, but thinking of time did seem blasphemous.

Glancing over the flame of the match he struck to a cigarette, he saw her fumbling for the compact and lipstick in her handbag.

"What the hell," was his unspoken thought, noticing the second hand cosmetic on the tip of his smoke, "do I have to take off a fresh layer, that she's just becoming good and kissable?"

Madeleine's fingers were deft, but Farrell, watching time on his own account, was a shade more vigilant than he would ordinarily have been. Thus he saw her palming a small glass vial.

That was an odd note.

"This light is terrible," she complained.

He unsuccessfully tinkered with the shade. The result was glaring.

"There's a goose neck lamp on the living room table," she suggested.

He was gone only for a moment, and it took no longer to plug it in.

The tiny bottle did not feature in the complexion repairs. It had disappeared. A swift, appreciative glance told him that her hose tops were not concealing it. Presently he was certain that the flimsy brassiere had not entered the play—no, he didn't *look*...

He made a dive for an ashtray, knocked the handbag to the floor, cursed his own clumsiness. As he stooped to retrieve it, back turned toward Madeleine, he unsnapped the clasps.

The glance was revealing. A small automatic pistol and an emptied vial were nestled among a tangle of feminine odds and ends. His finger tips brushed the smeared stopper.

The smell identified it: tincture of opium. But why lull him to sleep? She had a pistol, if she wanted to make it permanent.

Farrell, certain that his mission in Singapore was already kicking back at him, had to compliment the unknown master of intrigue for fast work. Hell's fire, he'd been wise to Farrell ever since that day in Penang!

Madeleine's glass was full. He reached for the decanter and filled his own. The heavy-bodied, tawny port masked all but the scantiest trace of the opiate. He sipped a bit, appreciatively smacked his lips.

"Say—" He set the glass down. "I must be getting absent-minded. I'm nuts about this port myself, but maybe you'd like a drop of *oloroso* sherry. "It's topside number one."

"Well...just a drop," she agreed. "My head's fairly spinning."

In a moment he was uncorking the *oloroso*. The stopper yielded with a jerk. He tipped the filled glass from the table, and knocked the empty one to the floor.

"Awfully sorry," he apologized, noting the moist glisten of her skin through the wine-soaked hosiery. "Maybe—"

"Think nothing of it," she laughed.

"I'll rinse them."

Madeleine headed for the bath. Farrell emptied the decanter and goblet out the window. He refilled the former with *oloroso*. It was about the color of the tawny port. The dark glass of the sherry bottle concealed the shortage.

When she returned to hang the stocking in front of the fan, Farrell was setting down a glass and smacking his lips.

"Try the *oloroso*," he invited. He refilled his own goblet from the decanter, which Madeleine of course assumed contained drugged port.

"To a nicer evening than we could possibly spend anywhere else!" she proposed, smiling over the edge of her glass.

As she watched his drink go down the hatch, Madeleine fairly smothered him with breath-taking kisses...

He responded nobly, until he became drowsy and languid. She stroked his hair, and whispered sleepy nothings...

Finally, she gently drew away, letting him slump back among the cushions. She listened to his slow breathing, then stealthily retrieved the dried hosiery.

Farrell's lids parted, but he did not watch the tempting display. He was looking at the brilliance just below the lamp shade. He continued staring at the eye-straining glare. His lids did not drop until Madeleine, giving her ensemble a final hitch and a pat, stepped over to listen and look.

Very gently she lifted an eyelid. The pupil was contracted—not from opium, as she thought, but from staring at the glaring light. Satisfied, she slipped softly from the room.

Before Farrell dared follow Madeleine. He heard a low, trilling whistle, then the creaking wheels of a *ghari* outside the compound.

He had not counted on such complete preparation. No chance of following; not after that slap across the pony's rump! Yet he was undrugged, and he had business at Crosby's house.

Farrell donned a dark suit and set out on foot. He had covered less than half a mile when he hailed an unoccupied rickshaw which he directed out Balestier Road.

A hundred yards from his destination, he dismissed his vehicle. He stealthily approached the palisade that enclosed the compound. With a thin, strong cord to lasso a paling, scaling the barrier was but a moment's work.

Farrell crept through the luxuriant vegetation and toward the tree that commanded the window of Crosby's study. But as he worked his way along the limb, a light flashed on within.

Under his breath he cursed the unexpected occupancy of the room. Then admiration checked his wrath.

A strikingly lovely Malay girl in European dress was following Crosby into the study. She had a pert little nose, great smouldering dark eyes, and lips like a pomegranate blossom; but her voice was low and wrathful.

"Tûan," she said, reaching into her bosom and producing a packet of bank notes which she slapped on the desk, "what manner of thing is this? Why this marked money? By Allah, you are trying to betray us!"

"Who sent you?" snapped Crosby.

"Look at the markings!" she challenged. Her voice and gesture were an accusation.

Was she one of the crew of spies and intriguers who represented the Claw of Iblis?

Crosby hunched forward to examine the money. A silvery flicker darted from the girl's side. Her knife was buried hilt deep between Crosby's shoulders.

Like a tigress, she was behind him, looping a scarf about his face, throttling his outcry and gurgling gasp. For a moment there was a hoarse, muffled choking and the girl's panting breath as she tensed to her grim task. Then Crosby slumped forward, shuddered, and was still.

That one deftly driven stroke had done its work.

"Damn it," muttered Farrell, "nothing more to learn from Crosby!"

If he paused to loot the dead man's files, he could not follow the girl. She was worth trailing as a lead to Crosby's background. She might even serve the Claw of Iblis; but if he followed her, he would not be able to return and search the office. Once the police learned of the crime, Farrell's task was blocked.

Before he could approach the problem, it became worse. A door silently opened into the room. A woman entered: Madeleine, pistol in hand.

"Back away from that desk, but don't raise your hands, or I'll shoot." Her rice was low and venomous.

She spoke fluent Malay! Farrell's teeth gritted. She had made a sap out of him from the start, with that honeyed, "Oh, it's so sweet of you to show me the sights."

She was reaching for the telephone on the desk. Farrell's hot wrath turned to cold chills. Madeleine had drugged him, and now she was holding the Malay girl a prisoner. Could she be a police spy?

Farrell needed action. He opened his penknife, leaned toward the plantain cluster at his side and snipped one from the bunch.

A plantain is something like a banana, only three times as large, and so wooden a horse couldn't eat one raw.

As Madeleine's lips shaped a number, the plantain zipped through the window, knocking the pistol from her grasp.

Farrell followed through; but the Malay girl had the situation in hand before his feet were fairly on the carpet.

"Hang on, *sitti*," encouraged Farrell, bounding into action. "By Allah, I am your friend."

His timely intervention was all the proof the little brown sister needed at the moment. Between them, they took a drape cord and lashed Madeleine to a chair, then gagged her with the scarf that had choked Crosby's outcry.

"Next time you put opium into my wine, darling," whispered Farrell, "be damn' sure I'm not looking. That was *oloroso* I was drinking, the same as you."

Madeleine could not answer, but her eyes were blistering.

"Where are the servants?" Farrell demanded, turning to his lovely ally. "And who the devil are you?"

"*Mûnah,*" she answered, "and don't worry about the servants."

He plucked the keys from Crosby's pocket, opened the filing cases, rapidly sifted the contents. In a few moments he had assembled a thick sheaf.

"That is odd plunder, *tûan*," observed Mûnah.

Despite his haste, Farrell was fascinated by that delicate oval face and the lithe, sweetly rounded figure which he could not help trying to visualize in a silken sarong, and frail jacket whose transparency a many colored shawl would only make more alluring.

She reminded him of a young tigress when she said, "It is not good to leave this woman alive—she will talk—"

Another knife blossomed in her hand.

"Forget it!" snapped Farrell. "We'll be out of town before she's loose."

He followed her to the rear. A light car was parked behind the estate. She had entered by a wicket used by the servants.

"I am going to Johore Bahru," she said, "where there is less law. A *sampan* will take me across the straits."

* * * *

She drove cross town and out the Serangoon Road. Farrell's mission bad blown up before it started. His intervention in favor of Mûnah had made him an accessory after the fact of murder, and the records he had taken were merely clues to Crosby's evil background, not blueprints leading to the Claw of Iblis. With luck he might get to Siam, and finally to the states with the data that some other investigator could follow up.

Mûnah pulled up at the Moslem cemetery at the outskirts of Serangoon Village. She slipped out of her trim ensemble. For a moment she was a slender length of amber-tinted loveliness in the moonglow, a fascinating anomaly: Malay flesh adorned by ultra-western step-ins!

Then she deftly wrapped a sheer silken sarong about her hips. It was something like a skirt, only better. At one side the edges would part at every step, revealing a shapely leg from ankle to hip.

In a moment, all her European finery was in a compact bundle at her feet.

"Tûan," she said, coming so close that her warmth and fragrance made him forget both peril and business for a moment, "The white woman you so foolishly let live thinks we are accomplices. It would be dangerous for us to be seen together."

"Where's your *sampan*?" he demanded.

"Waiting under cover," Mûnah answered. "I will paddle it myself."

He seated himself in the shadow of a headstone shaped like a hitching post capped by a turban, then drew her to his side.

"Listen, Mûnah," he said, "suppose I don't let you go?" She fearlessly regarded him, then replied, "You are not one to put me back in peril."

"Why did you hate Crosby?"

"What have *you* against him?" she countered. "Why did you take those papers?"

Farrell's job was to learn things, not reveal them. And Mûnah's caution might yield to persuasion. He was certain she was holding out plenty—referring to information, not what she kept packed in silk.

"Let us speak of something else," he evaded. "What difference does anything make except that presently you go your way and I go mine, and only Allah knows what our end may be."

He gathered an armful of Mûnah. She was firm-fleshed and supple. The tremor of his voice seemed to strike a responsive chord. But for him, she would still be looking into a pistol muzzle.

She returned his kiss, clung to him with a fervor that sent thrills chasing each other all the way to his toenails. Farrell's thoughts rapidly shifted to mysteries only indirectly pertaining to the Claw of Iblis.

Mûnah was rapidly responding to treatment. Though slender to the eye, he learned through other senses that she was plump as a young partridge, and, like Madeleine, slender where a woman should be slim...he began to wish he had four arms, like the great god Siva...no wonder the Hindus called him a god... who wouldn't be, with four hands to cover practically everything of interest, and all at once!

But Mûnah kept her head. She had slipped clear of his embrace and drew together the edges of her *sarong*, effectively blocking his ardor.

"Please don't—not now. Let me for a change speak of something else," she protested. A long, smouldering, speculative glance. Then, "Perhaps you could help me again? Though it is dangerous, and the reward will be nothing."

That last was an outright mistake, Farrell told her.

"My father, Nureddin Ali," resumed Mûnah, "is a prisoner in a house on Jalan Penang, in the hands of an enemy trying to force him to equip a pirate boat. I also was a prisoner, but I escaped and went to Crosby's bungalow to exact vengeance. Crosby trapped my father."

Vengeance was meat and drink to a Malay. Mûnah's knife work was reasonable. But if she thought that she was using Farrell as a sap, the laugh was on her. The specifications sounded like the Claw of Iblis! This was a break.

"But why not notify the British police?" Farrell countered, catching the joker in the deck.

"My father," Mûnah explained, "already has a price on his head. He is unjustly accused. His only hope is escape and flight to Sumatra."

It was a bit too reasonable! Farrell, however, could not decline the risk. However dangerous, it must lead from Crosby to the sinister Claw.

"I'll go," he agreed; then he listened as Mûnah gave him detailed directions.

"My father's enemy has followers of all races," she concluded, "and it will be easy for you to enter. No one knows his name. He is called the Great Lord. Take this token, and use it as I described."

She handed him a Straits dollar with two of the date numerals obliterated, leaving only a nine and a three. Mûnah, resisting the advances of one of her captors, had knifed him and taken his identification tag.

"I would go myself," she added, "except that my face is too familiar, and I am only a woman. Now take this thin bladed knife. Conceal it. It may serve you."

"And you, in the meanwhile?" queried Farrell.

"To Johore Bahru," she answered. "Take my hired car. Abandon it when it has served you."

* * * *

Farrell drove back to Singapore, parked at the gas works, and set out for the native quarter on foot.

Jalan Penang was a rankly scented darkness through which turbaned figures slunk like ghosts. From a nearby courtyard came the muffled clanging of gongs, whining of moon fiddles, and the sputter of firecrackers: a Chinese funeral procession about to set out.

Farrell shuddered as he heard the eerie wailing and thumping, and muttered, "If this don't work, there's going to be another funeral, and not Chinese…"

Then he squared his shoulders. The amiable Farrell grin that had fatally fooled many an enemy crinkled his face. Fate, that blind idiot, was jerking the strings.

He tapped at the door. A wrinkled Malay with betel juice drooling from the corners of his mouth answered him with an iron stare.

"Ninety-three reporting," announced Farrell, presenting the dollar.

"The third nail," recited the Malay.

"Of the ninth claw," answered Farrell, wondering if Mûnah had been right about the password. One hand was on the butt of the Webley in his coat pocket.

The Malay led him into a murky den crowded with drunkards gurgling at flasks of arrak, and hopheads pulling at the stems of opium pipes.

The Claw had a sweet place.

Farrell's guide stalked toward a blank, dirty wall. There was no perceptible opening, but many bare feet had worn a slick streak across the rough floor. He tapped in peculiar rhythm; there was an answering tap; then he said, "*Ya* Abbas! Ninety-three reporting!"

A panel opened. Farrell crossed the threshold. A pistol prodded his ribs.

"Not a move, brother of a pig!" growled a voice from his side. The speaker probed his pockets, removed his pistol. "Miss Fortesque as well as the Master would like to see you."

The pistol at Farrell's back urged him into the murky glow of a single kerosene lamp suspended from the ceiling.

Madeleine Fortesque sat on a dais beside a thin, hook-nosed Arab with a henna-reddened beard and a mouth hard as a sword blade. Ignoring Mûnah's counsel had been a fatal mistake! He should have let her knife Madeleine!

Her face was drawn, pallid even in that murky yellow glow. He was trapped as surely as though he had taken the drugged wine she had set out for him.

"The third nail of the ninth claw," mocked the leather-faced Arab, "spent too much time toying in graveyards. We trailed you from Crosby's house, shortly after releasing Miss Fortesque. Despite her failure to trap you, we give her another chance to prove herself.

"If she succeeds, she will take the number you have borrowed! Pa'Bak! Gendut! Come forward!"

Two short, thick-muscled Malays appeared from a shadowed doorway. They bound Farrell's ankles with cords of hard spun silk. Then they stepped away, and so did the man whose pistol had prohibited resistance.

The last named approached the Claw and presented Farrell's Webley. The master of the show handed it to Madeleine.

"We have admitted you on probation. We cannot trust you until you have become an outlaw. Your fingerprints on the pistol that kills Farrell will guarantee your fidelity.

"The British law will not suspect you—until you fail me. Then there will be whisperings to the police.

"And you, Farrell, *Sahib*—though your feet are bound, you can hop. If you gain that door at your left before she hits you, you are free and she dies. Feminine marksmanship in this poor light will give you a chance."

Sweat cropped out on Farrell's forehead, and his lips became dry as the red dust of Singapore.

But for those spies who had followed Madeleine, his bluff would have worked. He could have gotten within arm's reach of the Claw, nailed him with Mûnah's dagger—

"Fire at will, Miss Fortesque!" murmured the Claw, smiling maliciously as her face became a tense white mask.

Madeleine, embarking on a career of adventure, was enjoying it no more than Farrell. For just an instant, the misery on her face made him sorry for her. Then he cursed women, brown and white alike. Two in one evening, through malice and bungling, had put him on the spot.

"If I ever get out of this, I'm getting a job as a eunuch—" The grotesque thought flashed through his mind even though he knew that he could not get clear.

Madeleine's pistol was rising. He stared at the gaping muzzle, his glance catching her agonized eyes. He watched the silent motion of her lips. The guards were at her elbow, ready to block a false move.

She was trying to give him a break, trying to tell him how they could both escape! But how?

He couldn't get it. The Claw was grinning and stroking his beard.

Farrell knew the mocker's promise was vain. He hopped, but not toward the door of safety. He purposely tripped, fell face forward. The Claw laughed at the sprawling intruder.

"It's jammed," complained Madeleine, vainly tugging the trigger. She handed the gun to the Claw. He reached for it. His henchman, enjoying the spectacle, crowded closer.

Then the fun ended in a hell blaze. Farrell, snatching Mûnah's dagger, hurled himself forward, instead of toward the exit. Though his ankles were bound, he sailed toward the dais in a long arc.

A pistol crackled. Not the heavy thunder of a Webley, but the spiteful smack of Madeleine's tiny weapon spraying fire and lead into the Claw! She had snatched it from her bag. His move, distracting the guards, had given her a chance.

Farrell, knife drawn, landed in the melee. The henchmen, dazed by the unexpected turn of their jest, yelled and drew blades. Farrell's dagger ripped upward. The Claw toppled over, his grin becoming a surprised gape.

Madeline, overwhelmed by the guards, was shooting wildly as Farrell made the most of the distraction. He slipped his red knife between his ankles, slashed the cord.

They were both swamped by tramping feet and probing knives. Additional ruffians came pouring in from the front room. And then Farrell recovered the Webley. It was far from jammed. Its iron thunder blasted holes into the tangle.

And then came the pounding of heavy footfalls, booming oaths in Hindustani. Turbaned Sikhs ploughed into the melee. The Singapore police were taking charge.

Strange, how quickly they had arrived! But it was not until hours later that Farrell, back in his bungalow, realized just how odd it was that his mad raid had tripped up the Claw of Iblis and earned him and Madeleine the thanks of the Governor General of the Malay States.

"Darling," Madeleine was explaining as they regarded each other through a tangle of bandages, "What you heard me tell the police was as synthetic as your story.

"I'm really Madeleine Millwood. The corporation that sent you here is managing my late father's estates. I suspected them of pulling crooked work to make me sell out, so I came to Malaya. Dad and I lived here, years ago, which made it easy for me to scout around.

"In Penang I made contact with you as well as the agents of the Claw. I was going to join the outfit. I suspected you of being part of his organization on account of your visit to Crosby, which I timed in on, from the compound. Seeing you dicker with him led to my play against you. That also led me to think that perhaps I'd not have to go through with the risk of meeting the Claw. But you forced that on me."

"Funny," muttered Farrell, "the police didn't find any records of the Claw's doings—"

And then the number one boy broke in to announce a visitor. Mûnah, resplendent in silken *sarong* and embroidered jacket.

"Tûan," she said, "I came to beg your pardon and Allah's—"

She stopped short. Her face froze as she saw Madeleine. Farrell reassured her, then gave her a long, pointed look. She smiled and continued, "I lied to you. My father was not a prisoner. I was working in behalf of my uncle. Raja Mahmud, of Batu Gaja. The Claw has blackmailed him on account of his anti-British activities during the world war. He forced my uncle to permit those crimes against planters and mine owners.

"So I used you as a catspaw to create a disturbance. I knew that while you slew those dogs, I could slip in by the rear and set fire to the evidence with which he extorted money and service from criminals, rajas, and white men alike! I succeeded, thanks to you and the police I called."

Then, with a malicious little smile at Madeleine, she added, "And as I promised you, there is no reward for your service... But do you forgive me?"

"For the sake of that knife, yes," admitted Farrell.

Before he could find further words, she turned toward the hallway.

"So that," murmured Madeleine, who had not missed Mûnah's flash of Malay wrath at the sight of a white woman in Farrell's arms, "is the heroine of that graveyard scenario the Claw mentioned?"

Farrell's face darkened a cozen shades.

"Yes, damn it!" he growled. "Which makes me a double catspaw—once for Mûnah, once for you. To hell with Millwood Industries—they can mail me a check—I'll write 'em a report—no use going back—"

"Don't be stupid, darling," smiled Madeleine. "I might have been annoyed if you'd waited in that graveyard for...well, sunrise...but how would you like to manage the Millwood Industries in Malaya?"

While Farrell had an aversion to conventional jobs, Madeleine's dark eyes were a promise of more than employment.

"I might play, if you'll forget to put opium into the wine," he agreed.

PIT OF MADNESS

Originally published in *Spicy Mystery Stories*, April 1936.

Bayonne seemed incredibly ancient and lovely to Denis Crane as he headed from the wine shop to the Biarritz Highway and across the sombre parkway toward the Gate of Spain. The cathedral spires were silver lance-heads reaching into the moonglow, and the city was a pearl gray enchantment afloat on a sea of writhing river mists: yet that blood soaked soil whispered to Denis Crane as he walked.

This was unholy ground, honeycombed with crypts in which Roman legionnaires had worshiped Mithra, and watched frenzied devotees slash and mutilate and emasculate themselves in honor of bloodthirsty Cybele. This corner of France was the home of witch and wizard and warlock.

A shiver rippled down Crane's lean, broad-shouldered body as he glanced to his left and saw the ominous cluster of ancient trees that overshadowed the low gray cupola of the spring where Satan and Saint Leon once had met—

Another medieval legend. Well, and here is the causeway, and just ahead, rue d'Espagne, with the yellow glow from the windows of Basque wine shops breaking its narrow gloom.

But the scream that came from his left told him how far from warm humanity he was, however near the lights might be. It was the sobbing, desperate outcry of some woman whose last gasp could not quite voice her terror.

Crane's suntan became a sickly yellow in that spectral, mist-filtered moonlight. He wheeled, stared into the swirling grayness of the dry moat that girdled the thirty-foot city wall. His face lengthened, tightened into grim angles, and his eyes narrowed as he listened. Silence—sinister…poisonous…

Then that dreadful wail again. It was closer now, and though it was inarticulate he knew that the woman was crying for help and despaired of getting it.

An everlasting instant, and she burst from the mist and into the foreground at the foot of the causeway that blocked the moat. Her abrupt appearance shocked Crane, though he knew that it was but the illusion of fog and moonlight.

Her hair was a streaming blackness, and her body a pearl-white glow. Her feet and legs were as bare as her torso. All she wore was a flimsy shawl caught at the shoulder, draping slantwise to veil one breast, and flaring out, to shroud the opposite hip. Crane distinguished no feature but her mouth. It was distorted in a cry she could not utter.

He plunged down the steep slope of the causeway and into the moat. Her legs gave way, pitching her headlong to the sand. She lay there, arms sprawled out. As he reached her side, she shuddered and slumped flat, no longer making instinctive efforts to protect herself.

Crane rolled her over into the crook of his arm. He saw then what mist and motion had masked: her throat was savagely torn, her breast and stomach clawed and lacerated. Her face was a gory crisscross of bruises and slashes. The filmy fragility of the shoulder-to-hip shawl had not hampered her assailant enough for him to tear it from her body.

Neither pulse nor breath was perceptible. Though her sweetly curved body was blood-splashed, her wounds could not have killed her; but terror and despair could have.

Her face must have been as lovely as her body; but horror blinded him to the sleekness of her hips and the shapeliness of her legs and firm young breasts. His eyes narrowed as he recovered sufficiently from the shock to interpret certain significant signs.

Her hands had the incredible softness of one utterly a stranger to the lightest work; but what she still clenched in her fingers was a startling revelation.

It was similar in shape to a military campaign badge; purple, with a rosette of the same color. A decoration awarded to an elect few.

But most revealing of all was the silken shawl. It placed her beyond any question. There was only one house in Bayonne where the girls paraded in such costume; and that place was on the street that ran along the city wall.

Then he noted that she was breathing; and a slash on her inside arm was bleeding. It might not be dangerous, but it was near an artery. He drew a clean handkerchief from his breast pocket, and devised a tourniquet.

The town was asleep, and he'd have to carry her to the house on the wall; but first give that tourniquet a twist. He fumbled for a pencil—

But Crane's first aid was not completed.

The sand of the moat bottom gave no betraying crunch; the mist thinned moonlight cast no warning shadow; and Crane's intuition was an instant too late. He dropped the battered girl, but before he caught more than a fleeting glimpse of the dark figure which loomed monstrously above him in the grayness, a flying tackle carried him crashing to the ground.

The impact knocked him breathless. Iron hands clutched his throat; but Crane's fist hammered home. Splintered teeth lacerated his knuckles, and blood gushed, drenching his face. His opponent, snarling scarcely articulate curses, jerked back. Crane's boot lashed out.

But the moonlight was blocked by another figure with monstrous, outspread wings. Bat wings, it seemed. It dropped, boring headlong, toppling Crane backward. A spicy, pungent odor, an odd blend of incense and cosmetics stung his nostrils. Then, still grappling with the thing which had swooped out of the upper mist, he crashed against the gray masonry of the bastioned wall. Crane's hard head had not a chance against a fortress built to defy a battering ram, but his shoulders absorbed enough of the terrific impact to save his skull Some lingering vestige of wits told him that once out of action, he no longer interested the enemy.

Minutes elapsed before he could fight off the numbness and inertia that clogged his will. But he finally rolled over and clambered to his knees.

He was alone in that gray, ghoulish moonglow. The girl was gone. He saw the prints of his own feet and those of the mysterious assailants that had swooped down on him. Blood flecked the sand, and one untrampled spot still held the imprint of that savagely slashed girl's breasts. It had not been illusion; but for a moment Crane's blood became ice.

The laundry marks and monogram on the handkerchief he had bound to the girl's arm would damn him beyond redemption when her body was found. And aside from that, he could not hope to obliterate the traces of the struggle in the moat.

The French police, inhumanly efficient, would inevitably connect him with the outrage. When he returned to his quarters, the *concierge* would note the time of his arrival. The proprietor of the wine shop on the Biarritz Road would remember when he had left, and the direction he had taken. And every foreigner is conspicuous in sleepy Bayonne.

Damn those experts with their omniscient microscopes! Their chemical tests which would detect the faintest trace of blood on his clothing.

And someone, watching from some darkened window of a house on the wall, might observe him as he left the moat, might already have heard and noted the encounter.

Only one move for Crane: find that girl, dead or alive. Hit first before the merciless *Sûreté Générate* connected him with the work of night-roving ghouls. And find the man whose decoration she had clutched.

As he hastened down the moat, he followed the girl's small, shapely footprints along the sand. Wrath burned him as his first fear left. Though that gaudy shawl branded her, she was still a woman, and the victim of something monstrous and deadly; something too eager for her torn flesh to bother with Crane beyond hammering him out of action.

Or had the two spectral assailants already arranged to frame him?

Half way to the sombre Lachepaillet Gate he noted the spot where her bare feet first marked the moat-bottom sand. He entered the walled city and hastened to his room at the Panier-Fleuri. The concièrge regarded him with bleary eyes that suddenly sharpened. But she said nothing.

Once in his room, he cleaned up, then stretched long legs toward rue Lachepaillet. He should report to the police; but who would believe such a story, told by an insane American, trying to implicate one who wore that coveted purple decoration the size of an A.E.F. campaign badge?

Crane jabbed a pushbutton. A trim, sharp-eyed girl in black admitted him and led the way to a spacious hall whose walls and ceiling were a solid expanse of mirror.

A bell tinkled, and a half a dozen girls lounging on upholstered benches lined up on parade as several others emerged from a rear apartment to join them.

They wore satin slippers and knee length silk hosiery. Their professional smiles, and the flimsy chiffon shawls draped from right breast to left hip completed their costume. Not a bad array; though some had over-plump legs, and breasts that would have been the better for a brassiere. A few were lovely in face and body, but there was something infinitely repulsive about that grotesque multiplication of bare flesh in those mirrored panels whose angles probed the concealment of chiffon shawls and made the glaring room a patchwork of feminine curves.

Crane caught a freshly mirrored whiteness and turned toward the door. The shock for an instant numbed him. A full moment elapsed before he realized that he was not looking at the girl who had vanished from the moat.

She had the same gracious inward dip at the waist, the same heart-warming flare of the hips, and one lovely breast peeped alluringly through the heavy strands of hair that trailed down over her left shoulder. Her blue eyes were almost black. Their troubled darkness matched the sombre droop of her lips.

Tears had smudged the mascara of her lashes and a trace of redness lingered. Crane perceived the tensity of her body and saw her fingers twisting the trailing fringe of her shawl.

Why had she been reserved from the lineup? Why that startling resemblance to that savagely mutilated girl in the moat? Why that black fear in her eyes?

The girl's fingers sank insistently into his wrist, and he felt the firm pressure of her hip and shoulder against him as she paused in the doorway.

More than her resemblance to the girl in the moat told Crane that this was the one who could give him the most help—or damn him soonest. He followed his hunch.

"Allons!" he whispered. "Let's go."

He tossed the three hundred pound keeper of the house a purple Banque de France note, and followed the girl in the scarlet shawl up a flight of stairs and into a sombrely furnished room.

Her name was Madeline, but all the coquetry of the game was missing, though she contrived a friendly smile as her fingers plucked the shoulder knot of her shawl.

Crane checked her.

"What's wrong?" he demanded.

"Diane—my sister," she answered. "I'm terribly worried. She hasn't come back. That awful Arab—or Turk—"

Crane frowned. That was an odd touch. Who ever heard of an Algerian wearing that decoration?

As she spoke, she abstractedly kicked off her slippers and leaned back among the cushions. She regarded Crane curiously, seeing that his face was gray and grim.

"What's the matter…don't you like me?"

"That will keep!" His voice was harsh and low. "Tell me about that Arab. What was wrong with him?"

"Some of the things he did, the first night he was here. Before he took Diane —wherever he's taken her. It was in the room next door, No, he didn't hurt her at all—I mean the other girl, not Diane. But he frightened her terribly. I saw him leave. His pupils were like black saucers. *Mon Dieu!* Such eyes. Like Satan eating opium."

She was wrong. Opium contracted the pupils, but her very intensity gave Crane the picture.

"Are you sure he didn't wear the Order of Saint Léon?"

"Mumm…no, of course not! But he dropped something in her room, and she showed it to me, and left it here." Madeline slid to her feet and stepped to the dresser. She returned with a small silver watch charm. It was a tiny peacock with ruby eyes; an exquisitely tooled bit of metal.

"A soldier who'd served in Syria once told me," explained Madeline, "that that is a symbol of the devil-worshipers. That's what's been worrying me. If I'd known in time, I'd never have let her go. But why should you care?"

"I'm a damn' fool who can't mind his business," Crane smiled grimly. "I've got to find your sister." She sceptically eyed him.

"Then you don't want me? But you paid—"

Crane shrugged. "If you knew, you'd understand."

"Oh..." Very slowly, like a dying echo. She caught him by the shoulders, stared him full in the face; and bit by bit she read that the sombre riddle in his gray eyes concerned her missing sister.

"I didn't realize you knew Diane..." Her arm slipped about his neck and she drew closer as she continued, "I'll go with you. I'll help."

She had guts. Crane's smile lost his bleakness. For a long moment their glances blended. She sighed, and her breasts crept through their screen of dark curls. Her smile was a revelation, and suddenly Crane's blood quickened from the soft caress of her arm and the warmth of her body.

"Tenez!" protested Crane. "Stop it, you damn' little fool. I've got some business to attend to—"

"You wouldn't buy me," she whispered. "Somehow, that's rather wonderful... but you like me just a little, don't you? Wouldn't that make it different?"

Somehow, it did; and Crane's sensible effort to break away failed. She was lonely and worried. He couldn't repulse her friendliness.

"Cut it out!" he growled, though his protest was weakening. He laughed harshly, thinking of the one about the mail-carrier who hiked on Sundays; but Madeline seemed no longer one of those who lined up in that mirrored hell glare. She had become a bright flame in the foulness that crept through the mists of that fiend-haunted gray city.

Those were not bought lips that clung thirstily to Crane's mouth, and the shudder that rippled down her throbbing body was instinctive...and as her arms closed about him, Crane defied the peril that was gathering outside. He could not repulse the first glow of friendliness in that drab lupanar...

Madeline's eyes were tear-sparkling when she slipped from Crane's arms and said, "I know now that she is dead."

"The devil you do!"he snapped, feeling decidedly stupid about the interlude that might in the end cost him all but his head—literally, as they use the guillotine in France.

"Yes. Or you'd not have lingered, with that wrath in your eyes. So I know you can't find her alive."

No use explaining his true motives. He took a key from his pocket.

"Go to the Panier-Fleuri. Stay under cover. What you told me about an Arab has entirely upset my assumption. I thought you could tell me about someone wearing the Order of Saint Léon. But no matter—I've got a fresh hunch. Now run along."

They waited for the cessation of laughter and footsteps in the hall. A latch click. Silence, except metallic voices from the reception room on the ground floor.

Crane watched Madeline slip toward the further stairway. A moment later, looking from the window that overlooked the narrow black alley that skirted the rear of the house, he saw the white blur of her face, and caught the gesture of her hand.

She was on her way. He slammed the door and strode down the main stairway. He forced a laugh at the doorkeeper's vulgar farewell; but as he crossed the threshold, he began to see that his investigation, despite the delay, had gained him an ally if the police should catch up with him.

But that silver peacock was an ominous hint. Devil worship...some damnable Asiatic cult. He'd heard it existed in the mountains of Kurdistan.

Yet for all that thickening menace, the riddle in some respects was less baffling in the light of reflection.

Diane had been headed off by the monsters that had swooped down on Crane from the lip of the moat. They must have held to a straight line across the parkway. That gave him a start toward tracing the point from which she had made her futile break.

The mist was thinning, yet enough remained to envelop Crane in a spectral veil that protected and at the same time hampered him. He was unarmed; but he paused long enough to remove his socks, stuff one inside the other, and then slip in a rock the size of his fist. Very pleasant, if he got the edge on the two who had laid him out.

For half an hour he circled, trying to pick a course that the two monsters would have used to head off the mangled fugitive.

"Her instinct would drive her to the closest route to safety," he reasoned. "To her sister. Then if the Gate of Spain was the closest, her direction must have been more to my left. Otherwise she'd have gone through the Lachepaillet Gate."

Half an hour search vindicated the hunch. A shred of scarlet chiffon. A splash of blood.

He looped left. He found footprints heading toward the Gate of Spain—her pursuers, eager to cut off a flight that would betray their rendezvous.

Ahead of him a masonry lunette loomed low in the mist. One of the outer defenses erected by Vauban—or perhaps something much more ancient, and conceived by no honest engineer.

Crane now crept through the mists until a whiff of stale tobacco warned him of a watcher's presence.

He rose and boldly stalked toward the lunette. A jet of light flared in his face, blinding him. He was challenged in French.

"I've got to see the *émir* at once!" Crane bluffed, using a plausible Arabic title that would flatter anyone of lower rank.

The sentry protested. The *émir* was not to be disturbed. The ceremony had started. Crane shrugged and offered him the silver peacock.

"Hurry, idiot!" growled Crane. "Tell him I'm here!"

The flash shifted toward the silver token. The drawn pistol was holstered and an empty hand reached for the symbol. And then Crane's bludgeon cracked down. The guardian collapsed. Crane caught him and the flashlight.

The fellow was wearing a gown, and a hood from which hung a mask to conceal his face. Crane donned the disguise. This was no time for qualms.

The memory of that mangled girl nerved his arm. He raised the pistol, smashed down with the barrel. Then he picked his way down a narrow casemate inclining sharply into the earth.

Furtive flashes of his light guided Crane. He descended a stairway of archaic masonry, crumbled treads whose rubbish litter had been swept against the walls. A splash of fresh blood guided him.

Finally there was an indirect glow ahead. Drums were thumping, and voices muttered in eerie rhythm. Some satanic ritual was in progress.

Reasonably, Crane should now notify the police; but that brained sentry left him with no retreat. More than ever, his story had to be good.

He halted at the jamb of an arch opening into a vaulted chamber illuminated by flickering wax tapers. Its circular walls were pierced with other arches that led to further and darker crypts.

Upward of a score of scarlet-robed and hooded figures were informally gathered in groups. They sat on low wooden tripods the size of coffee tables. Their muttered conversation was low-voiced and unintelligible, but Crane sensed the tension that gripped them, felt their awe and soul-stabbing anticipation.

There was one, tall and commanding, who strode from group to group. Red-masked faces jerked abruptly upward at his approach.

But most revealing of all was the blank arch opposite Crane. Stretched out on a massive block of stone lay a woman, bound hand and foot: Diane, recaptured for the ritual from which she had escaped. Her body was to serve as an altar, perhaps to feel the thrust of a sacrificial knife. Black candles burned about her, diffusing acrid fumes which half obscured her; but Crane saw that she breathed. The tourniquet with his initials, however, had been removed.

Since Diane was alive; he need not find that damning handkerchief, provided that he could extricate her. But though he was armed with the sentry's pistol, the odds were far too great for open attack.

Then he saw that the figure on the two foot, brazen crucifix behind that altar of bare, lacerated flesh was inverted. That final detail sent frost racing through his blood. Those hooded figures had gathered for the Black Mass, the evil ritual of modern satanism, utterly different from the oriental devil-worship. Crane wondered how that silver peacock fitted into the tangle.

From one of the passages at the left came bestial snarls and half human mutterings: some monster held in reserve for the ultimate horror of that mad gathering.

The lordly figure in black clapped his hands. The devotees shifted into crescent formation. Crane joined them as they moved toward the altar.

The Black Monster was donning a priest's stole and cope. Six red-robed acolytes filed from a passageway. Three carried thuribles from which poured blue-black, pungent fumes; the others had trays of hammered copper, all heaped with diamond shaped lozenges. They passed among the gathering, swinging their thuribles and offering wafers to the devotees.

Crane tasted one of the confections; but instead of swallowing, he palmed it. It reeked with hasheesh and datura, blended with other oriental drugs he could not identify; but the two he recognized warned him. Both were brain-searing aphrodisiacs. Those wafers of illusion would make the partaker a crazed beast gnawed by outrageous fancies and delusions. That would give Crane his chance to act.

And all the while that bestial mumbling and groaning and the vibration of pounded iron echoed from the further crypt.

Crane watched the high priest of Satan make a foul mockery of the genuflections of the Mass, saw him spit upon the reversed crucifix, heard him chanting in a high, malignant voice.

Crane could scarcely understand the ritual, but some phrases of ultimate blasphemy were all too clearly burned into his reeling brain.

"Satan, Lord of the World, defend us against an unjust god who created only to damn…defend us against hypocrisy that mocks with the lure of redemption… hear the voice of the damned, O Lucifer, Son of the Morning! Satan, to you we make our prayer, Just and Logical God…"

Finally, the priest faced about and mocked the caricatured crucifix.

"And You, O Thief of Homage and Deceiver of Mankind, I compel you to become incarnate in this bread…by the mockery you have ordained, I who am ordained command you and you will obey…yea, while we draw blood anew from your wounds…and press fresh thorns of vengeance on your brow…this I can and this I will do… Accursed Nazarene… Traitor Son of a Traitor God…"

A low rumbling mutter drowned his amen; then with an inverse gesture of his left hand, the priest blessed the gathering and in mocking accents completed the blasphemy: *"Hoc est enim corpus meum!"*

He spat upon the consecrated bread, stolen from some consecrated altar: he scattered the fragments among the frothing, slavering devotees. They closed in, maddened with blasphemy and Asiatic drugs. They groveled, clawing and growling as they fought for the fragments.

Crane joined them. It was too early for a break. He had to outwit the undrugged acolytes.

First voices, then the tearing of the scarlet robes told him that women were among those who writhed and panted and grappled on the floor. Hoods and masks yielded to clawing fingers. Soon they forgot blasphemy. The Asiatic drugs were biting deep.

In a moment the vault had become an animation of the bestial carvings of a Tantric temple, Women in jewels and costly gowns, and men in formal evening dress were clawing each other with a fury that stripped clothing to shreds.

A golden-haired fiend with crazed eyes and hungry red mouth emerged unpaired from the tangle and twined eager arms about Crane. A few scraps that glittered with green sequins trailed from her hips and what remained of a brassiere clung to breasts that throbbed from her fierce, drugged passion. Her legs were white serpents and her quivering body was a multitude of consuming flames, and her loose hair blinded and choked Crane as he swallowed his horror of that uncontrollable madness.

Yet he had to play his part. That black-robed demon's eyes glittered fiercely from behind his mask as he circled the arena, watching their ever fouler fancies cropping out…

That golden-haired woman's madness was cleaner than what was on every side. And despite his qualms, Crane's blood surged in irrepressible response to her savage frenzy...

Yet even as he yielded to that vortex of passion, a remote corner of his brain remained untainted. He plied her with answering kisses, felt the shudder of her hot flesh, but that one sane morsel was wondering. And at times he saw what was about him.

He recognized a black-bearded man whose face had appeared in every major newspaper of the world...another, who had led a victorious army...and one who from the sidelines told premiers what to say...

The Master gestured, and an acolyte dashed to the passageway at the left.

Crane's fist smashed home, driving away a black-haired woman who sought to displace his companion. Her body was raked and bitten and slashed, but she was seeking more savage company... Crane saw how Diane had been mangled. Her terror hinted that she had not been drugged...

Then Crane saw what had been released when those unseen iron bars clanged open. A tall, gray-haired man whose deeply lined face had once been handsome and commanding. He wore what remained of full evening dress. The ribbon that had crossed his shirtfront trailed like a streamer as he approached; and on it Crane saw the ribbons of civil and military decorations.

He recognized the man. He knew now from whose formal garb that purple rosette had been torn. His mouth frothed, and his eyes burned insanely. He snarled bestially and plunged into the surging orgy.

This was a man whose whispers shook Europe. Now he rolled vilely in that tangle of writhing flesh.

But why—Great God, *why?*

The Master laughed and gestured. The sullen ruddy glow of the tapers was drowned in a blue white, dazzling radiance, pitilessly revealing what shadows had shrouded.

Then Crane saw and understood.

A motion picture camera was covering the hideous show. That damnable film would place those drugged dignitaries forever in the power of that master of blasphemy. He had tricked them from Biarritz with hints of sensational ritual, drugged them, and the record of their unspeakable wallowings would doom them. Satanism had a logical purpose: political blackmail.

Time to move. The Master was distracted by his own show. Crane kicked clear of his companion, reached for his pistol.

It was gone! Lost in that writhing vortex.

He bounded to the altar, snatched that mockery of a crucifix, and whirled toward the Master. A pistol crackled. Crane felt the stab of hot lead, hurled himself aside as bullets spattered the masonry. The acolytes closed in. The brazen crucifix crunched home. But the survivors overwhelmed him, hammering and kicking and grinding him into the flagstones.

The Master joined them. Crane, battered and stunned, heaved up out of the gory tangle, clawed the mask aside. He slashed at that swarthy, aquiline face. He missed, ducked a knife thrust, and closed in. This was the *émir*, the Asiatic enemy whose grip on the drugged dignitaries would buy state and army secrets, upset an African colonial empire.

Crane bored in, but the enemy was fresh and he was dizzy and battered. They crashed to the floor, Crane underneath, vainly trying to drive home one good blow. He jerked clear of a second knife thrust; but the next raked his ribs. The vault became a roaring redness until he perceived nothing but those implacable eyes and that savage, brazen leer.

But that last stroke did not fall. The surging tangle of madmen, sated of all but blood lust, swept Crane and his enemies against the wall. As the acolytes strove to club them into reason, Crane made the most of his respite.

He snatched an abandoned thurible by the chains, swung it like a flail, flattening the Master's skull. He swung again, but the chains whipped athwart a devotee who intervened, and the weapon was jerked from Crane's grasp. He turned toward the altar, ploughing through the writhing tangle. He tripped and was dragged back into the whirlpool of madness, a yard short of his goal.

A pistol roared as he struggled to his feet.

Madeline had followed him.

Crane jerked the weapon from her fingers and blasted the acolytes back as she struggled with her sister's bonds.

Another shot. The cameraman toppled from his perch behind the altar. The pistol was empty. Crane seized the machine and smashed it across the head of a surviving enemy. The film reservoir spewed out its reel of yellow celluloid, fogged beyond redemption in an instant.

The knots yielded. Crane seized the half conscious girl and with Madeline at his heels, skirted the groveling tangle of drugged devil-worshipers. There were no acolytes left to pursue. And presently they reached the mist and moonlight...

"As you learned," explained Diane, hours later, in Crane's rooms, "I was just frightened helpless by your dashing down to meet me. The *émir* didn't intend for me to be clawed to ribbons. But *Monsieur le Général* Mar—"

"Forget his name!" interrupted Crane, "Later, I'll tell you why."

"Eh bien," resumed Diane, "through error he prematurely took some of those drugs sooner than the *émir* intended. Before the ritual started. And you saw—"

"Plenty." Crane shuddered. Then he glanced at Madeline. "You little fool, you had to follow me!"

"But yes. I suspected that through no fault of your own you had been involved and were following some insane American impulse to do what you thought the right thing. So I followed, to help if I could. I feared she was dead, so I hesitated to call the police."

"Damn lucky you didn't!"

And then Diane interposed, "Monsieur Denis, how can I ever express my gratitude—"

"Madeline," interrupted Crane, "has already taken care of that. And having had my fill of sunny France, I think I'll leave for Spain in the morning."

PALE HANDS

Originally published in *The Magic Carpet Magazine*, October 1933.

As Davis Lawton glanced up from the tall glass before him to gaze across the plaza just outside the gray-walled city of Bayonne, he saw that his friend Georges Joubert was approaching the table. Joubert was now a member of the *Sûreté Générale*; but instead of avoiding him, Lawton cultivated their wartime friendship. A subtle and audacious touch, that, maintaining cordial relations with a member of the French Secret Service!

"Sit down and have a drink," invited Lawton.

Although he declined the drink, as he usually did, Joubert accepted a place at Lawton's table.

"My friend," he began abruptly, after a marked and awkward silence, "there has been very much surmise about your connections, here in Bayonne, and else-where—in Morocco, for instance—"

Joubert paused again, groping for words. But further speech was not necessary to tell Lawton that his connections in Morocco were about to lead him to a stone wall in a courtyard, and a firing-squad primed with a stiff drink of cognac and grumbling with forced gruffness at small-arms practice at sunrise. Lawton knew that the *Sûreté* never made an open move until it had enough evidence to condemn a man. The trial would be only a matter of form. But Lawton eyed Joubert very calmly: for in the beginning. Lawton had been a soldier and he would be one again, in the end.

"Very well, Georges," he replied. "Read me the papers."

"Mon ami," came the answer, "I have no papers. That is, not yet. But I know that in twenty-four hours I shall have them. Maybe tomorrow morning. Some one has babbled. Not much, but more than enough. As for your being an agent of Abd el Krim, that is nothing to me, for personally, I don't think France has any right in Morocco. But once the information reaches me officially I shall be compelled to forget that day on the front, when you carried me safety through that hell of machine-gun fire.

"So get out of Bayonne and across the border as soon after sunrise as you can. There is an early express to Spain.

"Yesterday's paper," he continued, "told all about Abd el Krim's successful advance all along the front. So if I have to arrest you it will be either a firing-squad, or Devil's Island, which is much worse. *Au revoir, mon ami!*"

Then Joubert released Lawton's hand, turned, and abruptly strode across the plaza toward the Bridge of Saint Esprit.

* * * *

"Someone has babbled…"

Joubert's words still burned into Lawton's brain like hot irons. But before making his escape, he would have to find out what or who had betrayed him. Perhaps Madeleine had said too much in a careless moment. At the very most, she knew very little; but that would suffice. Perhaps, in a flare of jealousy—but that simply couldn't be the case! Of all lovers, Lawton had been the most devoted. Madeleine wouldn't have betrayed him, though she might have been indiscreet. And even though he escaped the *Sûreté*, thanks to Joubert, he would have to face the unforgiving wrath of Abd el Krim for blundering and wasting time. The problem of the moment was to find out who had betrayed him. Only the evening remained: but the Gray Goddess would tell him. She knew everything.

The law in France prohibited the sale of absinthe; but the Gray Goddess was subtle, so that she now materialized when the contents of two separate and distinct bottles, each in itself legal, were suitably blended. First a pony of *anis del oso*, then one of *cordiale gentiane*; and then the tall glass was filled with seltzer, which clouded, becoming gray and pearly. The result was insipid to taste, but when one had an abundance of time in which to court the lady of fancies, the innocuous flavor was worth enduring for the glamour that came stealing over one's senses.

Lawton paid for the afternoon's drinking, and then crossed the street to go up rue Port Neuf. He halted at a store near the corner, and after regarding its window display for a moment, stepped in. In a few minutes he emerged with a basket laden with all manner of exotic delicacies; and, among the several bottles of Oporto and Malaga, whose necks projected from their nest of parcels, there were as many more whose contents would insure the presence of the Gray Goddess during his last night in Bayonne.

Through continued evocation of the Gray Goddess, Davis Lawton had shaken off the fetters that bound him to earth and its restricting three dimensions. She had at last become a Presence, not visible, but none the less a distinct personality whose inspiration whipped Lawton's brain to uncanny agility, so that the most profound riddles became lucid as water. No reasoning was too intricate for his acuteness; and tonight she would tell him very certainly how he had been betrayed.

As he reached the head of rue Port Neuf, where the old cathedral lifts its tall spires like great, slim lance-heads, he wondered how much Madeleine had lost at Biarritz that day, and what new systems he would have to devise for her.

Madeleine lived in an apartment rue Lachepaillet, a street that ran along the walls of the city, and overlooked the park whose broad, tree-clustered green rolled away from the moat, far below. The door opened before Lawton could pick the key from its companions on his ring.

"I've had the most thrilling day," said Madeleine between kisses. "I do wish you could have been along—but what's in the basket? Oh, aren't those grapes just wonderful! Why, you've brought *everything!* Tinned duck, and *confiture d'abricots*, and—you know, I've got a new way to fix that caviar, with little tomatoes—and even my favorite pastries. Looks like one of your large evenings! Do tell me, have you had some good luck, too?"

Lawton smiled cryptically at that last. And as Madeleine, all enthusiastic about the indicated celebration, began her preparations for the feast, Lawton found a tall glass and mixed his libation to the Gray Goddess. To invoke her the more swiftly, he doubled the portions of liqueurs and diminished the quantity of selzer.

"You know, the pelota matches were wonderful today!" chattered Madeline. "And I won a bet of five louis from a charming old fellow. *Terribly* old, you understand, but he had the keenest eyes! Every once in a while he made a funny little gesture as if he were going to stroke his beard, then suddenly remembered that he was clean-shaven. He must have a history, that one, with the sudden shave he's not yet accustomed to!

"Oh, yes, and do you remember that bracelet we saw at Mornier Frères?" she continued as she set out an array of glasses. "That fascinating thing of green gold and platinum filigree, all set with diamonds and little sapphires—you didn't even notice I'm wearing it! You never notice *anything*, you with your pious meditations."

"It really is beautiful, sweetheart," admitted Lawton as he inspected the bracelet that glittered on her extended wrist. "You must have had a lucky day."

"You'd be surprised," replied Madeleine as she went on with her work. "But I'll tell you later. You'd never guess!"

And then the Gray Goddess, who had returned to Lawton's side, began whispering in his ear.

"Probably," she interposed, "she had it charged, so she can go back tomorrow with all her winnings and play them on double zero. You'll get the bill for the bracelet—"

"I know it was terribly expensive," continued Madeleine, pausing long enough to run her slim white fingers through his hair. "But—no, I won't tell you, yet. That's going to be a surprise." Lawton stared for a moment at her slender, exquisite hands. They had all had pale hands, that succession of ruinous adored ones of which Madeleine was the last. And each time that he rose from the wreckage of his duty they daintily plucked the foundation from beneath his feet again. Lawton sighed wearily, and felt very old at the recollection: but only for a moment. The Gray Goddess was weaving her web of sorcery and the Power was returning to Lawton. It pulsed and throbbed in his veins, and streaked in tiny flashes of fire down his spine, and tingled in his toes. The patterns of the Bokhara rug became exceedingly clean-cut, and then they clouded, islands of old ivory and deep blue in a sea of red that shimmered in the sultry glow of the tall floor lamp at his side. His head reeled ever so slightly with exaltation and all-knowingness. "Tomorrow," Madeleine was saying, "we'll drive to Saint Jean de Luz. Do you remember that day—"

"That first day?" interpolated Lawton, ignoring for a moment the silver-clear syllables of the Goddess whispering in his ear.

"Our first day," said Madeleine, "when we paused on that crest and saw the gulf sparkling, far off, through a cleft in the Pyrenees?"

"Little stupid!" chided Lawton fondly; "do you suppose that I could ever forget? There was never such a day before—"

There was a moment's silence, in which both she and Lawton half smiled to themselves at the memory.

"Do you know," she finally resumed, "I've often feared that some day you might leave. You're such a nomad. And I'm so glad that you remember. It might make you return, that memory."

"But suppose," suggested Lawton, "that I did return and didn't find you? Then what of remembrance?"

"Don't be absurd, darling," she reproved. "You know I'm perfectly foolish about you, and I'll always love you. But let's not even think of parting!"

To which Lawton nodded and smiled; for the Goddess at his side had taken form from the mist which always heralded her presence. She was tall when he stood, and she was tiny when he sat: always at a height just right for her to whisper in his ear, so close that no one else could overhear. And of course, no one else ever saw her.

Madeleine was chattering merrily. Lawton hated to cloud her gaiety by telling her of his departure in the morning. The evening was too lovely to mar with bad news. Later, he would tell her; but now, he would respond to her high spirits. It was easy to smile, and have his lips reply for him. And this would be agreeable to the Goddess, for Lawton now spoke to her in the language of the little gray gods, some of whom were standing respectfully in the corners of the room. He could not see them, yet, but he could feel their presence.

Madeleine was eating now, picking dainty bits of tropical palm hearts from their garniture of mayonnaise. Her great, smoldering eyes regarded him amorously. Then she would smile, and murmur affectionate fanciful things as she offered him morsels of cold fowl, and jelly, and curiously adorned pastries and sips of Malaga.

The enchantment was complete. He paid more and more attention to Madeleine, and yet was not distracted from the crystal-clear, thin voice of the Goddess. Lawton knew that she was not offended because Madeleine did not offer her a bit of pastry or a sip of wine, or even one of those honey-sweet and honey-colored grapes from Spain. Goddesses did not eat; and neither did gods, but Lawton tactfully ignored his divinity long enough to accept the tidbits that Madeleine offered him; for that was their last night, and he wished to make it so memorable and perfect that she would never forget him, no matter who sought her during his absence.

"You've been so patient all evening," Madeleine was saying, "I'm going to tell you the secret I've been saving. I know you couldn't even guess—"

"Do tell me and end the suspense," Lawton replied with surprising animation, in view of his speaking at the same time to the shadow presence at his side.

"I broke the bank today, really and truly! Can you believe it?"

As she spoke, Madeleine drew a great roll of Bank of France notes from her handbag, and then another, and still another roll, until the fine gold mesh, emptied, clung caressingly to her knee.

"Now, silly aren't you sorry you growled so much about my playing roulette?" demanded Madeleine triumphantly.

"Sweetheart, that's perfectly wonderful, and I'm repentant already," replied Layton. "Won't ever growl again."

The Goddess was still at Lawton's side, silent and smiling at her own thoughts. He could see her, without even turning his head, or lifting his glance from Madeleine's exquisite, slim hands and their rosy nails that glowed warmly in the rose-hued light. And then he saw that her eyes were amorous with heavy wine from Lisbon and the thin, ethereal vintage of France. In due course she would become very sleepy, and then Lawton could continue his conversation with the Goddess: but in the meanwhile—the girl beside him was exceedingly lovely and desirable.

Lawton dismissed the riddles of the early evening. They would keep. Nothing in the world, either this one or the next, could compare with his love for this girl and her supreme beauty that was enriching their farewell. Then he remembered that his voice was deep and resonant; and so he sang:

"Pale hands I loved, beside the Shalimar,
Where are you now…"

As the last word passed his inspired lips, he leaned back against his cloud-bank of cushions and accepted Madeleine's ecstasy of approval, and her wine-perfumed kiss.

"Oh, but that was lovely! And now, do tell me what it means, that song in English."

He should have remembered that Madeleine did not understand English. He could compose long speeches in Tamil and Gujarati when he tired of Arabic; but he should not expect her to have his gift of language. So he translated.

"The words are lovely, too," said Madeleine. "And you really do love me that much?"

"Ever so much, and your pale hands also," replied Lawton, as he kissed her fingers one by one.

"And you won't ever leave me, you incurable wanderer?"

Lawton smiled, and his eyes spoke the lie that his lips could not achieve. Then a somber fancy possessed him, and he recited:

"When I am dead, open my grave and see
The smoke that curles about thy feet;
In my dead heart the fire still burns for thee:
Yea, the smoke rises from my winding-sheet."

"That *is* beautiful," observed Madeleine. "Only, just a bit ghastly. You have the strangest fancies, my dear."

"Nothing strange about that," murmured the Gray Goddess to Lawton. "Very appropriate. You love her to distraction. And she's sold you to the enemy, and then showed you the price of your head. Only you won't be in your grave when she opens it. But she did get a good price for digging it, didn't she? One of those rolls would have been enough…"

Lawton watched Madeleine stuffing the notes back into the handbag, and saw her smile at his audible words.

"That was clever," whispered the Goddess at Lawton's side, "getting all that money as the price of your head. They couldn't possibly have known how much your head is worth…that's *our* secret.

"Maybe," continued that fine, thin voice, "maybe they just wanted to make an example of you."

"The chances are," suggested Lawton, "that they suspected I'd completed a rather brilliant plan to lead Abd el Krim's troops all the way to the sea, and drive the French out of Morocco. They must have known I had perfected my plan while I was pretending to be working on the Communists to collect funds for Abd el Krim. Shrewd fellows, to know that I was squandering all that money as a blind, and pretending to sit around the cafes, everlastingly drunk…"

"But you shouldn't blame her too much," murmured the fountain of wisdom. "Think of the temptation! All those thousands of francs! Anyway, she knew you were clever enough to escape."

"But I object to the principle of it!" protested Lawton.

Through the swirling hazes before him, Lawton saw the sparkle of a bracelet.

"She's sold me out, and I'm not ready to leave. Abd el Krim won't understand that I spent all that money as a subterfuge…"

Madeleine was clinging closely to him, now, and her eyes were very dark and lustrous. She was so near that he feared she might after all sense the presence of the Goddess, and be annoyed; so he cut short the conversation, caressed Madeleine's hair, and kissed her full on the lips. But he couldn't take too much time from the oracle that murmured in his ear.

No, it was Madeleine who murmured amorously as she caressed him.

"I'm not the least bit sleepy, sweetheart," he replied. "Well, then…but I'll have another drink first…"

With exquisitely precise gestures Lawton blended the final potion. That last one would give him the power to cross the Border and peer through ethereal vistas deep beyond reckoning. He would see with a keenness he had never before achieved. Then She would reveal the final secret.

Madeleine stood there between the parted draperies, all shimmering in an apricot-colored negligee. She paused for a moment to smile at him as she drew the drapes together. And then the Gray Goddess resumed her speech in a voice somewhat louder, now that they were alone.

"Lawton, you are still terribly stupid! In just another moment she'd have charmed you out of your senses, this fascinating girl who sold you to the *Sûreté*. Think, Lawton, you will face a firing-squad unless you leave by sunrise.

"But go into the next room," taunted that thin, clear voice, bitter and vibrant. "You love her to distraction. Wake her and sing once more of the pale hands you loved…

"Of *all* the pale hands," concluded the Gray Goddess with venomous emphasis.

"No, by God! I'll not sing. I'll choke her!" retorted Lawton, stung by the memory of all his follies. "They've been my damnation all these past dozen years."

"But you can't change," murmured the Gray Goddess with a softness more enraging than the previous sardonic piping. "So leave quietly. Don't wake her, or her arms will hold you until Joubert comes in the morning to arrest you."

"No, Gray Goddess," replied Lawton solemnly. "For once you are wrong. This is the first one to take the price of my head. And this time I shall redeem myself."

His glance roved up and down the wall, and in the ruddy glow of the floor lamp he saw the picture he had once hung for Madeleine. Lacking wire at the time, he had used a cord of hard-spun silk, a relic of old days in Asia. Madeleine had shuddered as he told its history, and showed her the swift gesture used by Indian *dacoits* in their stranglings.

"Look, Gray Goddess, how simple it will be."

But she mocked him for a braggart as the drapes closed about him. Then she followed him, lest his courage fade before the loveliness asleep in the moonlight that streamed in through the drawn curtains and caressed the curved throat.

As Lawton knelt beside her, Madeleine stirred slightly and her shapely arms twined about his neck to draw him to her.

"Pale hands," mocked the Goddess at his side. "They will hold you for Joubert in the morning…"

A whiteness of searing flame swept through his brain as the hard-spun cord cut short the kiss that sought his lips.

"You have proved yourself, Lawton," exulted the Gray Goddess as they emerged again into the sultry glow of the floor lamp. "And there in that mesh bag is the price of your head. It will redeem you and your broken faith in the eyes of Abd el Krim. Now hurry, Lawton, hurry!"

The Goddess led him into a gray world. Lawton strode triumphantly down rue Port Neuf and past the deserted plaza, and across the bridge of Saint Esprit. Dawn was almost at hand. In the distance he heard the whistle of the express that would take him across the border of Spain.

Lawton heard footsteps behind him. Perhaps it was Joubert coming to the station to assure himself that Lawton was leaving on time. He turned; but it was not Joubert who faced him. He stared for a moment, perplexed by the familiarity of the man who confronted him. Then he saw that it was Mahjoub, the right-hand man of Abd el Krim. No wonder that for a moment he had not recognized Mahjoub attired in European clothing, and without his long beard.

"Joubert didn't fail me," said Mahjoub. "By Allah! But I had to do it! You made such an ass of yourself. Abd el Krim gave me full authority; so I solved it my own way.

"Too bad it took that girl so long to learn to win," continued Mahjoub, ignoring Lawton's puzzled frown. "My heart stood still when I saw her take the winnings of the first play and stake them all on single zero. *But she won!*"

"What was that?" said Lawton, enunciating very slowly, like a mechanical toy that has just achieved speech.

"She won enough thousand-franc notes to stuff a saddle-bag. But…"

Mahjoub paused, and made a gesture of stroking his beard, then remembered he was clean-shaven.

"But I guess it was just as well that I did tell the *Sûreté*…"

"*You* told the *Sûreté*?" demanded Lawton.

His voice rang in his own ears as from a great distance.

"By Allah! Of course I did. Then I told your friend Joubert to scare you out of town. But Abd el Krim loves a good soldier, so he'll forgive a worthless secret agent."

"Then *she* didn't sell me?" Lawton's voice was husky and trembling. Exultation fought with despair, so that he could barely pronounce his question.

"No, she didn't," replied Mahjoub. "Nor did I. That was just the only way to get you out of town before Abd el Krim's wrath overcame him. If *he* had told the Sûreté...

"Mafeesh!" concluded the old man with a gesture of finality. "Finish for you."

The express was pulling into the station. But Lawton had turned, and was walking toward the bridge.

"Forgotten of Allah!" cried Mahjoub. "Where are you going?"

Lawton halted, faced about, but made no move to retrace his steps.

"I'm going back to town," he replied. His voice was strong and steady now, as though he commanded troops. "And my salaam to Abd el Krim!"

Then he turned and strode toward the bridge of Saint Esprit.

"Gray Goddess," he said bitterly, "you have mocked me. Her life is on my hands."

"Repentance is vain," murmured that sweet thin voice of the enchantress. "And you acted in good faith. So swallow your misery and your regrets. Be a man. Catch that express. Abd el Krim will give you a high command when he sees that money. You had reason to believe she betrayed you."

"Gray Goddess," replied Lawton, "I refuse to betray what little good there is left in me."

As he passed the second span of the bridge, his right hand swept out in a wide arc. A thick bundle of thousand-franc notes soared high into the morning light, fell into the river, and was sucked out of sight by an eddy. Then, as with lengthening stride he marched across the bridge, he sang in his rich, deep voice:

"Pale hands I loved, beside the Shalimar,
Where are you now..."

It was but a short walk to Joubert's house.

"Georges," said Lawton to his astonished friend, "place me under arrest. And tell the Prefect of Police to call at 34 rue Lachepaillet. He will find her with a cord about her throat. I thought that she sold me. But I met an old man at the station, who told me..."

"I understand," replied Joubert, as he heard the final whistle of the express clearing the yards for Spain.

LIVE BAIT

Originally published in *Alibi*, April 1934.

Davis P. Barrett's mother, who had died when he was six, doubtless thought that he was a beautiful child; but then, she was his mother, and something like thirty odd years may have changed little Davis. Mrs. Barrett's youngest son's face was now the Rock of Gibraltar done in that shade of bronze which comes from long exposure to the breath of blistering deserts and tropical jungles. His broad mouth was a thin, straight line no wider than the edge of an officer's dress-sword, and somewhat harder. His blue eyes glowed with ominous, volcanic mirth as they watched two perfectly barbered, tailored, and manicured gentlemen whose tables were at the corner of the tiny dance floor, and to Barrett's left.

The two racketeers were inseparable friends. They had assumed—somewhat erroneously, as it later developed—that their being at Club Martinique was pure coincidence, and they had agreed to combine their tables when their feminine companions arrived.

A waiter was bringing a note to the gentleman whose table was nearest Barrett: Guido Pichetti. Barrett's shaggy, reddish brows rose just perceptibly. His chin, which he fingered abstractedly, was thrust forward. There was something tense and expectant about Barrett, as though he were a panther about to spring. His interest seemed centered on the note, rather than on the perceptible bulge of the left breasts of the nicely fitted dinner jackets of Messieurs Pichetti and Spud Malone.

Club Martinique was a mirthful madhouse of blatant music, alcoholic laughter, and tinkle of ice against the sides of many tall glasses. White arms and shoulders, and whiter shirt fronts stared spectrally through the bluish glare of the spotlight that made the shifting bands of smoke seem like phantom serpents writhing in the warmth of a ghostly sun. The reek of gin, perfume, cosmetics, and unextinguished cigarette butts was the odor of gaiety to most of those assembled: but to Davis Barrett it was the exhalation of death, and the end of a story…

Guido Pichetti had opened the note. His swarthy features flushed with rage, then bleached sallow as he leaped from his table. What he said to Malone, and what Malone replied was not audible above the blare of the music; but Barrett's expectancy was not in vain. There was an almost simultaneous flashing of hands to shoulder holsters—

Barrett's lips relaxed enough to reveal a glimpse of his teeth as two pistols blazed into the satanic bluish moonlight, and their roar, almost a single, prolonged report, bellowed above the brazen clang of the orchestra. Barrett ignored the ensuing uproar and confusion as a glance, before the crowd became too dense about the fallen, assured him that the theretofore bosom friends had killed each other. He sighed deeply, slouched against the back of his chair, and for the first time realized how highly keyed he had been for the past half hour.

Justice that was beyond the power of the law.

Vengeance…and the end of the story…

* * * *

A burly, red-faced, grim mouthed man emerged from the gaping, babbling, hysterical crowd that pushed in as close as it could to the double X's that marked the respective spots where Guido Pichetti and Spud Malone had become public benefactors. In his hands he had a letter and an envelope, both of which he thrust before Barrett.

"Dave," he demanded, "what do you know about this? One look tells me it's fishy as kippered herring—even if Damon and Pythias were too dumb to realize it."

Barrett regarded first the envelope, then the letter, then John Healy, Chief of the Detective Bureau, who was beginning to understand why he had received a tip to be present, though unseen, at Club Martinique.

"End of the story, John. It's been a strain, figuring out ways of making these rats kill each other."

Healy grunted, nodded, then said, "Pretty good, Dave. Only, it's not the end of the story by a big damn sight! You've not finished something, you've started something. Watch your step."

Mrs. Barrett *might* have been right, some thirty years ago. Her lean, broad shouldered son, while far from handsome, in his lighter moments had a pleasant smile, and an engaging friendly manner.

"Thanks, John," he said quite affably as he rose from his seat. "Come out to the house some night soon. I have some mighty interesting jig-saw puzzles."

And a few moments later, Barrett was at the wheel of his Issotta, driving up Saint Charles Avenue toward Audoubon Place. He was smiling to himself at the gullibility of two dear friends whose lurking suspicion of each other had been detonated by the note Barrett had prepared and planted.

Two days later—thirty-six hours, to be accurate—Barrett's smile vanished. What he had called the end of a story had become the beginning of a longer and grimmer tale. His blue eyes were hard as sword points as he paced up and down the wine-red Boukhara rug in his library.

"Marie," he demanded abruptly as he halted and faced the girl who sat buried in the depths of an over-stuffed chair, "are you sure Lee hasn't just left town suddenly on urgent business?"

Marie Simpson shook her blonde head and dabbed her tear-reddened eyes. She had never learned the art of effective weeping.

"No, Dave. He'd have wired or phoned me by this time." She swallowed a sob, then said pointedly, "And I don't think you believe he's left on a business trip, either."

Barrett's features tensed. Vengeance was bearing bitter fruit.

"Suppose you run along home," he suggested with a gentleness that seemed out of keeping with his rugged features and the usually incisive snap of his voice.

"You know I'd go through hell and high water for Lee. And if there's anything off color about his being missing for the past twelve hours, I'll tear the roof off."

As he spoke, he helped Marie Simpson with her coat.

"Dave, do you think—"

"I'm not thinking anything," he evaded. "But I'm going to see. Now run along, and pull yourself together."

As the door clicked closed behind Marie Simpson, Barrett's eyes flashed to the half opened desk drawer. During the brief interview he had feared that his very effort not to think of what the drawer contained, not to let his eyes stray toward it would betray him to Marie's intuition. His hand halted midway as it reached for the envelope.

"Jackass!" he said aloud. "Healy was right." Barrett's bitter thoughts were interrupted by the arrival of John Healy. He indicated the chair that Marie Simpson had left but a few moments ago—or how long had it been that he had stared at that desk drawer?

"What's new and good, John?"

"About Lee Simpson, and it's not good," said Healy as he selected a cigar from Barrett's humidor and jammed his bulk into the spacious chair. "You're his number one friend. Where is he?"

"God knows," replied Barrett. "And I will if I live long enough. Has his wife —"

"Uh-uh. Run me ragged," interrupted Healy. "But no sign of him."

"Where do I come in?"

"Simpson's not got two nickels to click together," answered Healy. "And no enemies. The way I got it doped out, someone is getting at you for that job you pulled at Club Martinique. Somebody took a tumble."

Barrett flinched as at the thrust of a red hot iron.

"Right, John. I'd rather face a machine gun than this."

"Don't worry. You probably will, before it's over. Have you gotten any demands for ransom or the like?"

Barrett shook his head.

"You're a damn liar," declared Healy with the license of friendship.

"Have it your own way. And if you've any dope, pass it along. I'm on the job myself."

"No good, Dave," said Healy with a peremptory gesture. "That's the trouble. You've been on the job too much. You smoked out so many of these rats—and now they're pulling your teeth by snatching Simpson."

"My teeth," countered Barrett with an ominous glitter in his eyes, "aren't pulled yet. I want you to keep your hands off. None of your men following me around when I take the warpath. Will you give me a break? Stand clear?"

Healy saw Barrett's glance shift and linger on a rack of firearms that made the library look very much like an arsenal.

"Sold."

"Thanks, John. And remember, I've got my reasons for playing a lone hand."

Upon Healy's departure, Barrett re-read for the twentieth time the letter he had received that morning: *Bring $20,000 in new, unmarked hundred dollar bills to the main entrance of the Crescent Compress Company at midnight. If* *there is any sign of police interference, or if my men do not report by one A.M., we'll ship Simpson's head to join his finger. Come alone and unarmed."*

There was no signature. None was needed. Jake Moroni had made a final counterattack that would not fail as the others had. A small parcel which had accompanied the letter bore witness that the enemy meant business. It contained the fourth finger of Simpson. The blackened nail, recently crushed by a hammer tap, identified it beyond any doubt.

Barrett knew that the demand for the ransom was camouflage. Moroni had based his *coup* on the friendship of Simpson and Barrett. He knew that Barrett would willingly and knowingly walk into an ambuscade for the sake of Simpson.

"The—!" muttered Barrett as he thrust the letter back into his desk. "Using live bait..."

He grinned sourly, and added, "I'll do the same."

* * * *

At about the same hour of that same morning, Jake Moroni was holding high court in his armored office in an otherwise deserted warehouse near the river front. Moroni's swivel chair was a throne, and his well-tailored suit of imported worsteds was the imperial purple that had slipped from the shoulders of his predecessor when the muzzle of a .25-3000 reached through a loophole in a brick wall and snapped a tiny slug through a pistol proof vest.

In front of Moroni was a mahogany desk entirely suitable to an executive whose payrolls were as great as those of the city, and whose revenues were greater. At his left was a gaudy Japanese screen that added to the grotesquerie of the crude office. The screen, however, was no evidence of the house beautiful; it served a useful purpose. The center of one of its painted chrysanthemums had been neatly cut out with a knife.

Moroni's swarthy features smiled unpleasantly as his dark eyes bored coldly into the pudgy, evil faced ruffian before him.

"Orders are orders," he declared with ominous evenness of tone.

"I don't give a damn!" exclaimed Moroni's lieutenant, and commander in chief of the Praetorian guard of hop heads, and assorted assassins, "Tinkering with Barrett is like boxing with a tiger. Shaking him down for twenty grand to save Simpson's hide is one thing. That's easy. But trying to grab Barrett when he delivers the jack is plain foolishness."

"Mmmm...hm," breathed Moroni. His snake eyes flickered to the right. He seemed for an instant to be peering through and past the thugs who sat on a bench along the wall. "Carver! Are *you* man enough?"

A tall, rangy fellow whose bony features wore a warped, perpetual grin, fidgeted for a moment with the brim of his hat. His glance switched from Moroni to the lieutenant on the carpet, and back to Moroni again.

"Jeez, that ain't a fair question," he protested. "I'm workin' for you, but I'm directly under Schwartz. Ya know—"

He made a gesture of resignation.

"Mmm...discipline," murmured Moroni. "Yes. Discipline is splendid." Then he snapped a question: "How about you other punks?" The other two on the bench started, frowned ponderously, nodding and rubbing their chins as though a portentous decision was on the verge of birth. The atmosphere of the tiny, sound-proof office became electric from the tension.

"Yellow from your back bone to your belly!" crackled Moroni. "Just like this slob."

The slob on the carpet flushed.

"Who's yellow, you—"

His hand made a swift gesture; but it was not fast enough. A spurt of flame poured from the loophole of the chrysanthemum. As the pudgy lieutenant reeled crazily and collapsed, a pistol appeared in Moroni's hand. The three along the wall kept their hands rigidly motionless.

"You bastards gimme a headache," said Moroni pleasantly. "Mike—Otto! Get the hell outa here while I talk to Carver."

As the pair left the office, audibly sighing their relief at dismissal, Moroni beckoned to Sam Carver.

"I been fed up with him for a long time. You got guts enough to take this job?"

Carver swallowed just once.

"Sure thing. Only I'd like to know just what you want done."

"That's the talk," approved Moroni as he replaced his pistol. "When Barrett shows up tonight, I want you birds to nab him, tie him, and bring him to the *Carlotta*. And I don't want you to croak him—"

Sam Carver frowned perplexedly.

"Jeez, that's a contract. He's a fighting fool, and—" He saw Moroni's eyes shifting speculatively toward the man who lay on the floor. "But I'll make it—but it won't hurt to tap him on the nut just to keep him quiet, without really *hurtin'* him?"

Moroni nodded and smiled thinly.

"Just remember that a dead man can't sign an order for fifty grand. But *after* we get the dough…"

Carver grinned.

"Sorta double play, eh, Mr. Moroni?"

"Right. And just a bit of advice, Sam. You been getting too friendly with my secretary."

His voice was low, confidential, and alarming.

"Honest, I ain't done—I mean, I didn't mean a thing. Just bein' friendly to Nor—Miss Arradonda."

Moroni stroked his bluish jaw and smiled affably.

"I understand that, Sam. But it just don't look right. She's nothing to me a-tall, only…"

"I got ya, Mr. Moroni," Carver hastened to assure his chief.

"Okay. And no slips tonight. I'm counting on you. Twenty grand, and Barrett in shape to sign an order for fifty more, and then we'll have no more phony letters and civil war."

* * * *

Despite his chiefs warning, Sam Carver phoned Norma Arradonda, and after being assured that the coast was clear, called at her apartment. He came to the point at once.

"You and me are strangers from now on. Positively farewell appearance."

Norma was dark and shapely, and lived up to the exotic ear pendants she affected. Her full lips were red as a sabre slash against the transparent, creamy pallor of her skin.

"Matter, Sam?" Her delicately penciled brows rose in Moorish arches.

"Moroni's set on rubbing me out," Carver explained somberly. "That Barrett job—"

"You have been buying me too many drinks at Club Martinique," mused Norma.

"So I heard. And here I am."

"Still," resumed Norma, "I think you're heated up about nothing."

Carver shook his head.

"Barrett has been on the spot half a dozen times—and each time he's beaten it, with a surprise party of his own. And when he pulls a dumb one, his luck saves him.

"I'm scared of that guy's luck. He's a hoodoo. And he's filled a private graveyard with mugs that tried to get him. Snatching his best friend is like spitting in a tiger's eye."

Norma shook her head.

"Wrong, Sam. Him and Simpson are old buddies. And if you don't return by a certain time, it's Simpson's head. He knows it. That's going to make a boy scout out of Barrett."

"I don't care if it's supposed to make a good Christian of him," countered Carver dolefully. "I'm bein' framed—just like Dutch—"

Carver checked himself abruptly, swallowed, said nothing.

"Yes?" murmured Norma.

"Nothing!" snapped Sam. "I'm doing this job, and then I'm going to the country to raise chickens. There's no percentage."

He reached for his hat. Norma stopped him at the door.

"Since you're not going to see me any more," she said, "you might at least kiss me good bye—you're a good egg, Sam, and I hope you get the breaks…oh, just a minute…"

He paused as she scribbled an address and a telephone number on a slip of paper.

"Call me here, once in a while—*but disguise your voice*. Someone might be listening in on an extension. Don't say too much. Just enough so I'll know you're thinking of me. He's got his guts, trying to keep you from even being friendly in a nice way… Bye, Sam."

Norma was part of the dictator's intricate web of evasion and espionage. While terming her a secretary was perhaps a shade too figurative, hers was an important part in Moroni's system of seeming to be in several places at once, and proving it by answering, from one point, calls to half a dozen offices. Norma was much of the brain of the organization—but Norma was, after all, human—

* * * *

360

That night Barrett dressed very deliberately, as though for a dinner engagement instead of a rendezvous with kidnappers.

"Damn your black hide, Amos," he said reproachfully, as he regarded the tie that his white haired old colored handyman had laid out. "Do you think that goes with this suit?"

"Yas suh, Mistah Dave! Ah thinks it's jes go'geous," the old man insisted with a nod and a grin. Then he turned to the rack to replace his favorite among Barrett's array.

Barrett was content with the amendment submitted by Amos. As he adjusted it, he fondly regarded the Colt .45 that lay in his dresser drawer, and regretfully shook his head.

"That black scarf, Amos," he said abstractedly, as he detached a gold penknife from his chain. He took the scarf, snapped it several times, whip-like; and all the while, one eye half closed, he pondered as though considering a hitherto unweighed element of the evening's dangerous work. Barrett finally knotted the penknife into a corner of the scarf, then stuffed several packets of hundred dollar bills into his pockets.

"Amos," he said, "here is the key to the Ford. In case I don't come back, you can have it."

The old man's eyes widened, and his black face lengthened.

"Whhhh-y, Mistah Dave," he sputtered.

"Stick around and watch the phone," said Barrett. "And you don't know where I've gone—not even if the President calls!"

"Yas, suh, Mistah Dave. An' ain't nuthin' goin' a happen to you."

"I wish," reflected Barrett as he took the wheel of the heavy sedan that was next to the Ford coupe, "that I could be sure Amos is right."

Barrett parked near the corner of Munn and Tchoupitoulas Streets. Even by daylight, the vicinity seemed to have been blighted by a lurching vengeance that had doomed to failure the warehouses and ship's chandleries that line the river front.

"Munn Street...one block long—but it may take me the rest of my life to reach the end of it," was Barrett's thought as he sought to accustom his eyes to the blackness. The moon was still so low that the shadows of the buildings on the right blended with black bulk of those on the left. He shivered as the penetrating wind bit like a bayonet. Barrett drew his top coat about him. His fingers, grasping the lapels, touched the hard silk of his scarf.

"One concealed weapon, anyway..."

A gold penknife. If he had brought a pistol, he might be tempted to use it, and thus surely kill Lee Simpson as well as the one who received his fire.

"God, but it's dark..."

Barrett was used to the haunted blacknesses of Asiatic jungles, vibrant with the silent slinking of the eater in search of the eaten; yet Munn Street, which led to the river, was shrouded by an obscurity more malignant than any he had ever penetrated. Barrett shivered again, but this time, not from cold. He smiled, and his gait became fluent as that of the hunter.

Barrett forced himself to consider the moment at hand rather than the other life which hung in the balance. It was his fault that Simpson was in danger, and his duty to extricate him, regardless of the cost.

Twenty paces into the darkness. Then someone emerged from a doorway and said in a low, decisive voice, "Stick 'em up, Jack."

But it was the muzzle of a pistol that someone else jammed into the small of his back that gave force to the command. Barrett's hands rose.

"Now back into this doorway—Mike, frisk him, right now!"

Deft fingers went through his pockets. There was a mutter of satisfaction as Mike drew out four packets of bills. For an instant the beam of a tiny fountain pen flashlight winked at the numerals that marked the denomination. The reflected glow, however, revealed more than the direct light: Barrett noted that his captors were not masked. It seemed to make no difference to them that Barrett had in that moment's illumination seen enough to identify them.

There was an unavoidable conclusion that Barrett had to draw—unless he could convince himself that his captors had been careless, and had not realized that Barrett would ever afterwards recognize them.

"All right, fellows," said Barrett pleasantly. "You've got your money—now where's Simpson?"

"Ain't that a hot one, Sam?" chuckled the one who had searched Barrett.

"Simpson is in a safe place," came the reply. "And you're coming with us. Think we're going to turn you loose before this money's been checked to see nothing's phony?"

"Reasonable," admitted Barrett. "I'll sort of be taking Simpson's place, so you can turn him loose right away."

"Uh-uh," grunted Sam, apparently pleased by the prisoner's ready acquiescence. But to Barrett the arrangement was confirmation of his first suspicions.

"Mike, tie this bird," commanded Sam. "Lower your arms, you—but don't try any funny work."

"How is he going to climb down to the boat if his hands are tied?" wondered Mike. "And that Jacob's ladder up the *Car*—"

"Shut up, you boob!" snapped Sam Carver. "Grab that cord!"

"Aw what if he does—" countered Mike, then checked himself.

But that slip sufficed to assure Barrett that he was destined to board one of the many abandoned ships, war-time built merchant marine, moored along the opposite bank of the river. The secreted penknife might enable him to cut his bonds; but a doubt had risen in Barrett's mind: would Simpson be released, now that the ransom had been delivered, or would he be executed as part of the reprisal?

Barrett's captors were indifferent to future identification; and that could betoken but one thing other than gross carelessness.

A desperate scheme crystallized; and in an instant Barrett made his decision.

Sam, pistol in hand, was a blur in the darkness a yard ahead. Mike was fumbling in the gloom at Barrett's left, seeking a coil of rope. Surprise can work wonders. Barrett felt the enemy's assurance, and hoped that they did not sense his own.

Barrett's fingers closed on the end of the scarf about his neck and dragged it clear. They thought that he was unarmed; yet that folded square of silk was a silent, instantly fatal weapon which was invisible in the darkness.

As Mike rose and turned, Barrett moved with that catlike swiftness which had so often served him—and saved him. The silken scarf, weighted with the knife, whipped about Mike's throat. There was no warning in its touch. It seemed to be but the trick of a gust of wind; and in the obscurity of the doorway the gesture did not register.

The weighted end passed over Mike's shoulder as Barrett side-stepped, seized the enfolded penknife with his left hand and at the same time put all his weight behind his right, which grasped the free end of the scarf.

"Wh—"

Cut off before it was spoken; and the sharp cracking sound meant nothing to Sam Carver, least of all that Mike's neck had been broken.

All in one flashing instant; one fluent, continuous, deadly swift gesture. Had there been a blow, a shot, an outcry, Carver would have acted at once. He sensed that something deadly and inexplicable had happened before his eyes; but he had also to reconcile his intuition with the knowledge that Barrett's plays had always been accompanied by the flash of steel, the jetting flame of pistols, the impact of hard driving fists.

He lost an instant before he clubbed his pistol so that in accordance with orders he would not kill the fifty thousand dollar prisoner. And that instant sufficed for Mike's body to catapult out of the darkness, drive Carver crashing back against the wall.

Then savage fingers closed about his throat as the first blow of his pistol butt struck Mike's limp body to the ground. Carver writhed and struggled, smote blindly at the enemy within his guard. His feet were tramping on a man's body…

"Mike," he contrived to gasp hoarsely before his breath was utterly cut off.

Barrett's fingers sank relentlessly home. Lee Simpson's severed finger lent a murderous fury to Barrett's constricting grasp. He followed Carver to the paving. The blows of the pistol butt had ceased…*hours* ago, it seemed…

Finally he relaxed his grip, drew a deep breath, realized for the first time that glancing, misdirected blows had battered his head and shoulders. Barrett stretched out on the cold paving, dazed by his exertions and the slaying frenzy and the destructive nervous tension of his lightning assault.

In a moment, however, he recovered. He was trembling violently, seeking to reassemble the elements of the suddenly devised scheme. Then it all came back to him; but before going about what he intended to do, he paused to search the two who lay on the floor of the deep doorway recess. Dead, not merely out.

He scrutinized the contents of their pockets, piece by piece.

"Here's the touch!" he exclaimed as by the light of the fountain-pen flash lamp, fortunately undamaged, he read the notation on a slip of paper, in feminine script, *"Norma—Main 7771—blind listed, so learn it and then destroy this."*

That Sam Carver was a fair approximation of Barrett as to stature and conformation had already entered the plan; but this brief note suggested an interesting amendment, despite the fact that the open implication of an undercover friendship *might* be misleading. Yet, from his observation of Moroni's organization, he could at least be certain that the note was written by Norma Arradonda, and not by some obscure namesake.

Barrett's eyes glittered with that same fierce mirth of two nights ago, at Club Martinique. Then he remembered Lee Simpson's peril, and his mirth became exceedingly bitter. Barrett strode swiftly toward the ferry landing, a block further upstream, saw that the aged ticket taker was nodding at his post, and stepped into the telephone booth. He called Amos and gave the old negro two simple orders. This done, Barrett returned to the doorway on Munn Street and set to work exchanging clothing with the late Sam Carver.

In a few minutes the first move against the enemy was completed. With the flashlight Barrett checked his work to see that he had made no slips in the dark.

"If this don't work...good God, but it's *got* to work! It can't flop!" he told himself as he repressed a shudder at the thought of the dead man's apparel that now clothed him.

He heard the sound of a car pulling to the curbing. Old Amos...nevertheless Barrett advanced with drawn pistol until he was close enough to identify his servant.

"Go back home, Amos," he directed. "Leave the Ford here."

Barrett dashed back to the doorway of death, shouldered Sam Carver's body, and placed it at the wheel of the sedan. Mike was then stowed in the Ford coupe which Amos still had an excellent chance of inheriting. From the coupe Barrett took a double barreled, ten gauge shotgun. He lowered the window of the sedan...

A sheet of flame, a roar, the splintering of glass—Barrett knew that his work had been good, but he did not care to verify the fact by close inspection. He disconnected a gas line, let the ground beneath the car become drenched, then struck and tossed a match. As the flames rose in a lurid column, he turned toward the Ford coupe, to drive down town.

"It's got to work," he reiterated as he banished, by sheer force of will, the panic that assailed him at the thought of failure.

Barrett, hard bitten, and seasoned as he was by the World War, was shaken by the gruesome work of the past few minutes—and then he remembered Lee Simpson's severed finger, and Moroni's characteristic duplicity as revealed by the two who did not know that a silken scarf was a deadly weapon.

"Live bait, eh?" he muttered grimly.

Barrett drew up to the curbing some ten blocks short of Canal Street. He dragged Mike from the coupe, supporting him as though he were hopelessly drunk. The vicinity, though bustling during the day with trucks approaching and leaving the establishments of the produce dealers and commission merchants, was utterly deserted at night. Nevertheless, Barrett played his part by muttering incoherently as though he were as intoxicated as his burden was supposed to be.

Barrett knew that there was a telephone pay-station in the entrance that led to the second floor of the building. He maneuvered Mike into position, supported him with his elbow, then called Norma Arradonda. Barrett made an effort to disguise his voice to resemble the husky rasp of Mike.

"Norma... This is Mike," he began hurriedly. "You know—Sam's buddy—"

"Yes?" came the voice of Norma, with a peculiar, rising inflection that sent chills creeping up his spine. Warning? Anxiety? Dawning suspicion? A host of fatal possibilities trooped home in an instant. Lee Simpson's life was at stake. And then—

"Sam croaked Barrett and took the twenty grand—"

Barrett distinctly caught Norma's gasp of amazement and consternation. But what else? Concern for Sam's fate when Moroni learned of the trickery—*per-haps*.

"We're checkin' out. Meet us at Ponchartrain Junction! Quick! Yeah, hurry like—"

Barrett dropped the receiver, drew a pistol, and at the same time broke off his conversation to cry out in terror, "Sam—fer Chris—"

The crackle of the pistol cut short the shriek. Over the wire, the deception must have been perfect.

"That, and Mike full of lead," was Barrett's thought as he leaped to the coupe, "ought to convince them I'm dead and Sam's skipped with the ransom. Now let's see what they'll have at Ponchartrain Junction."

Barrett headed for the first city station beyond the main L & N depot.

Simpson, in view of Barrett's supposed death, would have no further vengeance-appeal for Moroni. But if Moroni suspected that it was not Barrett who was at the wheel of the flame warped sedan—!

* * * *

Barrett was grateful that he knew of several readily accessible public phones which were inconspicuous. There was one on Decatur Street, across from the French Market coffee stall. Made to order! He called John Healy at his residence.

"I've been bumped off. You'll find my body at Munn and Tchoupitoulas Streets," he informed the Chief of Detectives. "Land on Moroni and his boys for killing me. Right now, and for God's sake, shake it up! Stick to that story. It's foolproof. And it's Simpson's head if it flops."

Barrett smacked the receiver into place and drove on.

"That'll keep 'em off of Lee, wherever he is."

Barrett, whose successful campaigning had in the past been largely dependent on the proper interpretation of underworld whispers, had heard of Sam Carver's interest in Norma. Garrulity is the most fatal affliction of the racketeer. Thus, though Barrett inferred that Carver's interest had blossomed beyond mildness, he was not certain enough to predict her attitude toward Carver's supposed proposition. She might be loyal to Moroni—in which case there would be a reception committee awaiting Carver as represented by Davis P. Barrett; but that was a chance that could not be avoided.

Barrett parked in a side street, and taking full advantage of the darkness along the L & N tracks, made a careful reconnaissance. His wearing Carver's gray suit made him a good target; and Barrett was still uncertain as to what and who would meet him.

He saw a cab pull up across the tracks, heard the door slam, and watched its tail light disappear.

The passenger was a woman, and she was approaching the deserted station. The waiting room was in darkness save for a single feeble globe. By its dim glow he recognized the shapely figure, exotic coiffure, and graceful, confident gait of Norma Arradonda as she crossed the threshold.

Bait…live bait…who else might be there…

"Live bait it is," he told himself as he advanced. *"But which of us?"*

The girl, who had been watching his approach, emerged to meet him. She barely suppressed a cry of alarm as she realized that Sam Carver's gray suit did not contain Sam Carver. But Barrett's smile reassured her to a degree, so that she was perplexed rather than alarmed, Barrett, whatever he was, was not a woman killer.

"Sam didn't kill me," he explained. "That was just a handy stall. We made a bargain. Moroni thinks I'm dead. You know where Simpson is. Here's the twenty grand I'm giving you, from Sam, if you'll tell me where my buddy is held a prisoner."

It caught Norma off guard, but she quickly assimilated it.

"This money," she said, "is your security against Sam, and Simpson's our—"

"Right," said Barrett. "Now you get on that phone and get things going. The minute I know that Simpson is in the clear, you get the money. And don't worry about Sam—Moroni can't touch him."

"Dirty trick," was Barrett's thought as he caught a significant light in Norma's eyes. "She likes Carver…plenty."

But the memory of Simpson's severed finger stilled his qualms, and steeled him to carry on with his playing on the girl's obvious affection for Carver.

"But he'll know you're not dead," she objected.

"No. Mike's doubling for me—Sam didn't trust him, so—"

He made a gesture of finality. Norma understood. Despite her connection with the racket, she was for a moment taken aback by the grimness of Sam Carver's subterfuge.

As she paused for words, Barrett suddenly realized that he had been off guard for a moment, that his keen attention had relaxed. He glanced over his shoulder, caught a metallic glint. And before Norma could utter the words that were on her lips, Barrett's hand shot forward—not to his holster, but to the girl, striking her to the floor as Barrett himself plunged forward.

He made it with a split second to spare: a drumming fusillade rattled through the silence, and sent the panes beyond them splintering and tinkling to the floor.

"Wiggle clear!" hissed Barrett as he whipped his prone body to cover and flashed his pistol into line. The gunner was momentarily off guard, and certain that his volley had dropped Barrett and Norma. But the smack of Barrett's pistol sent him pitching backward. Another, coming from cover, returned Barrett's fire, spattering him with wood splinters, but doing no damage.

"Come out and take it, Carver," said a voice. "Or we'll chop the dump down and the Jane'll get it too."

"Smack!"

And a grunt of pain.

"Spill it!" urged Barrett in a low voice. "Don't be fussy about ratting! Can't you see somebody tapped your line, and Moroni's out for you and Sam?"

A siren screamed in the distance.

Barrett's pistol fire, now more accurate, halted the charge before it got a fair start.

"Here's the note you gave Sam. That proves I'm on the level."

He emptied his pistol, and drew the other salvaged weapon. Help was close; but the enemy could stick to the last second and still make a getaway. Some of them were slipping around to attack from the rear.

"Come across!" he barked above the deadly chatter of the automatic and the splintering of glass and wood. "You can't get away with this. You've got to leave town. And twenty grand—*crack-crack*—is a good stake."

"The *Carlotta*. Opposite Jackson ferry," she replied.

"Phone the police!" commanded Barrett as he jammed home a fresh clip, wondering as he did so whether he could hold the rush.

But the arrival of the police patrol spared Barrett the test. As the melee subsided, John Healy entered the station, alone.

"You jackass!" he demanded, "why didn't you tell me you were throwing a party here?"

"Cops hanging around would've crabbed the works. Send some men to the *Carlotta*. Get Simpson. And tell your outfit Sam Carver is here, dead. Don't let *anyone* get wise!"

Healy was perplexed, but he asked no questions.

"Duval! MacCarthy!" he bellowed. "Get this, and hop to it!"

He repeated Barrett's instructions, then added, "Don't lose a second—I'll hold this down—to hell with what's in here, hurry, damn it!"

* * * *

As the patrol car took off with a roar and a clash of gears, Healy turned to Barrett.

"Lord, Dave," he said, seeing Barrett's drawn, white features—white as his tropic tan allowed. "Did they get—"

"No. Didn't plug me, much—but if anything's slipped—Lee Simpson—"

Healy's eyes opened wide as Farrell explained a *few* things.

"But I don't quite understand," he protested.

"You're dumb!" snapped Barrett, giving him a hard glance. And then, "Norma, you don't have to wait here until Lee's in the clear—here's the dough. We'll drive to the airport and get you out of town right now!"

"But we found Mike Tomaso's body in a *phone booth*," Healy persisted, ignoring Barrett's murderous glance. "Not in your burned up car. Who—"

Norma's slender form jerked as from an electric shock. Her features twitched from the horror of sudden understanding. Then her hand flashed forward. Four packets of bills caught Barrett full in the face.

"You dirty —— ——!" she said with a deliberation that made the words even deadlier than their coming from a woman's lips.

Barrett nodded. Healy seized her wrists.

"I feel like one, Norma," he said solemnly. "But Lee Simpson was my friend. Had to do it. Now you get out of town, and take this dough—call it insurance money—anything you please."

"You big sap, are you giving her that jack?" demanded Healy.

His voice boomed above Norma's low, terribly calm reiterations of hatred, and contempt, and grief, grotesquely mingled.

Barrett started to answer, then changed his mind. He hardly expected the detective to understand his feelings regarding the evening's strategy.

"I hope they've killed him!" shrieked Norma, her calmness breaking.

The telephone in the closest booth rang. Healy, who had given his men the number, snatched the receiver. He listened for a moment; and during that moment Barrett felt strangely empty, and futile. He poised himself on the balls of both feet...his fists were clenching painfully tight...he forced himself not to think of anything...

"All clear, Dave!" roared Healy's voice after several age-long seconds. "Simpson's okay!"

Barrett slowly exhaled the breath he had been holding. He listened again to Norma's invective, once more low-voiced. Then he smiled, shook his head.

"John, drive her out to the airport and see she gets out of town—charter a plane if necessary, but get her out, or her life's not worth a dime."

He hitched his belt, redistributed the weight of the emptied pistols, and shrugged as he heard the grief stricken girl's final appraisal of him.

"*C'est la guerre!*—or something like that. They oughtn't have used live bait..."

THE CROOKED SQUARE

Originally published in *Strange Detective Stories*, February 1934.

Davis P. Barrett thrust back his chair and regarded his fellow directors of the First Trust Bank. They were assembled about a long, teak-wood table in the study of Barrett's town house, wondering who would be the next victim of the Square, that sinister criminal who had within the week reduced their number from nine to seven.

"Mr. Chairman," said Barrett, "the police are looking for the Square among professional criminals. But they will not find him."

Barrett's glance flashed from face to face.

"Because the Square is at this table. One of us is an assassin!"

Barrett's words rattled like an air hammer. The ensuing silence became oppressive. Then came a confused stirring, and false starts at speech.

"Why…er, Barrett, that's absurd!" exclaimed Simmons, the chairman of the board. His voice, when he found it, was outraged and incredulous. "Do you mean that one of *us* killed Dobson and Cartier, and sent Benton an extortion note demanding one hundred thousand dollars?"

Simmons rapped for order, and glared at Barrett, the recently appointed director.

"I mean just that, Mr. Chairman! Only, extortion is not the true motive. That was camouflage.

"The stock that Dobson and Cartier held in this bank, and in several other locally owned corporations—Crescent Chemical, for instance, and Gulf States Indemnity—will be scattered into small parcels when their estates are settled.

"The seven of us practically control those companies. Now, when this plot is completed by a few more deaths, one of the survivors will have absolute control without having purchased a single additional share."

They caught the point. While fifty-one percent of stock must *in theory* be held to secure absolute control, a much smaller percentage will suffice if the balance be scattered among small holders, hard to organize.

Barrett's eyes were hard as sword points. The directors stirred uneasily before the searching glance of that ex-hunter of men, beasts, and adventure. His hand slipped to his vest pocket. He produced a cardboard pill box which he set near the center of the table.

"This box contains a gelatin capsule of deadly, vegetable poison. When I switch out the lights we will pass in single file around the table. The Square—one of us—will take that capsule. On his way home, he will die, apparently of heart failure. A skilled toxicologist could scarcely detect the traces of poison unless he were forewarned of its presence.

"In this way the Square can escape the hangman. Otherwise, I'll continue my investigation and expose him. One more move, and he's through."

Barrett's gesture was eloquent, and inexorable. Those whose eyes followed its cutting finality noted the antique Oriental carpets and tapestries, and clusters of weapons from far off lands. The carpets came from Persian palaces; the weapons, from the hands of those who had made the error of hunting Barrett.

"Why...that's ghastly. Barrett, are you insane?... Whoever heard of such a thing!" they clamored, all finding their voices at once.

Barrett imperturbably regarded them, eye to eye, one by one. He gestured toward the cardboard pill-box and shrugged.

"One of us knows I'm not insane," he said evenly. "I offer that man a decent way out. If he declines, I will exact the uttermost vengeance. He will hang, despite his position."

The directors regarded each other in incredulous dismay. Their faces, some ruddy, some bronzed, some pasty, had all reached an equality in pallor. There was something sinister and chilling in Barrett's emphasis on the word *hang*. Taylor Hartley, shaken from his habitual self possession, glanced about.

"Mr. Chairman," he said, "even if one of us were guilty, this proposal carried into effect would make us all accessories to a private, extra-legal execution. Murder, no less."

"Right, Hartley," agreed Barrett grimly. "Or else one of us goes to the gallows, and the First Trust is sunk. Despite our precautions against the facts leaking out, there were dangerously heavy withdrawals today." Barrett paused, then added, "The cover of this pillbox is marked with luminous paint. Whoever wants it can easily find it in the dark."

"Good God! This is a damnable jest," protested the president, white haired James Kent.

Barrett's smile convinced the directors that the story of the Dyak whose long bladed kampilan and short bladed dagger adorned the wall was unvarnished truth. Then, as his hand reached for the switch: "Did you gentlemen ever hear me jest? Will you, or will you not?"

Barrett, towering over them in personality rather than stature, was compelling their belief, and goading them to desperation by the sheer force of his will.

"Mr. Chairman," said Taylor Hartley, "it sounds like a good way out for someone—if Barrett is right. Thus we'll have no rumors of suicide, or other scandal to complete the ruin. I move that we accept, and pledge ourselves to secrecy."

"Second it," faltered Benton, whose life was under the threatening shadow of the Square.

It was so ordered.

The lights snapped out. The shades had been drawn, and heavy drapes shrouded the windows, so that not a trace of light leaked in from without. The silent darkness was troubled by the breathing of those who for the first time felt the presence of death. They pictured the vengeful, panther-like Barrett smiling grimly in the blackness, and wondered whose life he held in his hand. None doubted any longer.

"Forward, march!" commanded Barrett. And then, as they filed around the table, he spoke again: "I will count to five, and then I'll snap on the lights as soon as I can reach the switch."

The phosphorescent glow of pill-box stared balefully from the darkness.

"One...two..."

Barrett's words dropped like earth upon a coffin.

"Three..."

For a moment the ominous glow was obscured. The tension became unbearable. Each wondered whether it had actually been a hand—a confession of guilt —that had masked the phosphorescence. Each dreaded the eye of his fellows when at the fifth count the light would flash on. But that solemnly pronounced "five" was not spoken.

A cry of pain and terror stabbed the murmur of hoarse breathing. Then a gurgling gasp, long drawn and agonized. A chair crashed, and then there was the *chunk* of a falling body. A moment later a switch clicked, and light flooded the room.

Benton lay at the foot of the table. The hilt of a dagger—one of Barrett's own weapons—projected from Benton's chest. A red stream trickled across his expanse of shirt front, and a red froth was gathering on his lips.

For a moment the directors regarded each other in voiceless horror. Even Barrett, the man hunter, had lost some of the tropic tan that had been burned into his lean cheeks by blazing, foreign suns. Then as one man they shifted their gaze toward the table.

The pill-box was gone. Someone had accepted the offer of death—and had struck his farewell blow.

"Christ," muttered the chairman as Barrett leaped from his post at the wall switch and knelt beside Benton, "you were right! Unless someone was lurking behind that tapestry..."

"Dead," pronounced Barrett. He rose and regarded the survivors. Then, solemnly, "That capsule gives painless, instant death. And I am still offering the assassin his chance, as I promised.

"Gentlemen, be pleased to remain while I call the police. And remember: not a word about that pill. The lights went out; someone who must have been hiding behind that tapestry snatched a dagger from the wall and got Benton. That, and no more. Do you get me?"

And it was that, and no more, which the police investigation uncovered that night, despite the questioning, the vain search for fingerprints, and a study of charts which showed the positions, seated, of the members of the Board.

"Barrett," said John Dolan, Chief of Detectives, as he glanced over his tabulated data, "this is fishy from the ground up. You're holding out."

Barrett nodded.

"I am, John, and you'll have to like it. This is a lot more than blackmail or extortion. And if you want to squash the Square, give me a free hand. You'll never make it, looking for anarchists, or other organized criminals."

"Cough up!" demanded Dolan, his broad, red face becoming stern. "Friendship has its limits. You're obstructing justice."

Barrett returned the glare, and shook his head.

"You're obstructing justice yourself. Give me a couple of days. A lot of depositors—men like yourself—have their last penny with us. If this story gets out, the bank, and working men's money goes glimmering.

"Will you play ball?"

"Never saw an Irishman with more blarney," growled Dolan. "I'll play."

* * * *

The following morning's mail brought Davis Barrett the usual heap of letters. One, marked "personal," was ominously familiar: while there was nothing striking about the size, shape, or texture of the envelope, the address, jammed into the lower right hand corner, with its letters so spaced as to make a perfect square, warned Barrett even before he broke the splash of black wax that secured the flap.

The Square, so called from the arrangement of his letters of extortion, was striking at the heart of the enemy.

Davis P. Barrett,
4644 Saint Charles
New Orleans, Louisiana.

The message, like those received by the three deceased, was pointed:

> *Go to Patio Moro tonight at nine o'clock sharp and wait at the third table on the right as you enter. Bring one hundred thousand dollars in new and unmarked thousand-dollar bills. At exactly nine fifteen put the money under the loose brick in the wall at the height of the table. Remain exactly five minutes, then leave. Be warned by the example of Benton and do not notify the police or trifle with THE SQUARE.*

Barrett scrutinized the note whose text, like the address, was carefully blocked off to make a perfect square in the lower corner of the sheet.

"Even if he has three of us to his credit, that hocus-pocus is still a hell of a waste of time and paper," muttered Barrett. "Probably no more finger prints or typewriter peculiarities than the others. But I guess his mind will be mathematically square to the last…"

Barrett grinned sourly, then added, "Unless I trip him up before he gets me!"

Whereupon Barrett took a cigar from the humidor on his desk, and settled down to sifting a collection of intangible clues which, by their nature, had not been accessible to the police. His reasoning involved an analysis of the circumstances and backgrounds of both the victims and the survivors. Barrett scrutinized the unaccountable recovery of a certain director from his 1929 losses; he sought the significance of a vote to approve an excessive loan to a cartage and warehousing company whose being bonded had little effect upon its activities; and he wondered at the revenue a member of the board received from sources as vague as they were inexhaustible. And finally, Barrett noted, each death had shifted the balance of power that existed between the survivors and their many interests.

Barrett had with ample reason demanded that the chief of detectives stand clear and give him a chance for a solution that would have the minimum of publicity. He had suspected Benton of having written himself an extortion letter as a means of deflecting possible suspicion: but Benton's death from a stab wound

372

that could not possibly have been self-inflicted, forced a revision —though not the discarding—of his original theory.

"The next time I buy an interest in a bank, I'll be sure it's not a madhouse I'm getting into!" he exclaimed wrathfully, as he looked up from his tabulated data and scrutinized the envelope which had contained the letter from the Square. He noted a detail that he had not thus far observed.

"I'll be double damned! *Postmarked an hour before Benton was killed*!"

He knew now that the Square had been so certain of Benton's death that the warning clause of Barrett's letter had been drafted at least several hours before the fatal meeting of the preceding night.

"And made a monkey of me, right under my nose. Used a dagger from my own collection!"

Barrett grimaced sourly, shook his head, and resumed his study. He made little progress, however, as his continued analysis was interrupted by the ringing of the telephone. Taylor Hartley was on the wire.

"...So the Square picked on you, eh?—Well, you should see what I got in the mail this morning.—Not notifying the police? Very good. Hartley. We'll fight this out in private. Stick to your guns, and don't let Dolan get a word out of you. —Suppose we deliver our ransoms together; we're scheduled ten minutes apart. —Okay, Hartley, see you this evening."

Barrett's face became long and thoughtful as he replaced the instrument.

"Two warned at the same time. The Square is changing his system. A fellow so mathematically inclined—Squares and the like—must have cause for a change —"

That evening, well ahead of the hour appointed for the payment of the hundred thousand dollar blackmail, Barrett called at Hartley's residence. He found Hartley in his library, an austere hall that served as a depository of the first editions which Hartley had accumulated. Hartley rose from the desk at which he had been engaged in studies which even an extortion letter had not been able to disturb.

"Paying off?" was Barrett's first remark following the exchange of greetings.

Hartley nodded and smiled cryptically.

"About the most prudent thing to do. How about yourself?"

Barrett took a packet of bills from his pocket and flipped them as he spoke. "Full count, brand new. But there are other ways of tricking this omnipotent Square. I might at the last minute change my mind and slip him a packet of cigar coupons!"

Hartley pondered for a moment.

"Maybe we could get away with that, and trap him before he could hit back."

Barrett followed Hartley to the paving.

"Want to drive down with me?" asked Barrett, pausing at the curbing and gesturing toward his car, a glittering, black Hispano.

"Thanks, no," replied Hartley. "I have a bit of running around to do when we are through with this errand. I'll meet you at Patio Moro."

Patio Moro is a courtyard in the *Vieux Carré*, or French Quarter of New Orleans, that section which lies erected by the Sieur de Bienville when he founded the city some two centuries ago. Patio Moro is literally a café: it is devoted exclusively to the serving of that chicory-tinctured, black coffee which in New Orleans is a ritual rather than a mere beverage.

When Barrett's Hispano drew up before the arched entrance of Patio Moro, he saw that Hartley's car was already at the curbing.

"Frost," he said to the grim faced, sturdy man at the wheel, "I want you to do a bit of prowling while I'm inside. Do you understand all the details?"

"Yes, sir."

And Barrett, as he strode down the vaulted passageway toward the dimness of the coffee court, knew that Frost, who had followed him on many a trail of adventure, would let little escape unnoticed.

At a table which was nestled close to the ivy-clad wall, and half concealed by a cluster of bamboo, Barrett saw Hartley, who was abstractedly marking dots on a cube of sugar and apparently unperturbed by keeping a rendezvous with the Square. Hartley, glancing up, smiled somberly and then looked at his watch as Barrett seated himself.

"In five minutes I am to put $100,000 into a crevice…"

Barrett followed Hartley's gesture and saw that one of the bricks of the old wall was loose, stripped of its mortar so that it could readily be lifted out with bare hands.

"Then put the brick on top of the packet and wait," he concluded.

"The time stated in my note," said Barrett, "is ten minutes later than yours. It seems that the Square will drag out your bundle to make room for mine. Got his nerve, lining us up two at a time!"

Hartley nodded.

"I wonder," continued Barrett, "how he can get the money without being detected, and when the penalty would be exacted if we tried to trick him? Or is he depending on our being scared stiff by the deaths of Hobson, Cartier, and Benton?" He glanced about, noting the clumps of broad leaved plantains that occupied the corners of the court, and the iron railed balcony of the house whose rear commanded the rear wall of the patio.

"He'd probably not shoot from ambush," suggested Hartley. "If that's what you had in mind. It would probably be something more daring. Look how the Square got Cartier: right on the steps of his own house, and…"

"To say nothing of Benton," added Barrett as he drew from his pocket a packet of notes which he laid on the table.

"I'm first," said Hartley, again glancing at his watch.

Barrett stuffed the crisp, new bills back into his pocket, then shivered as he remarked, "The Square must be a weather prophet! So chilly this evening there'd be no other customers."

The dim, bluish globes, hung high overhead, cast a satanic twilight over the patio. Death brooded over the silence that was interrupted only by the distant rattle of the street car going up Royal Street. Even the sounds from the kitchen were a subdued murmur. Barrett shivered again, and this time not on account of the evening chill. He was thinking of the relentless doom that laid wiped out one third of the directors of the First Trust Bank, and pondering on the unseen Square who was watching them as they awaited the appointed moment.

"Now," muttered Hartley. "We'll see."

A note of excitement had crept into his voice. He reached to the wall, plucked forth a brick—*the* brick—and laid into place a sheaf of bills.

"Wait a second," said Barrett as Hartley thrust the brick home. "Give me a look. I want to dope out this matter of the time between our deposits, when we might as well ante in together. Maybe…"

"Better not," counselled Hartley, shaking his head. "I've got an idea."

Barrett agreed, glanced at his watch.

"One hundred thousand for the privilege of living! Well, I guess it's worth it."

The succeeding minutes were interminable.

"Two more to go," observed Barrett. He noted that Hartley's saturnine features had become tense from suppressed excitement. The long fingers drummed nervously on the table.

A waiter approached. Barrett impatiently gestured for him to withdraw, but he did not heed.

"Sorry, sir," he apologized. "Gentleman out in front left this package and asked me to give it to Mr. Hartley, immediately. Seemed urgent."

"What did he look like?" demanded Barrett.

The waiter's description was so confused as to be worthless.

"Oh, all right," interrupted Hartley as he accepted the packet and handed the waiter a coin. "That'll be all. Thank you."

Hartley's dark brows rose to Gothic arches as he opened the parcel.

"Good lord!" he exclaimed. "Look!"

Barrett saw a bundle of paper cut to the size of bank notes, with a bill on top. A typewritten message accompanied it.

"Your roll, eh?"

"Yes. Returned with compliments and a warning," said Hartley somberly as he handed Barrett the note. "I wanted to try him by giving him a dummy—well, I know now."

"Don't try to trick us," Barrett read. *"You have just time to deliver the sum we demanded. Last chance. We are watching."*

He scrutinized the note for a moment, then: "Good God! Collected and checked up, right before our eyes! Dammit, that's impossible!"

Barrett removed the brick and explored the vacancy with his fingers. He felt the edge of a slot at the back, that would make it possible for someone to have drawn the packet to the other side of the wall.

"What are you going to do? Have you…"

Hartley drew from his pocket another sheaf of bills. "This time," he explained, "I'll give him what he demanded. I'm taking no chances!"

"Nor I either," echoed Barrett. "I'm off the cigar coupon idea. And—well, it's time for my contribution, so let's pay off together."

Hartley thrust his packet of bills into the bottom of the opening, then, as Barrett followed suit, he replaced the brick.

They sat in silence until Barrett, glancing at his watch, said, "Time's up. I think I'll risk a peep."

He withdrew the brick. Both packets were gone.

"Slick! Too slick!" muttered Barrett. "I begin to see why he ordered us to wait. Let's get out! This place gives me the creeps."

"Rather," agreed Hartley as he led the way to the entrance.

Frost was again at the wheel of the Hispano.

"Back to the house," directed Barrett. Then, with a gesture and a nod, he bade Hartley good night. They followed Hartley's tail light until they reached the rear of Saint Louis Cathedral. There, in response to Barrett's order, Frost pulled up at the curbing and stepped to the sidewalk.

"All right, Frost, I'm leaving it to you," was Barrett's remark, as he took the wheel. "And I'll be waiting for a call, unless I'm popped off."

He headed the Hispano uptown. As he crossed Canal Street, he smiled grimly and stroked the scar on his cheek.

"This guess," he muttered, "will finish the Square—or me!"

Barrett, rational and logical as he claimed to be, worked more by intuition than he realized. Several escapes by the very narrowest of margins had taught him not to ignore premonitions.

"A hunch," he declared, "is better than good sense."

And thus, less than half a dozen blocks past Canal Street, when Barrett sensed imminent peril, he knew better than to deny his instincts.

He glanced about him, and into the mirror, but saw no car following him, or paralleling him. He looked into the back of the Hispano to see that no one lurked, ready to strike him down. All was clear: yet the shadow of the Square hung over him.

As he approached Lee Circle, Barrett pulled up at the service station at his right. He knew he could not logically account for his action: but he knew also that the Square could not have foreseen it.

"Give me a tow, buddy," he requested.

"No use towing it," countered the service man. "We'll fix it right here."

"I want a tow," persisted Barrett, "and not advice. No, the steering gear isn't damaged, but I don't want anyone at the wheel. Lift 'er up with the crane and drag her on her tail!"

The service man eyed him curiously; then, noting Barrett's stern, thoughtful expression, and the cold gleam in his eye, nodded wisely and smiled to himself.

"Oh, all right," he agreed. "We won't have nobody at the wheel. I got you."

"Yes?" murmured Barrett as he seated himself beside the driver of emergency car. And to himself, "Maybe he's right—someone might have been figuring on pouring a charge of buckshot into me as I sat at the wheel...and this will throw them off the track."

Barrett had lost little time in getting a tow; but the wrecker was going at a leisurely pace and delaying his getting in touch with Frost.

"Step on it!" he snapped. "I'm in a hurry!"

The driver stepped. But the words had scarcely left Barrett's lips when a terrific concussion nearly blasted him from his seat. Shattered glass from the rear and sides of the cab rained about him.

Barrett, pistol drawn, leaped from the cab and into a wave acrid, black smoke which billowed about and overwhelmed them.

The Hispano was a smoking, tangled ruin. Flames were lapping up from the hood, and around the remnants of the wheel. A bomb had blown away the front seat, caved in the instrument panel, and set fire to the gas that ran from the shattered lines.

"Score one for the Square!" growled Barrett as he snatched a fire-extinguisher from the wrecker. Then, to the still speechless service man, "That's what I wanted to find out! Take 'er back—though there'll be damn little salvage."

"Nothing stirring! I'm through."

"Suit yourself." Barrett shrugged, discarded the extinguisher, and boarded a cab that had halted near the smoking ruin.

* * * *

As he approached the 4000 block, Barrett dismissed the cab and proceeded on foot. He paused at a pay station and called police headquarters.

"Dolan? Barrett speaking…now get this carefully…"

Barrett rapidly summarized the events of the evening, and concluded by saying, "Rush a man to my house to wait for a call from Frost—No, I'll warn Hartley myself. I'm just a few blocks from where he lives."

Hartley himself met Barrett at the door and led the way to the library, in the left wing.

"When you hear what the Square did for me," said Barrett as he seated himself, "you'll probably spend the rest of the evening in pious meditation."

Hartley listened without comment to Barrett's account of the bombing.

"Funny," concluded Barrett, as Hartley reached for a decanter, "that the Square would pick on me, when I paid off—whereas you did trifle with him."

Hartley regarded Barrett speculatively for a moment and shook his head.

"That is puzzling. I think I'll drive down town to stay at the Union Club until this thing has blown over."

Hartley's right hand toyed with the neck of the decanter. "Let's have a drink first," he suggested.

"Why not!" agreed Barrett easily. Then, in a low, tense voice, "And I think you'd better put that capsule into your drink, Hartley!"

Hartley stiffened and swayed forward, leaning on his desk.

"Easiest way out, Hartley," murmured Barrett with ominous smoothness. "You betrayed yourself by—"

Barrett's right hand flashed to his shoulder; but swift as the gesture was, Hartley's left hand had the advantage of an earlier start as it emerged from the table drawer with a pistol. The flash and the fumes blinded Barrett, and the bullet, boring into his right shoulder, paralyzed his arm before he could reach his shoulder holster. Hartley's second shot went wild as Barrett, recovering from the shock of the first, cleared the corner of the table and drove home with his left, sending Hartley crashing backward into a book case, pistol clattering to the hardwood floor.

The enemy was closer than the pistol; and Barrett's right arm was out of action. He closed in, empty handed, to counter-attack. His left doubled Hartley with a jab to the pit of the stomach; but a split second later the decanter crashed home. Barrett jerked his head, going with the blow, but though he thus kept his skull intact, he went down before the crushing impact, flattening out into a pool of bottomless blackness. He wondered, in his lingering vestige of consciousness, how the killer would dispose of his body: for Hartley would be the first to recover...

* * * *

To his considerable surprise, Barrett finally opened his eyes and realized that Hartley had not taken the logical course. His first sensation was in his splitting head and throbbing, bullet-bored shoulder; and then the tang of high-powered whiskey trickling down his throat. He heard the gruff voice of John Dolan, and saw, as he lifted himself up on his good elbow, that the leaded glass front doors of the house had been well scattered over an acre of Persian carpet. Dolan had entered unceremoniously, but in time.

"I knew it would take more than a banker to bust your thick head," said Dolan as he helped Barrett to his feet. Then, indicating Hartley who, handcuffed, battered, and still unconscious, lay on the floor, he said to the detective who had accompanied him "Lecoin, phone for the wagon."

"And so he is the Square, eh?" interjected Dolan, as he heard Barrett's account of the encounter. "How did you dope it out?"

"I knew that Benton couldn't possibly raise one hundred thousand dollars. Any businesslike blackmailer would also have known that fact. Thus I knew that there must be some other motive."

Barrett then explained how each death had concentrated the control of the bank and several local corporations in the hands of the survivors.

"And tonight, in the courtyard," continued Barrett, "Hartley put a dummy roll into the hole in the wall: this was to get a warning to scare me into line, so I'd not pull the same gag. I showed him a roll of bills, but actually substituted a packet of wrapping paper. And since I wasn't warned, it tipped me off that Hartley and the Square were the same person. The Square didn't know I'd fudged the play, because Hartley didn't know. Get it?"

Dolan nodded.

"As for that bomb—Hartley had plenty of chances to plant it. He had to do something. He knew that he'd be exposed unless I were wiped out."

"But how about the way those packets disappeared?" wondered Dolan. "And that warning?"

"The warning," explained Barrett, "was made up in advance, and delivered by a confederate who didn't know what it was all about. As for the packets—they were probably forced down into a space between the double wall. Frost will be able to tell us when he checks in with whatever he's found. That, and other details..."

A heavy, muffled explosion shook the house.

Dolan and Lecoin dashed to the rear to investigate. Barrett did not accompany them. Instead, he turned to the bound Hartley.

Hartley regarded him in baleful silence, beaten but defiant.

"The play is over," continued Barrett, "all except the final act, a solo dance with you on the end of a rope. Hartley, you will hang!"

"There's still a chance, Hartley," said Barrett. "Before they come back. Where's that pill-box—you took it, that night."

A flash of rage contorted Harley's features for an instant. Then he rose from the floor; and, as Barrett covered him with his own pistol he went to his desk, opened a drawer, and with his manacled hands picked out a small cardboard box. He seated himself just as Dolan and Lecoin returned from the rear.

"Lot of smoke and smudge, but not much damage," remarked Dolan, jerking his thumb over his shoulder.

Barrett, who had handed Hartley a glass of water, turned and stood between Hartley and the detectives. "Probably not," he said. "That shot was to complete his case by faking a bombing of his own house, to tie in with the explosion that was to tear me and my car to pieces."

"Don't see how we'll keep this mess under cover," said Dolan. "Sorry, but there's no way out."

"Don't worry about that, John," countered Barrett. "The coroner will find heart failure as the cause of his death."

"Death?"

"Look at him," was the laconic reply, as Barrett stepped aside. Hartley's saturnine features were pale. He sat slumped in his chair. The capsule had acted swiftly.

Then Barrett added, "Now that everything is all square again, suppose you drive me to the Emergency Hospital. My shoulder is giving me hell!"

www.ingramcontent.com/pod-product-compliance
Lightning Source LLC
Chambersburg PA
CBHW032225010726
47494CB00002B/351